INDIAN PRAIRIE PUBLIC LIBRARY
401 Plainfield Road
Darien, IL 60561

P9-EGB-084

DEC - 1 2021

Dragon Hoops

GENE LUEN YANG

Color by **LARK PIEN**

Art Assists by **RIANNE MEYERS** and **KOLBE YANG**

:01

First Second

New York

**Dedicated to the community of Bishop O'Dowd High School.
I will forever bleed black and gold.**

First Second

Copyright © 2020 by Humble Comics LLC

No references in this book to real individuals, entities, or brands are intended to suggest any authorization, endorsement, or sponsorship by such individuals, entities, or brand owners.

Published by First Second

First Second is an imprint of Roaring Brook Press,
a division of Holtzbrinck Publishing Holdings Limited Partnership
120 Broadway, New York, NY 10271

Don't miss your next favorite book from First Second! For the latest updates go to firstsecondnewsletter.com and sign up for our enewsletter.

All rights reserved

Library of Congress Control Number: 2018953556

ISBN: 978-1-62672-079-4

Our books may be purchased in bulk for promotional, educational, or business use. Please contact your local bookseller or the Macmillan Corporate and Premium Sales Department at (800) 221-7945 ext. 5442 or by email at MacmillanSpecialMarkets@macmillan.com.

First edition, 2020
Edited by Mark Siegel and Alex Lu
Cover design by Kirk Benshoff
Interior book design by Rob Steen
Color by Lark Pien
Art assistance by Rianne Meyers and Kolbe Yang

Printed in Malaysia

Penciled, inked, and colored in Clip Studio and Photoshop.

10 9 8 7 6 5 4 3

PROLOGUE:
MR. YANG

I've hated *sports* ever since I was a little kid.

Especially *basketball*.

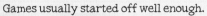

Games usually started off well enough.

Wow! A dragonfly!

BULLS 23

But inevitably--

?!

Gene! Heads up!

JAM!!

Ow!

And the pain wouldn't be limited to my fingers.

Ya gotta learn how to handle a *bullet pass*, Stick*!

BULLS 23

* My junior high nickname. I used to be really, really skinny.

What can I say?

I'm just not a *sports* kind of guy.

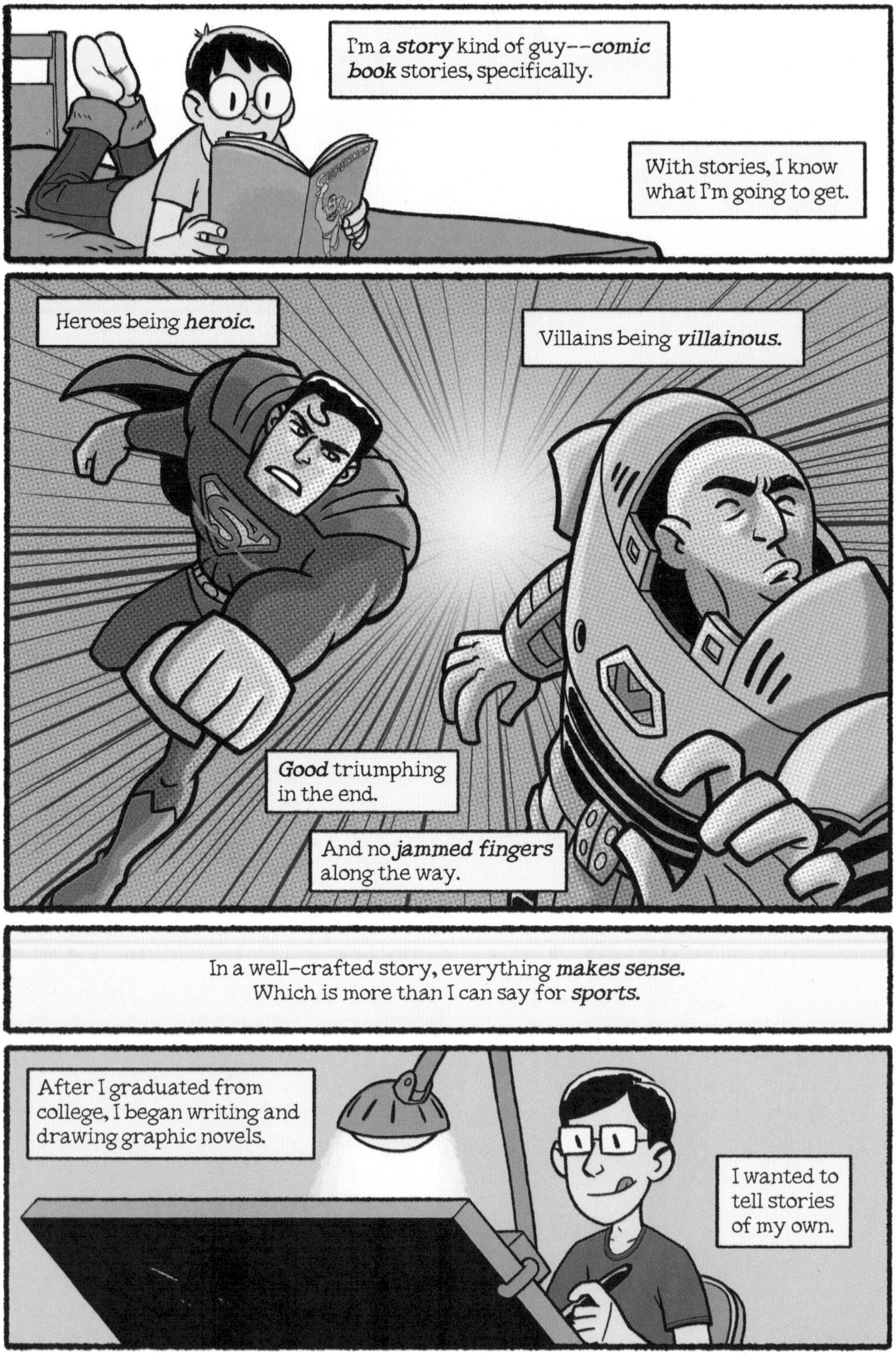
I'm a story kind of guy--comic book stories, specifically.
With stories, I know what I'm going to get.
Heroes being heroic.
Villains being villainous.
Good triumphing in the end.
And no jammed fingers along the way.
In a well-crafted story, everything makes sense. Which is more than I can say for sports.
After I graduated from college, I began writing and drawing graphic novels.
I wanted to tell stories of my own.

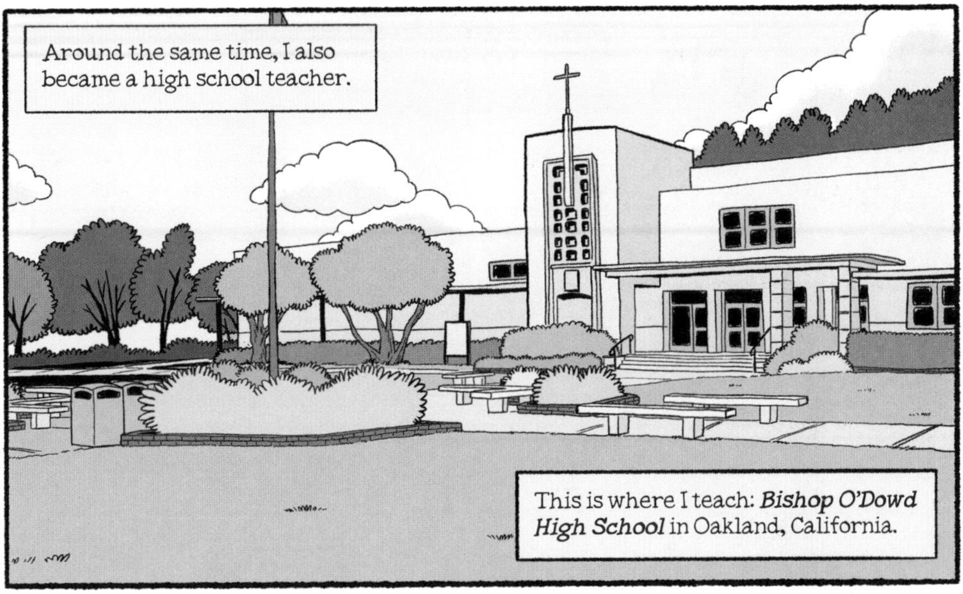
Around the same time, I also became a high school teacher.
This is where I teach: *Bishop O'Dowd High School* in Oakland, California.

So here's the thing about growing up: As you get older, you generally spend less and less time with people who aren't ***your kind*** of people.

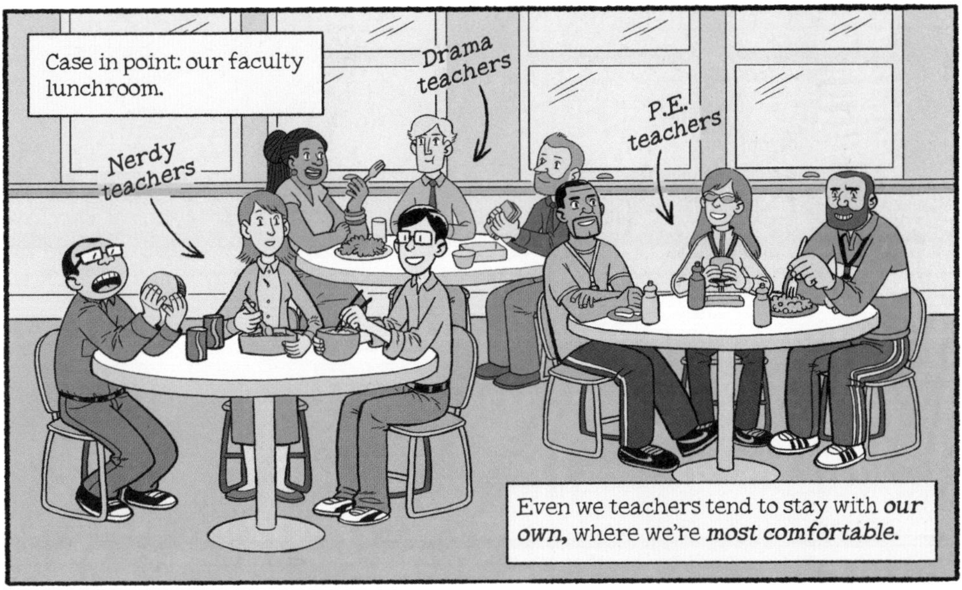
Case in point: our faculty lunchroom.
Nerdy teachers
Drama teachers
P.E. teachers
Even we teachers tend to stay with ***our own,*** where we're ***most comfortable.***

But every now and then, something makes you *leave.*

2013.
What's in the box, Daddy?
Something cool?
A present?
I think it might be . . .
. . . my new graphic novel!
Congratulations, honey!
Oh.
I wish it was a present.
Yay!
My last graphic novel took six years to finish.
Teaching!
84
2 2 3 7
Weekdays!
Comics!
Family!
Nights and Weekends!
It was an awful lot of work, but it also gave the last six years of my life a certain *balance.*
We should celebrate!
In-N-Out Burger?
Yay!
Everybody in the van!

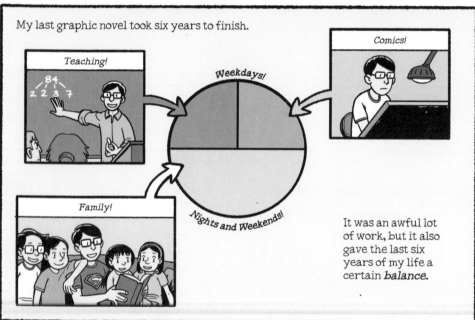

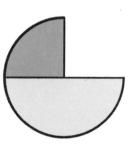

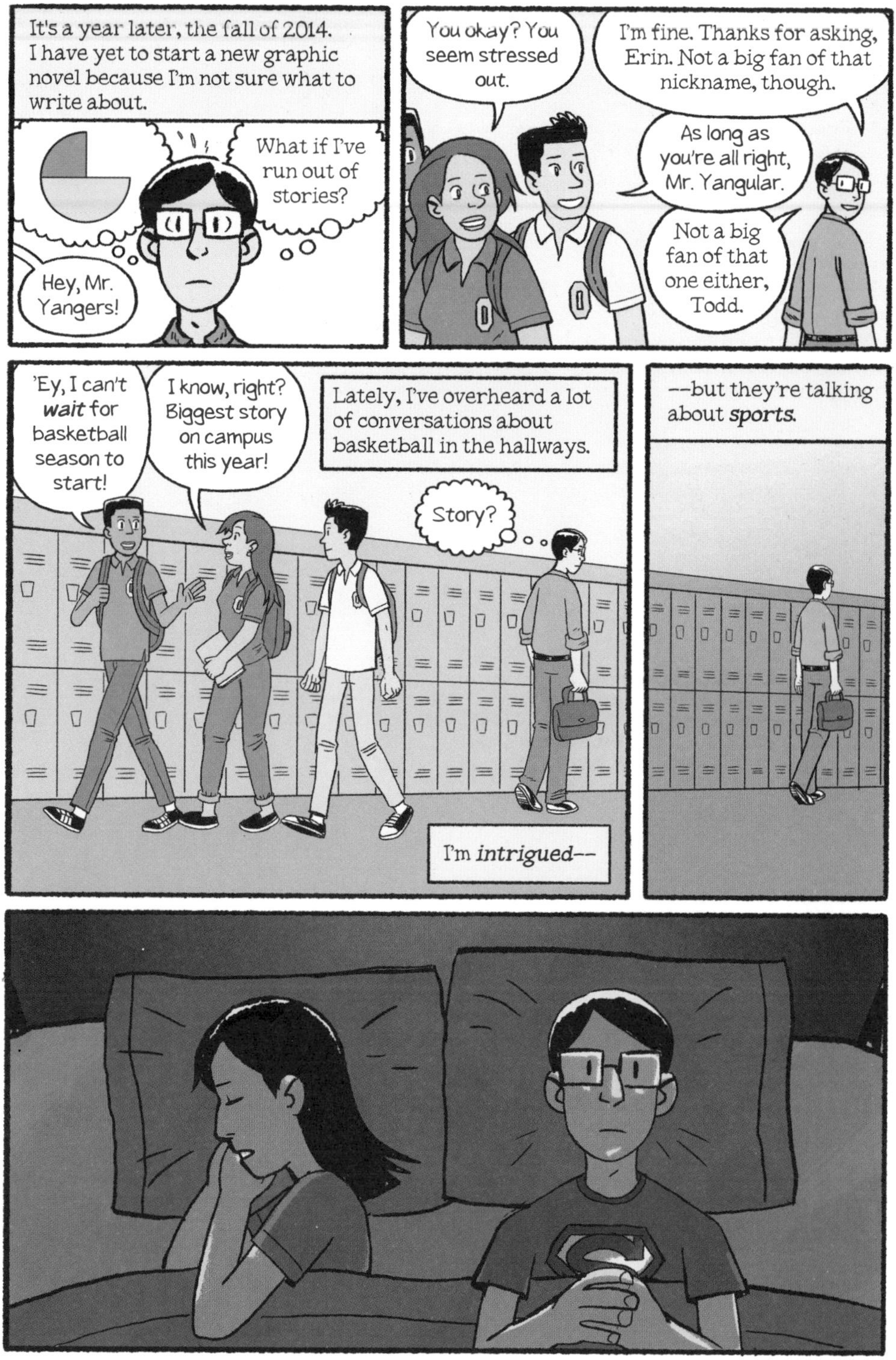

It's a year later, the fall of 2014. I have yet to start a new graphic novel because I'm not sure what to write about.
What if I've run out of stories?
Hey, Mr. Yangers!
You okay? You seem stressed out.
I'm fine. Thanks for asking, Erin. Not a big fan of that nickname, though.
As long as you're all right, Mr. Yangular.
Not a big fan of that one either, Todd.
'Ey, I can't *wait* for basketball season to start!
I know, right? Biggest story on campus this year!
Lately, I've overheard a lot of conversations about basketball in the hallways.
Story?
I'm *intrigued*--
--but they're talking about *sports*.

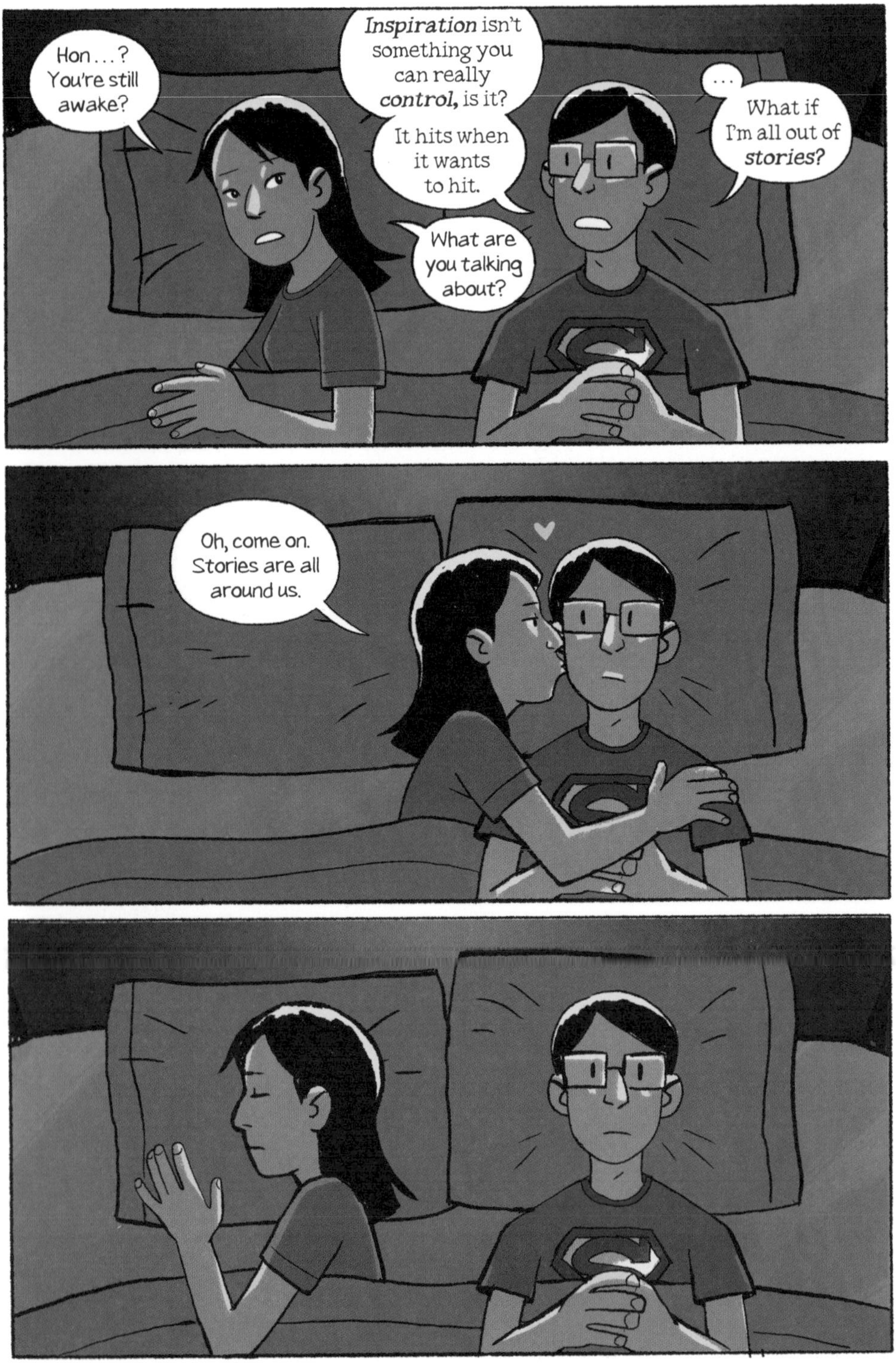
Hon...? You're still awake?
Inspiration isn't something you can really *control,* is it?
It hits when it wants to hit.
What are you talking about?
...
What if I'm all out of *stories?*
Oh, come on. Stories are all around us.

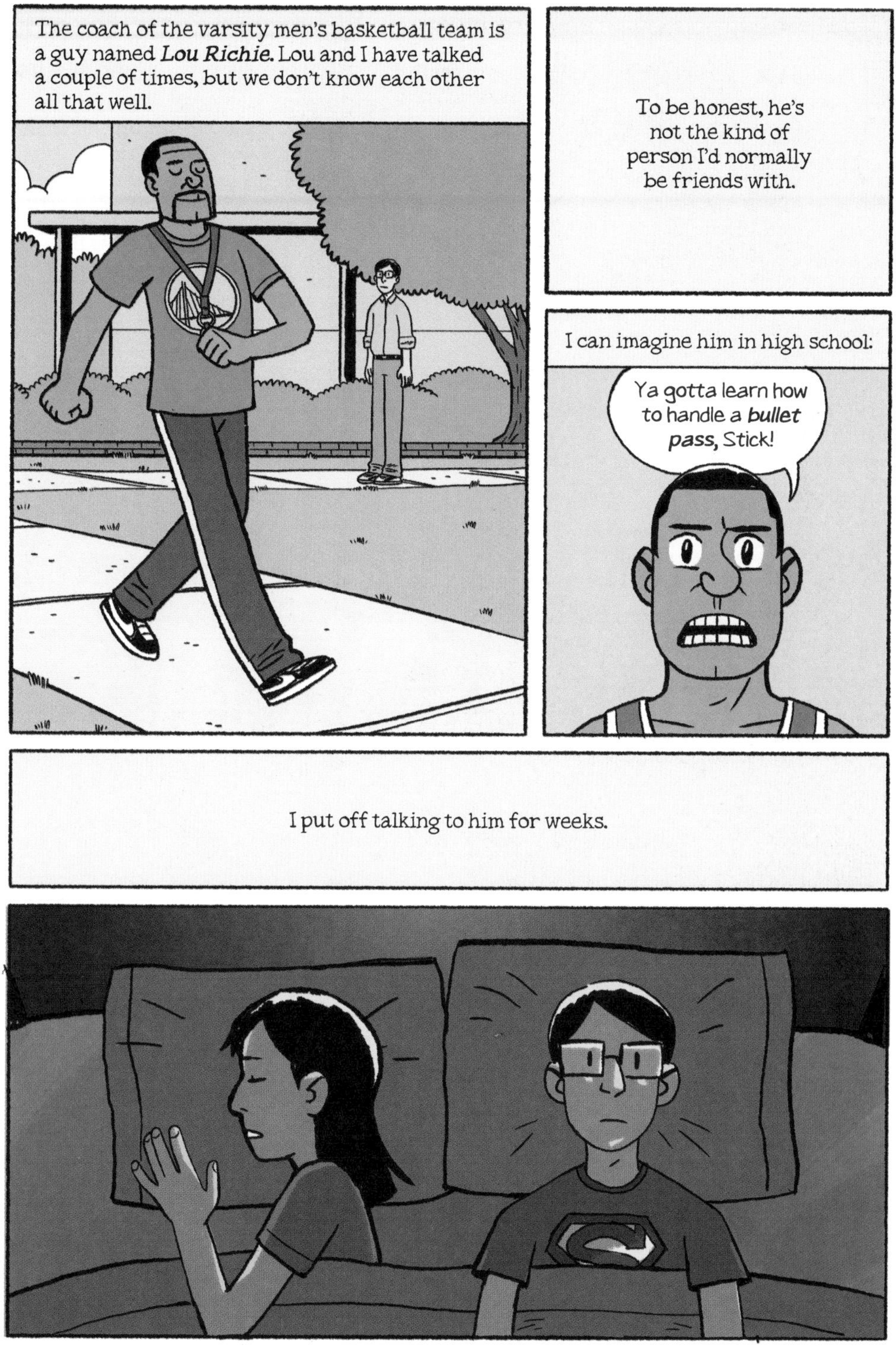
The coach of the varsity men's basketball team is a guy named *Lou Richie.* Lou and I have talked a couple of times, but we don't know each other all that well.
To be honest, he's not the kind of person I'd normally be friends with.
I can imagine him in high school:
Ya gotta learn how to handle a ***bullet pass,*** Stick!
I put off talking to him for weeks.

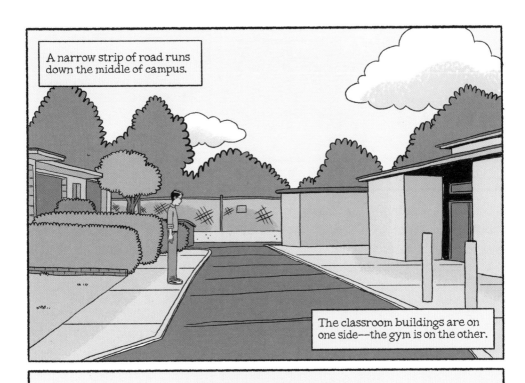

A narrow strip of road runs down the middle of campus.

The classroom buildings are on one side--the gym is on the other.

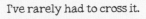

I've rarely had to cross it.

STEP.

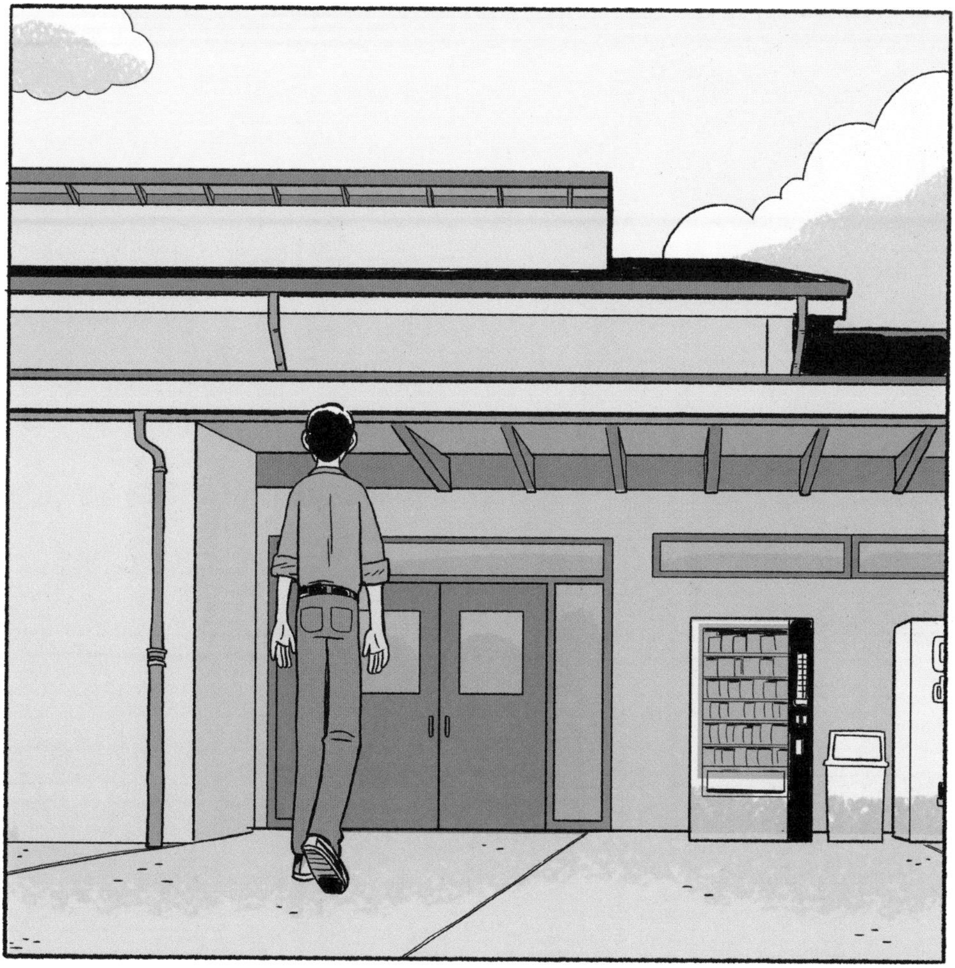

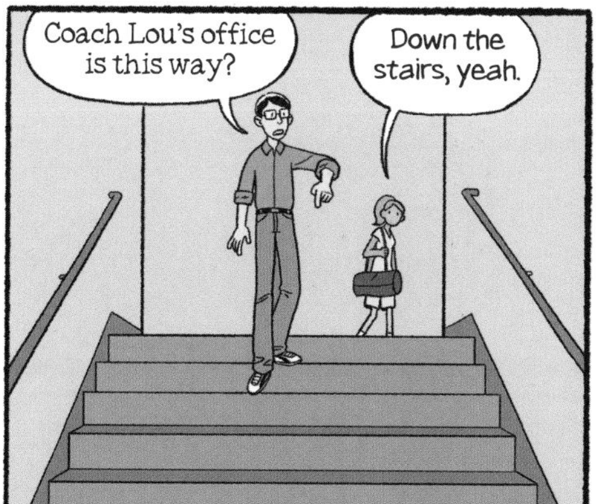
Coach Lou's office is this way?
Down the stairs, yeah.

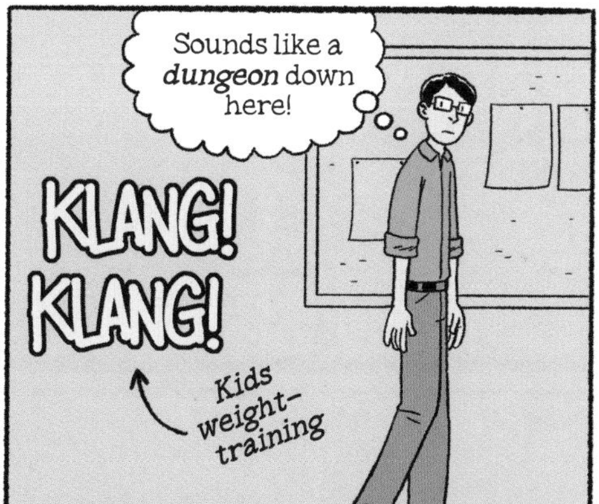
Sounds like a *dungeon* down here!
KLANG! KLANG!
Kids weight-training

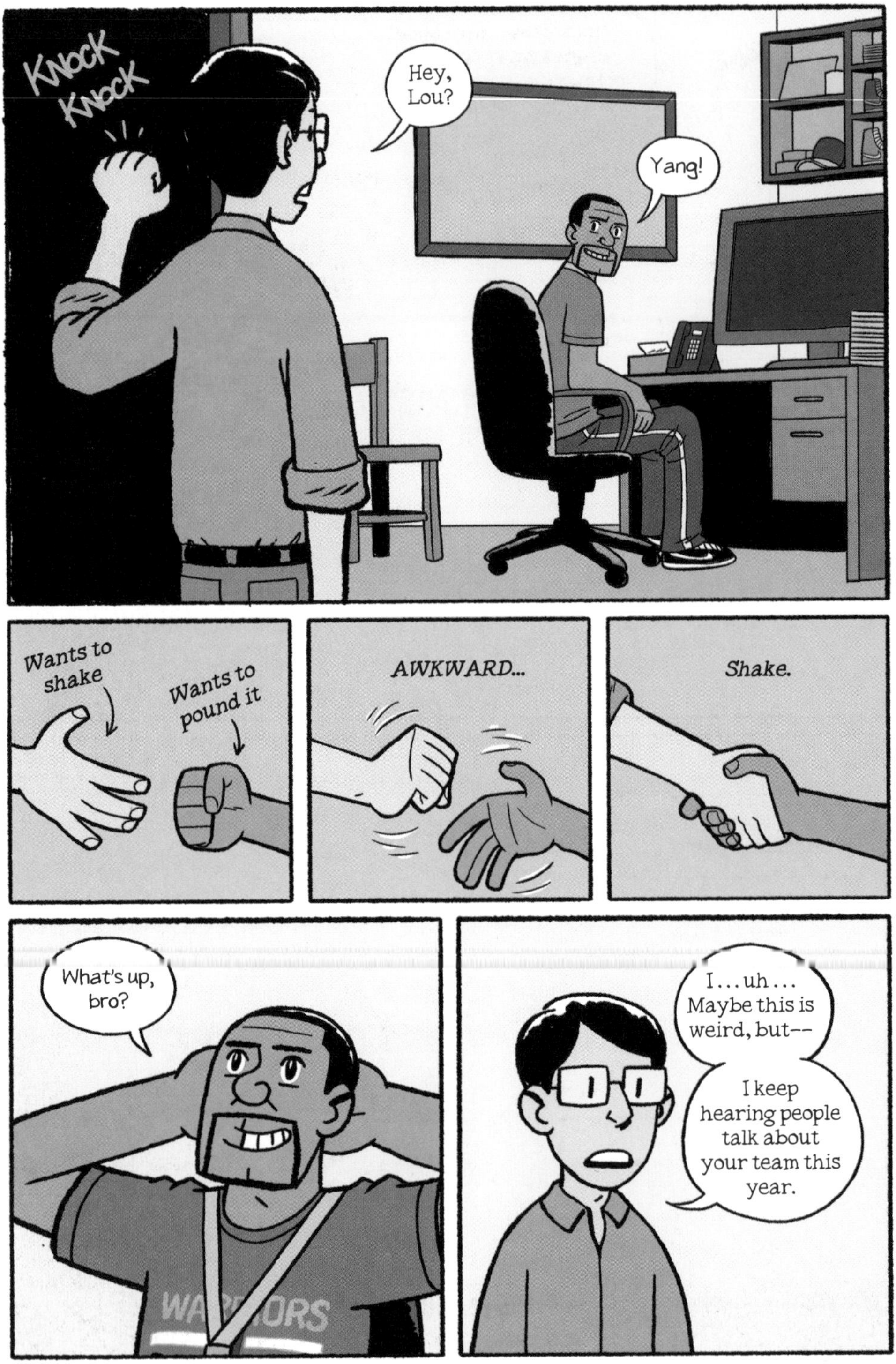
KNOCK KNOCK
Hey, Lou?
Yang!
Wants to shake
Wants to pound it
AWKWARD...
Shake.
What's up, bro?
WARRIORS
I... uh... Maybe this is weird, but--
I keep hearing people talk about your team this year.

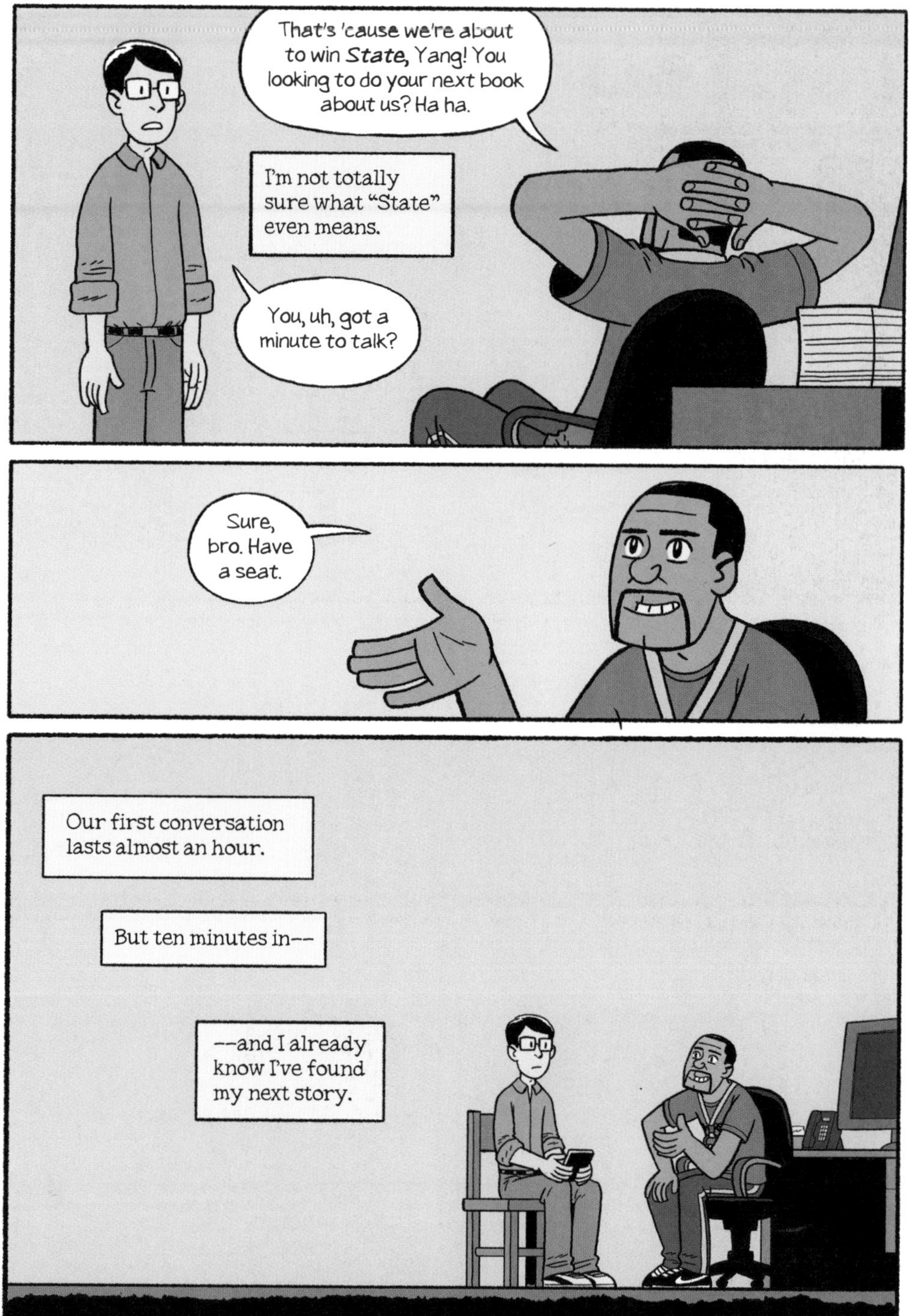
That's 'cause we're about to win *State,* Yang! You looking to do your next book about us? Ha ha.
I'm not totally sure what "State" even means.
You, uh, got a minute to talk?
Sure, bro. Have a seat.
Our first conversation lasts almost an hour.
But ten minutes in--
--and I already know I've found my next story.

CHAPTER 1:
COACH LOU

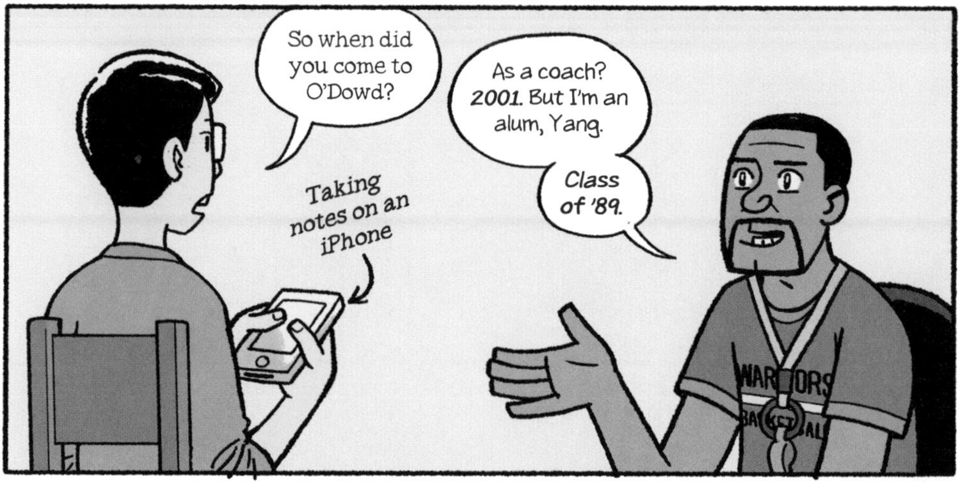
So when did you come to O'Dowd?
Taking notes on an iPhone
As a coach? 2001. But I'm an alum, Yang.
Class of '89.

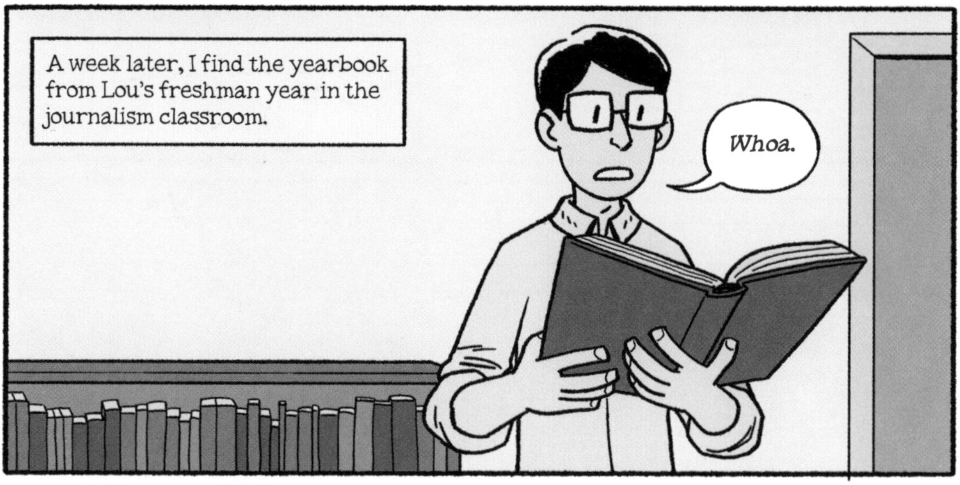
A week later, I find the yearbook from Lou's freshman year in the journalism classroom.
Whoa.

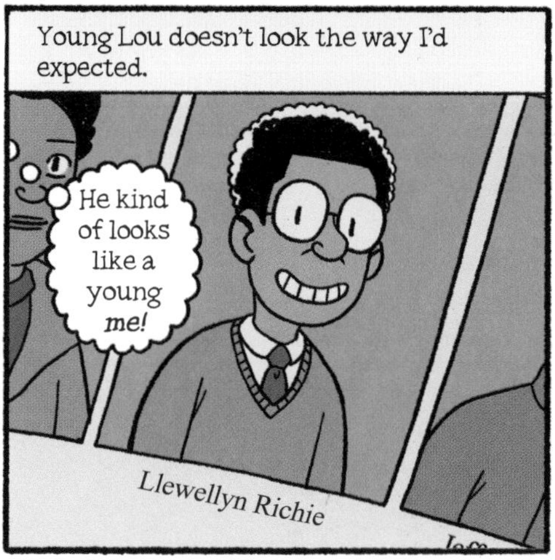
Young Lou doesn't look the way I'd expected.
He kind of looks like a young me!
Llewellyn Richie

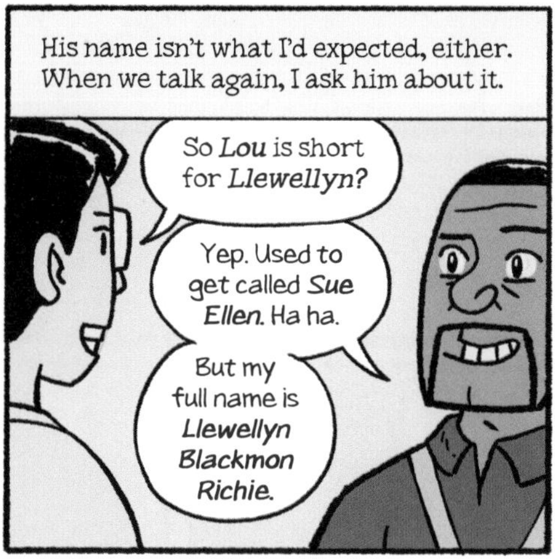
His name isn't what I'd expected, either. When we talk again, I ask him about it.
So Lou is short for Llewellyn?
Yep. Used to get called Sue Ellen. Ha ha.
But my full name is Llewellyn Blackmon Richie.

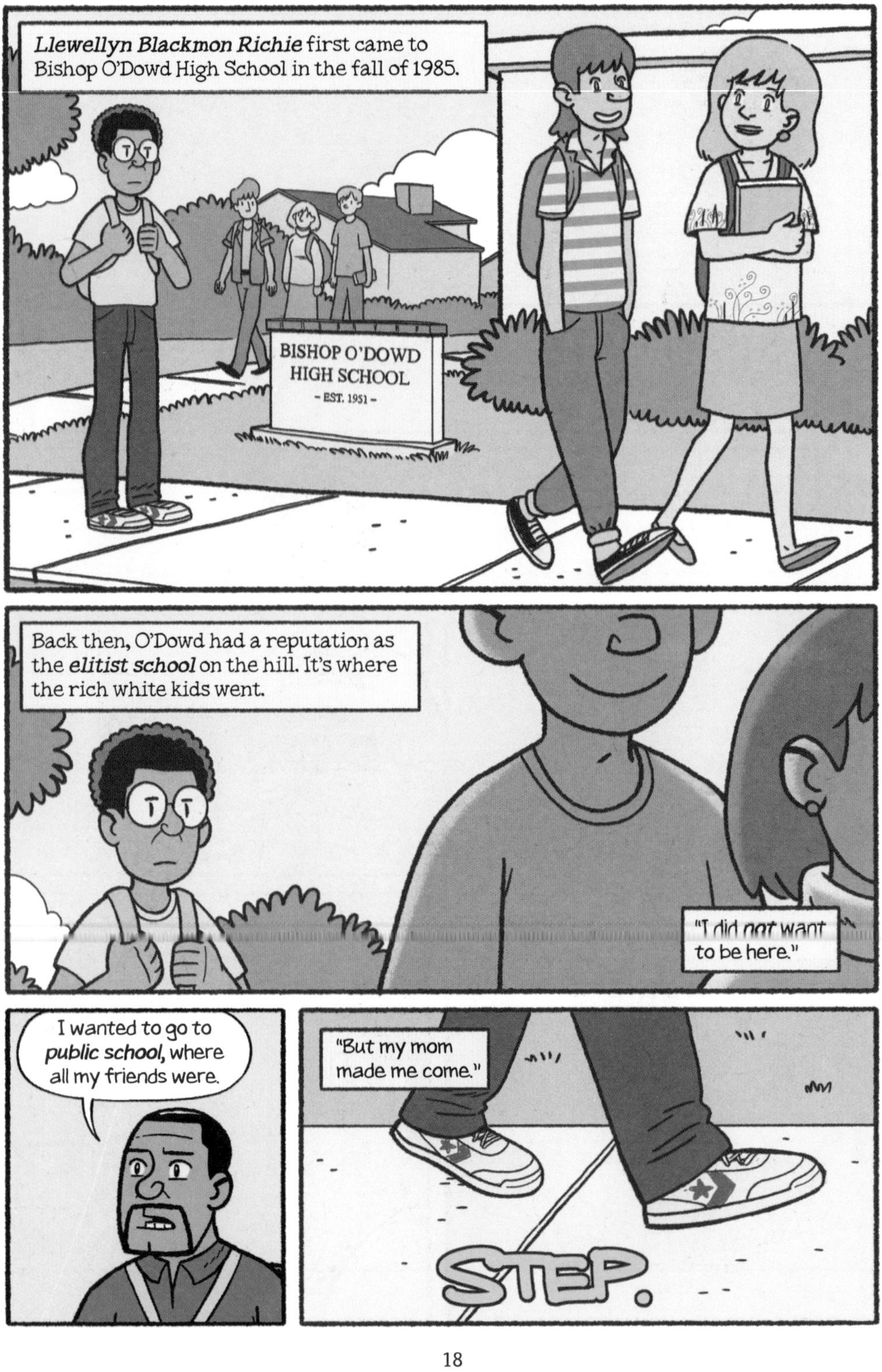
Llewellyn Blackmon Richie first came to Bishop O'Dowd High School in the fall of 1985.
BISHOP O'DOWD HIGH SCHOOL
- EST. 1951 -
Back then, O'Dowd had a reputation as the elitist school on the hill. It's where the rich white kids went.
"I did not want to be here."
I wanted to go to public school, where all my friends were.
"But my mom made me come."
STEP.

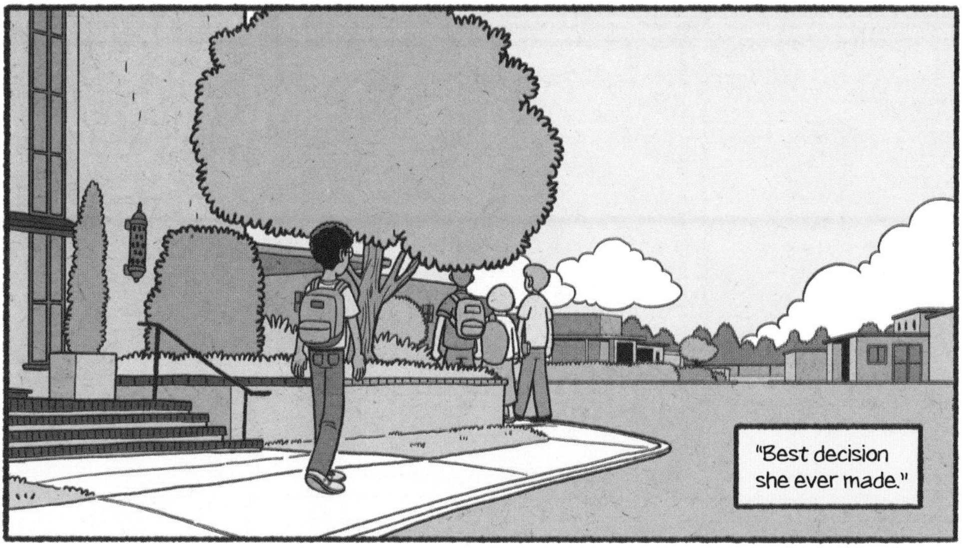
"Best decision she ever made."

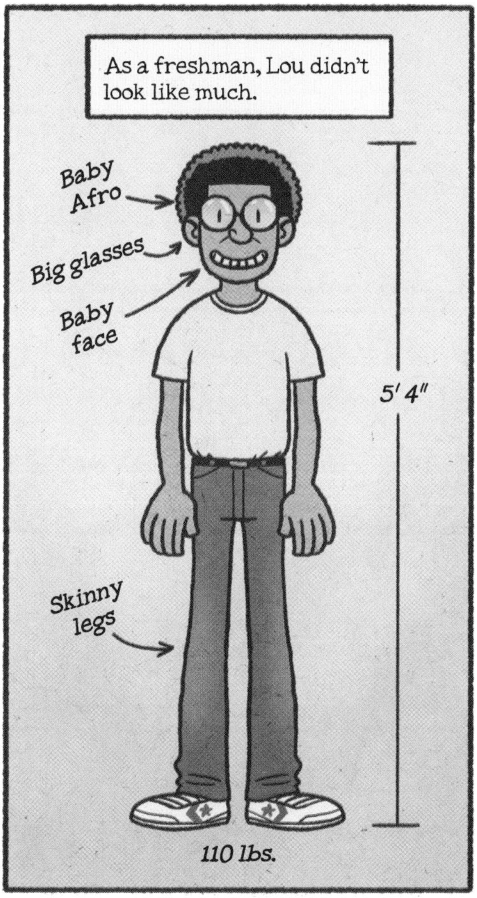
As a freshman, Lou didn't look like much.
Baby Afro
Big glasses
Baby face
Skinny legs
5′ 4″
110 lbs.

Some of the kids at O'Dowd liked to give him a hard time.

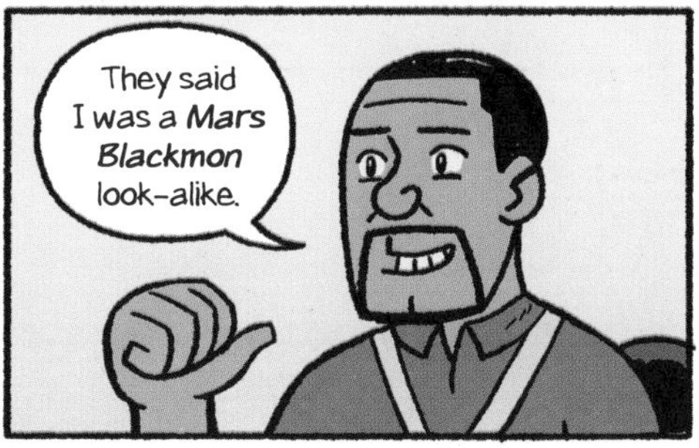
They said I was a *Mars Blackmon* look-alike.

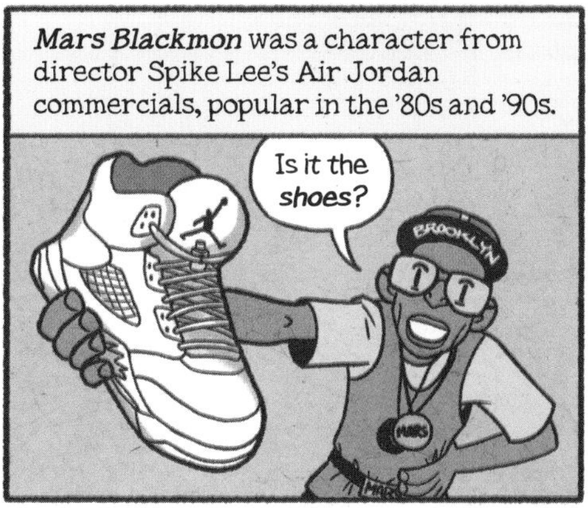
Mars Blackmon was a character from director Spike Lee's Air Jordan commercials, popular in the '80s and '90s.
Is it the *shoes?*
BROOKLYN
MARS

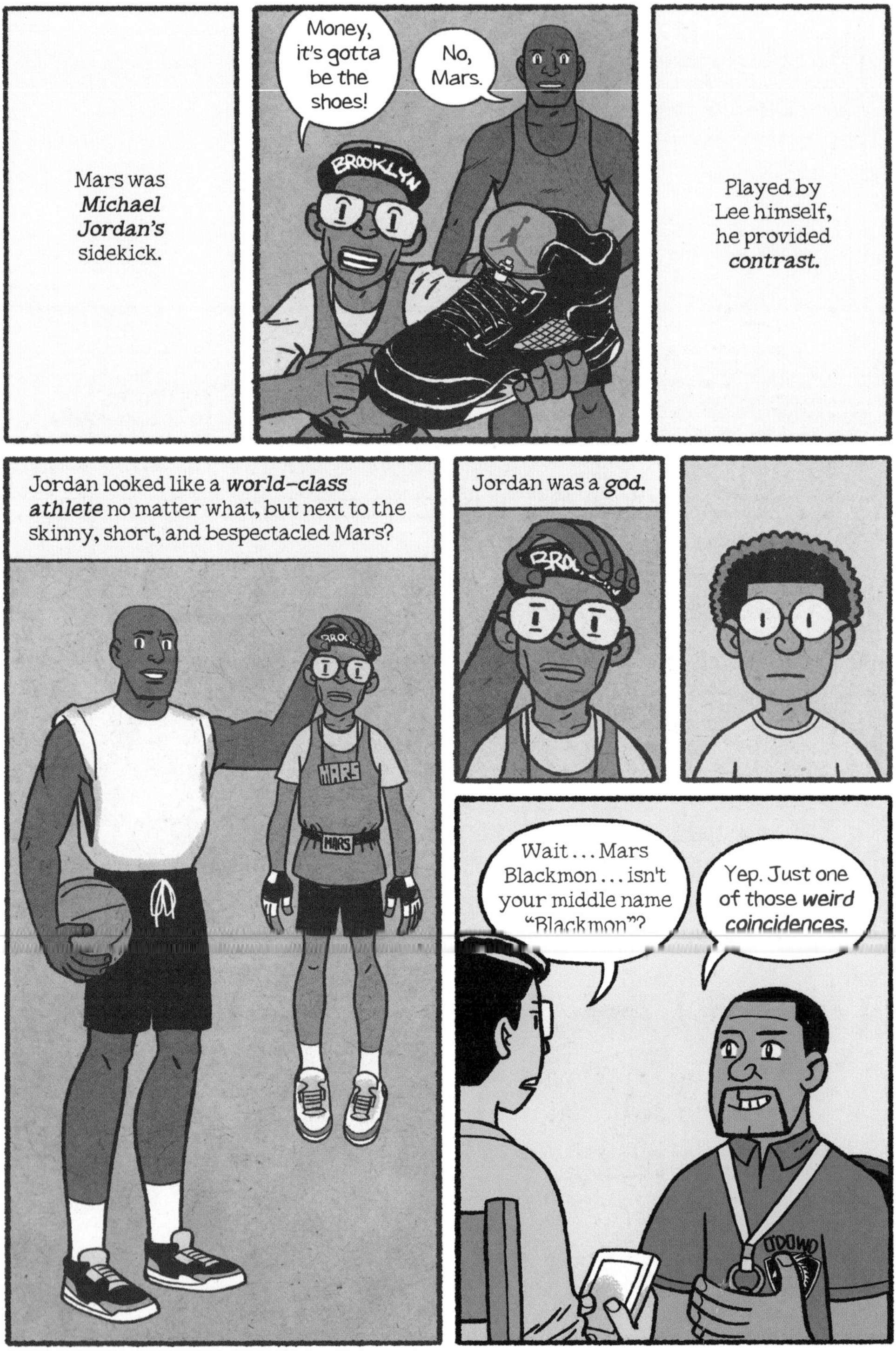

Mars was Michael Jordan's sidekick.
Money, it's gotta be the shoes!
No, Mars.
BROOKLYN
Played by Lee himself, he provided contrast.
Jordan looked like a world-class athlete no matter what, but next to the skinny, short, and bespectacled Mars?
MARS
MARS
Jordan was a god.
Wait . . . Mars Blackmon . . . isn't your middle name "Blackmon"?
Yep. Just one of those weird coincidences.

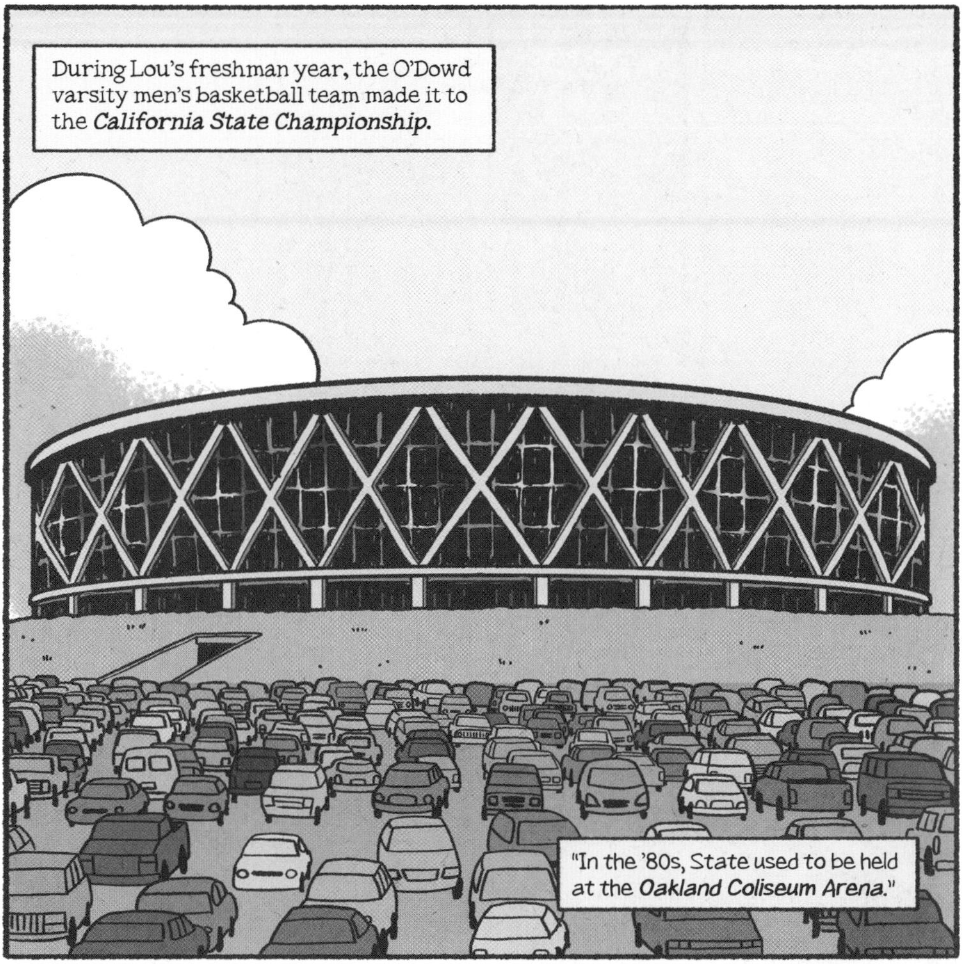
During Lou's freshman year, the O'Dowd varsity men's basketball team made it to the *California State Championship.*
"In the '80s, State used to be held at the *Oakland Coliseum Arena.*"

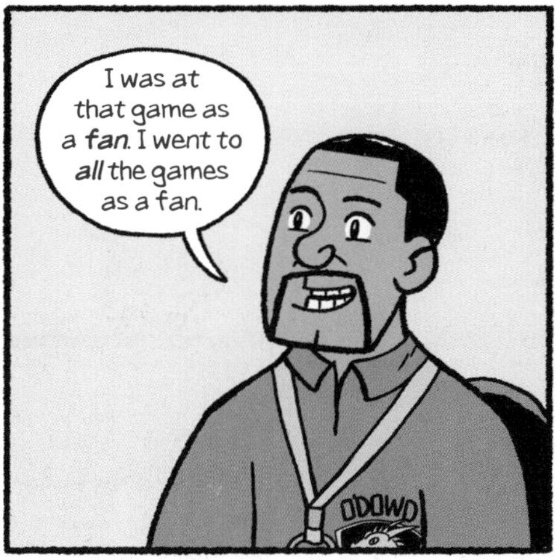
I was at that game as a **fan**. I went to ***all*** the games as a fan.
O'DOWD

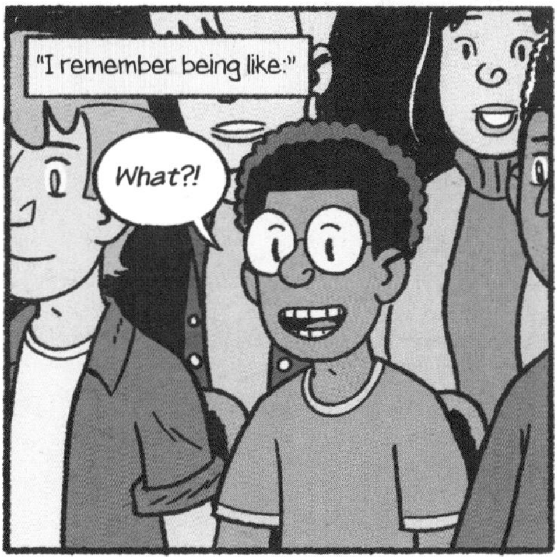
"I remember being like:"
What?!

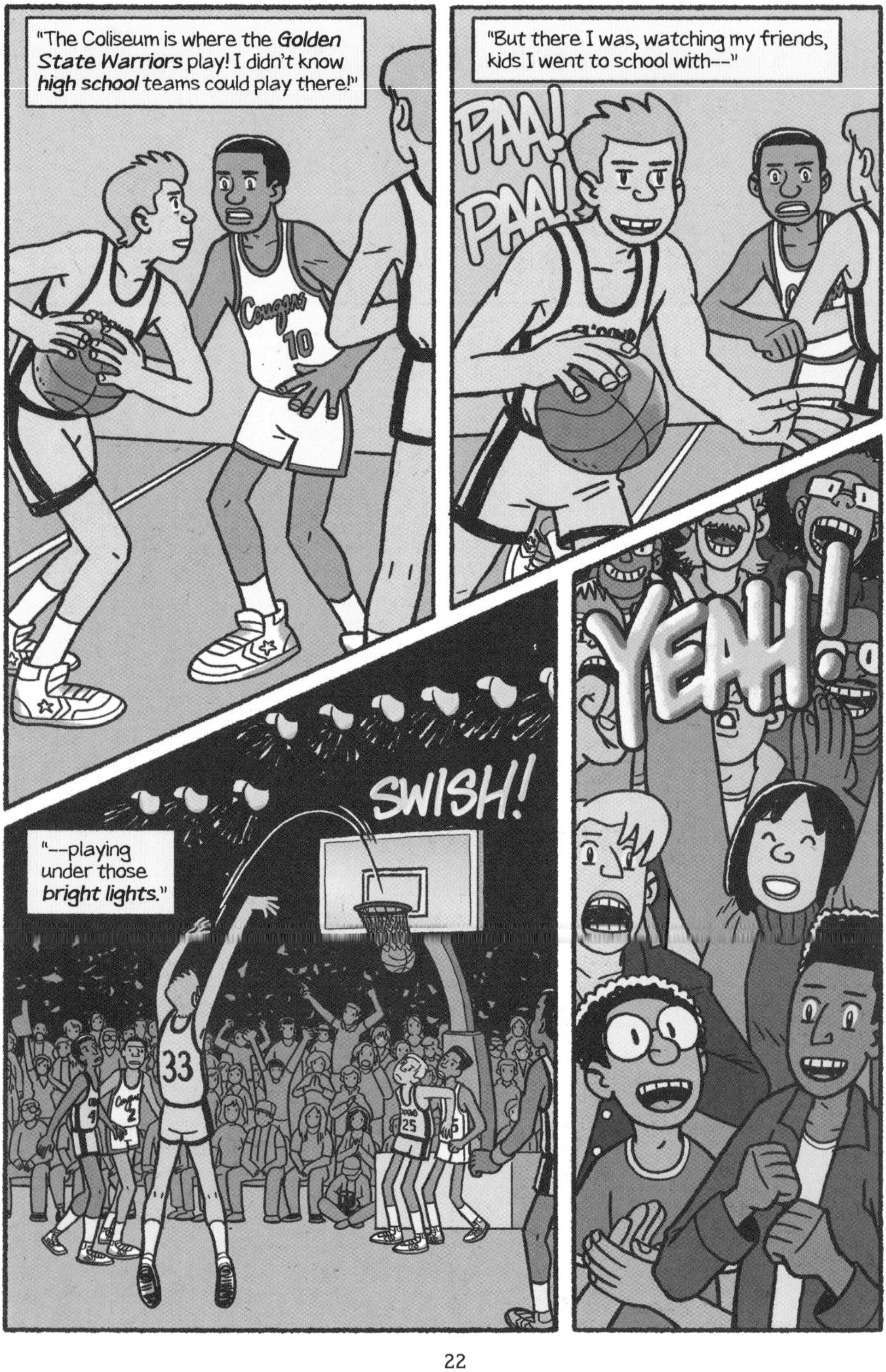
"The Coliseum is where the ***Golden State Warriors*** play! I didn't know ***high school*** teams could play there!"
Cougars
10
"But there I was, watching my friends, kids I went to school with--"
PAA!
PAA!
SWISH!
"--playing under those ***bright lights***."
33
25
YEAH!

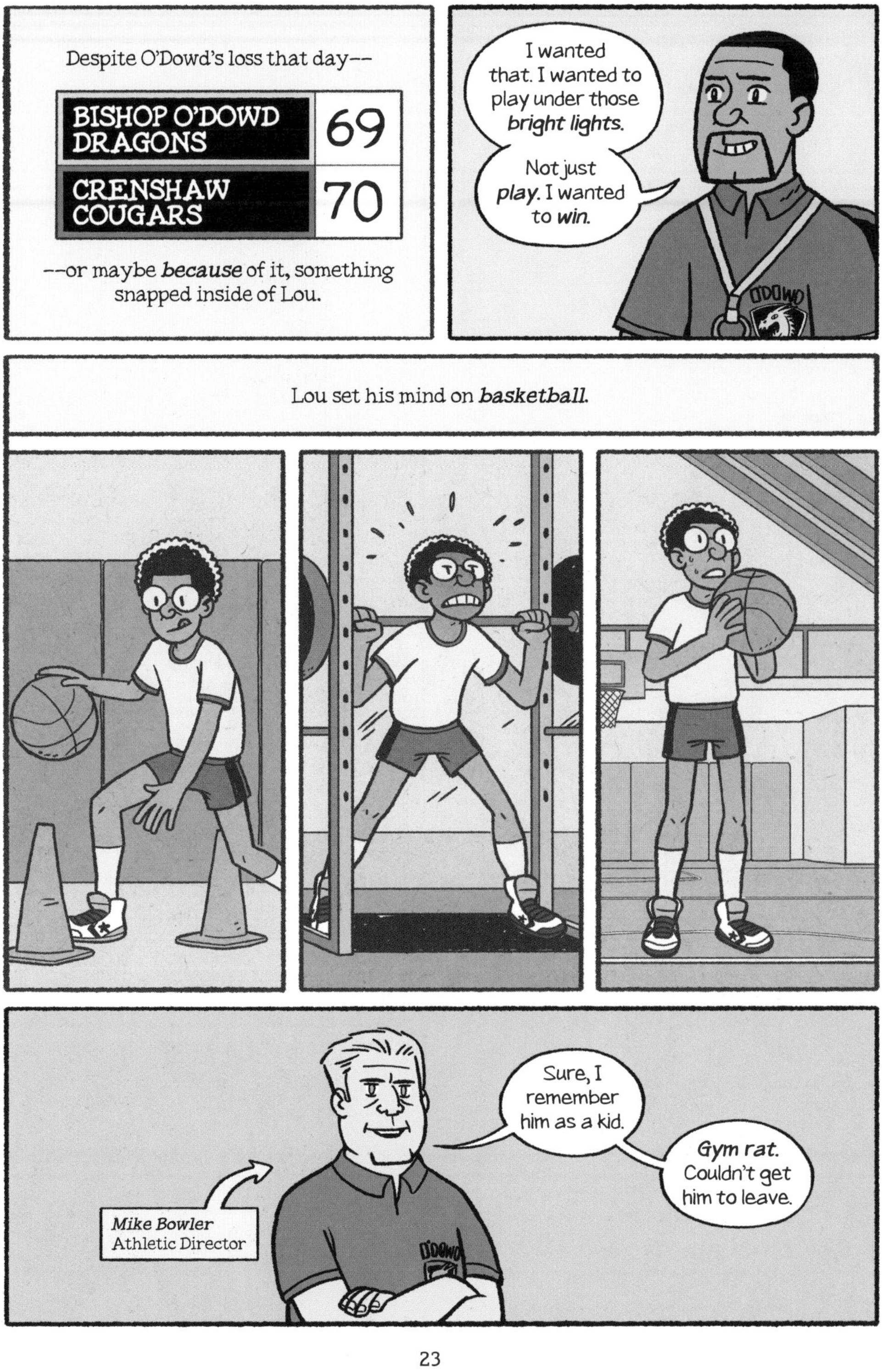

Despite O'Dowd's loss that day--
BISHOP O'DOWD DRAGONS 69
CRENSHAW COUGARS 70
--or maybe *because* of it, something snapped inside of Lou.
I wanted that. I wanted to play under those *bright lights*.
Not just *play*. I wanted to *win*.
O'DOWD
Lou set his mind on *basketball*.
Mike Bowler
Athletic Director
Sure, I remember him as a kid.
Gym rat. Couldn't get him to leave.

His hard work paid off.

By his junior year, Lou had grown a few inches taller and a whole lot stronger.

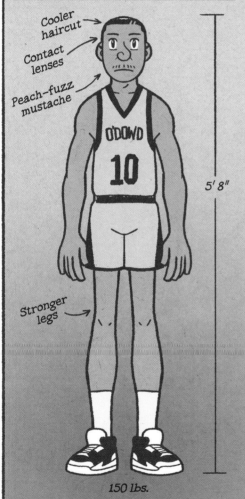

Cooler haircut

Contact lenses

Peach-fuzz mustache

O'DOWD 10

5' 8"

Stronger legs

150 lbs.

He'd earned a place on the varsity squad as a backup point guard.

He and his teammates fought hard all season long.

They made it.

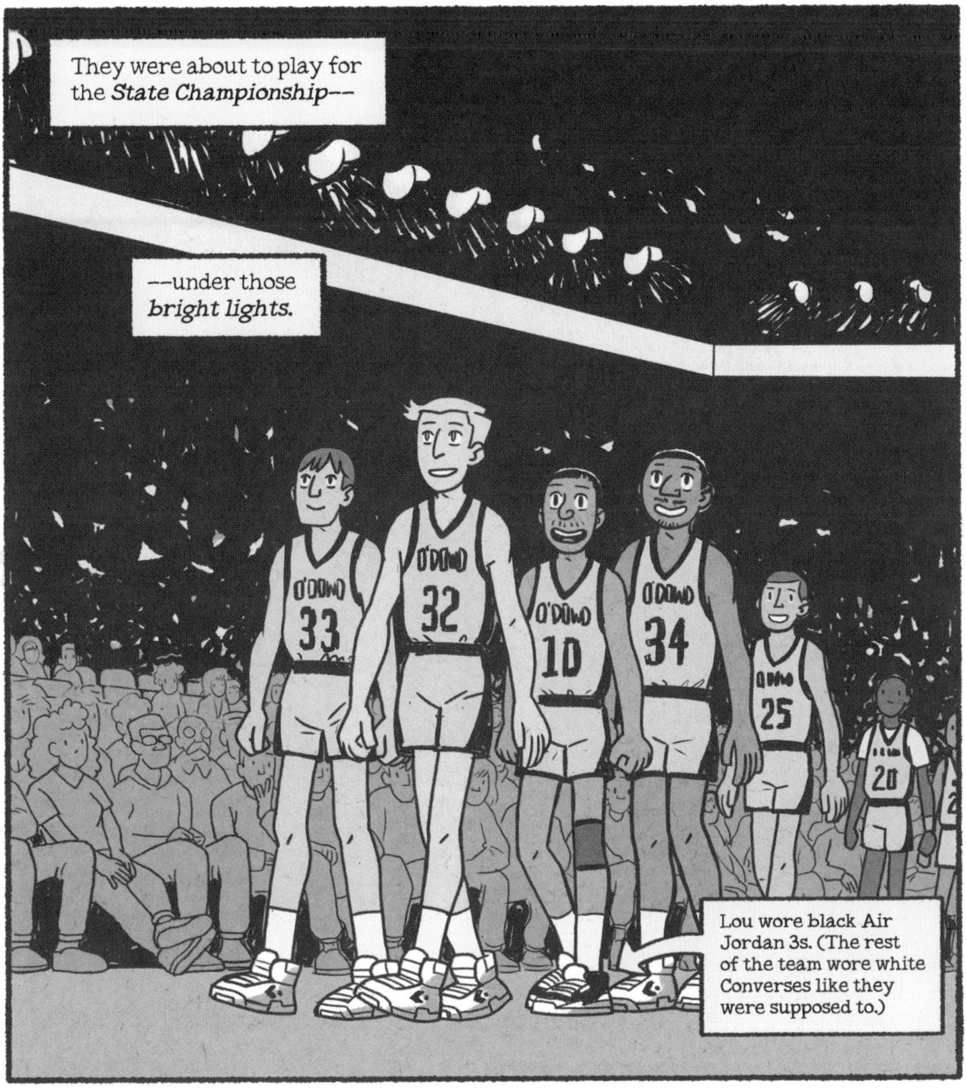
They were about to play for the *State Championship*--
--under those *bright lights.*
O'DOWD 33
O'DOWD 32
O'DOWD 10
O'DOWD 34
O'DOWD 25
20
Lou wore black Air Jordan 3s. (The rest of the team wore white Converses like they were supposed to.)

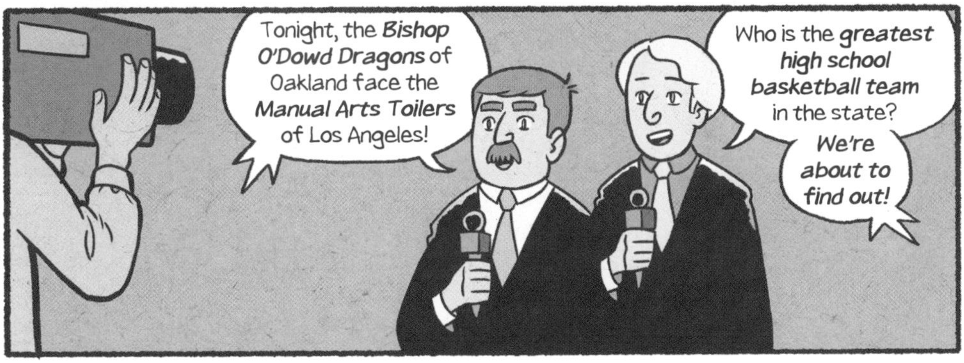
Tonight, the *Bishop O'Dowd Dragons* of Oakland face the *Manual Arts Toilers* of Los Angeles!
Who is the ***greatest high school basketball team*** in the state?
We're about to find out!

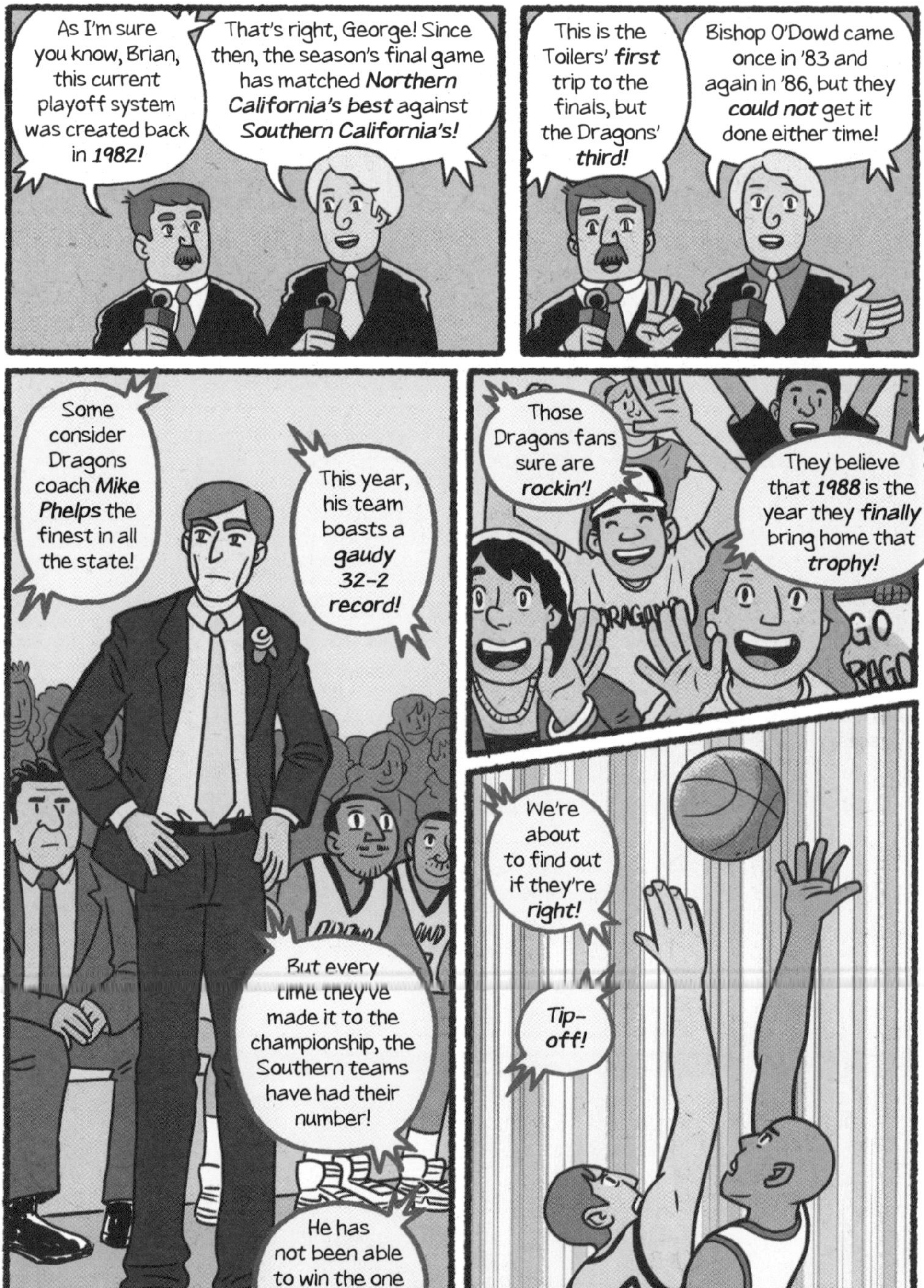
As I'm sure you know, Brian, this current playoff system was created back in *1982!*
That's right, George! Since then, the season's final game has matched ***Northern California's best*** against ***Southern California's!***
This is the Toilers' ***first*** trip to the finals, but the Dragons' ***third!***
Bishop O'Dowd came once in '83 and again in '86, but they ***could not*** get it done either time!
Some consider Dragons coach ***Mike Phelps*** the finest in all the state!
This year, his team boasts a ***gaudy 32–2 record!***
But every time they've made it to the championship, the Southern teams have had their number!
He has not been able to win the one game that counts ***most!***
Those Dragons fans sure are ***rockin'!***
They believe that ***1988*** is the year they ***finally*** bring home that ***trophy!***
We're about to find out if they're ***right!***
Tip-off!

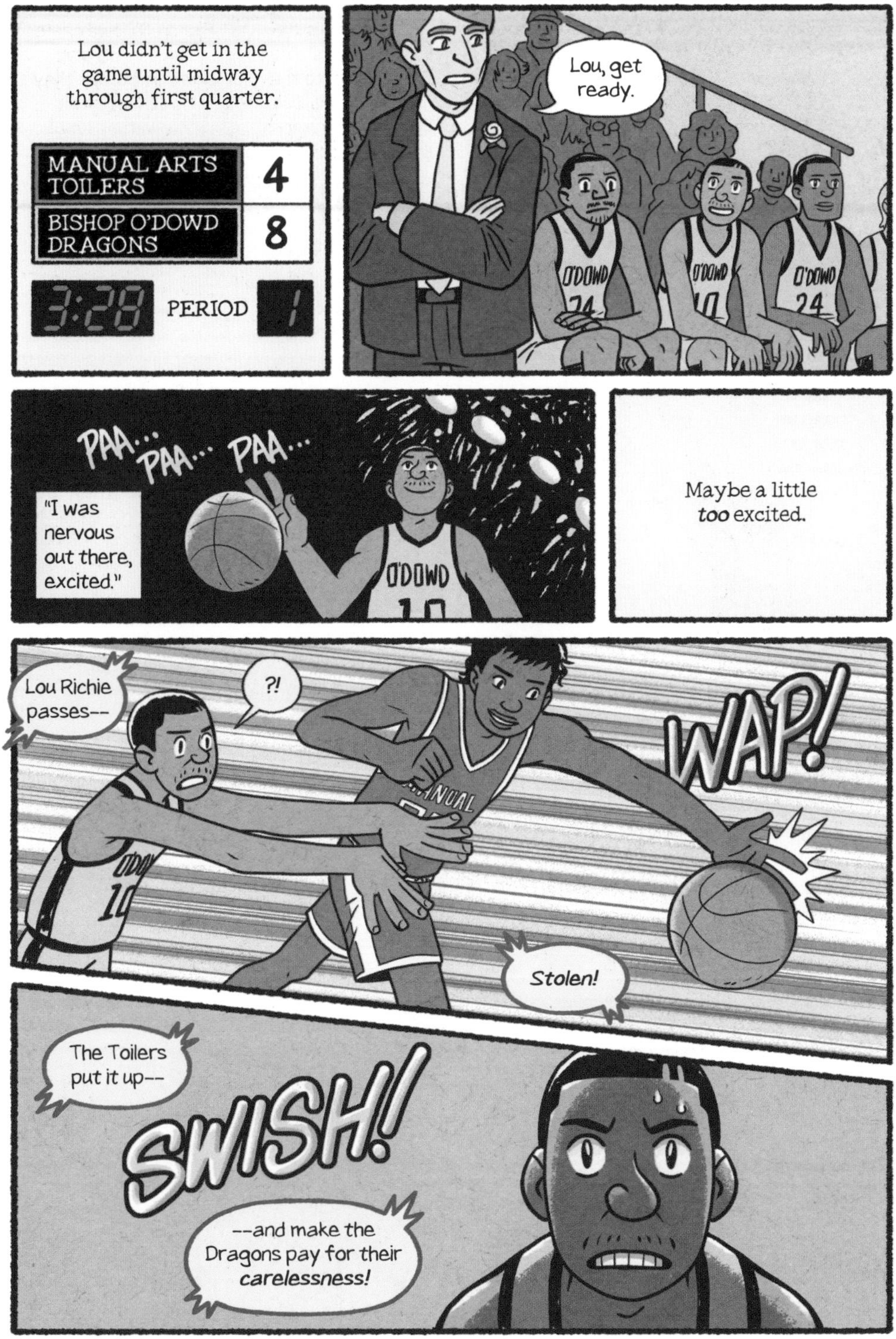
Lou didn't get in the game until midway through first quarter.
MANUAL ARTS TOILERS 4
BISHOP O'DOWD DRAGONS 8
3:28 PERIOD 1
Lou, get ready.
O'DOWD 24
O'DOWD 10
O'DOWD 24
PAA... PAA... PAA...
"I was nervous out there, excited."
O'DOWD 10
Maybe a little *too* excited.
Lou Richie passes--
?!
WAP!
Stolen!
The Toilers put it up--
SWISH!
--and make the Dragons pay for their *carelessness!*

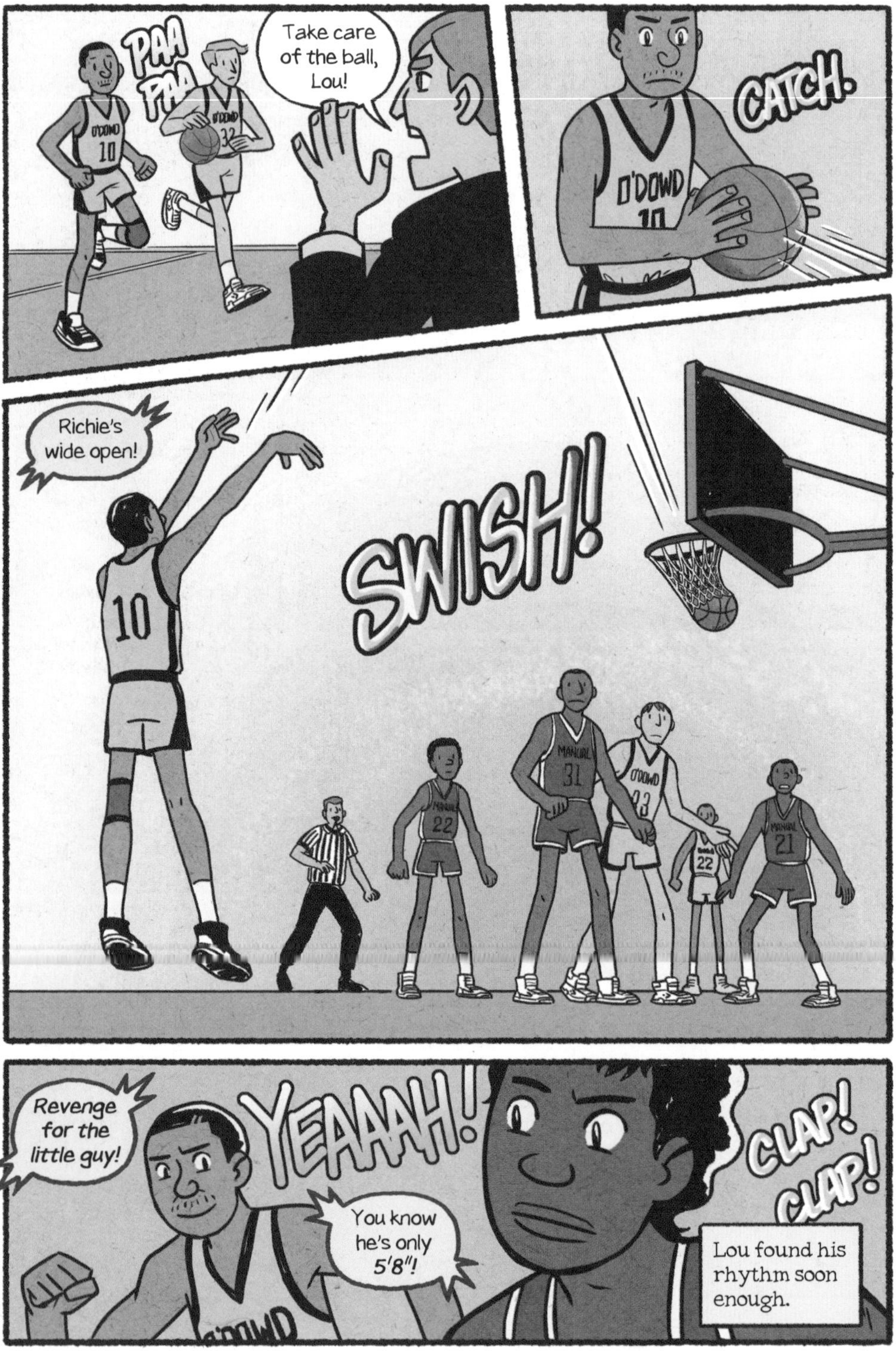
PAA PAA
Take care of the ball, Lou!
O'DOWD
CATCH.
Richie's wide open!
SWISH!
MANUAL
O'DOWD
Revenge for the little guy!
YEAAAH!
You know he's only 5'8"!
CLAP! CLAP!
Lou found his rhythm soon enough.

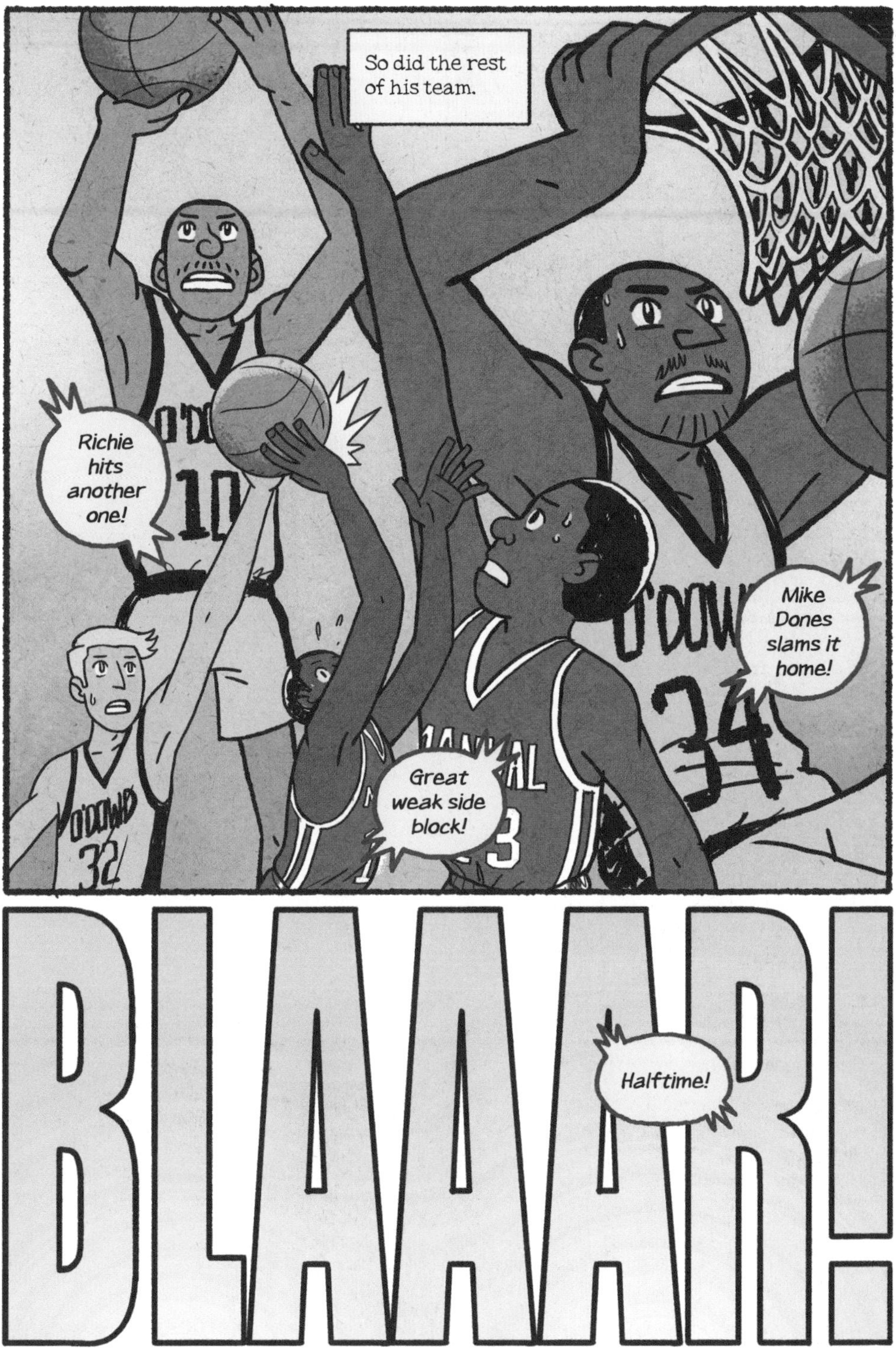
So did the rest of his team.
Richie hits another one!
Mike Dones slams it home!
Great weak side block!
BLAAAR!
Halftime!

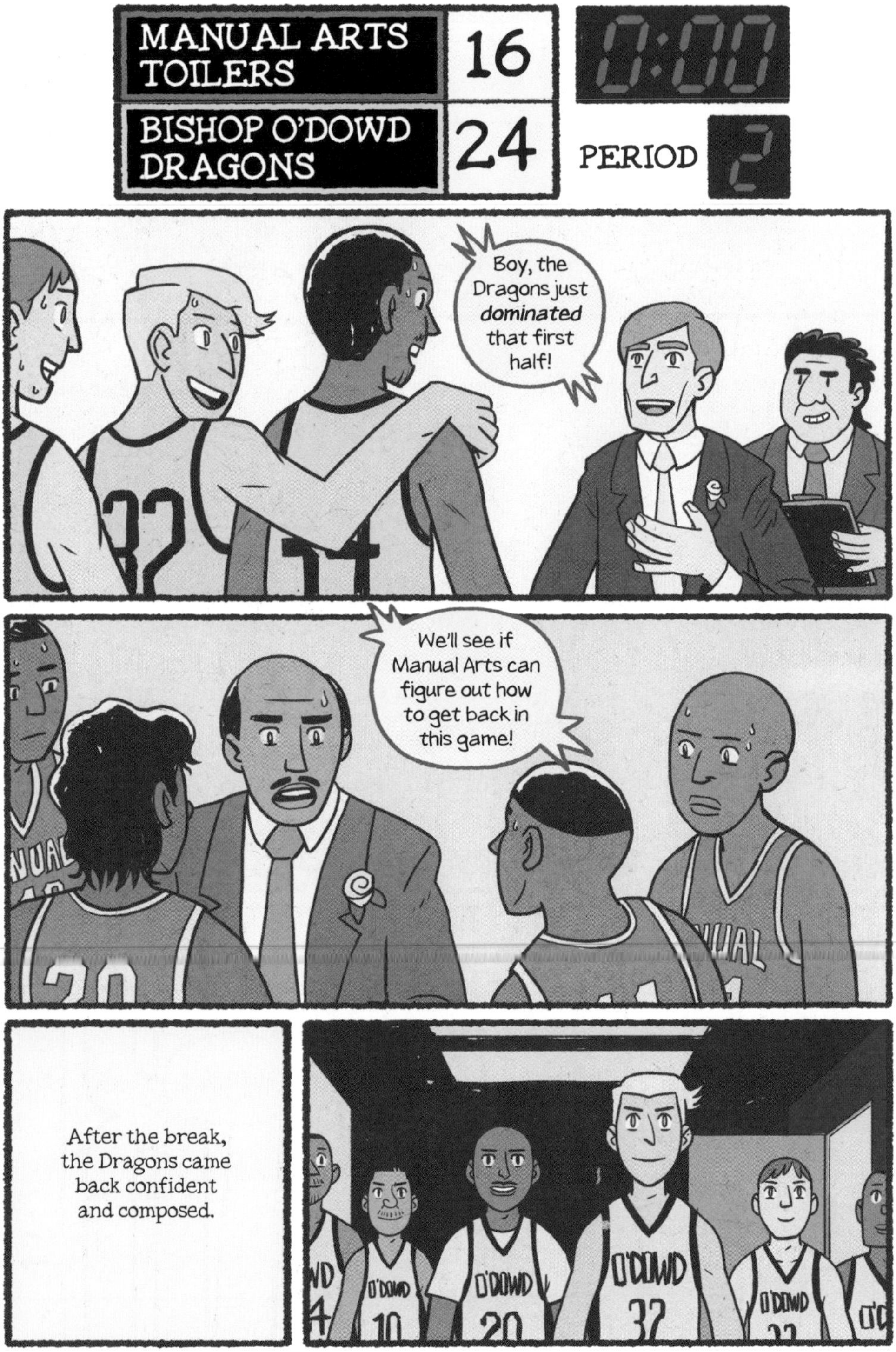
MANUAL ARTS TOILERS
16
BISHOP O'DOWD DRAGONS
24
0:00
PERIOD
2
Boy, the Dragons just *dominated* that first half!
We'll see if Manual Arts can figure out how to get back in this game!
After the break, the Dragons came back confident and composed.

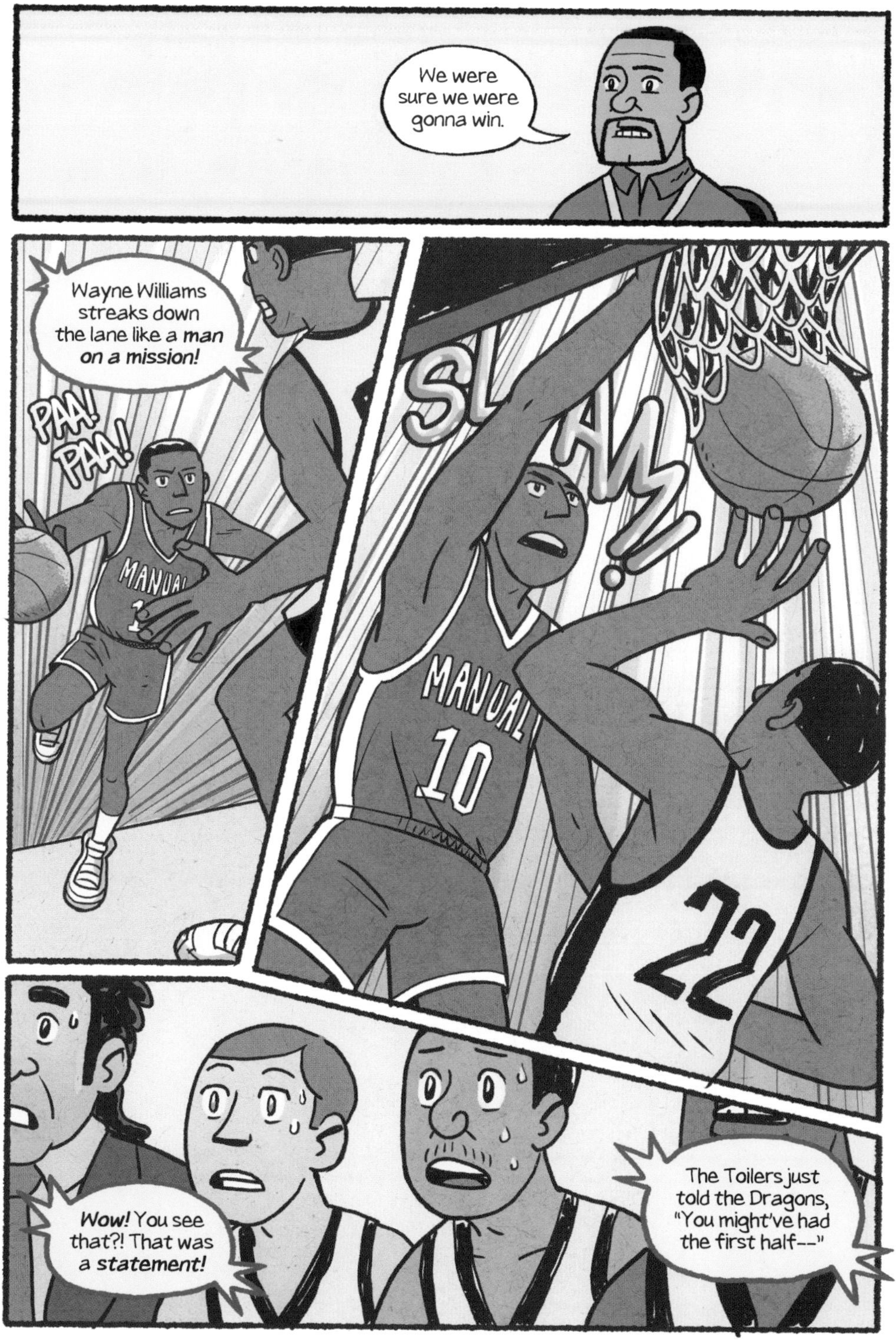
We were sure we were gonna win.
Wayne Williams streaks down the lane like a *man on a mission!*
PAA! PAA!
MANUAL 1
SLAM!!
MANUAL 10
22
Wow! You see that?! That was a *statement!*
The Toilers just told the Dragons, "You might've had the first half--"

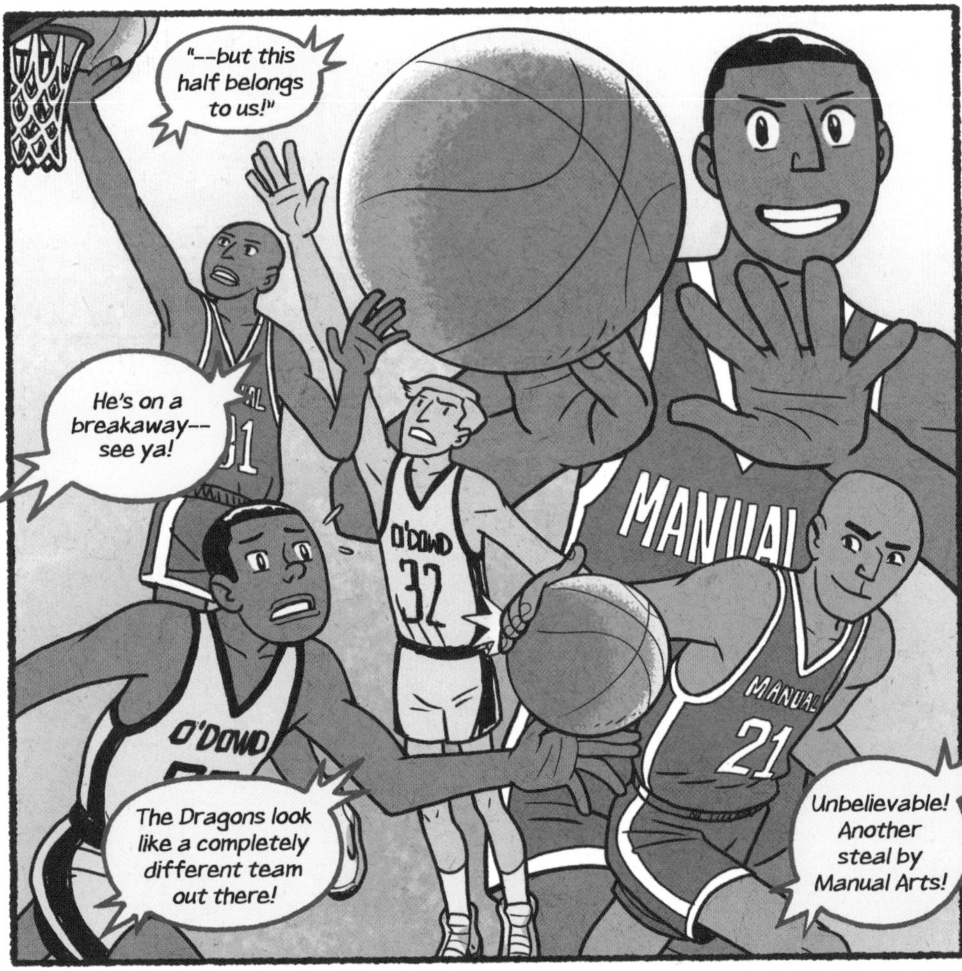
"--but this half belongs to us!"
He's on a breakaway-- see ya!
MANUAL
O'DOWD
32
MANUAL
21
O'DOWD
The Dragons look like a completely different team out there!
Unbelievable! Another steal by Manual Arts!

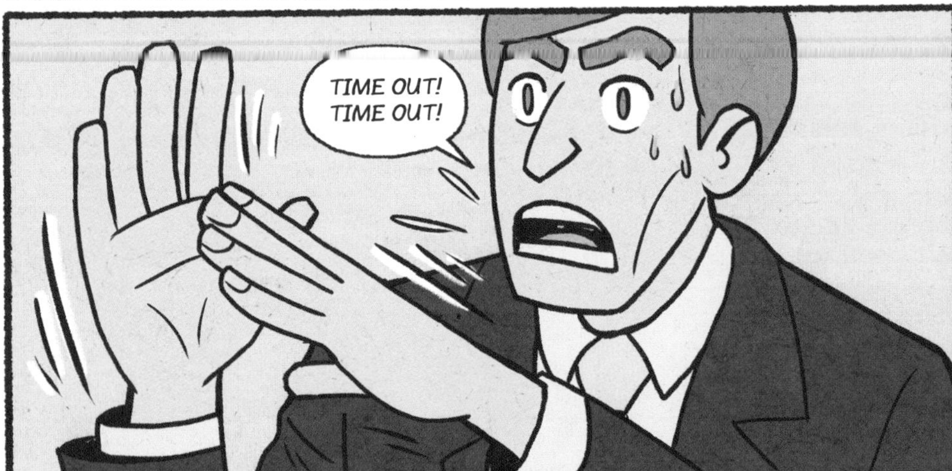
TIME OUT! TIME OUT!

MANUAL ARTS TOILERS	54
BISHOP O'DOWD DRAGONS	53

0:07

PERIOD 4

My good-ness!

What a game!

This is it, gentlemen! Every practice, every game, every *ounce of sweat* we've poured into this season--

--it all comes down to these *last seven seconds!*

Get that ball *inbounds!* Don't let 'em *touch it!* Then whoever gets it--

--*make something happen!*

33

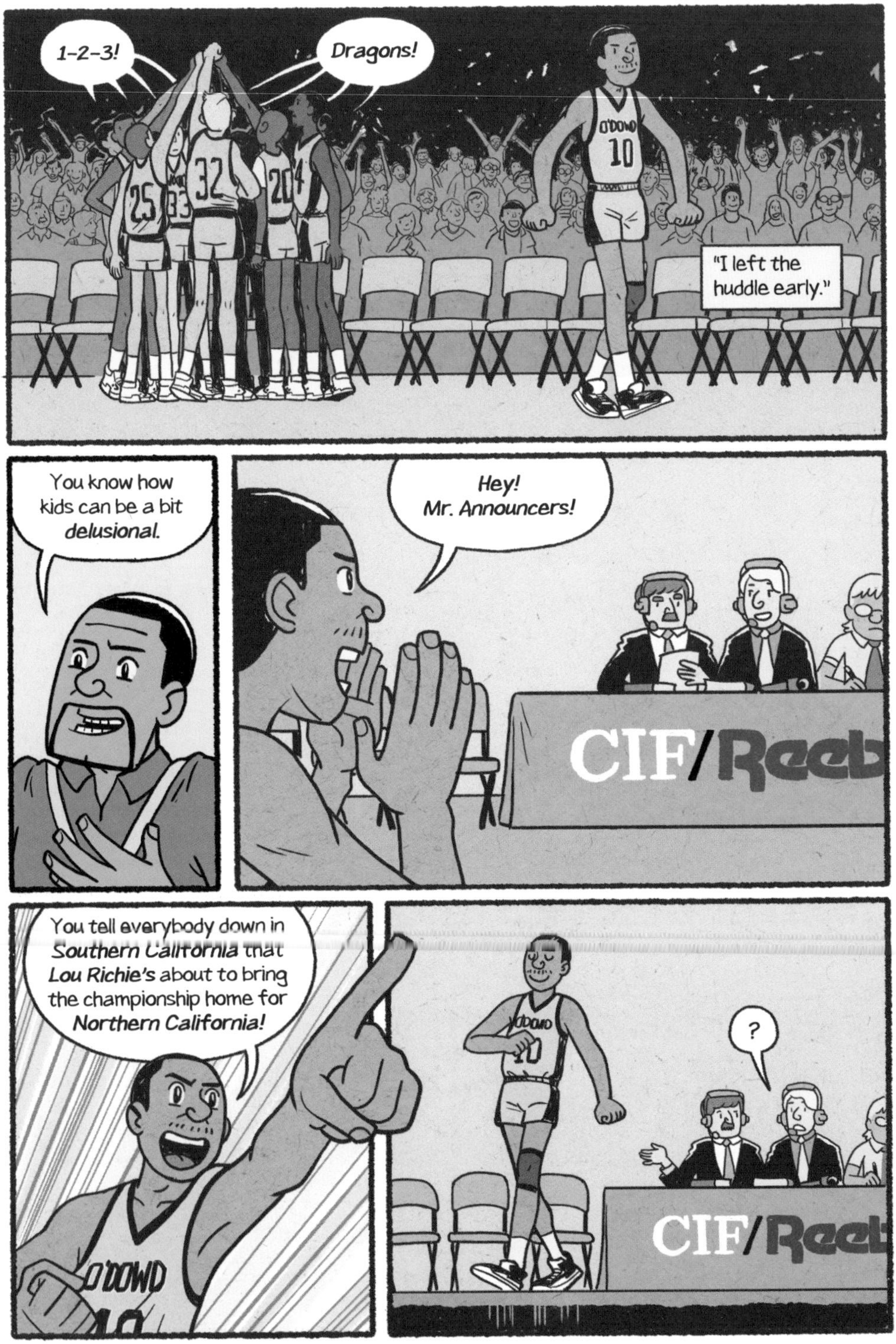
1-2-3!
Dragons!
"I left the huddle early."
You know how kids can be a bit delusional.
Hey! Mr. Announcers!
CIF/Reeb
You tell everybody down in Southern California that Lou Richie's about to bring the championship home for Northern California!
?
CIF/Reeb

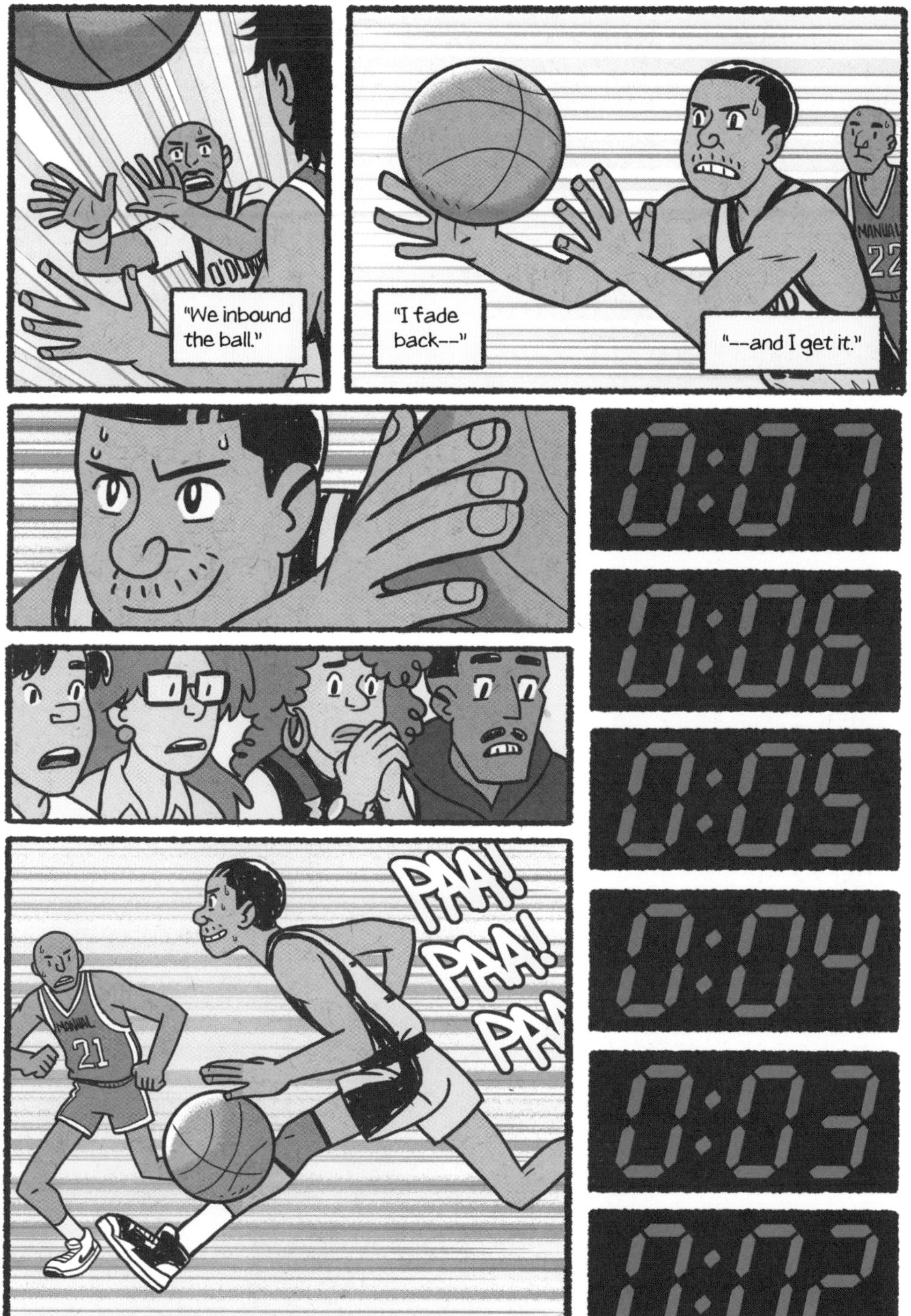
"We inbound the ball."
"I fade back--"
MANUAL
22
"--and I get it."
0:07
0:06
0:05
0:04
0:03
0:02
MANUAL
21
PAA!
PAA!

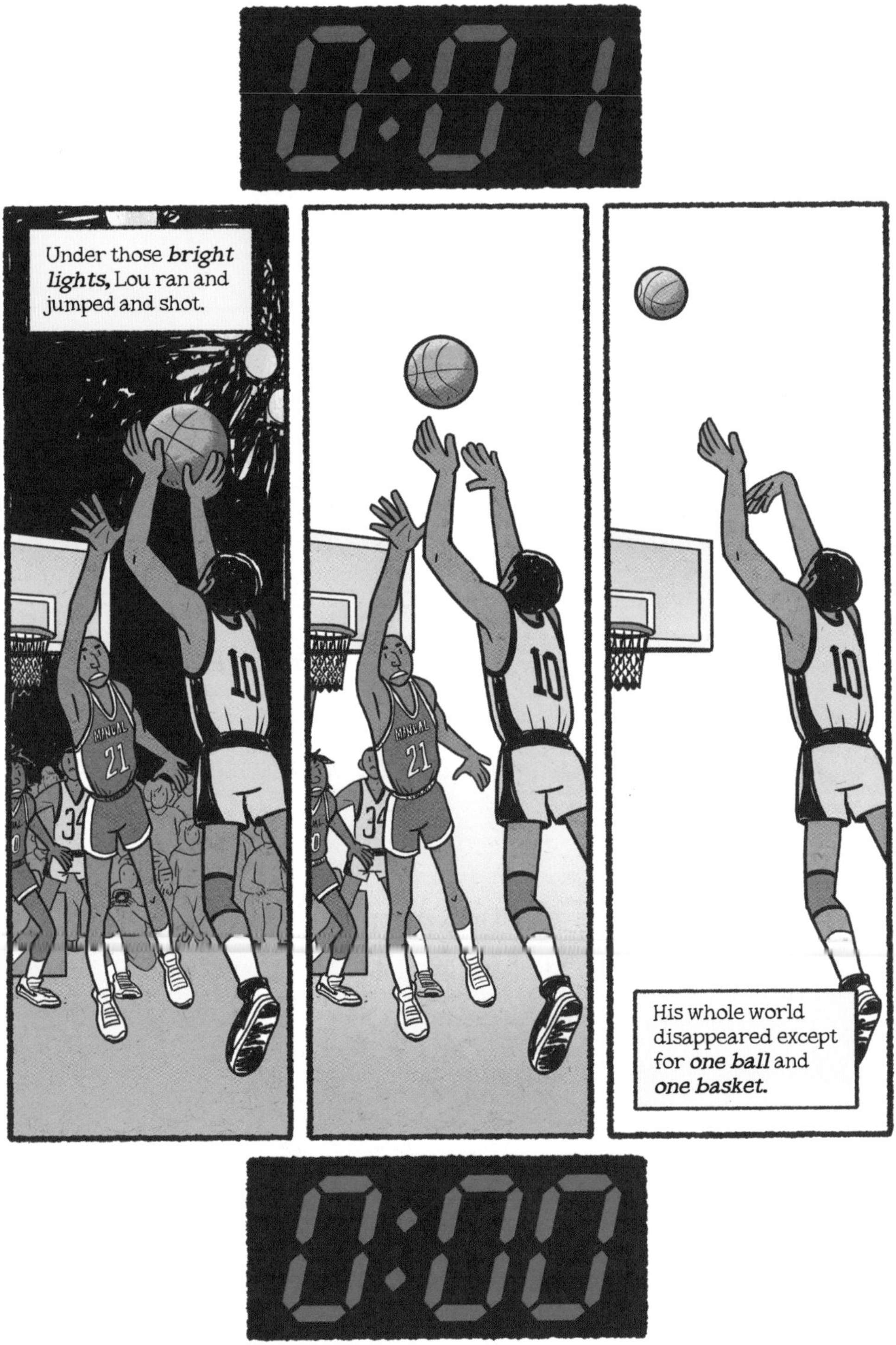
0:01
Under those *bright lights,* Lou ran and jumped and shot.
10
21
34
10
21
34
10
His whole world disappeared except for *one ball* and *one basket.*
0:00

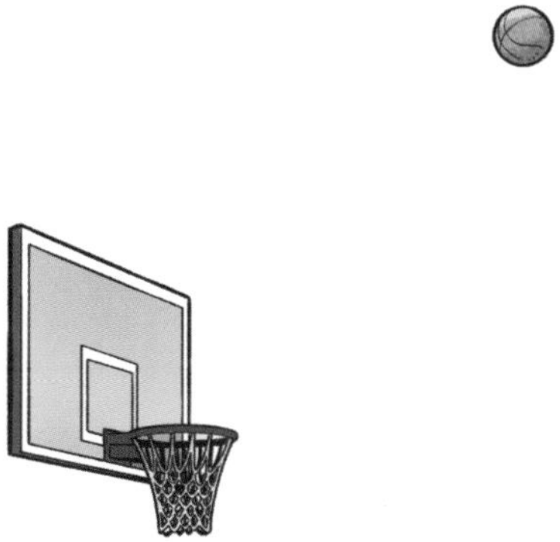

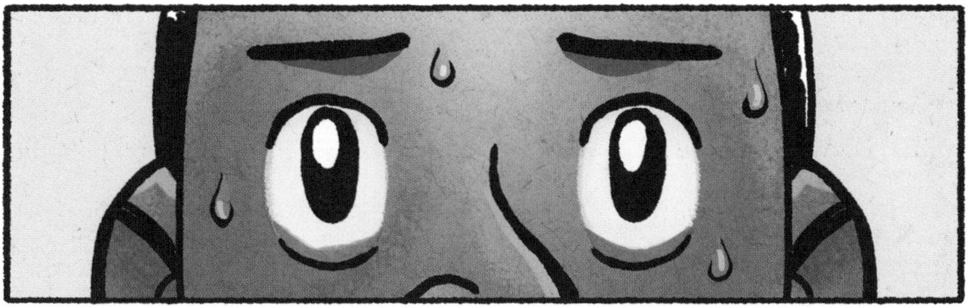

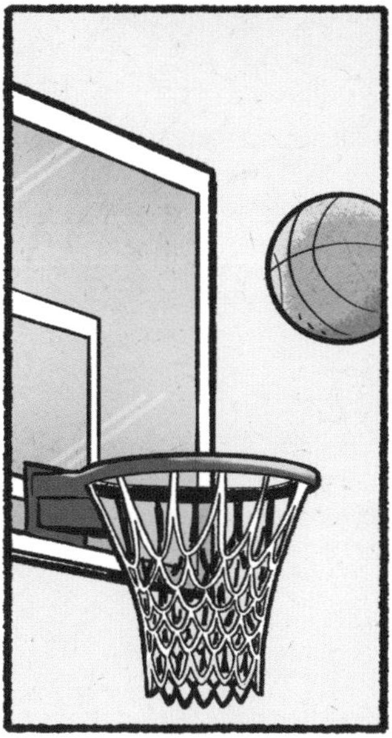

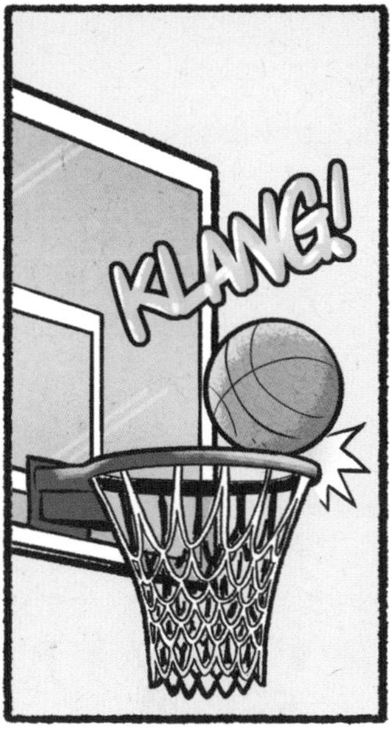
KLANG!

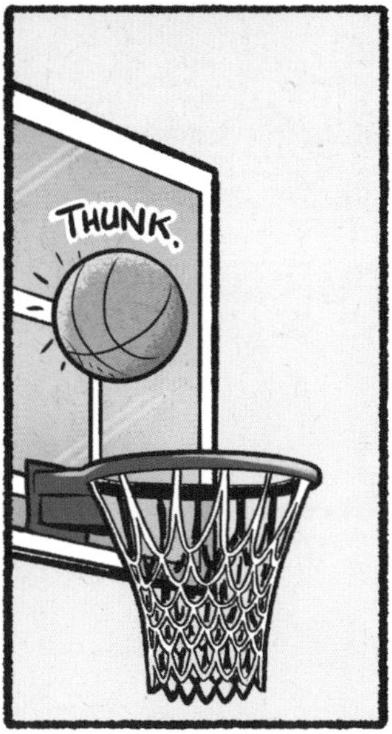
THUNK.

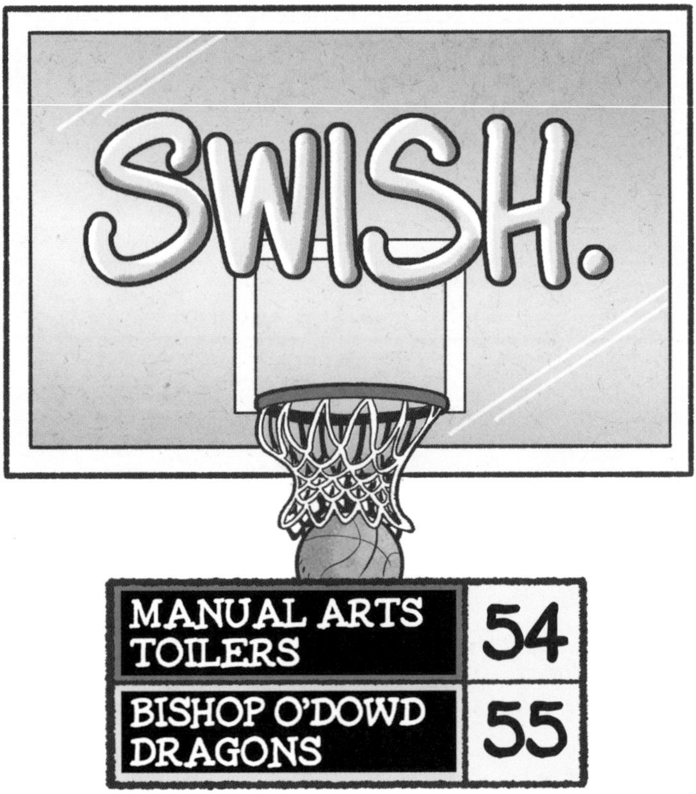
SWISH.
MANUAL ARTS TOILERS 54
BISHOP O'DOWD DRAGONS 55

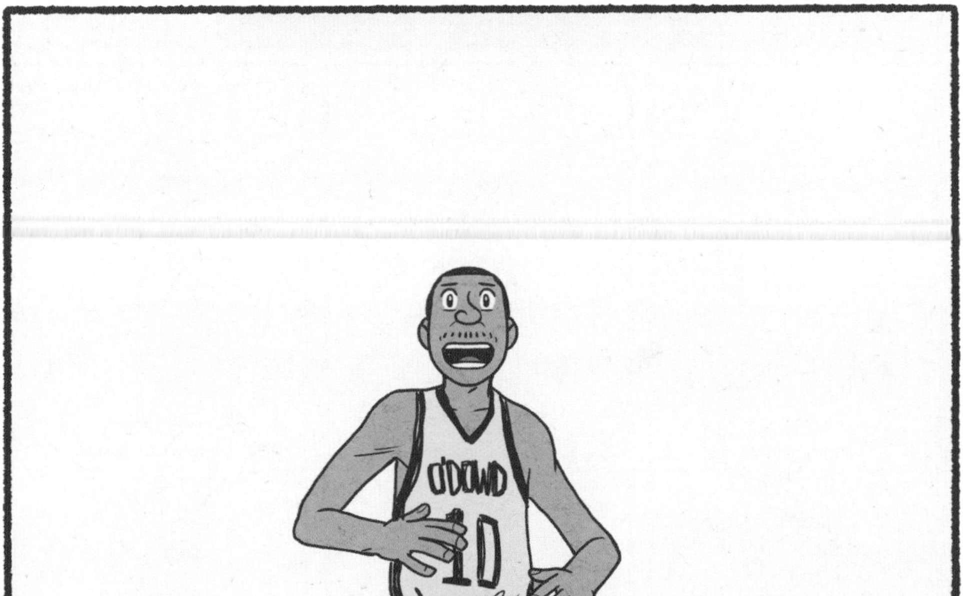
O'DOWD
10

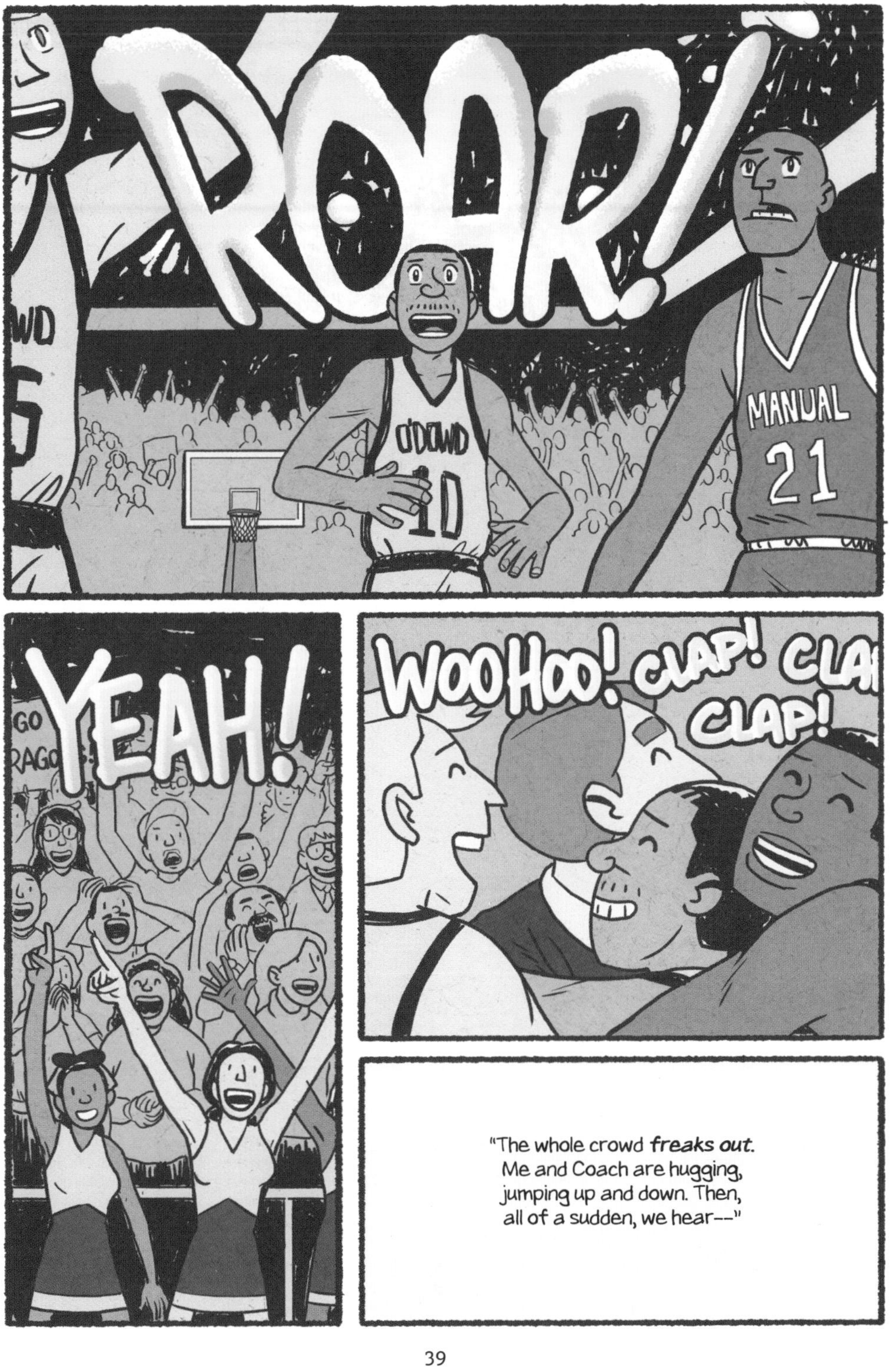
ROAR!
O'DOWD
10
MANUAL
21
YEAH!
WOOHOO!
CLAP! CLA
CLAP!
"The whole crowd **freaks out**.
Me and Coach are hugging,
jumping up and down. Then,
all of a sudden, we hear--"

NO BUCKET! OFFENSIVE GOALTENDING!

In the game of basketball, the *cylindrical space* above the basket is considered *sacred*.

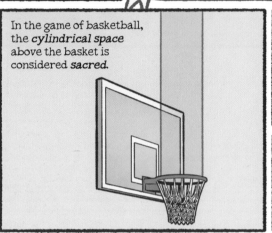

When the ball is there, no *human* is allowed to touch it or the *rim* below it.

The ball is given the chance to decide *fate* on its own.

Unfortunately for the Dragons, there *was* a human hand near-- or possibly even *on*--the rim while the ball was in its sacred space.

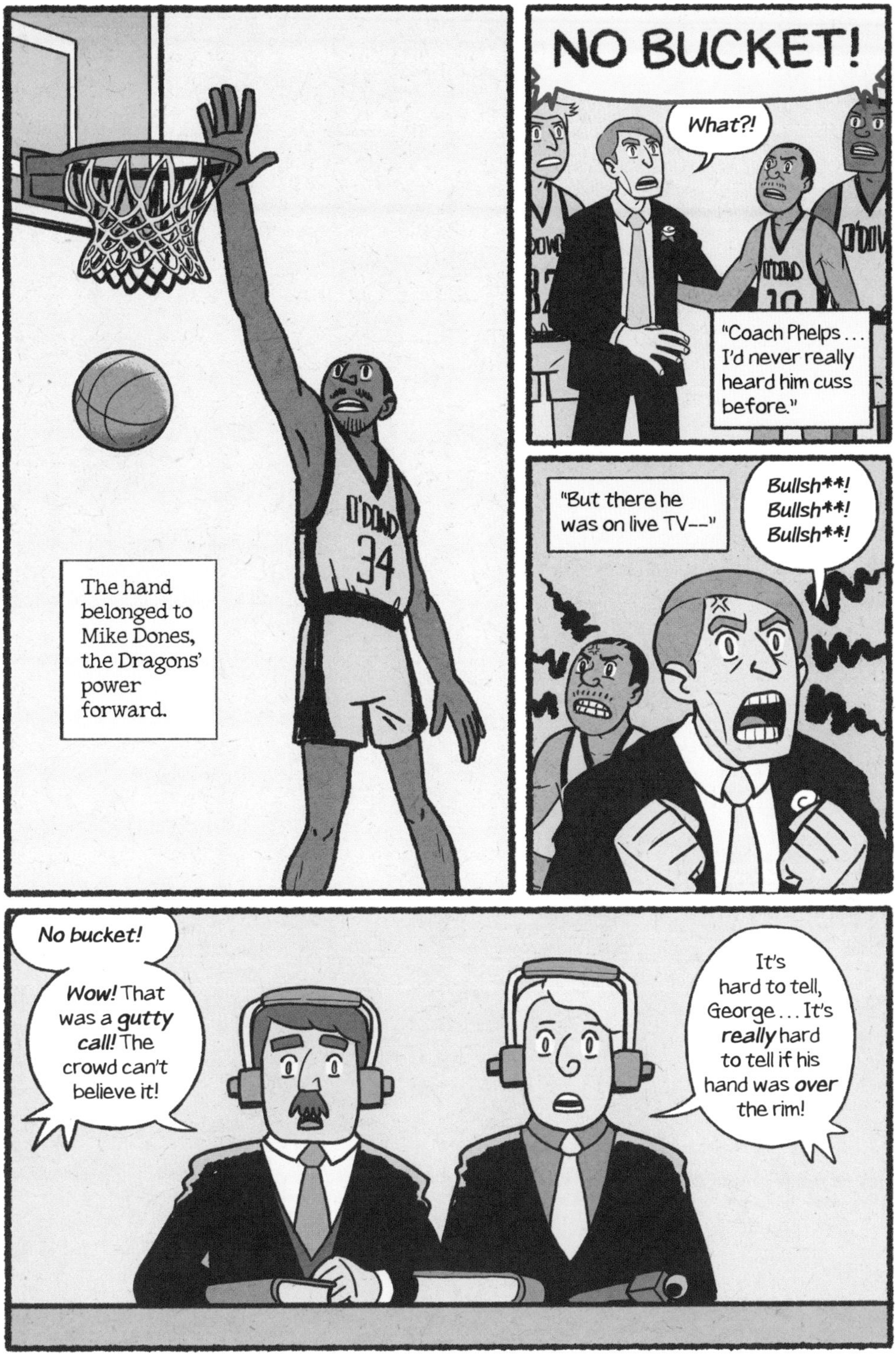
The hand belonged to Mike Dones, the Dragons' power forward.
NO BUCKET!
What?!
"Coach Phelps . . . I'd never really heard him cuss before."
"But there he was on live TV--"
Bullsh**! Bullsh**! Bullsh**!
No bucket!
Wow! That was a gutty call! The crowd can't believe it!
It's hard to tell, George . . . It's really hard to tell if his hand was over the rim!

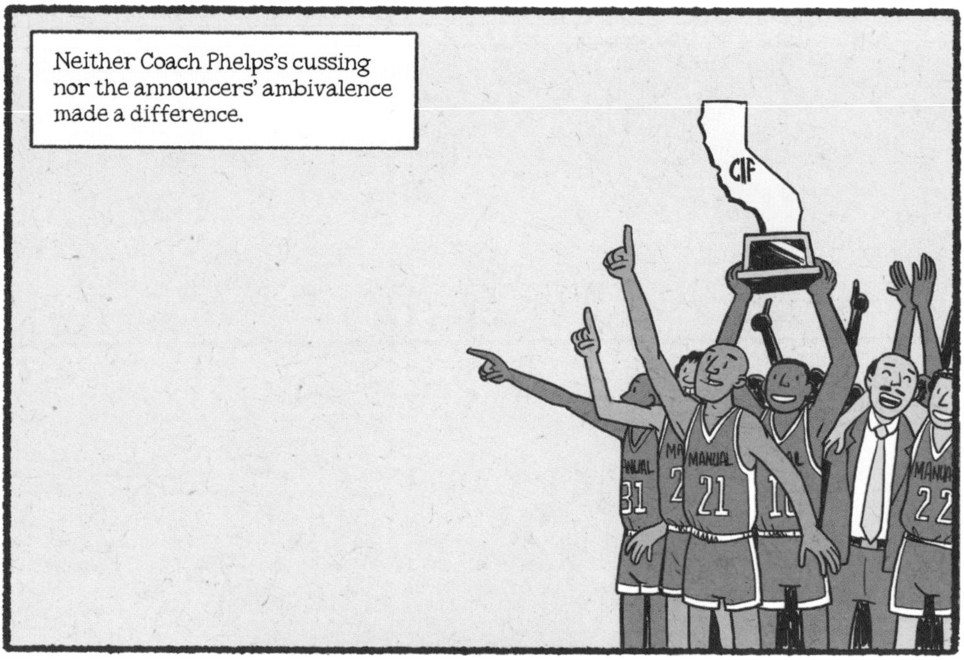
Neither Coach Phelps's cussing nor the announcers' ambivalence made a difference.
CIF
MANUAL
21
22
31

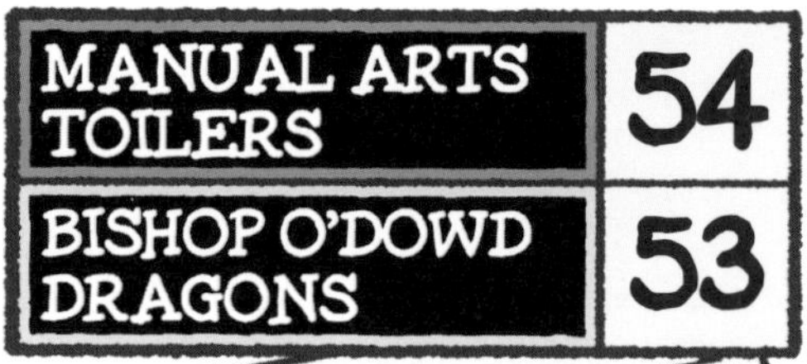
MANUAL ARTS TOILERS
54
BISHOP O'DOWD DRAGONS
53

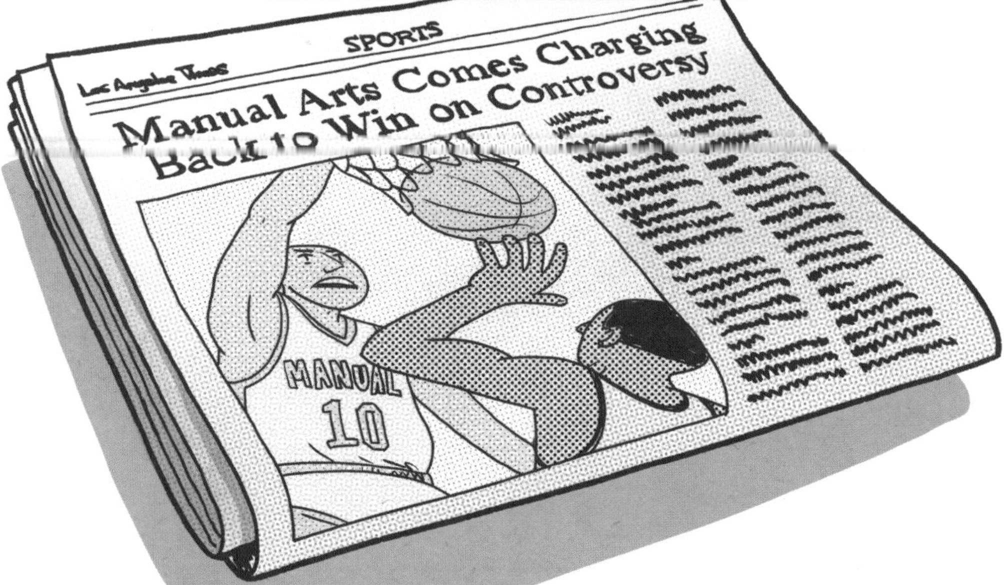
SPORTS
Los Angeles Times
Manual Arts Comes Charging Back to Win on Controversy
MANUAL
10

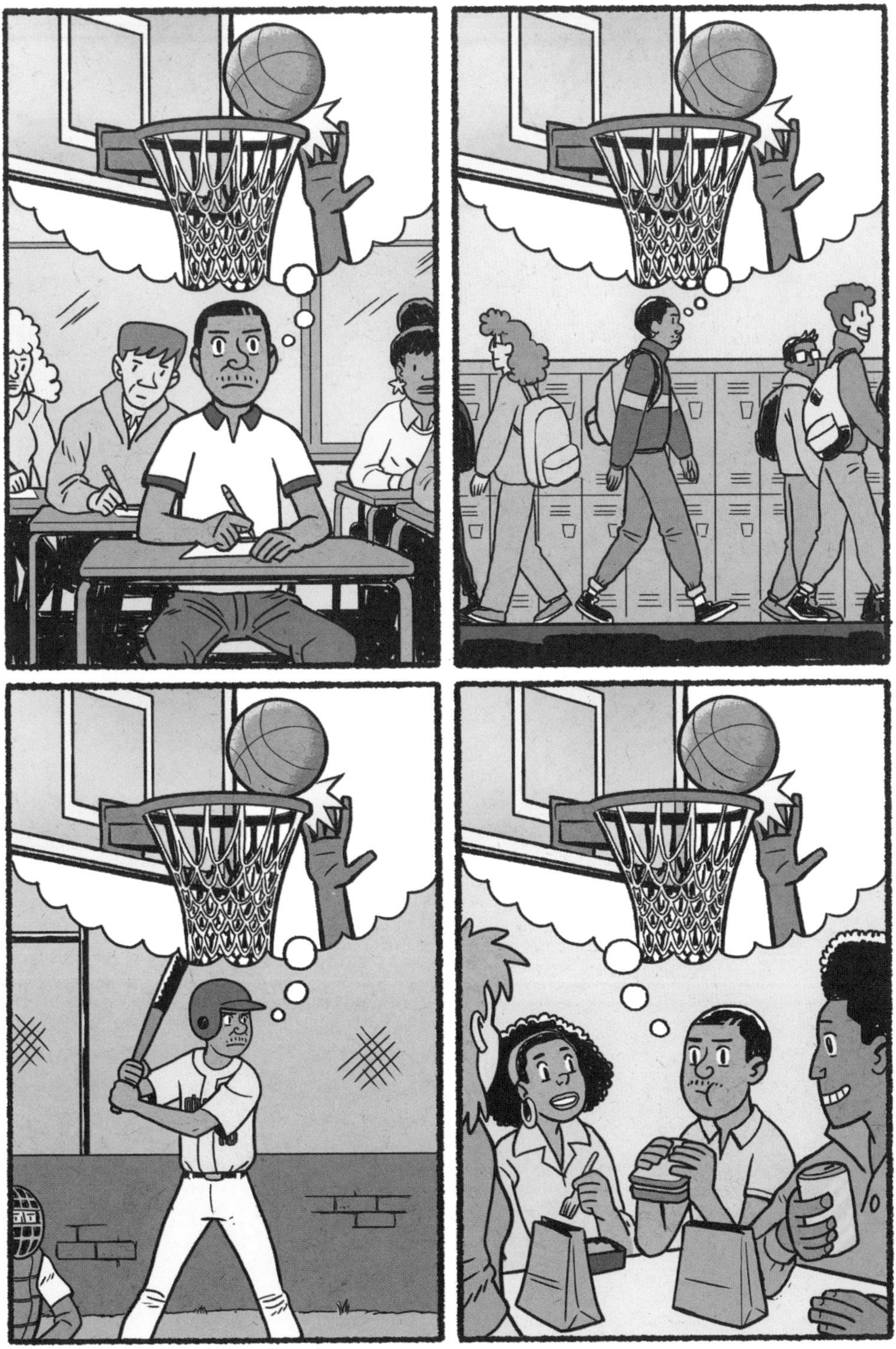

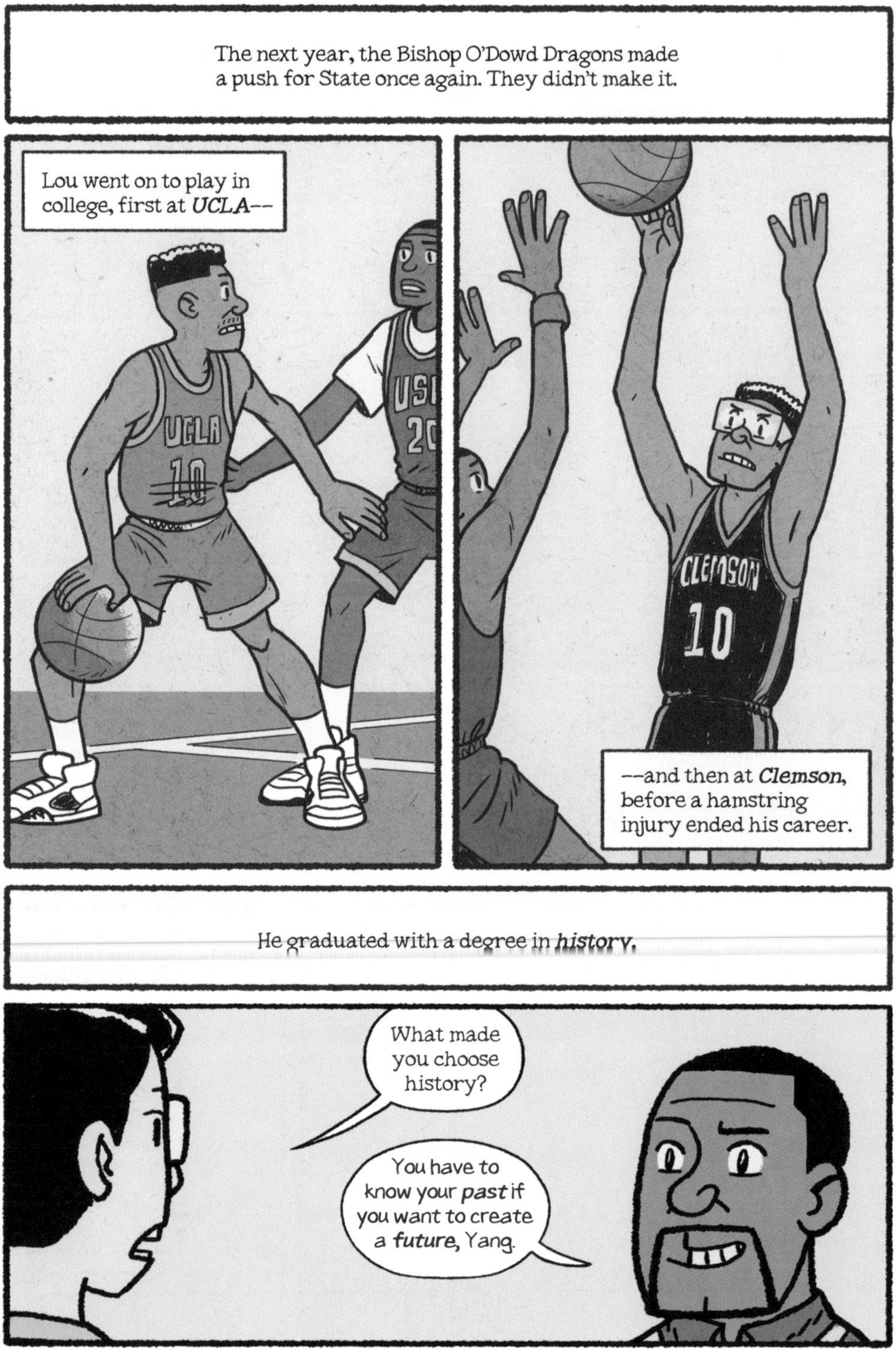

The next year, the Bishop O'Dowd Dragons made a push for State once again. They didn't make it.
Lou went on to play in college, first at *UCLA*--
UCLA 10
USC 20
CLEMSON 10
--and then at *Clemson*, before a hamstring injury ended his career.
He graduated with a degree in ***history***.
What made you choose history?
You have to know your ***past*** if you want to create a ***future***, Yang.

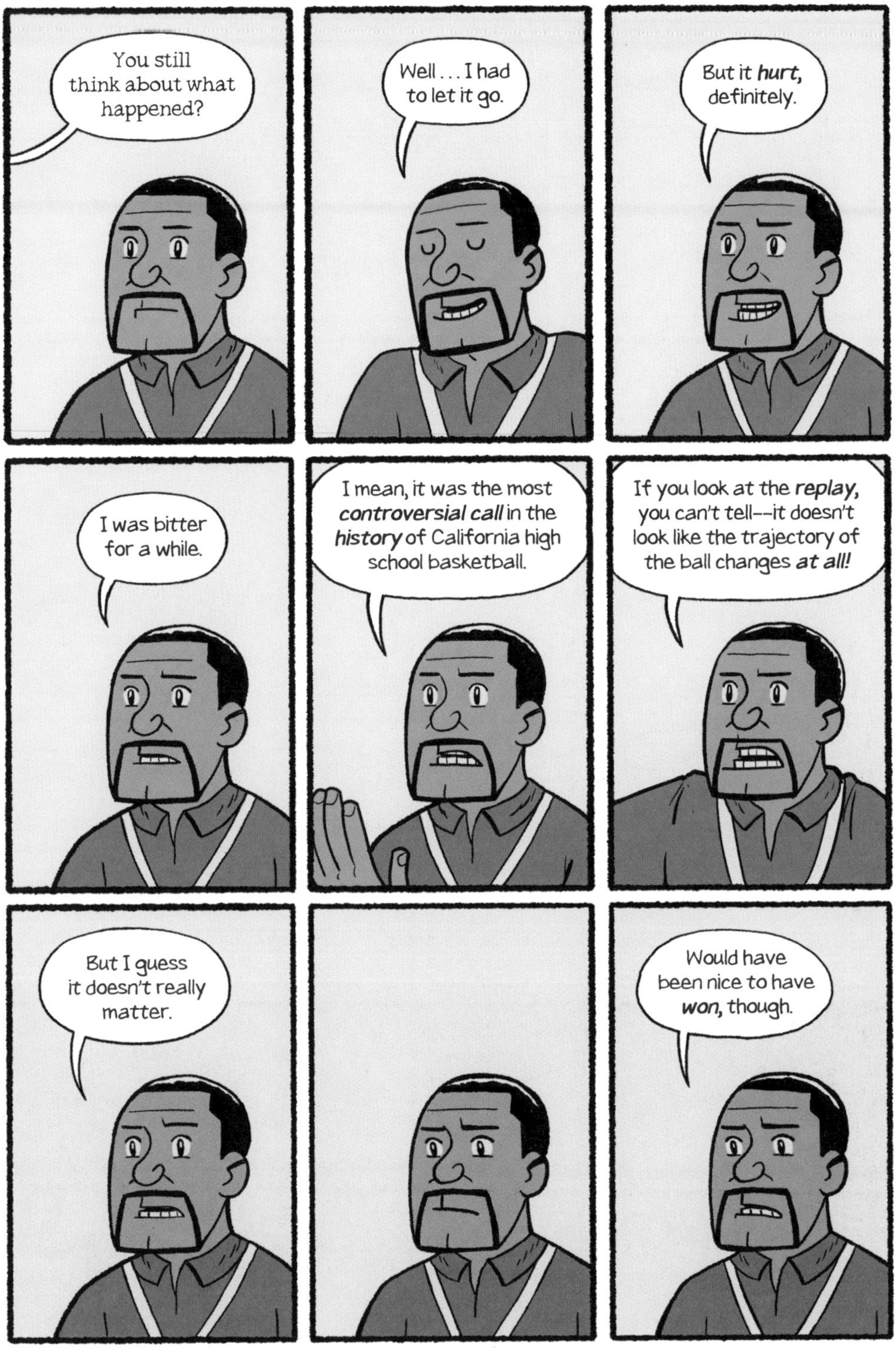
You still think about what happened?
Well . . . I had to let it go.
But it hurt, definitely.
I was bitter for a while.
I mean, it was the most controversial call in the history of California high school basketball.
If you look at the replay, you can't tell--it doesn't look like the trajectory of the ball changes at all!
But I guess it doesn't really matter.
Would have been nice to have won, though.

In the fall of 2001, Lou Richie came back to Bishop O'Dowd High School for the first time in more than a decade.

STEP.

This time, he came as a *coach*.

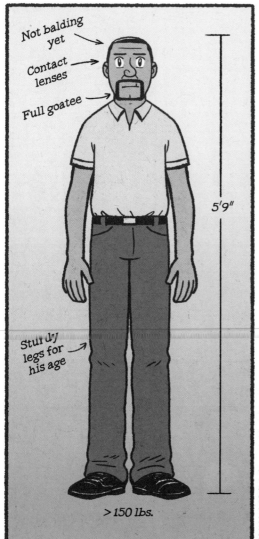

Not balding yet

Contact lenses

Full goatee

5'9"

Sturdy legs for his age

> 150 lbs.

He began as an **assistant** to Mike Phelps.

Then in 2012, he was promoted to *head coach*.

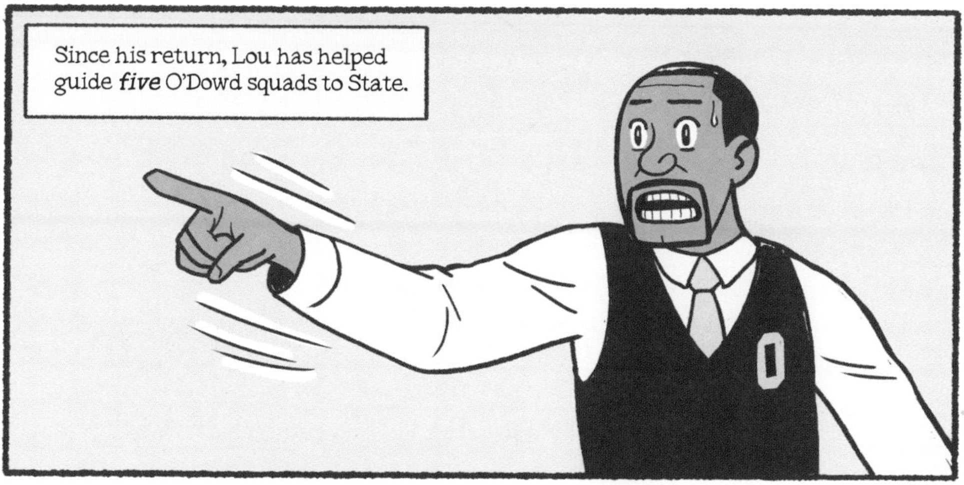
Since his return, Lou has helped guide *five* O'Dowd squads to State.

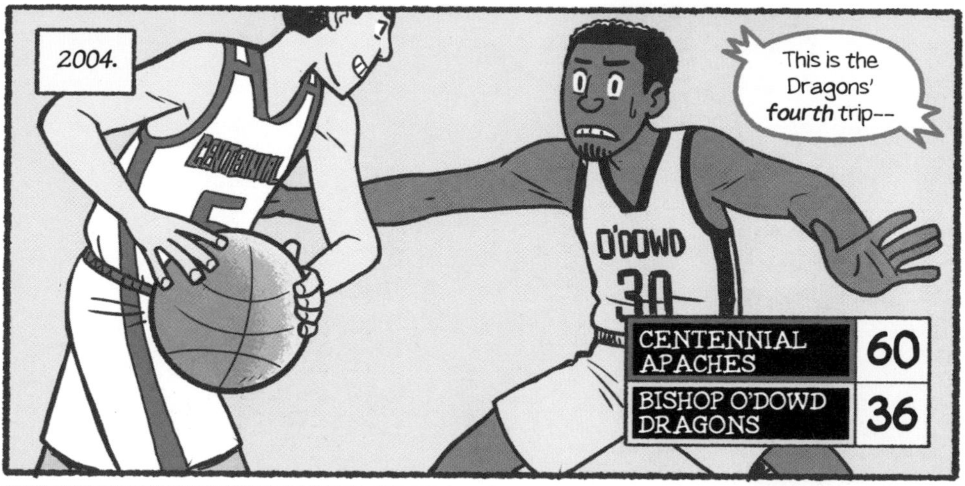
2004.
This is the Dragons' *fourth* trip--
CENTENNIAL APACHES 60
BISHOP O'DOWD DRAGONS 36

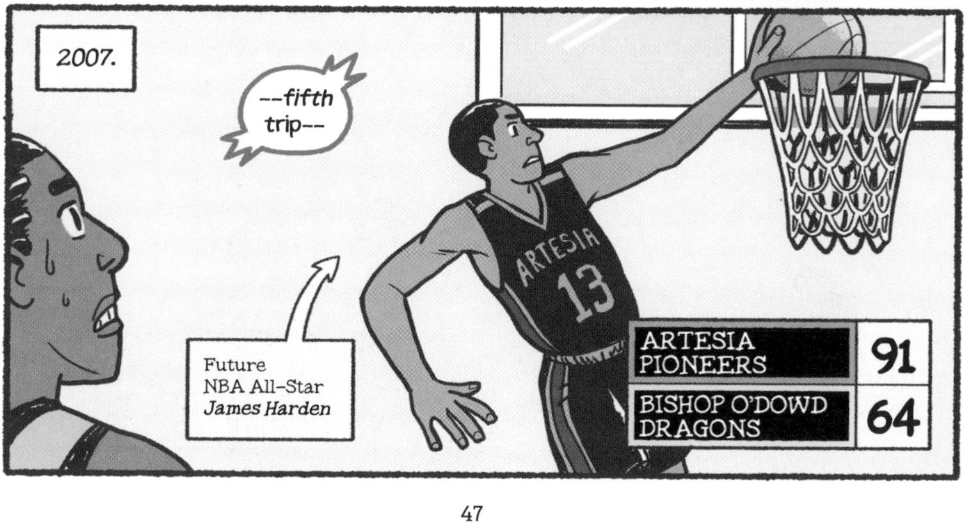
2007.
--*fifth* trip--
Future NBA All-Star *James Harden*
ARTESIA PIONEERS 91
BISHOP O'DOWD DRAGONS 64

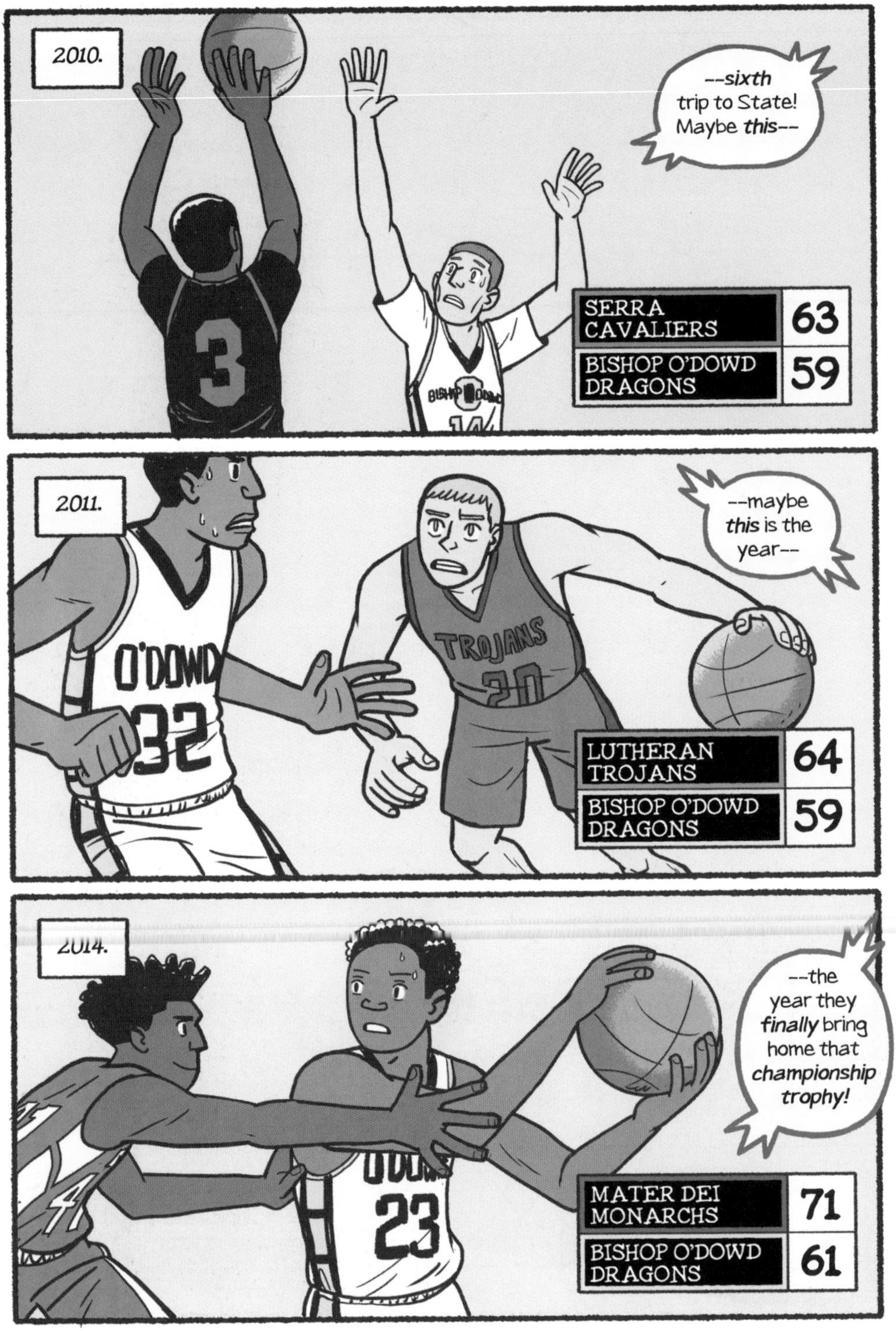
2010.
--*sixth* trip to State! Maybe *this*--
3
SERRA CAVALIERS 63
BISHOP O'DOWD DRAGONS 59
2011.
O'DOWD
32
TROJANS
20
--maybe *this* is the year--
LUTHERAN TROJANS 64
BISHOP O'DOWD DRAGONS 59
2014.
23
--the year they *finally* bring home that *championship trophy!*
MATER DEI MONARCHS 71
BISHOP O'DOWD DRAGONS 61

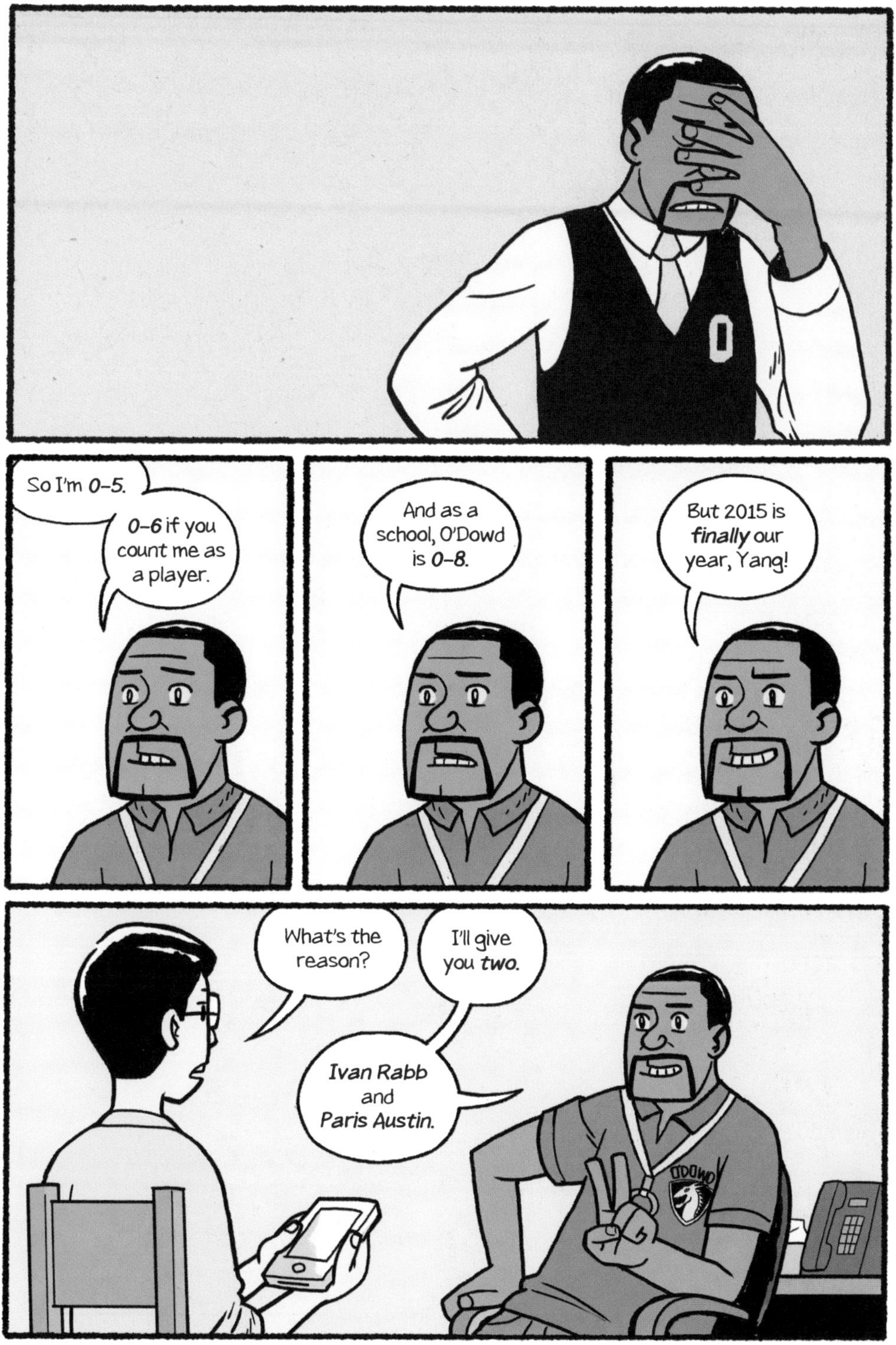
So I'm *0–5*.
0–6 if you count me as a player.
And as a school, O'Dowd is *0–8*.
But 2015 is ***finally*** our year, Yang!
What's the reason?
I'll give you ***two***.
Ivan Rabb and ***Paris Austin***.
O'DOWD

CHAPTER 2:
IVAN AND PARIS

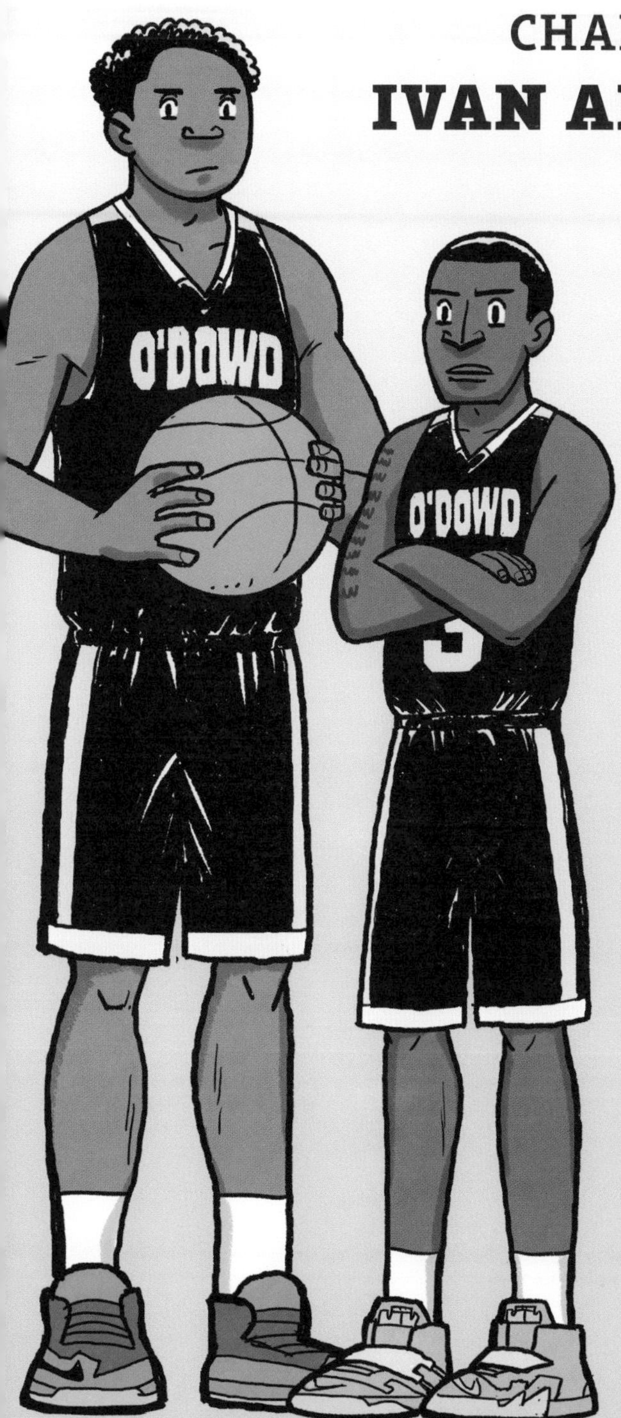
O'DOWD
O'DOWD

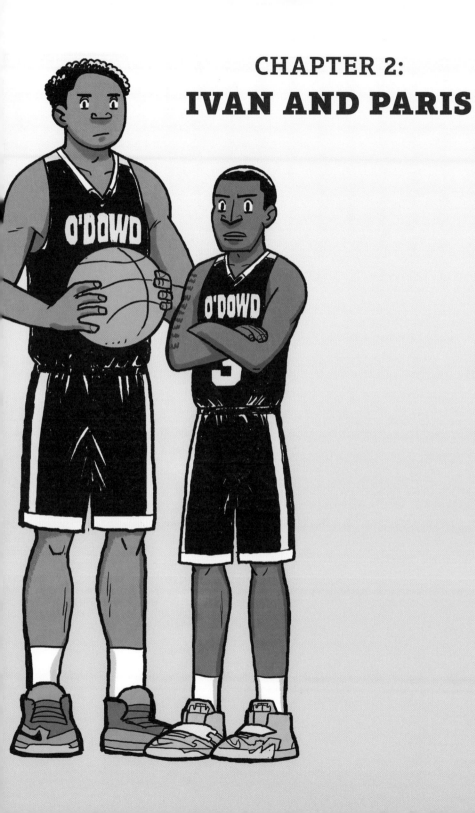

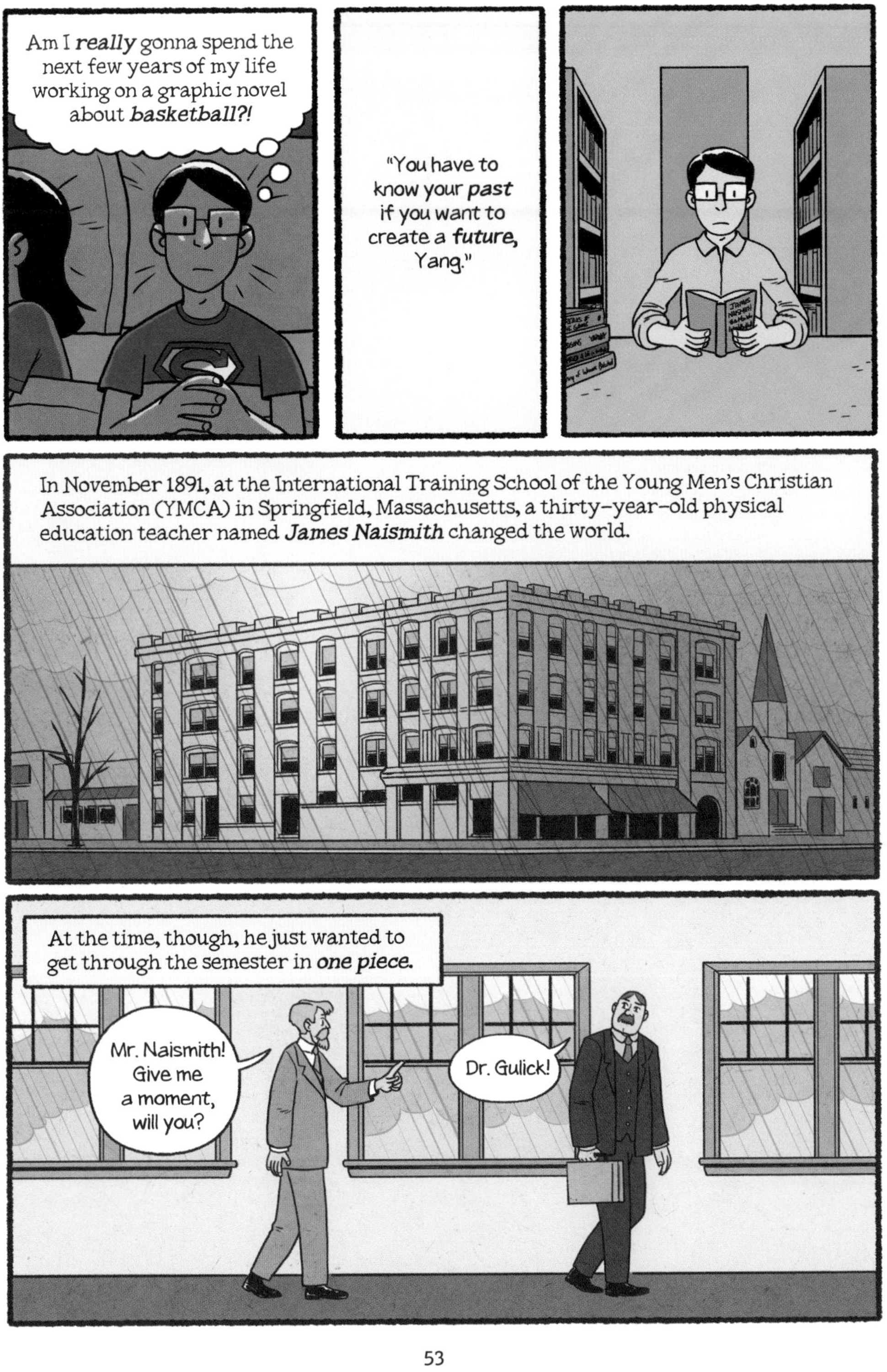
Am I *really* gonna spend the next few years of my life working on a graphic novel about *basketball?!*
"You have to know your *past* if you want to create a *future,* Yang."
In November 1891, at the International Training School of the Young Men's Christian Association (YMCA) in Springfield, Massachusetts, a thirty-year-old physical education teacher named *James Naismith* changed the world.
At the time, though, he just wanted to get through the semester in *one piece.*
Mr. Naismith! Give me a moment, will you?
Dr. Gulick!

I know you're upset about your new assignment.

That class has a reputation of being the most *incorrigible* in the institution!

Two instructors have already tried to engage them. **Both quit!** I don't believe I'll do much better!

Take the class, Mr. Naismith. I want to see what you can do with it.

The students in James Naismith's new class were all *grown men*.

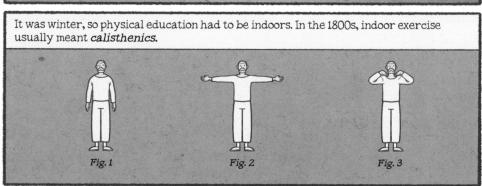

It was winter, so physical education had to be indoors. In the 1800s, indoor exercise usually meant *calisthenics*.

Fig. 1

Fig. 2

Fig. 3

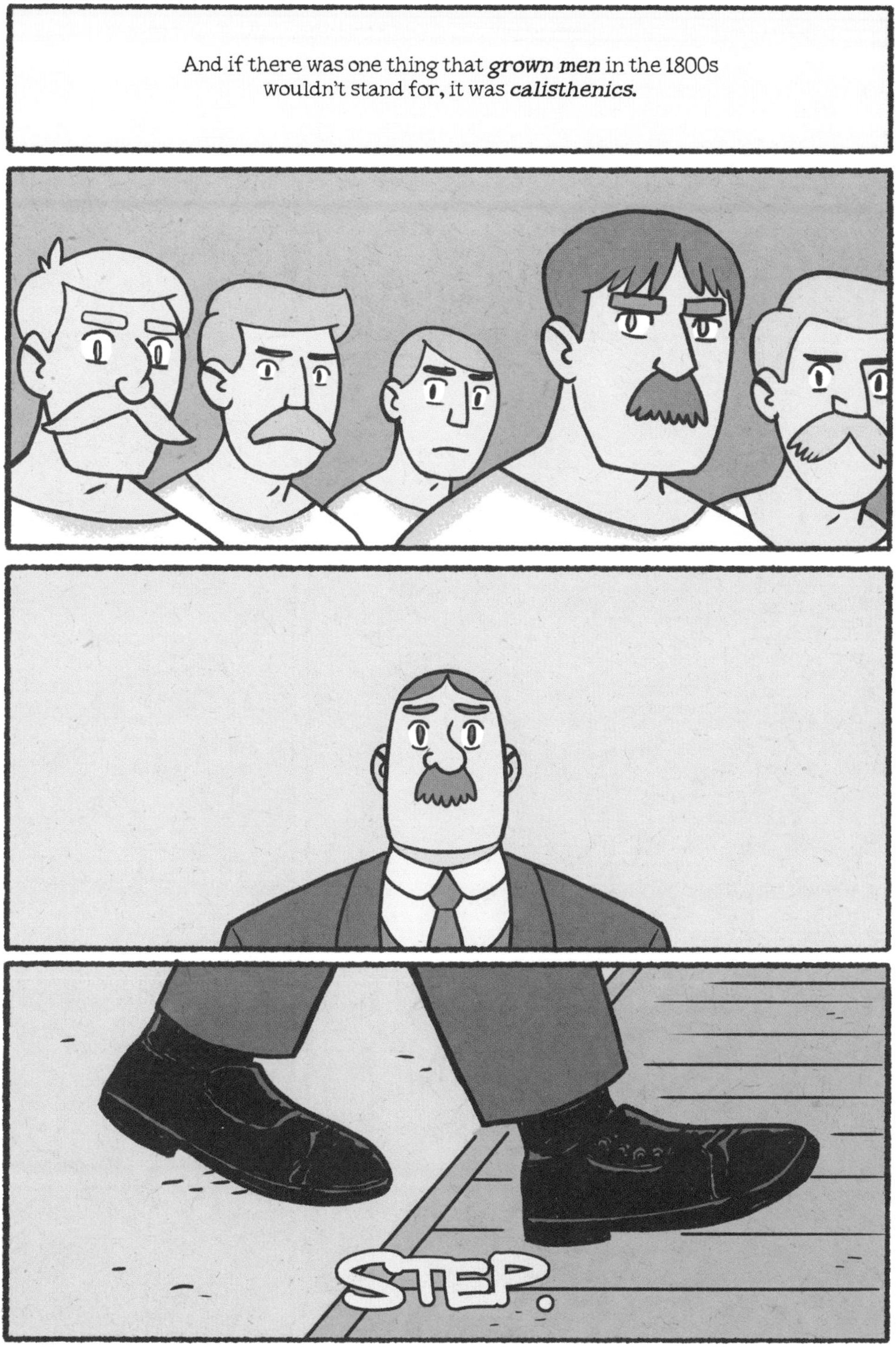
And if there was one thing that ***grown men*** in the 1800s wouldn't stand for, it was ***calisthenics.***
STEP.

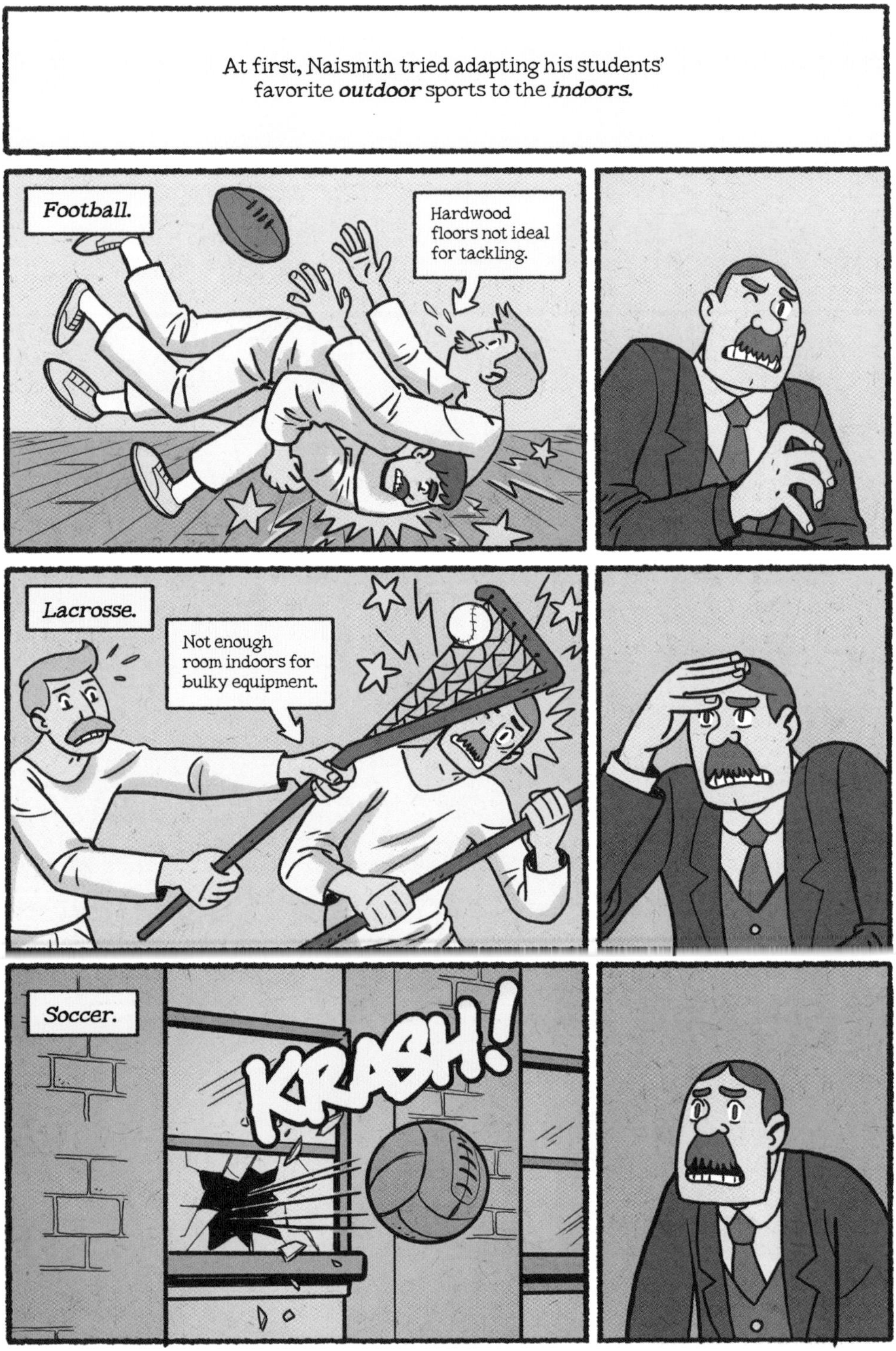
At first, Naismith tried adapting his students' favorite ***outdoor*** sports to the ***indoors.***
Football.
Hardwood floors not ideal for tackling.
Lacrosse.
Not enough room indoors for bulky equipment.
Soccer.
KRASH!

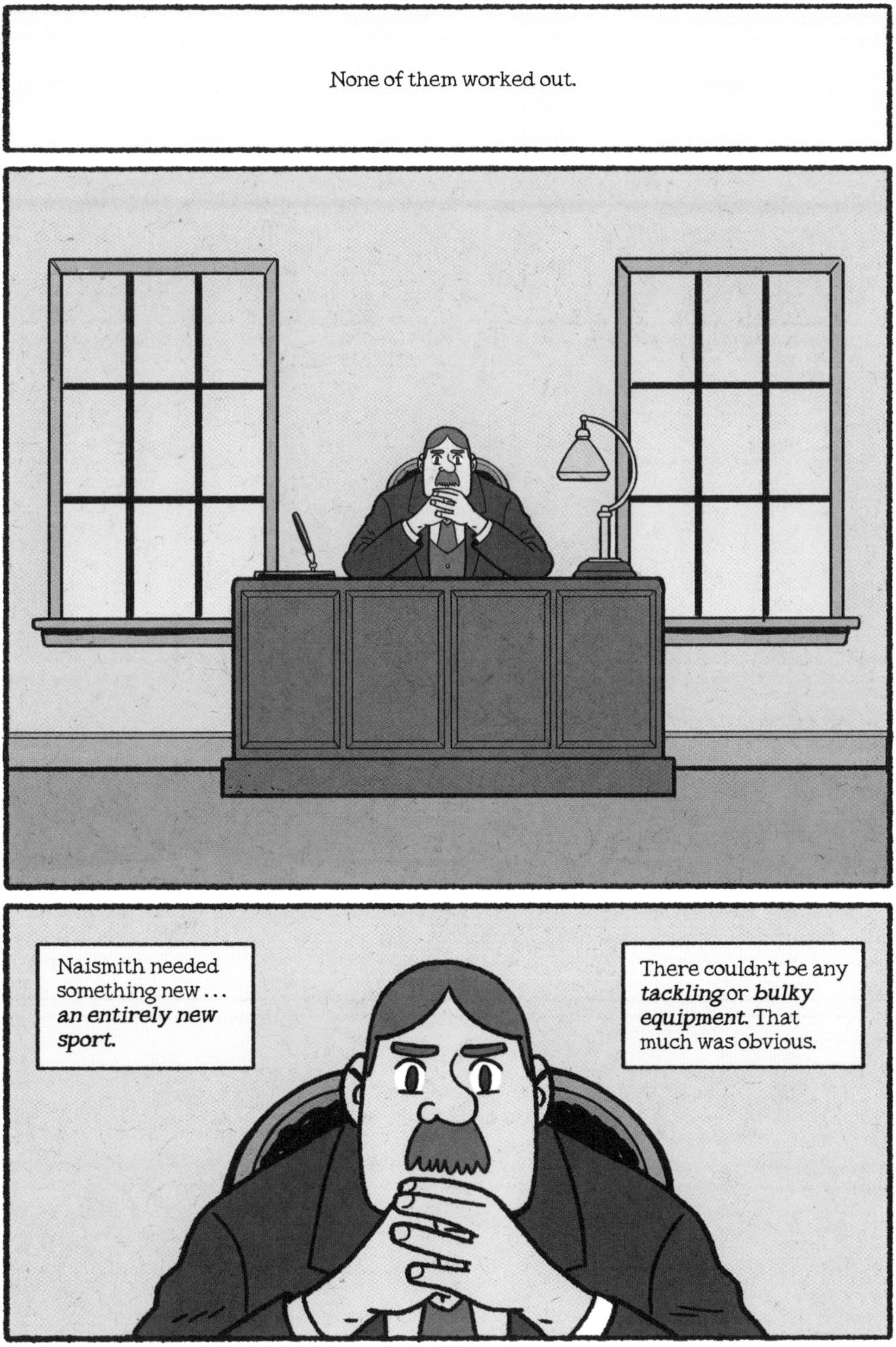
None of them worked out.
Naismith needed something new . . . ***an entirely new sport.***
There couldn't be any ***tackling*** or ***bulky equipment.*** That much was obvious.

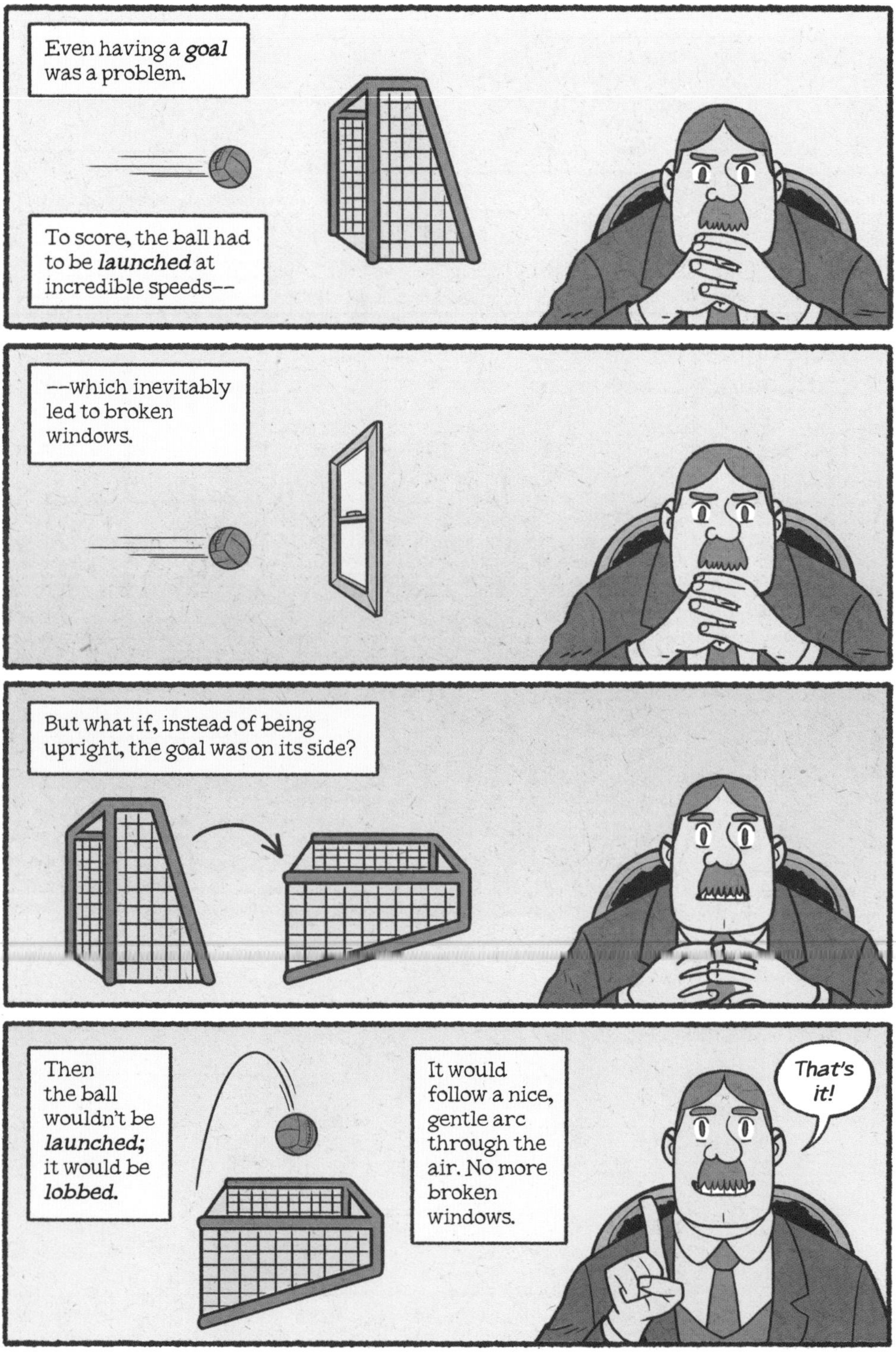
Even having a *goal* was a problem.
To score, the ball had to be *launched* at incredible speeds--
--which inevitably led to broken windows.
But what if, instead of being upright, the goal was on its side?
Then the ball wouldn't be *launched;* it would be *lobbed.*
It would follow a nice, gentle arc through the air. No more broken windows.
That's it!

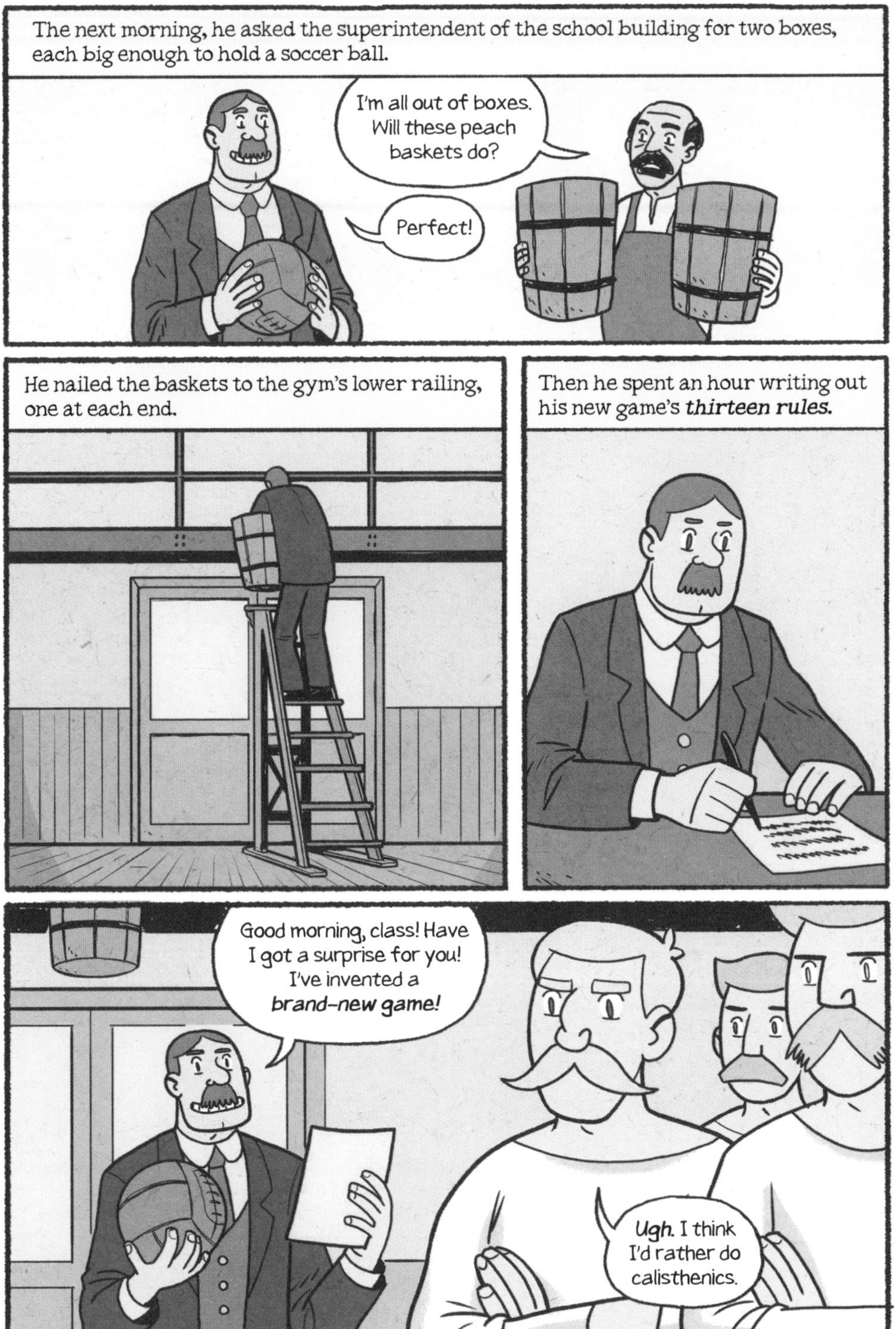
The next morning, he asked the superintendent of the school building for two boxes, each big enough to hold a soccer ball.
I'm all out of boxes. Will these peach baskets do?
Perfect!
He nailed the baskets to the gym's lower railing, one at each end.
Then he spent an hour writing out his new game's ***thirteen rules.***
Good morning, class! Have I got a surprise for you! I've invented a ***brand-new game!***
Ugh. I think I'd rather do calisthenics.

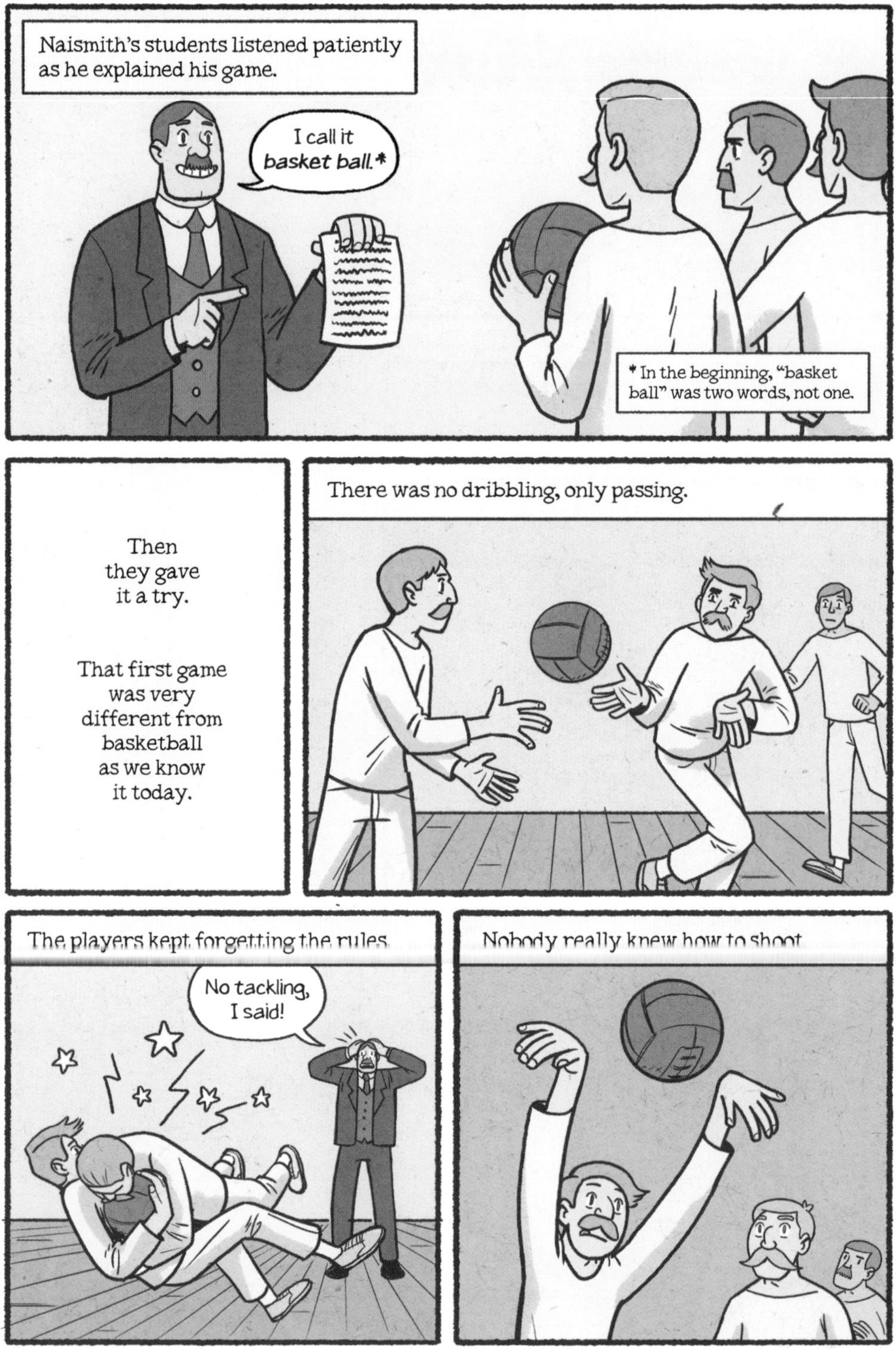
Naismith's students listened patiently as he explained his game.
I call it *basket ball.**
* In the beginning, "basket ball" was two words, not one.
Then they gave it a try.
That first game was very different from basketball as we know it today.
There was no dribbling, only passing.
The players kept forgetting the rules
No tackling, I said!
Nobody really knew how to shoot

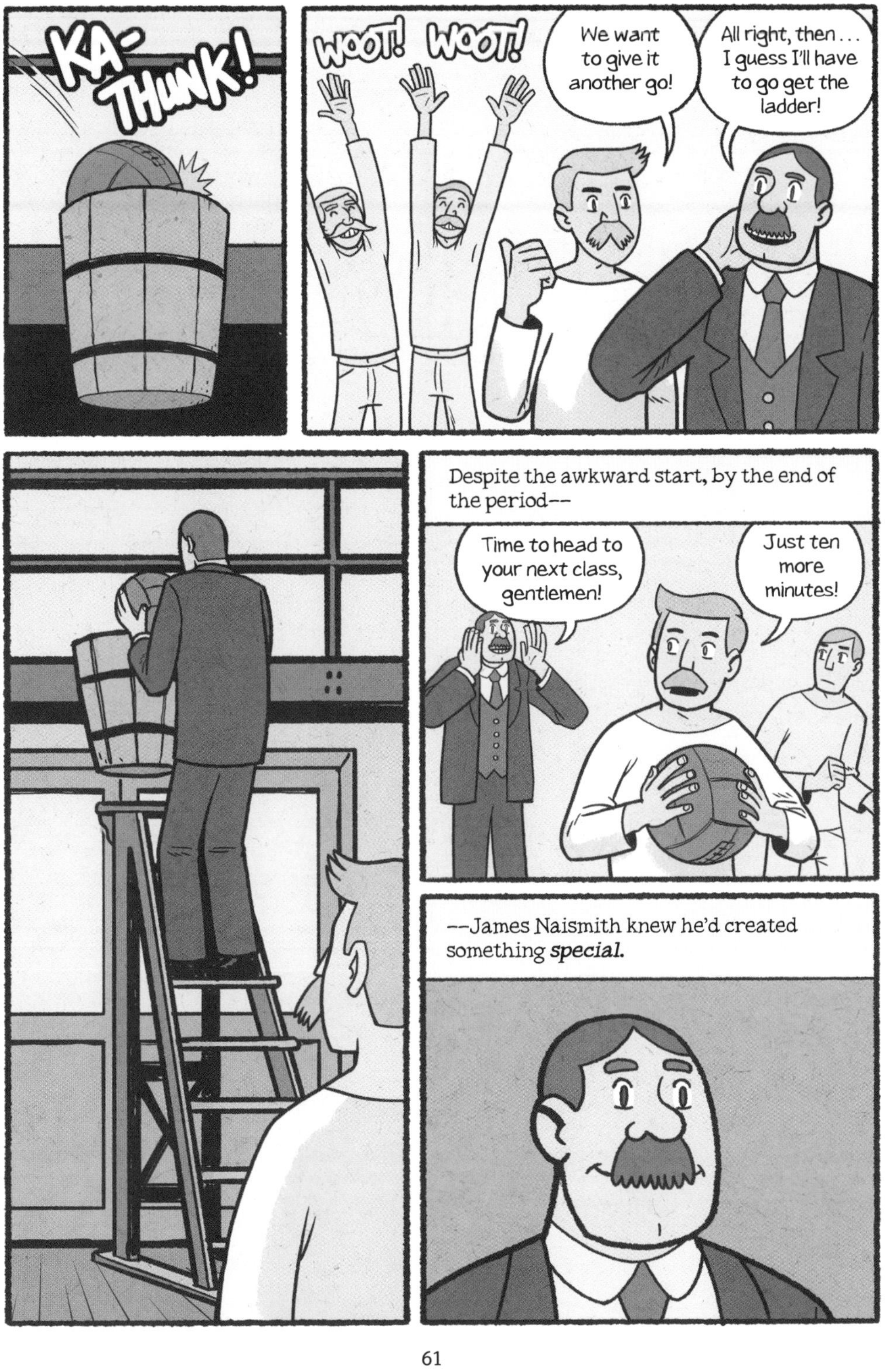
KA-THUNK!
WOOT! WOOT!
We want to give it another go!
All right, then . . . I guess I'll have to go get the ladder!
Despite the awkward start, by the end of the period--
Time to head to your next class, gentlemen!
Just ten more minutes!
--James Naismith knew he'd created something *special.*

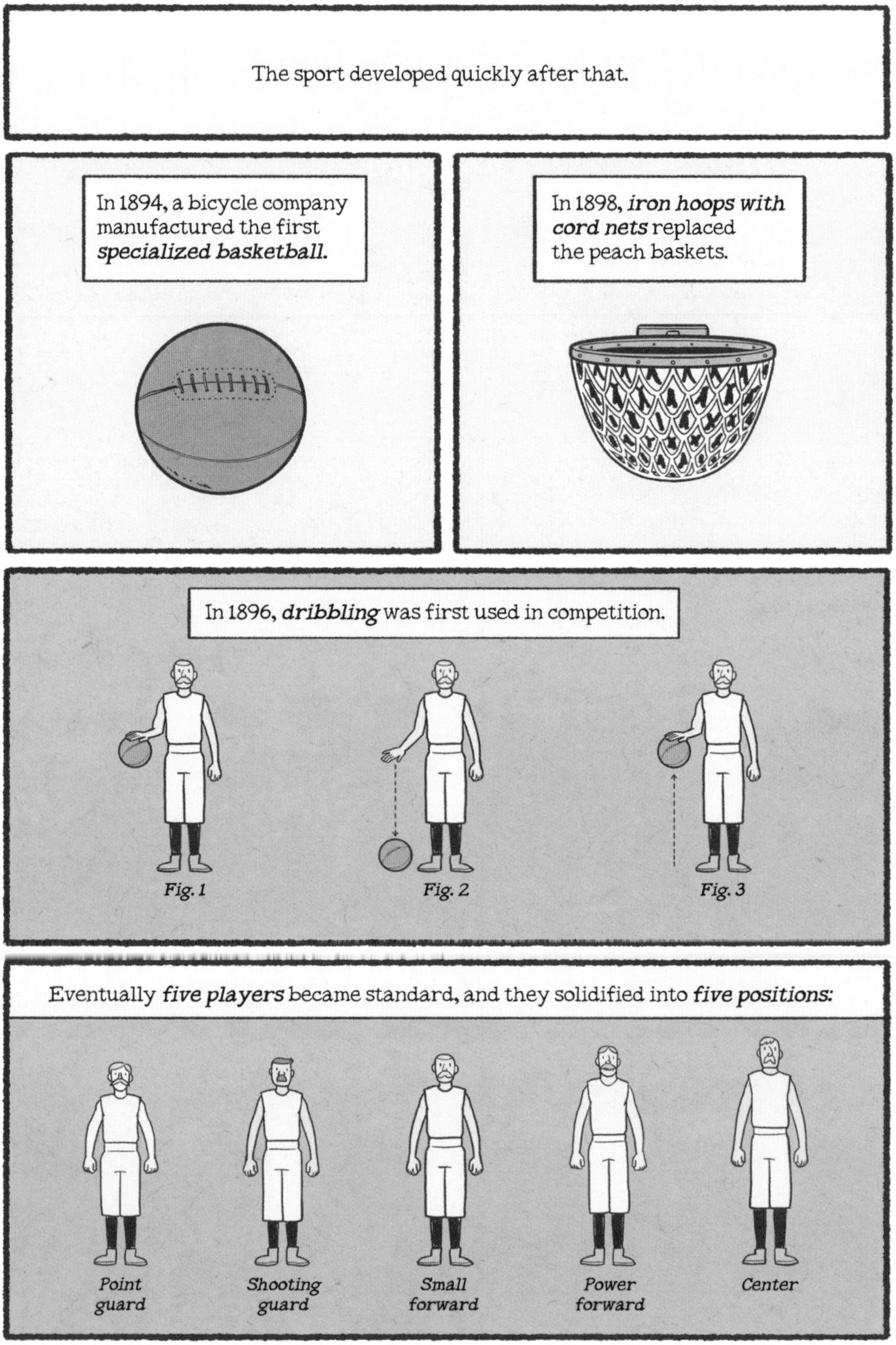
The sport developed quickly after that.
In 1894, a bicycle company manufactured the first *specialized basketball.*
In 1898, *iron hoops with cord nets* replaced the peach baskets.
In 1896, *dribbling* was first used in competition.
Fig. 1
Fig. 2
Fig. 3
Eventually *five players* became standard, and they solidified into *five positions:*
Point guard
Shooting guard
Small forward
Power forward
Center

Though it proved enormously popular at YMCAs around the world, early on, basketball had a hard time competing for crowds with the more established sports.

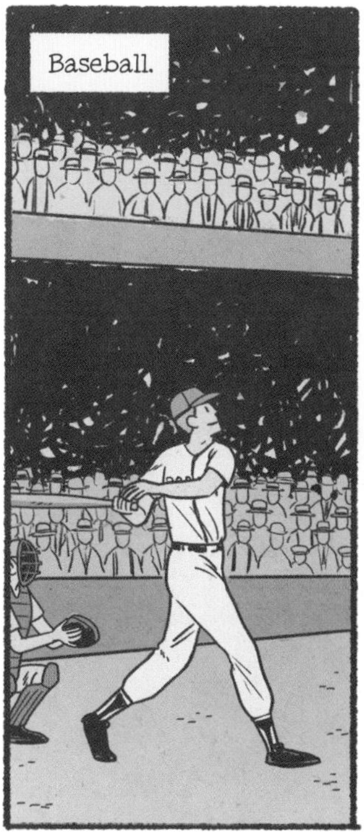
Baseball.

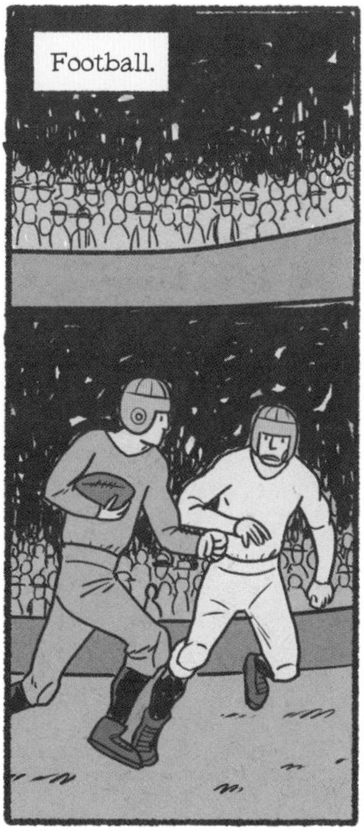
Football.

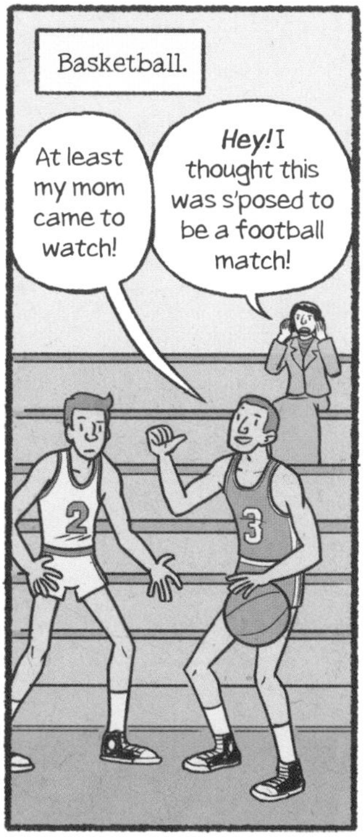
Basketball.
At least my mom came to watch!
Hey! I thought this was s'posed to be a football match!

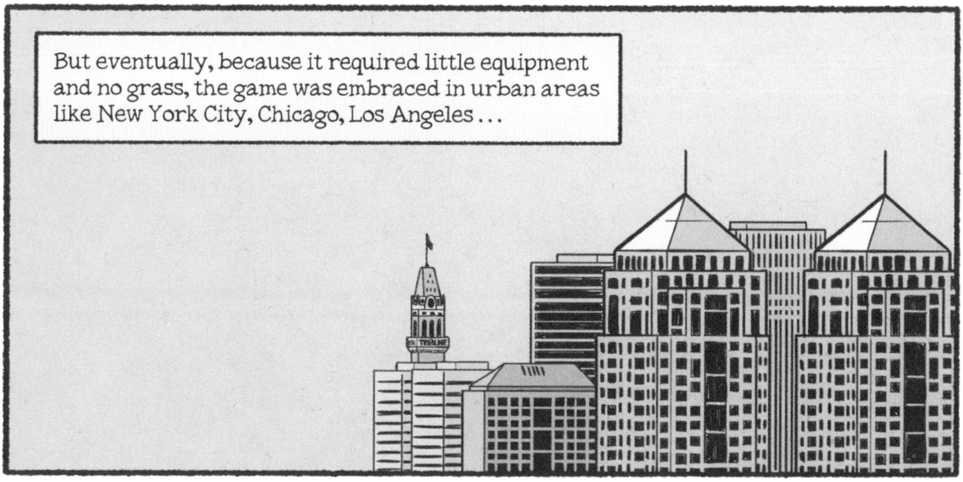
But eventually, because it required little equipment and no grass, the game was embraced in urban areas like New York City, Chicago, Los Angeles . . .

. . . and *Oakland.*

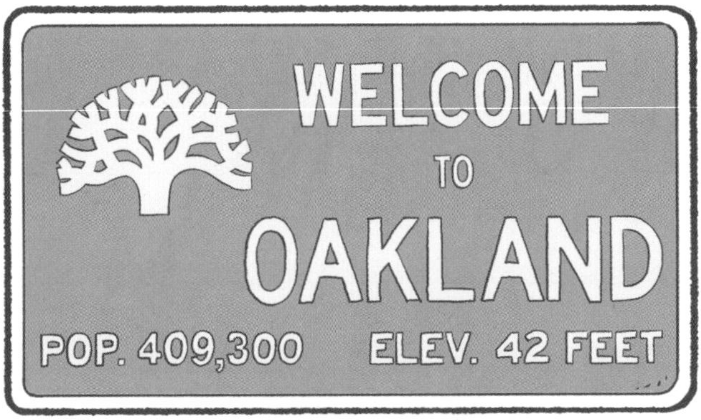
WELCOME
TO
OAKLAND
POP. 409,300
ELEV. 42 FEET

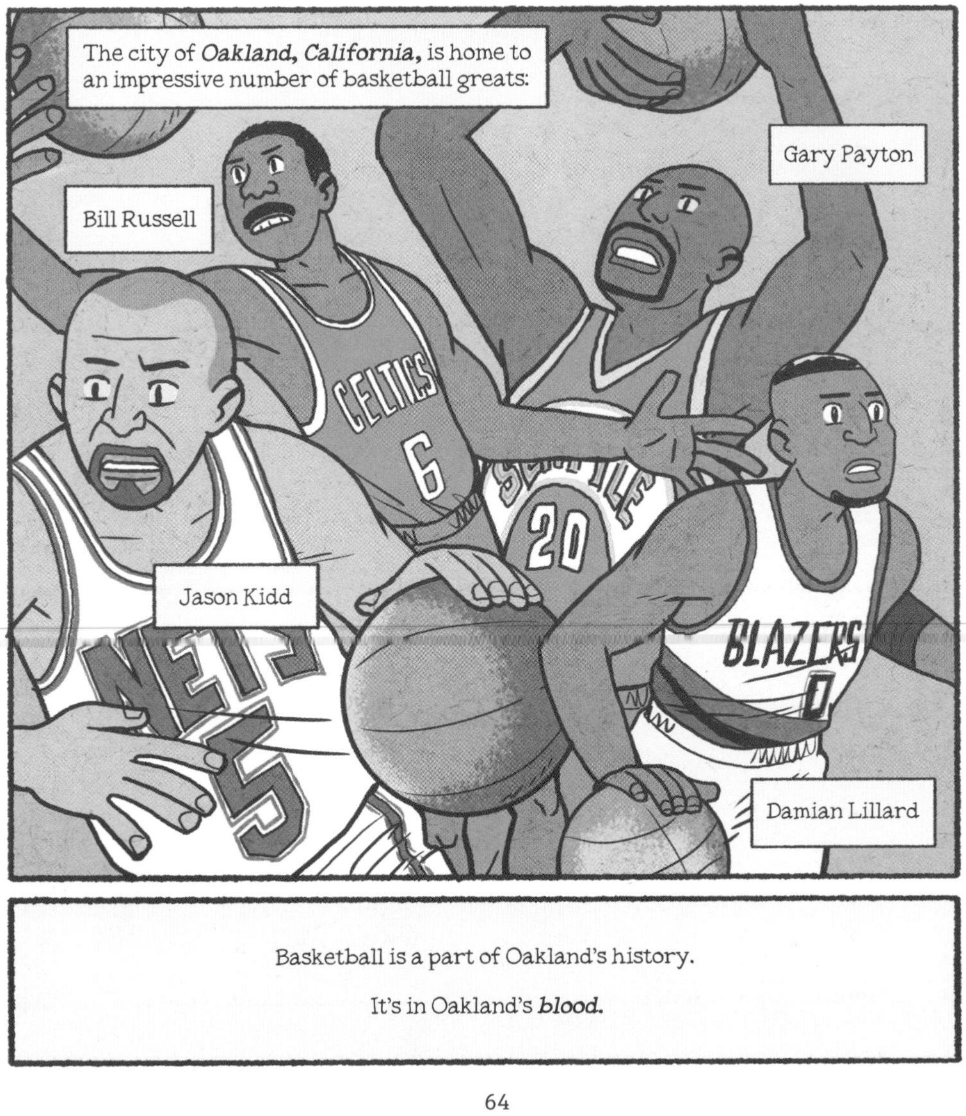
The city of *Oakland, California,* is home to an impressive number of basketball greats:
Bill Russell
Gary Payton
CELTICS
6
SEATTLE
20
Jason Kidd
NETS
5
BLAZERS
0
Damian Lillard

Basketball is a part of Oakland's history.

It's in Oakland's ***blood.***

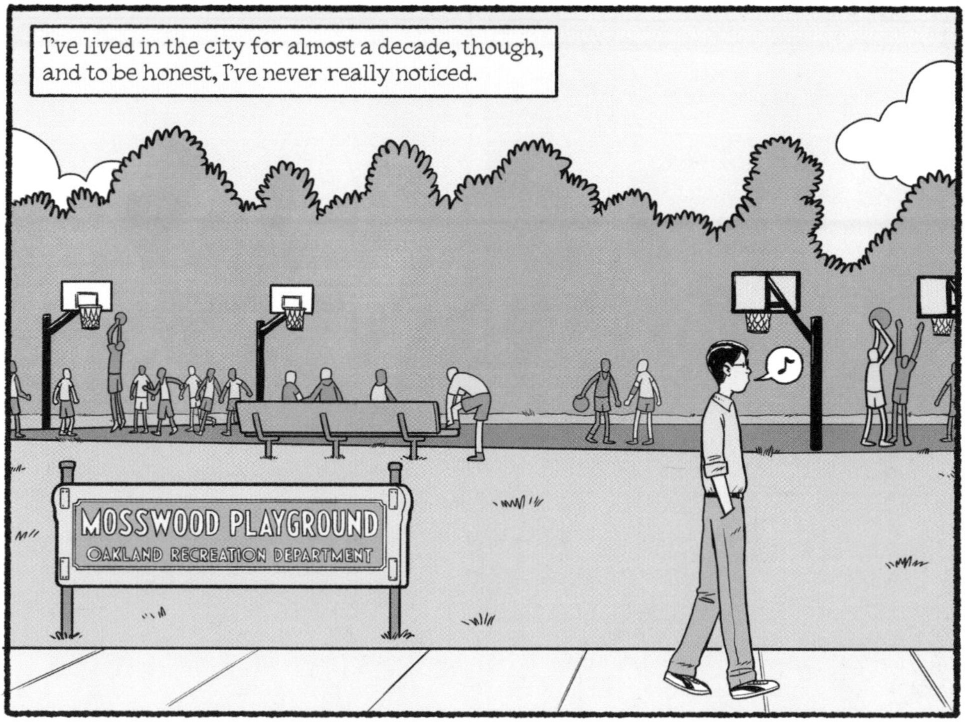
I've lived in the city for almost a decade, though, and to be honest, I've never really noticed.
MOSSWOOD PLAYGROUND
OAKLAND RECREATION DEPARTMENT

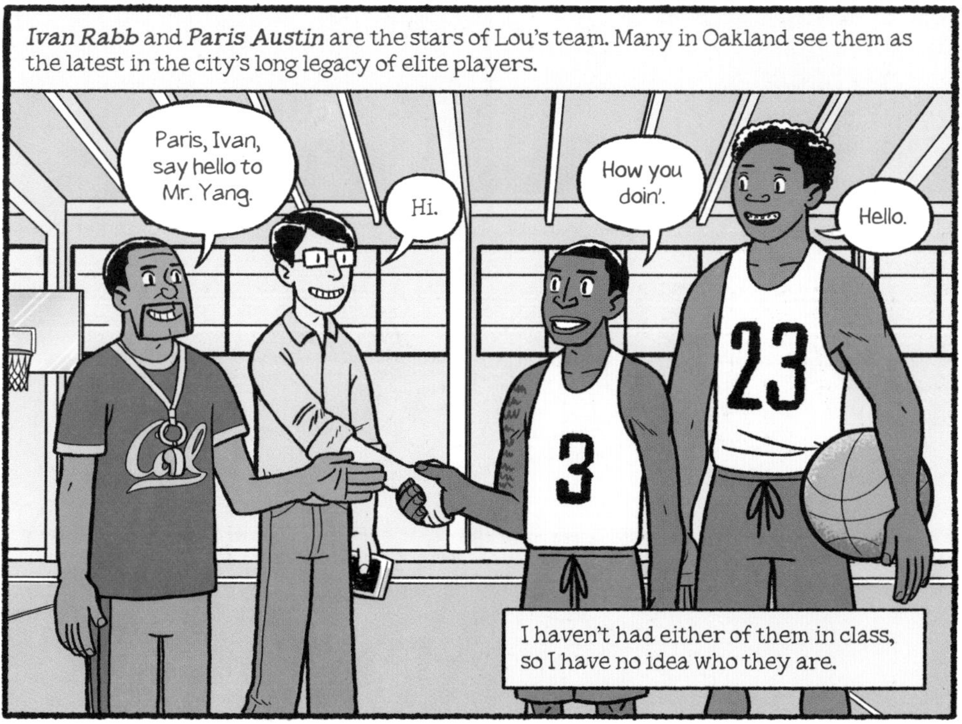
Ivan Rabb and *Paris Austin* are the stars of Lou's team. Many in Oakland see them as the latest in the city's long legacy of elite players.
Paris, Ivan, say hello to Mr. Yang.
Hi.
How you doin'.
Hello.
I haven't had either of them in class, so I have no idea who they are.

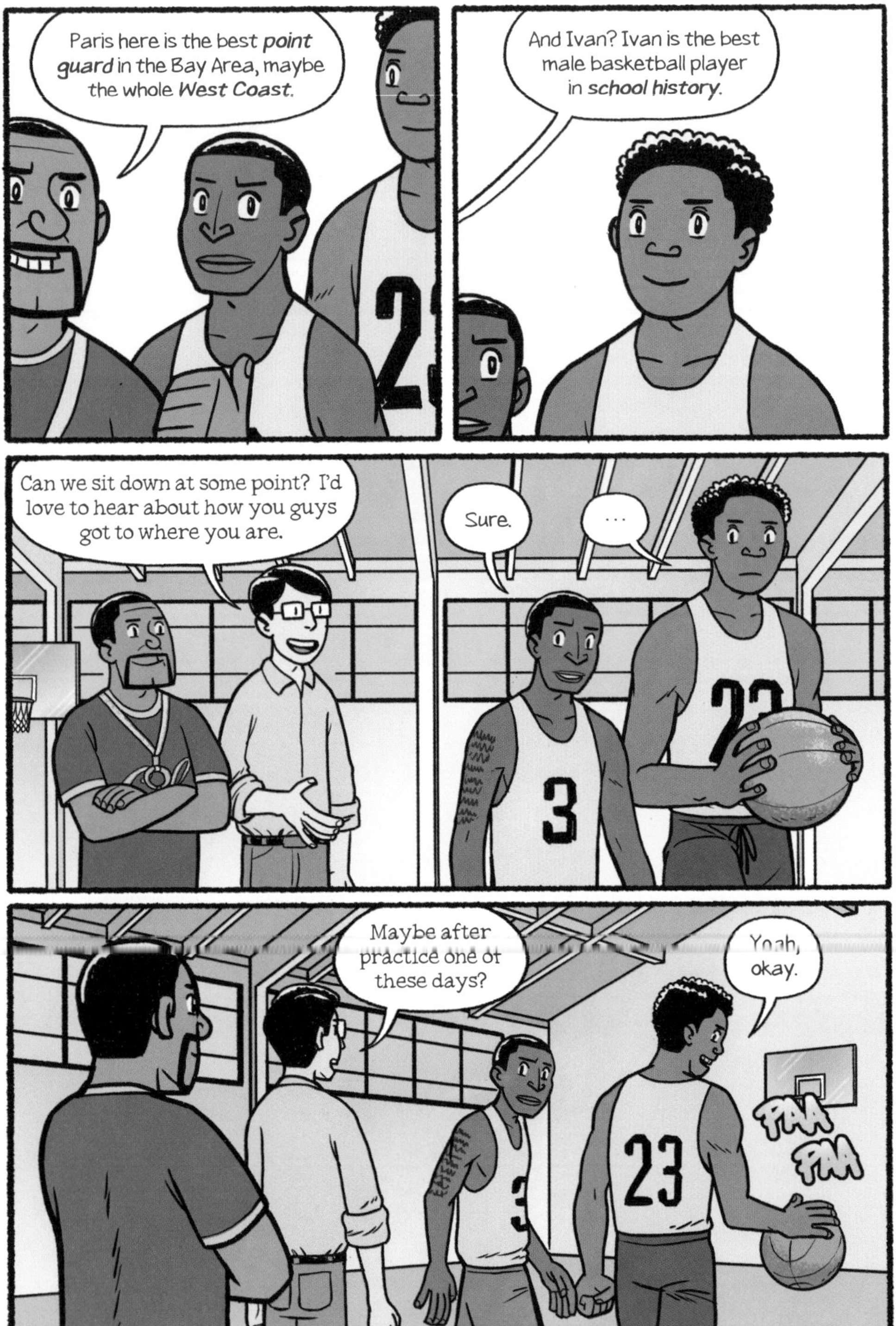

Paris here is the best *point guard* in the Bay Area, maybe the whole *West Coast*.
And Ivan? Ivan is the best male basketball player in *school history*.
23
Can we sit down at some point? I'd love to hear about how you guys got to where you are.
Sure.
...
3
23
Maybe after practice one of these days?
Yeah, okay.
23
PAA
PAA

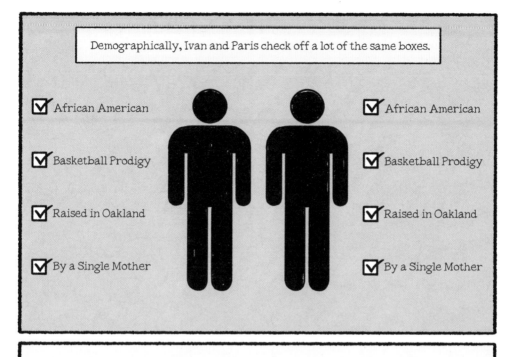

Demographically, Ivan and Paris check off a lot of the same boxes.

☑ African American

☑ Basketball Prodigy

☑ Raised in Oakland

☑ By a Single Mother

☑ African American

☑ Basketball Prodigy

☑ Raised in Oakland

☑ By a Single Mother

As people and as players, though, they couldn't be more different.

6' 10"

5' 10"

Ivan is one of the tallest members of the team.

Paris is one of the shortest.

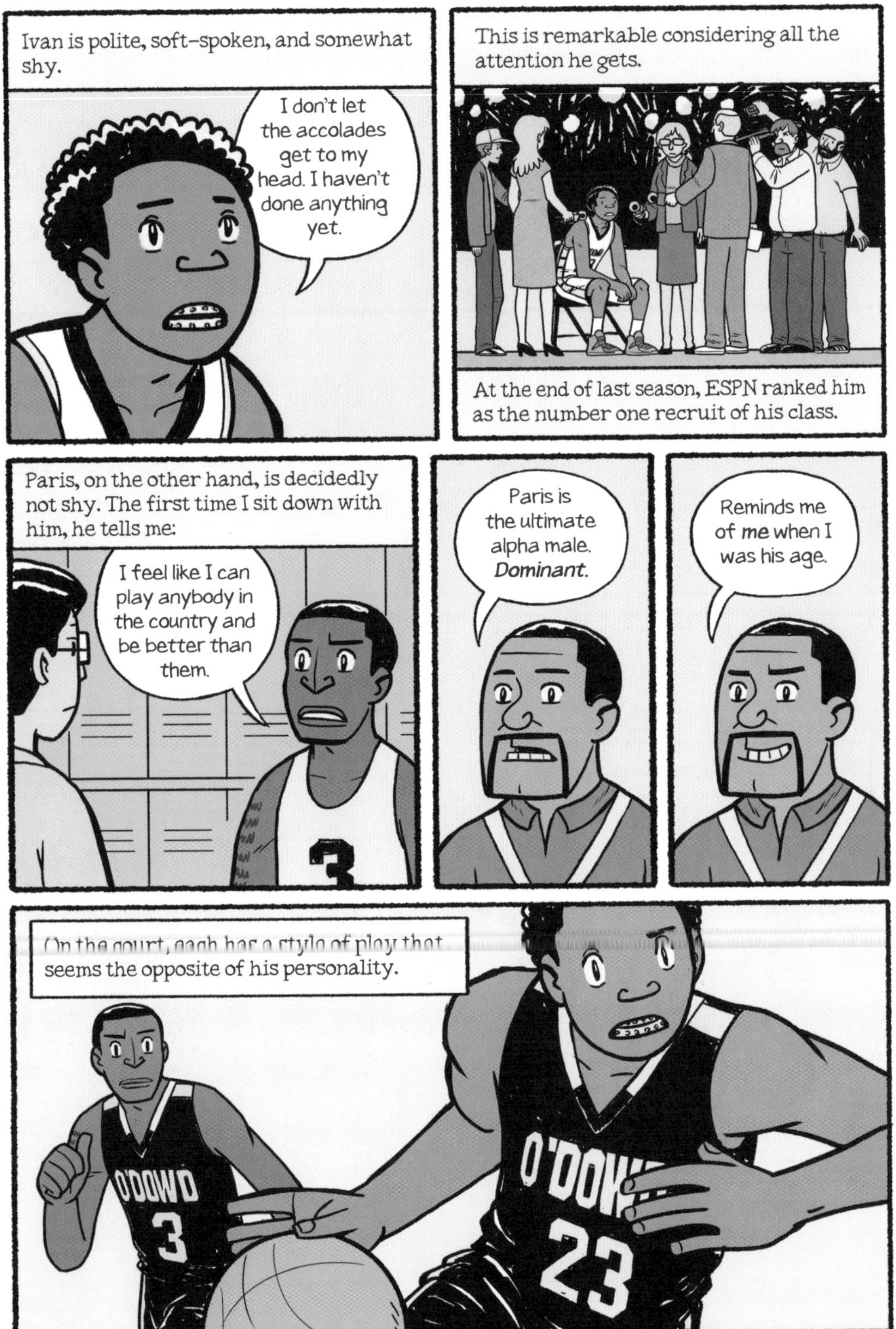
Ivan is polite, soft-spoken, and somewhat shy.
I don't let the accolades get to my head. I haven't done anything yet.
This is remarkable considering all the attention he gets.
At the end of last season, ESPN ranked him as the number one recruit of his class.
Paris, on the other hand, is decidedly not shy. The first time I sit down with him, he tells me:
I feel like I can play anybody in the country and be better than them.
Paris is the ultimate alpha male. *Dominant.*
Reminds me of *me* when I was his age.
On the court, each has a style of play that seems the opposite of his personality.
O'DOWD
3
23

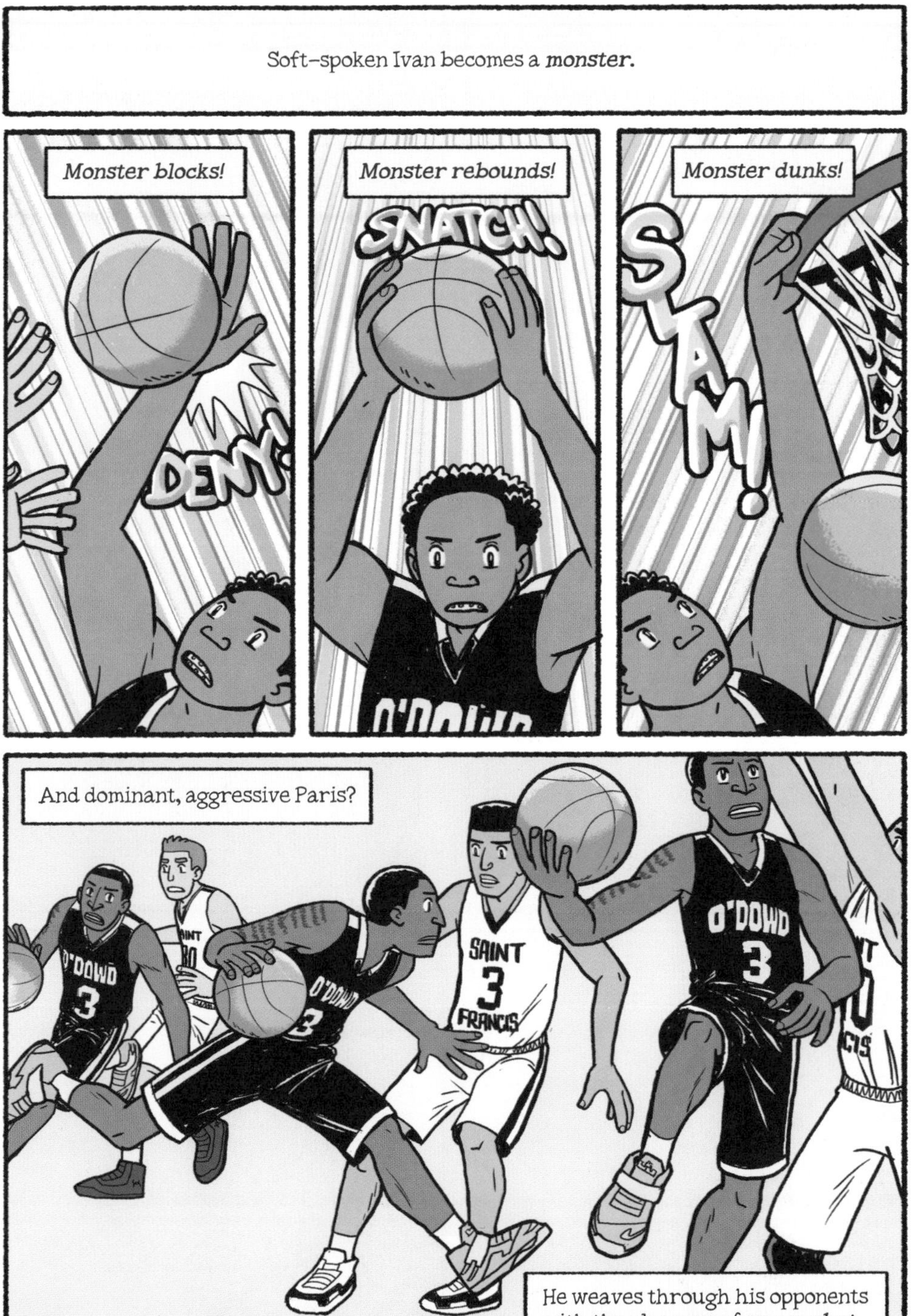
Soft-spoken Ivan becomes a *monster.*
Monster blocks!
DENY!
Monster rebounds!
SNATCH!
Monster dunks!
SLAM!
And dominant, aggressive Paris?
O'DOWD 3
SAINT 3 FRANCIS
He weaves through his opponents with the elegance of an *acrobat.*

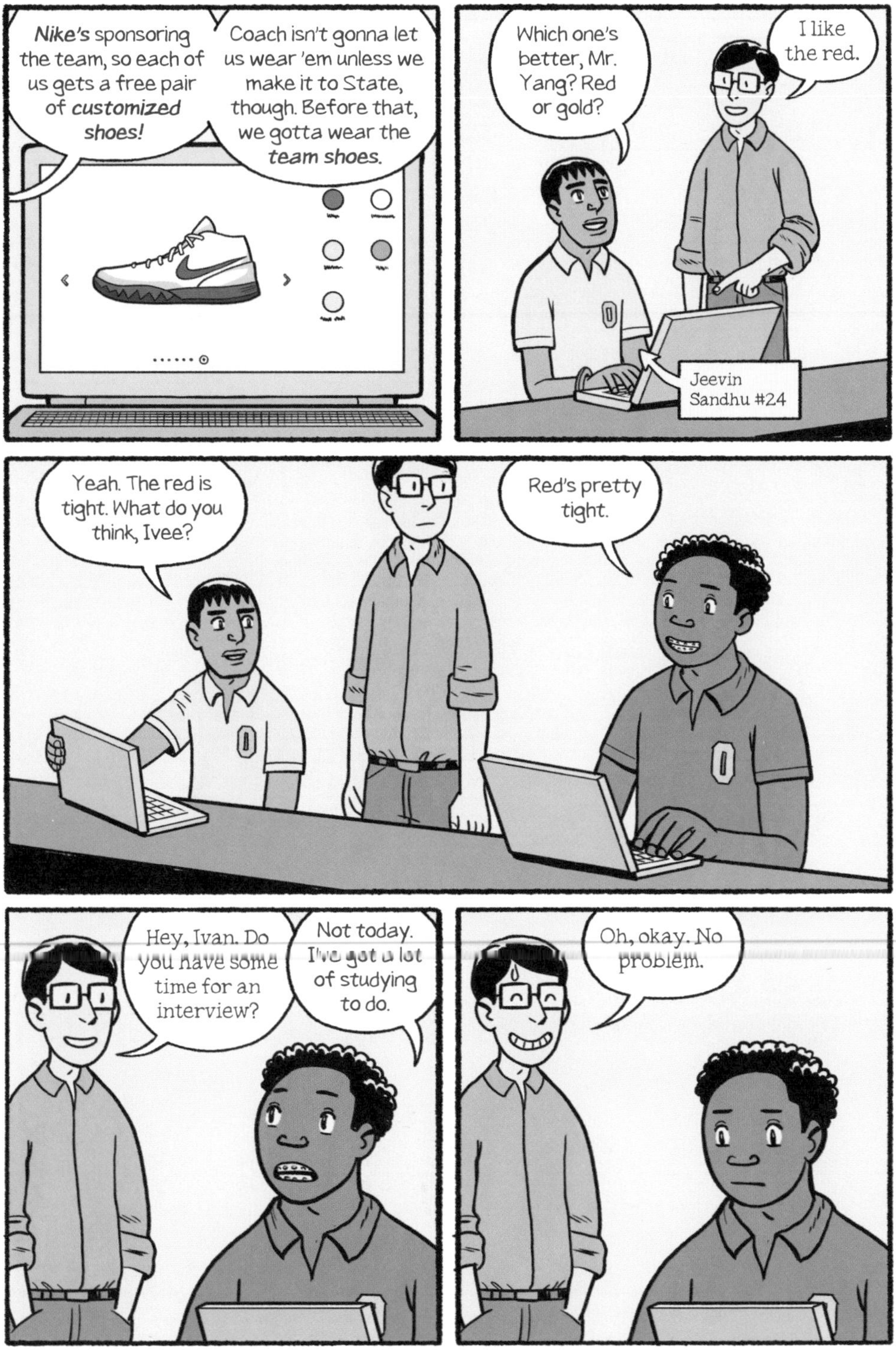
Nike's sponsoring the team, so each of us gets a free pair of ***customized shoes!***
Coach isn't gonna let us wear 'em unless we make it to State, though. Before that, we gotta wear the ***team shoes.***
Which one's better, Mr. Yang? Red or gold?
I like the red.
Jeevin Sandhu #24
Yeah. The red is tight. What do you think, Ivee?
Red's pretty tight.
Hey, Ivan. Do you have some time for an interview?
Not today. I've got a lot of studying to do.
Oh, okay. No problem.

Ivan and Paris played together at Montera, the public middle school down the road.

That's where they became *best friends*.

They both decided to come to Bishop O'Dowd High School.

BISHOP O'DOWD
HIGH SCHOOL
— EST. 1951 —

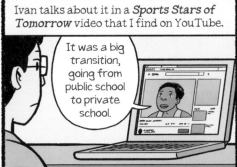

Ivan talks about it in a *Sports Stars of Tomorrow* video that I find on YouTube.

It was a big transition, going from public school to private school.

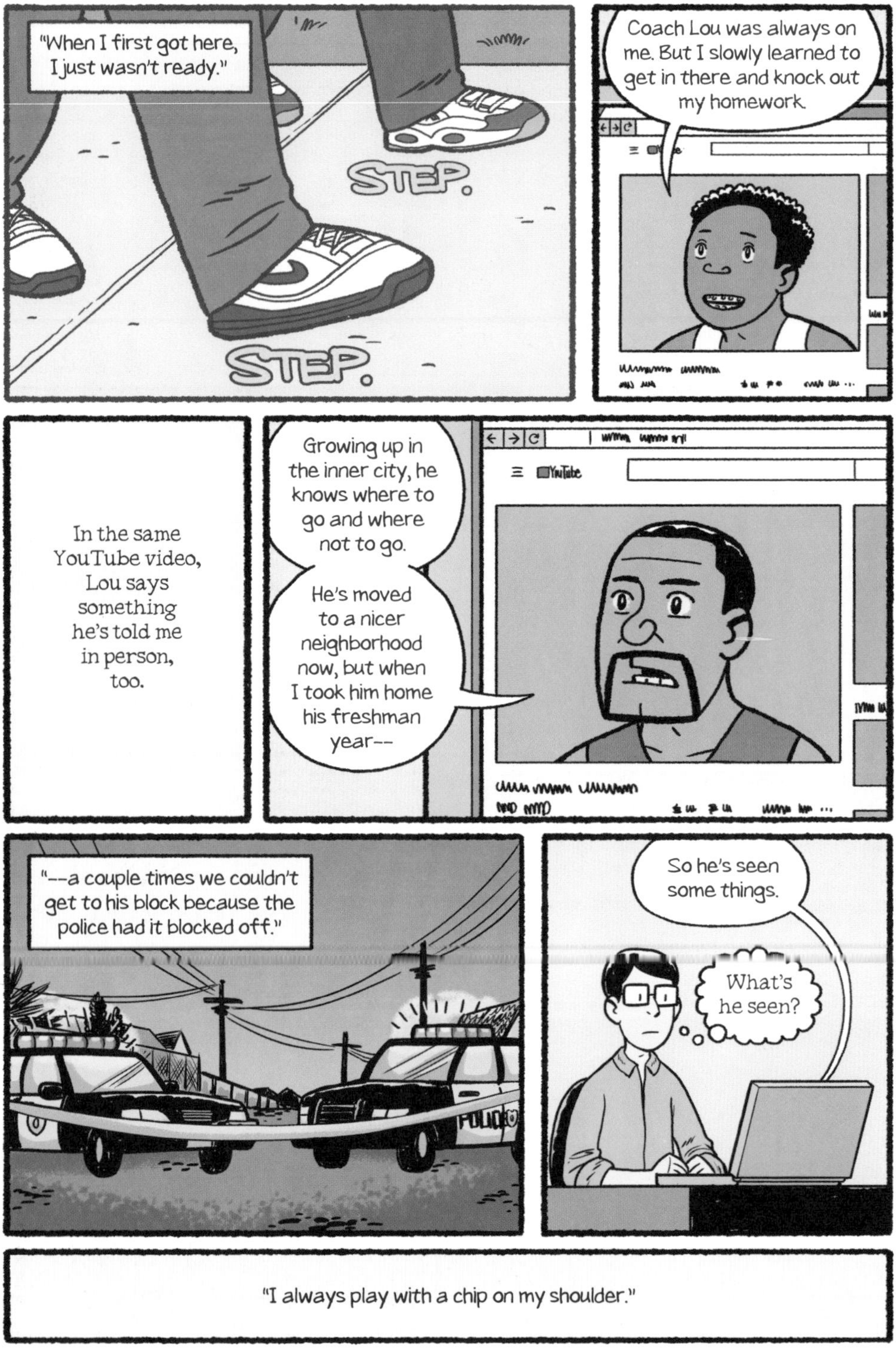
"When I first got here, I just wasn't ready."
STEP.
STEP.
Coach Lou was always on me. But I slowly learned to get in there and knock out my homework.
In the same YouTube video, Lou says something he's told me in person, too.
Growing up in the inner city, he knows where to go and where not to go.
He's moved to a nicer neighborhood now, but when I took him home his freshman year--
"--a couple times we couldn't get to his block because the police had it blocked off."
So he's seen some things.
What's he seen?
"I always play with a chip on my shoulder."

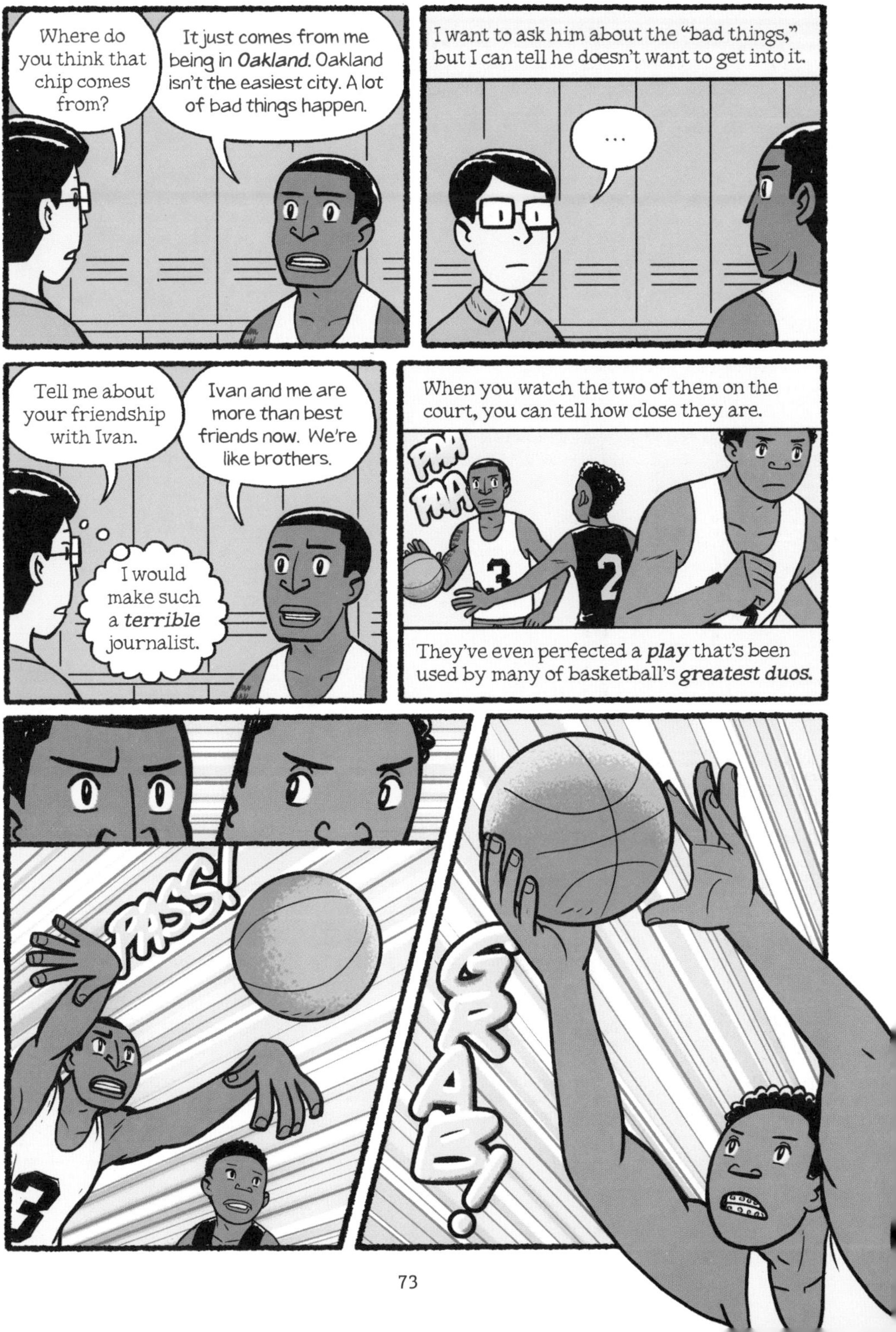

Where do you think that chip comes from?
It just comes from me being in Oakland. Oakland isn't the easiest city. A lot of bad things happen.
I want to ask him about the "bad things," but I can tell he doesn't want to get into it.
...
Tell me about your friendship with Ivan.
Ivan and me are more than best friends now. We're like brothers.
I would make such a terrible journalist.
When you watch the two of them on the court, you can tell how close they are.
PAA PAA
They've even perfected a play that's been used by many of basketball's greatest duos.
PASS!
GRAB!

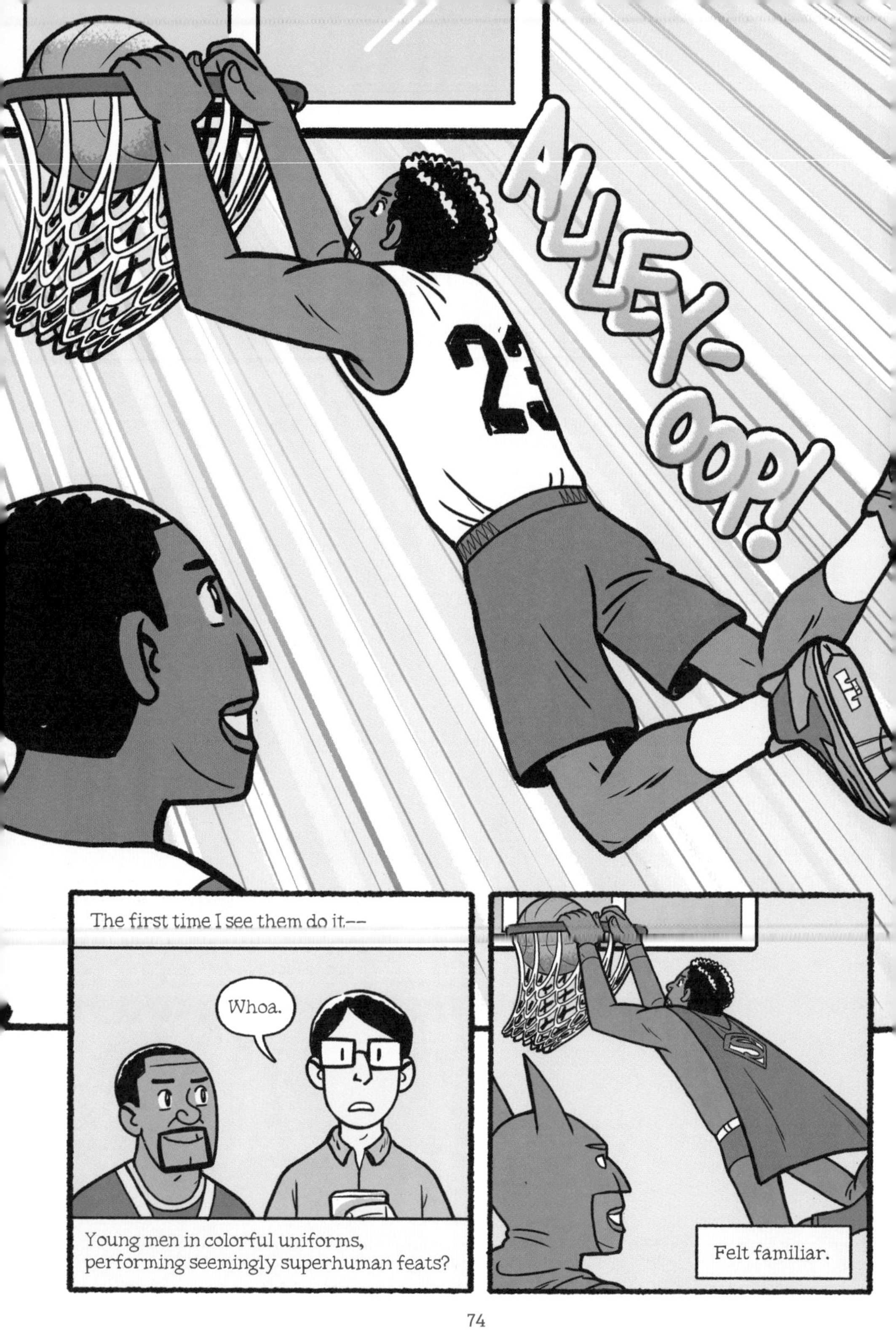
ALLEY-OOP!
The first time I see them do it--
Whoa.
Young men in colorful uniforms, performing seemingly superhuman feats?
Felt familiar.

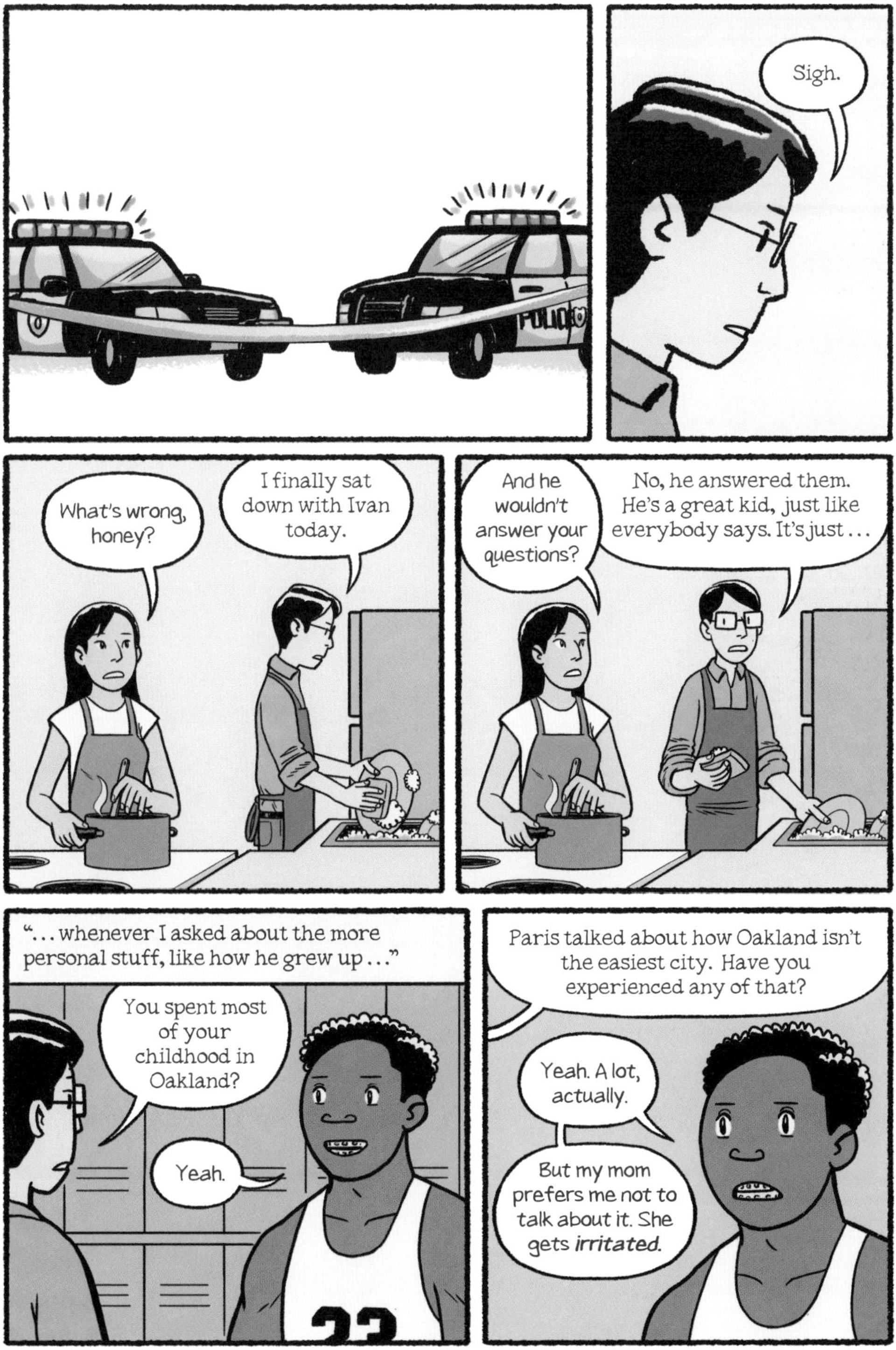

POLICE
Sigh.
What's wrong, honey?
I finally sat down with Ivan today.
And he wouldn't answer your questions?
No, he answered them. He's a great kid, just like everybody says. It's just . . .
". . . whenever I asked about the more personal stuff, like how he grew up . . ."
You spent most of your childhood in Oakland?
Yeah.
Paris talked about how Oakland isn't the easiest city. Have you experienced any of that?
Yeah. A lot, actually.
But my mom prefers me not to talk about it. She gets *irritated*.

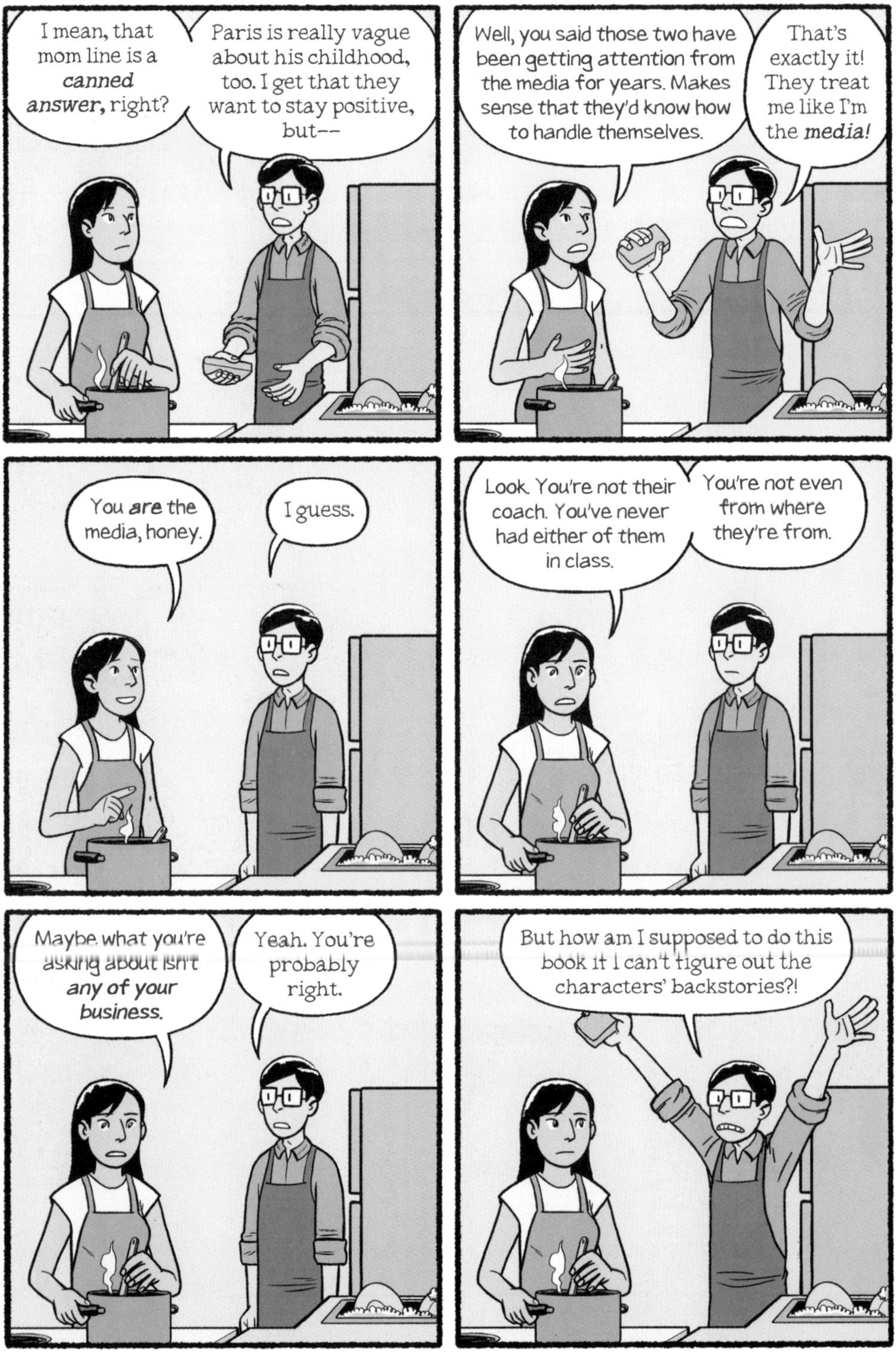

I mean, that mom line is a *canned answer,* right?
Paris is really vague about his childhood, too. I get that they want to stay positive, but--
Well, you said those two have been getting attention from the media for years. Makes sense that they'd know how to handle themselves.
That's exactly it! They treat me like I'm the *media!*
You **are** the media, honey.
I guess.
Look. You're not their coach. You've never had either of them in class.
You're not even from where they're from.
Maybe what you're asking about isn't ***any of your business.***
Yeah. You're probably right.
But how am I supposed to do this book if I can't figure out the characters' backstories?!

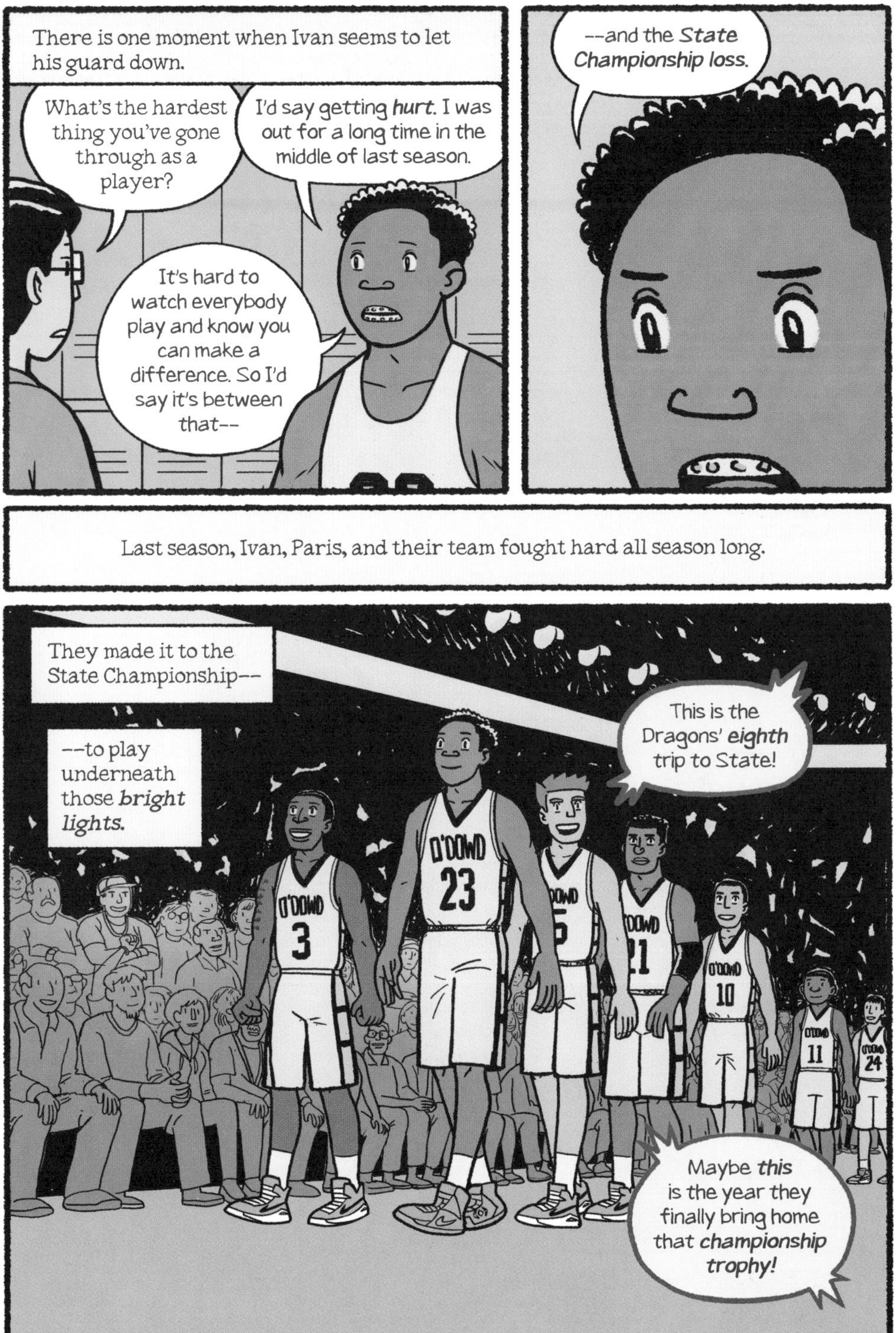

There is one moment when Ivan seems to let his guard down.
What's the hardest thing you've gone through as a player?
I'd say getting *hurt*. I was out for a long time in the middle of last season.
It's hard to watch everybody play and know you can make a difference. So I'd say it's between that--
--and the *State Championship loss.*
Last season, Ivan, Paris, and their team fought hard all season long.
They made it to the State Championship--
--to play underneath those *bright lights.*
This is the Dragons' *eighth* trip to State!
Maybe *this* is the year they finally bring home that *championship trophy!*

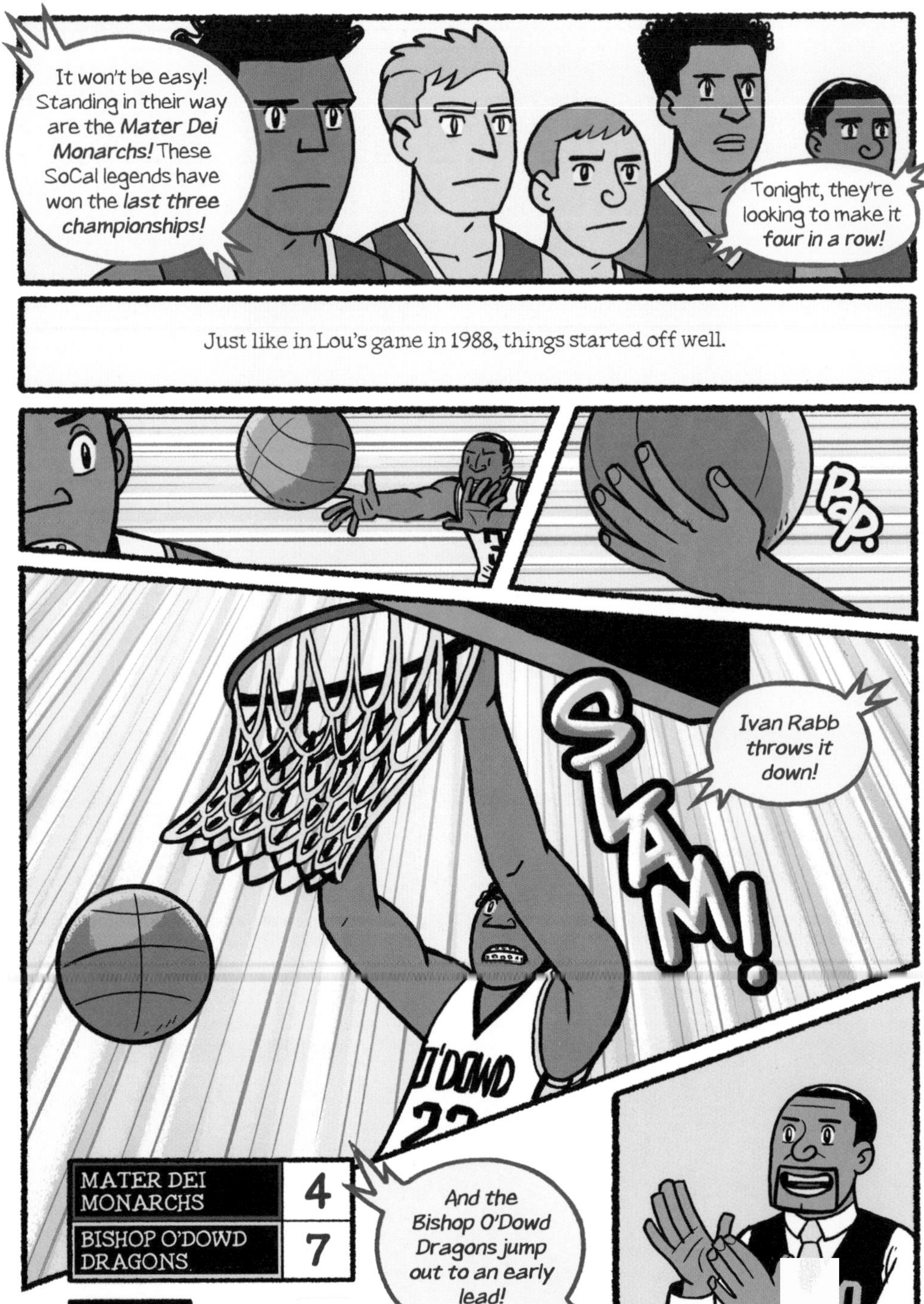
It won't be easy! Standing in their way are the *Mater Dei Monarchs!* These SoCal legends have won the *last three championships!*
Tonight, they're looking to make it *four in a row!*
Just like in Lou's game in 1988, things started off well.
PAP.
SLAM!
Ivan Rabb throws it down!
O'DOWD
MATER DEI MONARCHS 4
BISHOP O'DOWD DRAGONS 7
4:05 PERIOD
And the Bishop O'Dowd Dragons jump out to an early lead!

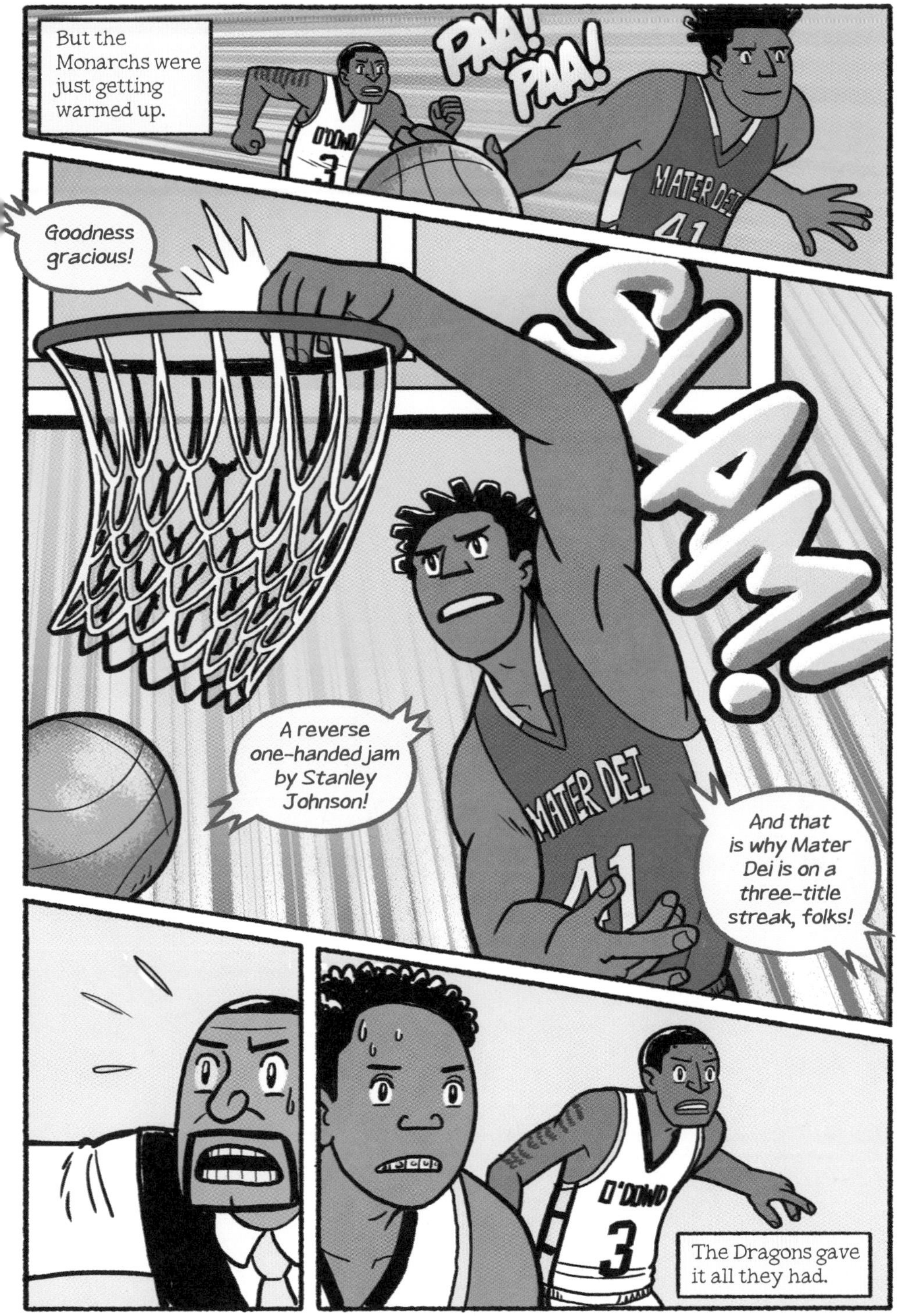

But the Monarchs were just getting warmed up.
PAA! PAA!
O'DOWD 3
MATER DEI 41
Goodness gracious!
SLAM!!
A reverse one-handed jam by Stanley Johnson!
MATER DEI 41
And that is why Mater Dei is on a three-title streak, folks!
O'DOWD 3
The Dragons gave it all they had.

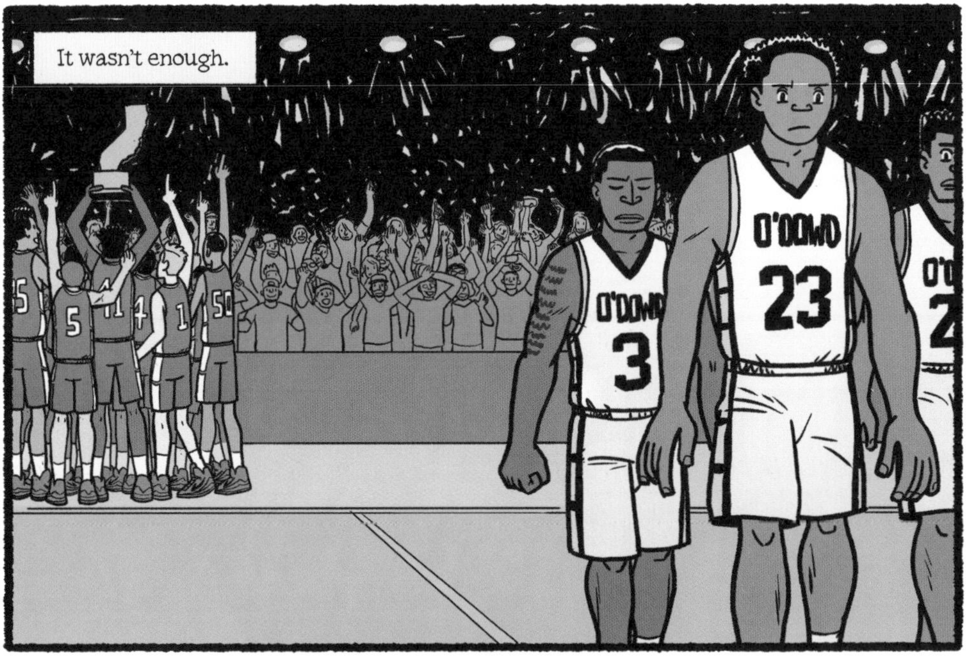
It wasn't enough.
O'DOWD
23
O'DOWD
3

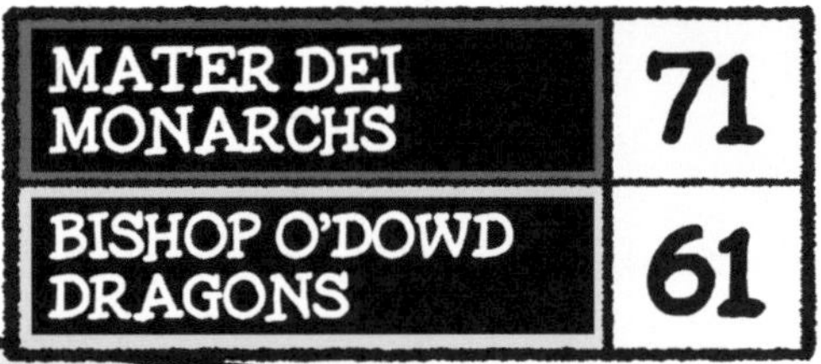
MATER DEI MONARCHS
71
BISHOP O'DOWD DRAGONS
61

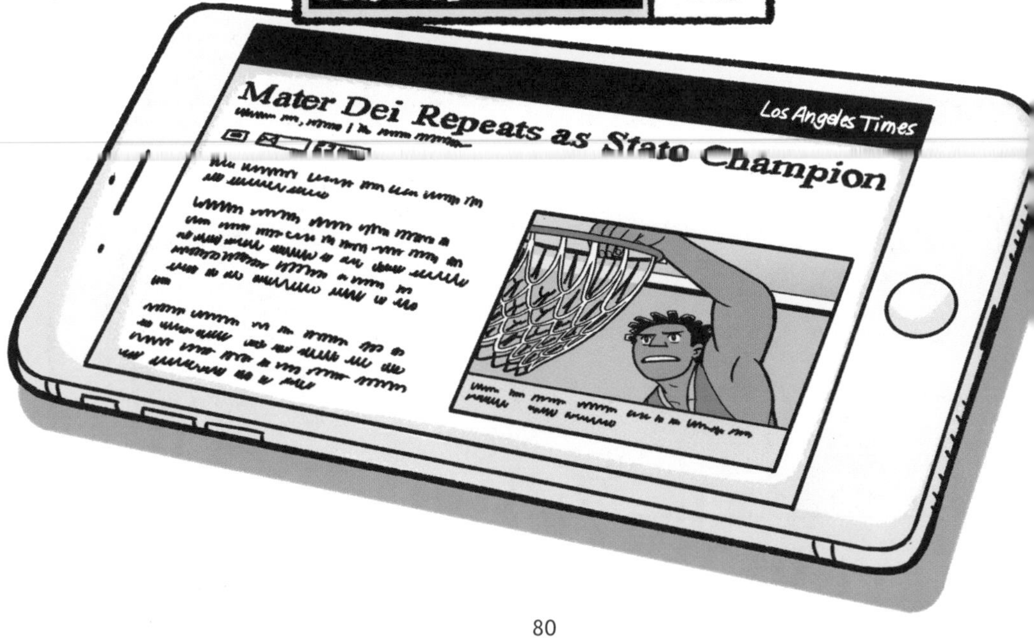
Mater Dei Repeats as State Champion
Los Angeles Times

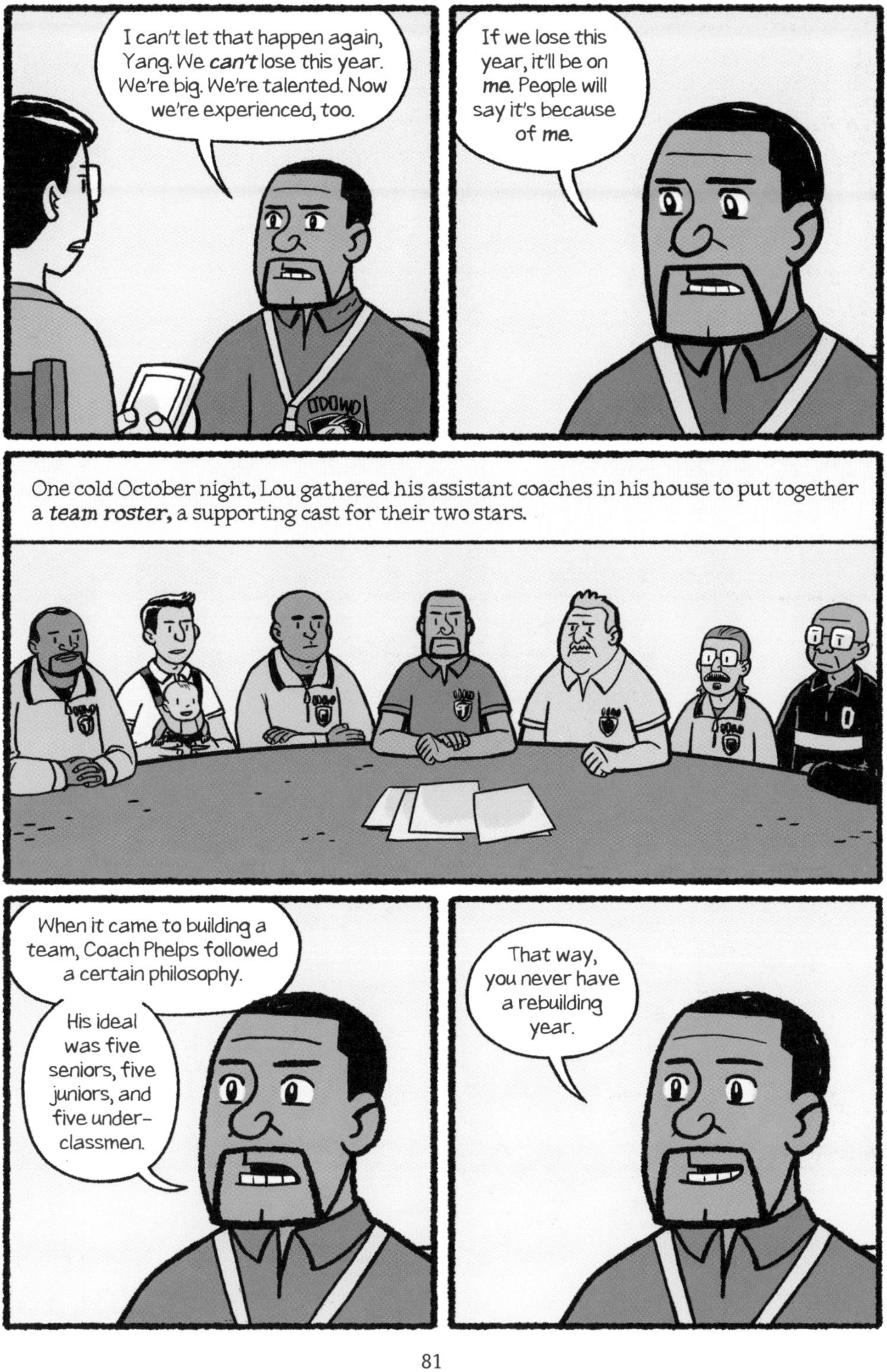
I can't let that happen again, Yang. We *can't* lose this year. We're big. We're talented. Now we're experienced, too.
If we lose this year, it'll be on **me**. People will say it's because of **me**.
One cold October night, Lou gathered his assistant coaches in his house to put together a ***team roster,*** a supporting cast for their two stars.
When it came to building a team, Coach Phelps followed a certain philosophy.
His ideal was five seniors, five juniors, and five under-classmen.
That way, you never have a rebuilding year.

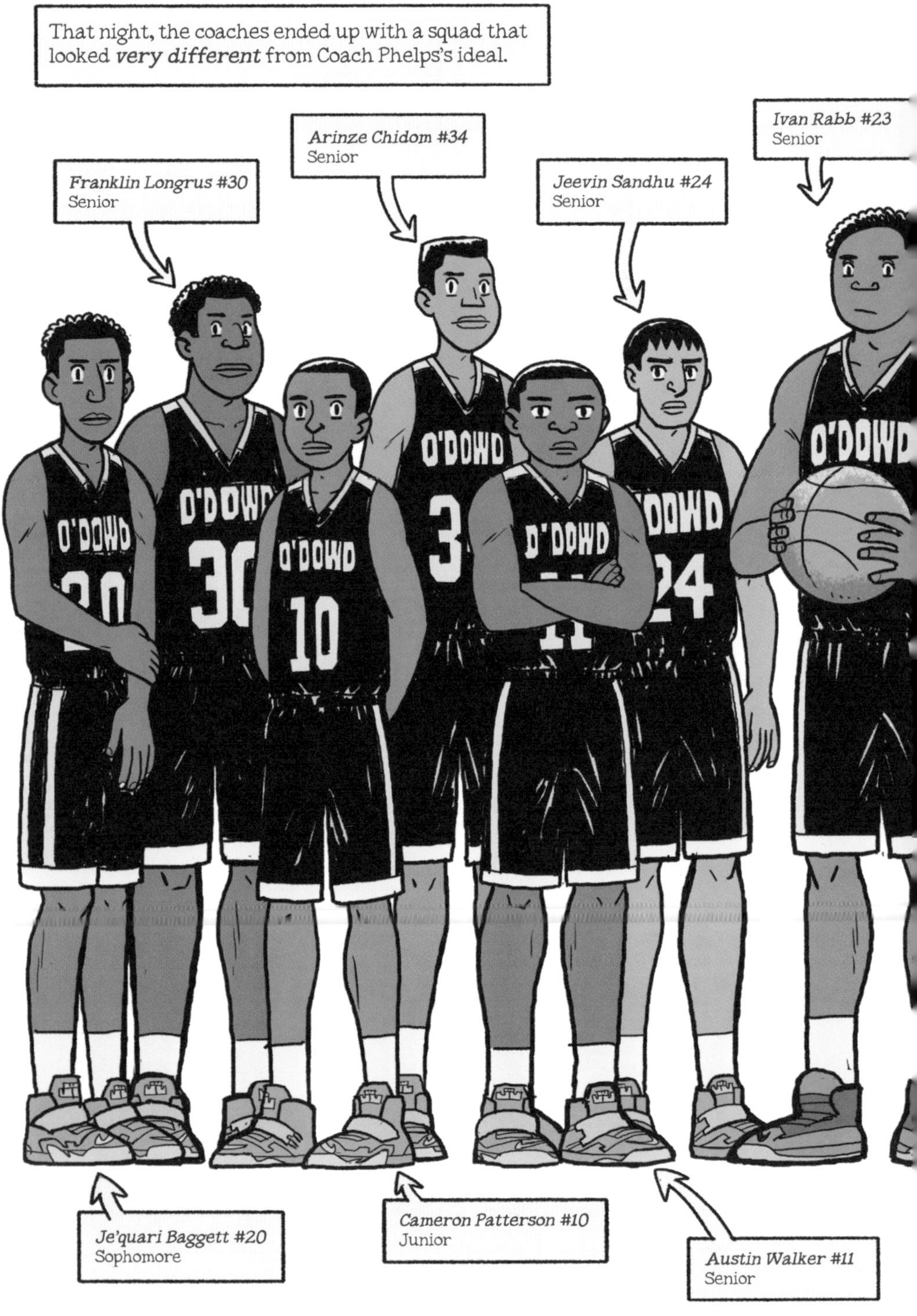
That night, the coaches ended up with a squad that looked ***very different*** from Coach Phelps's ideal.
Franklin Longrus #30
Senior
Arinze Chidom #34
Senior
Jeevin Sandhu #24
Senior
Ivan Rabb #23
Senior
O'DOWD
30
O'DOWD
10
O'DOWD
3
O'DOWD
O'DOWD
24
O'DOWD
Je'quari Baggett #20
Sophomore
Cameron Patterson #10
Junior
Austin Walker #11
Senior

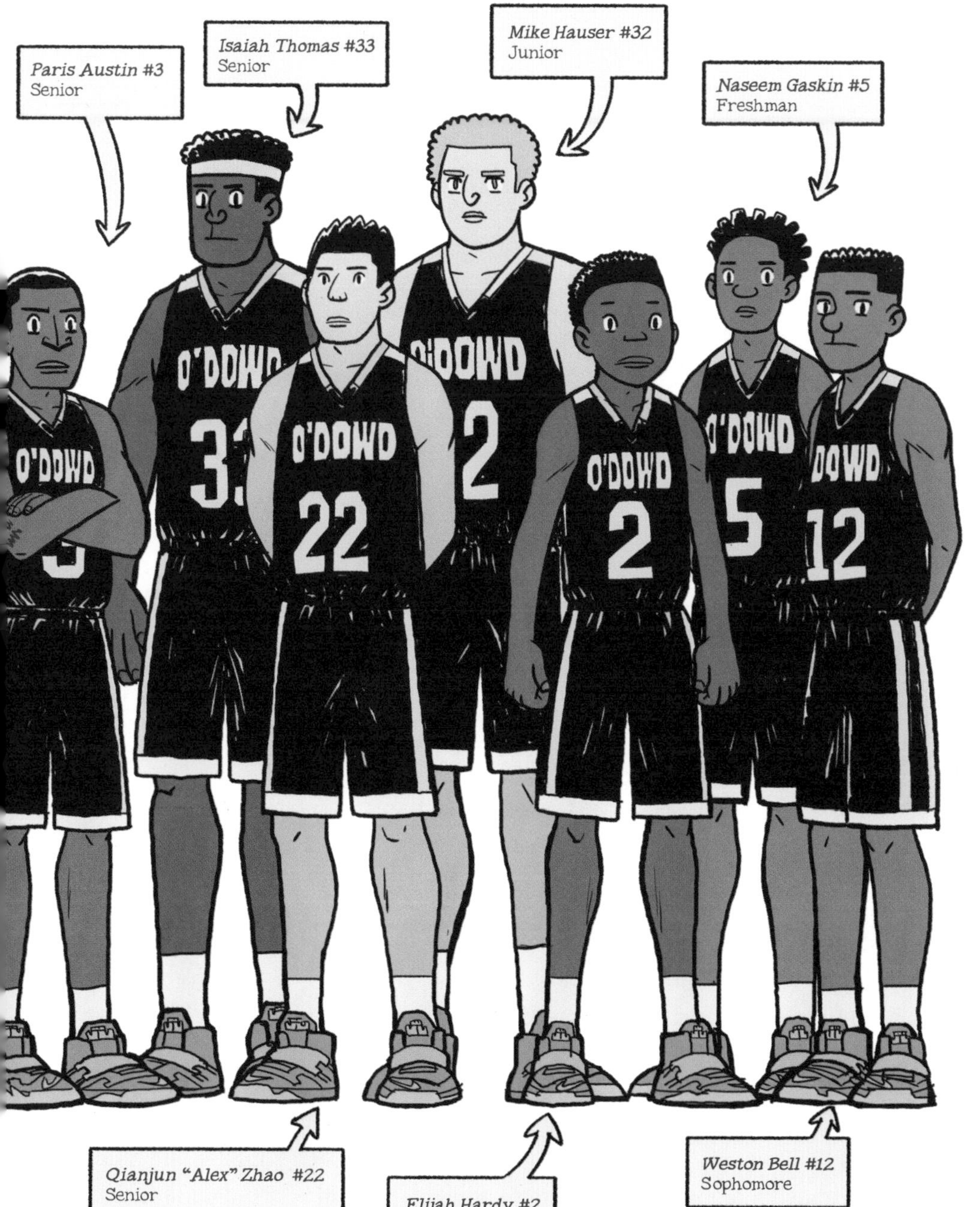

Paris Austin #3
Senior
Isaiah Thomas #33
Senior
Mike Hauser #32
Junior
Naseem Gaskin #5
Freshman
O'DOWD
O'DOWD
O'DOWD
O'DOWD
O'DOWD
O'DOWD
DOWD
33
22
2
2
5
12
Qianjun "Alex" Zhao #22
Senior
Elijah Hardy #2
Freshman
Weston Bell #12
Sophomore

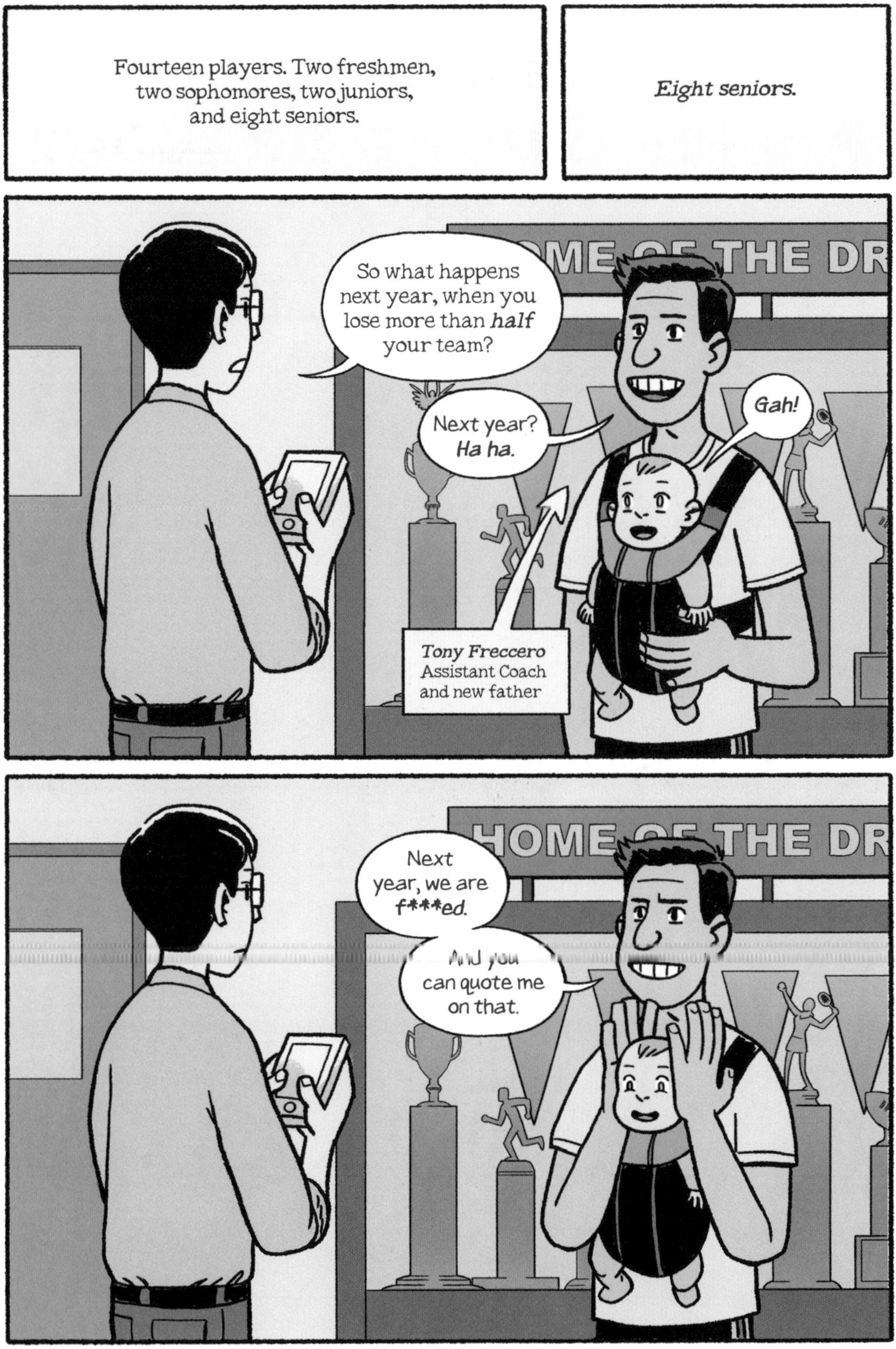
Fourteen players. Two freshmen, two sophomores, two juniors, and eight seniors.
Eight seniors.
HOME OF THE DR
So what happens next year, when you lose more than ***half*** your team?
Next year? ***Ha ha.***
Gah!
Tony Freccero Assistant Coach and new father
HOME OF THE DR
Next year, we are ***f***ed.***
And you can quote me on that.

CHAPTER 3:
BISHOP O'DOWD DRAGONS
VS.
DE LA SALLE SPARTANS

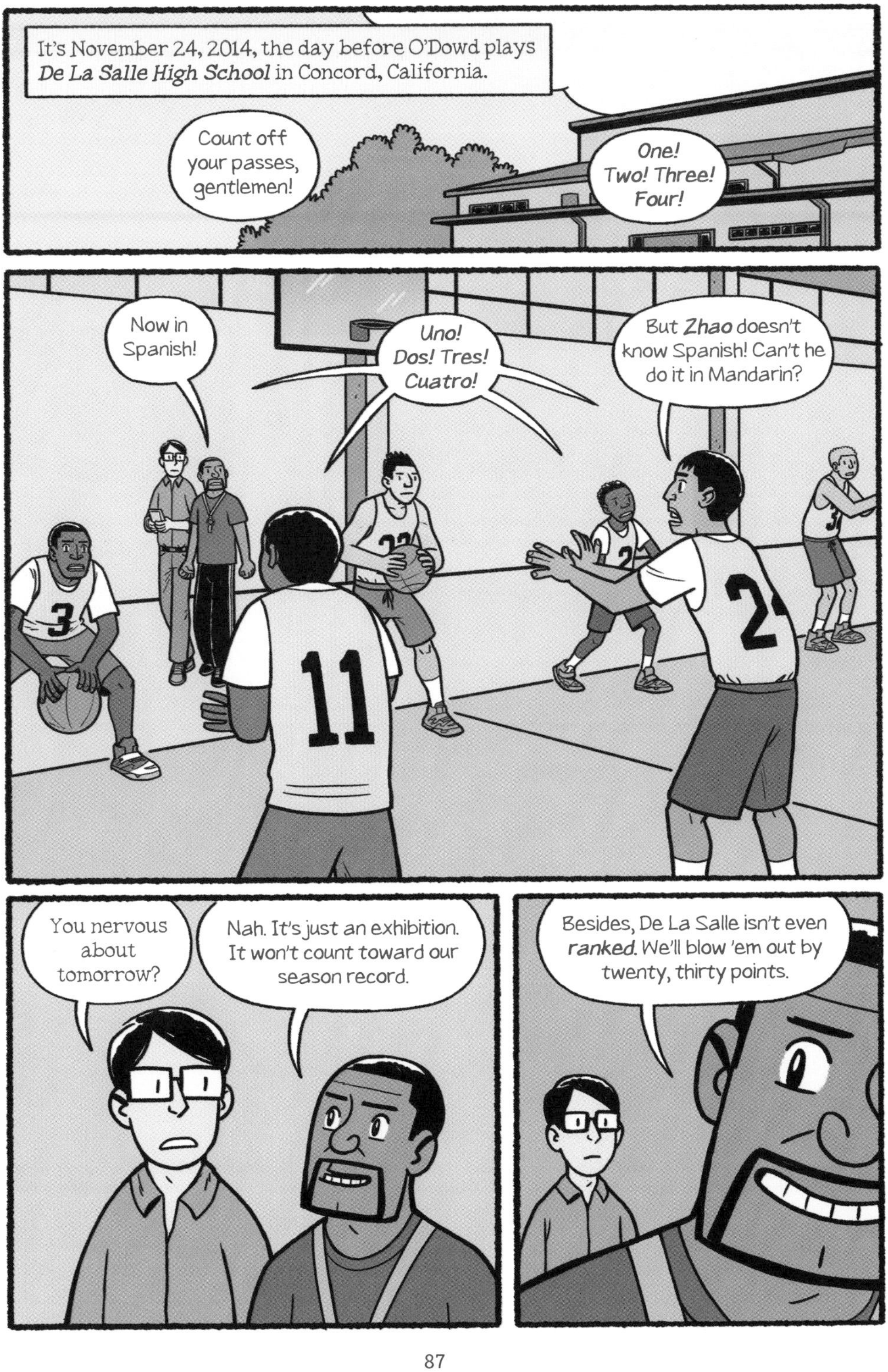
It's November 24, 2014, the day before O'Dowd plays *De La Salle High School* in Concord, California.
Count off your passes, gentlemen!
One! Two! Three! Four!
Now in Spanish!
Uno! Dos! Tres! Cuatro!
But Zhao doesn't know Spanish! Can't he do it in Mandarin?
You nervous about tomorrow?
Nah. It's just an exhibition. It won't count toward our season record.
Besides, De La Salle isn't even ranked. We'll blow 'em out by twenty, thirty points.

Later that evening, the *Ferguson decision* is announced.

Three months earlier, on August 9, 2014, an unarmed young African American man was *fatally shot* by a white police officer in Ferguson, Missouri.

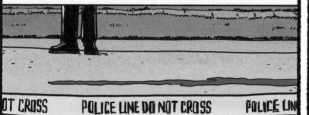

OT CROSS   POLICE LINE DO NOT CROSS   POLICE LIN

The victim's name was *Michael Brown.* He was the same age as the seniors are now.

The jury has determined that *no probable cause* exists to file any charge against Officer Wilson.

Protests erupt in cities all over the nation--

END POLICE BRUTALITY

BLACK LIVES MATTER

--including *Oakland.*

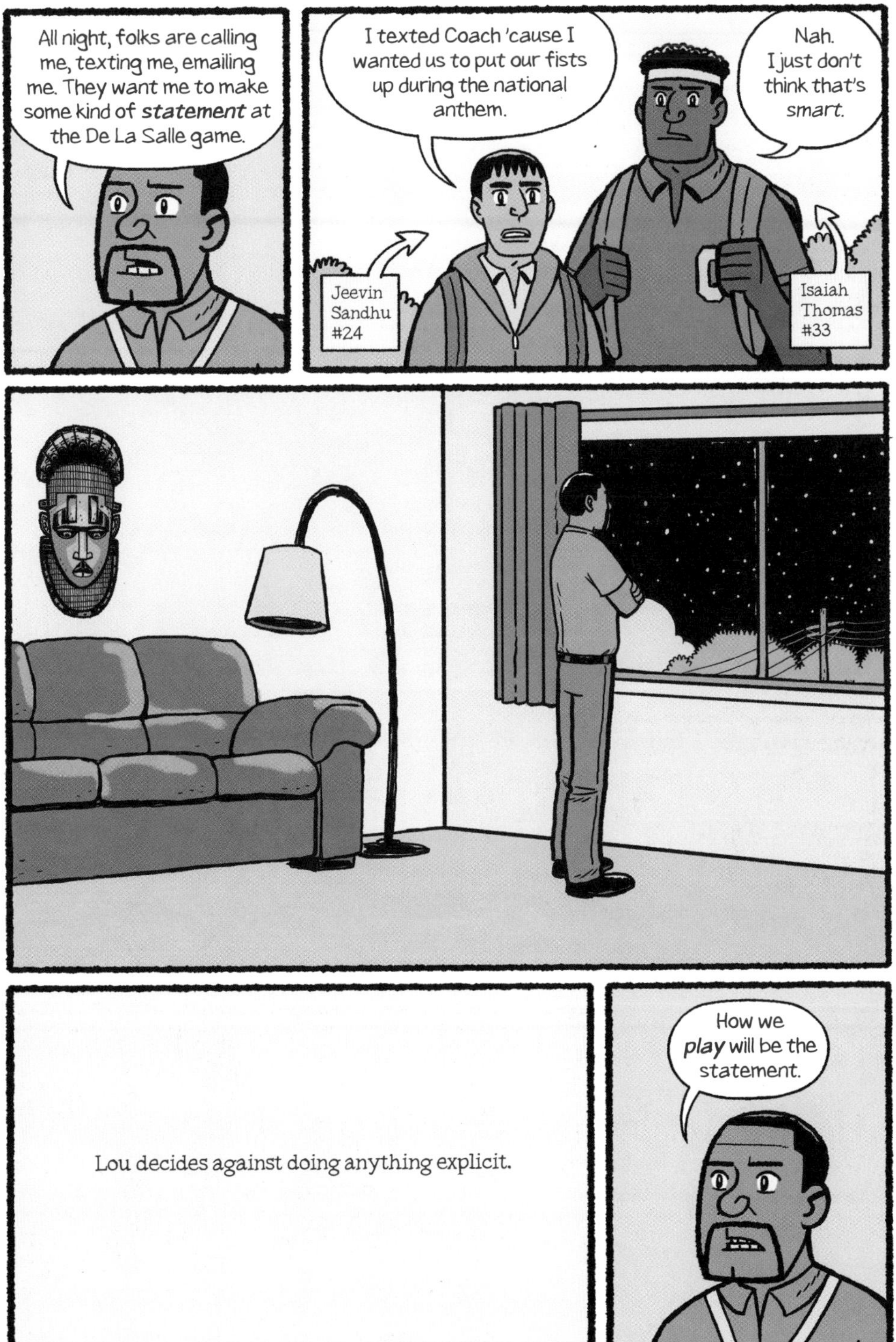
All night, folks are calling me, texting me, emailing me. They want me to make some kind of ***statement*** at the De La Salle game.
I texted Coach 'cause I wanted us to put our fists up during the national anthem.
Nah. I just don't think that's *smart*.
Jeevin Sandhu #24
Isaiah Thomas #33
Lou decides against doing anything explicit.
How we ***play*** will be the statement.

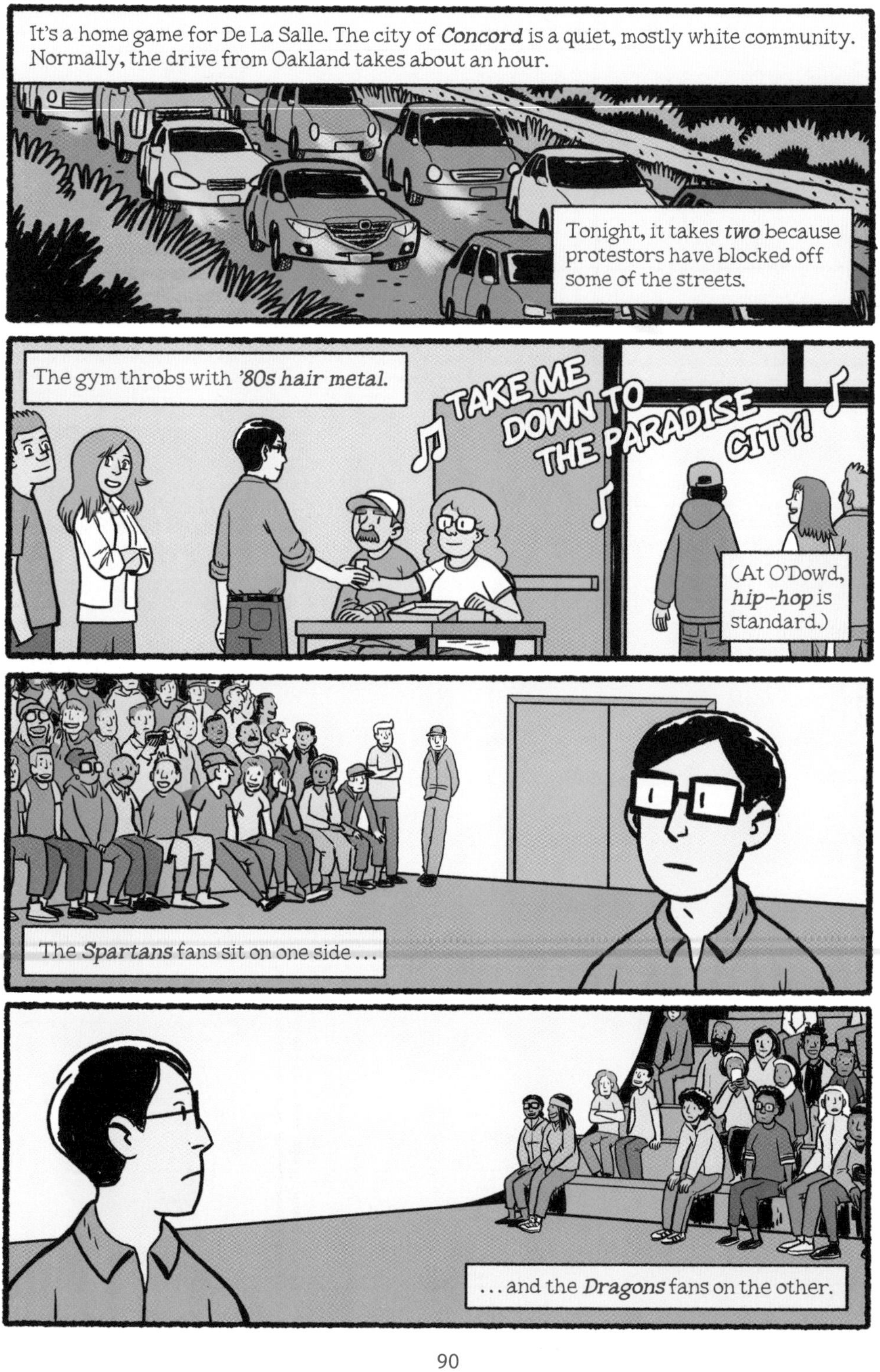
It's a home game for De La Salle. The city of *Concord* is a quiet, mostly white community. Normally, the drive from Oakland takes about an hour.
Tonight, it takes *two* because protestors have blocked off some of the streets.
The gym throbs with *'80s hair metal.*
TAKE ME DOWN TO THE PARADISE CITY!
(At O'Dowd, *hip-hop* is standard.)
The *Spartans* fans sit on one side...
...and the *Dragons* fans on the other.

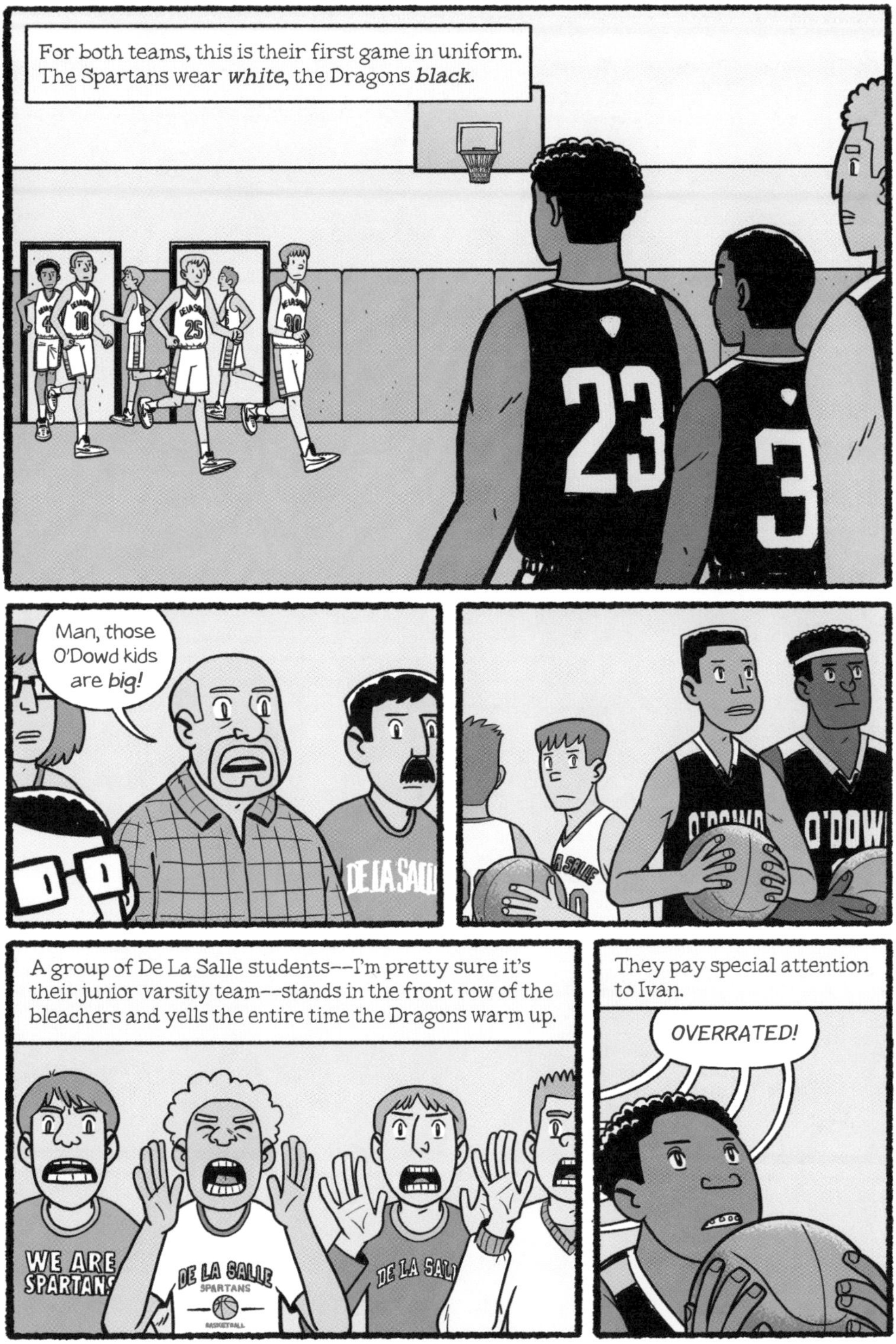

For both teams, this is their first game in uniform. The Spartans wear *white*, the Dragons *black*.
23
3
Man, those O'Dowd kids are *big*!
DE LA SALLE
LA SALLE
O'DOWD
O'DOW
A group of De La Salle students--I'm pretty sure it's their junior varsity team--stands in the front row of the bleachers and yells the entire time the Dragons warm up.
WE ARE SPARTANS
DE LA SALLE
SPARTANS
DE LA SALL
They pay special attention to Ivan.
OVERRATED!

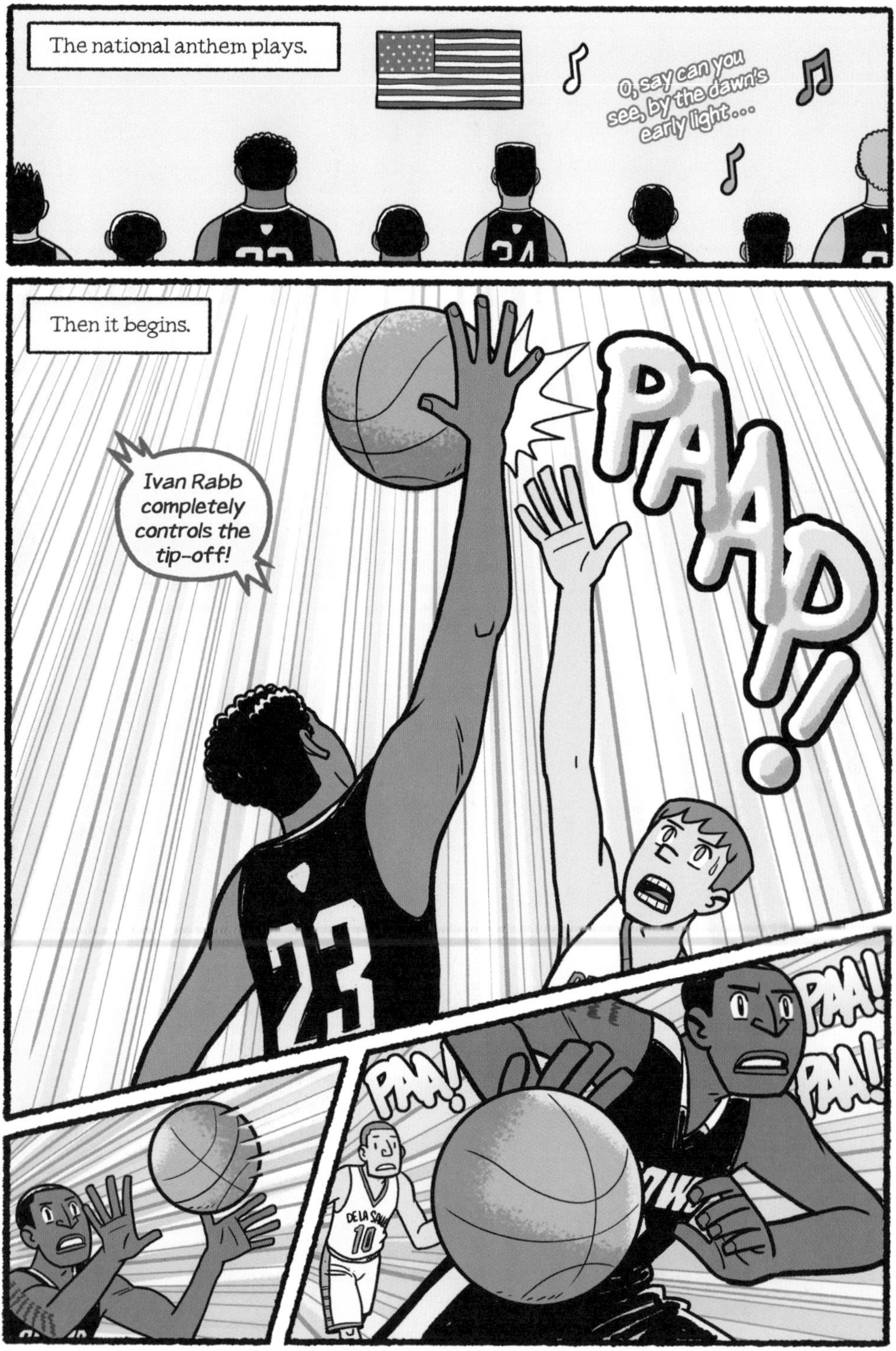
The national anthem plays.
O, say can you see, by the dawn's early light . . .
Then it begins.
Ivan Rabb completely controls the tip-off!
PAAAP!!
PAA!
PAA!
PAA!

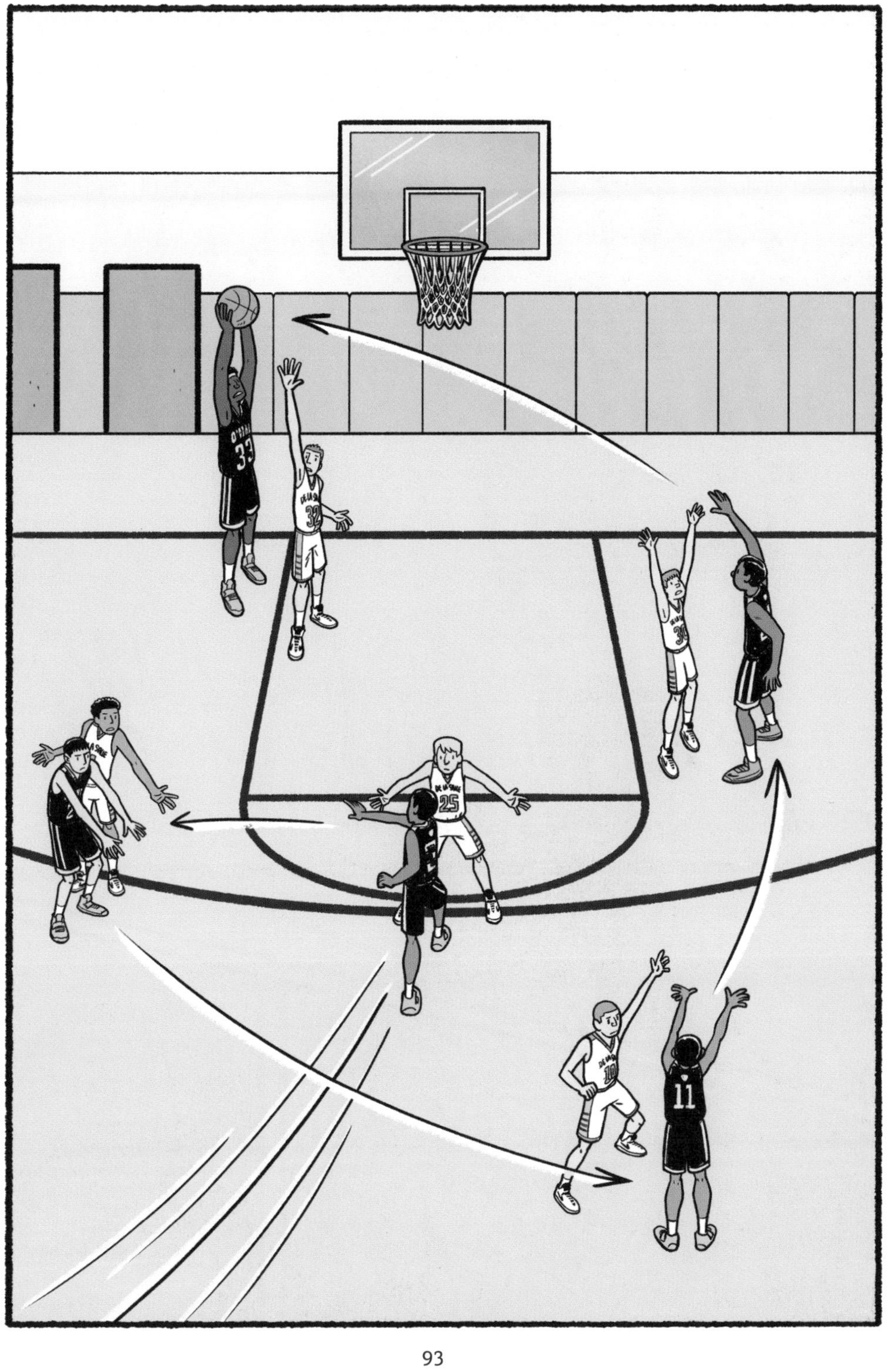

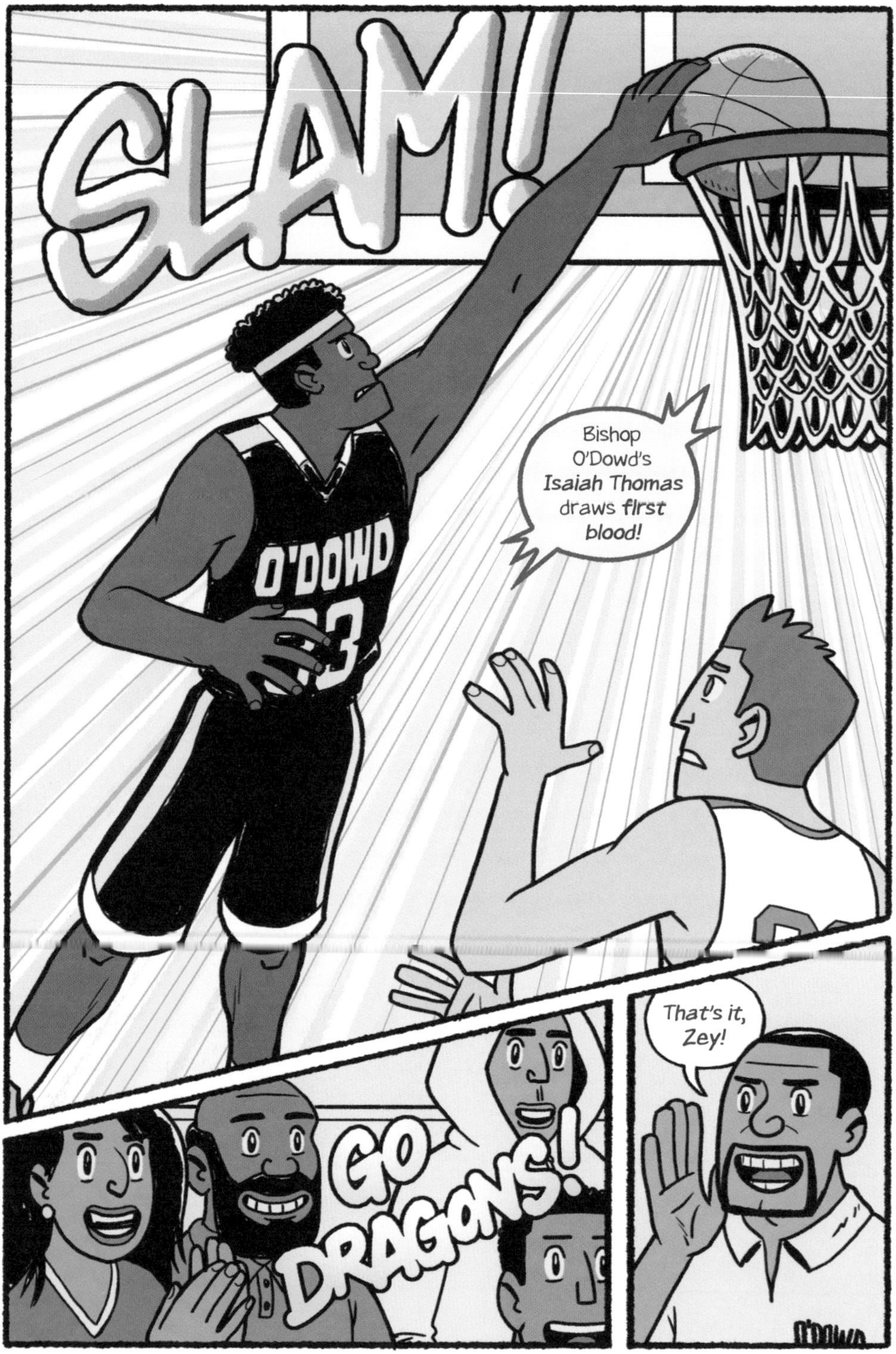
SLAM!
O'DOWD
Bishop O'Dowd's Isaiah Thomas draws first blood!
GO DRAGONS!
That's it, Zey!

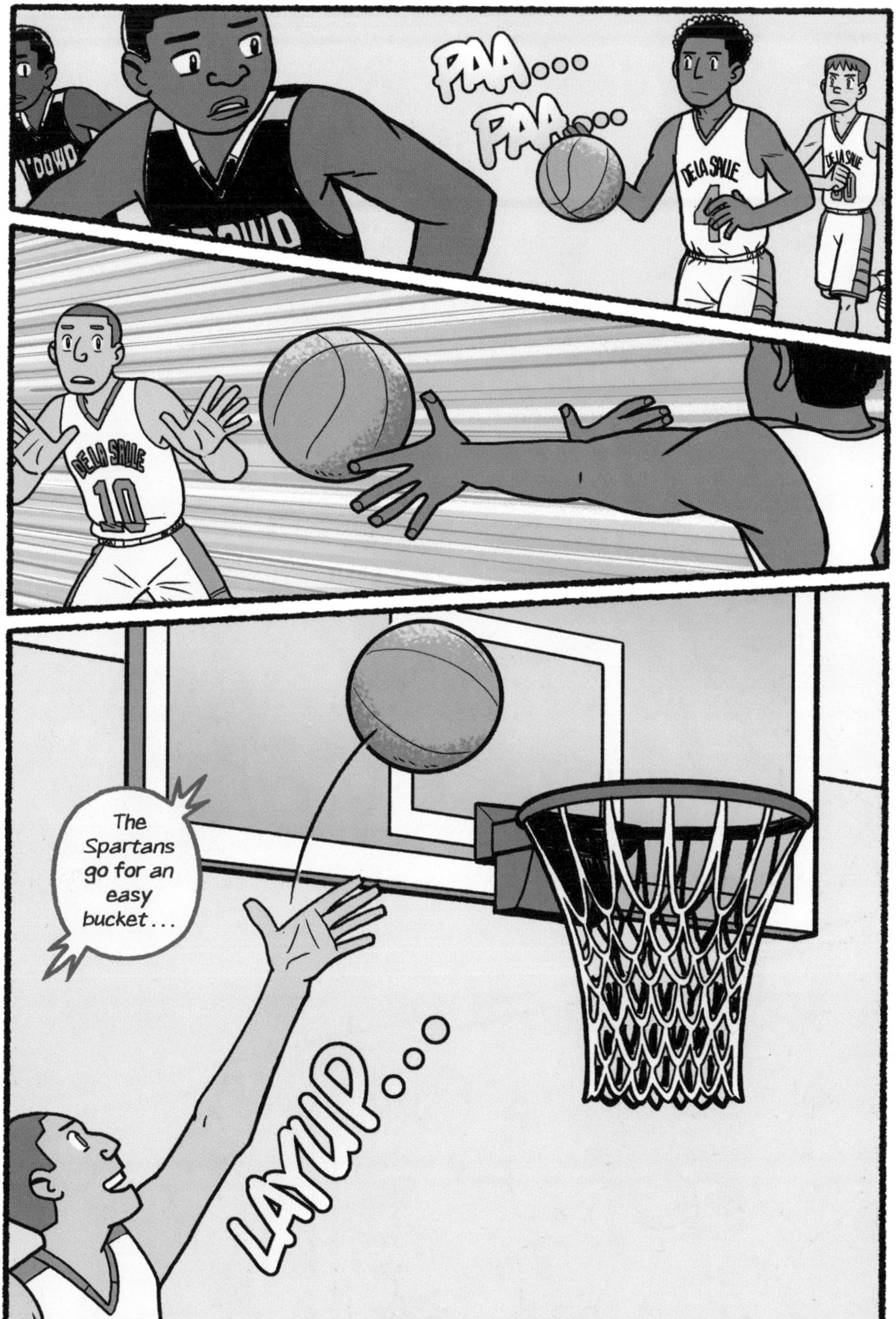
PAA...
PAA...
The Spartans go for an easy bucket...
LAYUP...

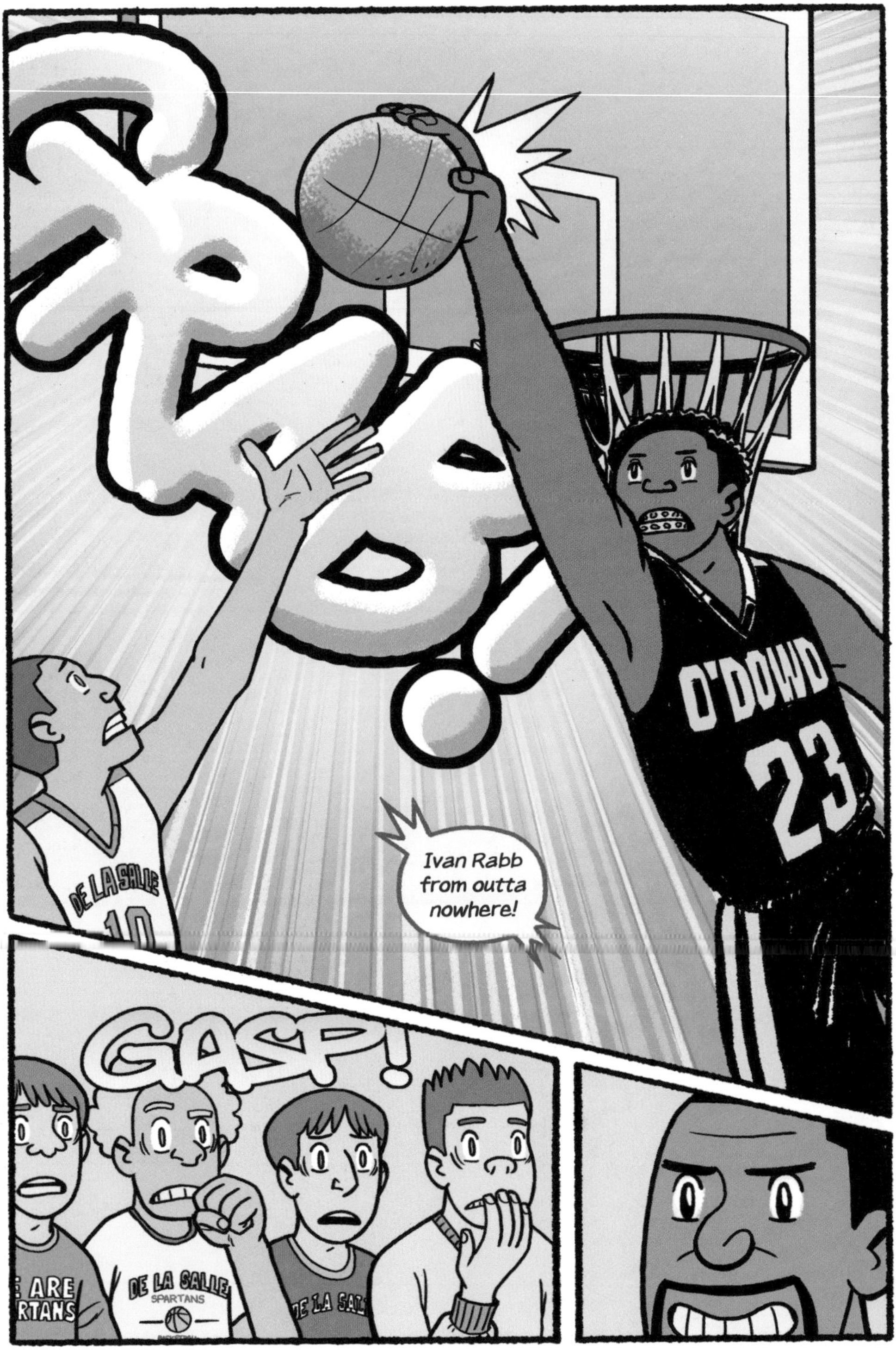
O'DOWD
23
DE LA SALLE
10
Ivan Rabb from outta nowhere!
GASP!
DE LA SALLE
SPARTANS

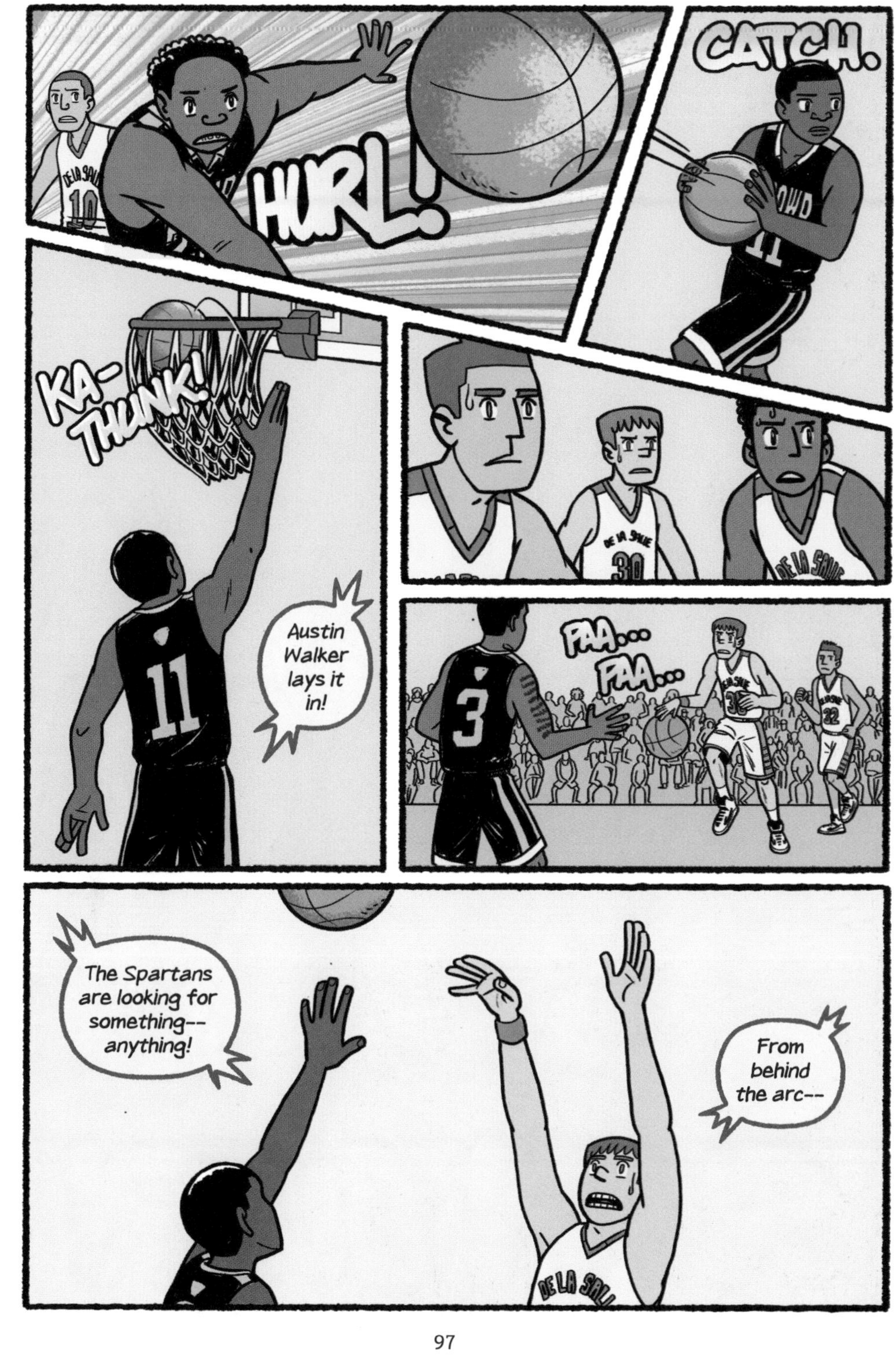
HURL!
CATCH.
KA-THUNK!
Austin Walker lays it in!
PAA... PAA...
The Spartans are looking for something--anything!
From behind the arc--

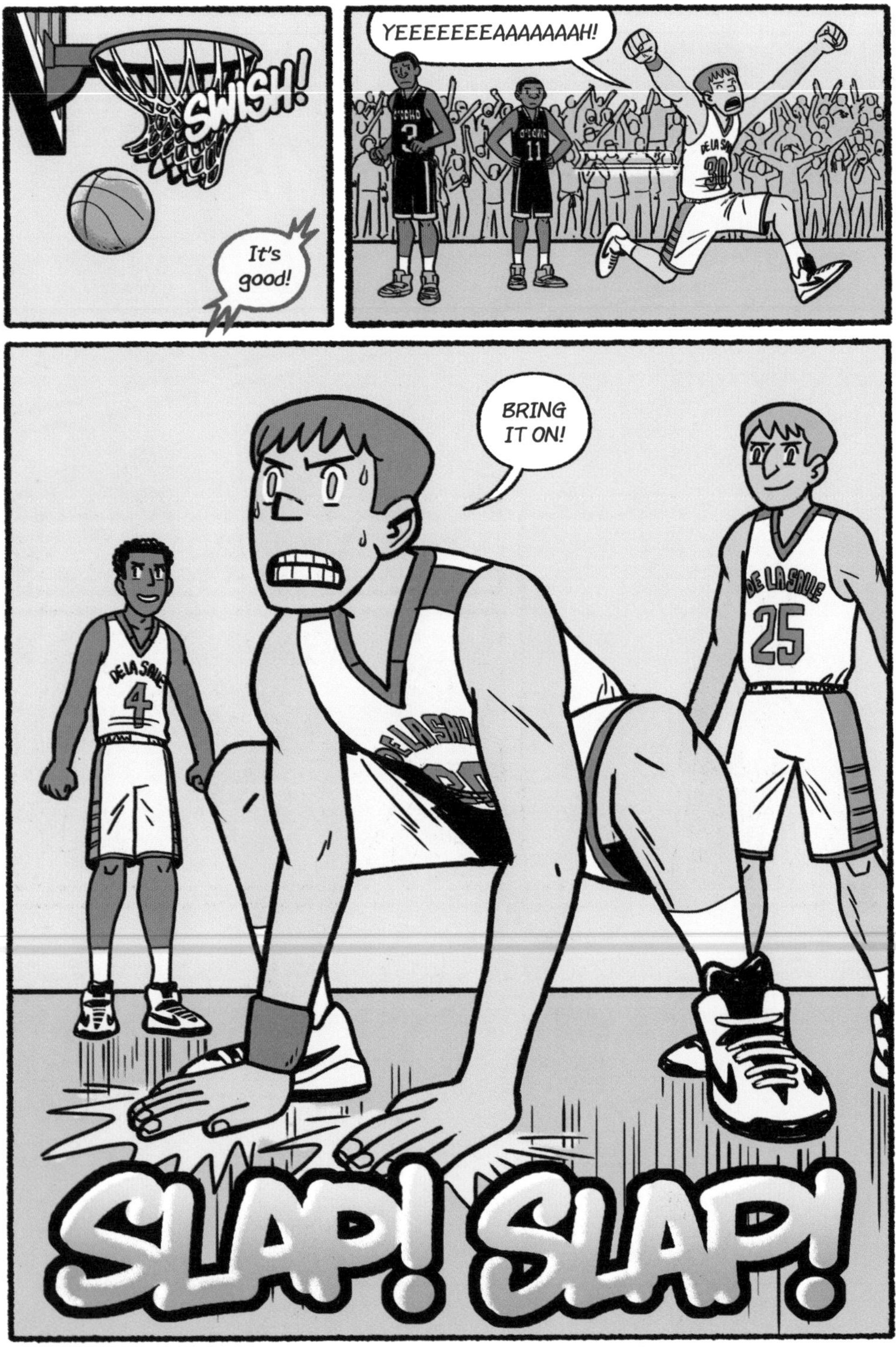
SWISH!
It's good!
YEEEEEEEAAAAAAAH!
BRING IT ON!
SLAP! SLAP!

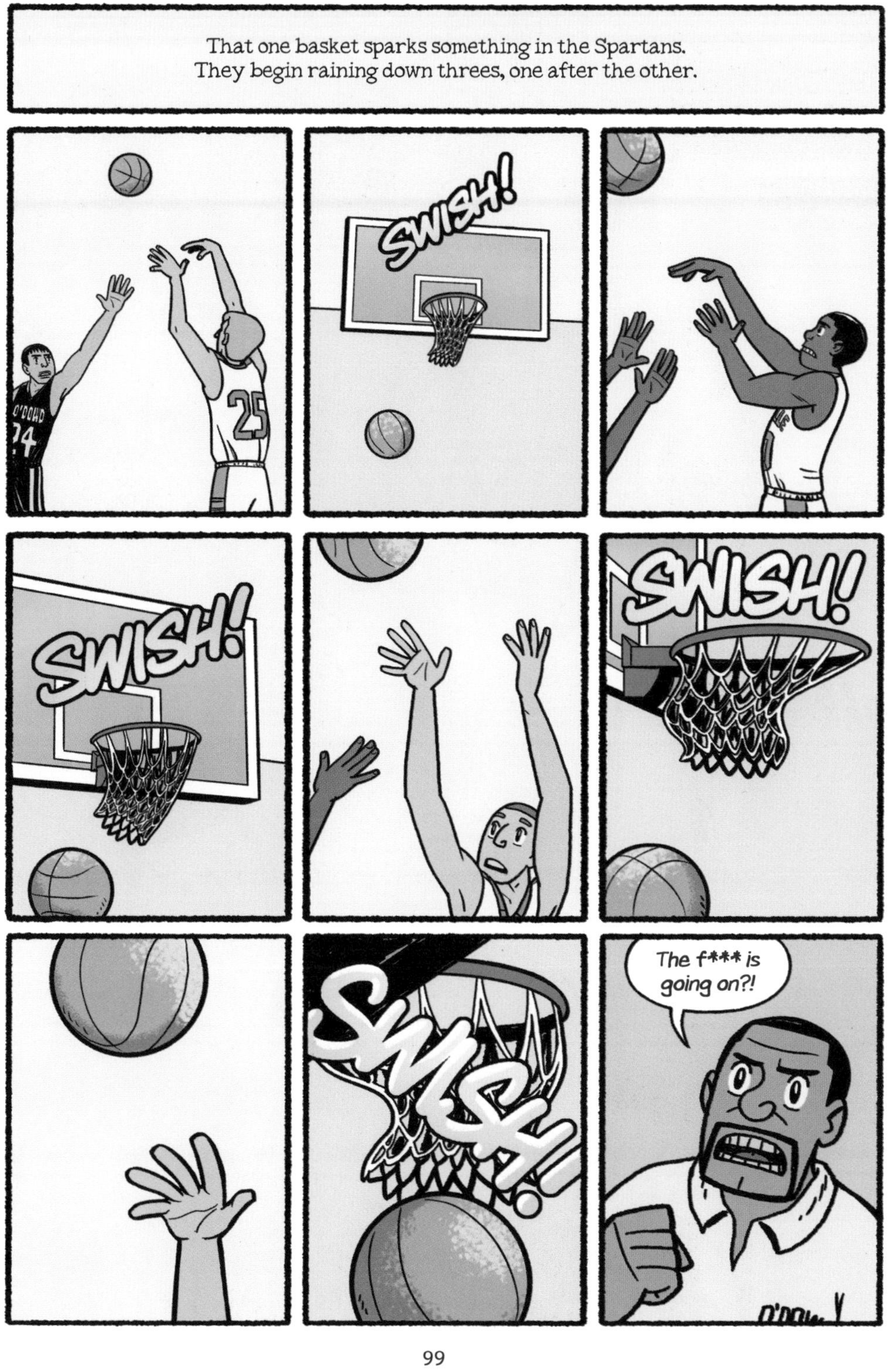
That one basket sparks something in the Spartans.
They begin raining down threes, one after the other.
SWISH!
SWISH!
SWISH!
SWISH!
The f*** is going on?!

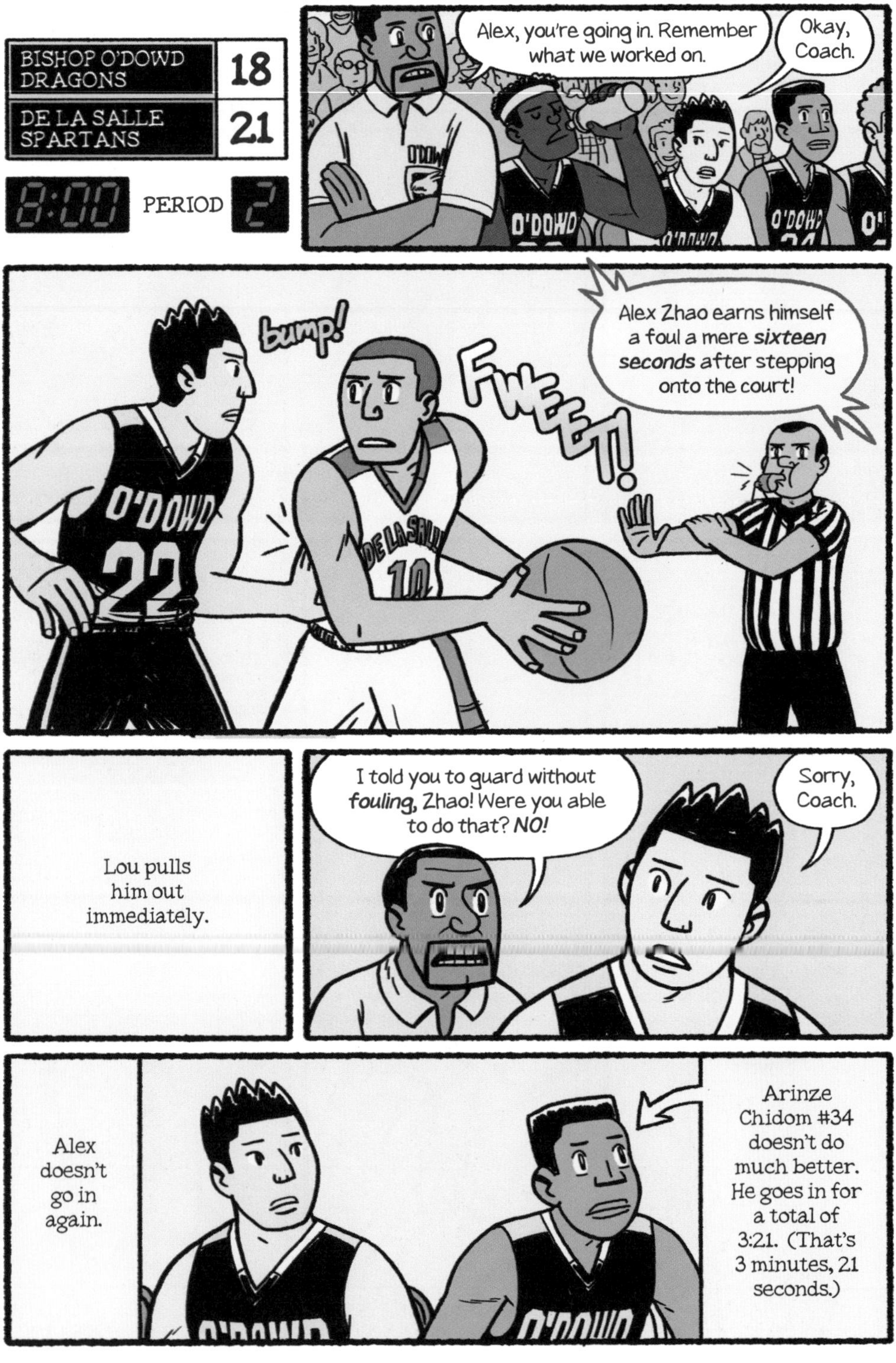

BISHOP O'DOWD DRAGONS
18
DE LA SALLE SPARTANS
21
8:00
PERIOD
2
Alex, you're going in. Remember what we worked on.
Okay, Coach.
O'DOWD
bump!
FWEET!
Alex Zhao earns himself a foul a mere *sixteen seconds* after stepping onto the court!
O'DOWD
22
DE LA SALLE
10
Lou pulls him out immediately.
I told you to guard without *fouling*, Zhao! Were you able to do that? *NO!*
Sorry, Coach.
Alex doesn't go in again.
Arinze Chidom #34 doesn't do much better. He goes in for a total of 3:21. (That's 3 minutes, 21 seconds.)

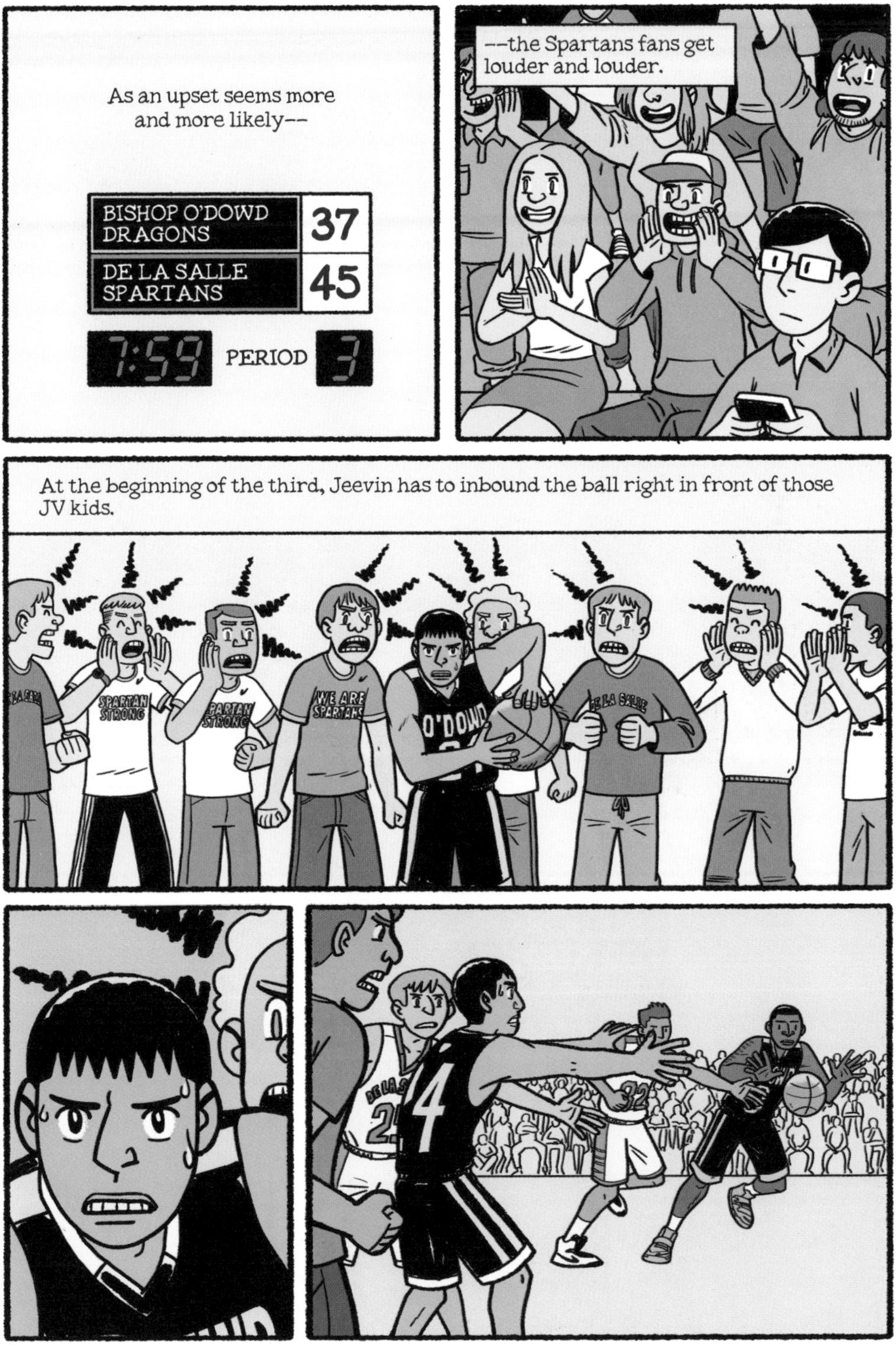
As an upset seems more and more likely--
BISHOP O'DOWD DRAGONS
37
DE LA SALLE SPARTANS
45
7:59
PERIOD
3
--the Spartans fans get louder and louder.
At the beginning of the third, Jeevin has to inbound the ball right in front of those JV kids.
SPARTAN STRONG
SPARTAN STRONG
WE ARE SPARTANS
O'DOWD
DE LA SALLE
4

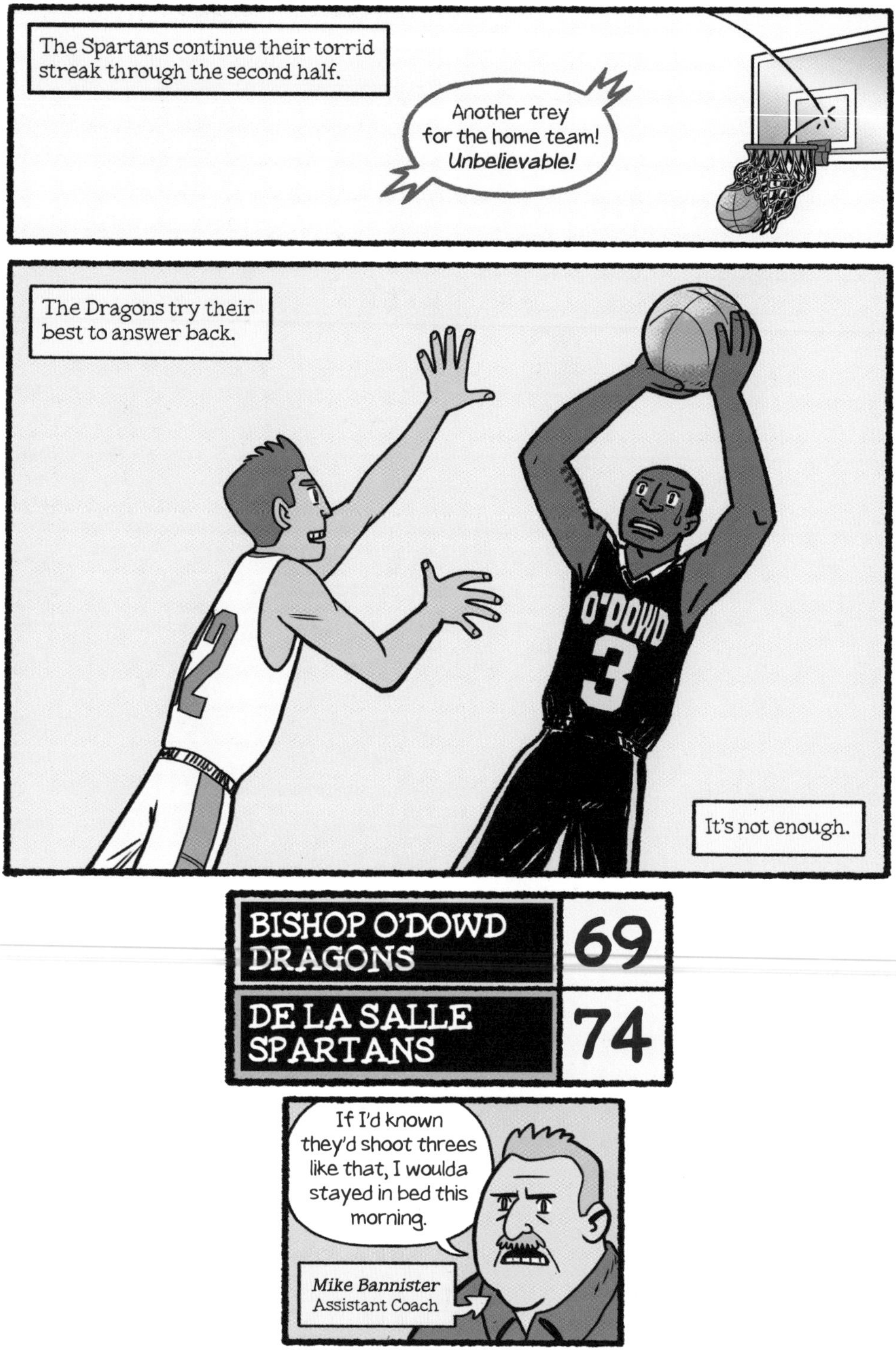
The Spartans continue their torrid streak through the second half.
Another trey for the home team! *Unbelievable!*
The Dragons try their best to answer back.
O'DOWD 3
It's not enough.
BISHOP O'DOWD DRAGONS 69
DE LA SALLE SPARTANS 74
If I'd known they'd shoot threes like that, I woulda stayed in bed this morning.
Mike Bannister Assistant Coach

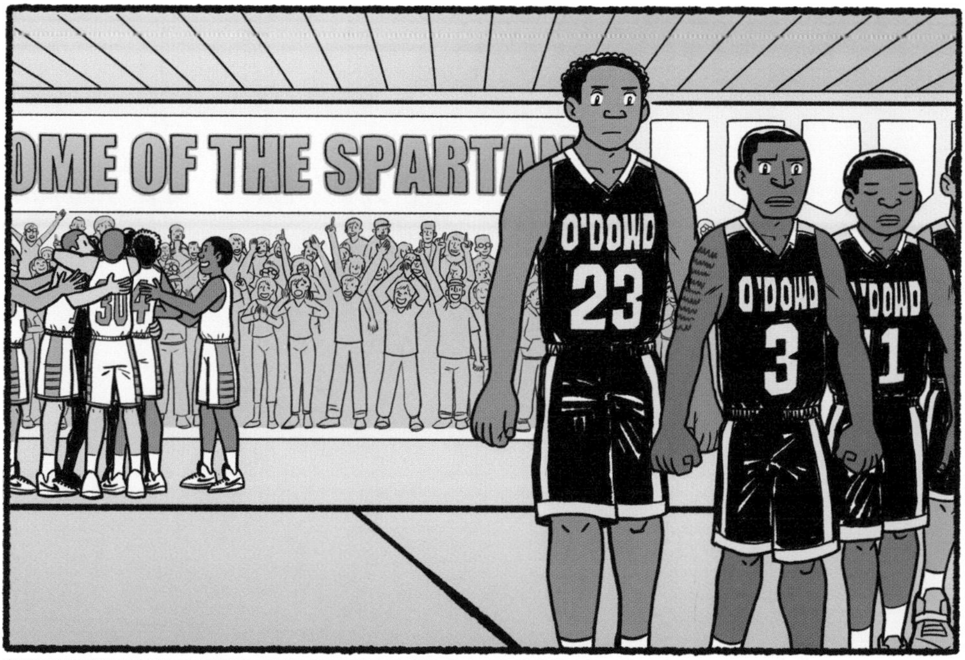
OME OF THE SPARTAN
O'DOWD 23
O'DOWD 3

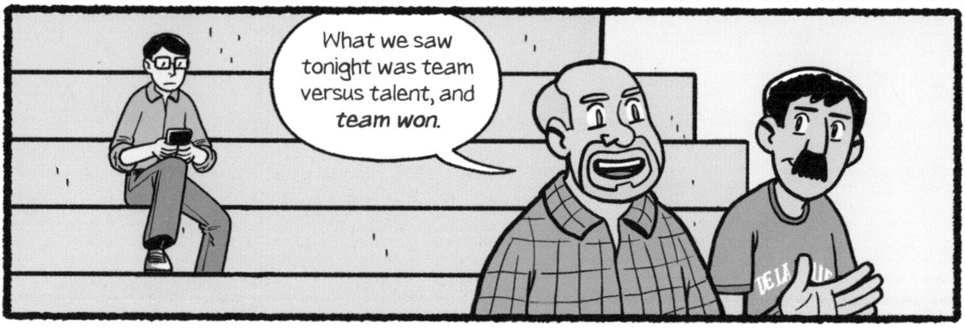
What we saw tonight was team versus talent, and *team won.*

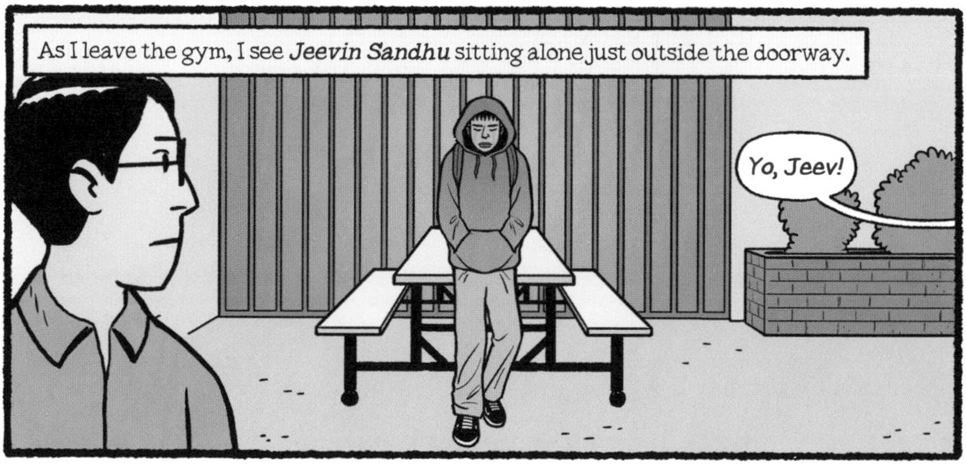
As I leave the gym, I see *Jeevin Sandhu* sitting alone just outside the doorway.
Yo, Jeev!

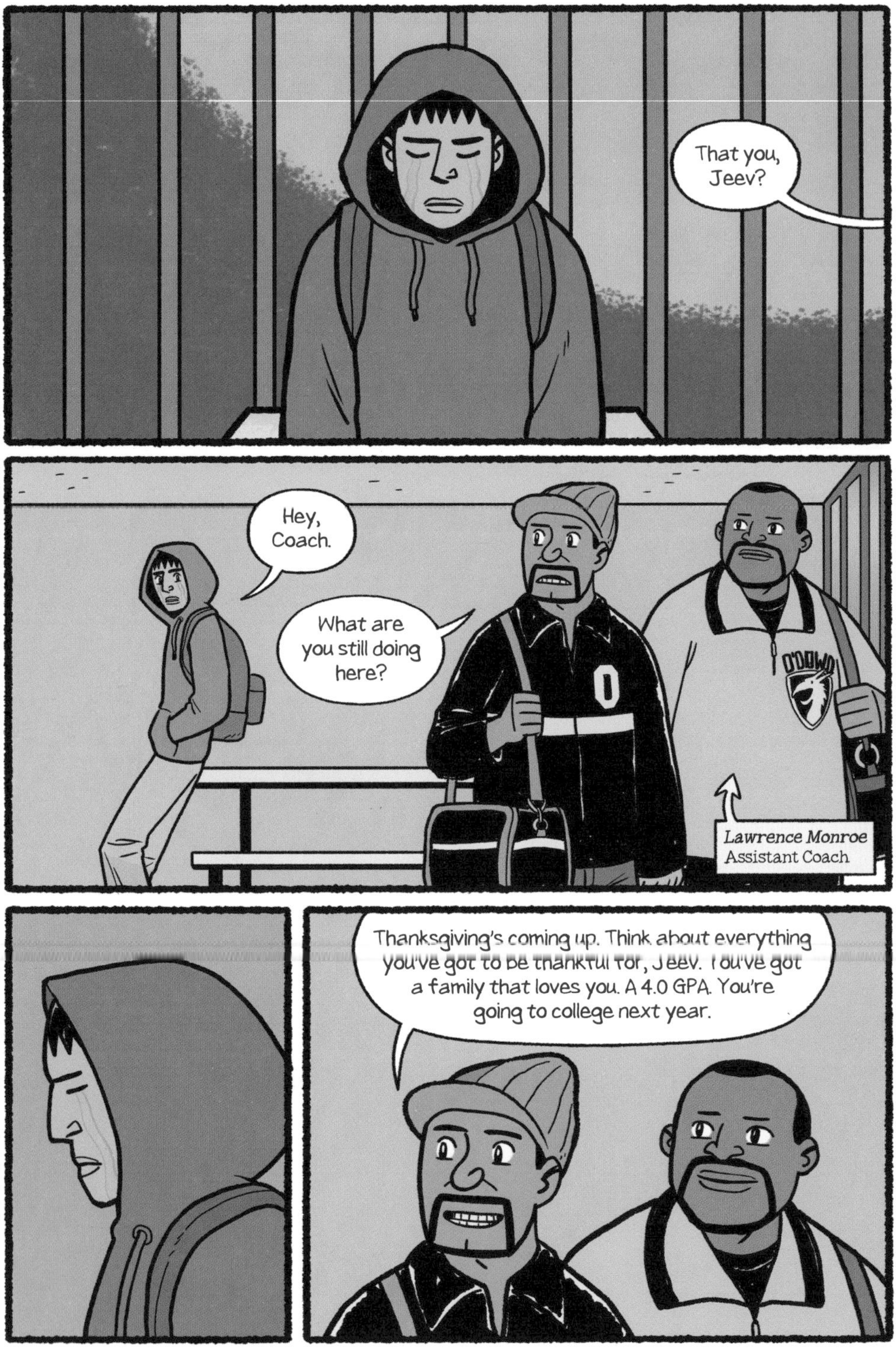
That you, Jeev?
Hey, Coach.
What are you still doing here?
Lawrence Monroe
Assistant Coach
Thanksgiving's coming up. Think about everything you've got to be thankful for, Jeev. You've got a family that loves you. A 4.0 GPA. You're going to college next year.

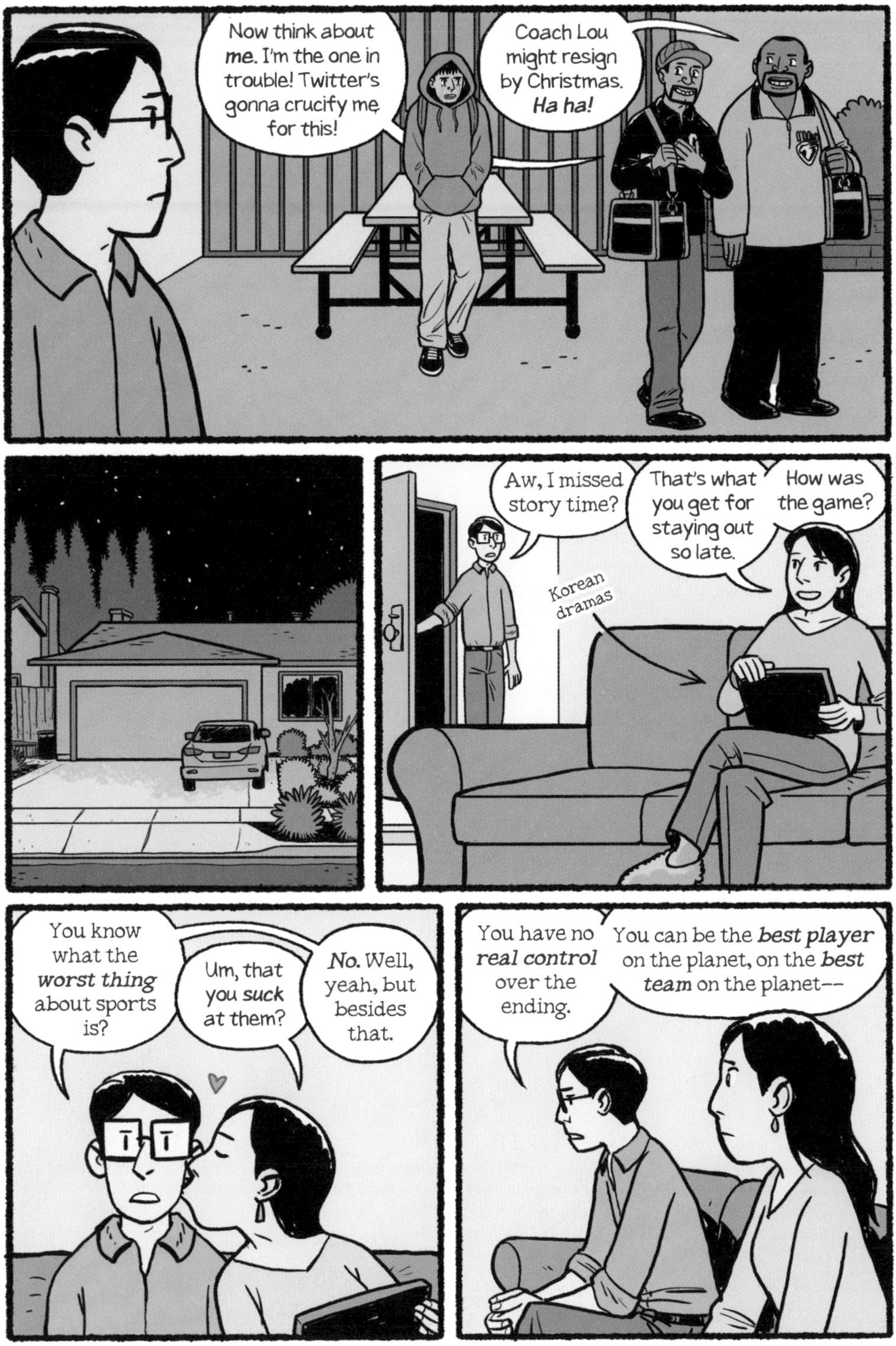
Now think about **me**. I'm the one in trouble! Twitter's gonna crucify me for this!
Coach Lou might resign by Christmas. ***Ha ha!***
Aw, I missed story time?
That's what you get for staying out so late.
How was the game?
Korean dramas
You know what the ***worst thing*** about sports is?
Um, that you ***suck*** at them?
No. Well, yeah, but besides that.
You have no ***real control*** over the ending.
You can be the ***best player*** on the planet, on the ***best team*** on the planet--

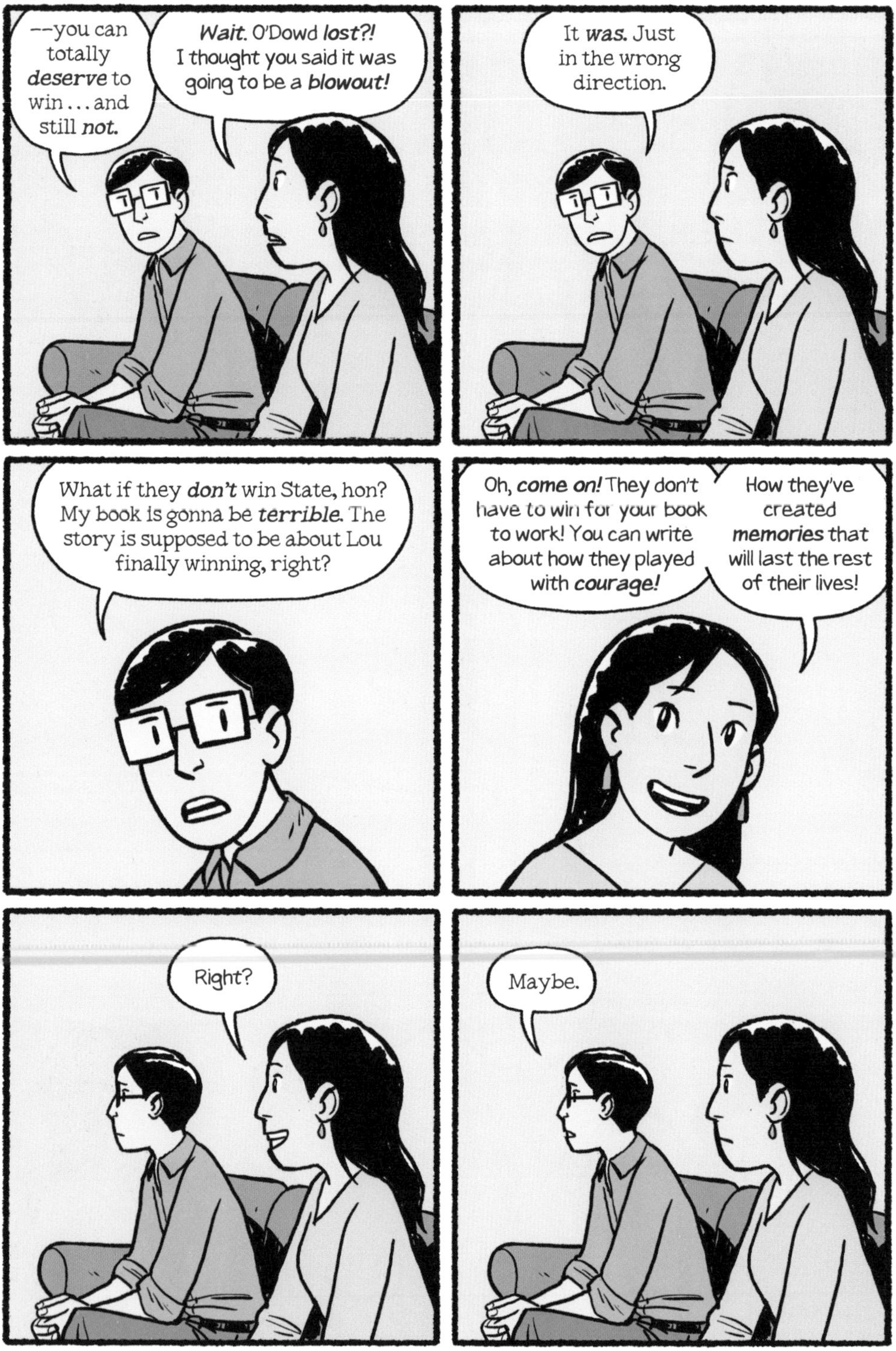
--you can totally *deserve* to win... and still *not.*
Wait. O'Dowd *lost?!* I thought you said it was going to be a *blowout!*
It *was.* Just in the wrong direction.
What if they *don't* win State, hon? My book is gonna be *terrible.* The story is supposed to be about Lou finally winning, right?
Oh, *come on!* They don't have to win for your book to work! You can write about how they played with *courage!*
How they've created *memories* that will last the rest of their lives!
Right?
Maybe.

CHAPTER 4:
COACH PHELPS

In the early days of basketball, there was no league at the national level. The leagues that did exist were ***small*** and ***regional.***

Many teams didn't belong to a league at all. They simply ***"barnstormed"*** from one town to the next, challenging local teams to matches.

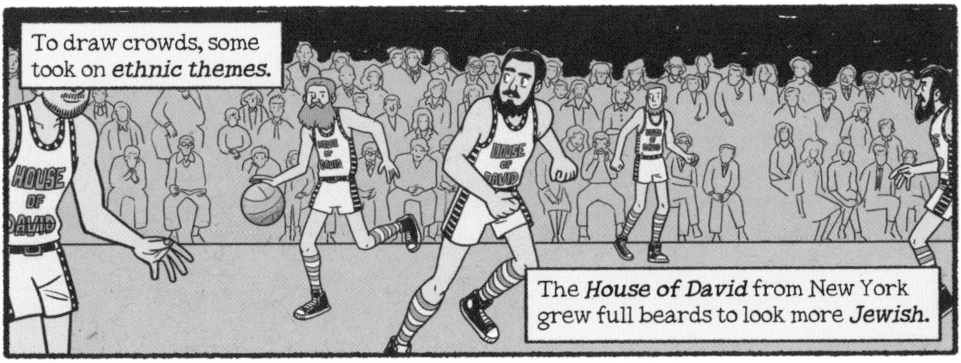
To draw crowds, some took on ***ethnic themes.***
HOUSE OF DAVID
The ***House of David*** from New York grew full beards to look more ***Jewish.***

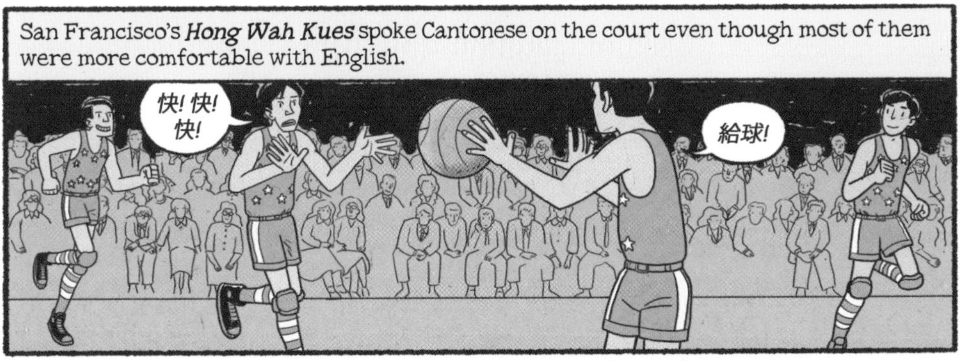
San Francisco's ***Hong Wah Kues*** spoke Cantonese on the court even though most of them were more comfortable with English.
快! 快! 快!
給球!

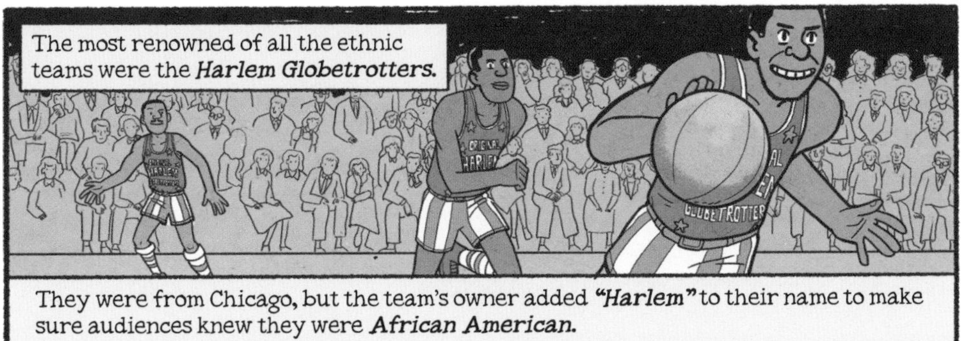
The most renowned of all the ethnic teams were the ***Harlem Globetrotters.***
GLOBETROTTERS
They were from Chicago, but the team's owner added ***"Harlem"*** to their name to make sure audiences knew they were ***African American.***

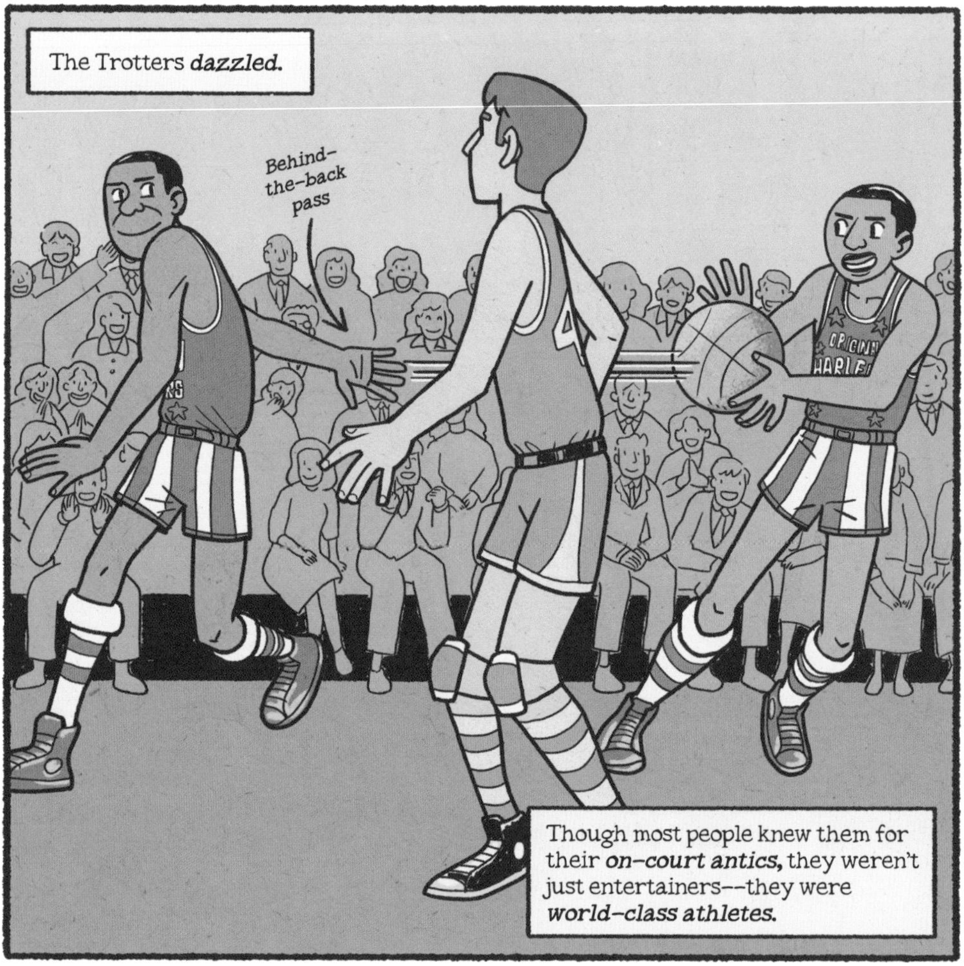
The Trotters *dazzled.*
Behind-the-back pass
Though most people knew them for their ***on-court antics,*** they weren't just entertainers--they were ***world-class athletes.***

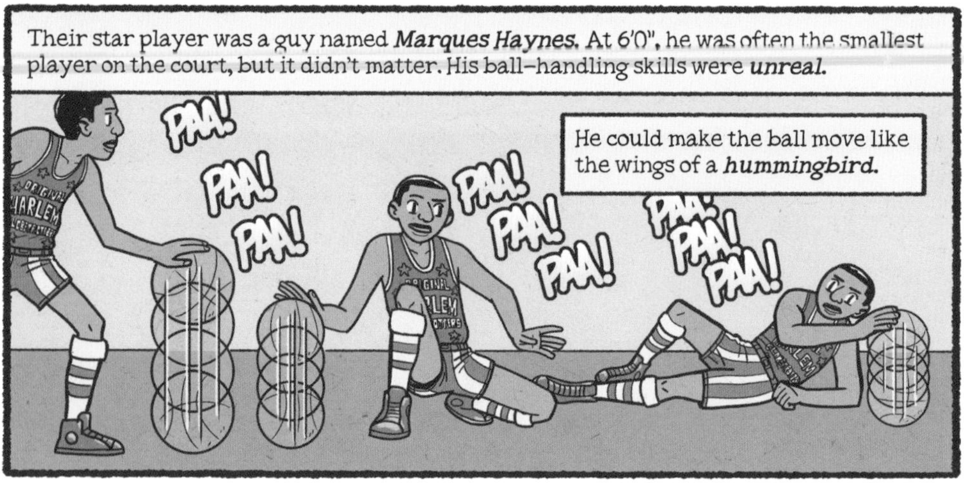
Their star player was a guy named ***Marques Haynes.*** At 6'0", he was often the smallest player on the court, but it didn't matter. His ball-handling skills were ***unreal.***
PAA!
PAA!
PAA!
He could make the ball move like the wings of a ***hummingbird.***
PAA!
PAA!
PAA!
PAA!
PAA!
PAA!

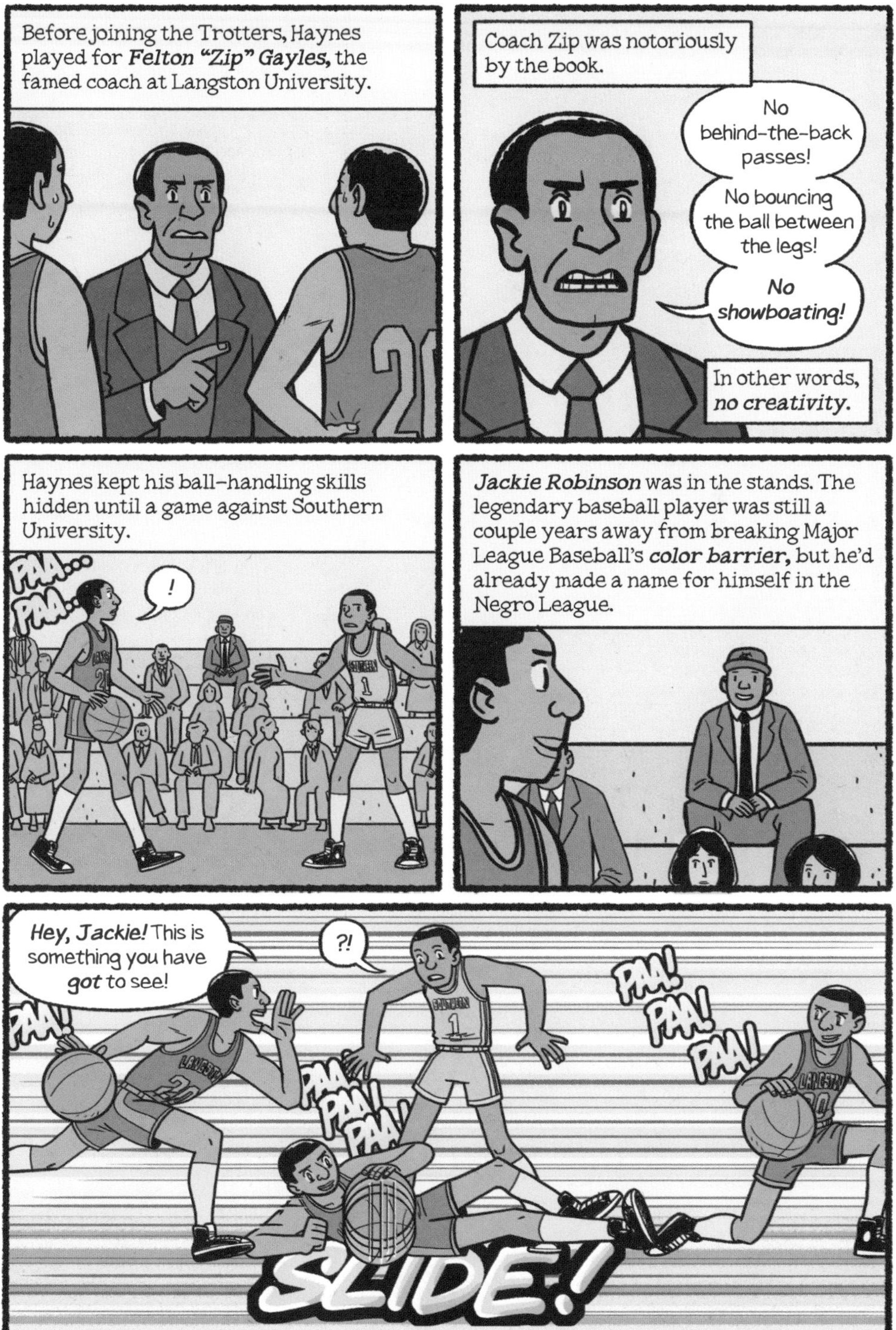
Before joining the Trotters, Haynes played for ***Felton "Zip" Gayles,*** the famed coach at Langston University.
Coach Zip was notoriously by the book.
No behind-the-back passes!
No bouncing the ball between the legs!
No showboating!
In other words, ***no creativity.***
Haynes kept his ball-handling skills hidden until a game against Southern University.
PAA... PAA...
!
Jackie Robinson was in the stands. The legendary baseball player was still a couple years away from breaking Major League Baseball's ***color barrier,*** but he'd already made a name for himself in the Negro League.
Hey, Jackie! This is something you have ***got*** to see!
PAA!
?!
PAA! PAA! PAA!
PAA! PAA! PAA!
SLIDE!

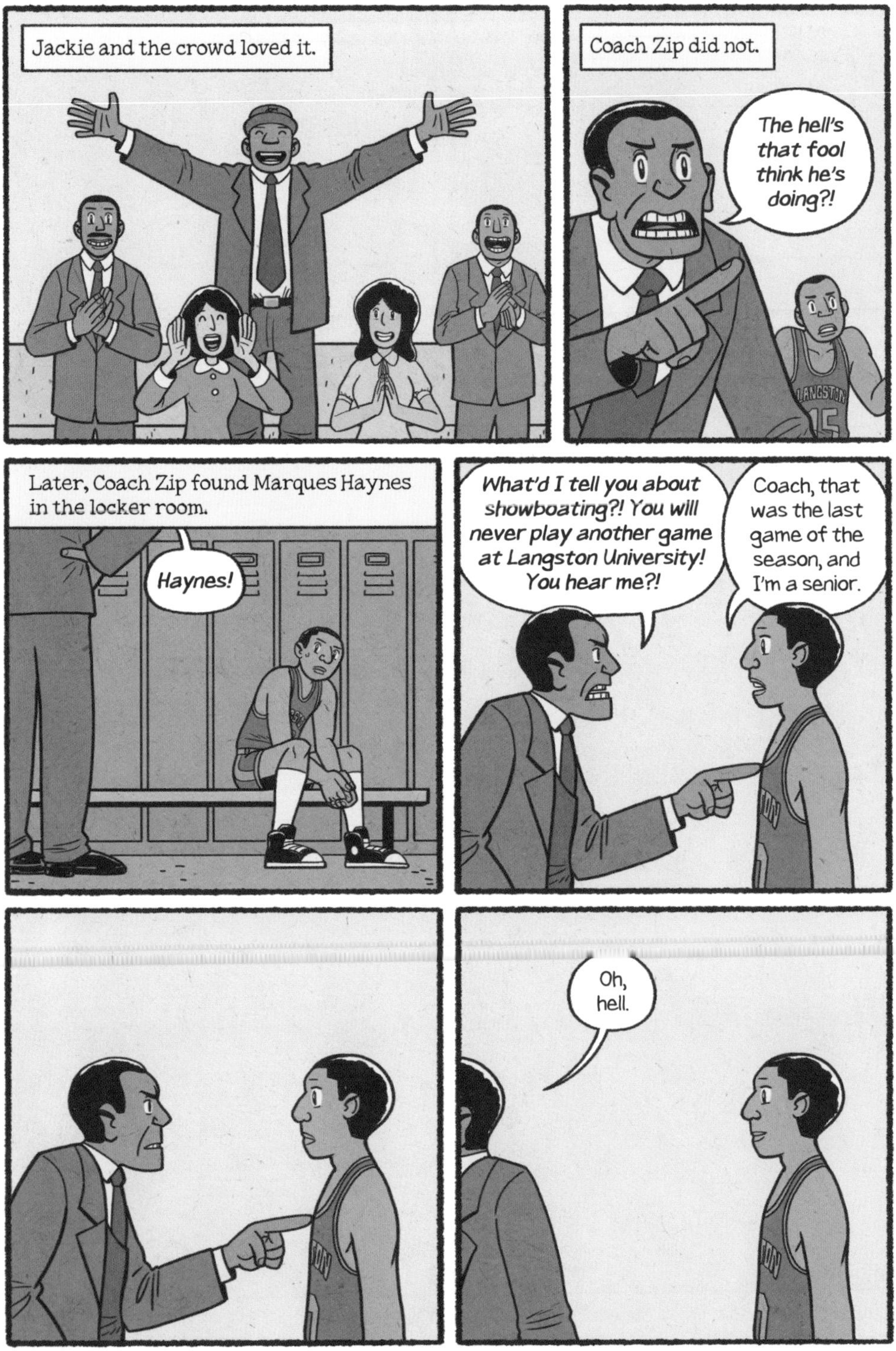
Jackie and the crowd loved it.
Coach Zip did not.
The hell's that fool think he's doing?!
Later, Coach Zip found Marques Haynes in the locker room.
Haynes!
What'd I tell you about showboating?! You will never play another game at Langston University! You hear me?!
Coach, that was the last game of the season, and I'm a senior.
Oh, hell.

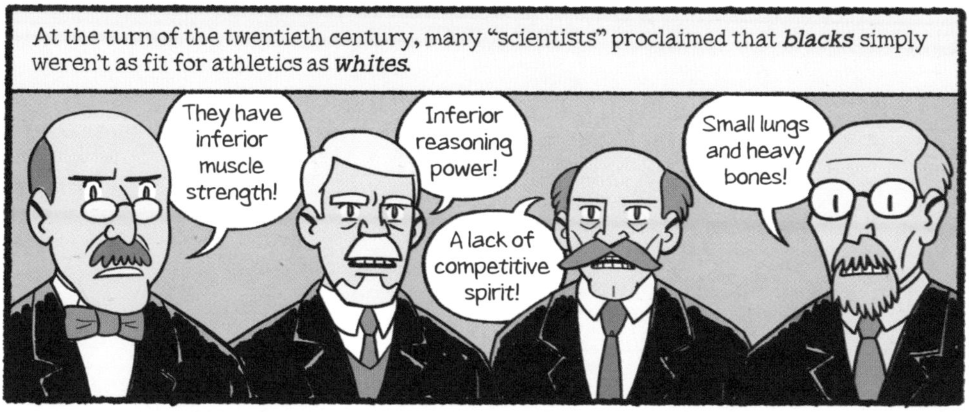
At the turn of the twentieth century, many "scientists" proclaimed that ***blacks*** simply weren't as fit for athletics as ***whites.***
They have inferior muscle strength!
Inferior reasoning power!
A lack of competitive spirit!
Small lungs and heavy bones!

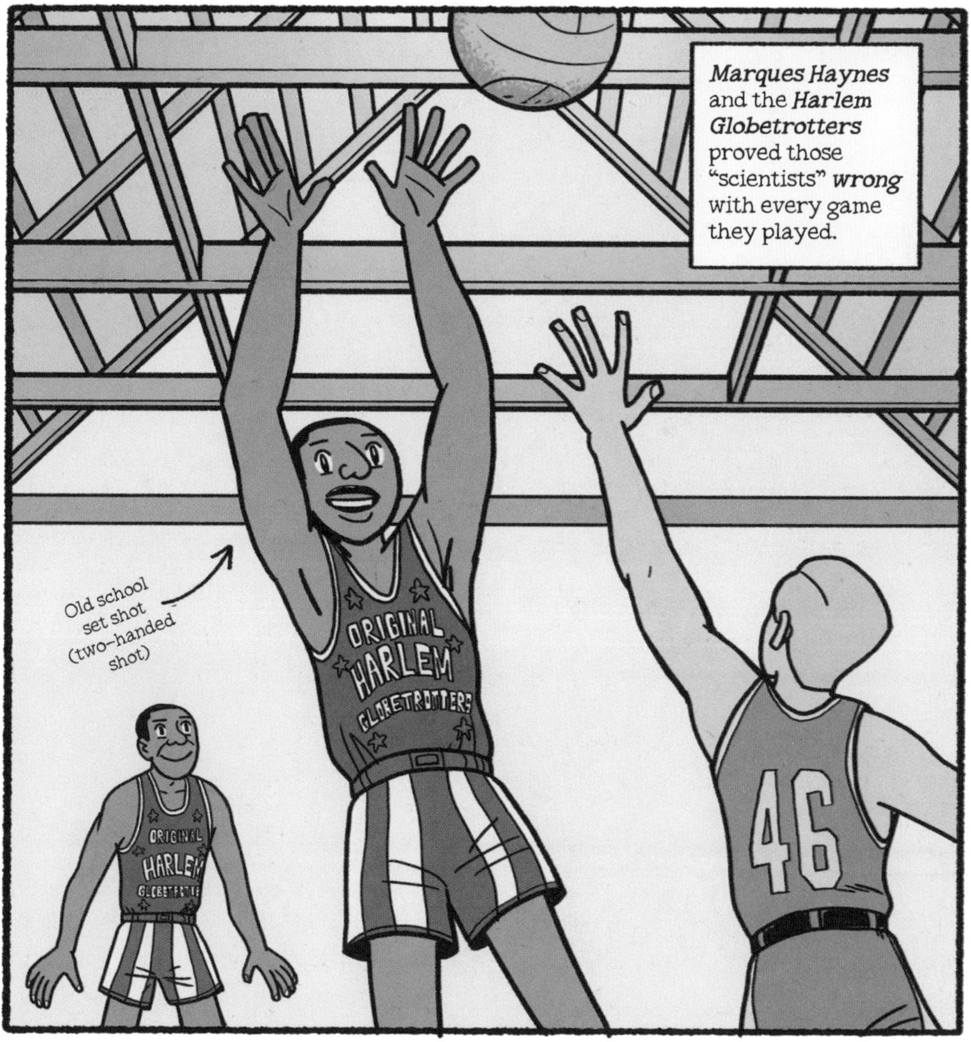
Marques Haynes and the ***Harlem Globetrotters*** proved those "scientists" ***wrong*** with every game they played.
Old school set shot (two-handed shot)
ORIGINAL HARLEM GLOBETROTTERS
46

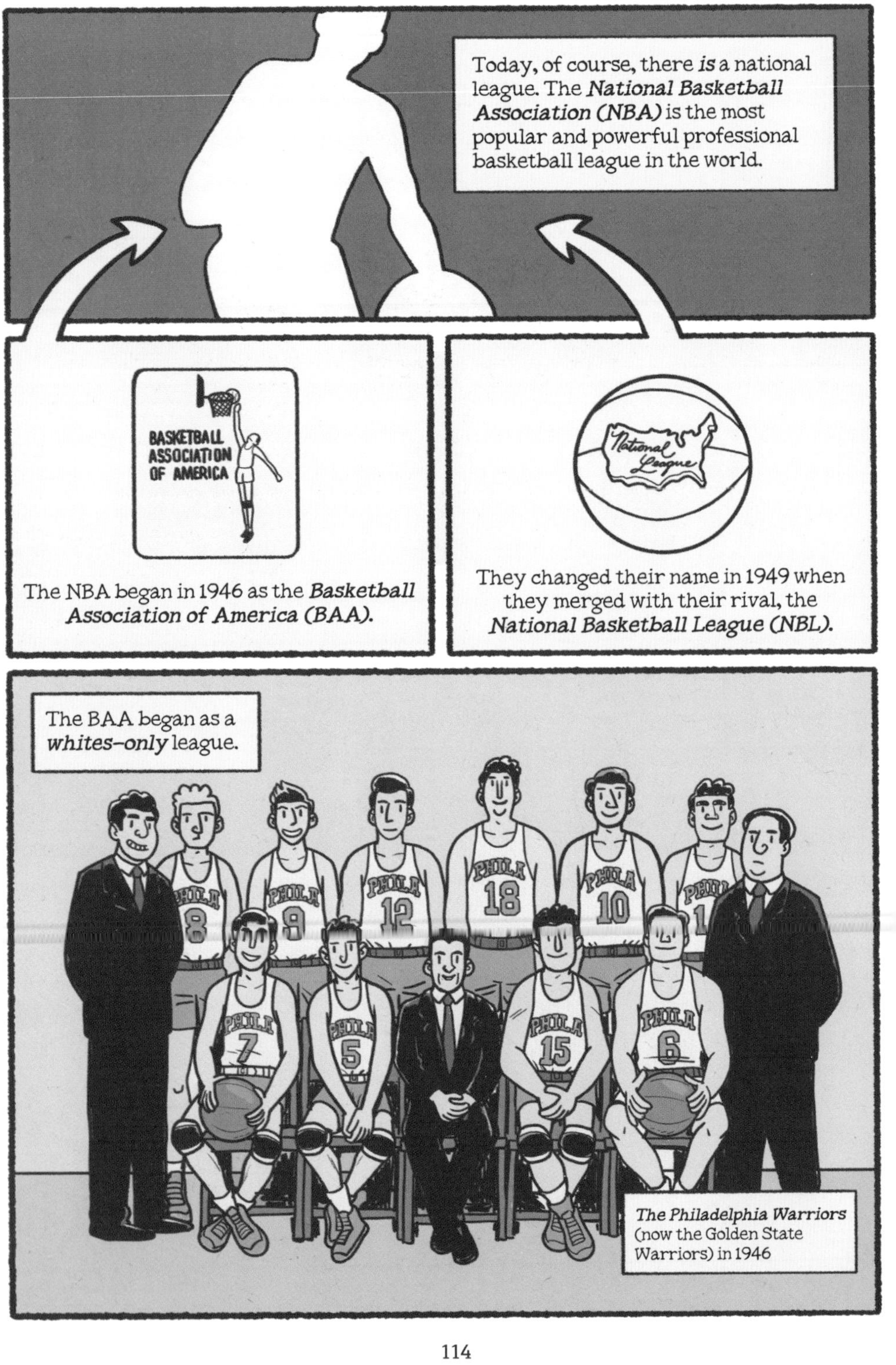
Today, of course, there *is* a national league. The ***National Basketball Association (NBA)*** is the most popular and powerful professional basketball league in the world.
BASKETBALL ASSOCIATION OF AMERICA
The NBA began in 1946 as the ***Basketball Association of America (BAA).***
National League
They changed their name in 1949 when they merged with their rival, the ***National Basketball League (NBL).***
The BAA began as a ***whites-only*** league.
The Philadelphia Warriors (now the Golden State Warriors) in 1946

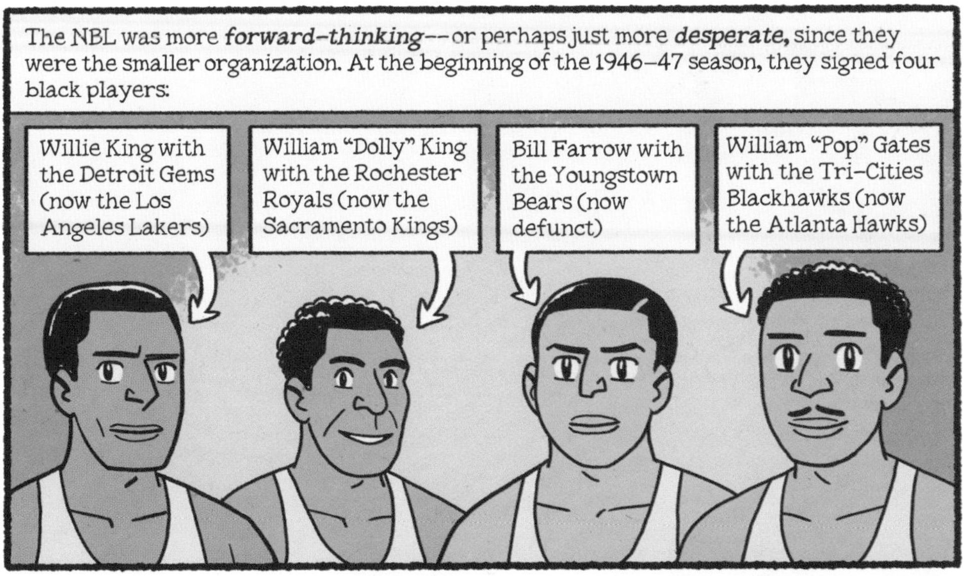
The NBL was more ***forward-thinking***-- or perhaps just more ***desperate,*** since they were the smaller organization. At the beginning of the 1946-47 season, they signed four black players:
Willie King with the Detroit Gems (now the Los Angeles Lakers)
William "Dolly" King with the Rochester Royals (now the Sacramento Kings)
Bill Farrow with the Youngstown Bears (now defunct)
William "Pop" Gates with the Tri-Cities Blackhawks (now the Atlanta Hawks)
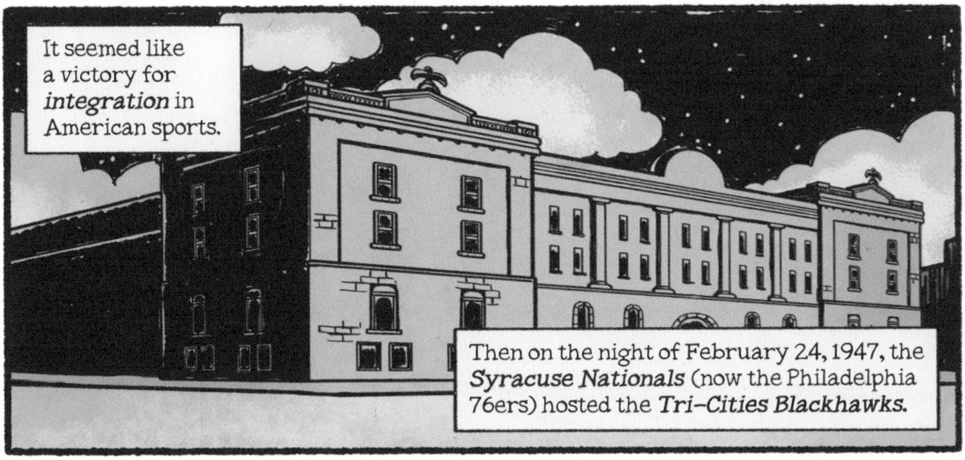
It seemed like a victory for ***integration*** in American sports.
Then on the night of February 24, 1947, the ***Syracuse Nationals*** (now the Philadelphia 76ers) hosted the ***Tri-Cities Blackhawks.***
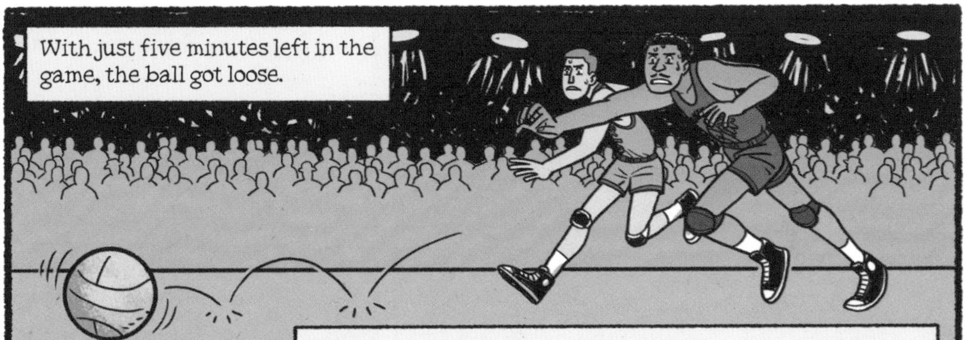
With just five minutes left in the game, the ball got loose.
Pop Gates and the Nats' ***Chick Meehan*** both went after it.

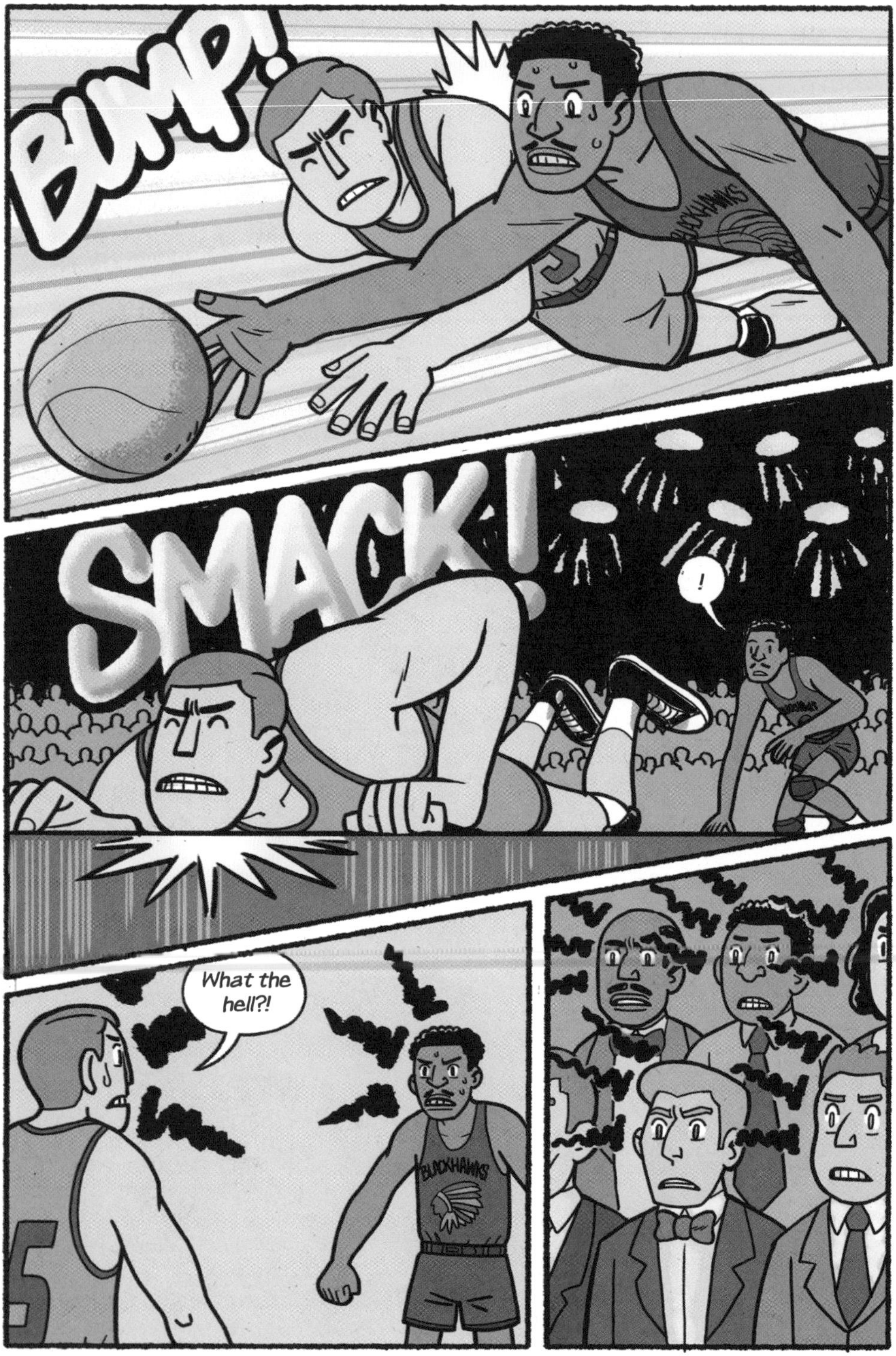
BUMP!
BUCKHAWKS
SMACK!
!
What the hell?!
BUCKHAWKS

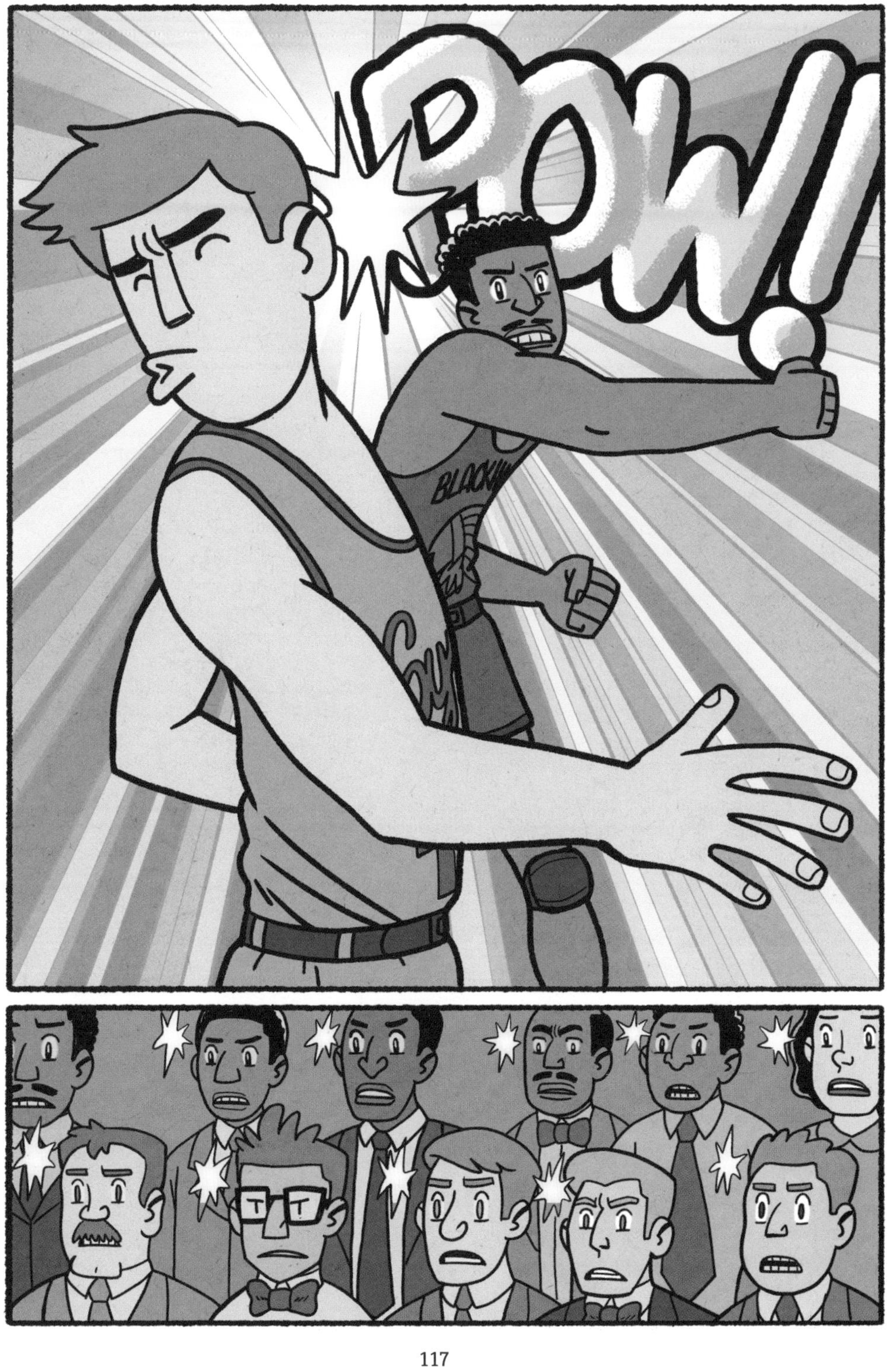
POW!!

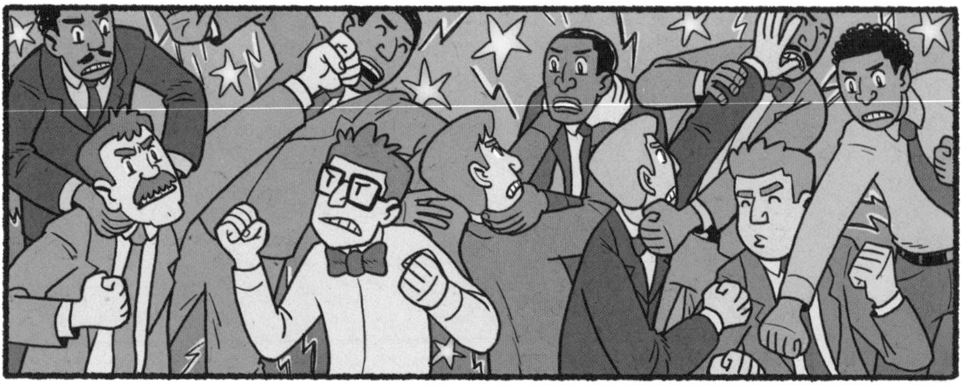

The National Guard had to be called in to restore order.

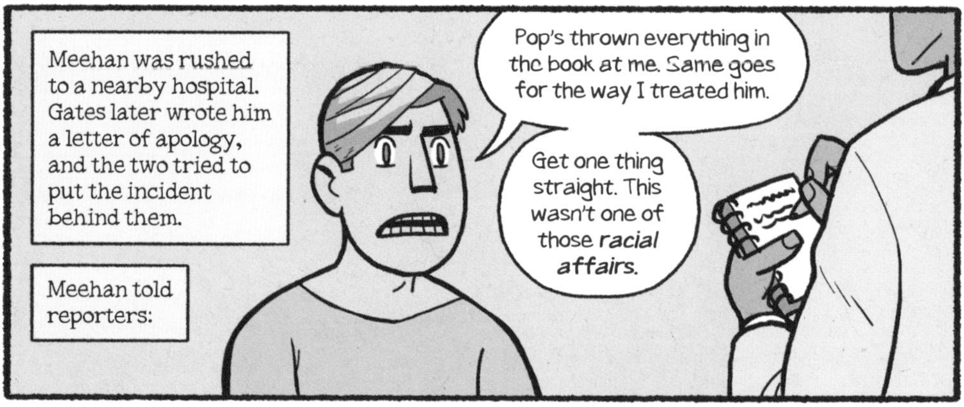
Meehan was rushed to a nearby hospital. Gates later wrote him a letter of apology, and the two tried to put the incident behind them.
Meehan told reporters:
Pop's thrown everything in thc book at me. Same goes for the way I treated him.
Get one thing straight. This wasn't one of those *racial affairs*.

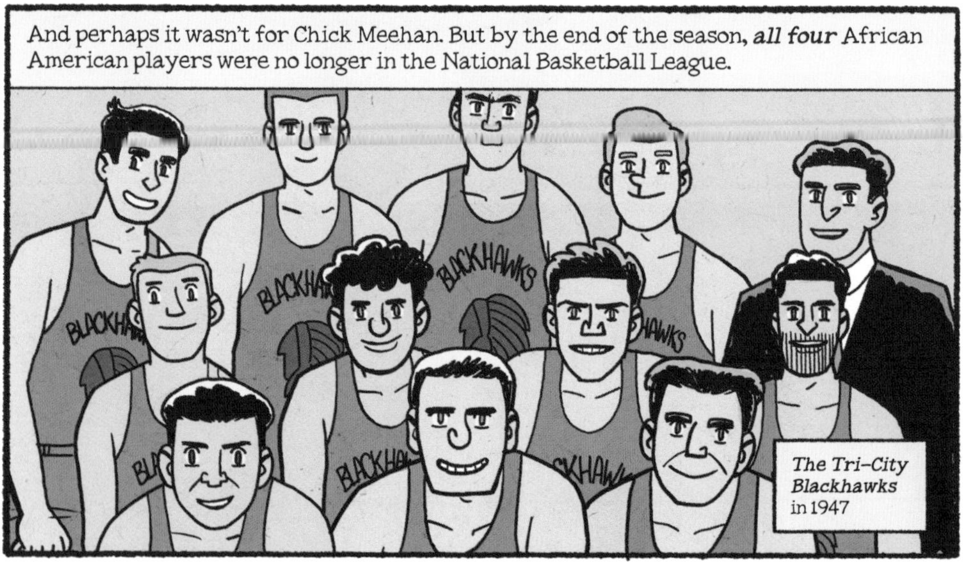
And perhaps it wasn't for Chick Meehan. But by the end of the season, ***all four*** African American players were no longer in the National Basketball League.
BLACKHAWKS
The Tri-City Blackhawks in 1947

Put blacks and whites on the same court, the thinking went, and sooner or later, ***violence*** would result.

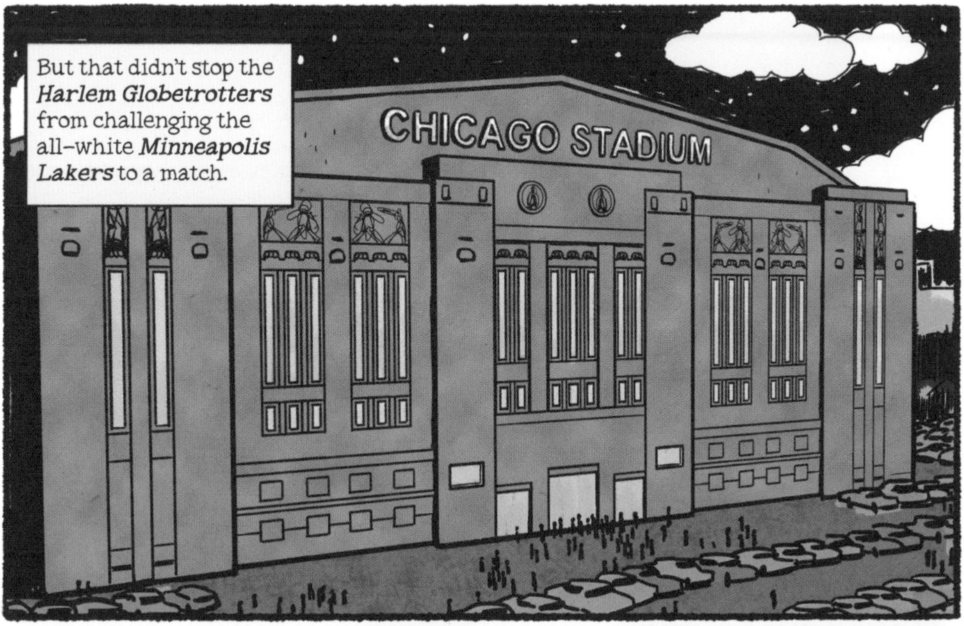
But that didn't stop the *Harlem Globetrotters* from challenging the all-white *Minneapolis Lakers* to a match.
CHICAGO STADIUM

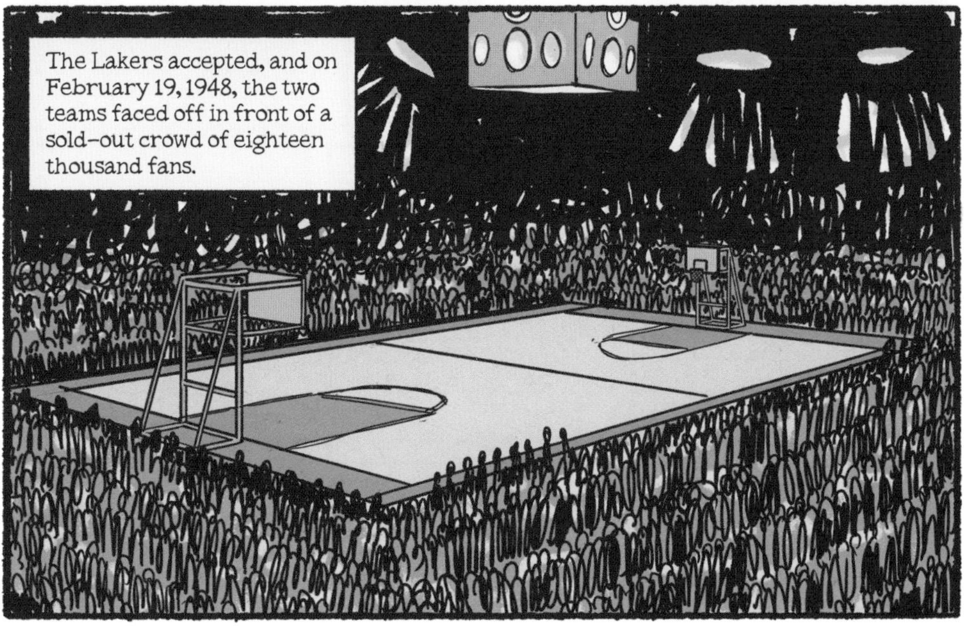
The Lakers accepted, and on February 19, 1948, the two teams faced off in front of a sold-out crowd of eighteen thousand fans.

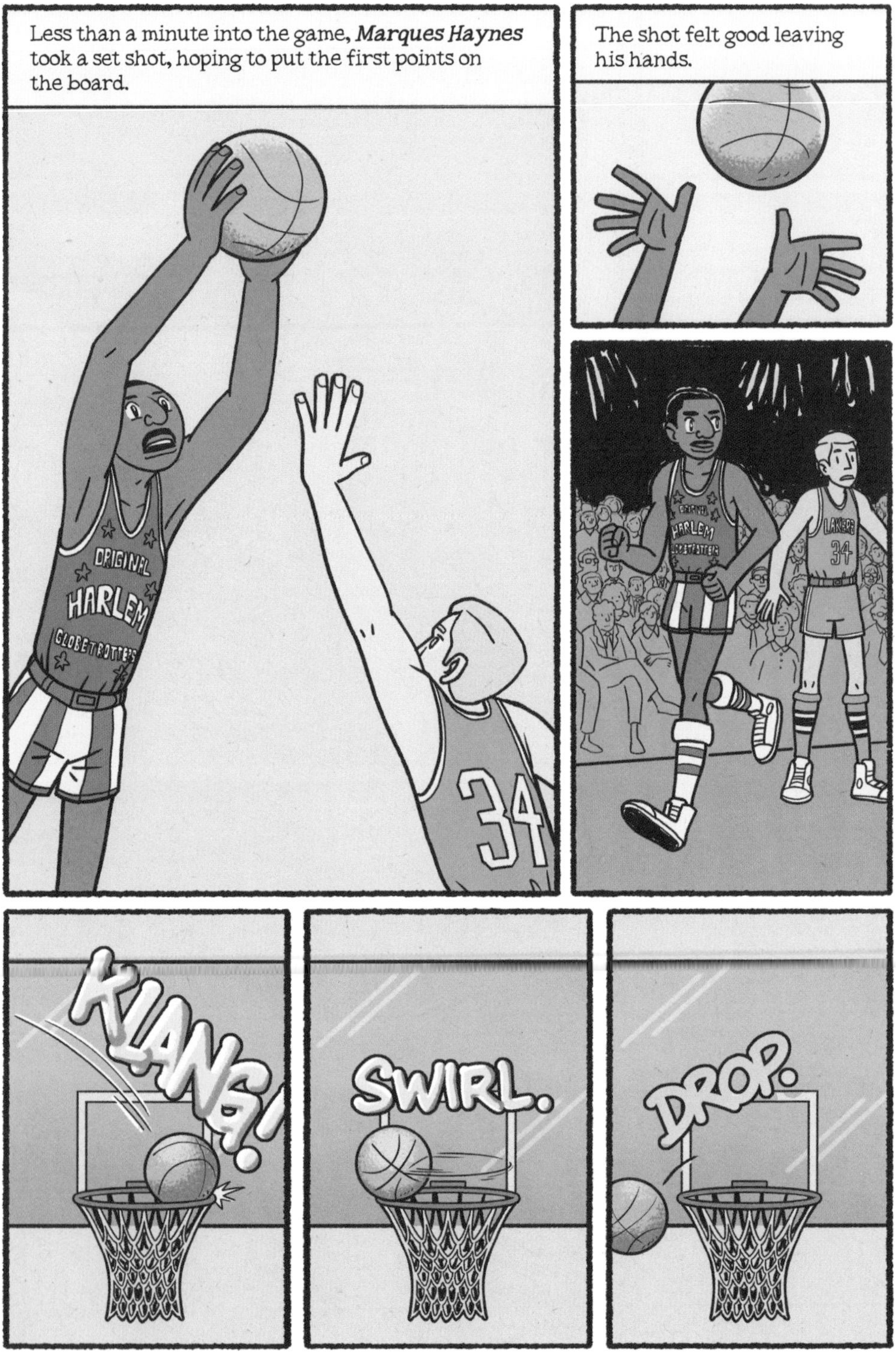
Less than a minute into the game, ***Marques Haynes*** took a set shot, hoping to put the first points on the board.
ORIGINAL HARLEM GLOBETROTTERS
34
The shot felt good leaving his hands.
ORIGINAL HARLEM GLOBETROTTERS
LAKERS 34
KLANG!
SWIRL.
DROP.

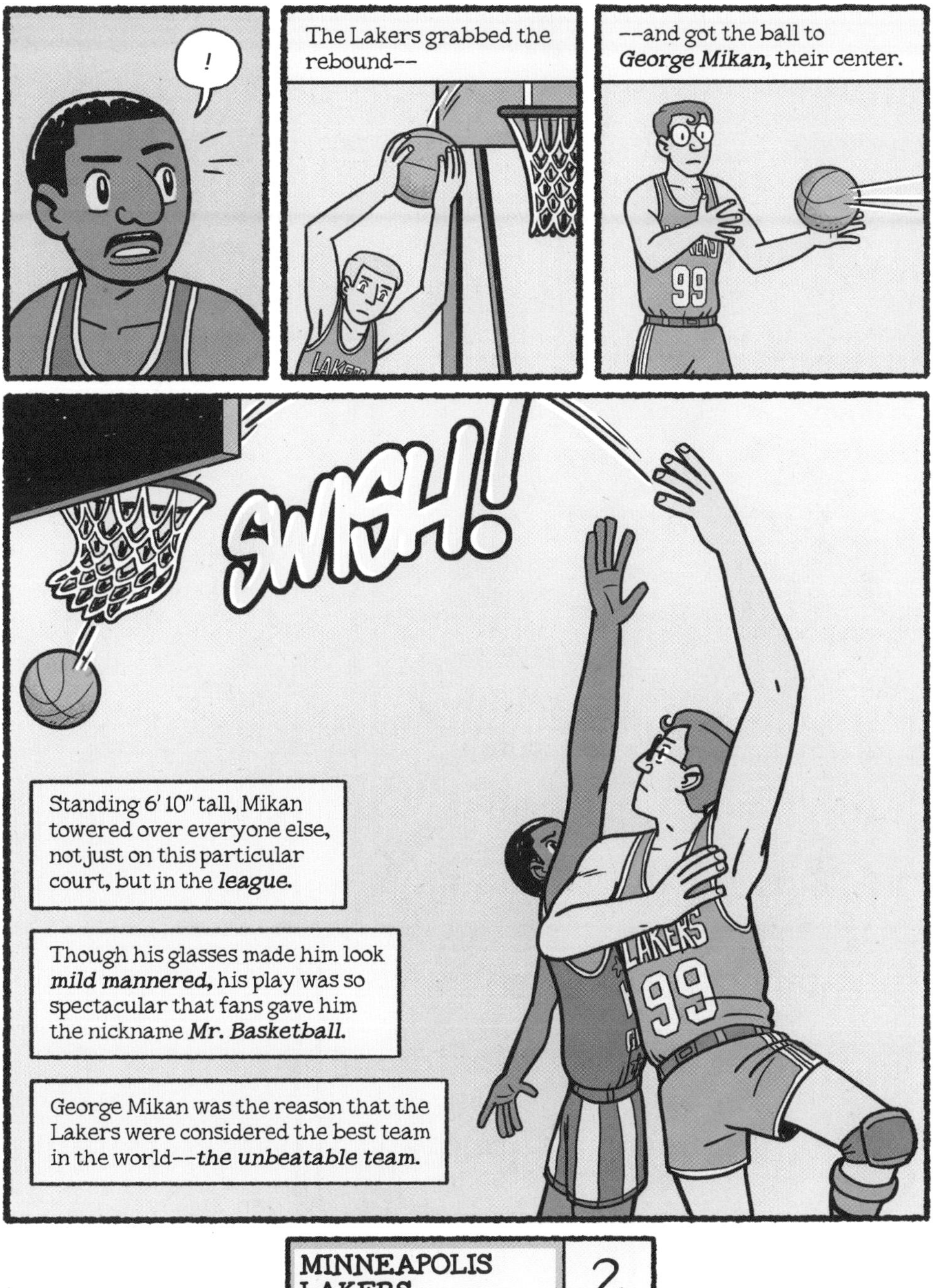
!
The Lakers grabbed the rebound--
LAKERS
--and got the ball to *George Mikan,* their center.
99
SWISH!
Standing 6' 10" tall, Mikan towered over everyone else, not just on this particular court, but in the *league.*
Though his glasses made him look *mild mannered,* his play was so spectacular that fans gave him the nickname *Mr. Basketball.*
George Mikan was the reason that the Lakers were considered the best team in the world--*the unbeatable team.*
LAKERS
99
MINNEAPOLIS LAKERS
2
HARLEM GLOBETROTTERS
0

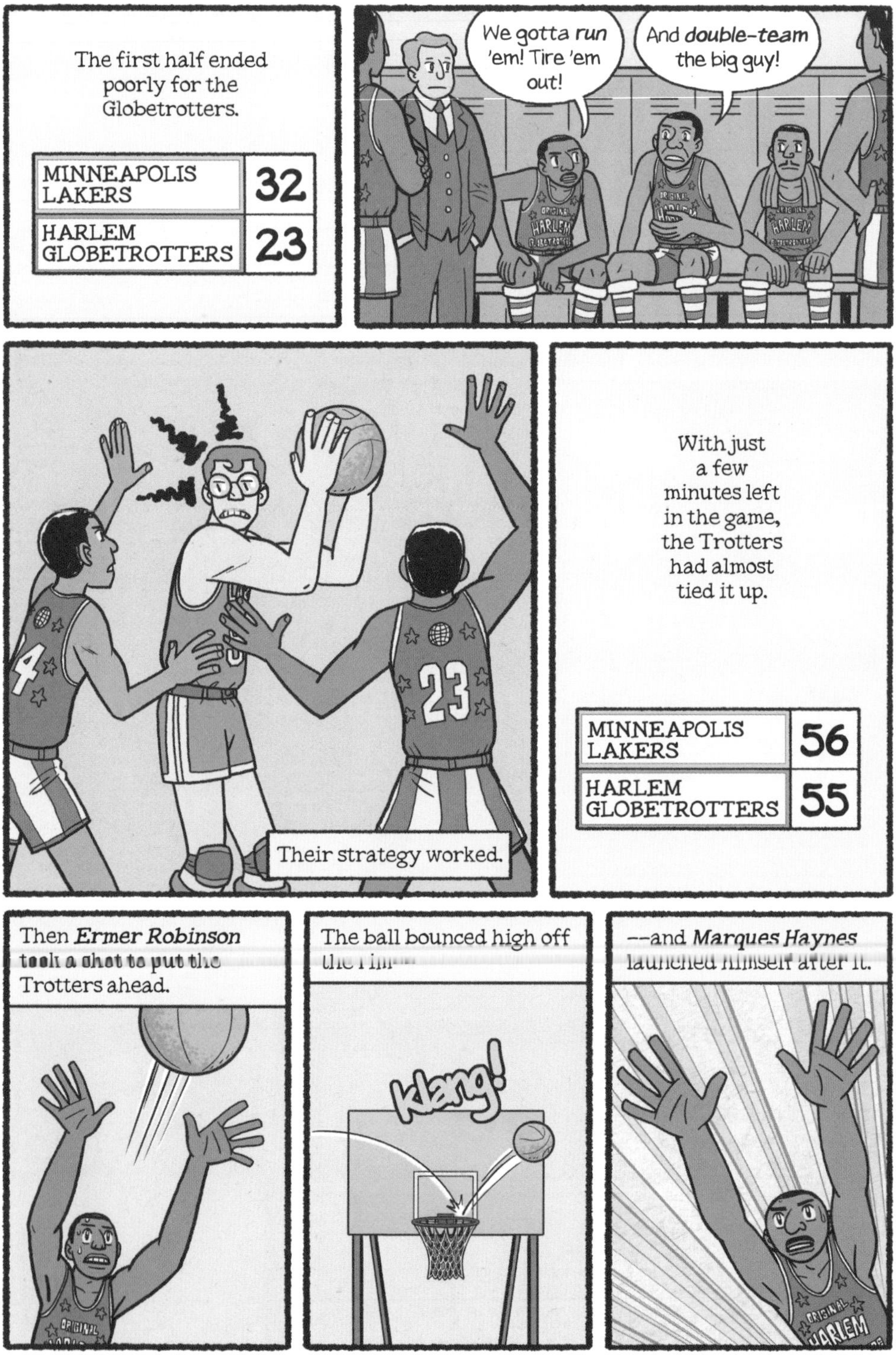
The first half ended poorly for the Globetrotters.
MINNEAPOLIS LAKERS 32
HARLEM GLOBETROTTERS 23
We gotta *run* 'em! Tire 'em out!
And *double-team* the big guy!
ORIGINAL HARLEM GLOBETROTTERS
Their strategy worked.
With just a few minutes left in the game, the Trotters had almost tied it up.
MINNEAPOLIS LAKERS 56
HARLEM GLOBETROTTERS 55
Then *Ermer Robinson* took a shot to put the Trotters ahead.
The ball bounced high off the rim--
Klang!
--and *Marques Haynes* launched himself after it.
ORIGINAL HARLEM

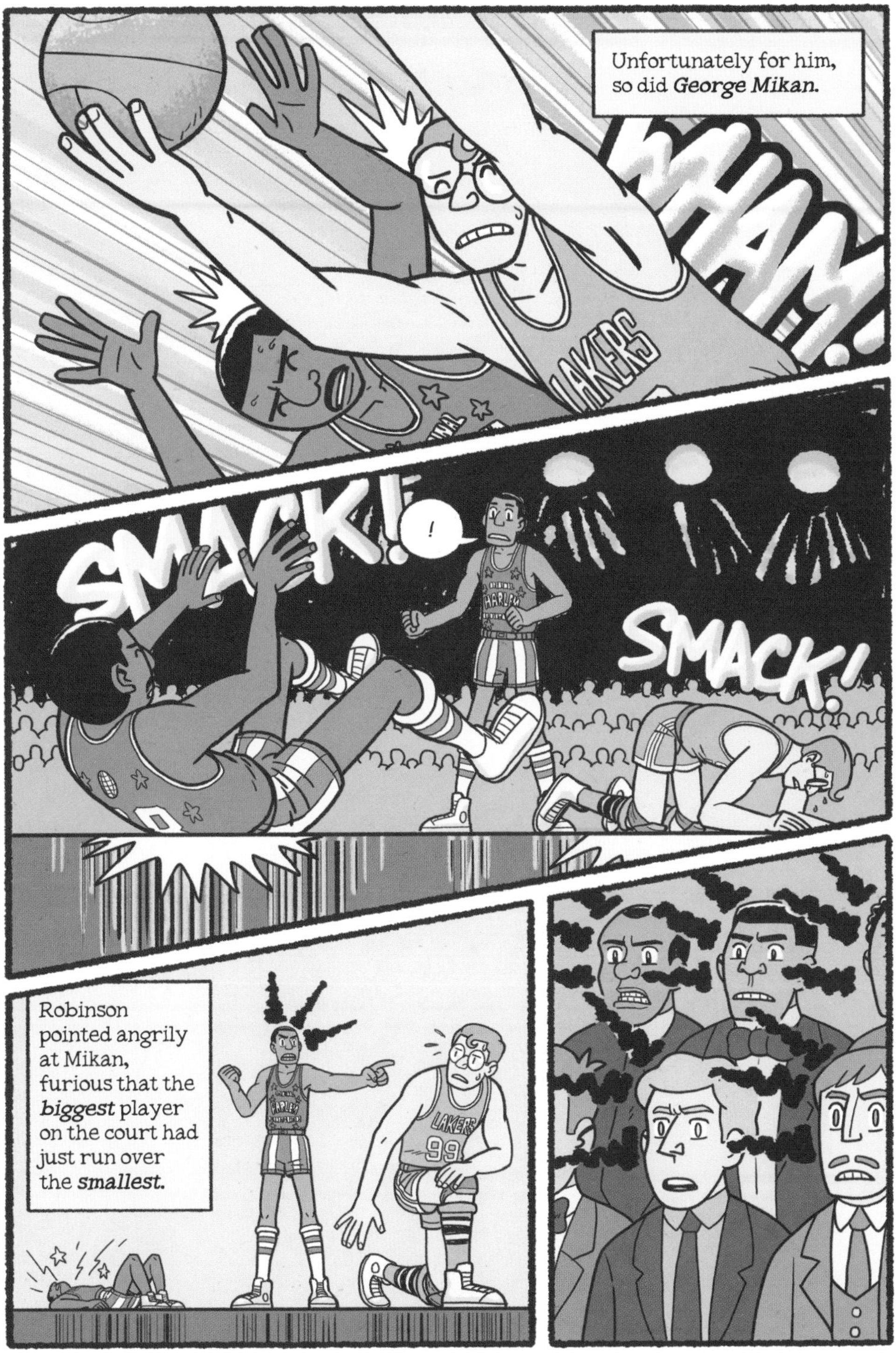
Unfortunately for him, so did George Mikan.
WHAM!!
LAKERS
SMACK!
!
SMACK!
Robinson pointed angrily at Mikan, furious that the biggest player on the court had just run over the smallest.
LAKERS
99

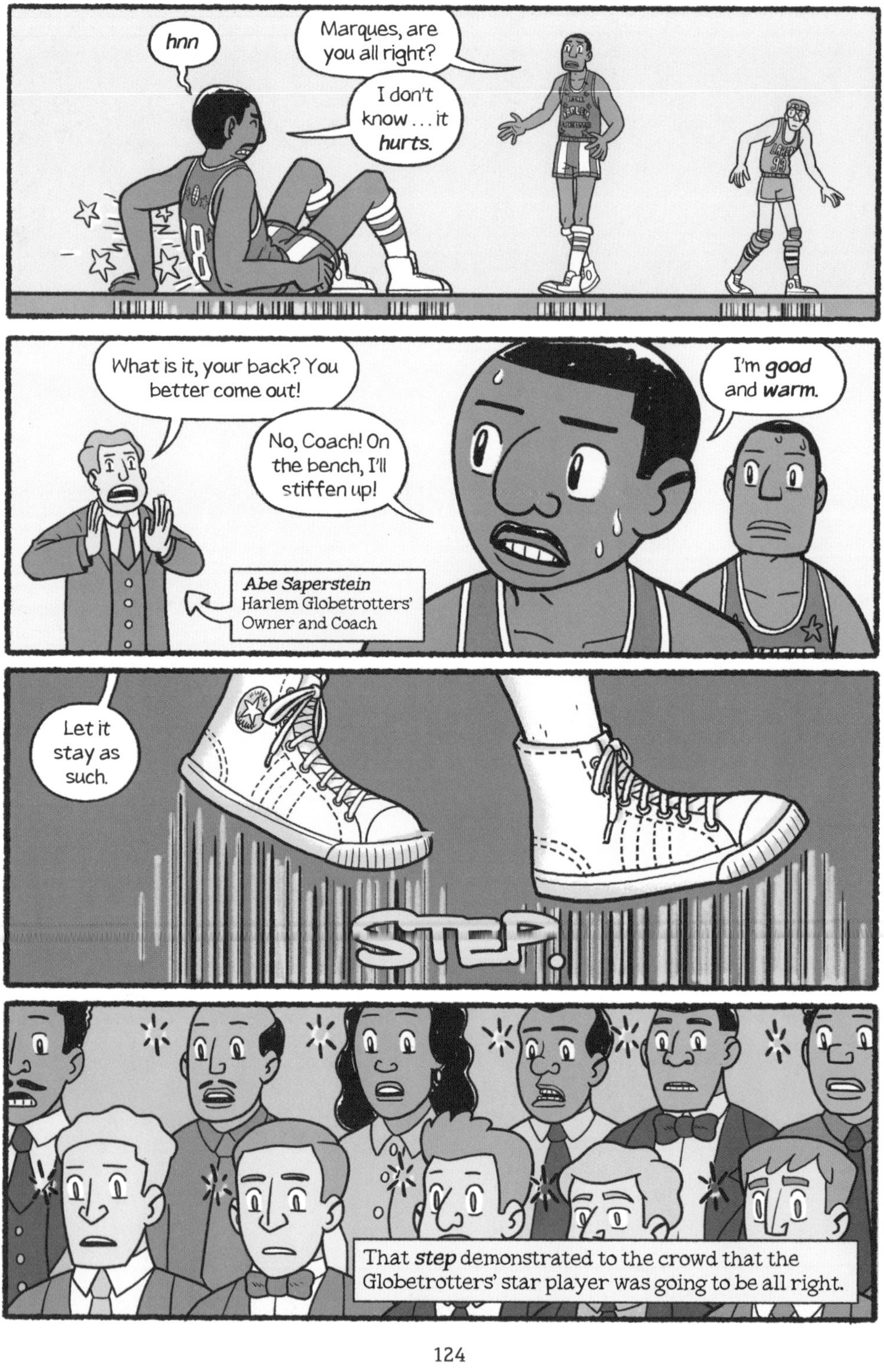
hnn
Marques, are you all right?
I don't know . . . it *hurts*.
What is it, your back? You better come out!
No, Coach! On the bench, I'll stiffen up!
I'm *good* and *warm*.
Abe Saperstein Harlem Globetrotters' Owner and Coach
Let it stay as such.
STEP.
That *step* demonstrated to the crowd that the Globetrotters' star player was going to be all right.

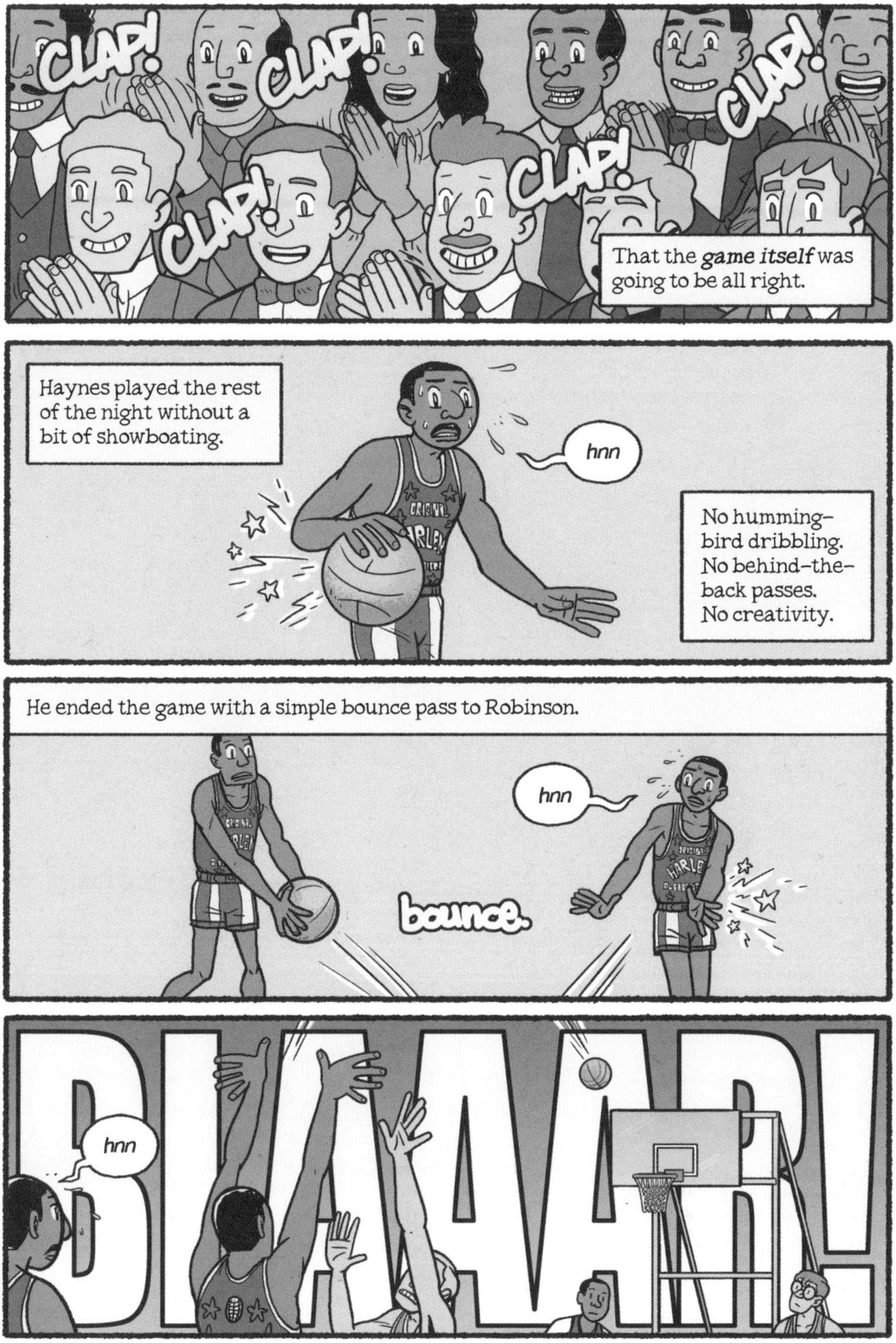
CLAP!
CLAP!
CLAP!
CLAP!
CLAP!
That the *game itself* was going to be all right.
Haynes played the rest of the night without a bit of showboating.
hnn
No humming-bird dribbling. No behind-the-back passes. No creativity.
He ended the game with a simple bounce pass to Robinson.
hnn
bounce.
BLAAR!
hnn

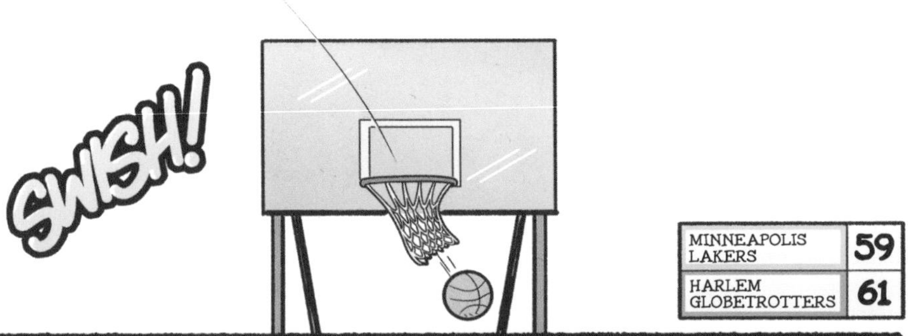
SWISH!
MINNEAPOLIS LAKERS 59
HARLEM GLOBETROTTERS 61

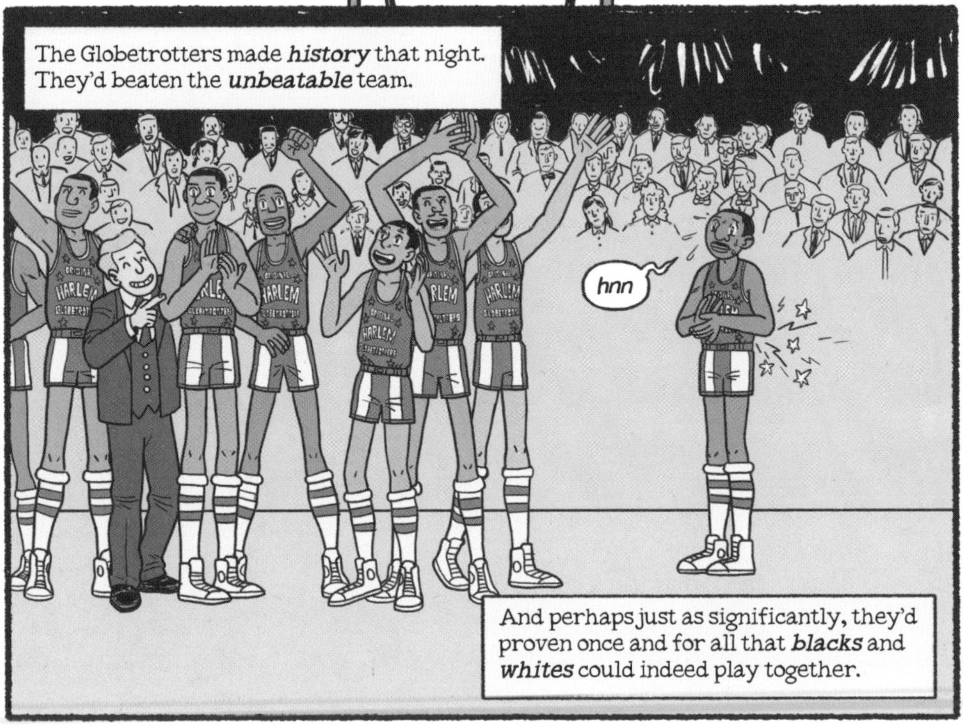
The Globetrotters made ***history*** that night. They'd beaten the ***unbeatable*** team.
hnn
And perhaps just as significantly, they'd proven once and for all that ***blacks*** and ***whites*** could indeed play together.

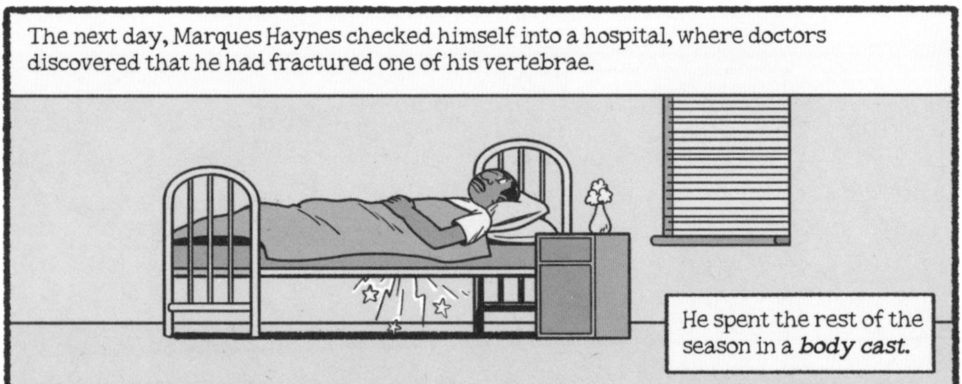
The next day, Marques Haynes checked himself into a hospital, where doctors discovered that he had fractured one of his vertebrae.
He spent the rest of the season in a ***body cast.***

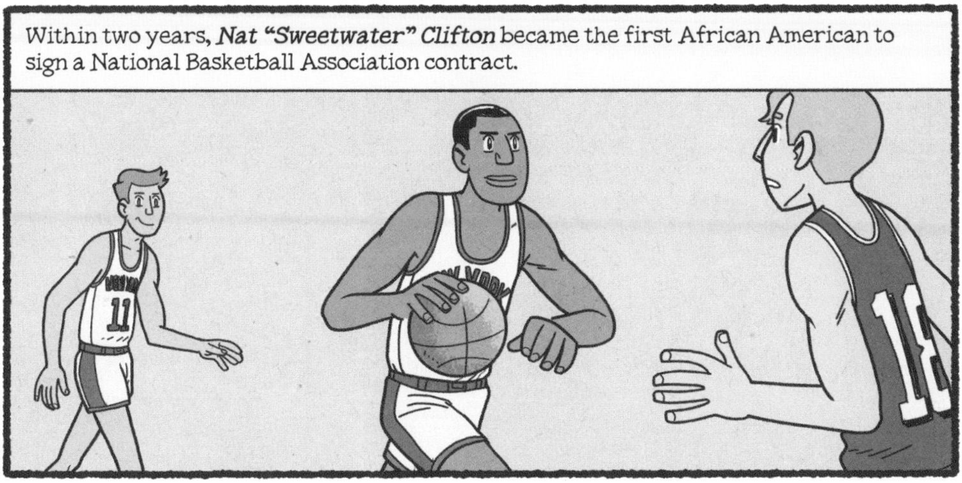
Within two years, ***Nat "Sweetwater" Clifton*** became the first African American to sign a National Basketball Association contract.
11
18

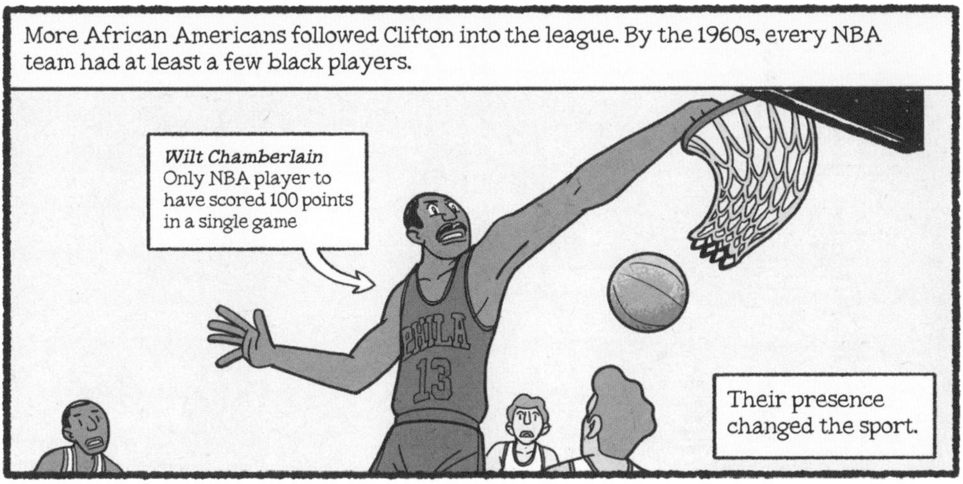
More African Americans followed Clifton into the league. By the 1960s, every NBA team had at least a few black players.
Wilt Chamberlain
Only NBA player to have scored 100 points in a single game
PHILA
13
Their presence changed the sport.

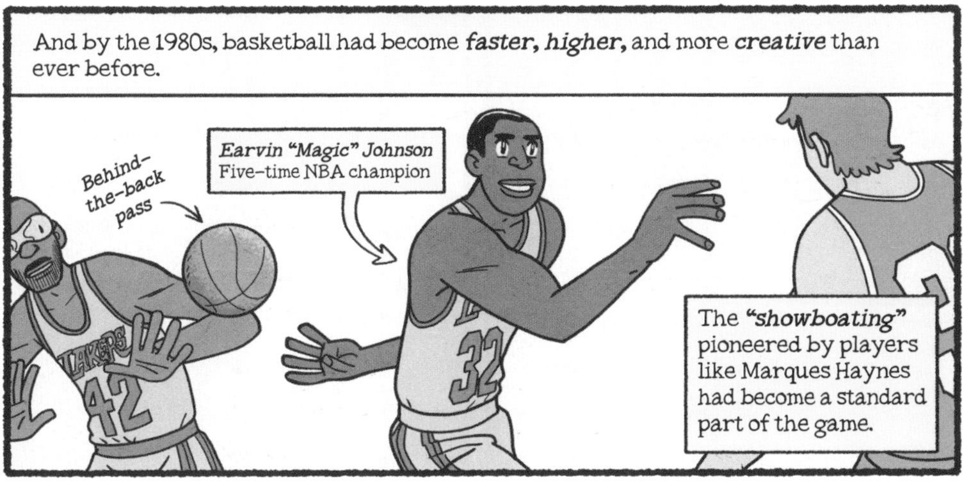
And by the 1980s, basketball had become ***faster, higher,*** and more ***creative*** than ever before.
Behind-the-back pass
Earvin "Magic" Johnson
Five-time NBA champion
LAKERS
42
32
The ***"showboating"*** pioneered by players like Marques Haynes had become a standard part of the game.

The entire world of basketball was changing, and *Bishop O'Dowd High School* was no exception.

Mike Phelps, Lou's coach from his high school years, took over the men's varsity basketball team in *1979.*

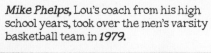

He retired in *2003.*

My freshman year, there were two *black* players on Coach Phelps's team.

My senior year, there were two *white* players.

So there was definitely a *changing of the guard.*

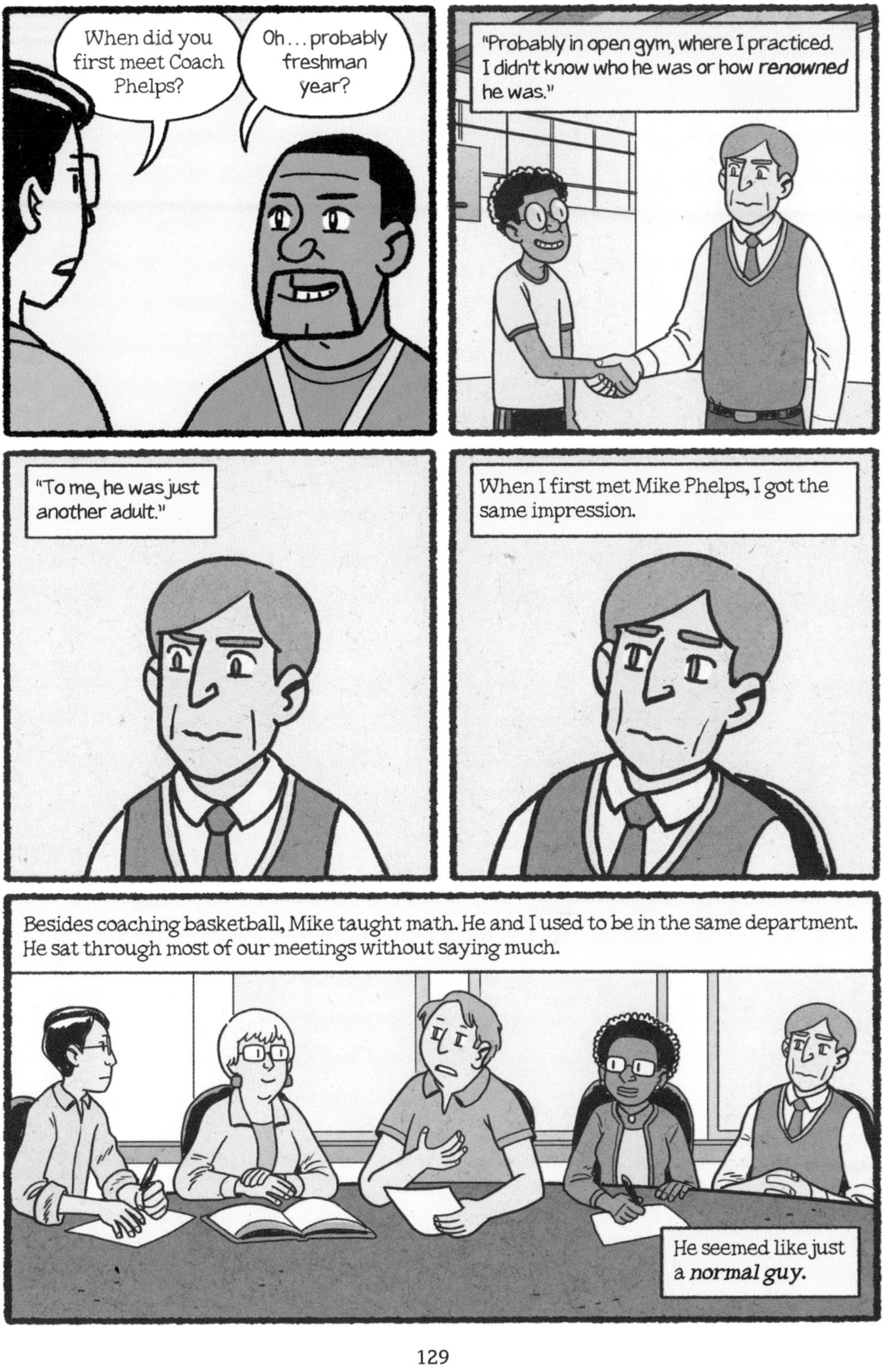
When did you first meet Coach Phelps?
Oh... probably freshman year?
"Probably in open gym, where I practiced. I didn't know who he was or how *renowned* he was."
"To me, he was just another adult."
When I first met Mike Phelps, I got the same impression.
Besides coaching basketball, Mike taught math. He and I used to be in the same department. He sat through most of our meetings without saying much.
He seemed like just a ***normal guy.***

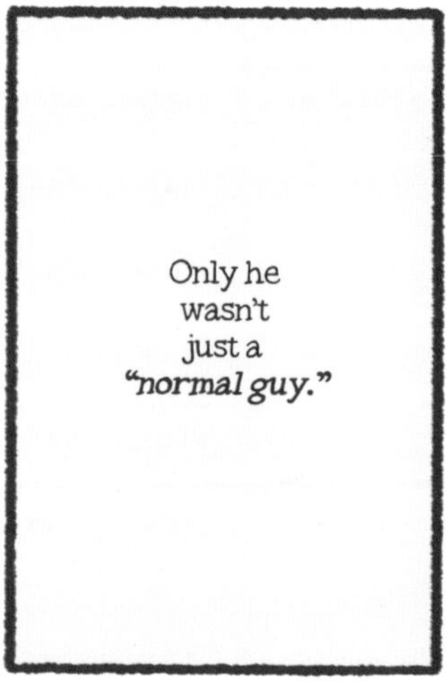
Only he wasn't just a *"normal guy."*

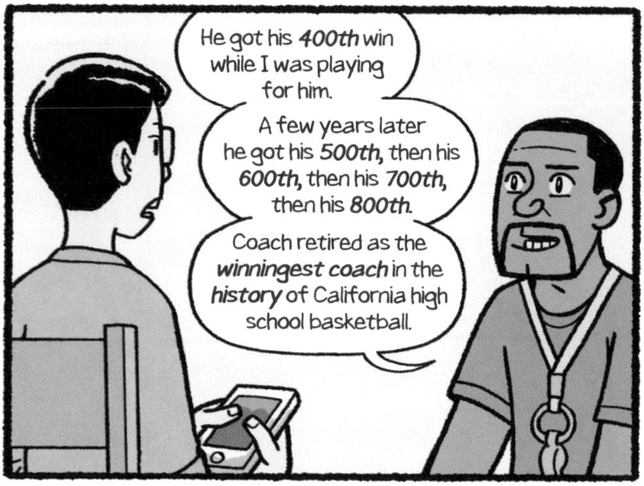
He got his **400th** win while I was playing for him.
A few years later he got his **500th,** then his **600th,** then his **700th,** then his **800th.**
Coach retired as the ***winningest coach*** in the ***history*** of California high school basketball.

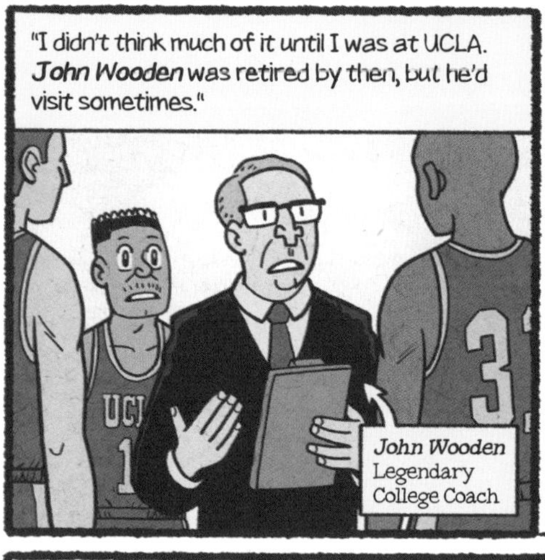
"I didn't think much of it until I was at UCLA. ***John Wooden*** was retired by then, but he'd visit sometimes."
UCLA
John Wooden
Legendary College Coach

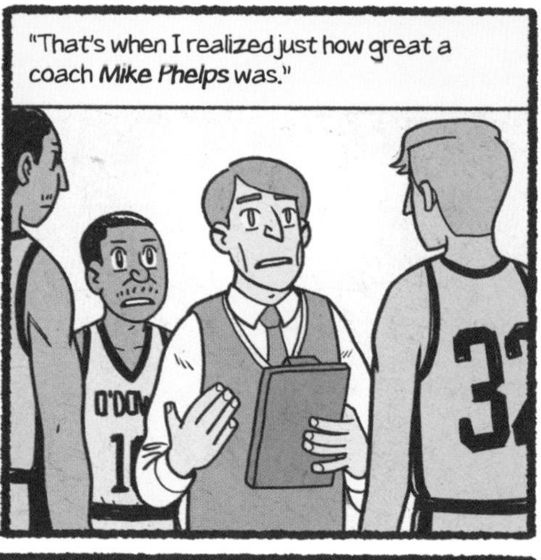
"That's when I realized just how great a coach ***Mike Phelps*** was."
32

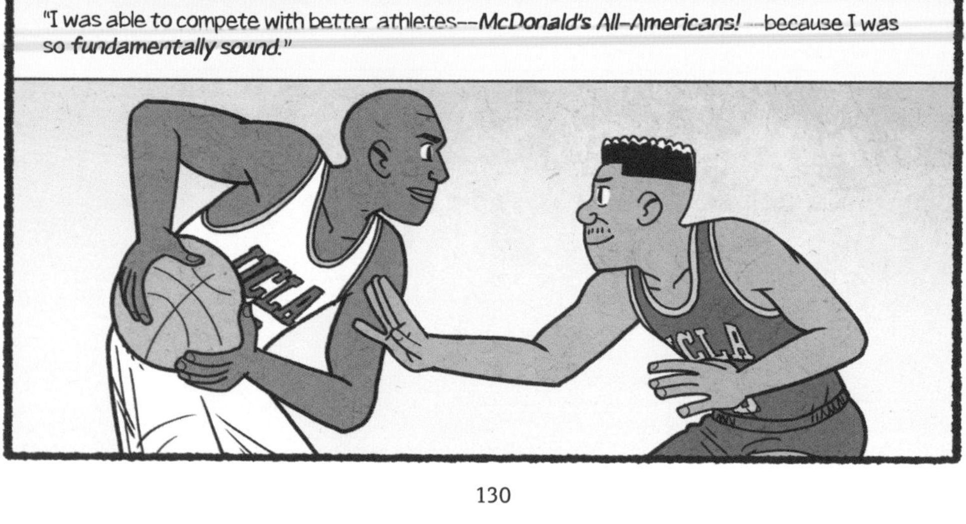
"I was able to compete with better athletes--***McDonald's All-Americans!***--because I was so ***fundamentally sound.***"
UCLA
UCLA

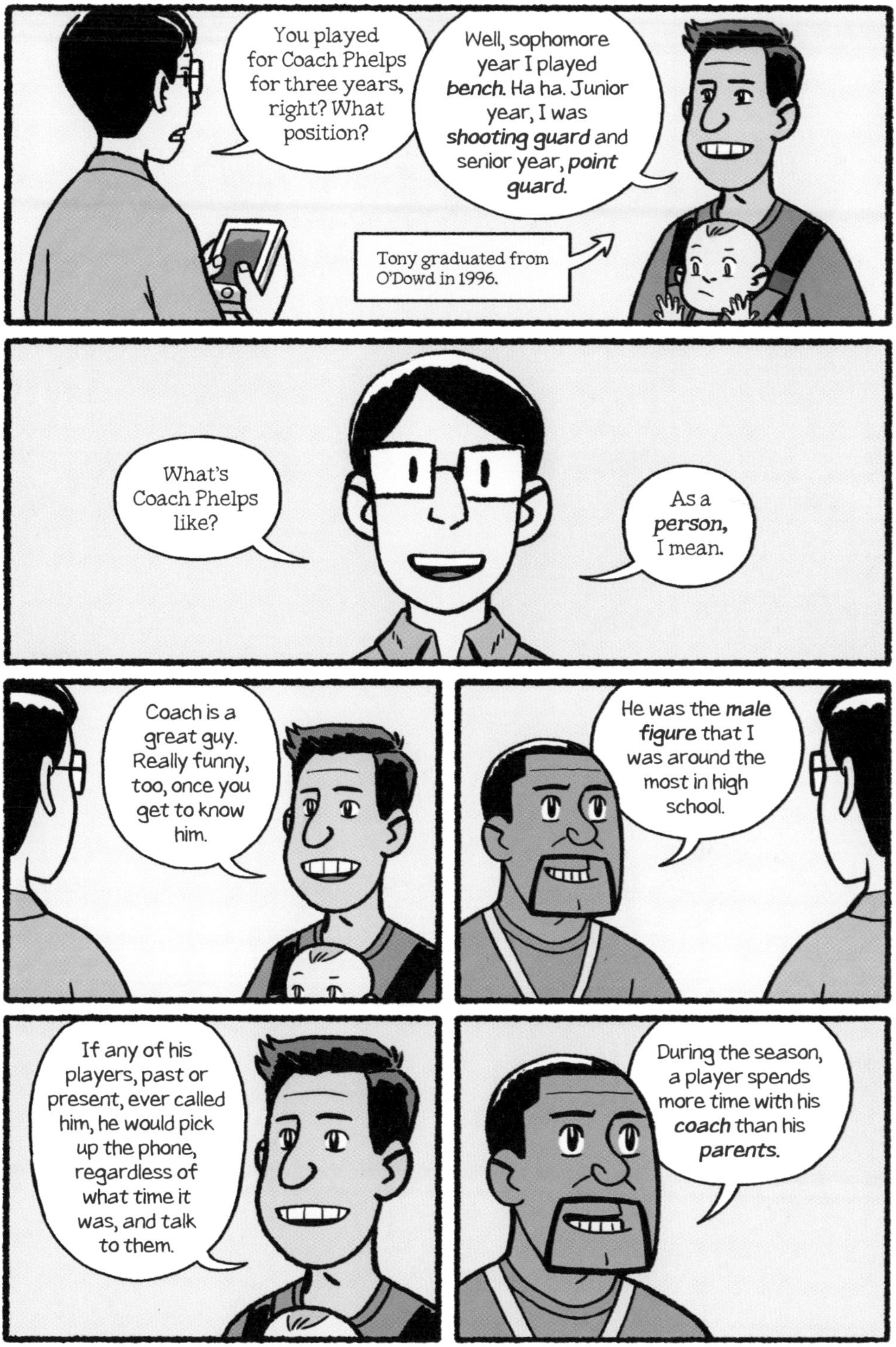
You played for Coach Phelps for three years, right? What position?
Well, sophomore year I played bench. Ha ha. Junior year, I was shooting guard and senior year, point guard.
Tony graduated from O'Dowd in 1996.
What's Coach Phelps like?
As a person, I mean.
Coach is a great guy. Really funny, too, once you get to know him.
He was the male figure that I was around the most in high school.
If any of his players, past or present, ever called him, he would pick up the phone, regardless of what time it was, and talk to them.
During the season, a player spends more time with his coach than his parents.

He had a way of making you feel important, no matter who you were.

"Coach would take the five kids at the end of the bench and make them the *'scout team.'* They'd learn the offenses of the opposing teams and run plays during practice."

"He made us feel like we were *contributing*."

My junior and senior year, my family lived in San Francisco.

"Coach used to give me rides to the BART station. I could have taken the bus, but Coach saved me time, plus we got a chance to *talk*."

"It's those little things, your coach giving you a ride somewhere, that's how you start to build a *bond*."

He was *always* there for us.

He became like a *father* to me.

Then when it came time for me to go to college, Coach found me a place to play.*

* Tony played for Cal State Hayward.

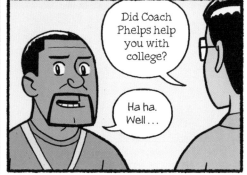
Did Coach Phelps help you with college?

Ha ha. Well . . .

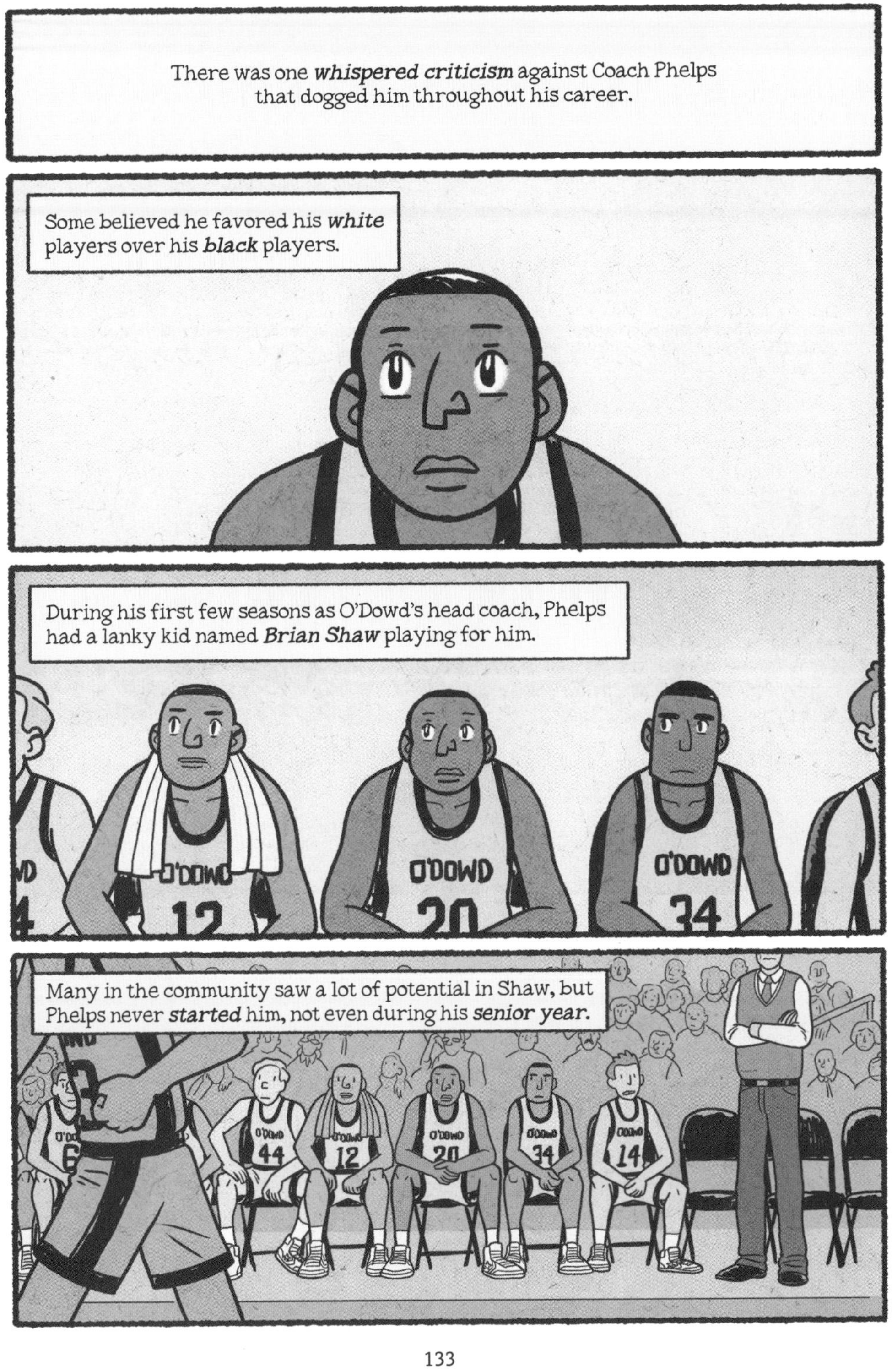
There was one ***whispered criticism*** against Coach Phelps that dogged him throughout his career.
Some believed he favored his ***white*** players over his ***black*** players.
During his first few seasons as O'Dowd's head coach, Phelps had a lanky kid named ***Brian Shaw*** playing for him.
Many in the community saw a lot of potential in Shaw, but Phelps never ***started*** him, not even during his ***senior year***.

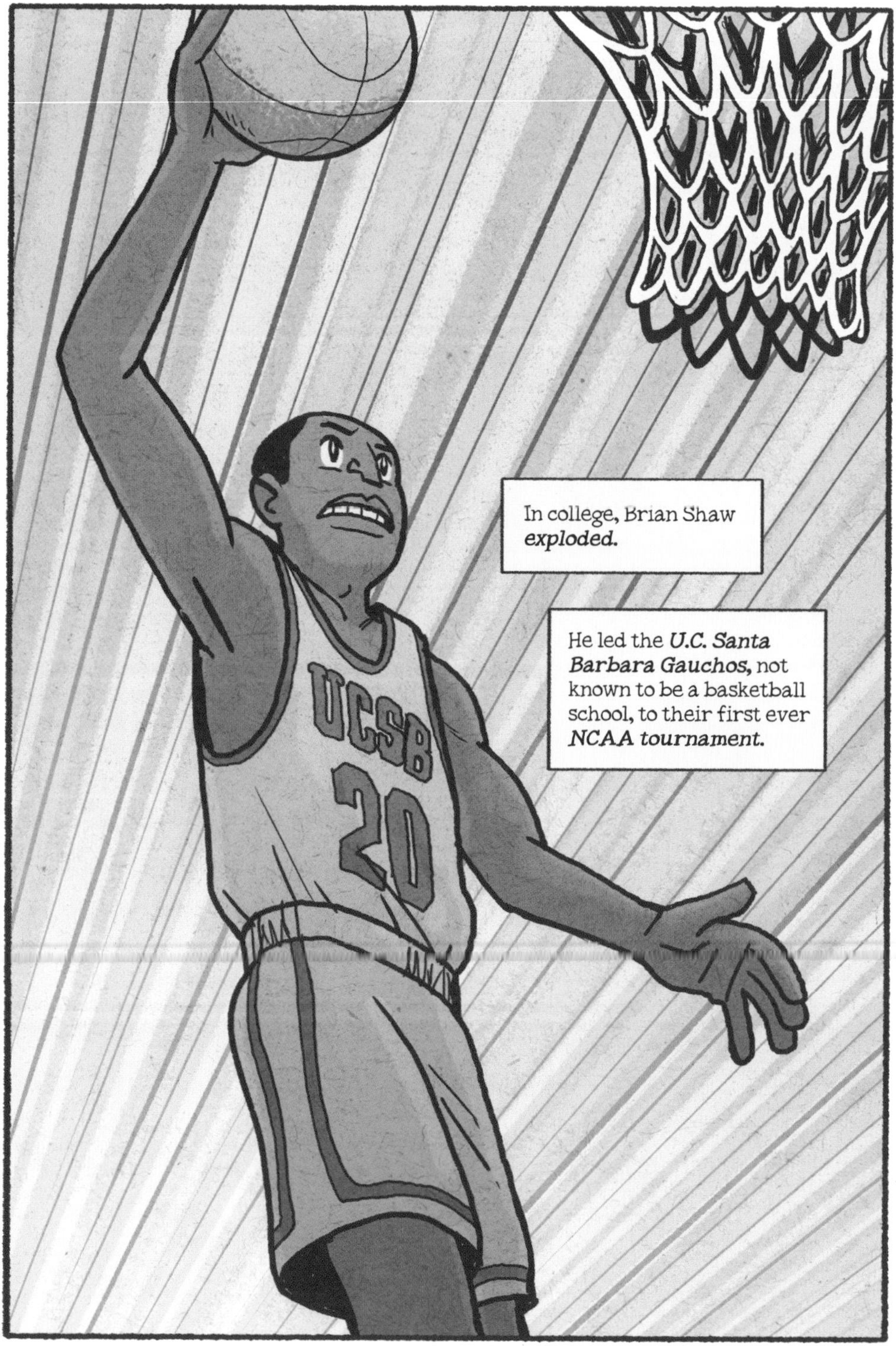
In college, Brian Shaw ***exploded.***
He led the ***U.C. Santa Barbara Gauchos,*** not known to be a basketball school, to their first ever ***NCAA tournament.***
UCSB
20

After graduation, Shaw was drafted into the NBA as the number twenty-four pick overall.

He went on to play in the league for ***fourteen years.*** His career was almost three times as long as the average NBA player's.

He played for seven teams.

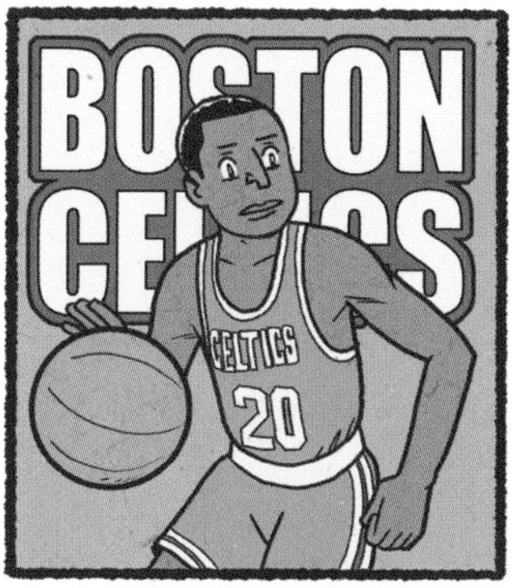
BOSTON
CELTICS
20

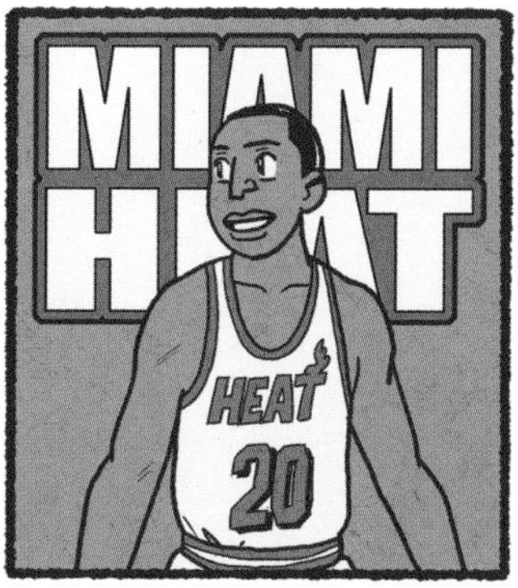
MIAMI
HEAT
20

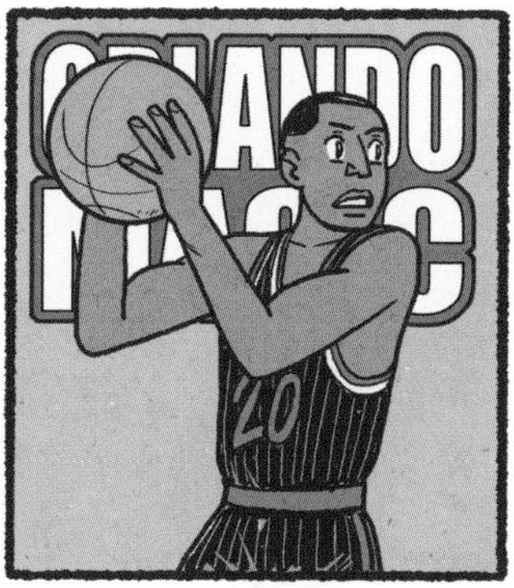
20

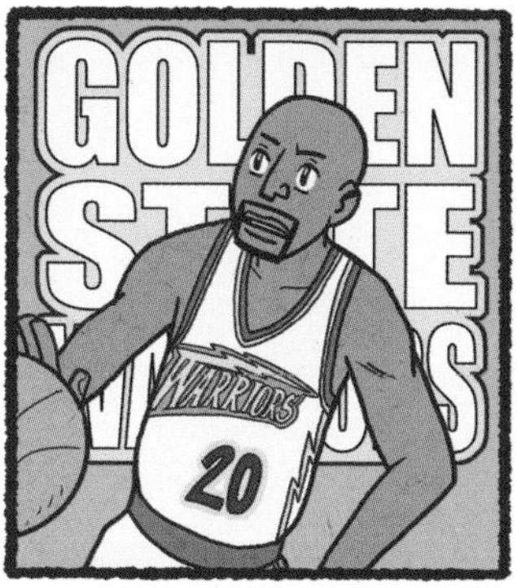
GOLDEN
WARRIORS
20

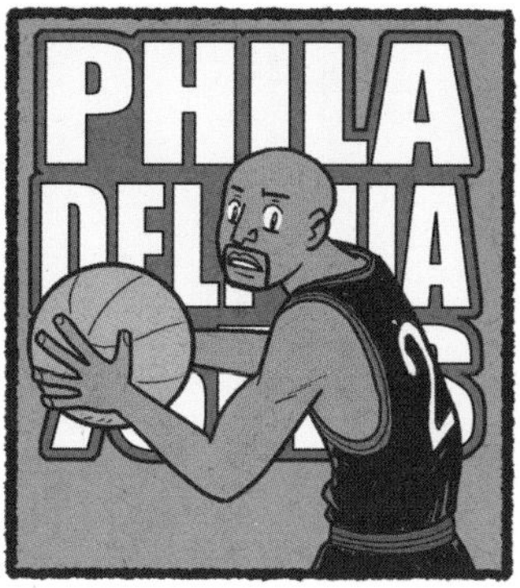
PHILA

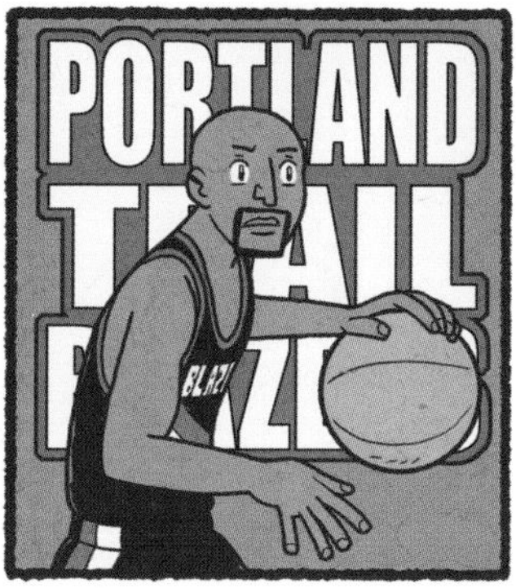
PORTLAND

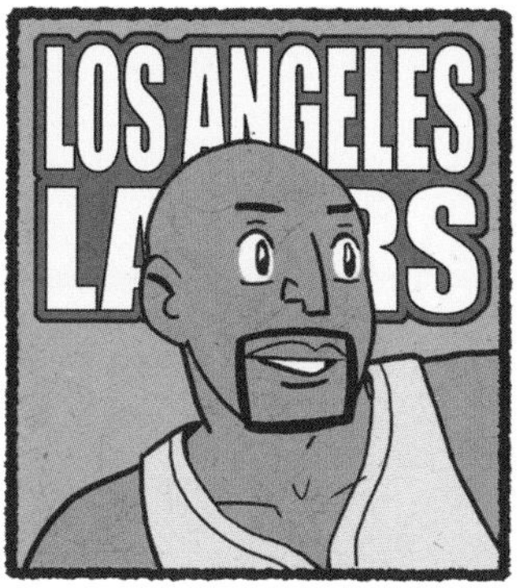
LOS ANGELES

He retired with three championship rings.

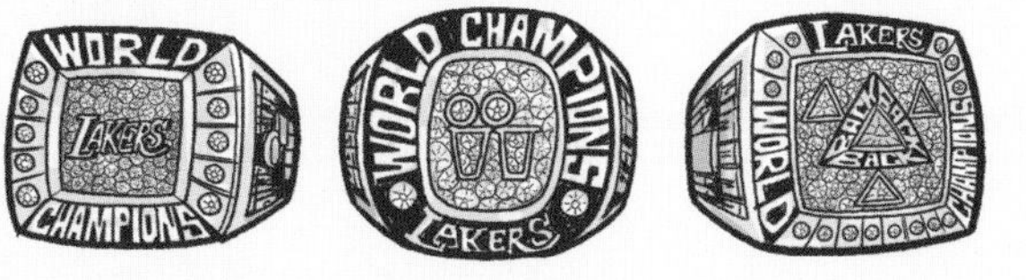
WORLD
LAKERS
CHAMPIONS
WORLD CHAMPIONS
LAKERS
LAKERS
WORLD
CHAMPIONS

Not bad for a kid who never started in high school.

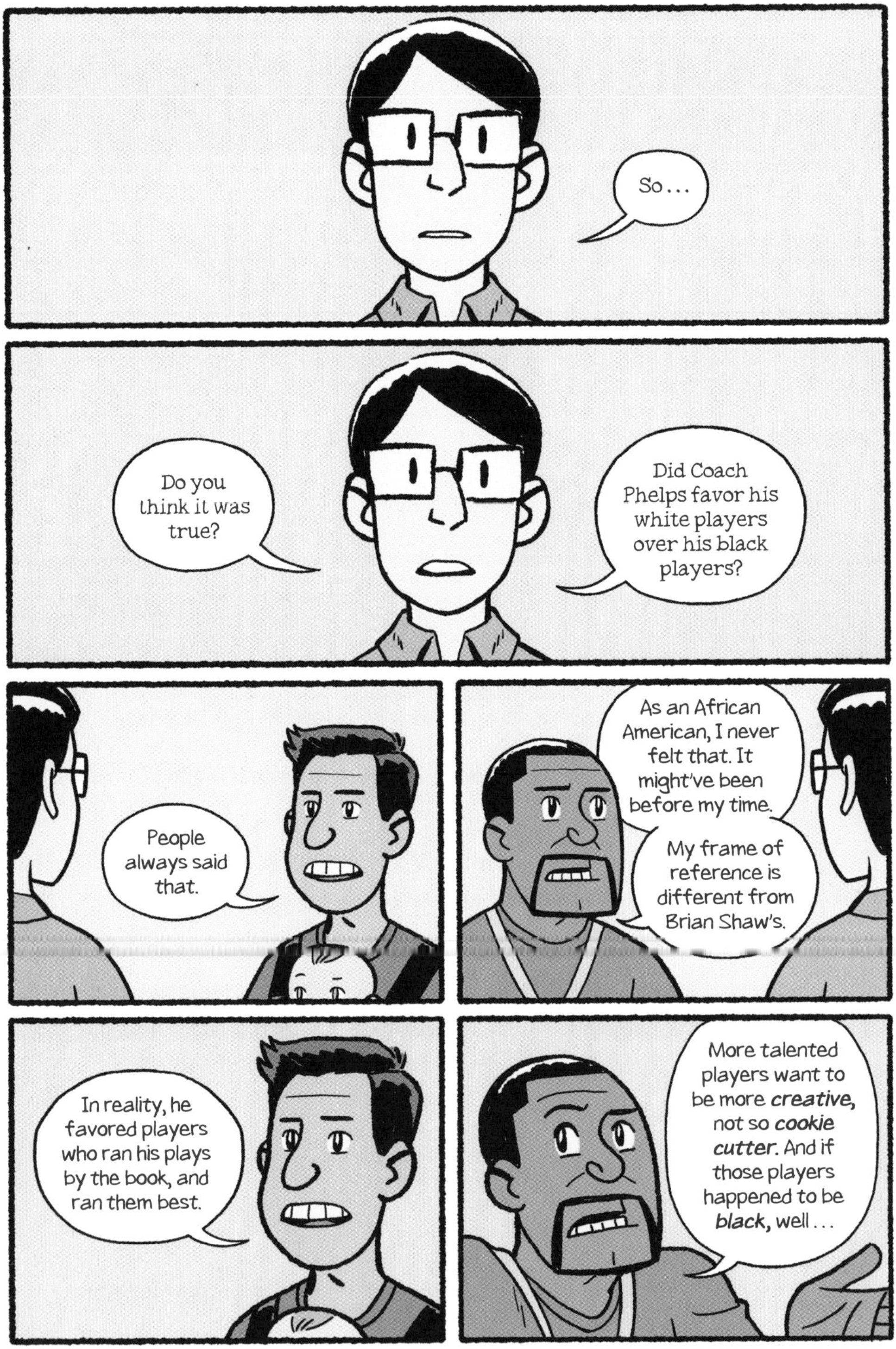
So...
Do you think it was true?
Did Coach Phelps favor his white players over his black players?
People always said that.
As an African American, I never felt that. It might've been before my time.
My frame of reference is different from Brian Shaw's.
In reality, he favored players who ran his plays by the book, and ran them best.
More talented players want to be more ***creative,*** not so ***cookie cutter.*** And if those players happened to be ***black,*** well...

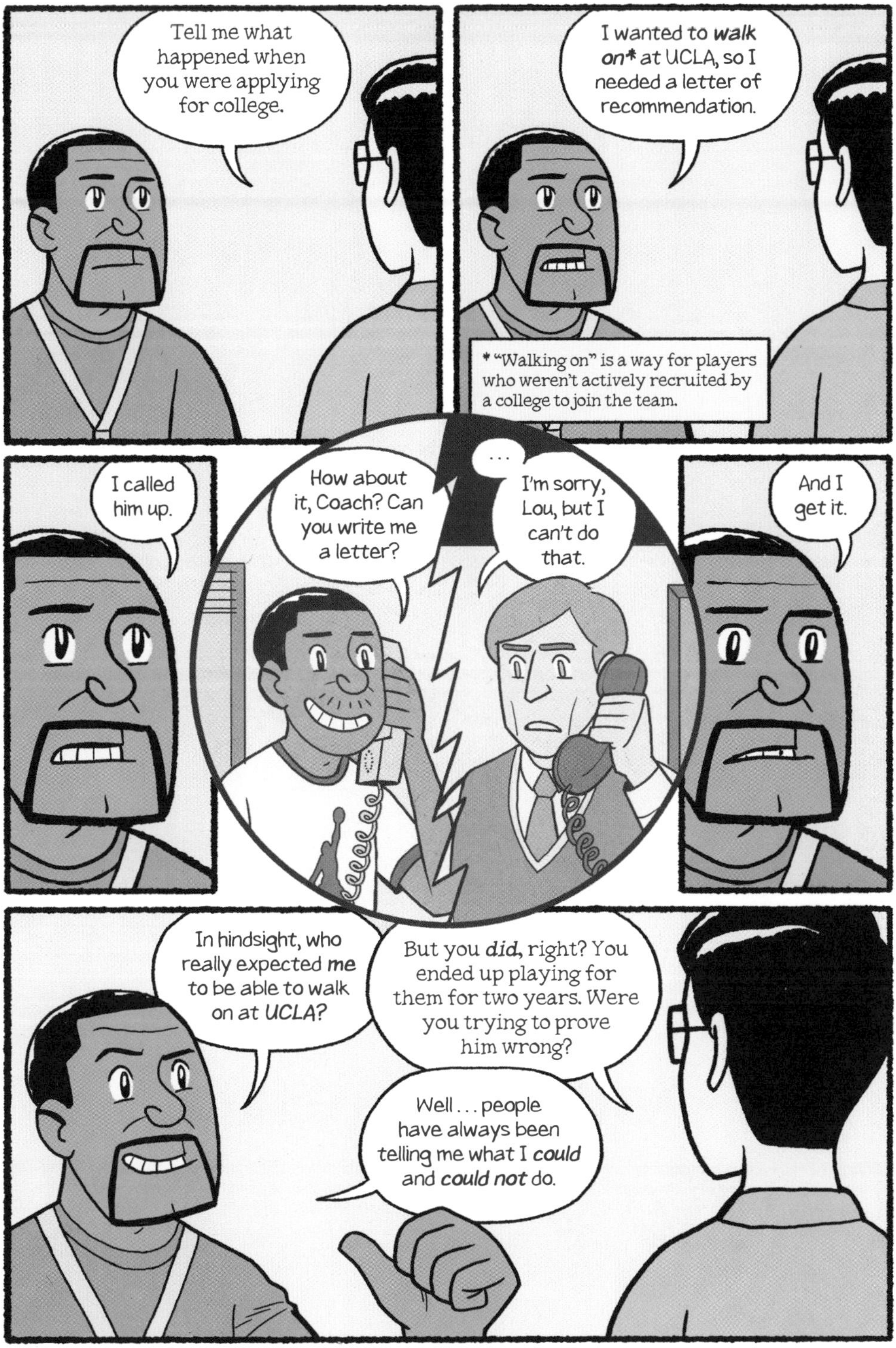
Tell me what happened when you were applying for college.
I wanted to **walk on*** at UCLA, so I needed a letter of recommendation.
* "Walking on" is a way for players who weren't actively recruited by a college to join the team.
I called him up.
How about it, Coach? Can you write me a letter?
...
I'm sorry, Lou, but I can't do that.
And I get it.
In hindsight, who really expected **me** to be able to walk on at *UCLA*?
But you ***did***, right? You ended up playing for them for two years. Were you trying to prove him wrong?
Well . . . people have always been telling me what I ***could*** and ***could not*** do.

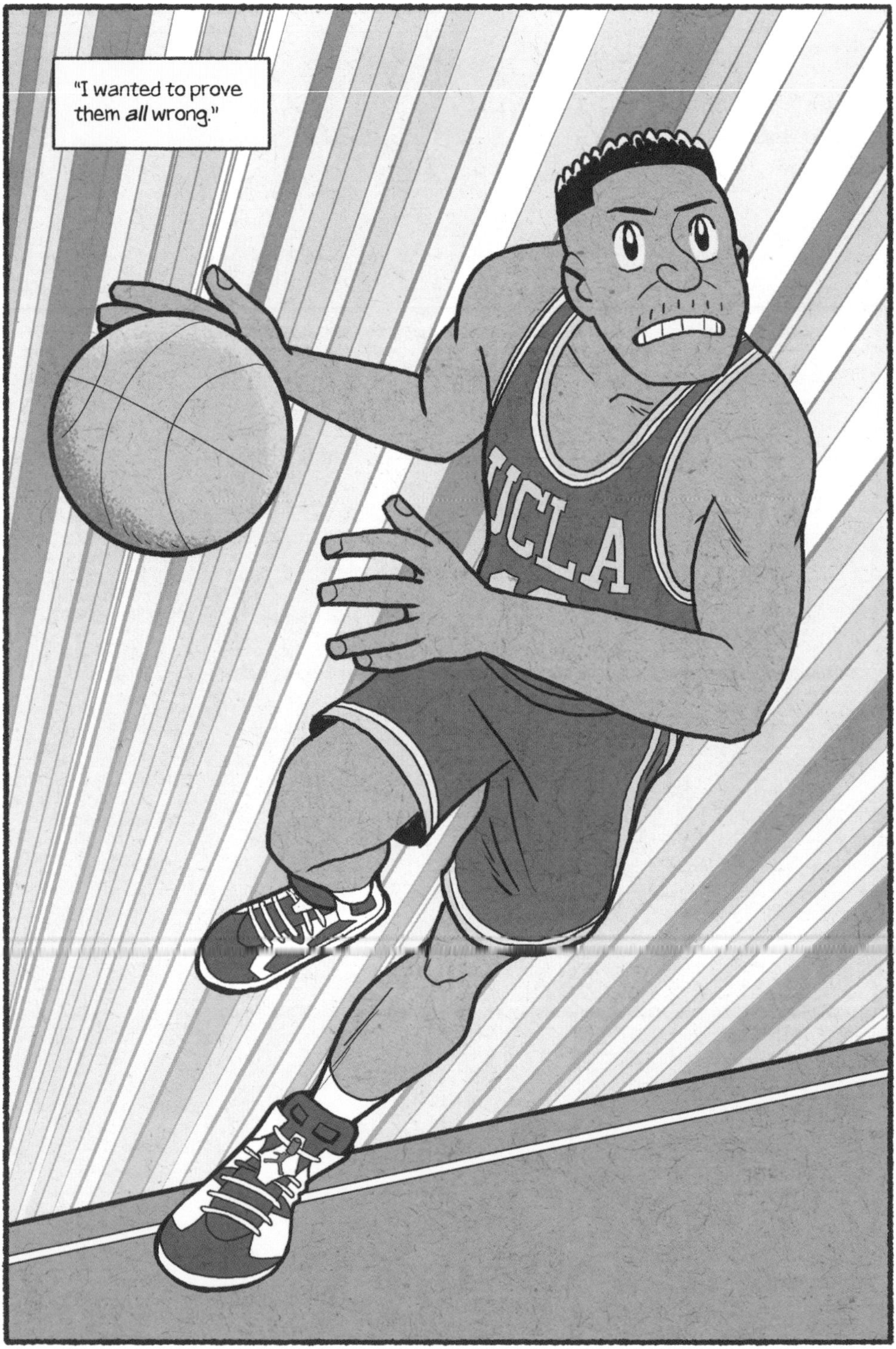
"I wanted to prove them *all* wrong."
UCLA

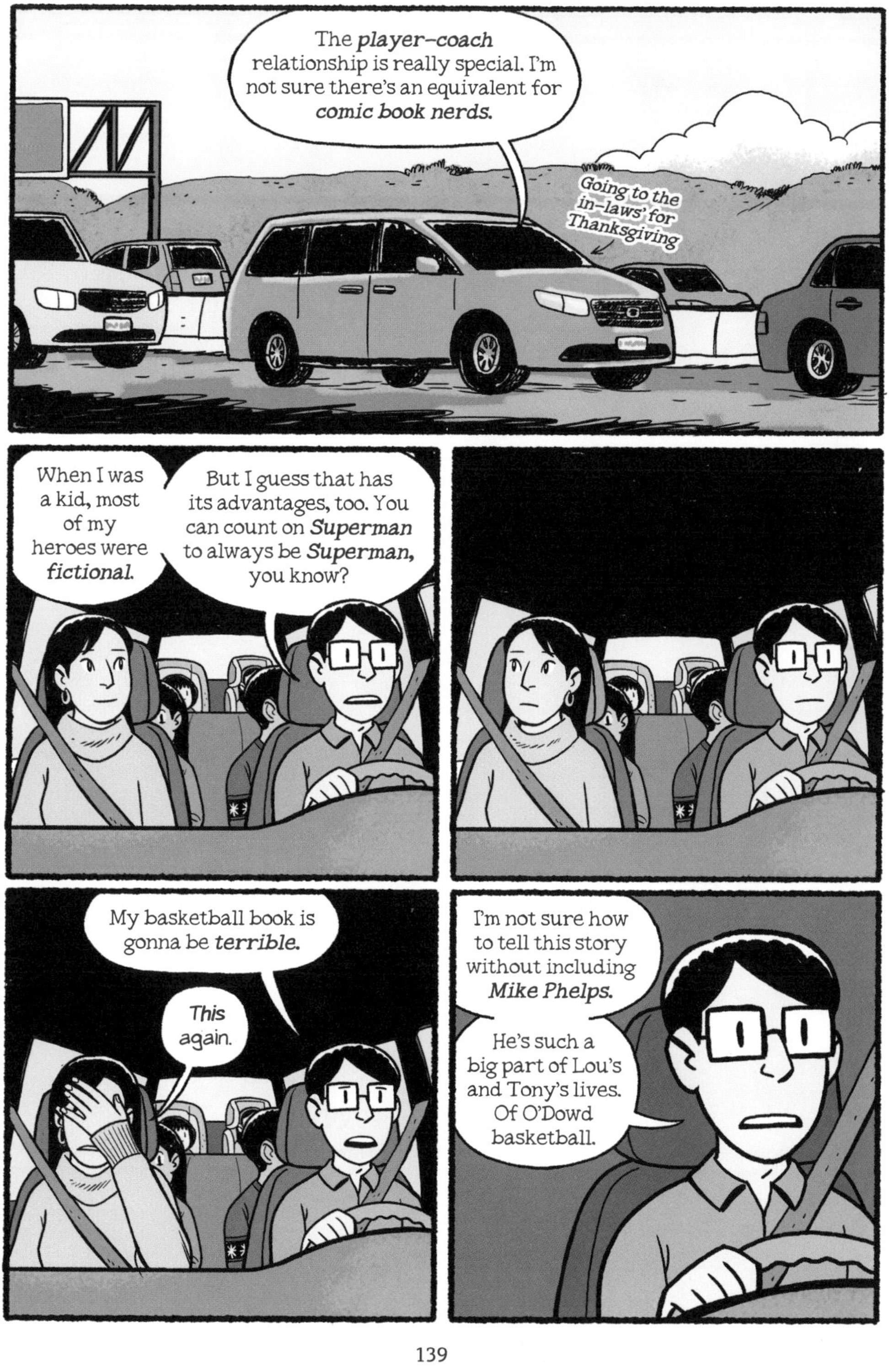
The player–coach relationship is really special. I'm not sure there's an equivalent for comic book nerds.
Going to the in-laws' for Thanksgiving
When I was a kid, most of my heroes were fictional.
But I guess that has its advantages, too. You can count on Superman to always be Superman, you know?
My basketball book is gonna be terrible.
This again.
I'm not sure how to tell this story without including Mike Phelps.
He's such a big part of Lou's and Tony's lives. Of O'Dowd basketball.

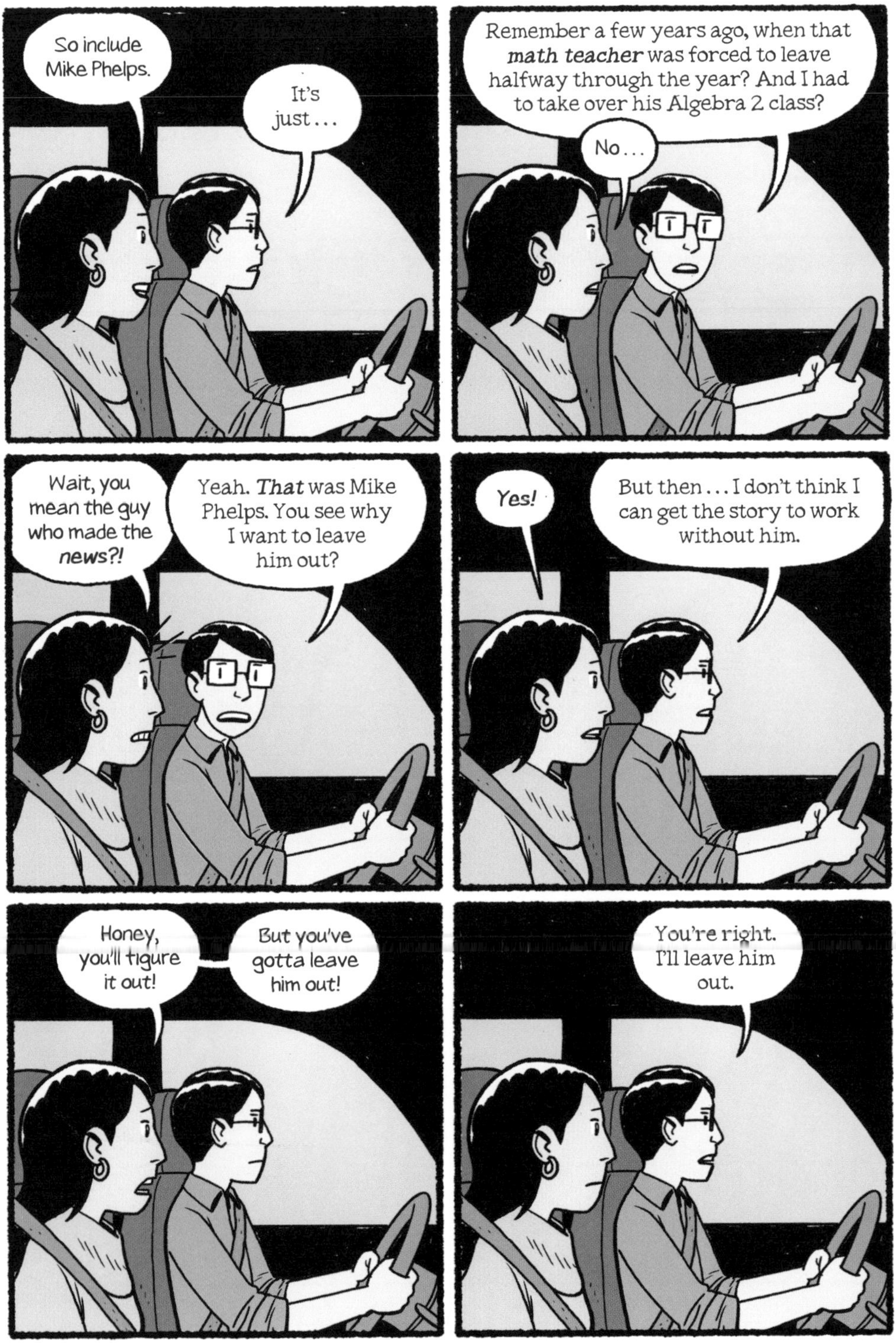
So include Mike Phelps.
It's just...
Remember a few years ago, when that **math teacher** was forced to leave halfway through the year? And I had to take over his Algebra 2 class?
No...
Wait, you mean the guy who made the *news?!*
Yeah. ***That*** was Mike Phelps. You see why I want to leave him out?
Yes!
But then... I don't think I can get the story to work without him.
Honey, you'll figure it out!
But you've gotta leave him out!
You're right. I'll leave him out.

CHAPTER 5:
BISHOP GORMAN GAELS
VS.
BISHOP O'DOWD DRAGONS

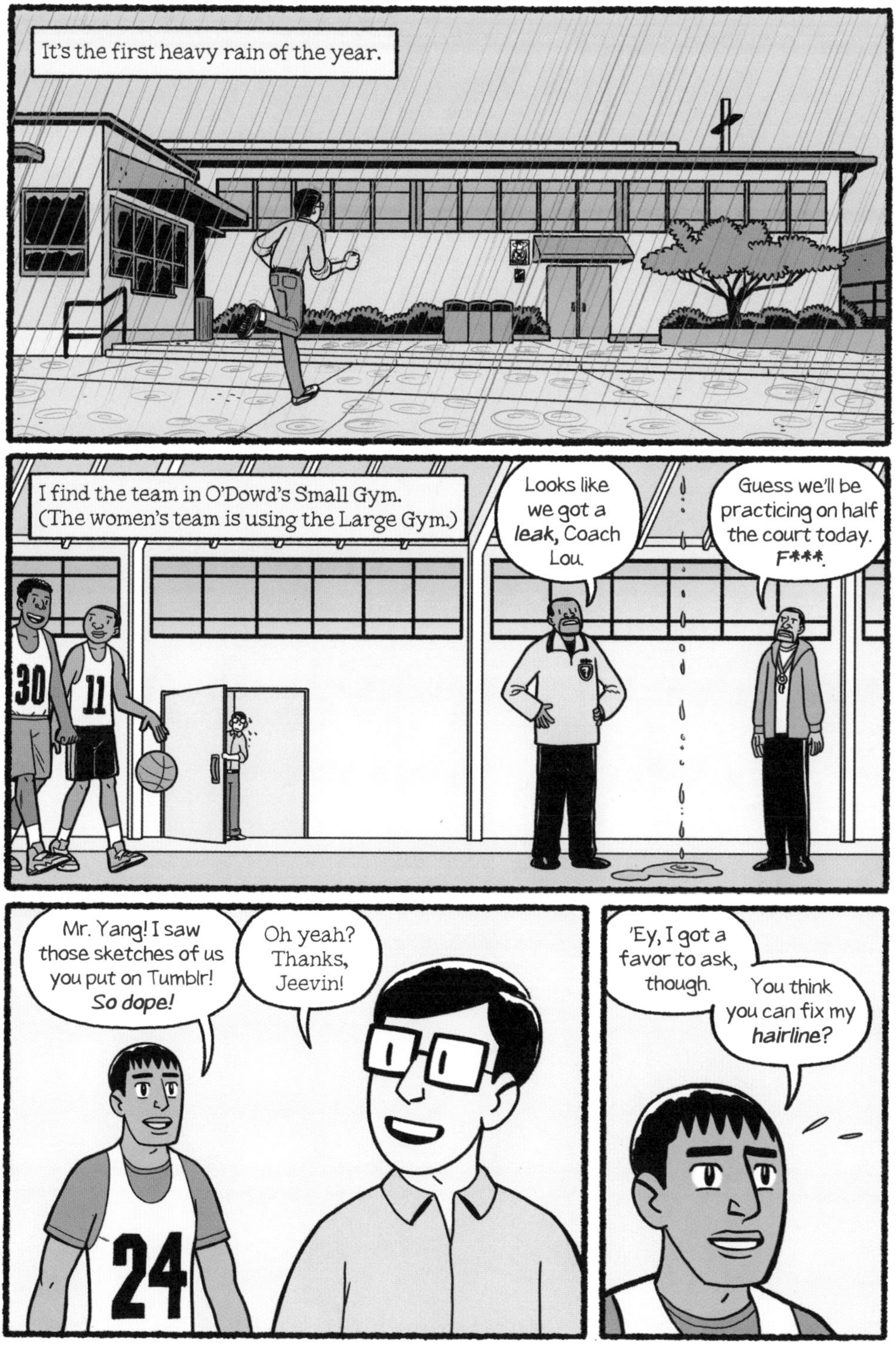
It's the first heavy rain of the year.
I find the team in O'Dowd's Small Gym. (The women's team is using the Large Gym.)
Looks like we got a *leak,* Coach Lou.
Guess we'll be practicing on half the court today. *F***.*
Mr. Yang! I saw those sketches of us you put on Tumblr! *So dope!*
Oh yeah? Thanks, Jeevin!
'Ey, I got a favor to ask, though.
You think you can fix my *hairline?*

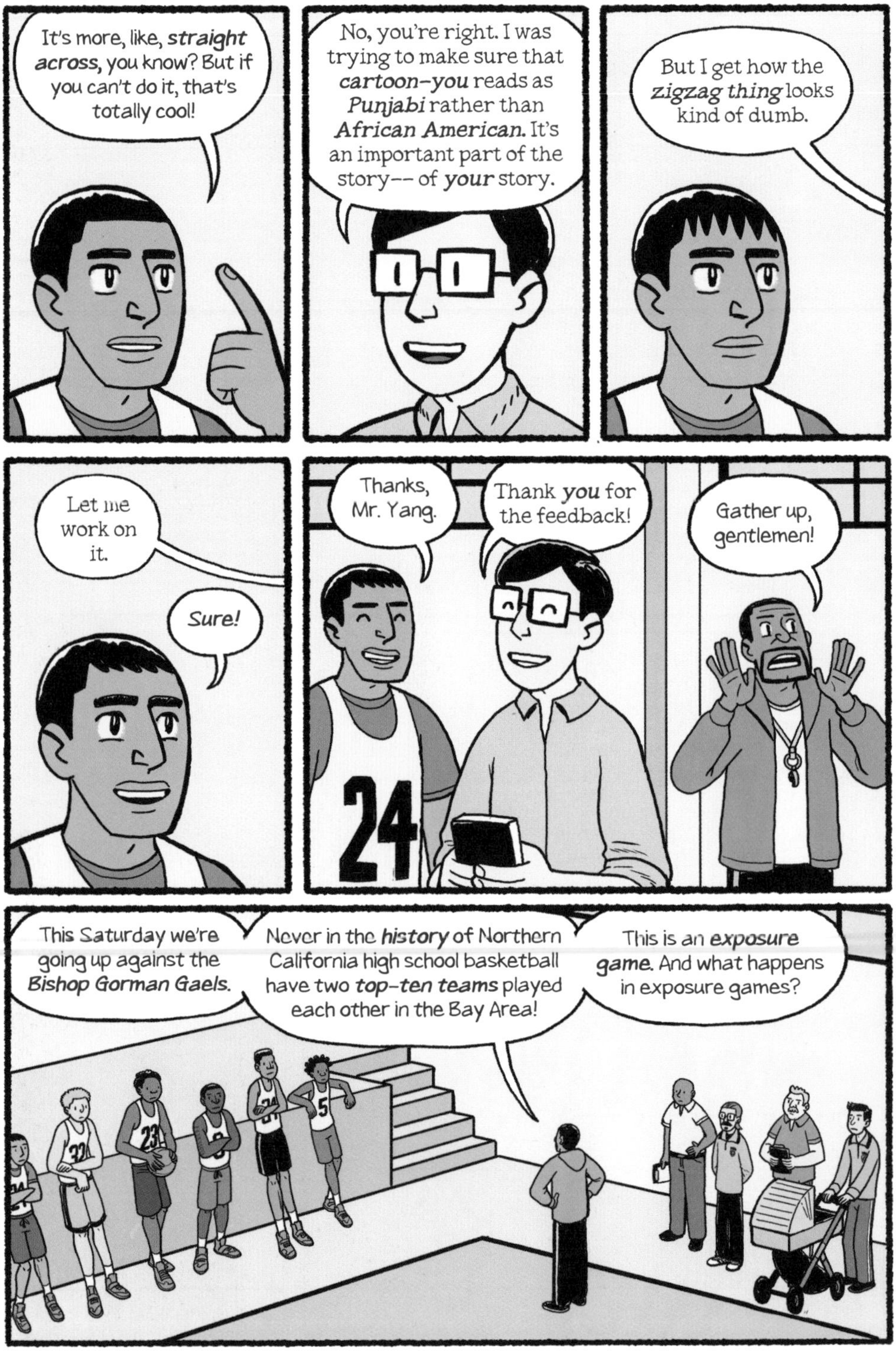
It's more, like, straight across, you know? But if you can't do it, that's totally cool!
No, you're right. I was trying to make sure that cartoon-you reads as Punjabi rather than African American. It's an important part of the story-- of your story.
But I get how the zigzag thing looks kind of dumb.
Let me work on it.
Sure!
Thanks, Mr. Yang.
Thank you for the feedback!
Gather up, gentlemen!
This Saturday we're going up against the Bishop Gorman Gaels.
Never in the history of Northern California high school basketball have two top-ten teams played each other in the Bay Area!
This is an exposure game. And what happens in exposure games?

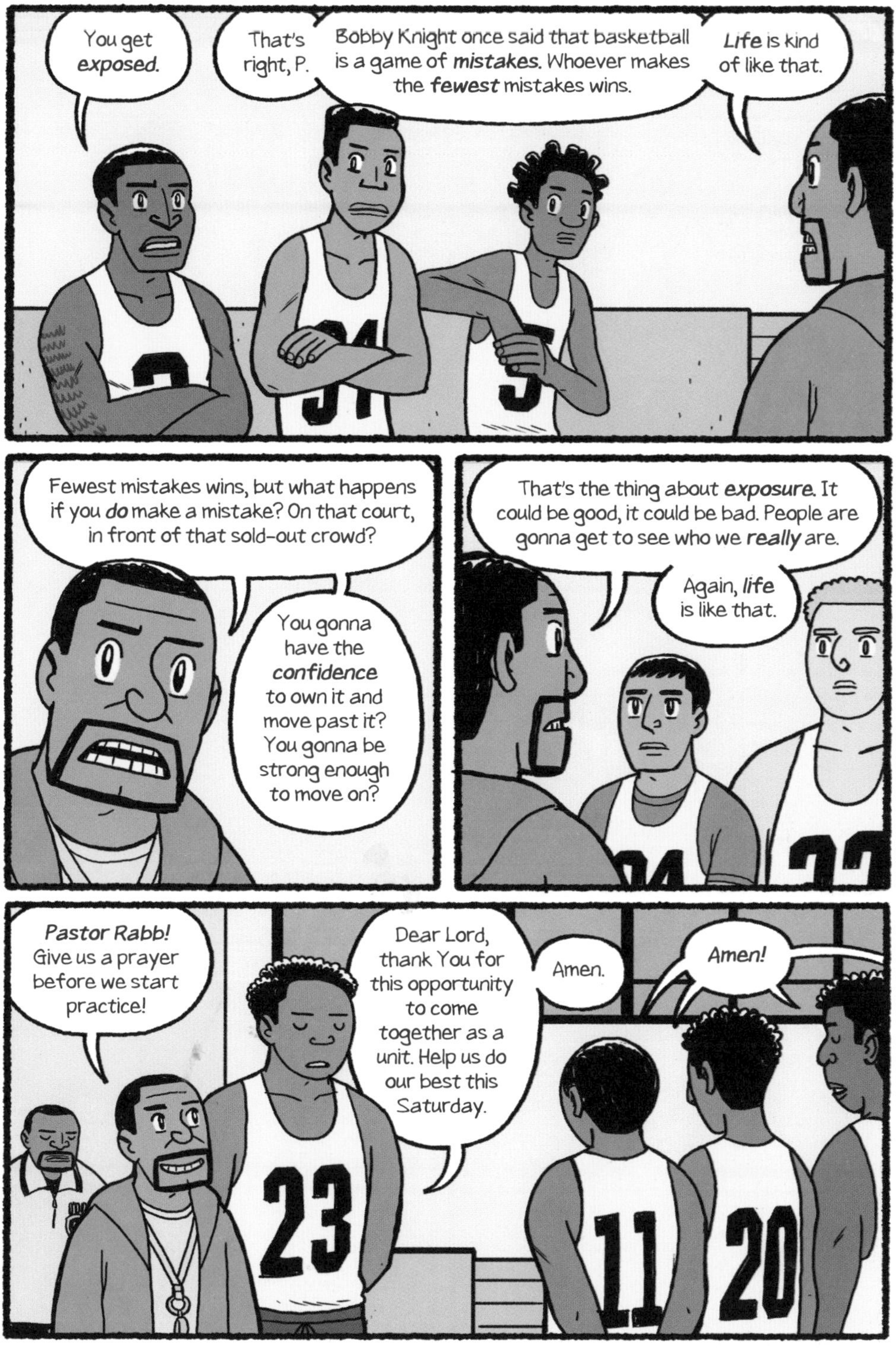
You get *exposed.*
That's right, P.
Bobby Knight once said that basketball is a game of *mistakes.* Whoever makes the *fewest* mistakes wins.
Life is kind of like that.
Fewest mistakes wins, but what happens if you *do* make a mistake? On that court, in front of that sold-out crowd?
You gonna have the *confidence* to own it and move past it? You gonna be strong enough to move on?
That's the thing about *exposure.* It could be good, it could be bad. People are gonna get to see who we *really* are.
Again, *life* is like that.
Pastor Rabb! Give us a prayer before we start practice!
Dear Lord, thank You for this opportunity to come together as a unit. Help us do our best this Saturday.
Amen.
Amen!

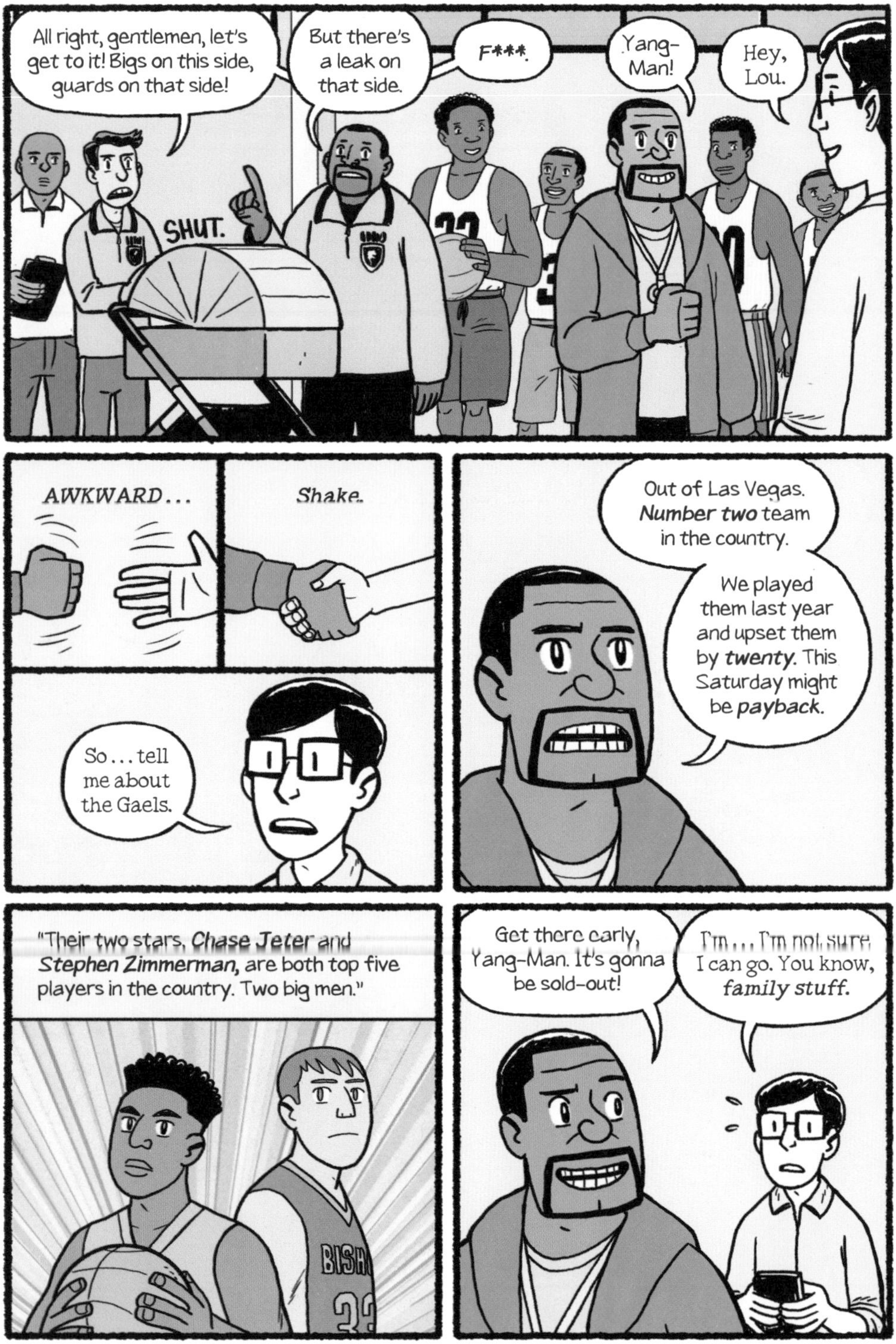

All right, gentlemen, let's get to it! Bigs on this side, guards on that side!
But there's a leak on that side.
SHUT.
F***.
Yang-Man!
Hey, Lou.
AWKWARD...
Shake.
So... tell me about the Gaels.
Out of Las Vegas. Number two team in the country.
We played them last year and upset them by twenty. This Saturday might be payback.
"Their two stars, Chase Jeter and Stephen Zimmerman, are both top five players in the country. Two big men."
Get there early, Yang-Man. It's gonna be sold-out!
I'm... I'm not sure I can go. You know, family stuff.

"Family stuff" isn't much of anything at all. We end up watching a superhero movie.

Daddy, is there *bad guys* in it? I don't like it when there's bad guys in it!

Don't worry, sweetie. The heroes always win. *Always.*

Isn't O'Dowd playing today?

Yeah, but it's raining... plus I get to spend time with you and the kids.

I gotta go pee.

Want us to pause?

No, it's okay.

It felt *so good* when I first decided to do this book.

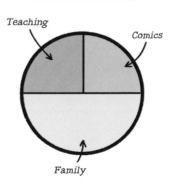

I felt *whole* again.

Teaching

Comics

Family

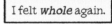

But now? There's so much *uncertainty.*
What happens if the team doesn't win?
How am I gonna get more of Ivan and Paris's backstory?
Is leaving Mike Phelps out really the right way to go?
Checking game updates
Doesn't really need to pee
I can't help but think about it even when I'm not supposed to.
Teaching
Comics
Family
I feel *out of control.*
Sigh. Maybe I should've gone.
Watching Ivan Rabb for Bishop O'Dowd - He is the REAL DEAL, ladies and gentlemen!!
Daddy! The bad guys just showed up!
Daddyyy!
knock! knock!
I'll be right out, Sweetie!

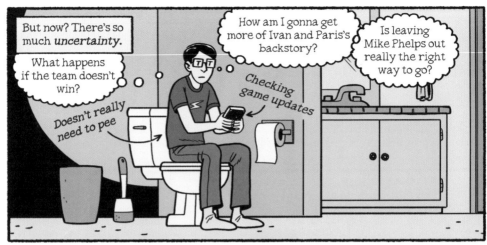

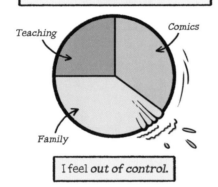

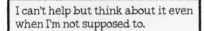

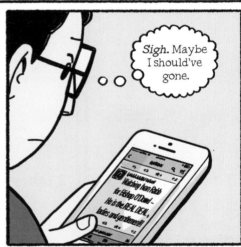

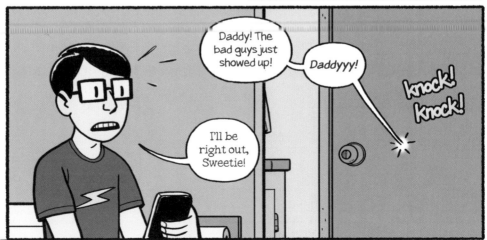

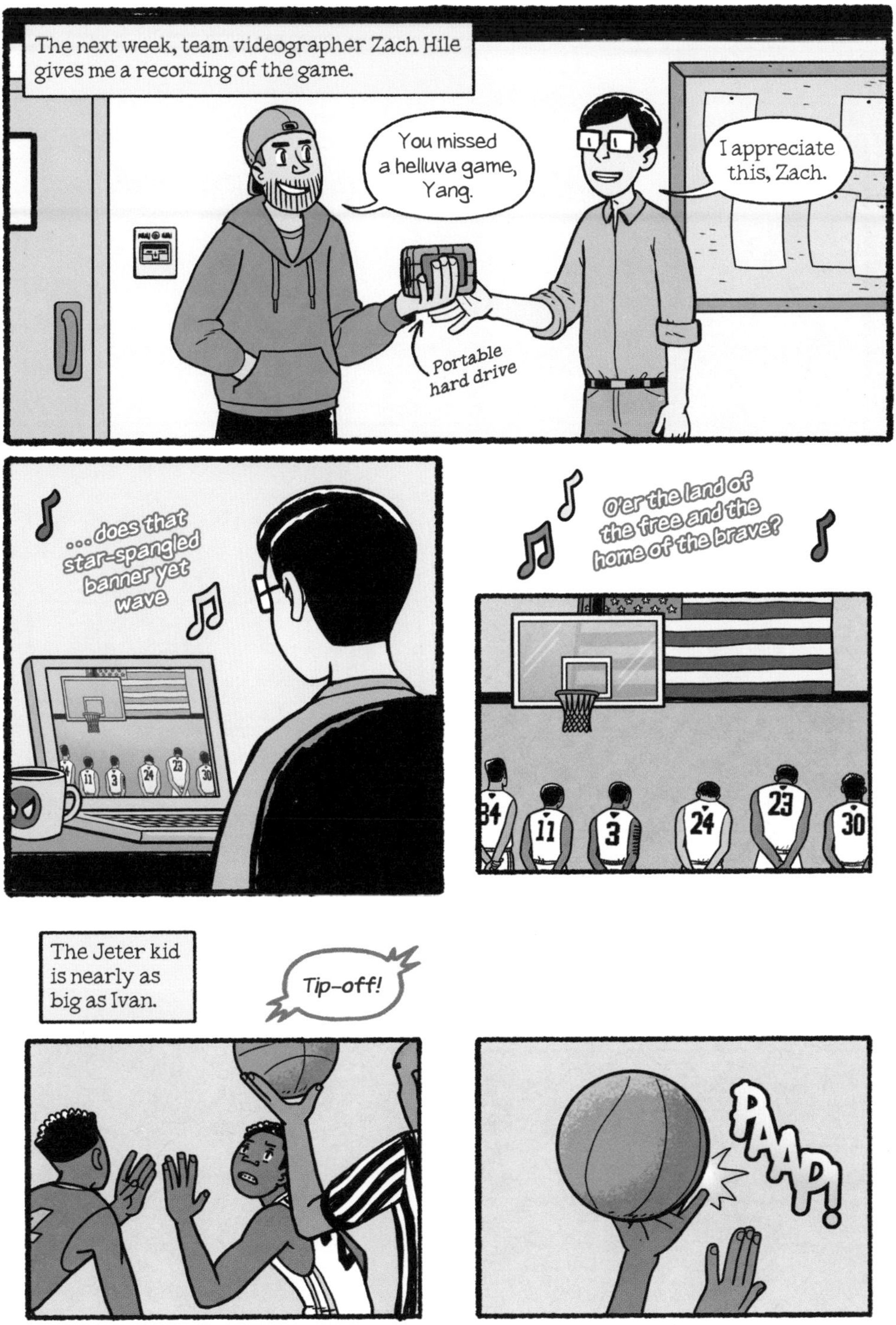
The next week, team videographer Zach Hile gives me a recording of the game.
You missed a helluva game, Yang.
I appreciate this, Zach.
Portable hard drive
...does that star-spangled banner yet wave
O'er the land of the free and the home of the brave?
34
11
3
24
23
30
The Jeter kid is nearly as big as Ivan.
Tip-off!
PAAP!

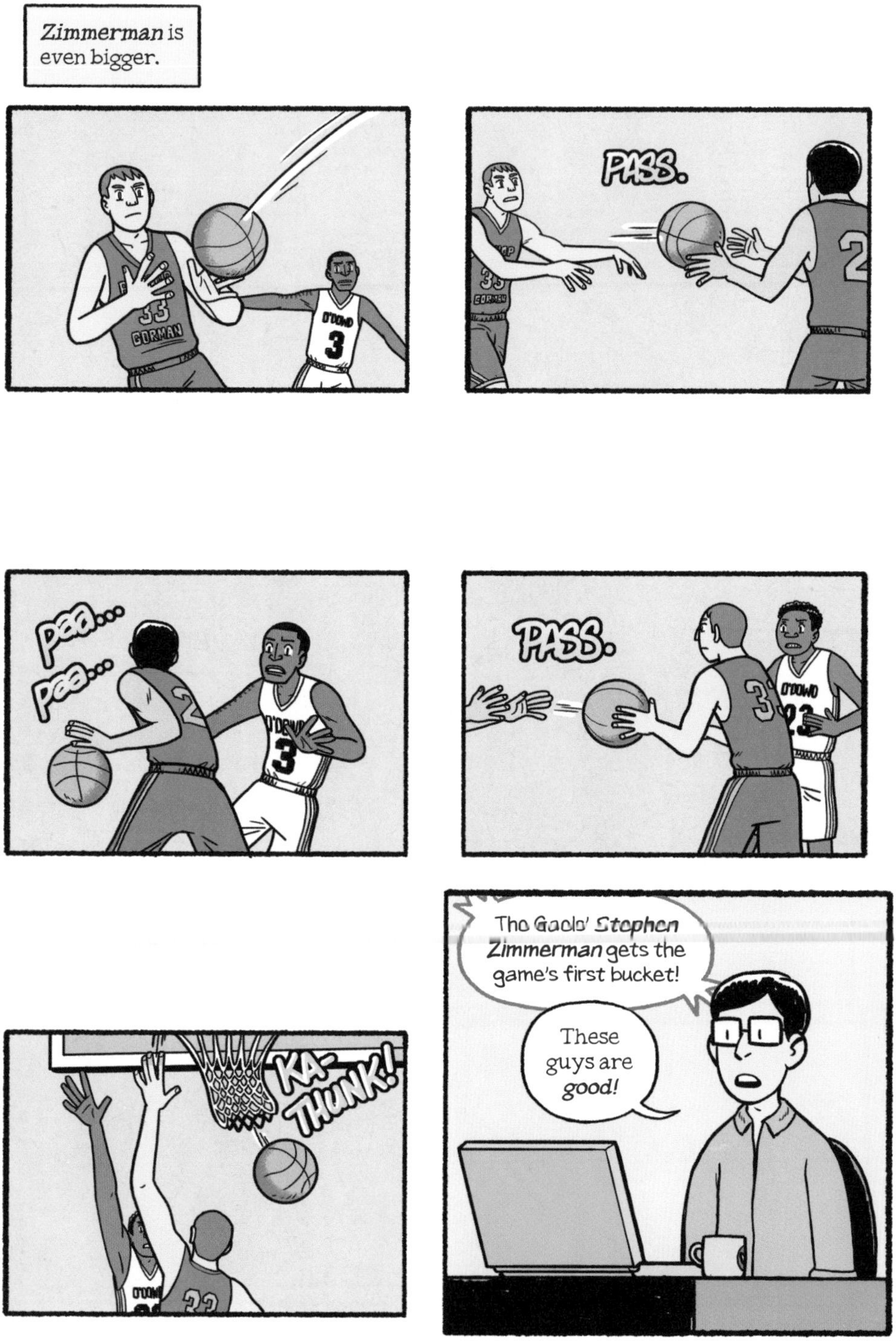
Zimmerman is even bigger.
PASS.
paa...
paa...
PASS.
KA-THUNK!
The Gaels' Stephen Zimmerman gets the game's first bucket!
These guys are good!

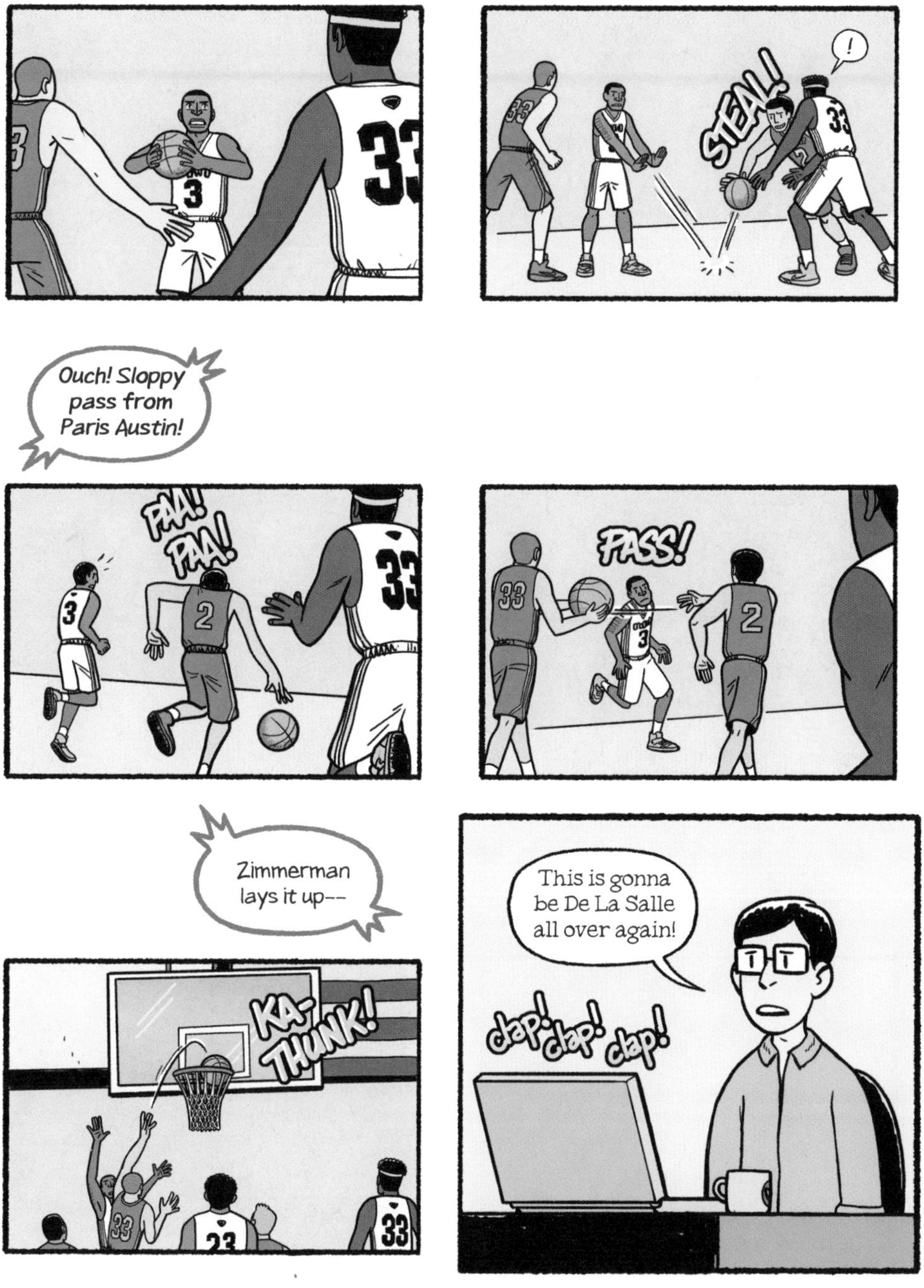
STEAL!
!
Ouch! Sloppy pass from Paris Austin!
PAA! PAA!
PASS!
Zimmerman lays it up--
KA-THUNK!
This is gonna be De La Salle all over again!
clap! clap! clap!

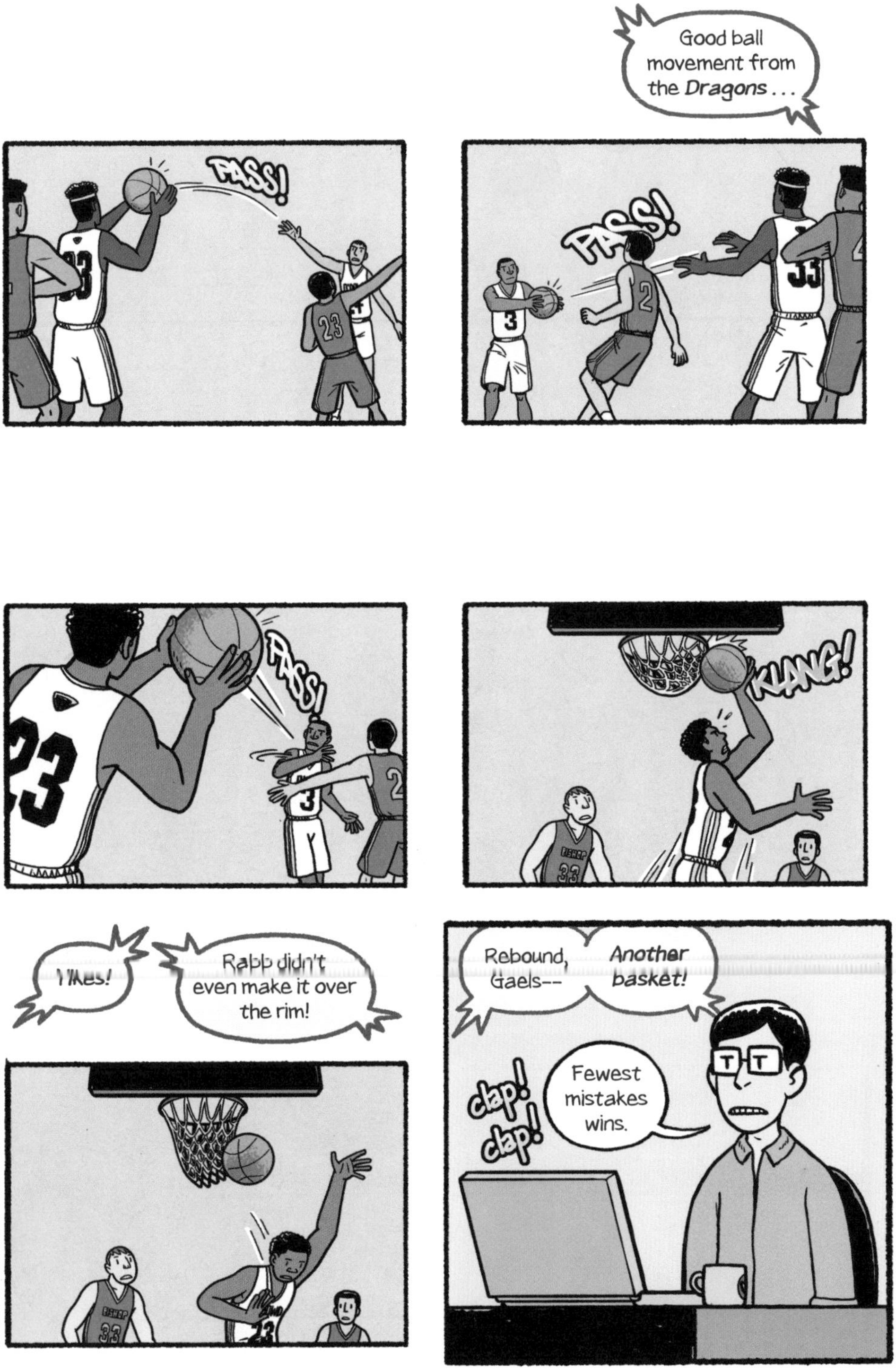

PASS!
Good ball movement from the *Dragons* . . .
PASS!
PASS!
KLANG!
Yikes!
Rabb didn't even make it over the rim!
Rebound, Gaels--
Another basket!
clap! clap!
Fewest mistakes wins.

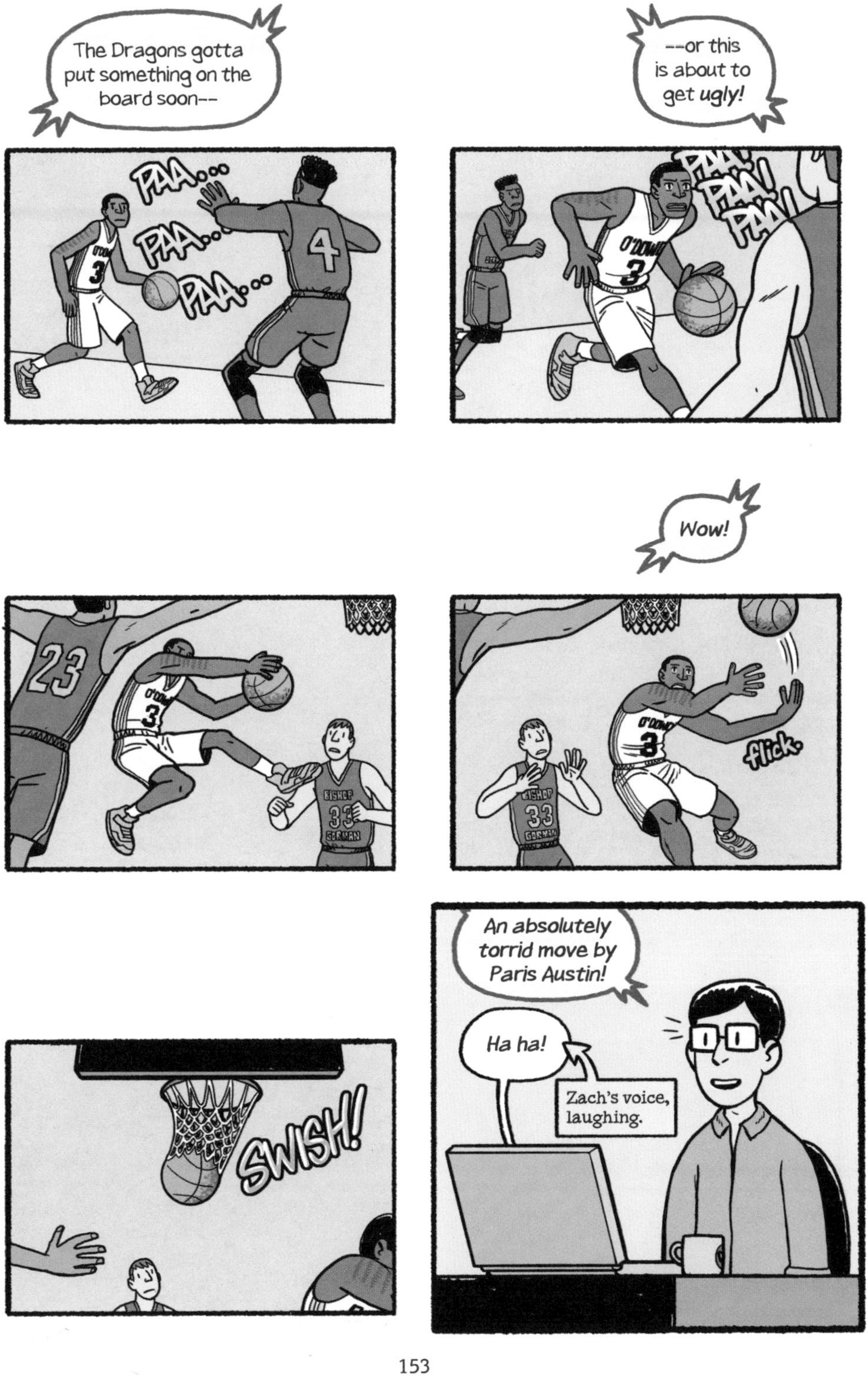
The Dragons gotta put something on the board soon--
PAA...
PAA...
PAA...
--or this is about to get *ugly!*
PAA!
PAA!
PAA!
Wow!
flick.
SWISH!
An absolutely torrid move by Paris Austin!
Ha ha!
Zach's voice, laughing.

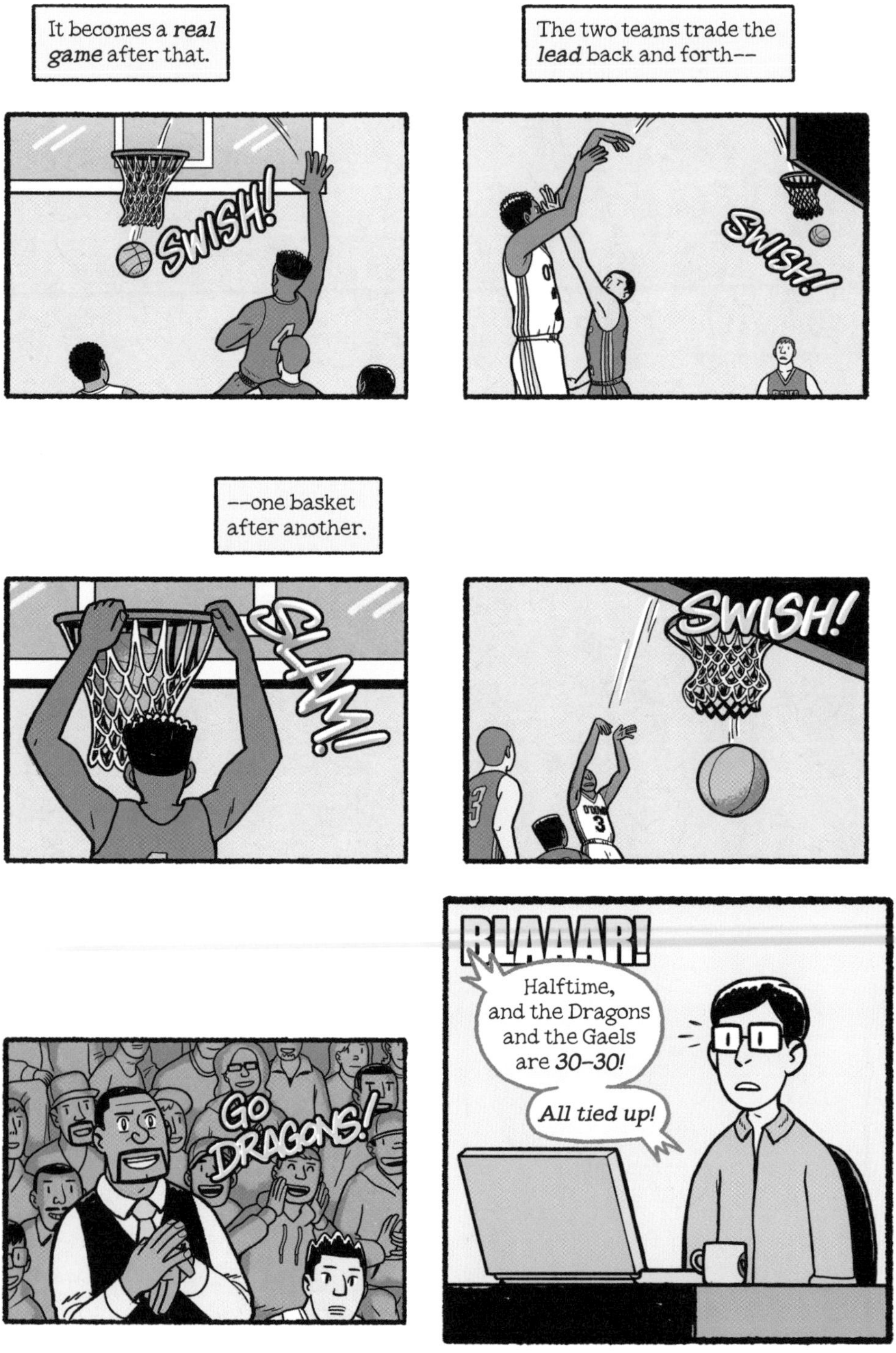
It becomes a real game after that.
SWISH!
The two teams trade the lead back and forth--
SWISH!
--one basket after another.
SLAM!
SWISH!
GO DRAGONS!
BLAAAR!
Halftime, and the Dragons and the Gaels are 30-30!
All tied up!

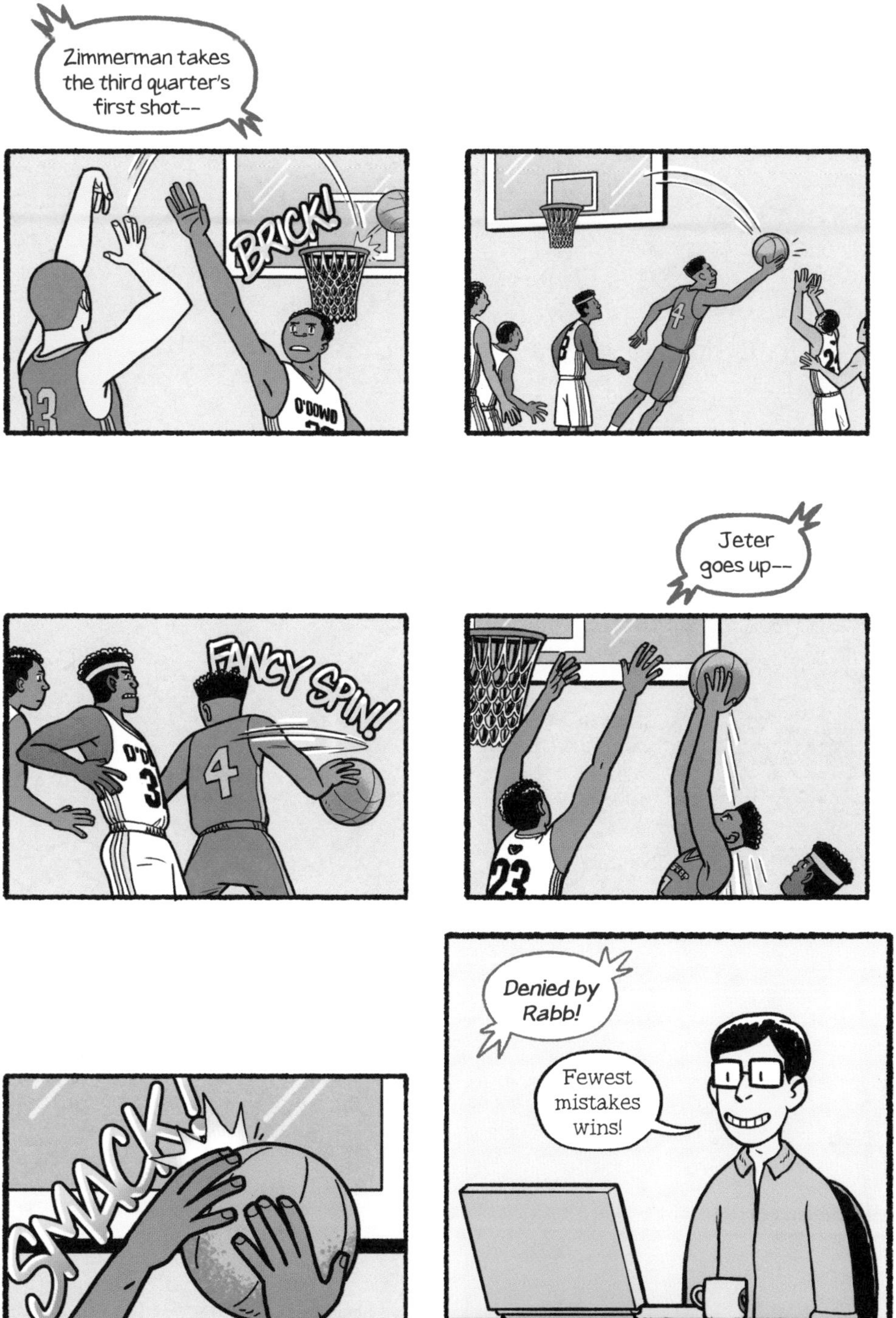
Zimmerman takes the third quarter's first shot--
BRICK!
FANCY SPIN!
Jeter goes up--
SMACK!
Denied by Rabb!
Fewest mistakes wins!

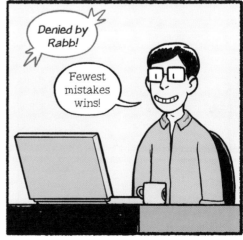

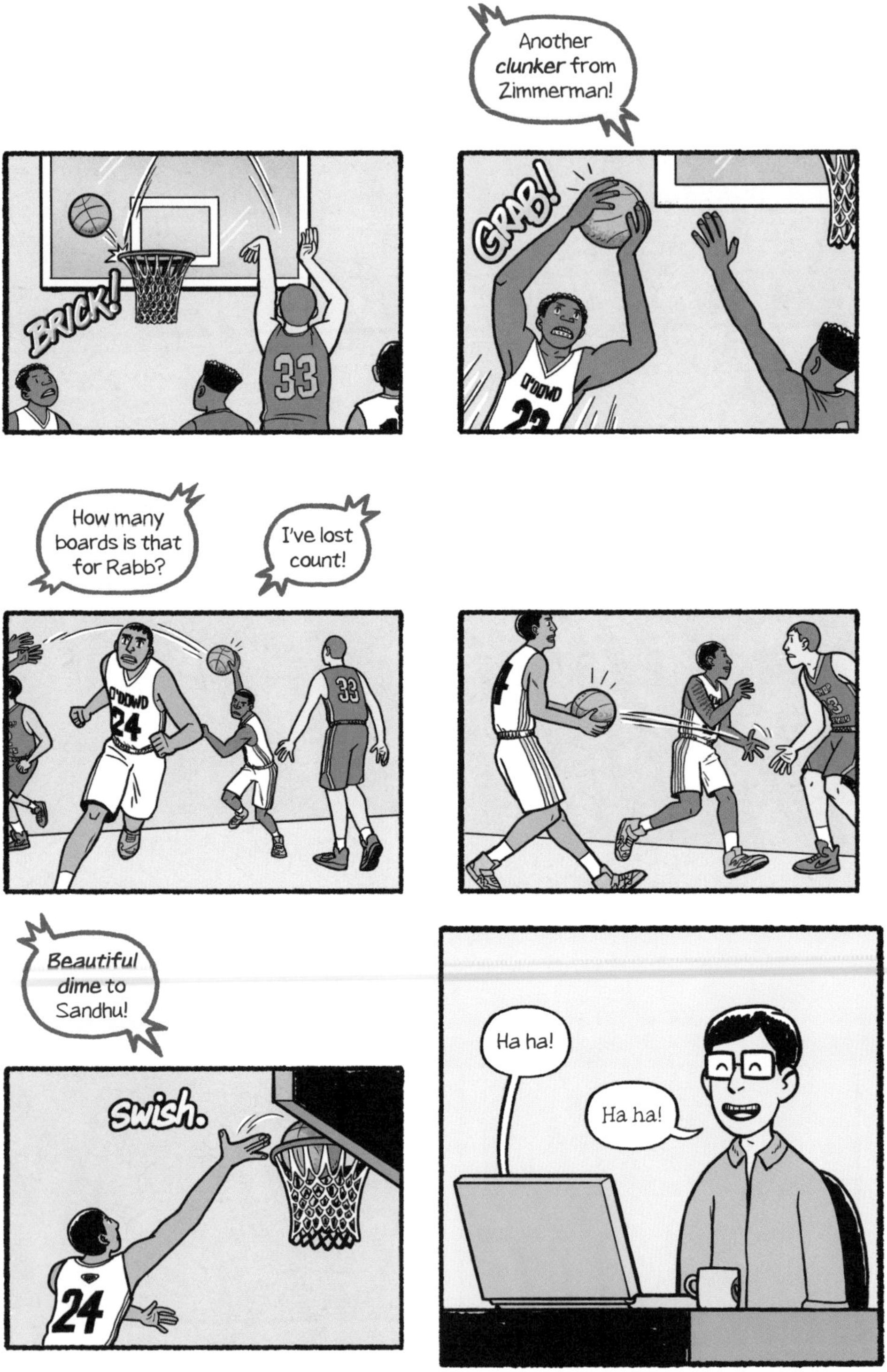
BRICK!
Another **clunker** from Zimmerman!
GRAB!
How many boards is that for Rabb?
I've lost count!
Beautiful dime to Sandhu!
Swish.
Ha ha!
Ha ha!

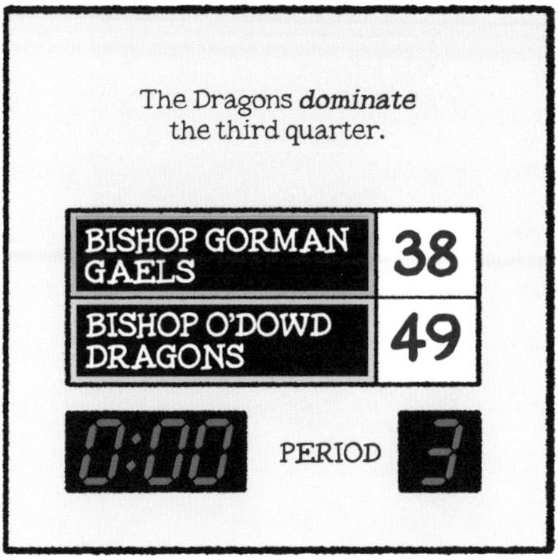
The Dragons *dominate* the third quarter.
BISHOP GORMAN GAELS
38
BISHOP O'DOWD DRAGONS
49
0:00
PERIOD
3

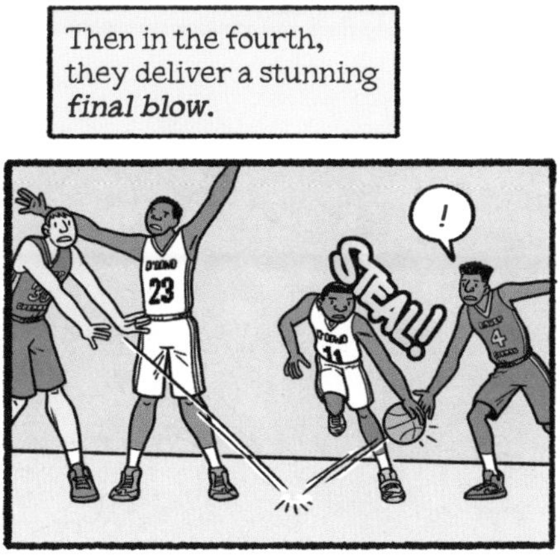
Then in the fourth, they deliver a stunning *final blow.*
STEAL!
!

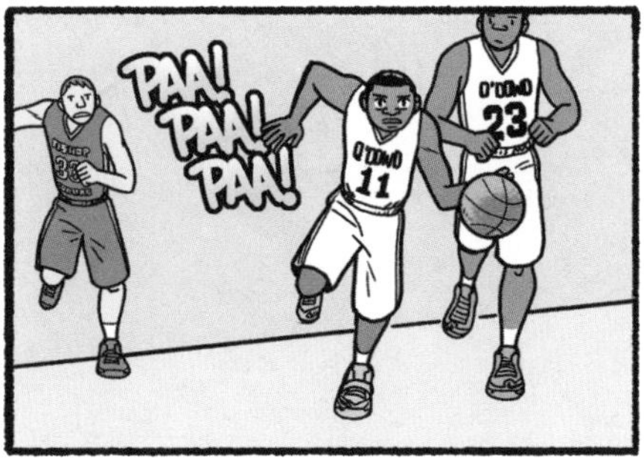
PAA! PAA! PAA!

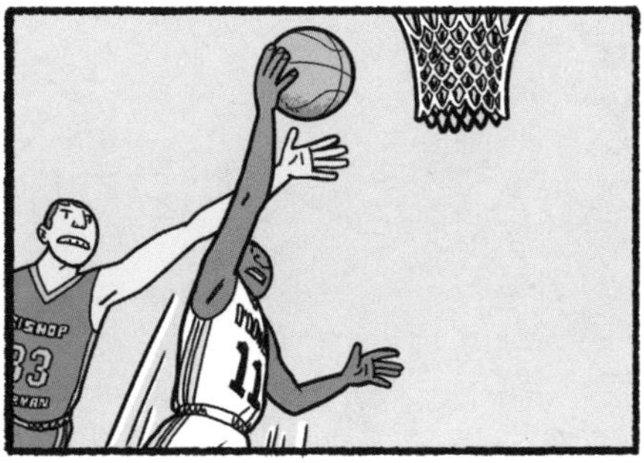

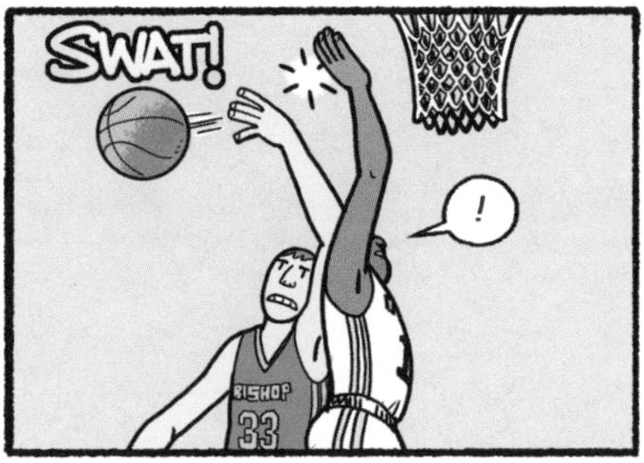
SWAT!
!

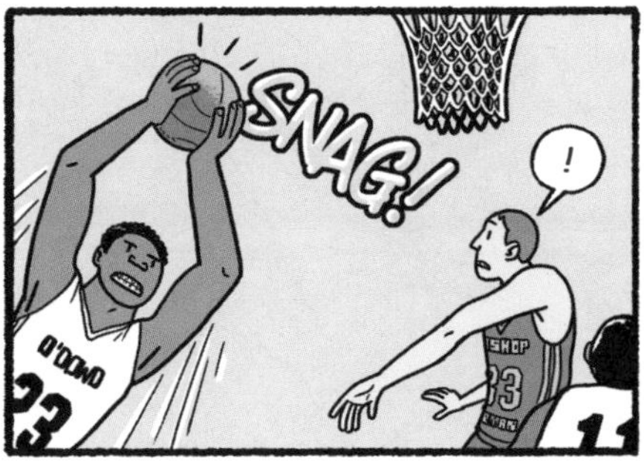
SNAG!
!

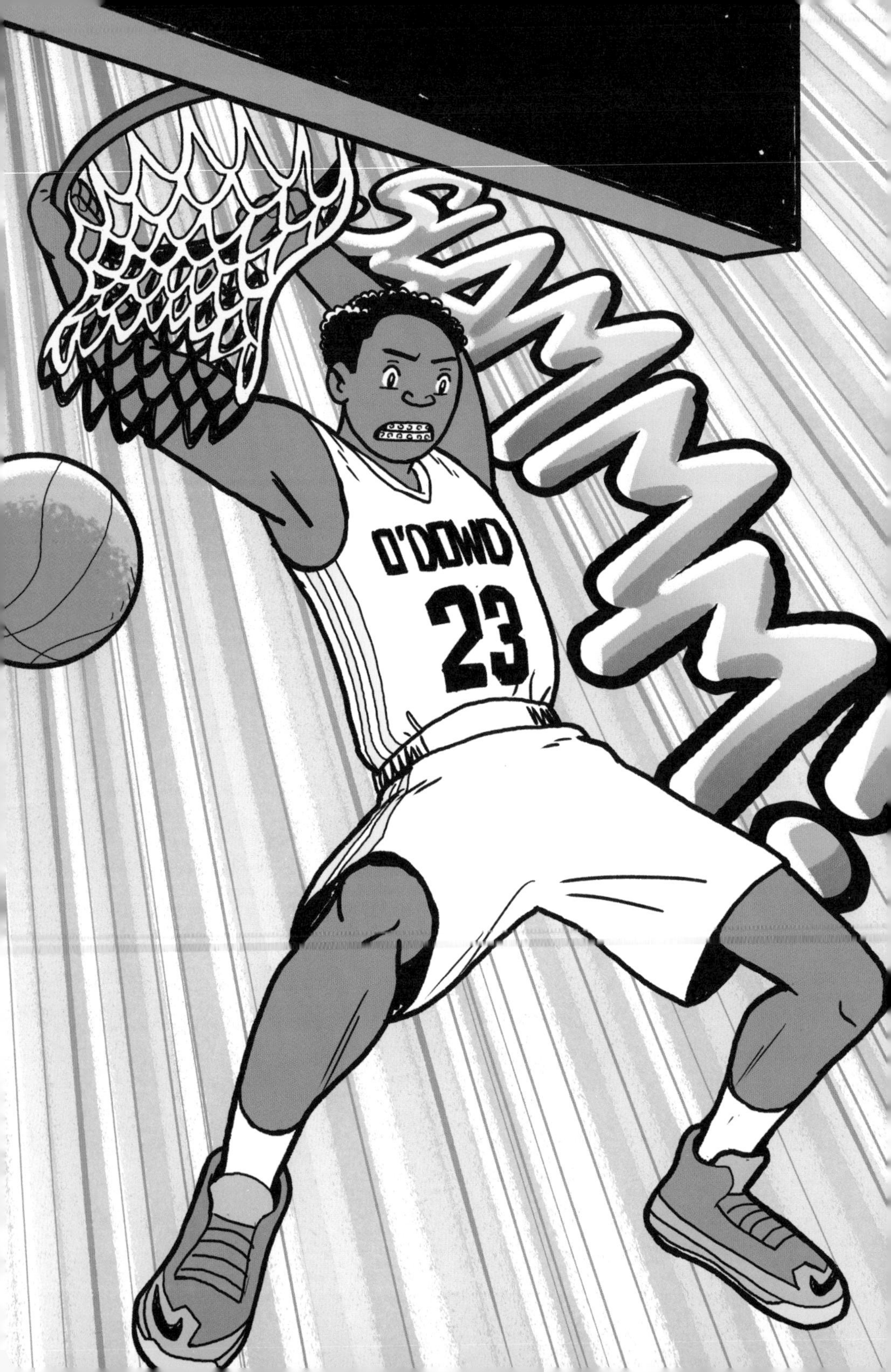
O'DOWD
23

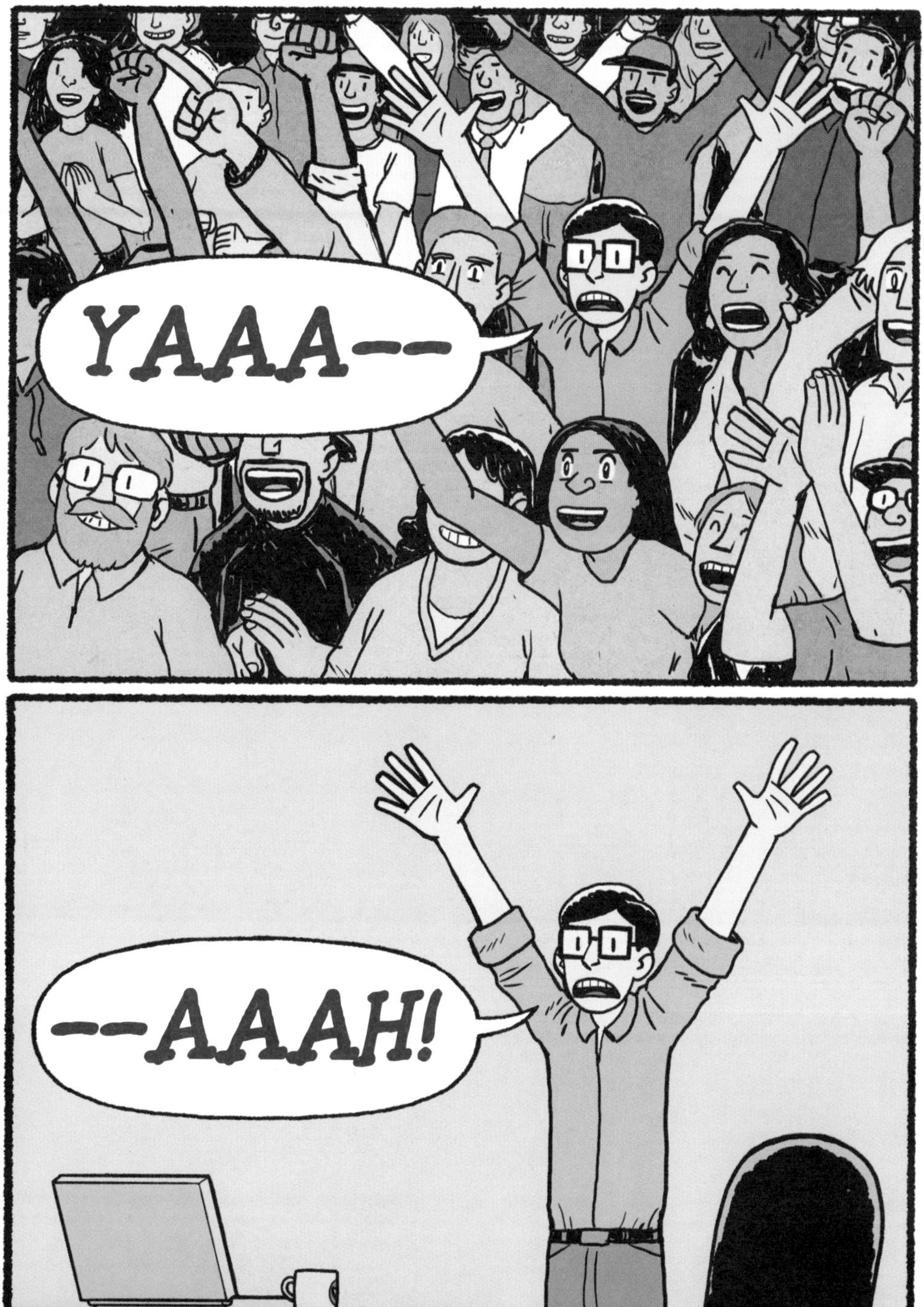
YAAA--
--AAAH!

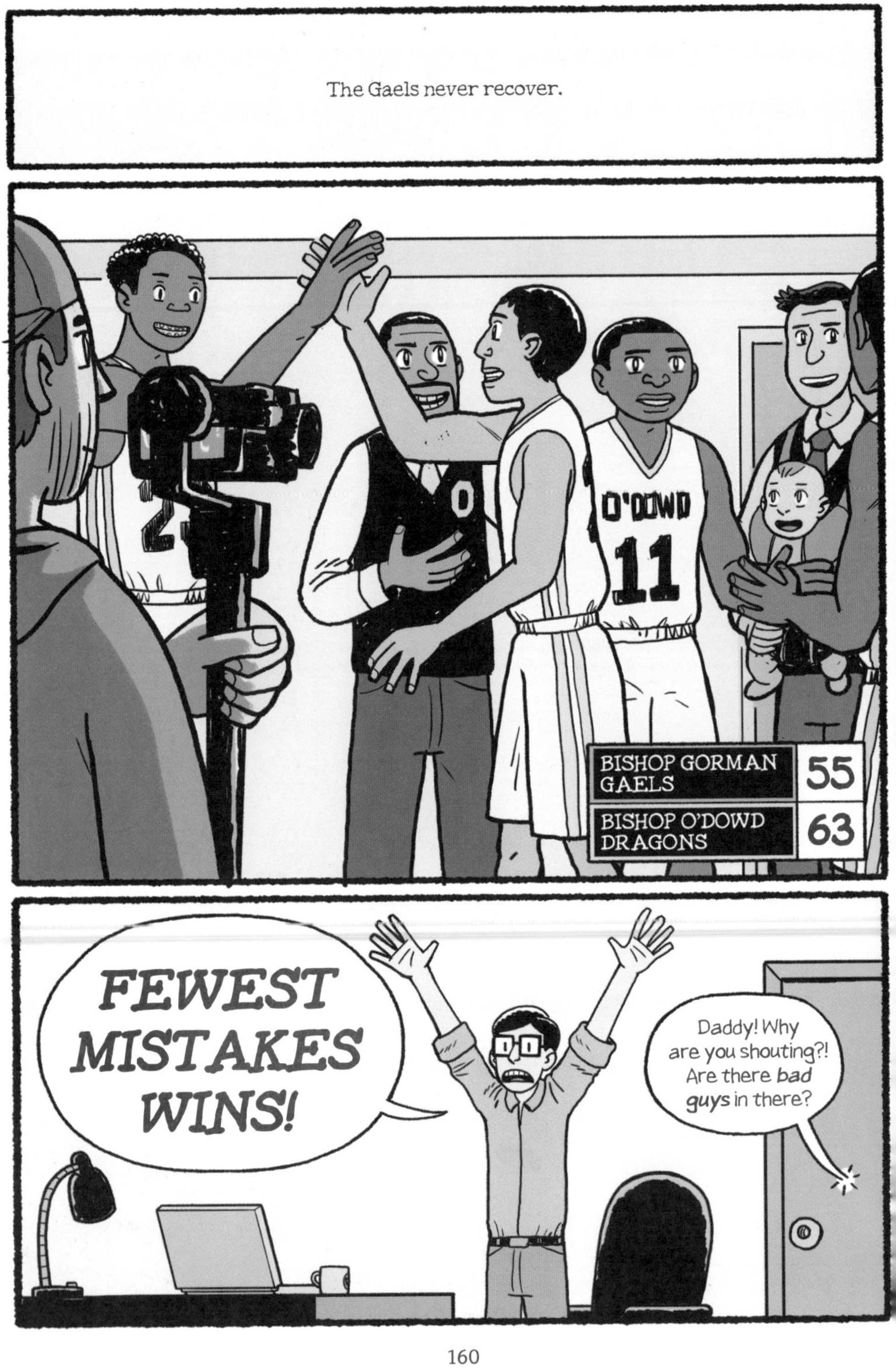

The Gaels never recover.
O'DOWD
11
BISHOP GORMAN GAELS
55
BISHOP O'DOWD DRAGONS
63
FEWEST MISTAKES WINS!
Daddy! Why are you shouting?! Are there *bad guys* in there?

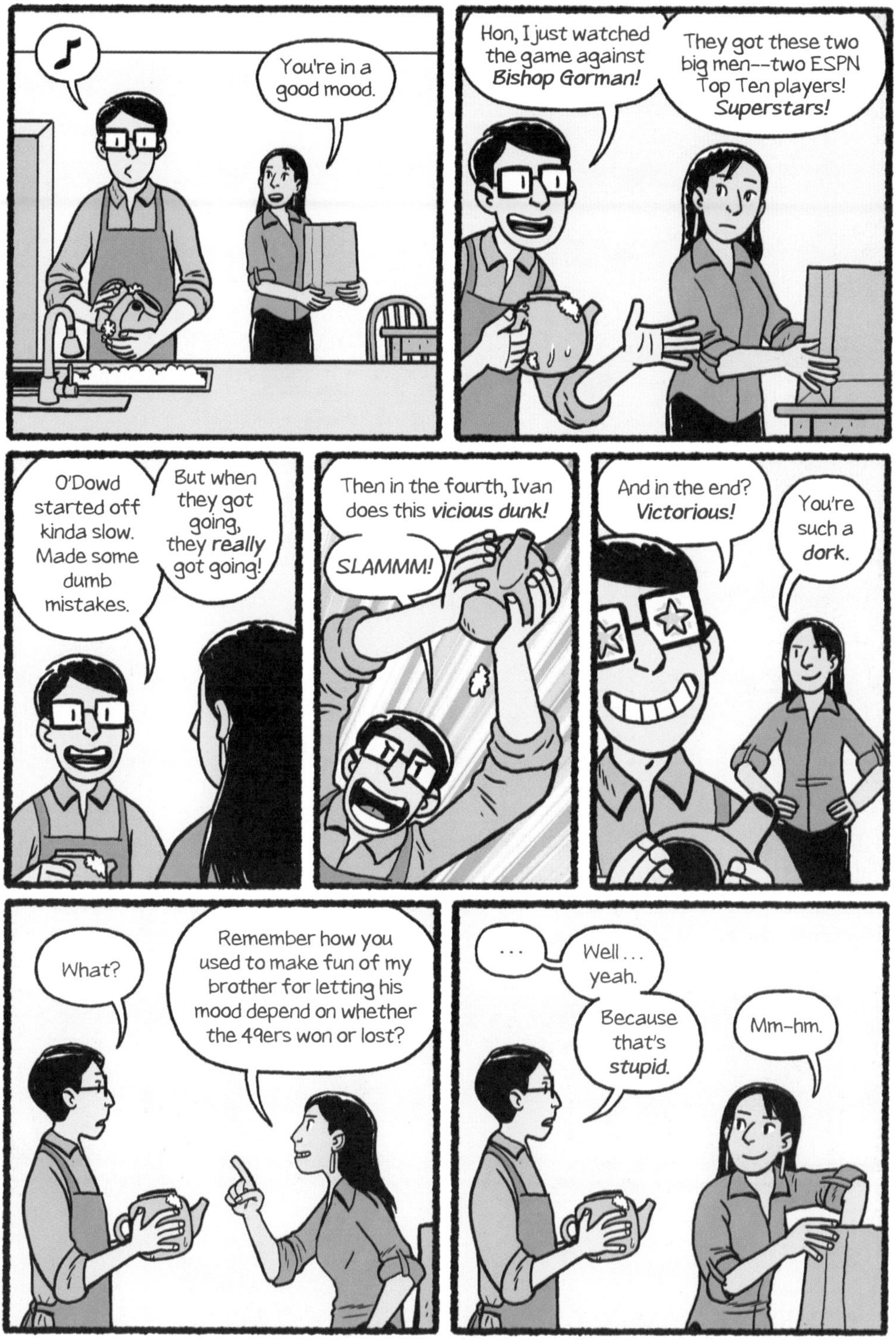
♪
You're in a good mood.
Hon, I just watched the game against *Bishop Gorman!*
They got these two big men--two ESPN Top Ten players! *Superstars!*
O'Dowd started off kinda slow. Made some dumb mistakes.
But when they got going, they *really* got going!
Then in the fourth, Ivan does this *vicious dunk!*
SLAMMM!
And in the end? *Victorious!*
You're such a *dork.*
What?
Remember how you used to make fun of my brother for letting his mood depend on whether the 49ers won or lost?
...
Well... yeah.
Because that's *stupid.*
Mm-hm.

Lou!

Yang-Man!

That game was *amazing!*

What was the locker room like after? Must've been *crazy!*

It was... *uneven.*

"The players who got good minutes were *shouting, celebrating.*"

O'DOWD 3

O'DOWD 11

O'DOWD 23

30:44

29:36

30:41

"Those who didn't, not so much."

O'DOWD 22

O'DOWD 24

O'DOWD 32

0:56

1:13

0:20

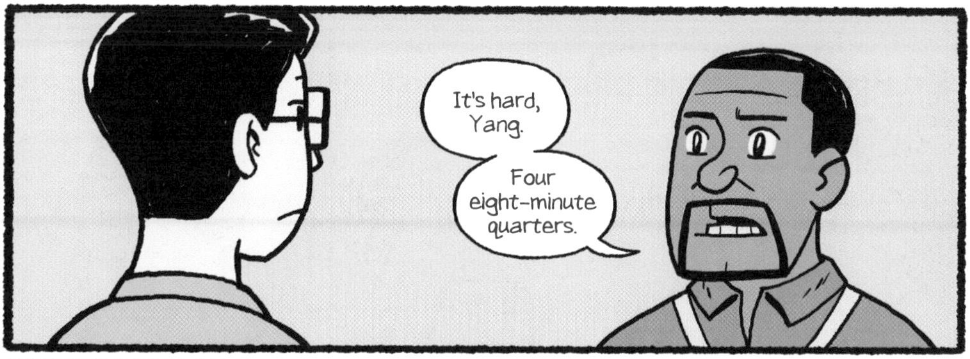
It's hard, Yang.
Four eight-minute quarters.

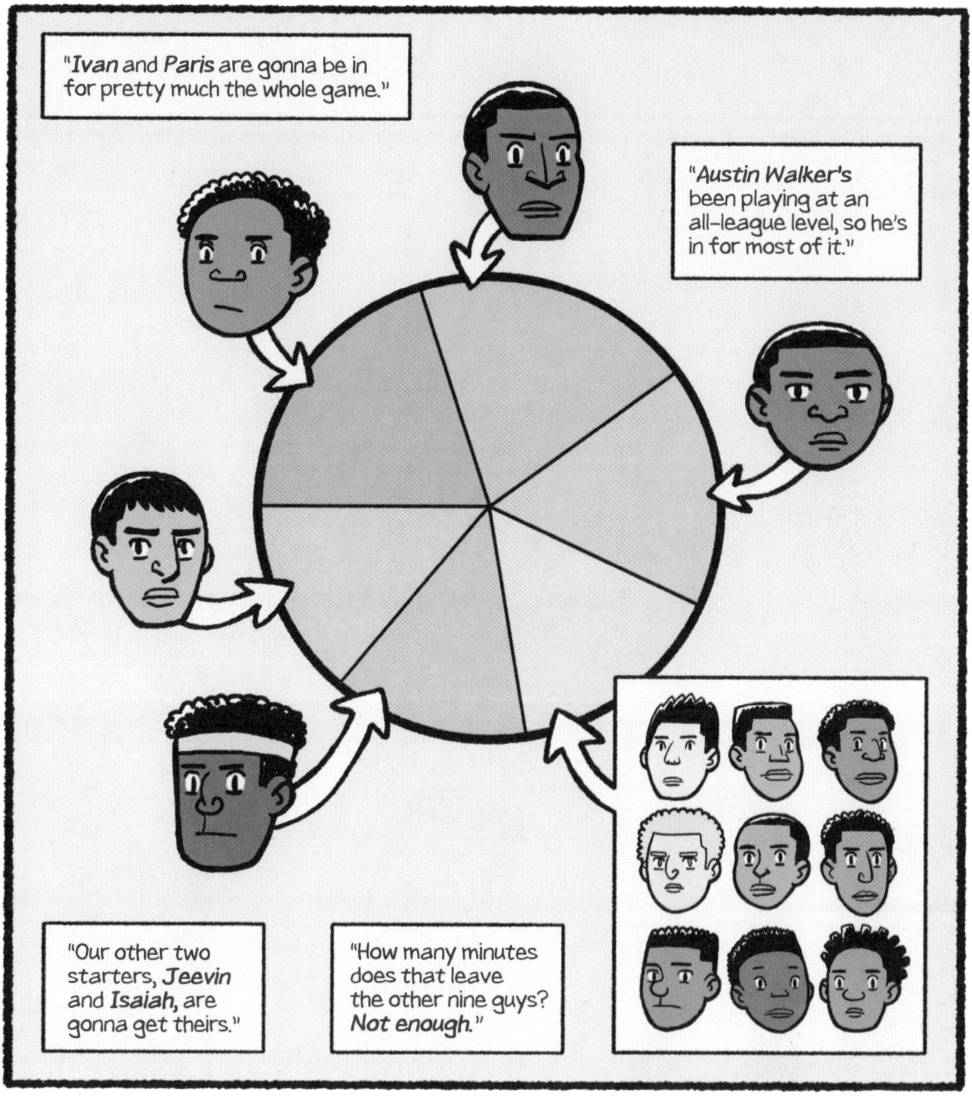
"*Ivan* and *Paris* are gonna be in for pretty much the whole game."
"*Austin Walker's* been playing at an all-league level, so he's in for most of it."
"Our other two starters, *Jeevin* and *Isaiah*, are gonna get theirs."
"How many minutes does that leave the other nine guys? *Not enough.*"

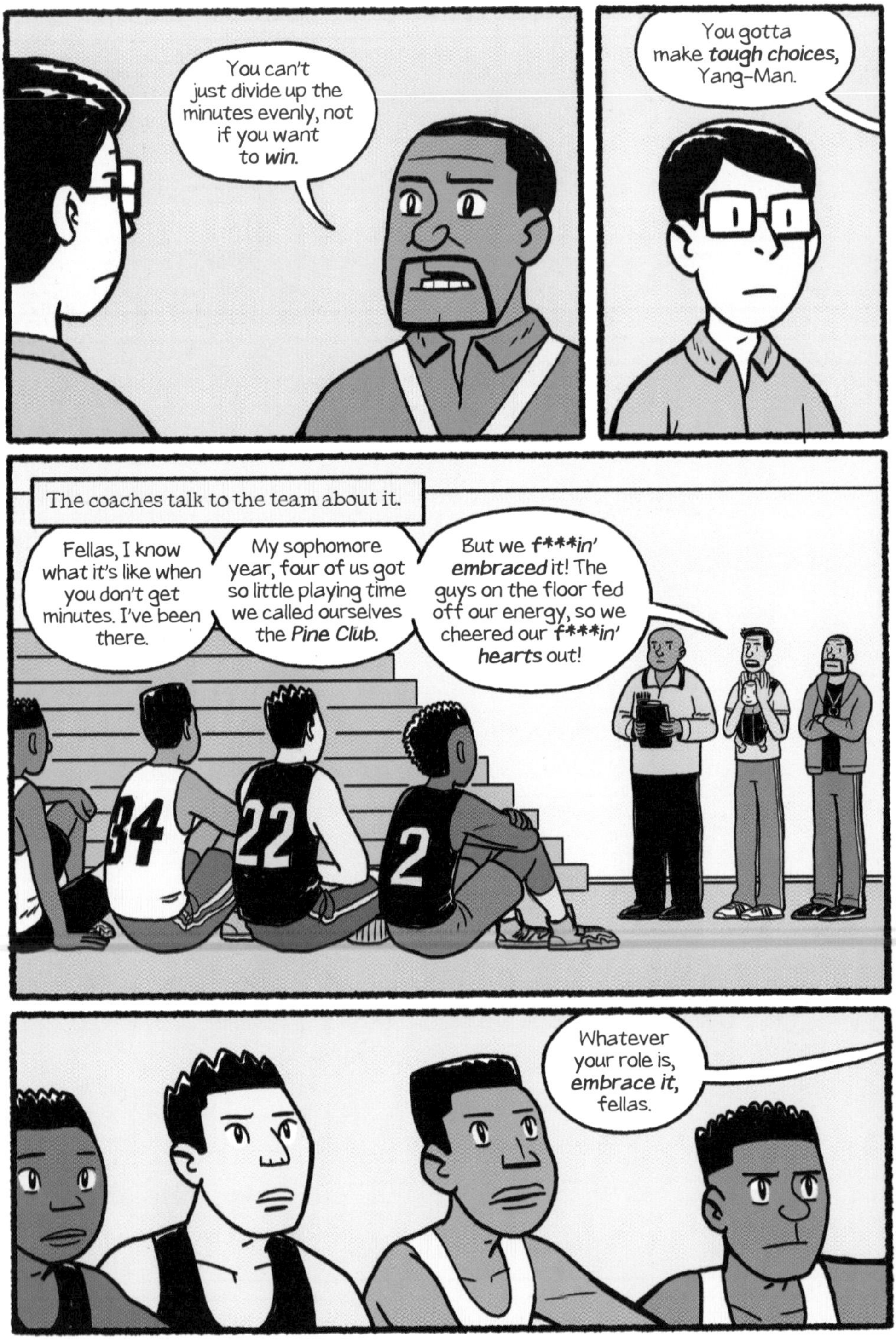
You can't just divide up the minutes evenly, not if you want to *win*.
You gotta make ***tough choices,*** Yang-Man.
The coaches talk to the team about it.
Fellas, I know what it's like when you don't get minutes. I've been there.
My sophomore year, four of us got so little playing time we called ourselves the *Pine Club*.
But we ***f***in' embraced*** it! The guys on the floor fed off our energy, so we cheered our ***f***in' hearts*** out!
Whatever your role is, ***embrace it,*** fellas.

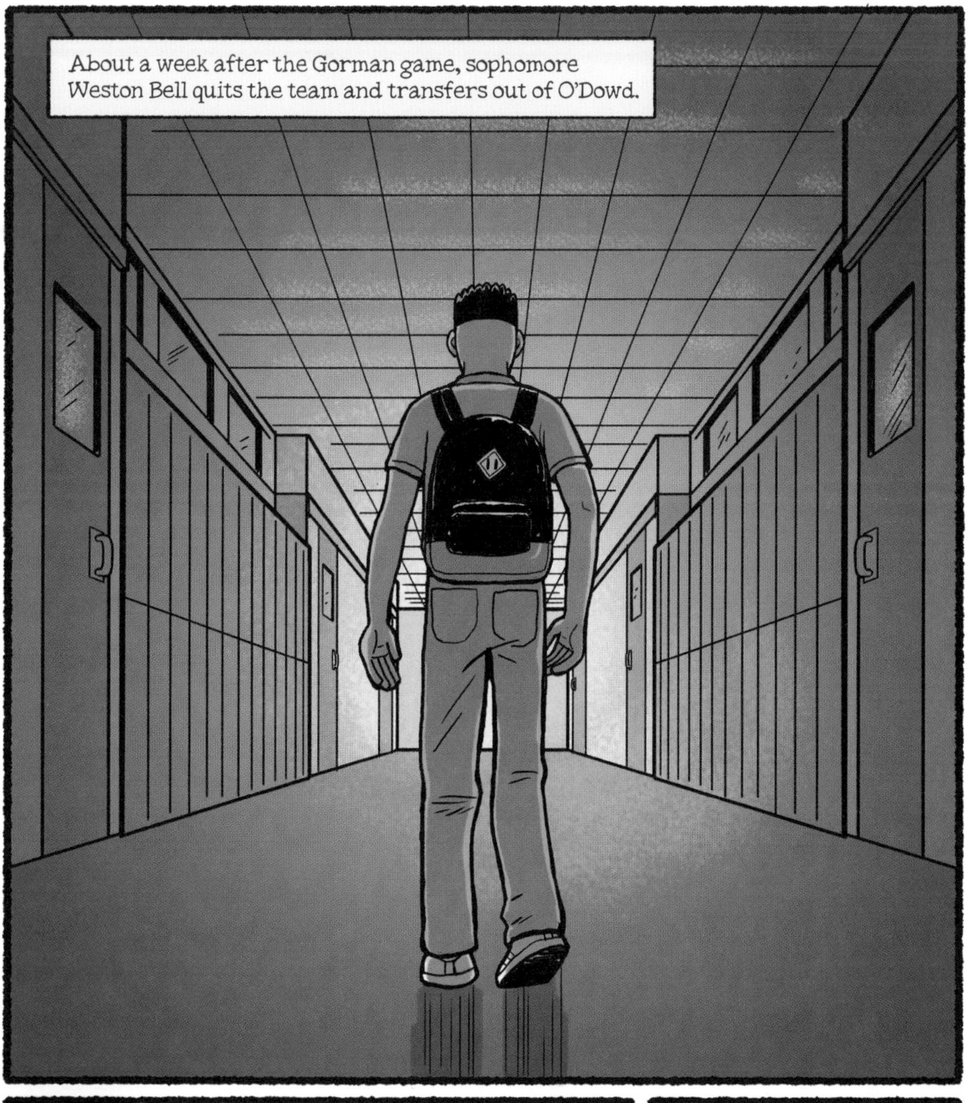
About a week after the Gorman game, sophomore Weston Bell quits the team and transfers out of O'Dowd.

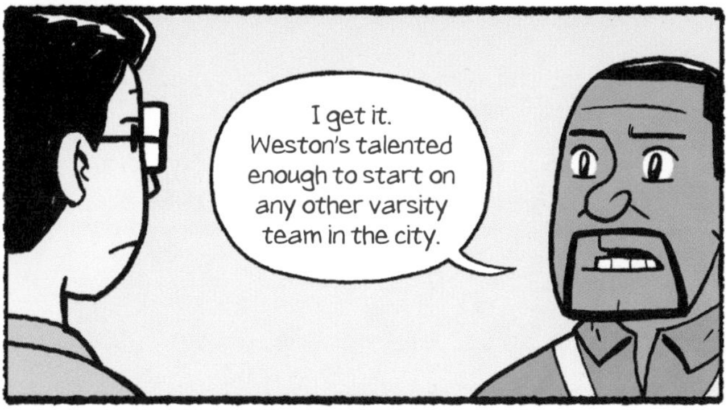
I get it. Weston's talented enough to start on any other varsity team in the city.

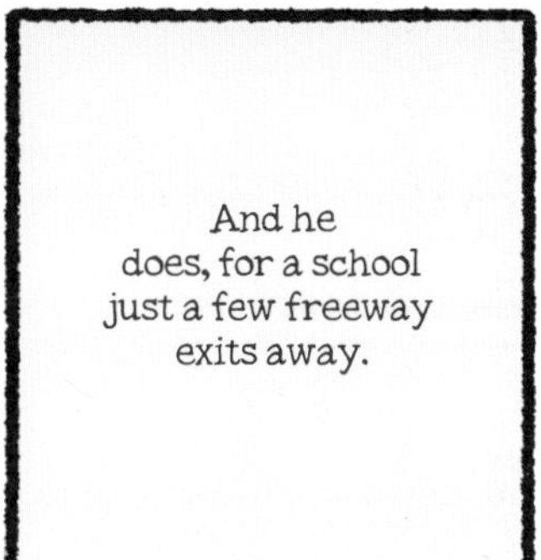
And he does, for a school just a few freeway exits away.

CHAPTER 6: **ODERAH AND ARINZE**

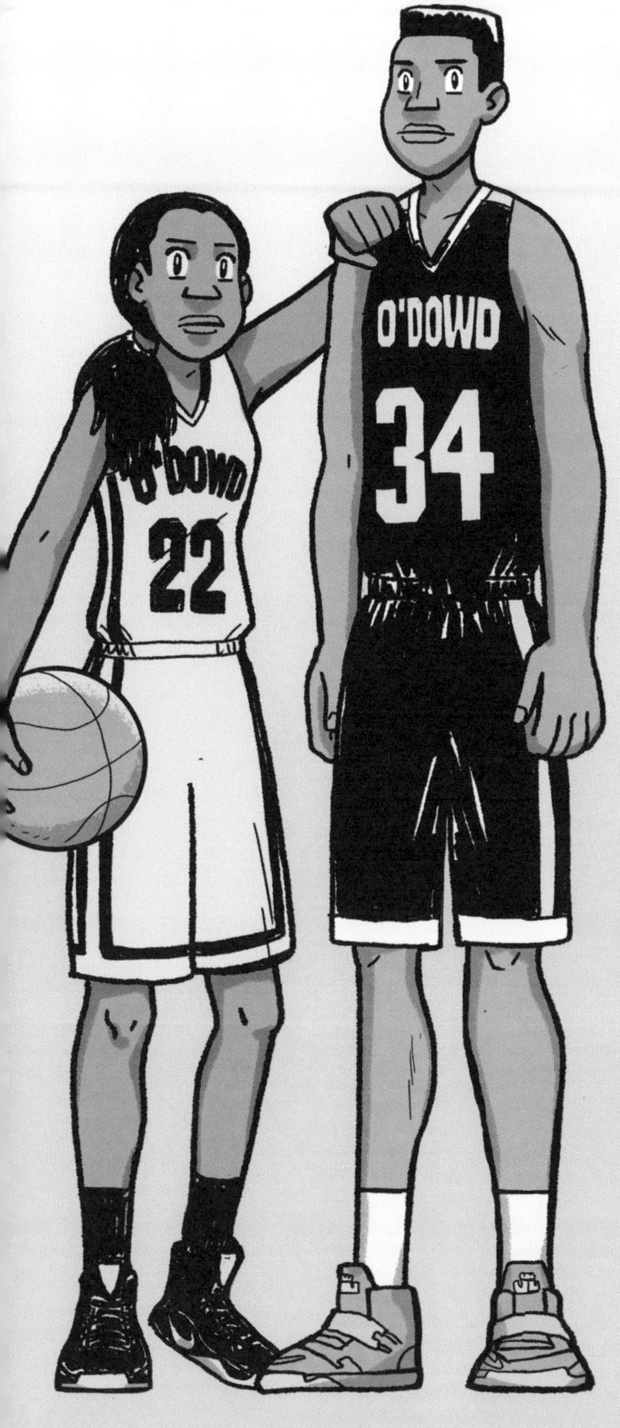
O'DOWD
22
O'DOWD
34

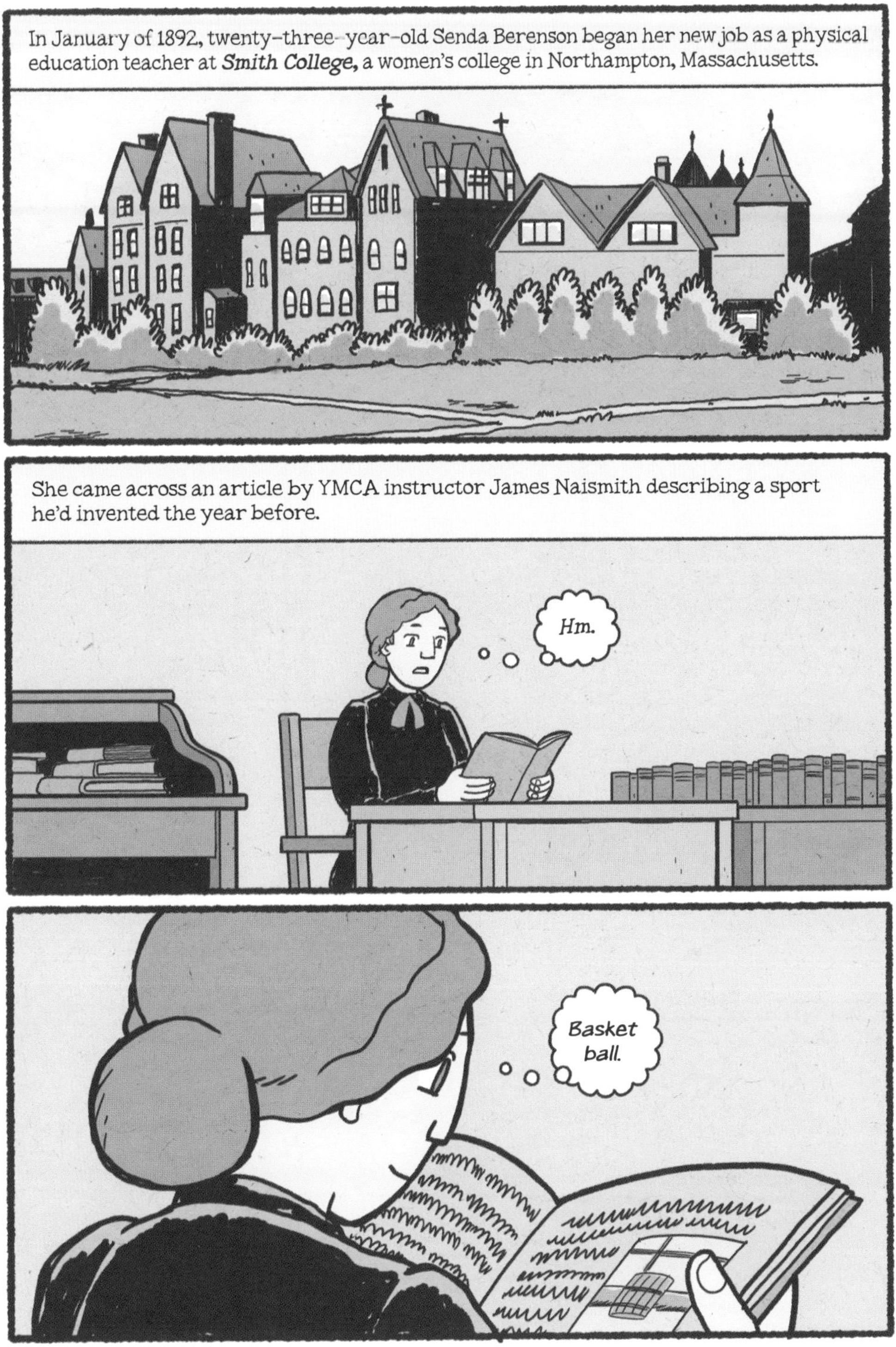
In January of 1892, twenty-three-year-old Senda Berenson began her new job as a physical education teacher at ***Smith College,*** a women's college in Northampton, Massachusetts.
She came across an article by YMCA instructor James Naismith describing a sport he'd invented the year before.
Hm.
Basket ball.

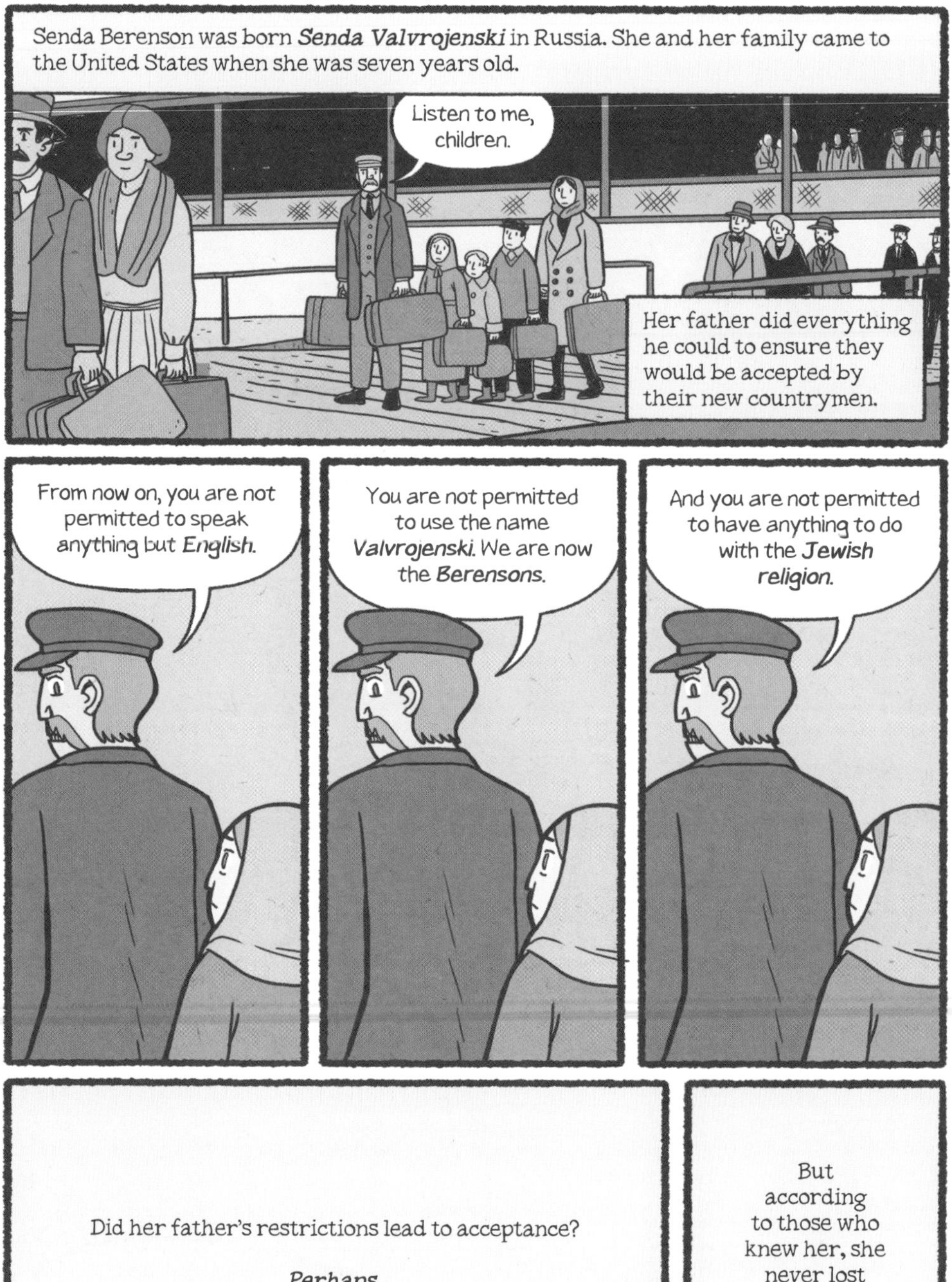
Senda Berenson was born *Senda Valvrojenski* in Russia. She and her family came to the United States when she was seven years old.
Listen to me, children.
Her father did everything he could to ensure they would be accepted by their new countrymen.
From now on, you are not permitted to speak anything but *English*.
You are not permitted to use the name *Valvrojenski*. We are now the *Berensons*.
And you are not permitted to have anything to do with the *Jewish religion*.
Did her father's restrictions lead to acceptance?
Perhaps.
But according to those who knew her, she never lost her Russian accent.

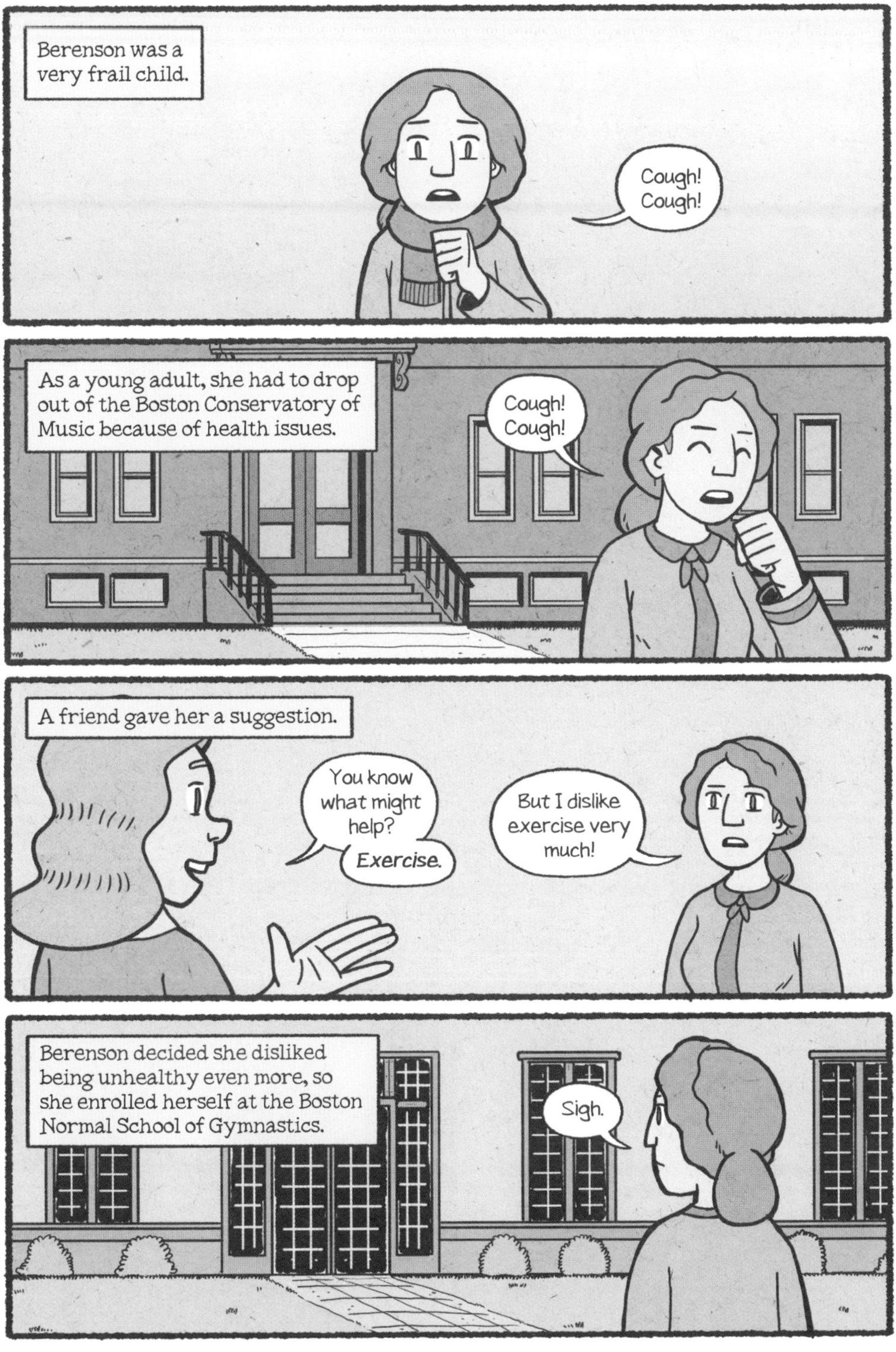
Berenson was a very frail child.
Cough! Cough!
As a young adult, she had to drop out of the Boston Conservatory of Music because of health issues.
Cough! Cough!
A friend gave her a suggestion.
You know what might help? *Exercise.*
But I dislike exercise very much!
Berenson decided she disliked being unhealthy even more, so she enrolled herself at the Boston Normal School of Gymnastics.
Sigh.

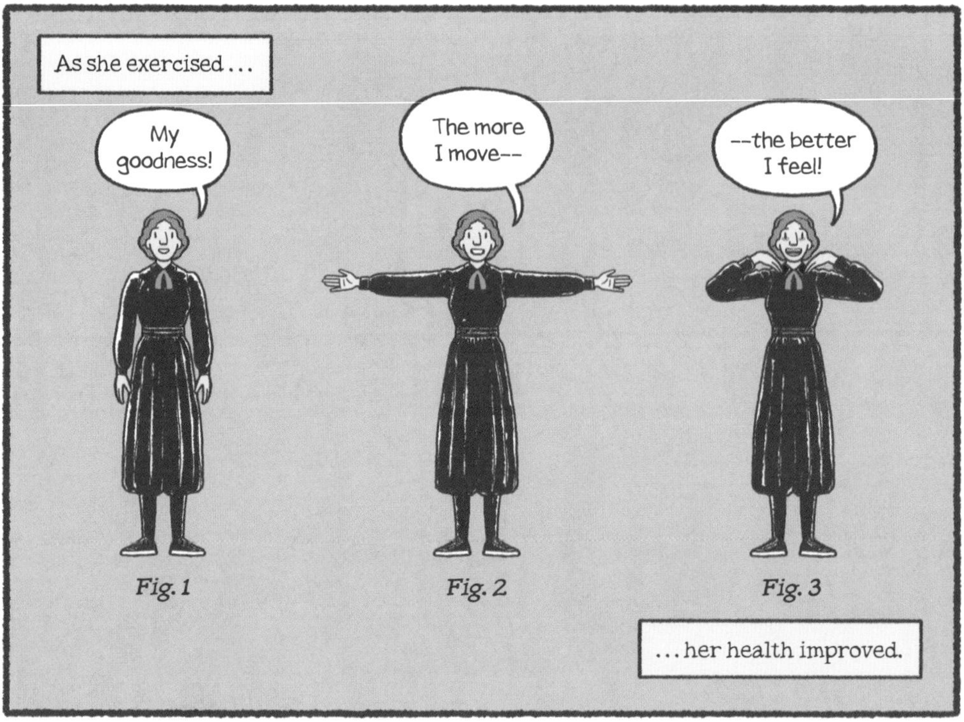
As she exercised . . .
My goodness!
The more I move--
--the better I feel!
Fig. 1
Fig. 2
Fig. 3
. . . her health improved.

Her health improved so much that her life ***completely transformed.***
She wanted to help other women experience that same sort of change--

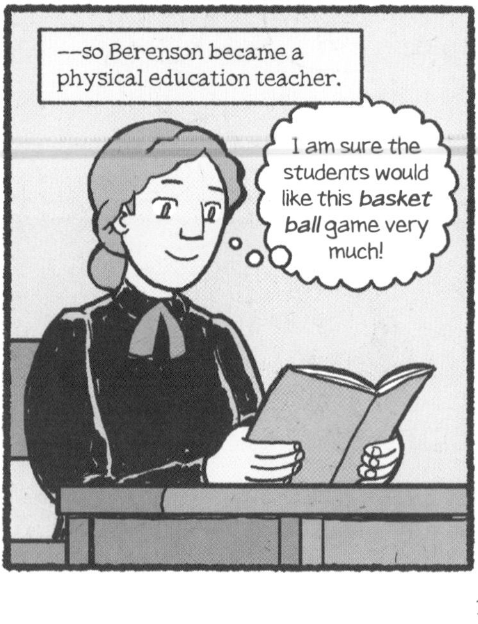
--so Berenson became a physical education teacher.
I am sure the students would like this ***basket ball*** game very much!

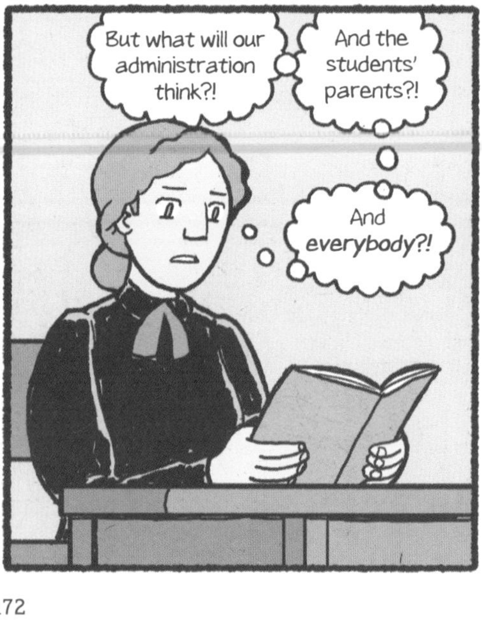
But what will our administration think?!
And the students' parents?!
And ***everybody?!***

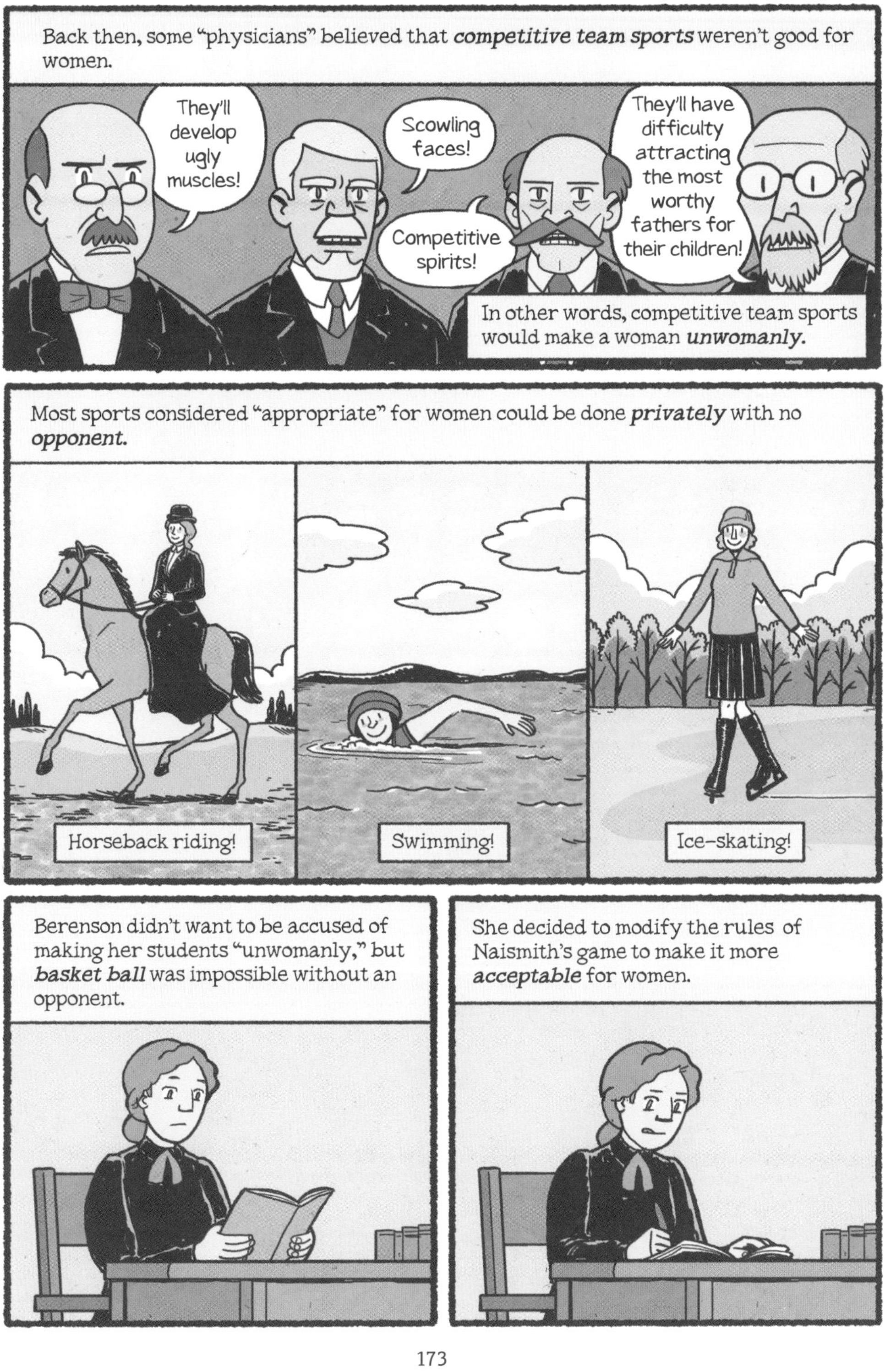
Back then, some "physicians" believed that ***competitive team sports*** weren't good for women.
They'll develop ugly muscles!
Scowling faces!
Competitive spirits!
They'll have difficulty attracting the most worthy fathers for their children!
In other words, competitive team sports would make a woman ***unwomanly.***
Most sports considered "appropriate" for women could be done ***privately*** with no ***opponent.***
Horseback riding!
Swimming!
Ice-skating!
Berenson didn't want to be accused of making her students "unwomanly," but ***basket ball*** was impossible without an opponent.
She decided to modify the rules of Naismith's game to make it more ***acceptable*** for women.

To keep players from *exerting* themselves too much, the court would be divided into three sections. Players would not be permitted to go outside their assigned section.

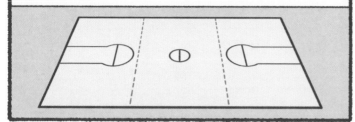

Avoids ugly muscles!

To keep players from getting too *combative,* they wouldn't be permitted to snatch the ball from one another.

Avoids scowling faces!

To make players *share* more often, they wouldn't be permitted to hold the ball for more than three seconds or dribble the ball more than three times.

Avoids competitive spirits!

All so they'll still be able to attract the most worthy fathers for their children!

174

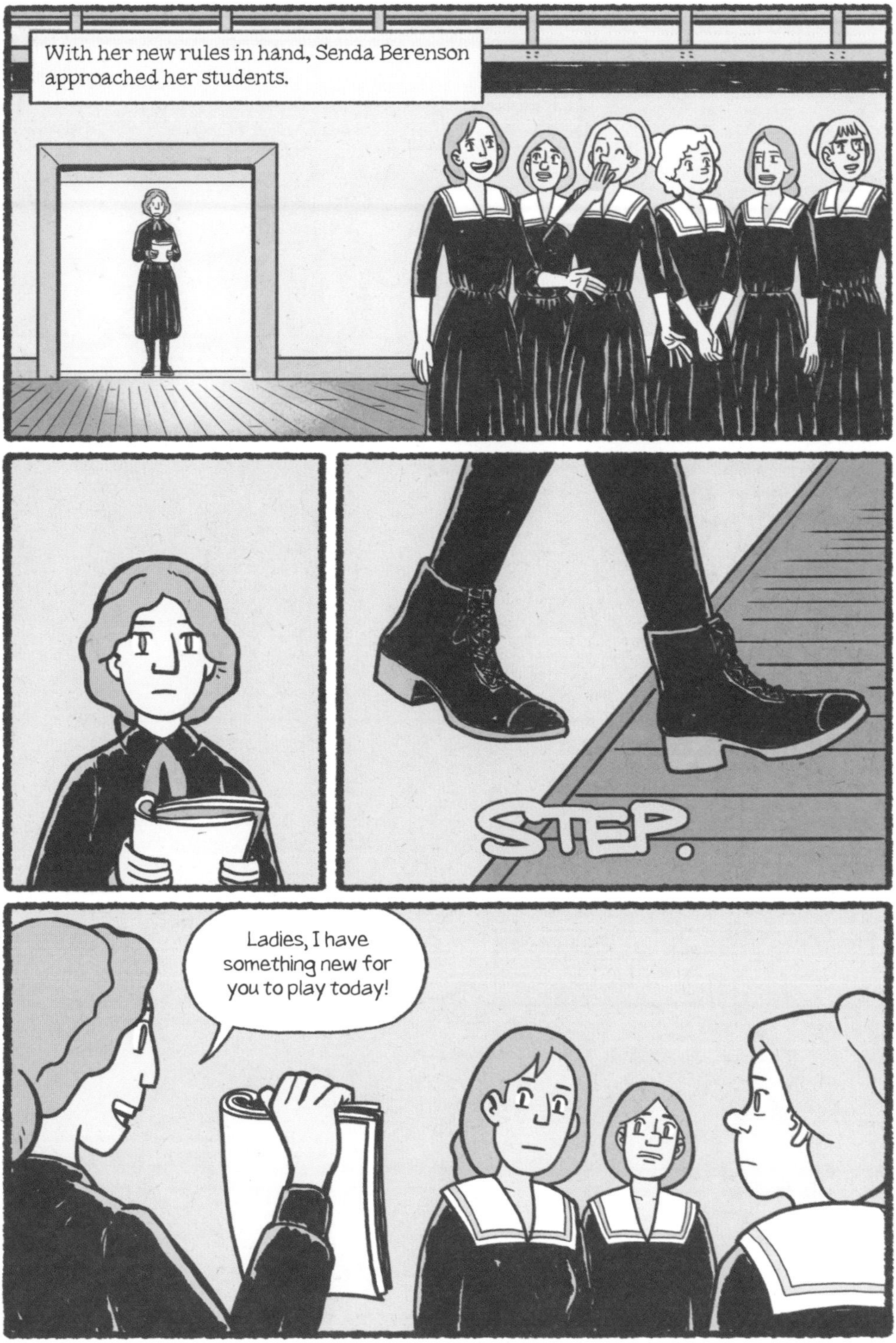
With her new rules in hand, Senda Berenson approached her students.
STEP.
Ladies, I have something new for you to play today!

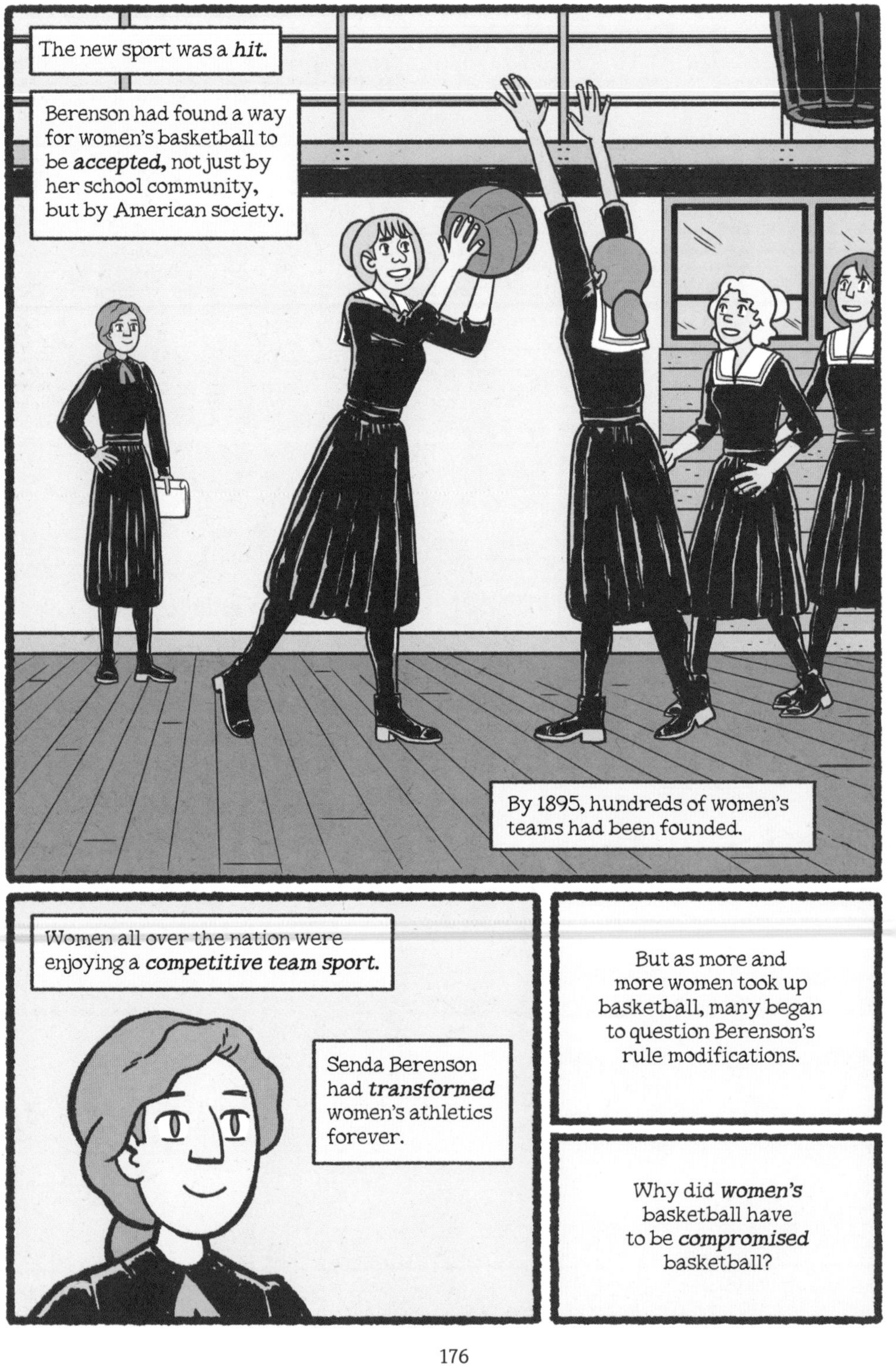
The new sport was a ***hit.***
Berenson had found a way for women's basketball to be ***accepted,*** not just by her school community, but by American society.
By 1895, hundreds of women's teams had been founded.
Women all over the nation were enjoying a ***competitive team sport.***
Senda Berenson had ***transformed*** women's athletics forever.
But as more and more women took up basketball, many began to question Berenson's rule modifications.
Why did ***women's*** basketball have to be ***compromised*** basketball?

They pushed for *change*.

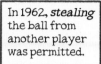 In 1962, *stealing* the ball from another player was permitted.

In 1966, *dribbling* restrictions were removed.

And in 1971, women players could finally run the *full length* of the court.

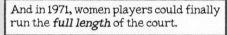

Today, women's and men's basketball are essentially the same game.

The size of the ball is one of the few differences.

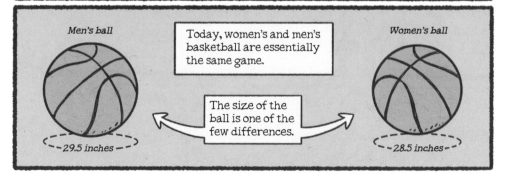

Men's ball

~ 29.5 inches ~

Women's ball

~ 28.5 inches ~

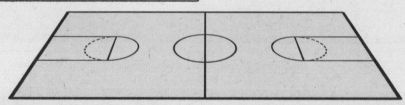

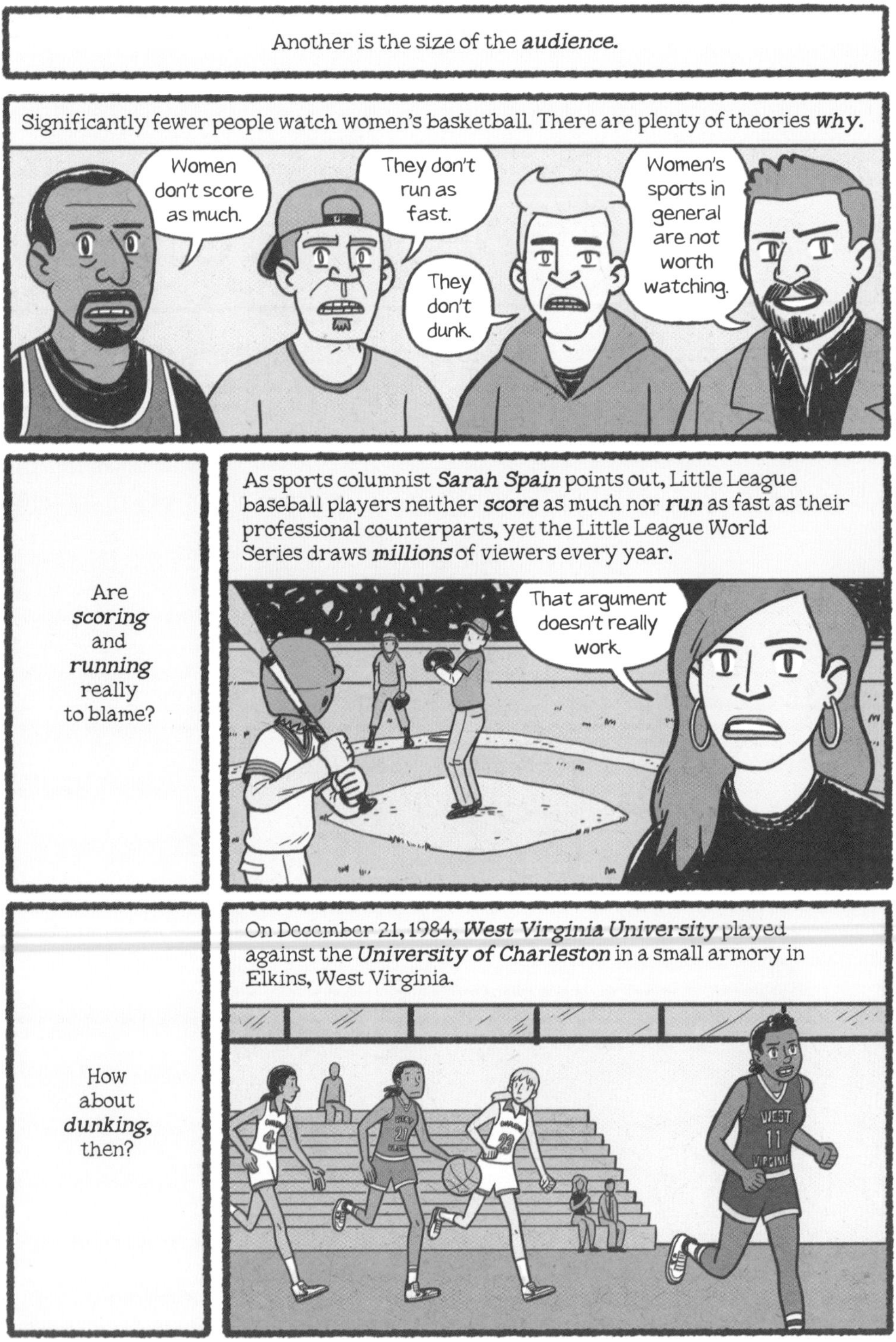

Another is the size of the *audience.*
Significantly fewer people watch women's basketball. There are plenty of theories *why.*
Women don't score as much.
They don't run as fast.
They don't dunk.
Women's sports in general are not worth watching.
Are *scoring* and *running* really to blame?
As sports columnist *Sarah Spain* points out, Little League baseball players neither *score* as much nor *run* as fast as their professional counterparts, yet the Little League World Series draws *millions* of viewers every year.
That argument doesn't really work.
How about *dunking,* then?
On December 21, 1984, *West Virginia University* played against the *University of Charleston* in a small armory in Elkins, West Virginia.

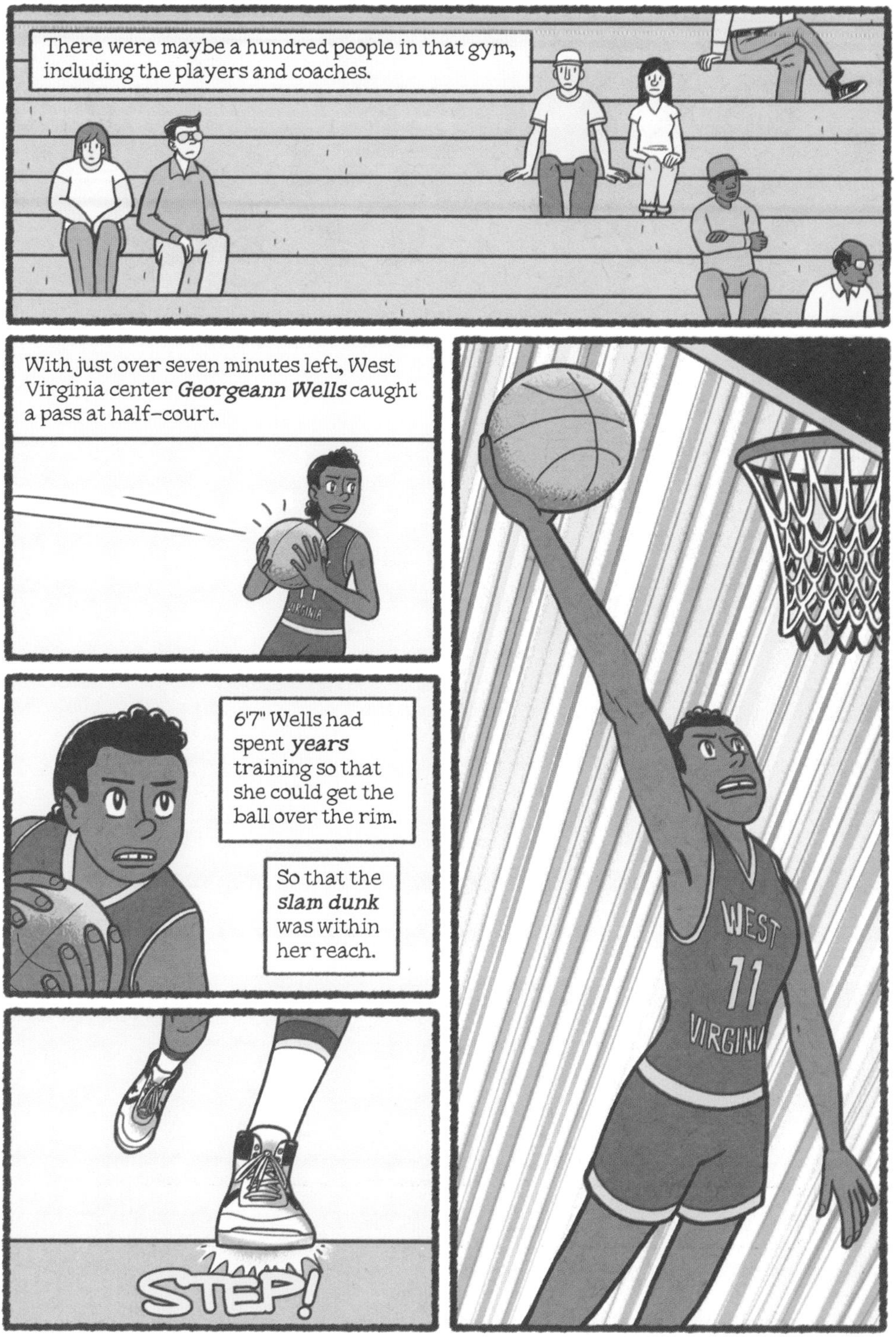
There were maybe a hundred people in that gym, including the players and coaches.
With just over seven minutes left, West Virginia center ***Georgeann Wells*** caught a pass at half-court.
6'7" Wells had spent ***years*** training so that she could get the ball over the rim.
So that the ***slam dunk*** was within her reach.
STEP!

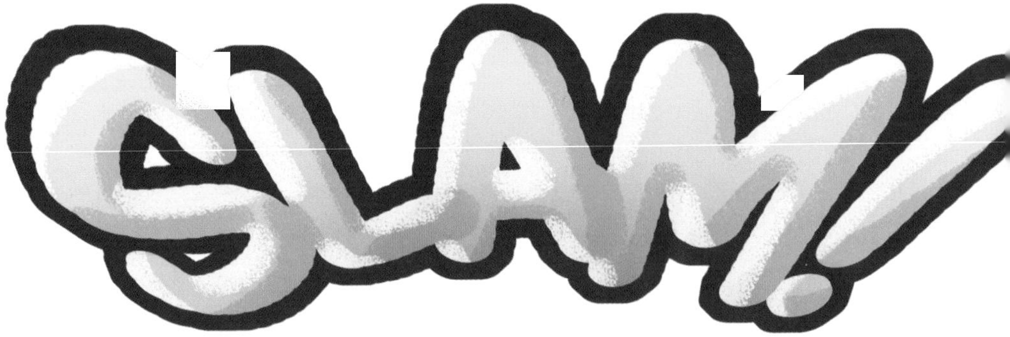
SLAM!

It was the ***first dunk*** by a woman in the history of college basketball.

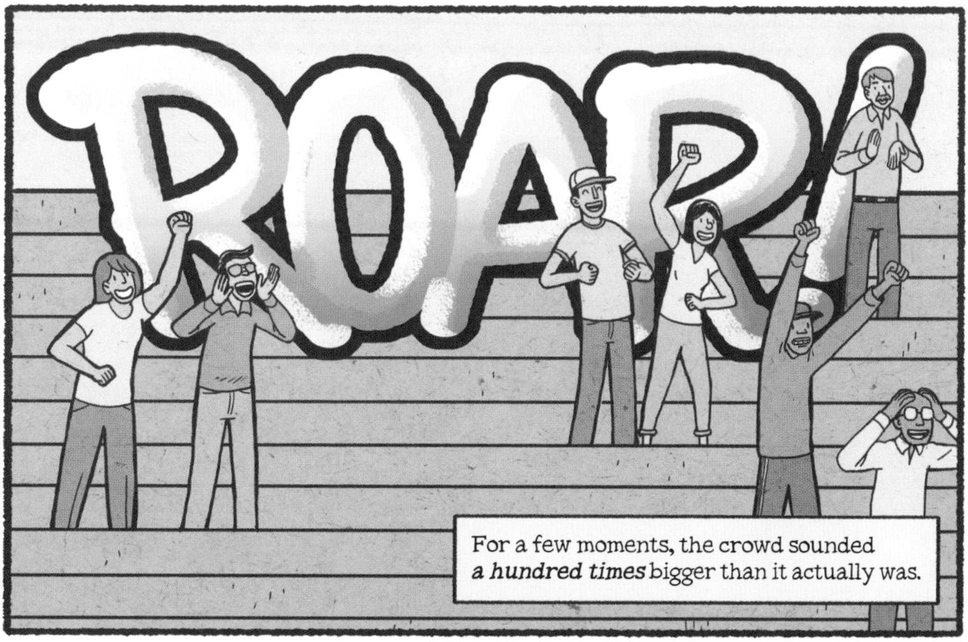
ROAR!
For a few moments, the crowd sounded *a hundred times* bigger than it actually was.

No one at West Virginia had caught the dunk on camera, but a videographer from Charleston had.

West Virginia coach Kittie Blakemore called up Charleston coach Bud Francis.

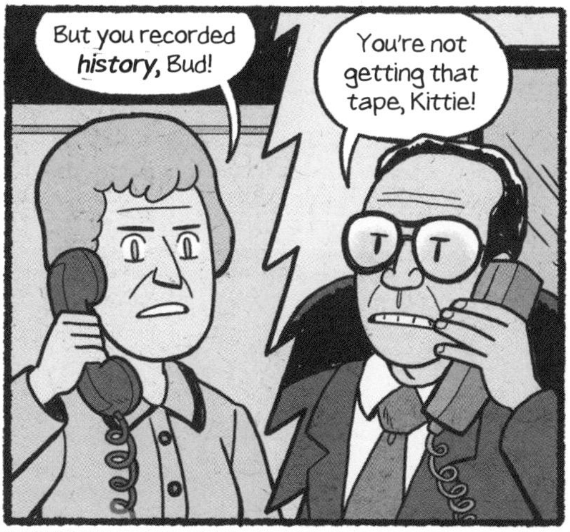
But you recorded *history*, Bud!
You're not getting that tape, Kittie!

Despite repeated requests from Blakemore and the media, Francis never released that tape.

He was unwilling to compromise his ***pride.***

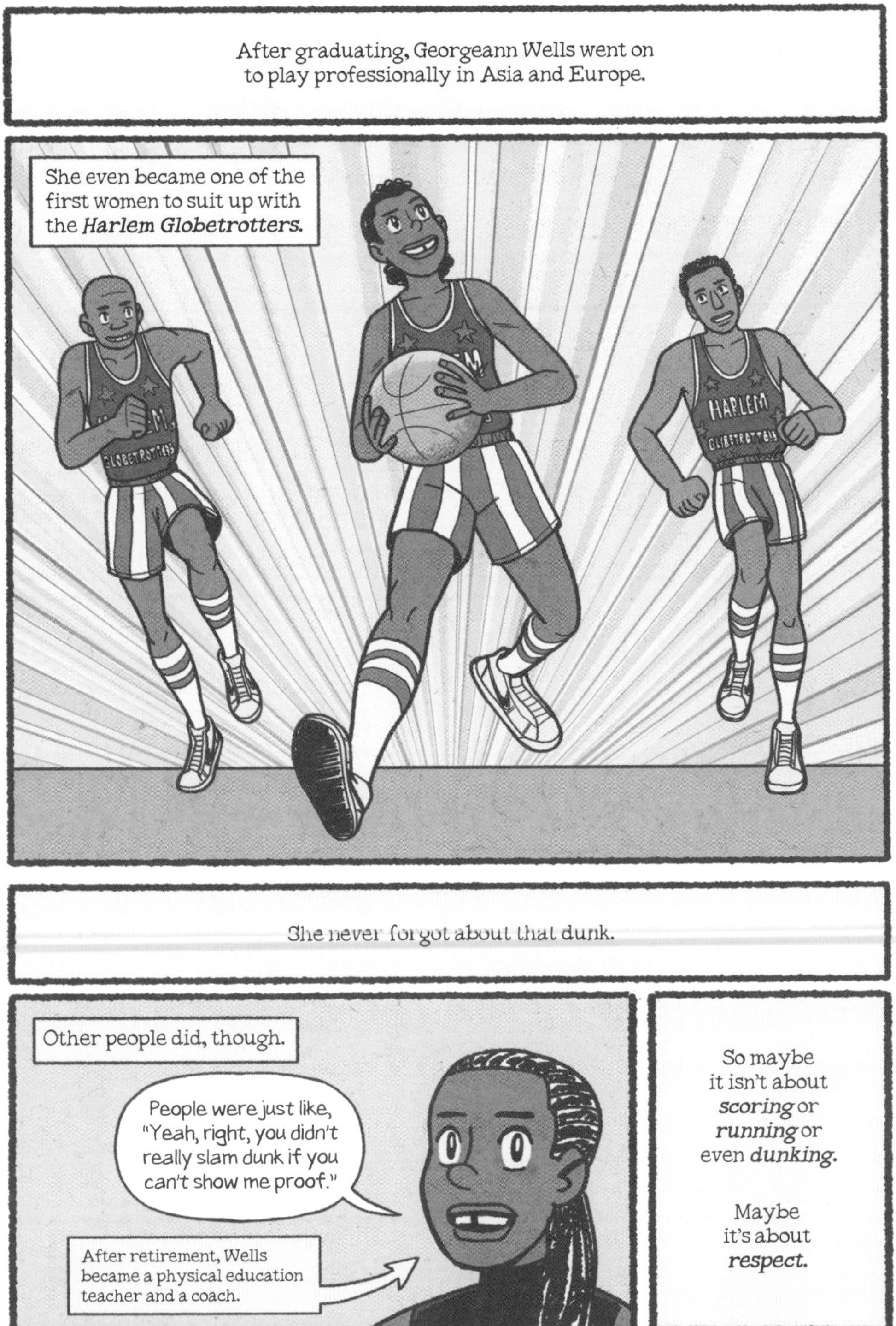
After graduating, Georgeann Wells went on to play professionally in Asia and Europe.
She even became one of the first women to suit up with the *Harlem Globetrotters.*
She never forgot about that dunk.
Other people did, though.
People were just like, "Yeah, right, you didn't really slam dunk if you can't show me proof."
After retirement, Wells became a physical education teacher and a coach.
So maybe it isn't about *scoring* or *running* or even *dunking.*
Maybe it's about *respect.*

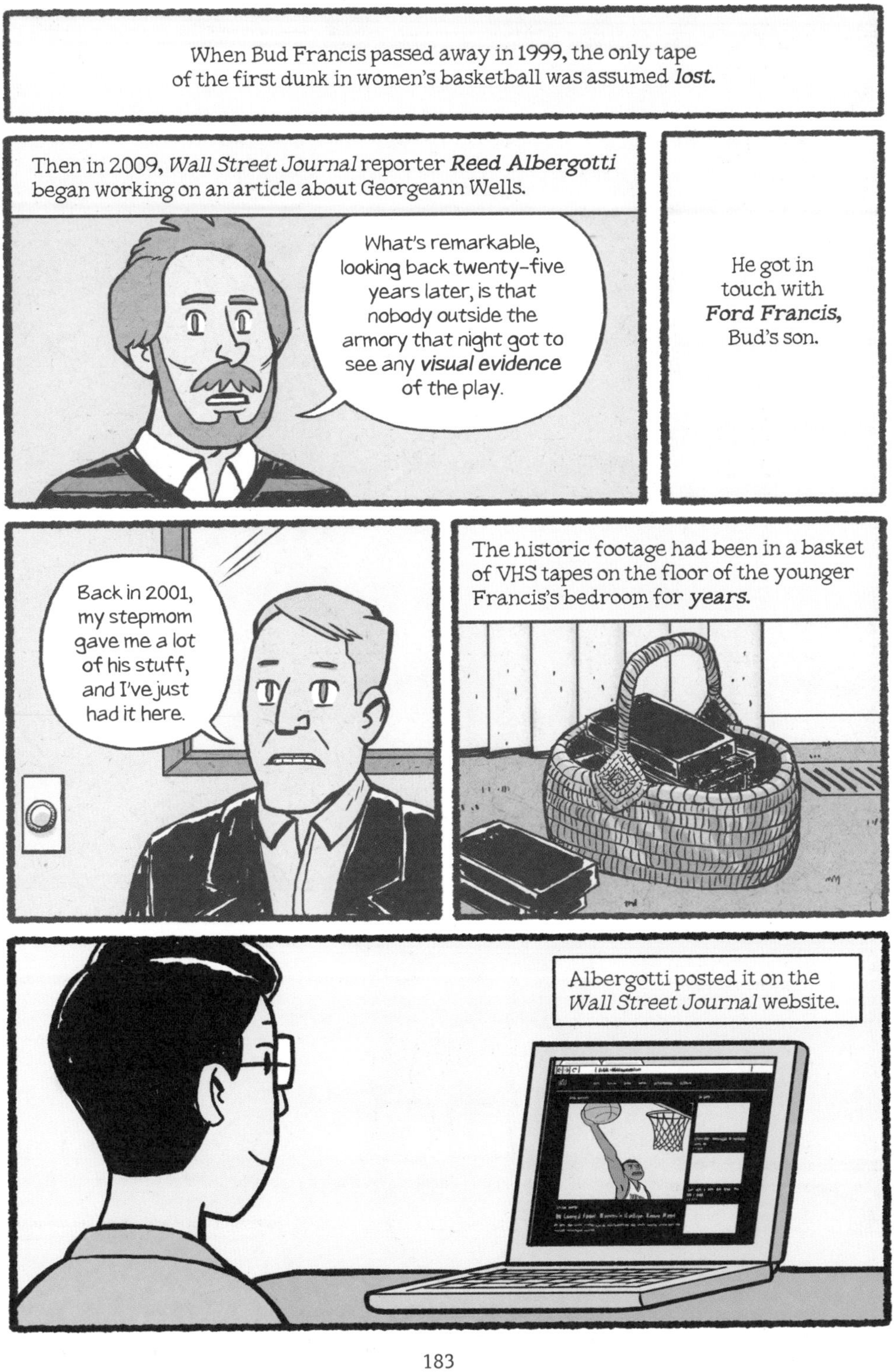
When Bud Francis passed away in 1999, the only tape of the first dunk in women's basketball was assumed *lost.*
Then in 2009, *Wall Street Journal* reporter ***Reed Albergotti*** began working on an article about Georgeann Wells.
What's remarkable, looking back twenty-five years later, is that nobody outside the armory that night got to see any ***visual evidence*** of the play.
He got in touch with ***Ford Francis,*** Bud's son.
Back in 2001, my stepmom gave me a lot of his stuff, and I've just had it here.
The historic footage had been in a basket of VHS tapes on the floor of the younger Francis's bedroom for ***years.***
Albergotti posted it on the *Wall Street Journal* website.

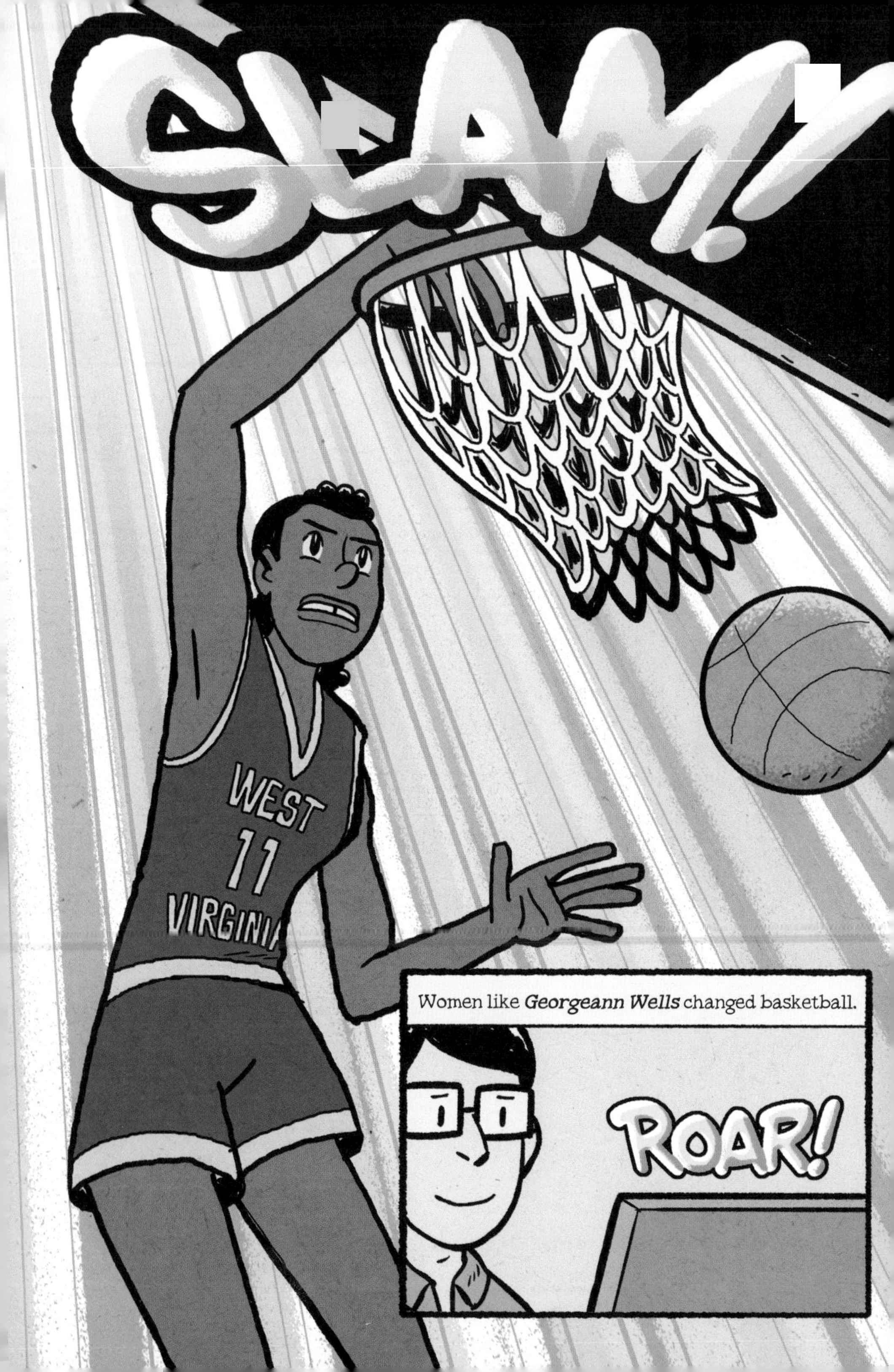
SLAM!
WEST
11
VIRGINIA
Women like *Georgeann Wells* changed basketball.
ROAR!

Change came to *Bishop O'Dowd High School,* too. When the campus was constructed in 1951, two gyms were built.

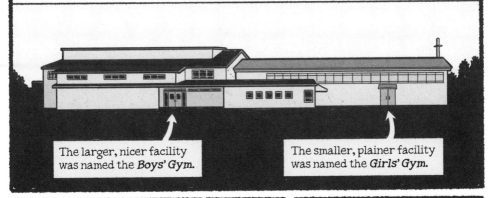

The larger, nicer facility was named the *Boys' Gym.*

The smaller, plainer facility was named the *Girls' Gym.*

The names stayed that way for decades.

We didn't change it to *"Large Gym"* and *"Small Gym"* until what ... 1982ish?

Today, the women's and men's teams rotate between the two gyms.

The women *thrived* on this newfound respect.

In 2011, they made it to the *State Championship* for the first time.

BISHOP O'DOWD
WOMEN'S BASKETBALL
NORCAL CHAMPIONS
2011

BISHOP O'DOWD
WOMEN'S BASKETBALL
STATE CHAMPIONS
2012

BISHOP O'DOWD
WOMEN'S BASKETBALL
STATE CHAMPIONS
2013

They lost.

But then they won the very next year.

And again the year after that.

It was *historic.*

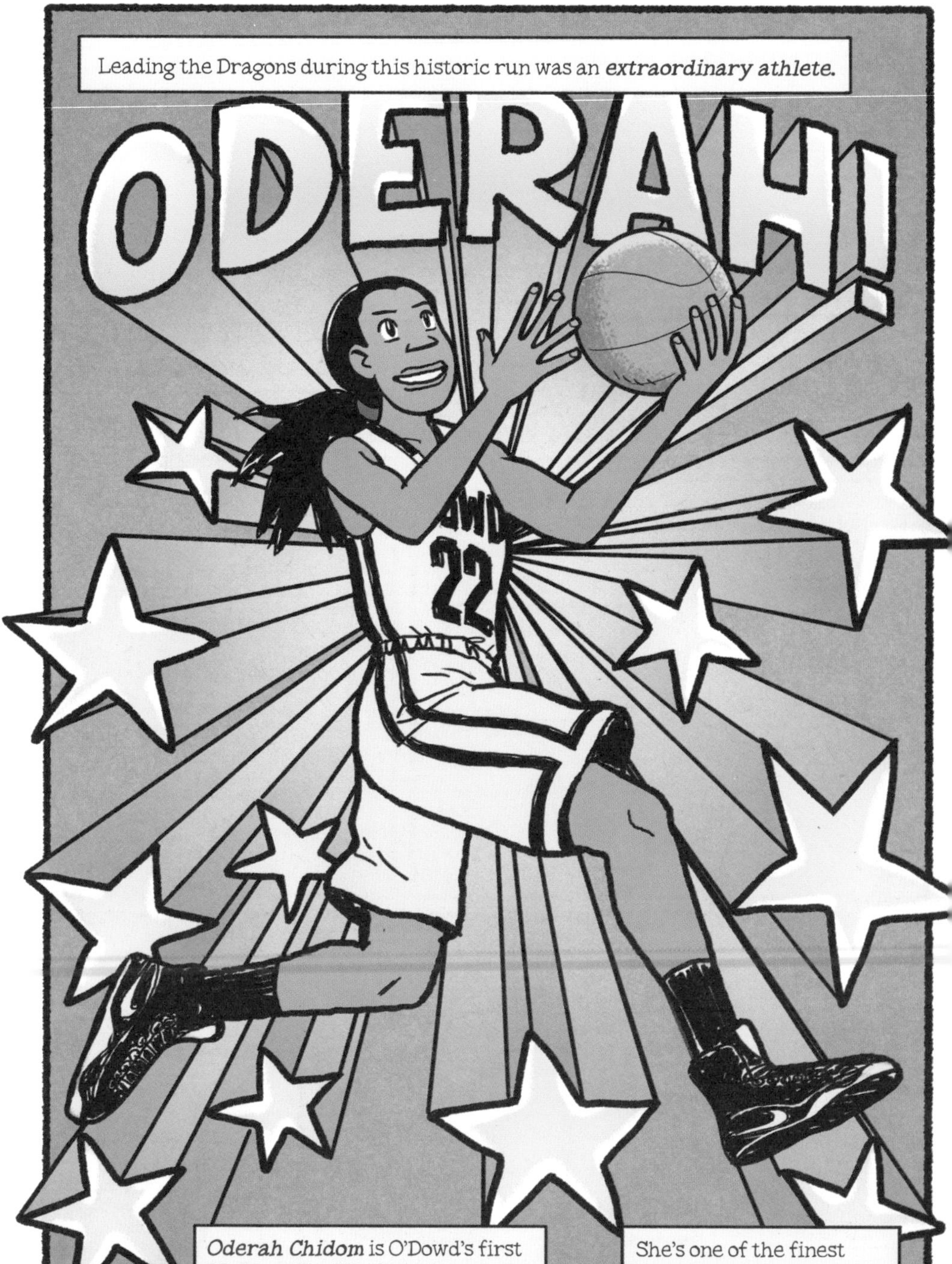
Leading the Dragons during this historic run was an *extraordinary athlete.*
ODERAH!
22
Oderah Chidom is O'Dowd's first *McDonald's All-American,* male or female.
She's one of the finest athletes to ever graduate from the school.

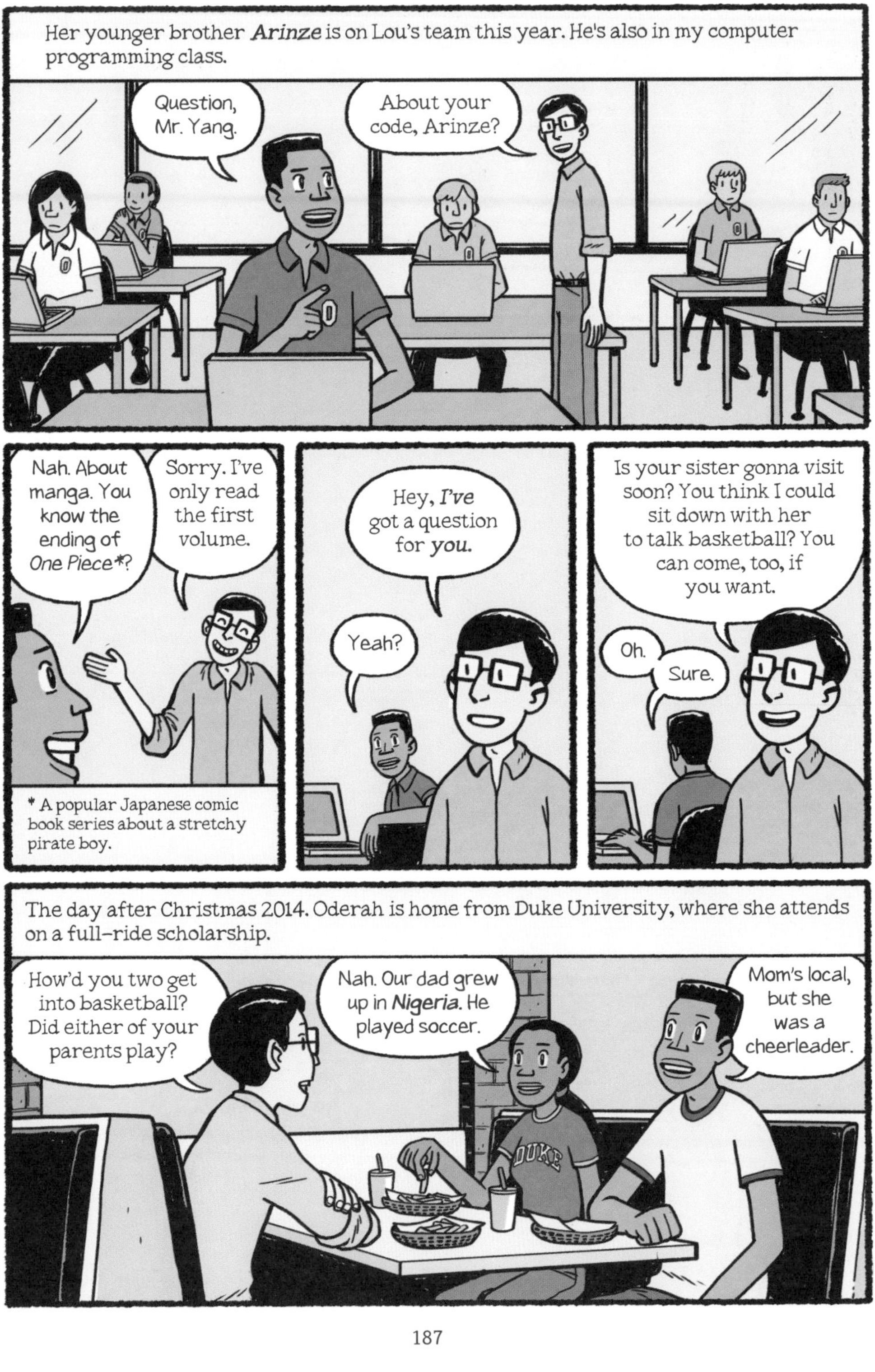
Her younger brother **Arinze** is on Lou's team this year. He's also in my computer programming class.
Question, Mr. Yang.
About your code, Arinze?
Nah. About manga. You know the ending of *One Piece**?
Sorry. I've only read the first volume.
* A popular Japanese comic book series about a stretchy pirate boy.
Hey, ***I've*** got a question for ***you.***
Yeah?
Is your sister gonna visit soon? You think I could sit down with her to talk basketball? You can come, too, if you want.
Oh.
Sure.
The day after Christmas 2014. Oderah is home from Duke University, where she attends on a full-ride scholarship.
How'd you two get into basketball? Did either of your parents play?
Nah. Our dad grew up in ***Nigeria.*** He played soccer.
Mom's local, but she was a cheerleader.

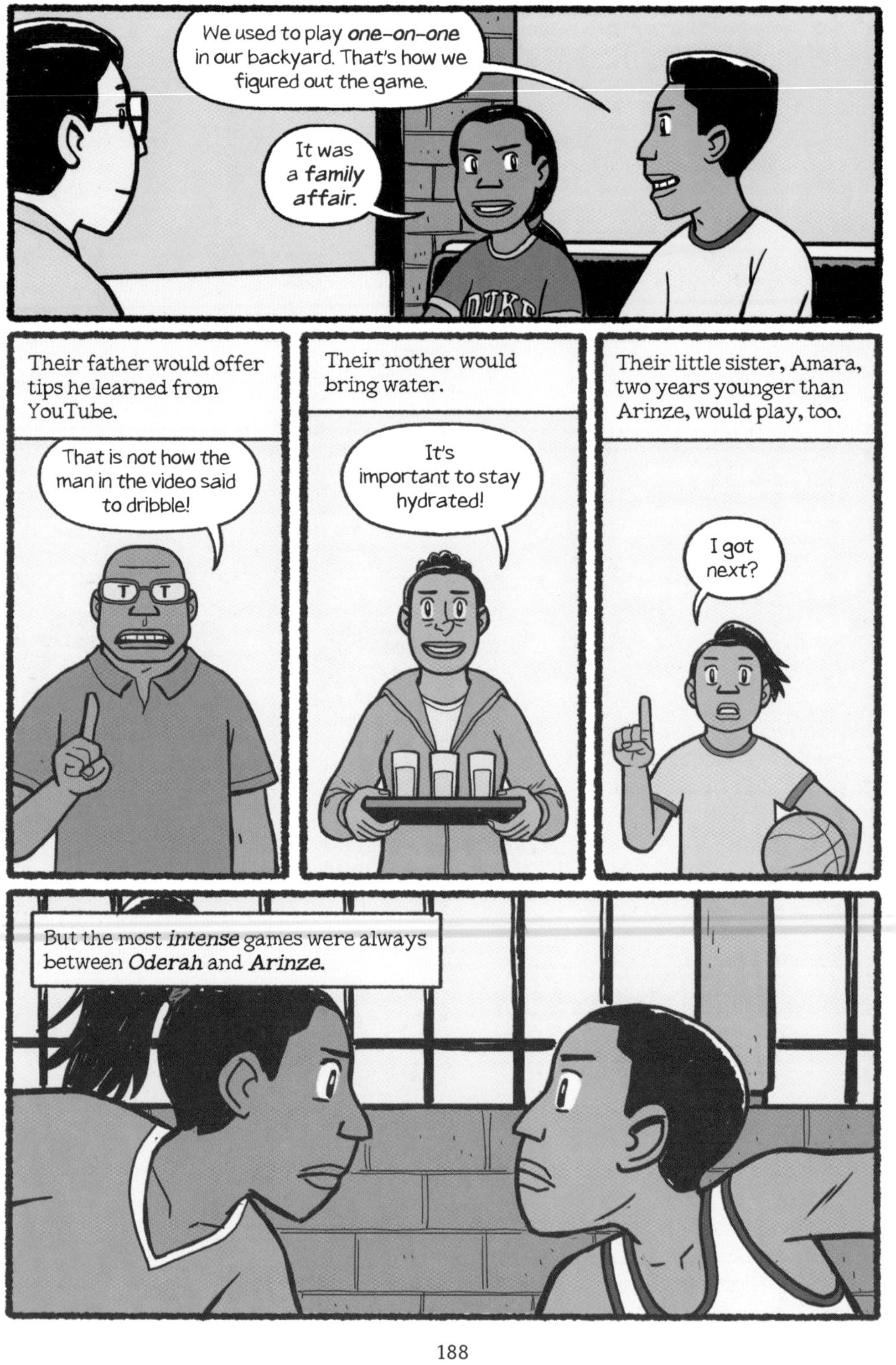
We used to play one-on-one in our backyard. That's how we figured out the game.
It was a family affair.
DUKE
Their father would offer tips he learned from YouTube.
That is not how the man in the video said to dribble!
Their mother would bring water.
It's important to stay hydrated!
Their little sister, Amara, two years younger than Arinze, would play, too.
I got next?
But the most intense games were always between Oderah and Arinze.

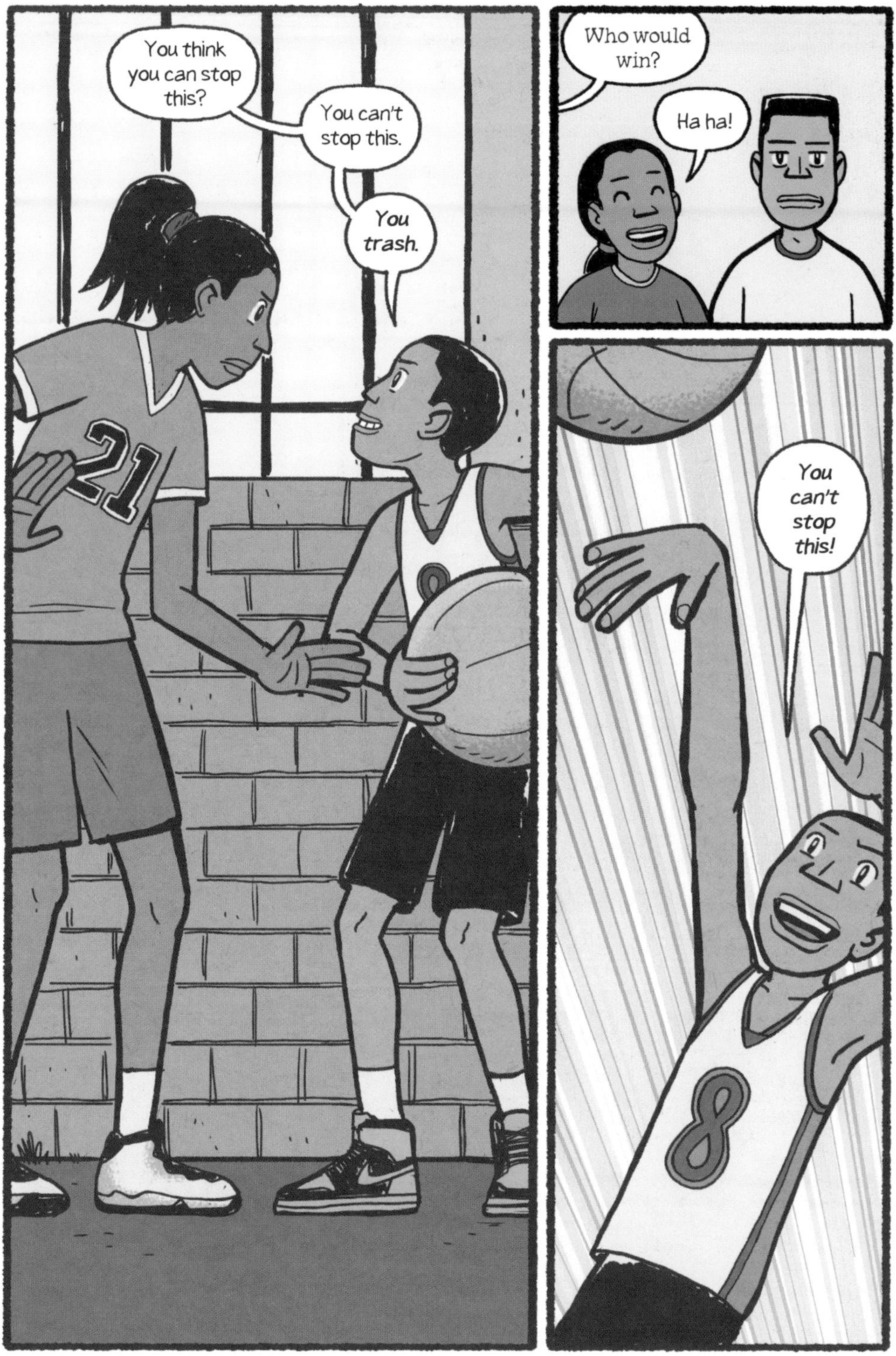
You think you can stop this?
You can't stop this.
You trash.
Who would win?
Ha ha!
You can't stop this!

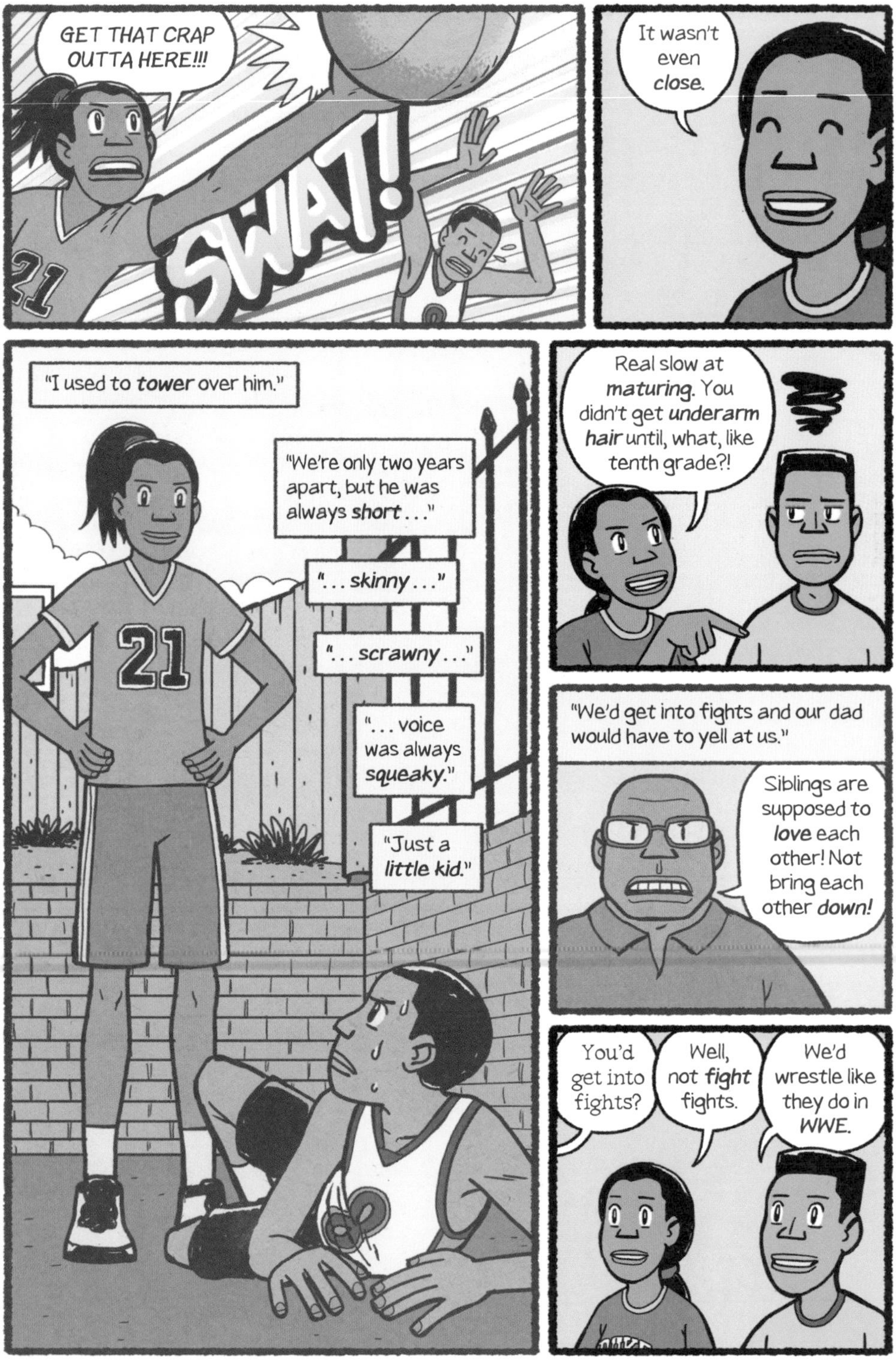
GET THAT CRAP OUTTA HERE!!!
SWAT!
It wasn't even close.
"I used to tower over him."
"We're only two years apart, but he was always short . . ."
". . . skinny . . ."
". . . scrawny . . ."
". . . voice was always squeaky."
"Just a little kid."
Real slow at maturing. You didn't get underarm hair until, what, like tenth grade?!
"We'd get into fights and our dad would have to yell at us."
Siblings are supposed to love each other! Not bring each other down!
You'd get into fights?
Well, not fight fights.
We'd wrestle like they do in WWE.

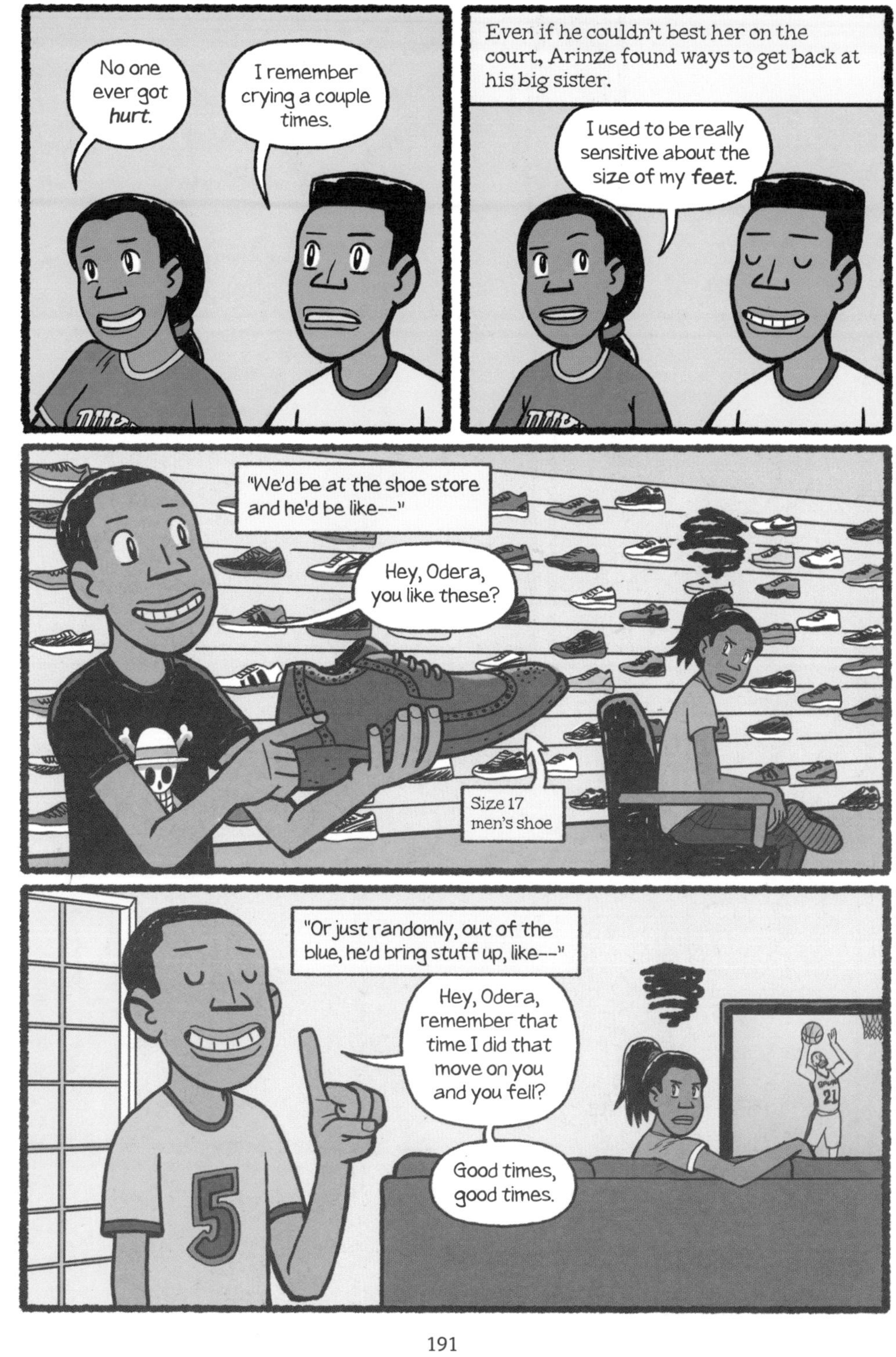
No one ever got *hurt*.
I remember crying a couple times.
Even if he couldn't best her on the court, Arinze found ways to get back at his big sister.
I used to be really sensitive about the size of my **feet**.
"We'd be at the shoe store and he'd be like--"
Hey, Odera, you like these?
Size 17 men's shoe
"Or just randomly, out of the blue, he'd bring stuff up, like--"
Hey, Odera, remember that time I did that move on you and you fell?
Good times, good times.

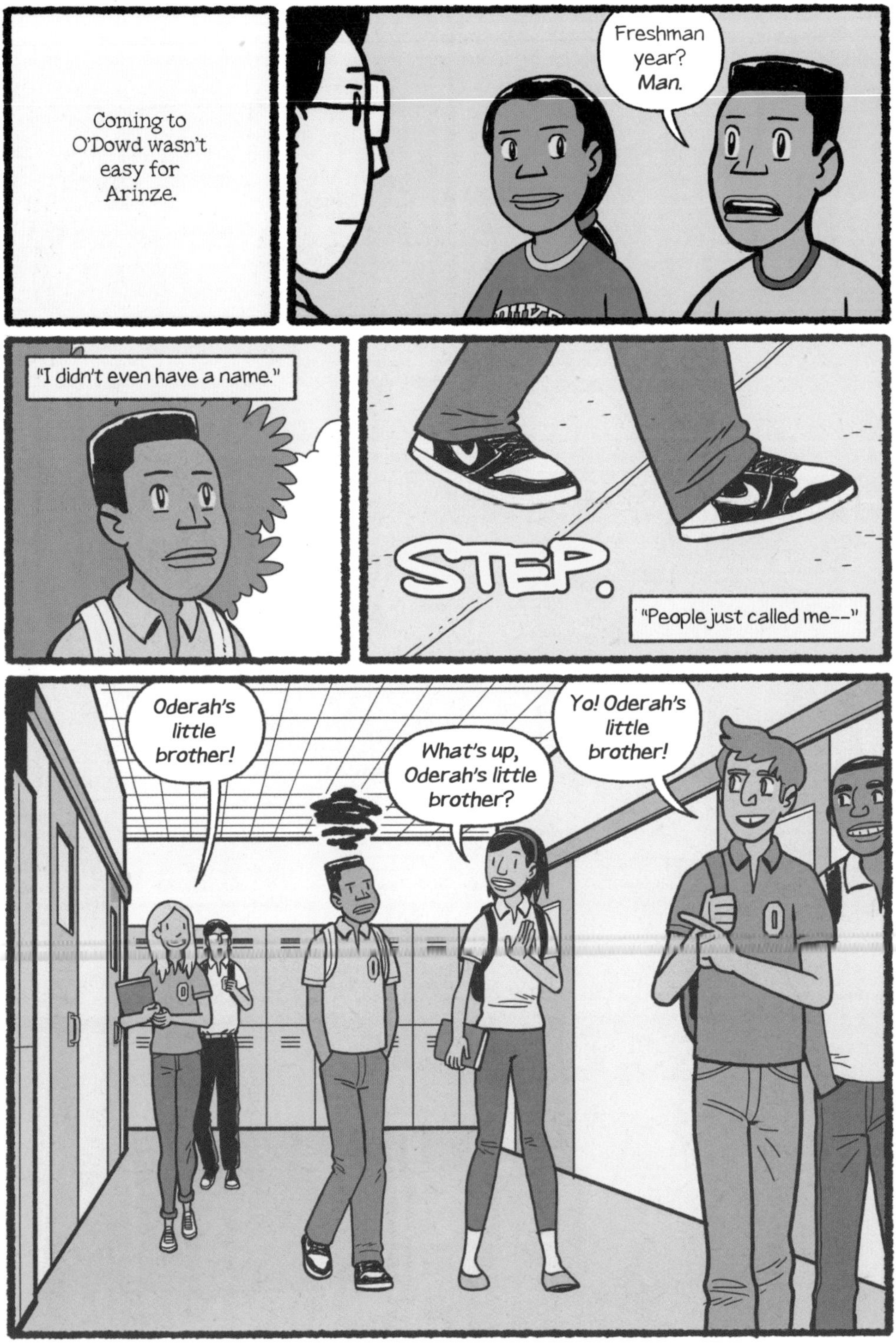
Coming to O'Dowd wasn't easy for Arinze.
Freshman year? Man.
"I didn't even have a name."
STEP.
"People just called me--"
Oderah's little brother!
What's up, Oderah's little brother?
Yo! Oderah's little brother!

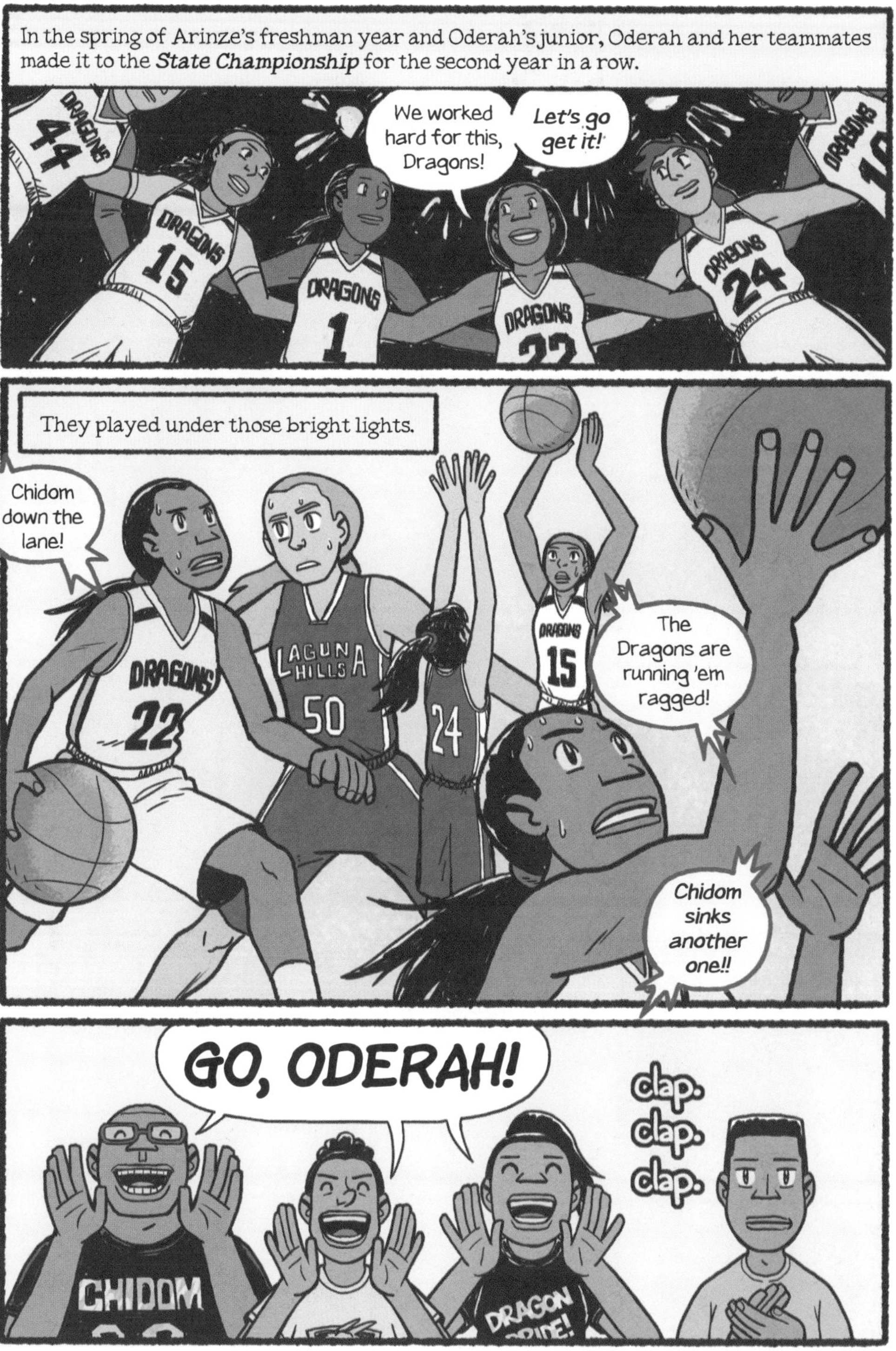
In the spring of Arinze's freshman year and Oderah's junior, Oderah and her teammates made it to the *State Championship* for the second year in a row.
We worked hard for this, Dragons!
Let's go get it!
They played under those bright lights.
Chidom down the lane!
The Dragons are running 'em ragged!
Chidom sinks another one!!
GO, ODERAH!
clap. clap. clap.

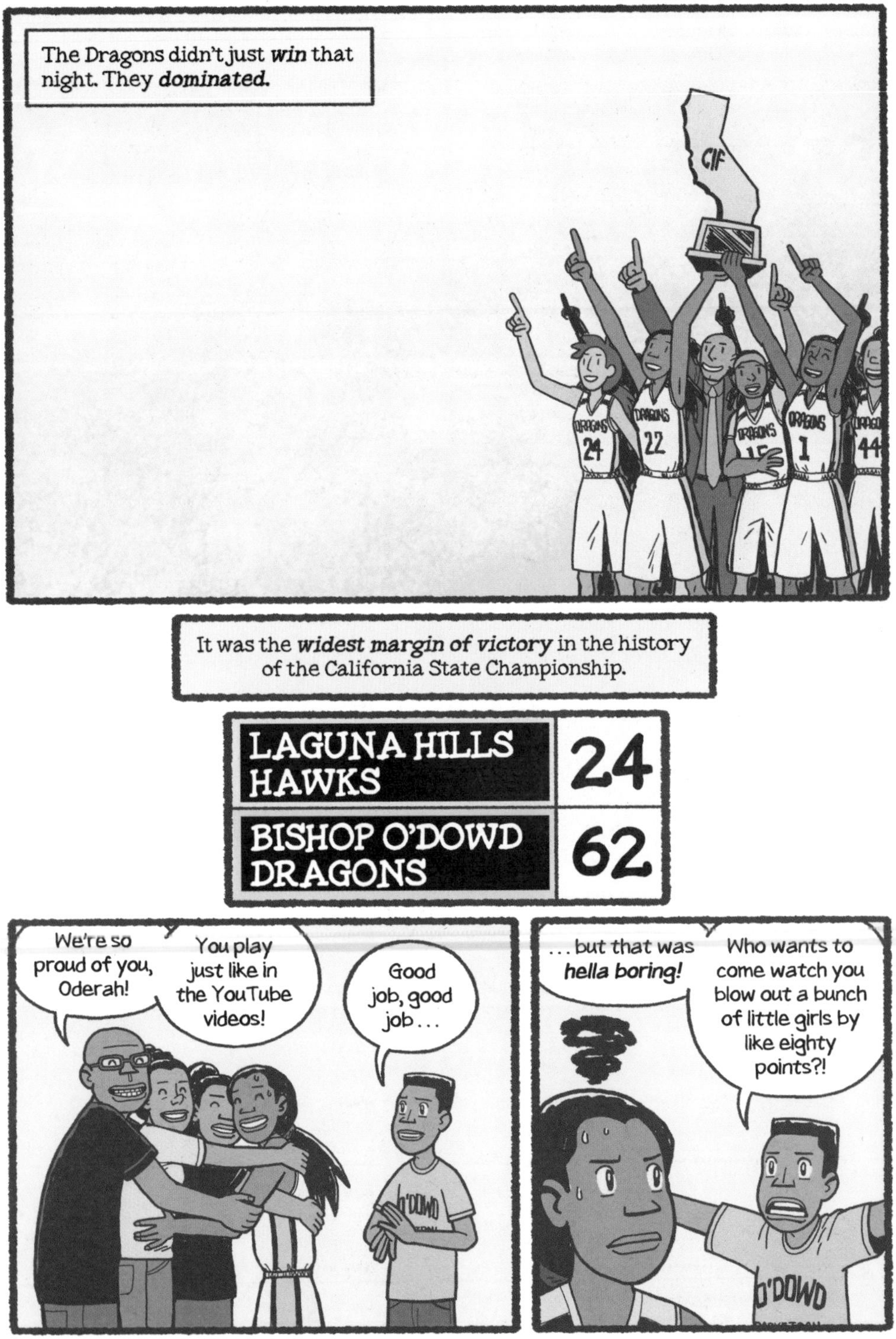
The Dragons didn't just *win* that night. They *dominated.*
CIF
It was the *widest margin of victory* in the history of the California State Championship.
LAGUNA HILLS HAWKS
24
BISHOP O'DOWD DRAGONS
62
We're so proud of you, Oderah!
You play just like in the YouTube videos!
Good job, good job . . .
O'DOWD
. . . but that was *hella boring!*
Who wants to come watch you blow out a bunch of little girls by like eighty points?!
O'DOWD

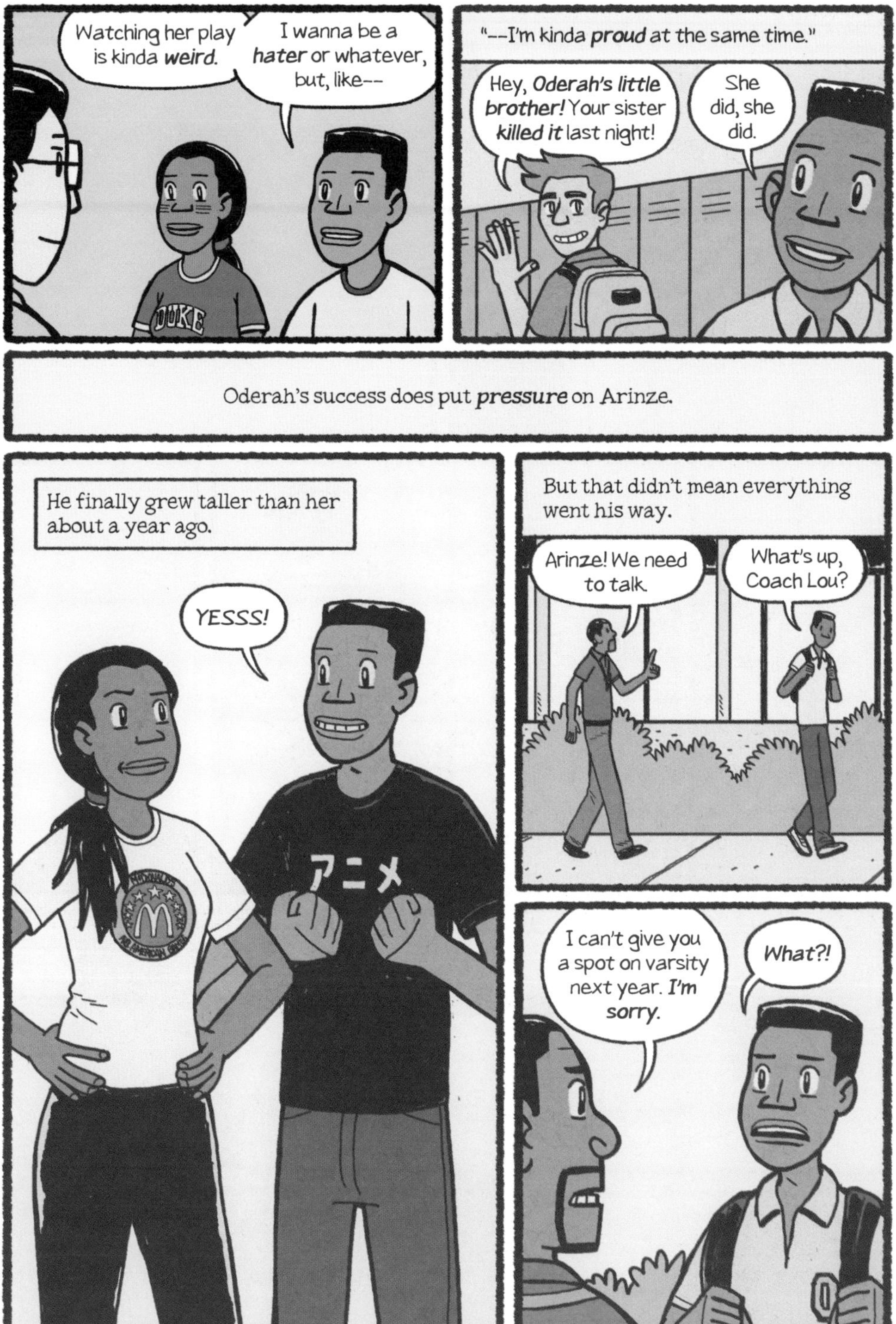
Watching her play is kinda *weird.*
I wanna be a *hater* or whatever, but, like--
DUKE
"--I'm kinda ***proud*** at the same time."
Hey, ***Oderah's little brother!*** Your sister ***killed it*** last night!
She did, she did.
Oderah's success does put ***pressure*** on Arinze.
He finally grew taller than her about a year ago.
YESSS!
アニメ
But that didn't mean everything went his way.
Arinze! We need to talk.
What's up, Coach Lou?
I can't give you a spot on varsity next year. ***I'm sorry.***
What?!

But don't worry, I'm not gonna hang you out to dry. I want you to play *junior varsity* one more year.

A junior on JV?!

It was an **unusual move.**

Usually, only freshmen and sophomores played junior varsity.

Arinze would be an *exception.*

A junior on JV?!

Amara's a **freshman,** and even she made varsity!

Fortunately, he wasn't the **only** exception.

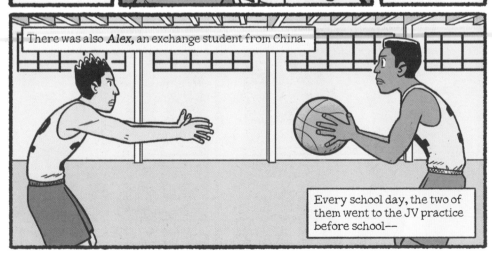

There was also **Alex,** an exchange student from China.

Every school day, the two of them went to the JV practice before school--

196

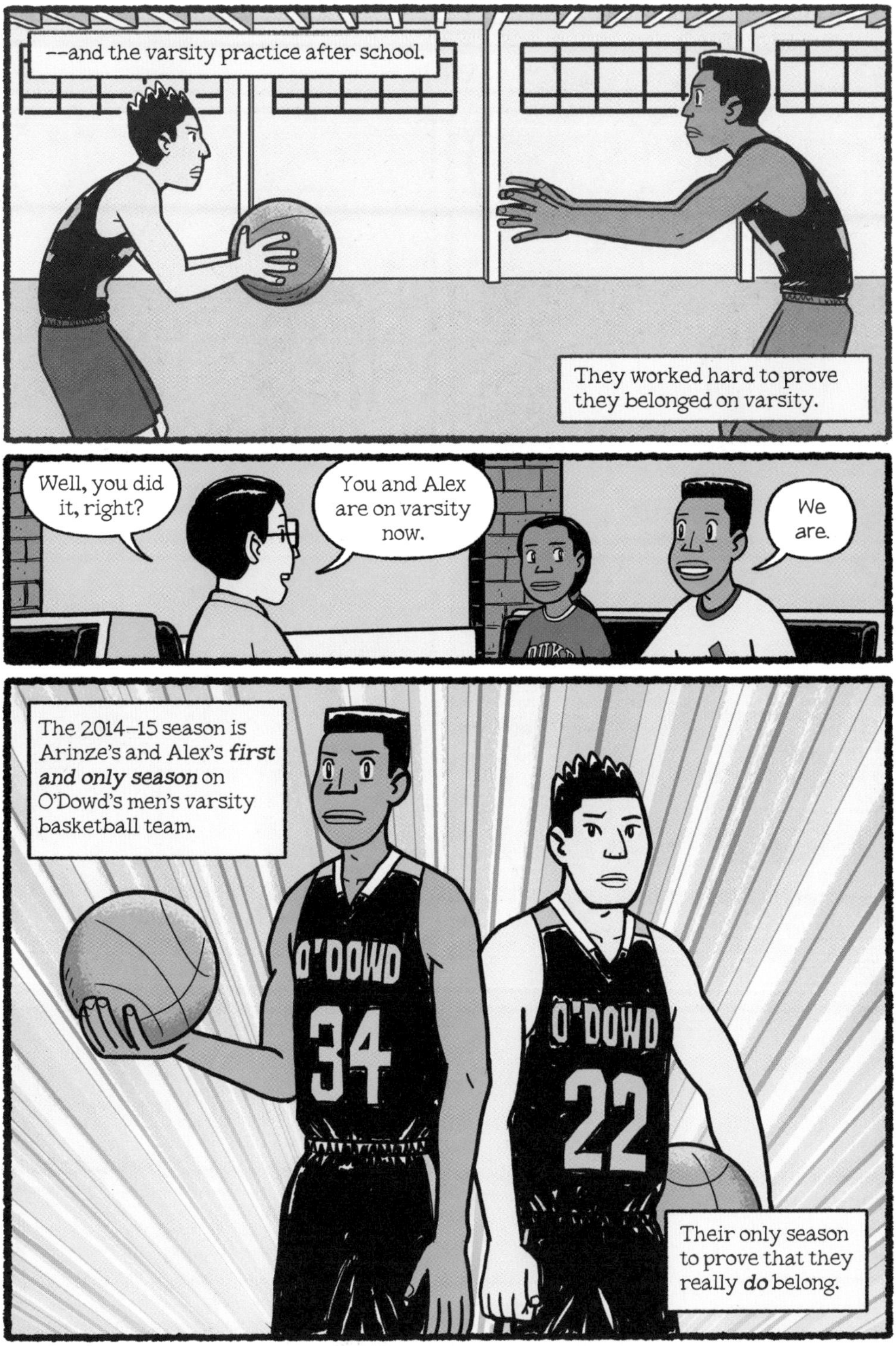
--and the varsity practice after school.
They worked hard to prove they belonged on varsity.
Well, you did it, right?
You and Alex are on varsity now.
We are.
The 2014–15 season is Arinze's and Alex's ***first and only season*** on O'Dowd's men's varsity basketball team.
O'DOWD
34
O'DOWD
22
Their only season to prove that they really ***do*** belong.

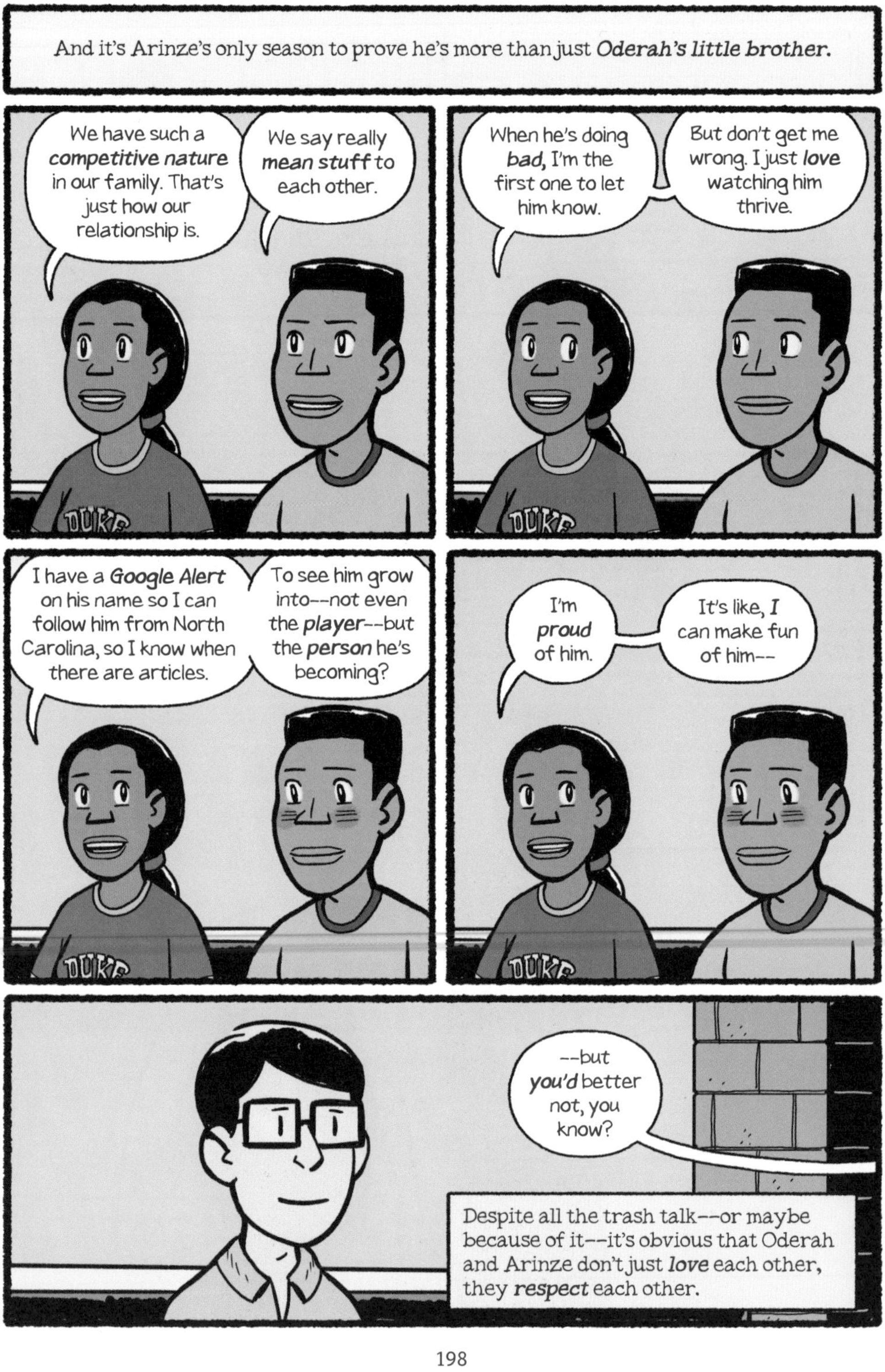
And it's Arinze's only season to prove he's more than just *Oderah's little brother.*
We have such a *competitive nature* in our family. That's just how our relationship is.
We say really *mean stuff* to each other.
When he's doing *bad,* I'm the first one to let him know.
But don't get me wrong. I just *love* watching him thrive.
DUKE
I have a *Google Alert* on his name so I can follow him from North Carolina, so I know when there are articles.
To see him grow into--not even the *player*--but the *person* he's becoming?
I'm *proud* of him.
It's like, *I* can make fun of him--
--but *you'd* better not, you know?
Despite all the trash talk--or maybe because of it--it's obvious that Oderah and Arinze don't just *love* each other, they *respect* each other.

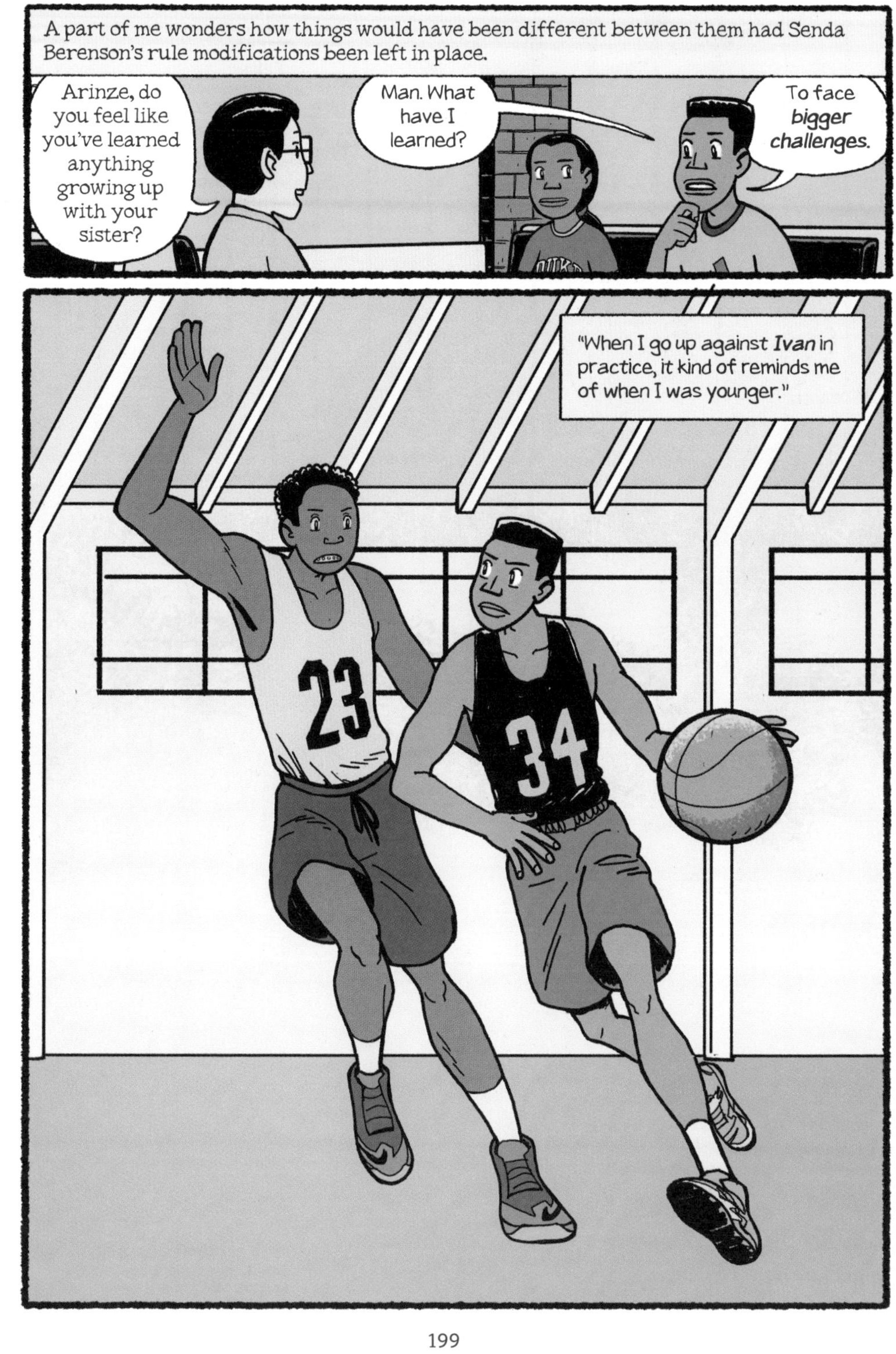
A part of me wonders how things would have been different between them had Senda Berenson's rule modifications been left in place.
Arinze, do you feel like you've learned anything growing up with your sister?
Man. What have I learned?
To face *bigger challenges.*
"When I go up against *Ivan* in practice, it kind of reminds me of when I was younger."
23
34

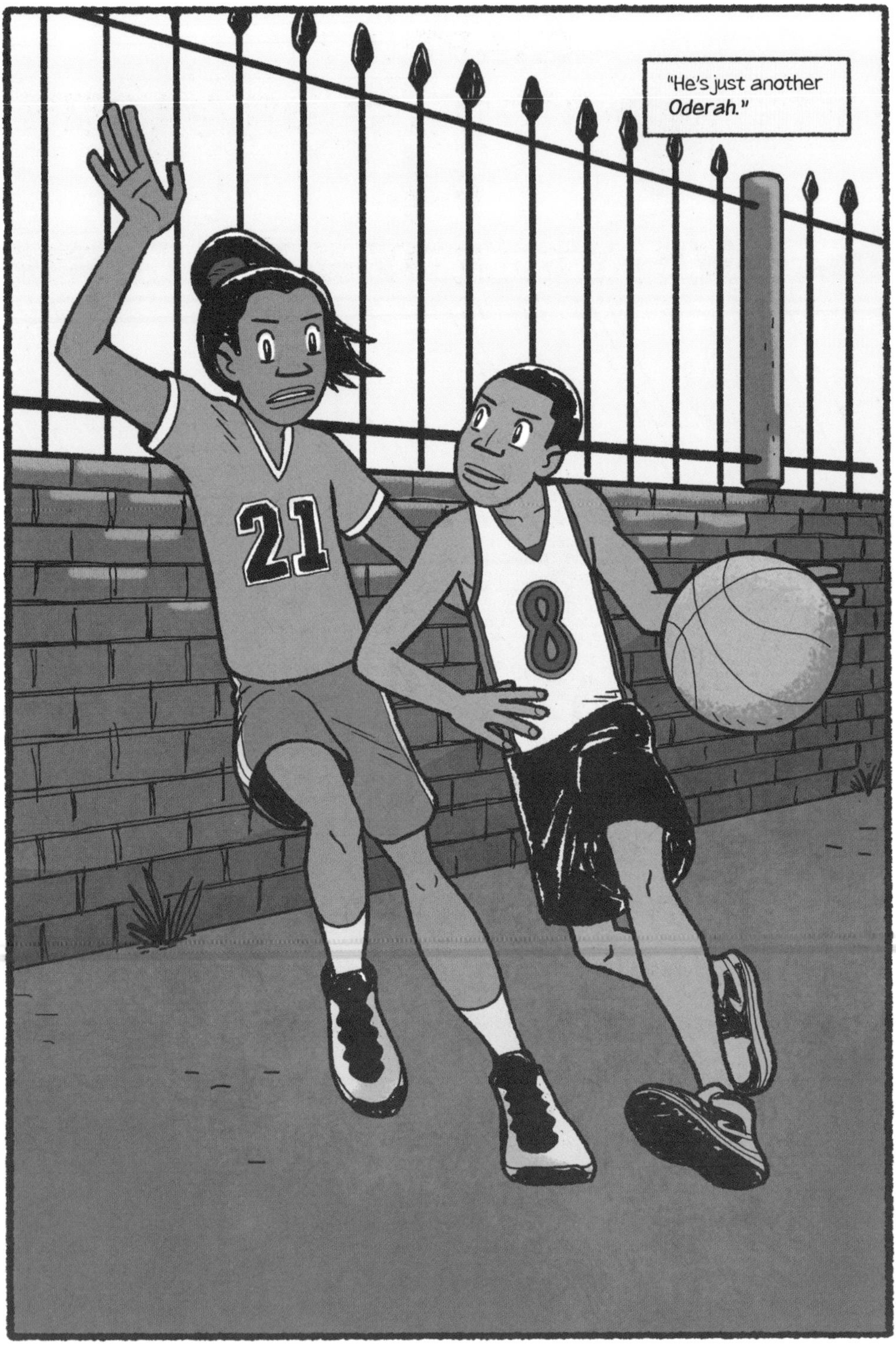
"He's just another
Oderah."
21
8

CHAPTER 7:
BISHOP O'DOWD DRAGONS
VS.
MONTVERDE EAGLES

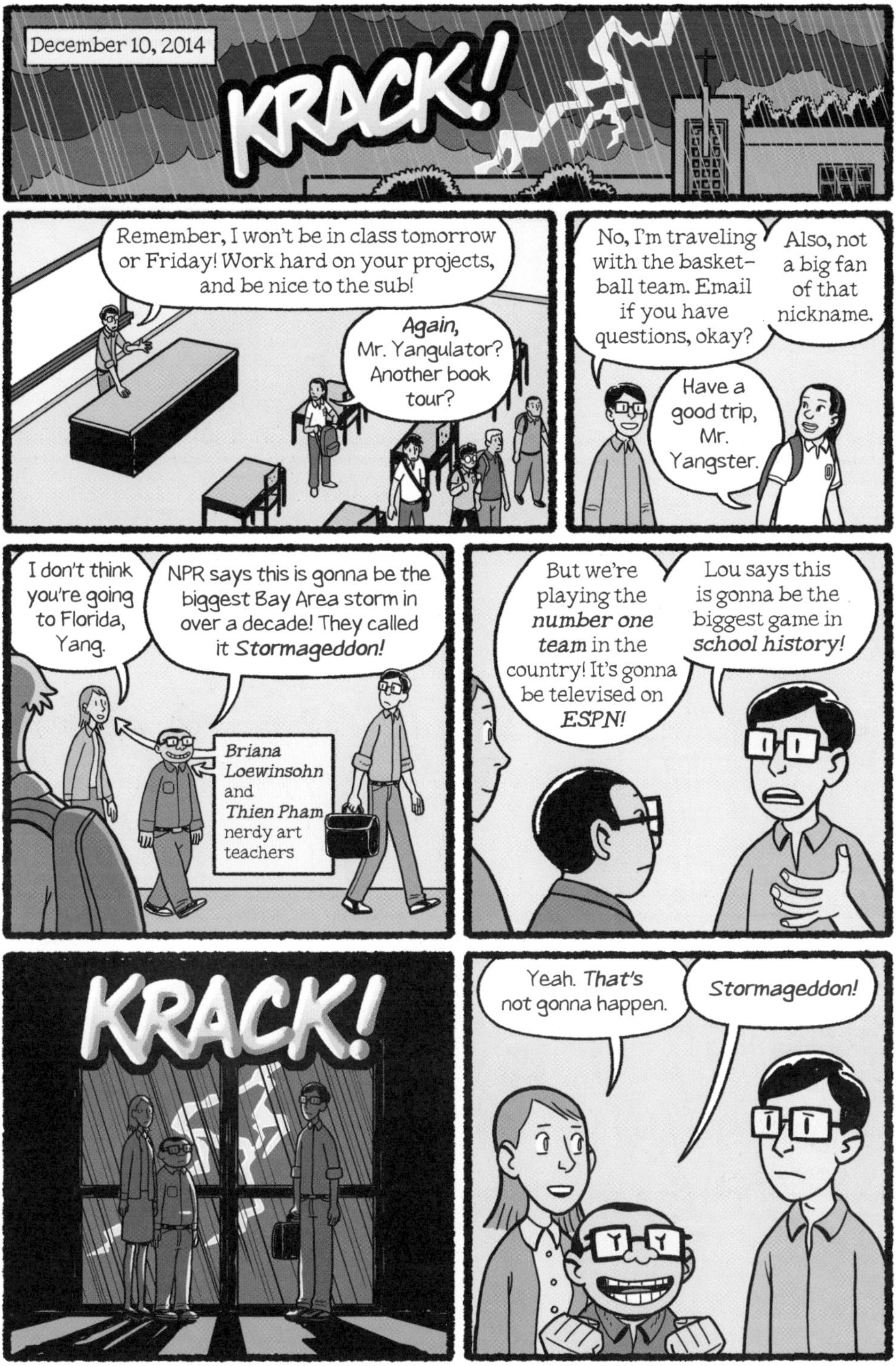
December 10, 2014
KRACK!
Remember, I won't be in class tomorrow or Friday! Work hard on your projects, and be nice to the sub!
Again, Mr. Yangulator? Another book tour?
No, I'm traveling with the basket-ball team. Email if you have questions, okay?
Also, not a big fan of that nickname.
Have a good trip, Mr. Yangster.
I don't think you're going to Florida, Yang.
NPR says this is gonna be the biggest Bay Area storm in over a decade! They called it *Stormageddon!*
Briana Loewinsohn and *Thien Pham* nerdy art teachers
But we're playing the ***number one team*** in the country! It's gonna be televised on ***ESPN!***
Lou says this is gonna be the biggest game in ***school history!***
KRACK!
Yeah. *That's* not gonna happen.
Stormageddon!

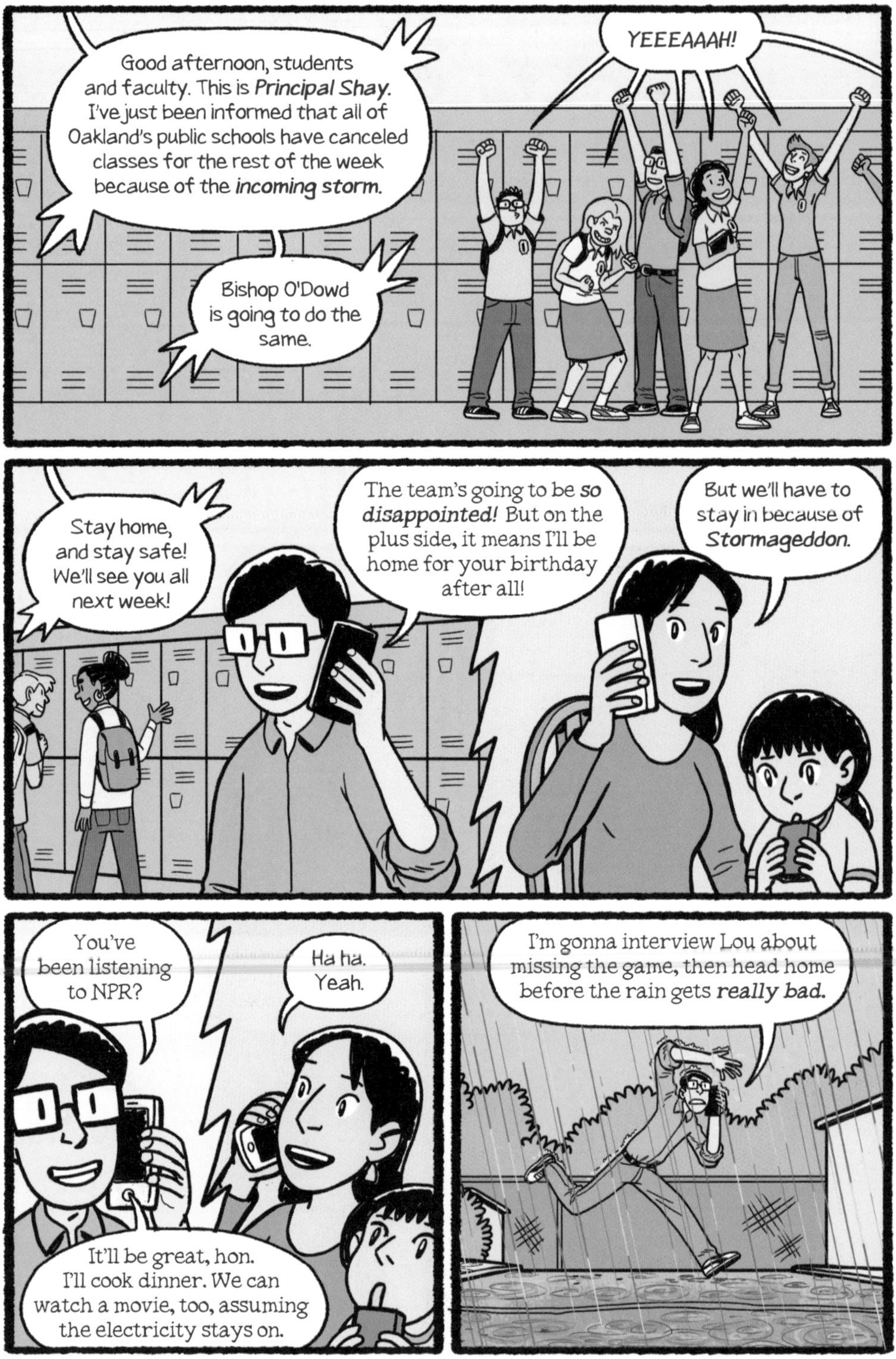
Good afternoon, students and faculty. This is *Principal Shay*. I've just been informed that all of Oakland's public schools have canceled classes for the rest of the week because of the *incoming storm*.
Bishop O'Dowd is going to do the same.
YEEEAAAH!
Stay home, and stay safe! We'll see you all next week!
The team's going to be *so disappointed!* But on the plus side, it means I'll be home for your birthday after all!
But we'll have to stay in because of *Stormageddon*.
You've been listening to NPR?
Ha ha. Yeah.
It'll be great, hon. I'll cook dinner. We can watch a movie, too, assuming the electricity stays on.
I'm gonna interview Lou about missing the game, then head home before the rain gets *really bad*.

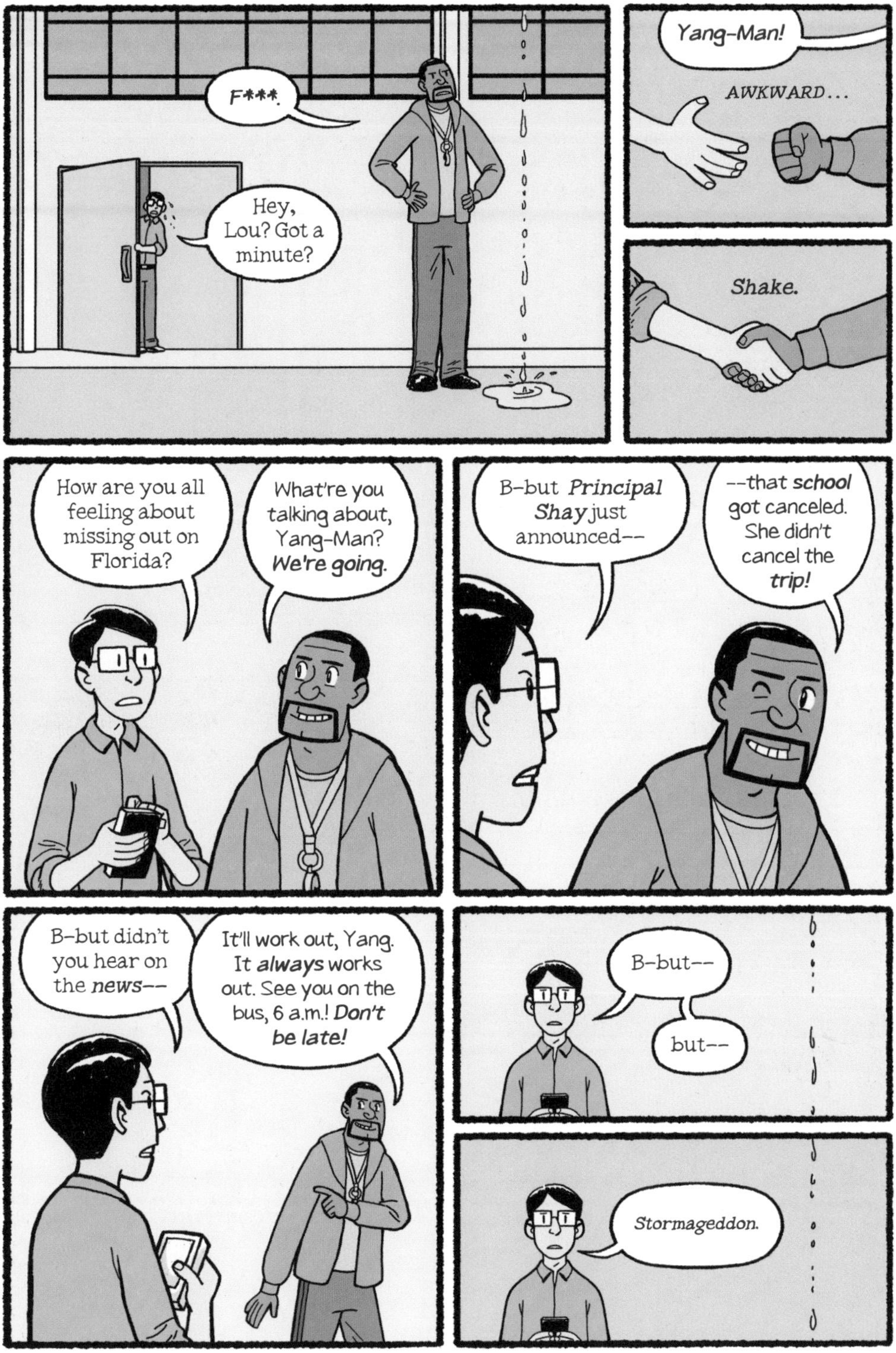
F***.
Hey, Lou? Got a minute?
Yang-Man!
AWKWARD...
Shake.
How are you all feeling about missing out on Florida?
What're you talking about, Yang-Man? *We're going*.
B-but *Principal Shay* just announced--
--that *school* got canceled. She didn't cancel the *trip!*
B-but didn't you hear on the *news*--
It'll work out, Yang. It *always* works out. See you on the bus, 6 a.m.! *Don't be late!*
B-but--
but--
Stormageddon.

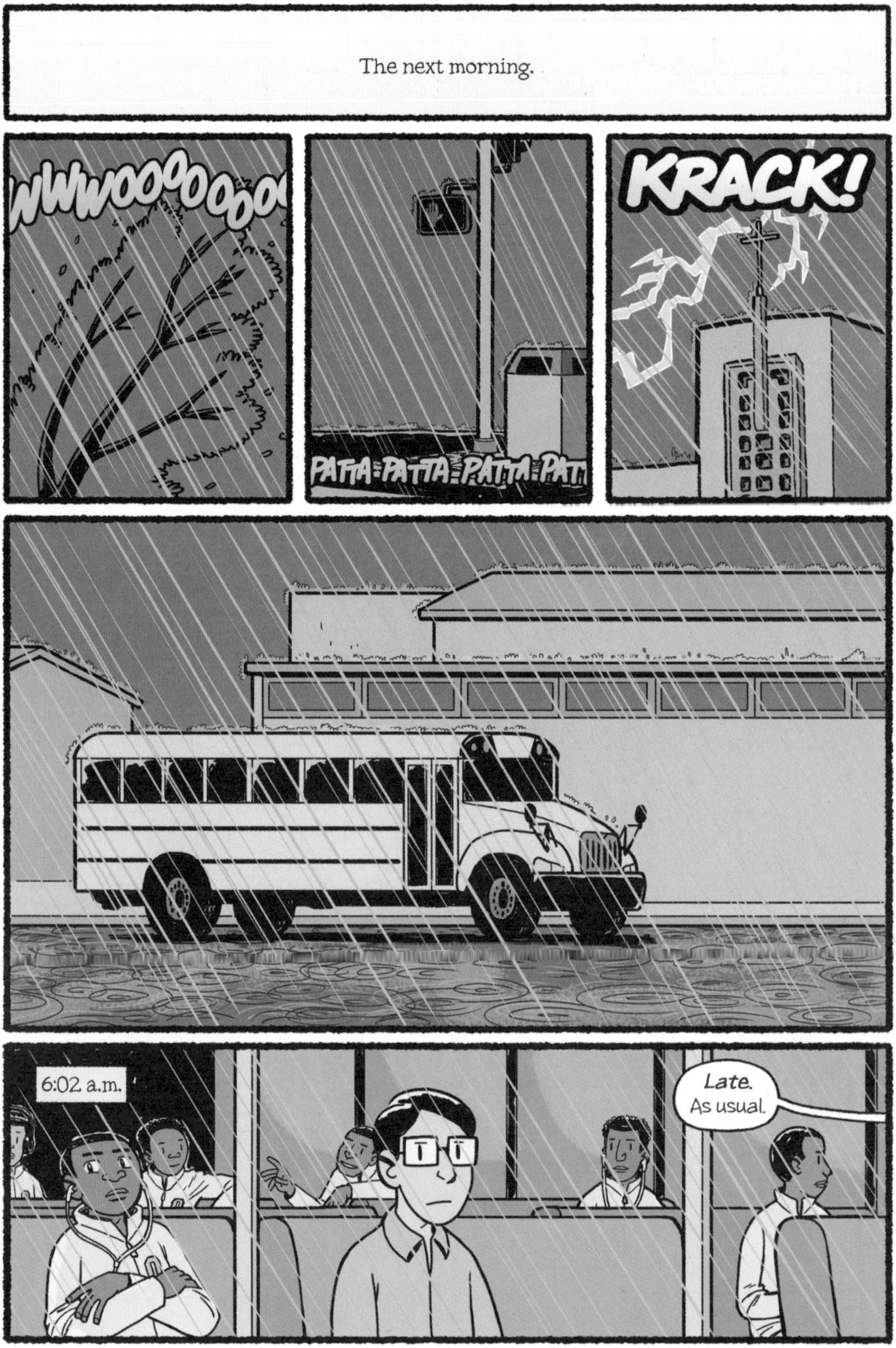
The next morning.
WWWOOOOOOOOO
PATTA PATTA PATTA PAT
KRACK!
6:02 a.m.
Late. As usual.

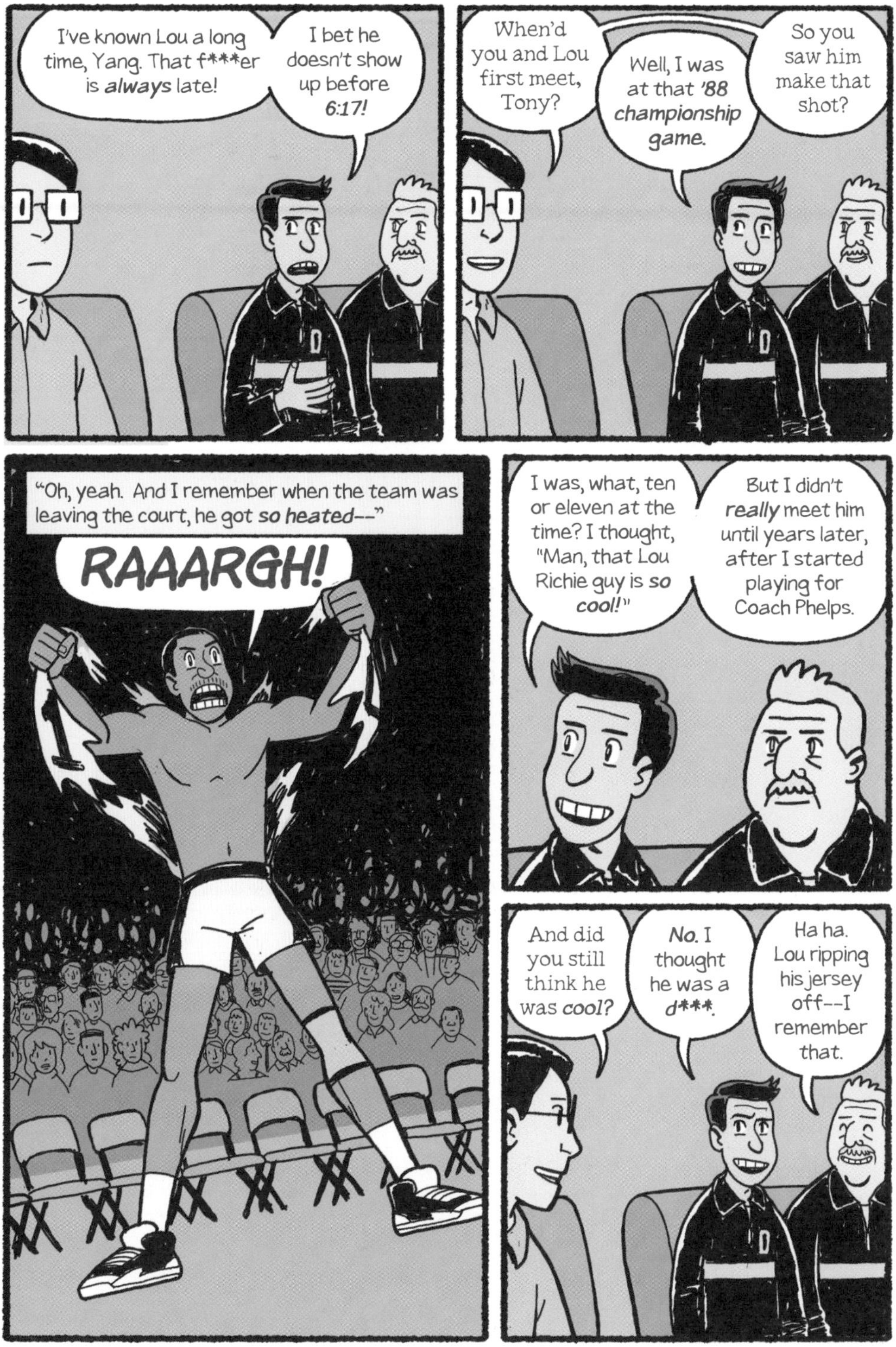
I've known Lou a long time, Yang. That f***er is *always* late!
I bet he doesn't show up before *6:17!*
When'd you and Lou first meet, Tony?
Well, I was at that *'88 championship game.*
So you saw him make that shot?
"Oh, yeah. And I remember when the team was leaving the court, he got *so heated--*"
RAAARGH!
I was, what, ten or eleven at the time? I thought, "Man, that Lou Richie guy is *so cool!*"
But I didn't *really* meet him until years later, after I started playing for Coach Phelps.
And did you still think he was *cool?*
No. I thought he was a *d****.
Ha ha. Lou ripping his jersey off--I remember that.

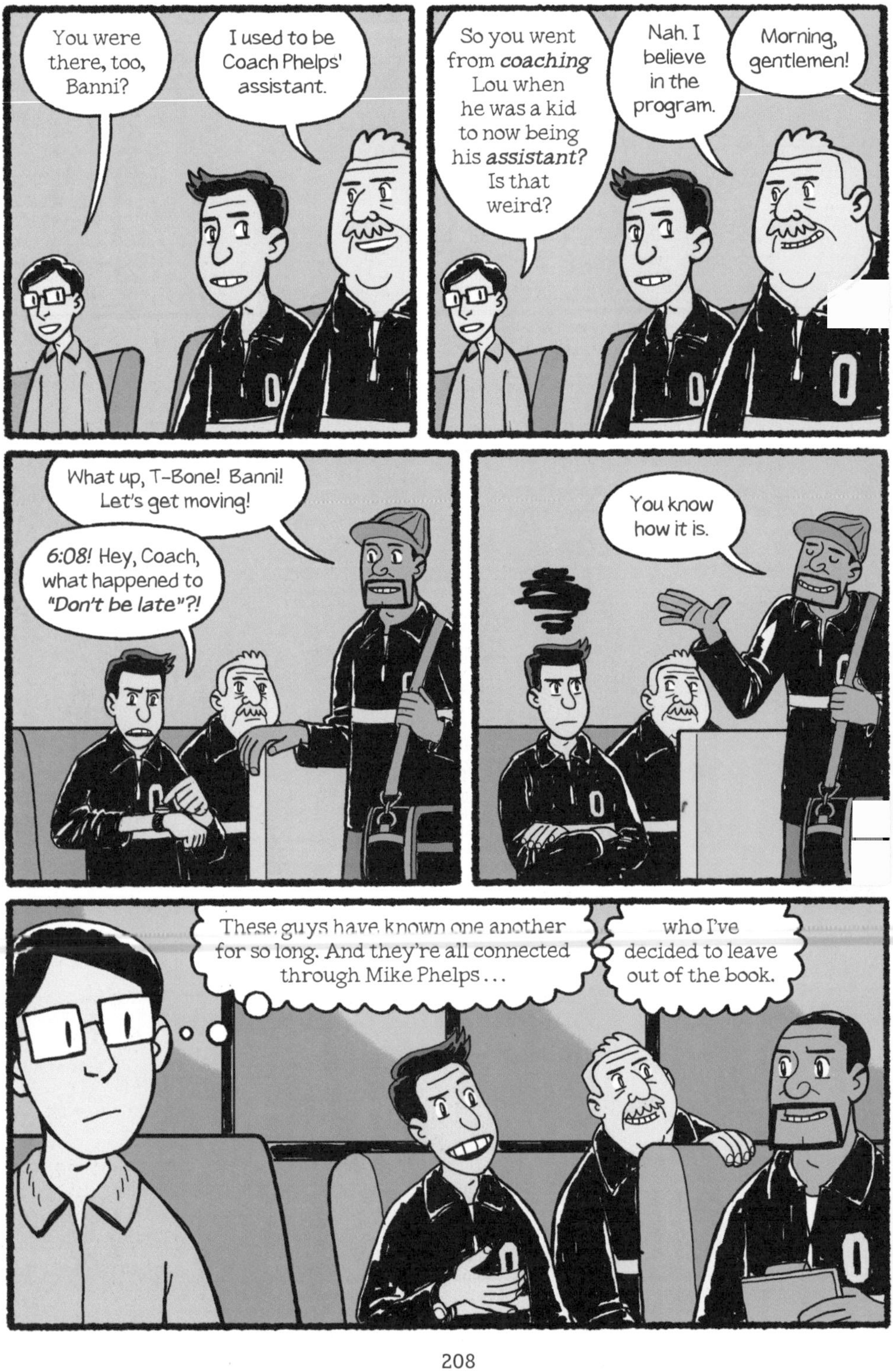
You were there, too, Banni?
I used to be Coach Phelps' assistant.
So you went from *coaching* Lou when he was a kid to now being his *assistant?* Is that weird?
Nah. I believe in the program.
Morning, gentlemen!
What up, T-Bone! Banni! Let's get moving!
6:08! Hey, Coach, what happened to *"Don't be late"?!*
You know how it is.
These guys have known one another for so long. And they're all connected through Mike Phelps . . .
who I've decided to leave out of the book.

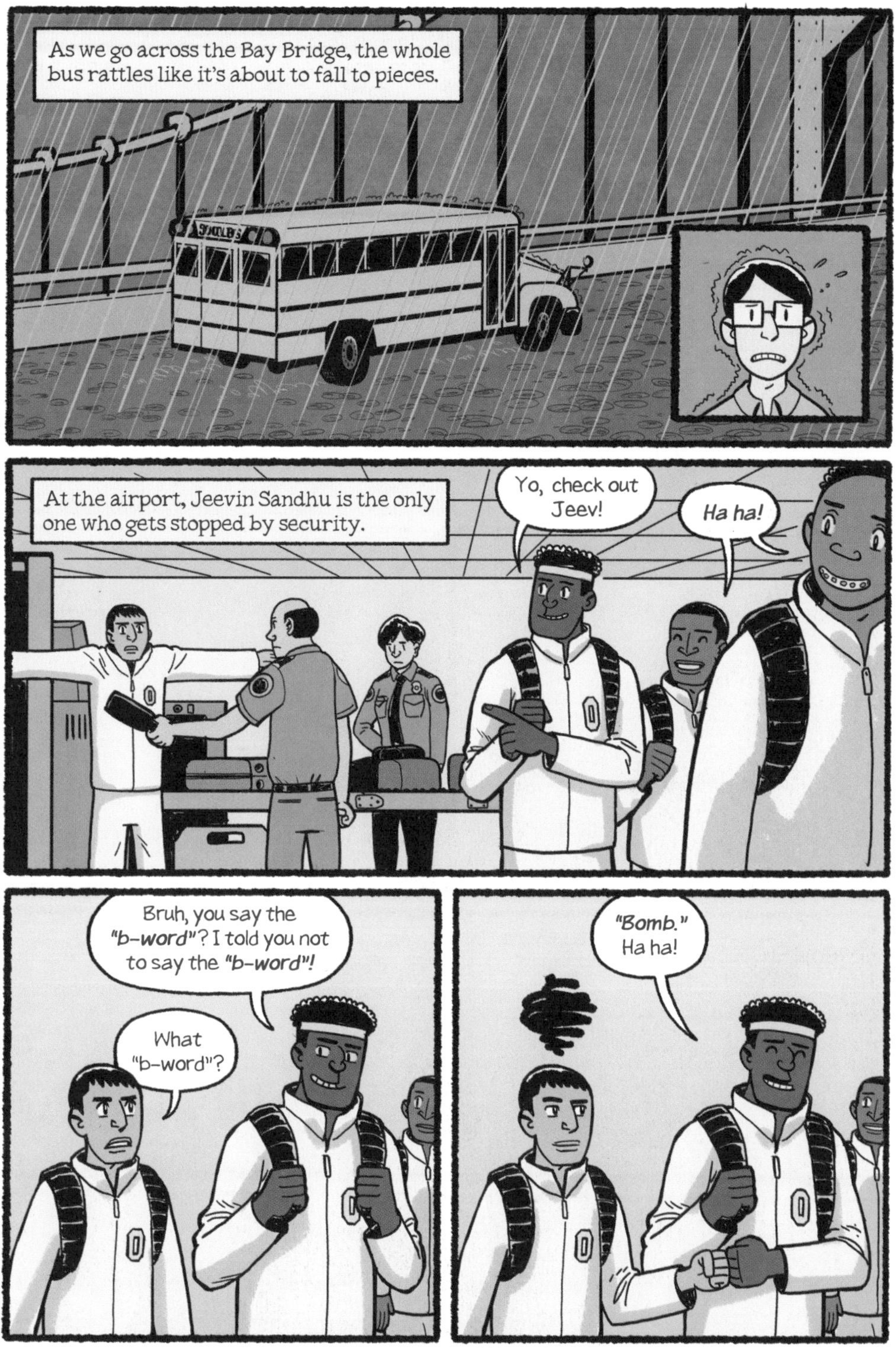
As we go across the Bay Bridge, the whole bus rattles like it's about to fall to pieces.
At the airport, Jeevin Sandhu is the only one who gets stopped by security.
Yo, check out Jeev!
Ha ha!
Bruh, you say the "b-word"? I told you not to say the "b-word"!
What "b-word"?
"Bomb." Ha ha!

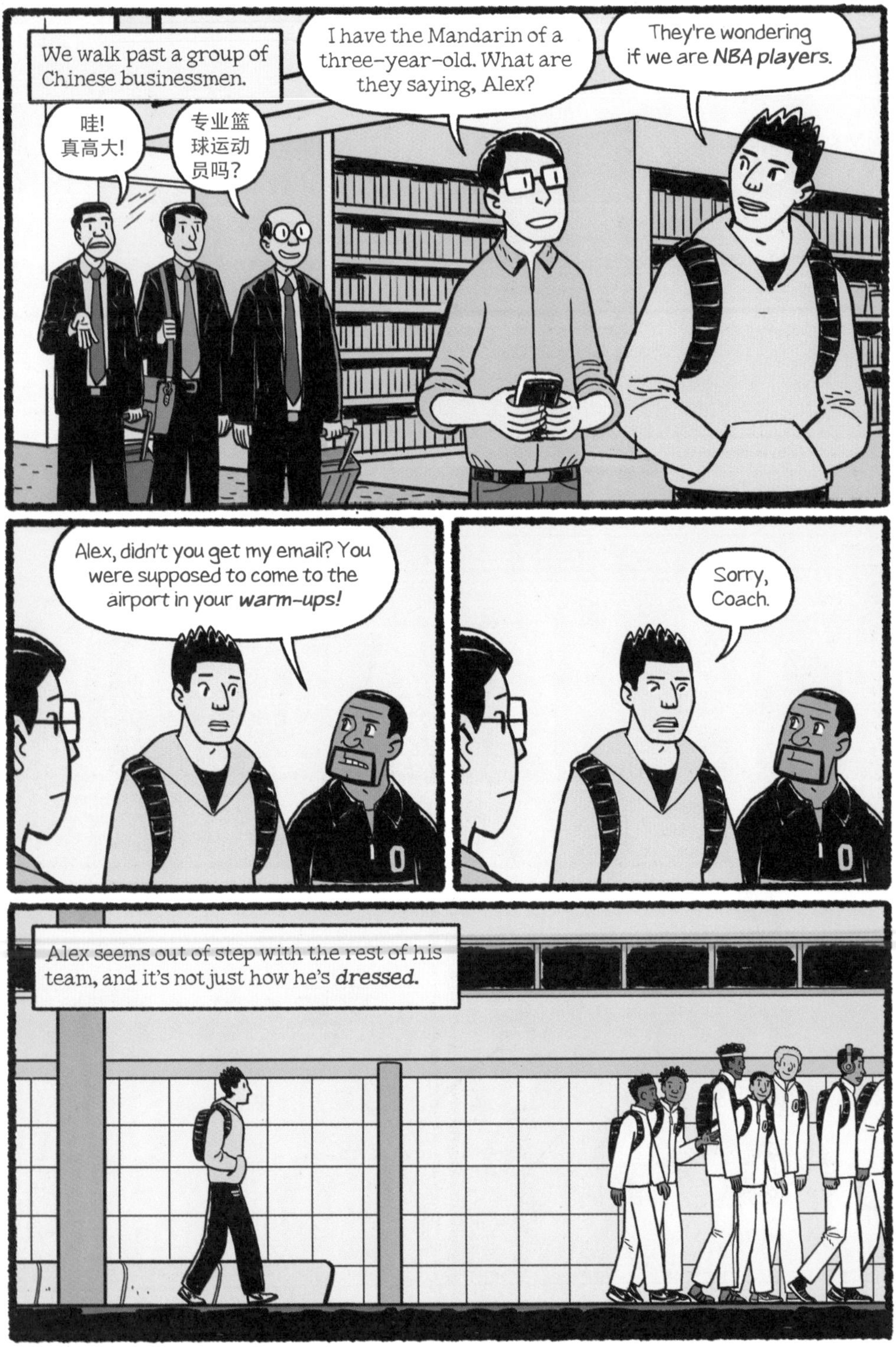
We walk past a group of Chinese businessmen.
I have the Mandarin of a three-year-old. What are they saying, Alex?
They're wondering if we are *NBA players*.
哇!真高大!
专业篮球运动员吗?
Alex, didn't you get my email? You were supposed to come to the airport in your *warm-ups!*
Sorry, Coach.
Alex seems out of step with the rest of his team, and it's not just how he's *dressed*.

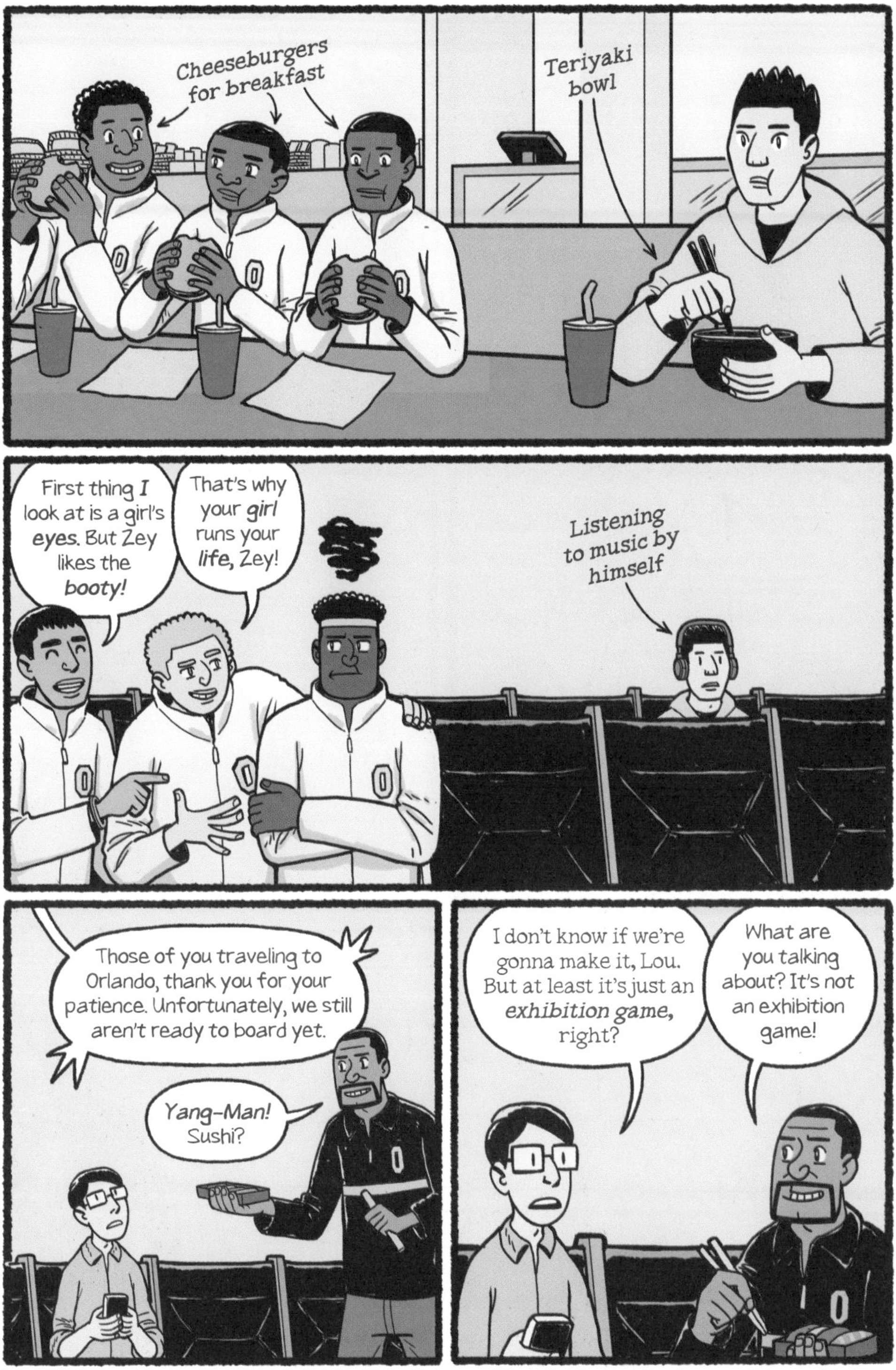

Cheeseburgers for breakfast
Teriyaki bowl
First thing *I* look at is a girl's *eyes*. But Zey likes the *booty!*
That's why your *girl* runs your *life*, Zey!
Listening to music by himself
Those of you traveling to Orlando, thank you for your patience. Unfortunately, we still aren't ready to board yet.
Yang-Man! Sushi?
I don't know if we're gonna make it, Lou. But at least it's just an *exhibition game*, right?
What are you talking about? It's not an exhibition game!

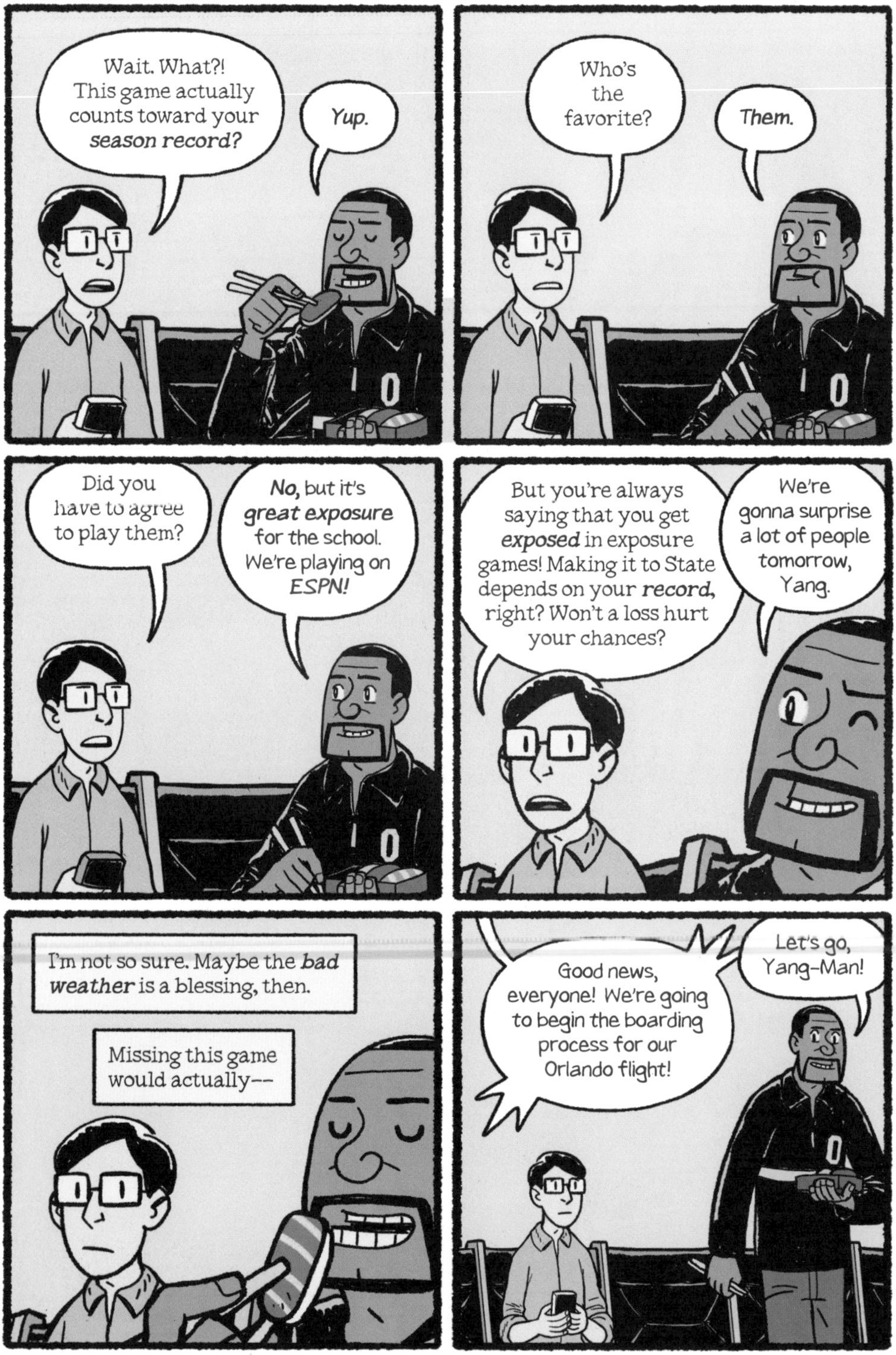

Wait. What?! This game actually counts toward your *season record?*
Yup.
Who's the favorite?
Them.
Did you have to agree to play them?
No, but it's *great exposure* for the school. We're playing on *ESPN!*
But you're always saying that you get *exposed* in exposure games! Making it to State depends on your *record,* right? Won't a loss hurt your chances?
We're gonna surprise a lot of people tomorrow, Yang.
I'm not so sure. Maybe the *bad weather* is a blessing, then.
Missing this game would actually--
Good news, everyone! We're going to begin the boarding process for our Orlando flight!
Let's go, Yang-Man!
0

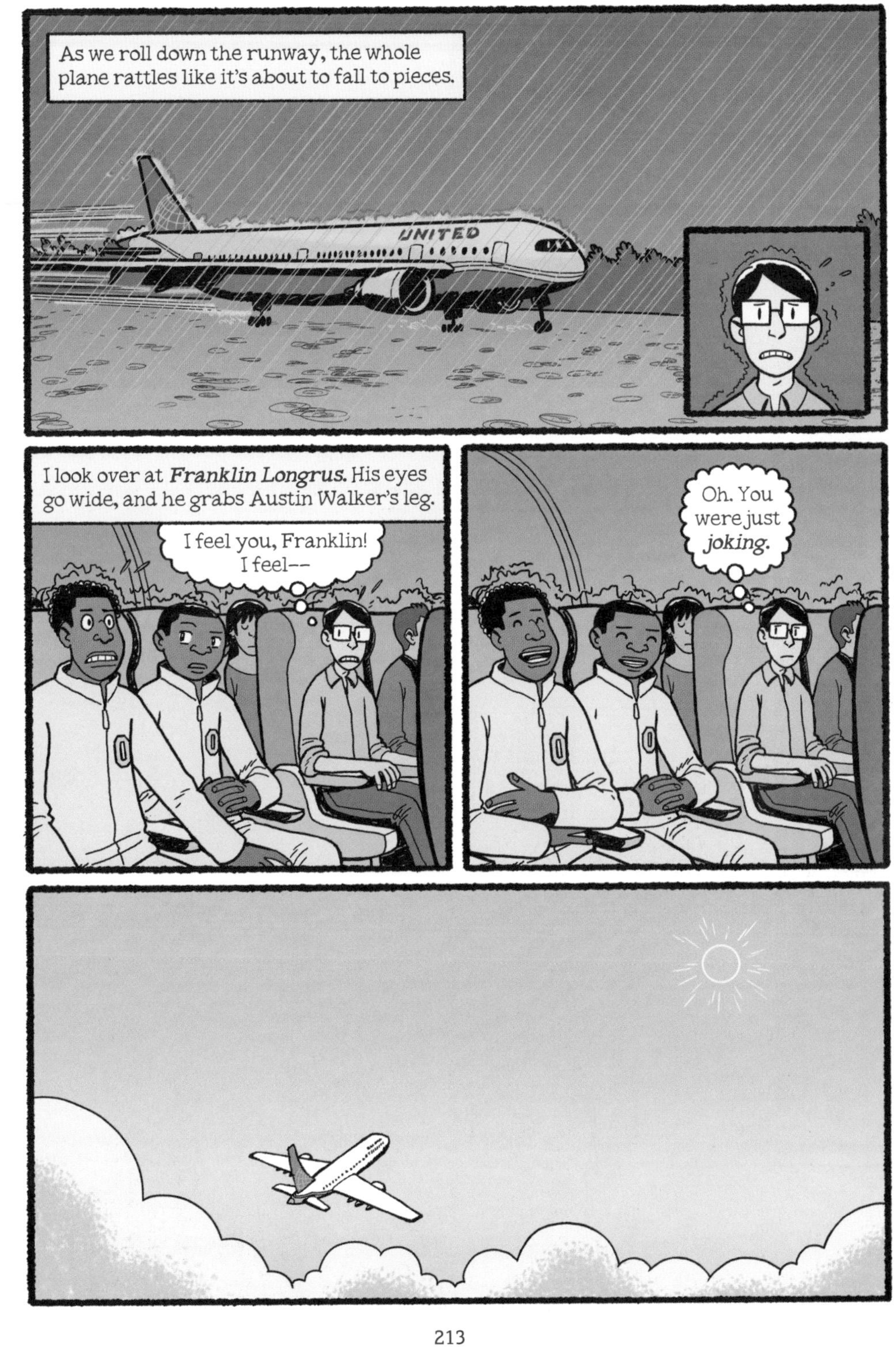
As we roll down the runway, the whole plane rattles like it's about to fall to pieces.
UNITED
I look over at ***Franklin Longrus.*** His eyes go wide, and he grabs Austin Walker's leg.
I feel you, Franklin! I feel--
Oh. You were just *joking.*

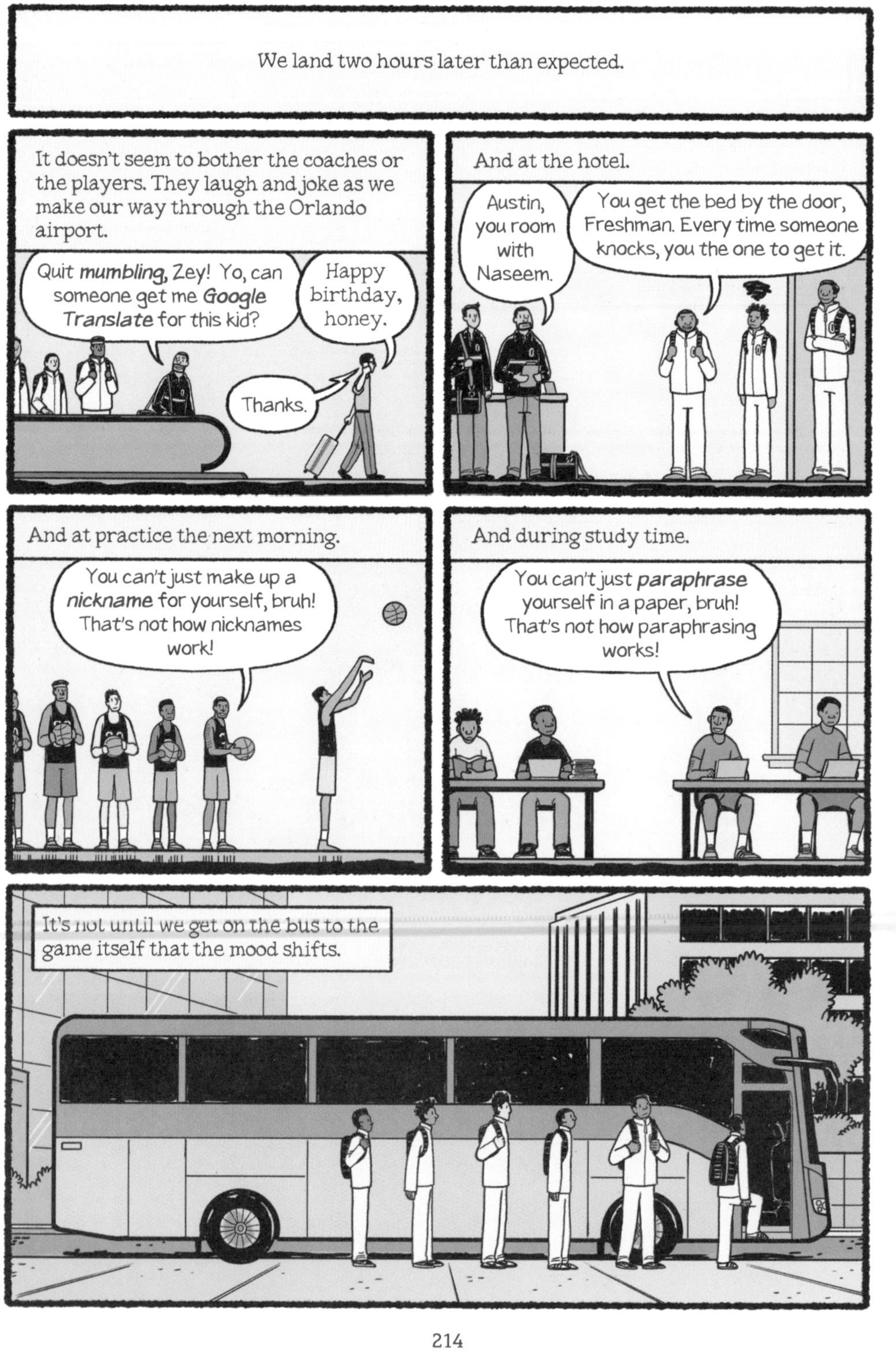
We land two hours later than expected.
It doesn't seem to bother the coaches or the players. They laugh and joke as we make our way through the Orlando airport.
Quit **mumbling,** Zey! Yo, can someone get me ***Google Translate*** for this kid?
Happy birthday, honey.
Thanks.
And at the hotel.
Austin, you room with Naseem.
You get the bed by the door, Freshman. Every time someone knocks, you the one to get it.
And at practice the next morning.
You can't just make up a ***nickname*** for yourself, bruh! That's not how nicknames work!
And during study time.
You can't just ***paraphrase*** yourself in a paper, bruh! That's not how paraphrasing works!
It's not until we get on the bus to the game itself that the mood shifts.

Without the coaches saying a word, the players stop talking to one another. They don't even sit next to one another.

Each of them puts on his headphones.

Only *Elijah* and *Naseem,* the two freshmen, bop their heads to their music. Everyone else sits perfectly still.

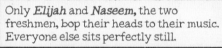

The bus is dead silent as we pull into **"The Nest,"** Montverde Academy's 6.5-million-dollar athletic facility.

THE MONTVERDE ACADEMY CENTER FOR SPORTSMANSHIP AND WELLNESS
"THE NEST"

215

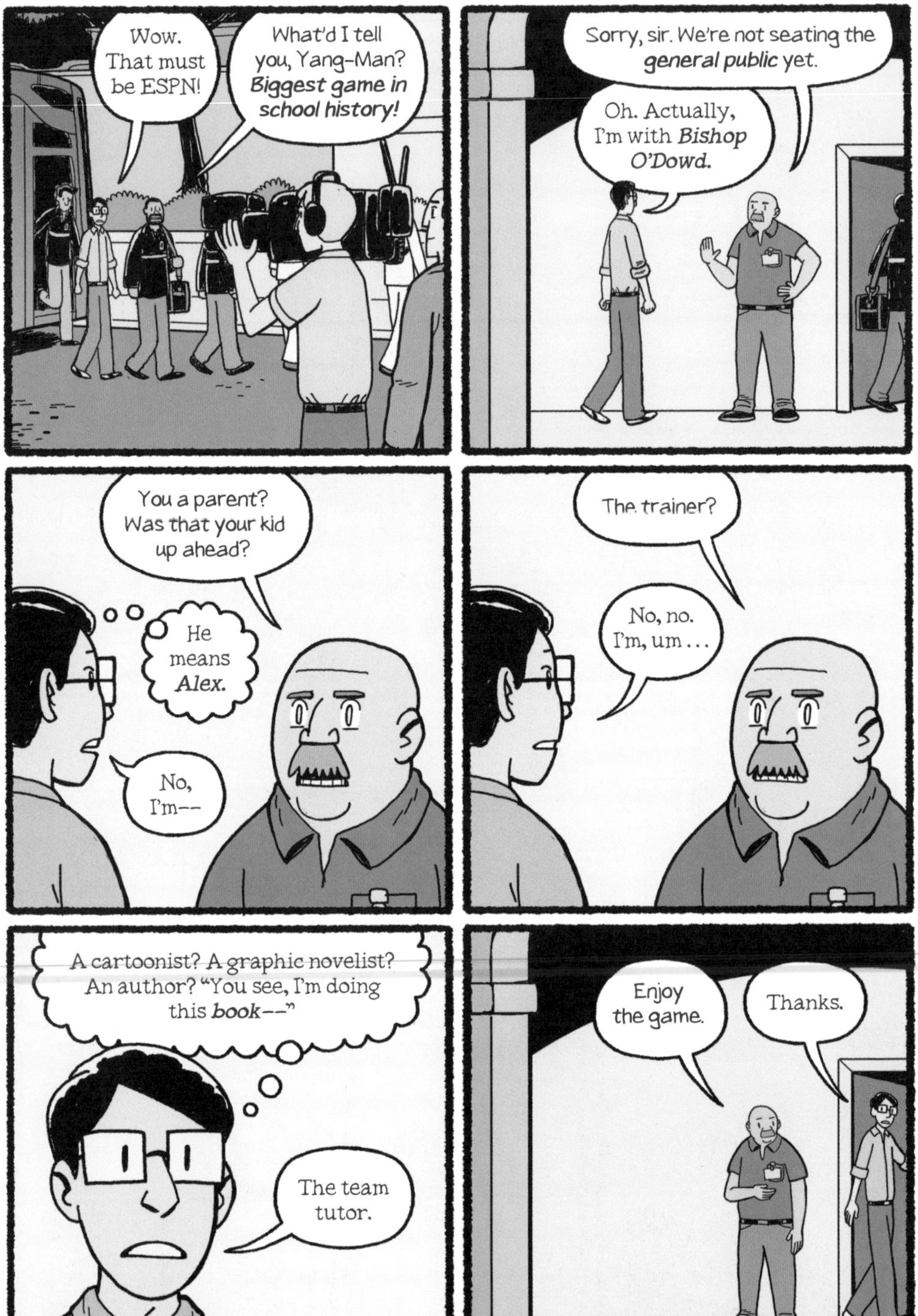
Wow. That must be ESPN!
What'd I tell you, Yang-Man? *Biggest game in school history!*
Sorry, sir. We're not seating the *general public* yet.
Oh. Actually, I'm with *Bishop O'Dowd.*
You a parent? Was that your kid up ahead?
He means *Alex.*
No, I'm--
The trainer?
No, no. I'm, um . . .
A cartoonist? A graphic novelist? An author? "You see, I'm doing this *book--*"
The team tutor.
Enjoy the game.
Thanks.

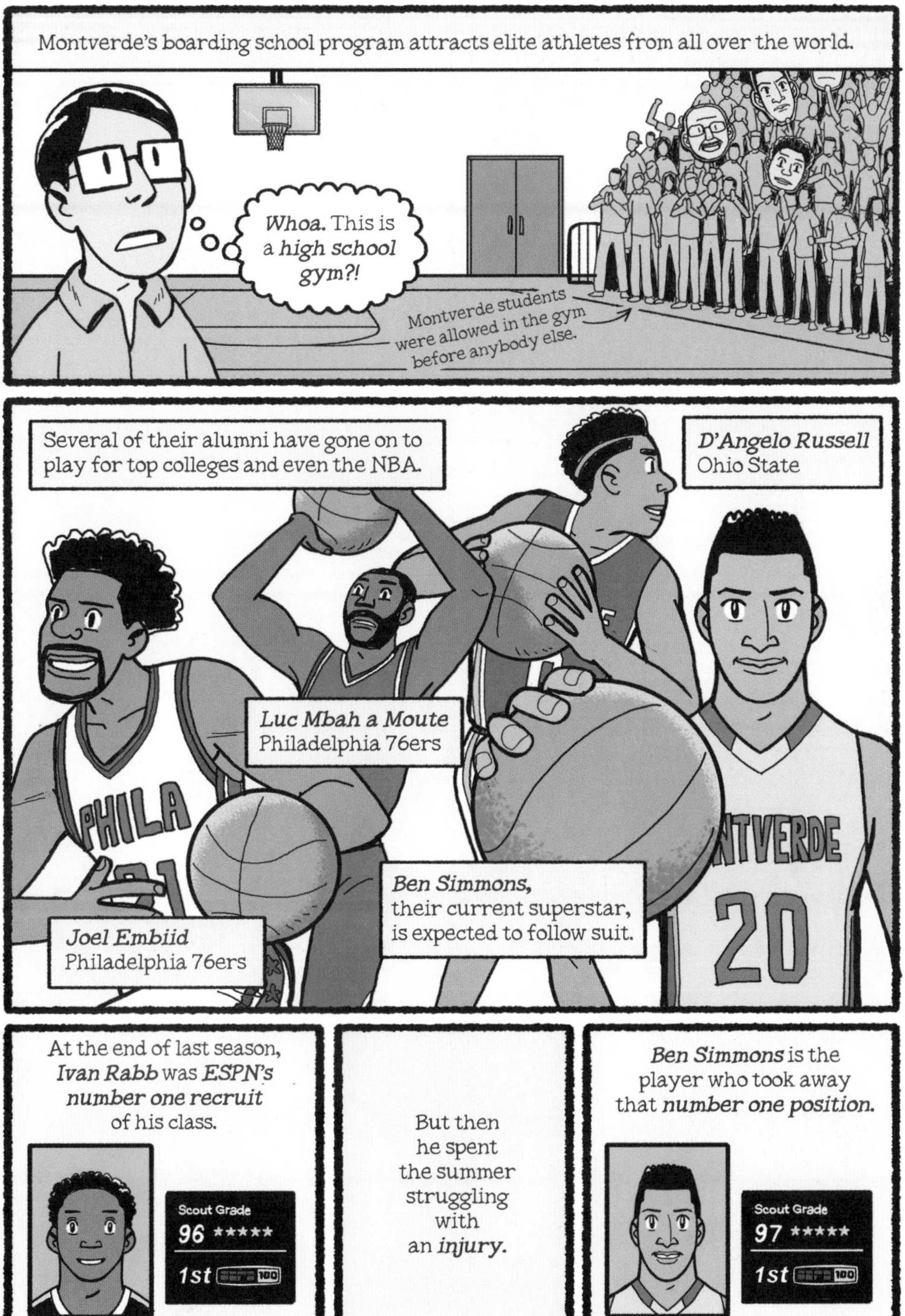
Montverde's boarding school program attracts elite athletes from all over the world.
Whoa. This is a *high school gym?!*
Montverde students were allowed in the gym before anybody else.
Several of their alumni have gone on to play for top colleges and even the NBA.
D'Angelo Russell Ohio State
Luc Mbah a Moute Philadelphia 76ers
PHILA
Ben Simmons, their current superstar, is expected to follow suit.
Joel Embiid Philadelphia 76ers
NTVERDE 20
At the end of last season, *Ivan Rabb* was *ESPN's number one recruit* of his class.
Scout Grade 96 ★★★★★ 1st
But then he spent the summer struggling with an *injury.*
Ben Simmons is the player who took away that *number one position.*
Scout Grade 97 ★★★★★ 1st

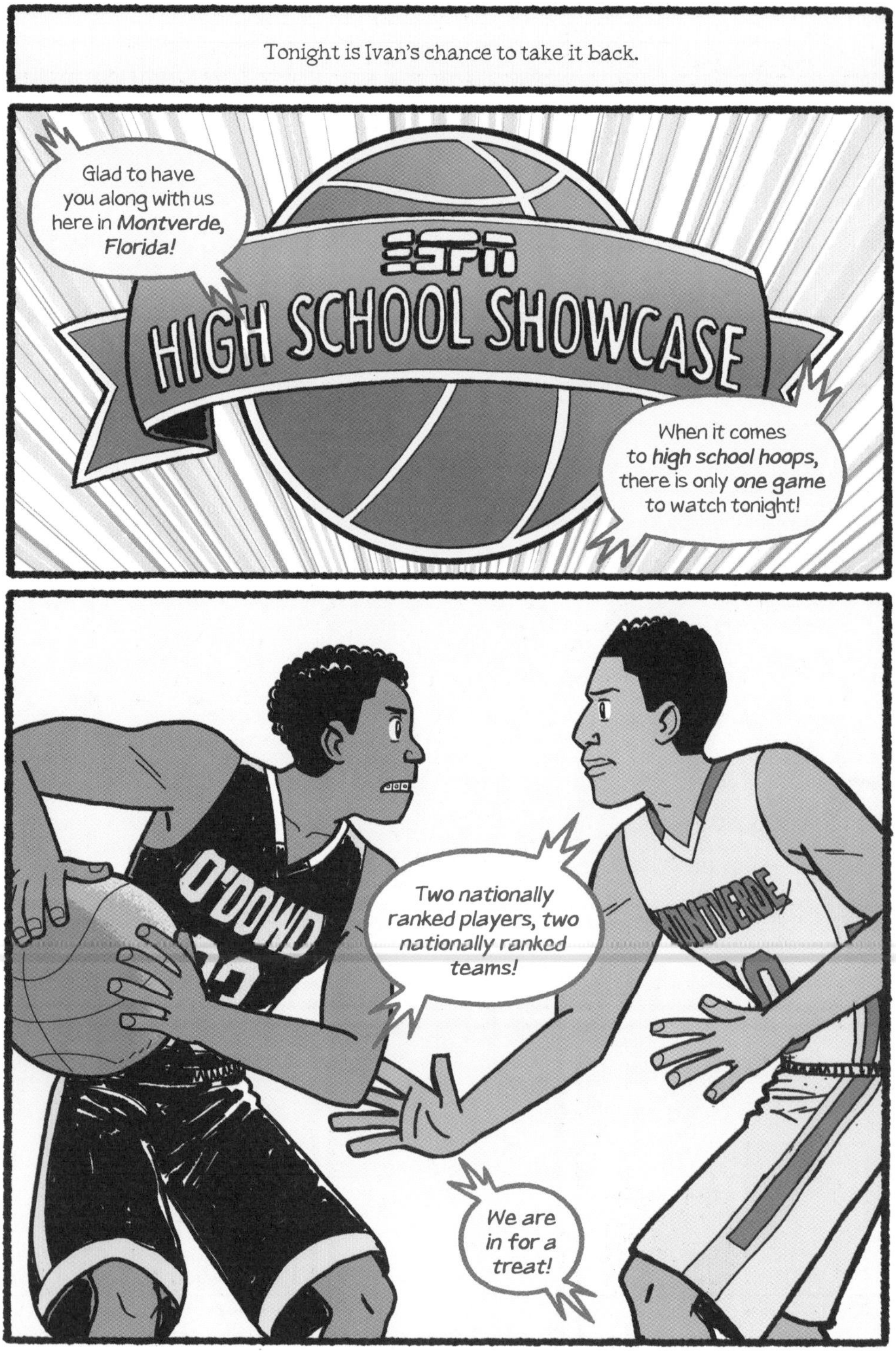
Tonight is Ivan's chance to take it back.
Glad to have you along with us here in *Montverde, Florida!*
ESPN
HIGH SCHOOL SHOWCASE
When it comes to ***high school hoops,*** there is only ***one game*** to watch tonight!
O'DOWD
MONTVERDE
Two nationally ranked players, two nationally ranked teams!
We are in for a treat!

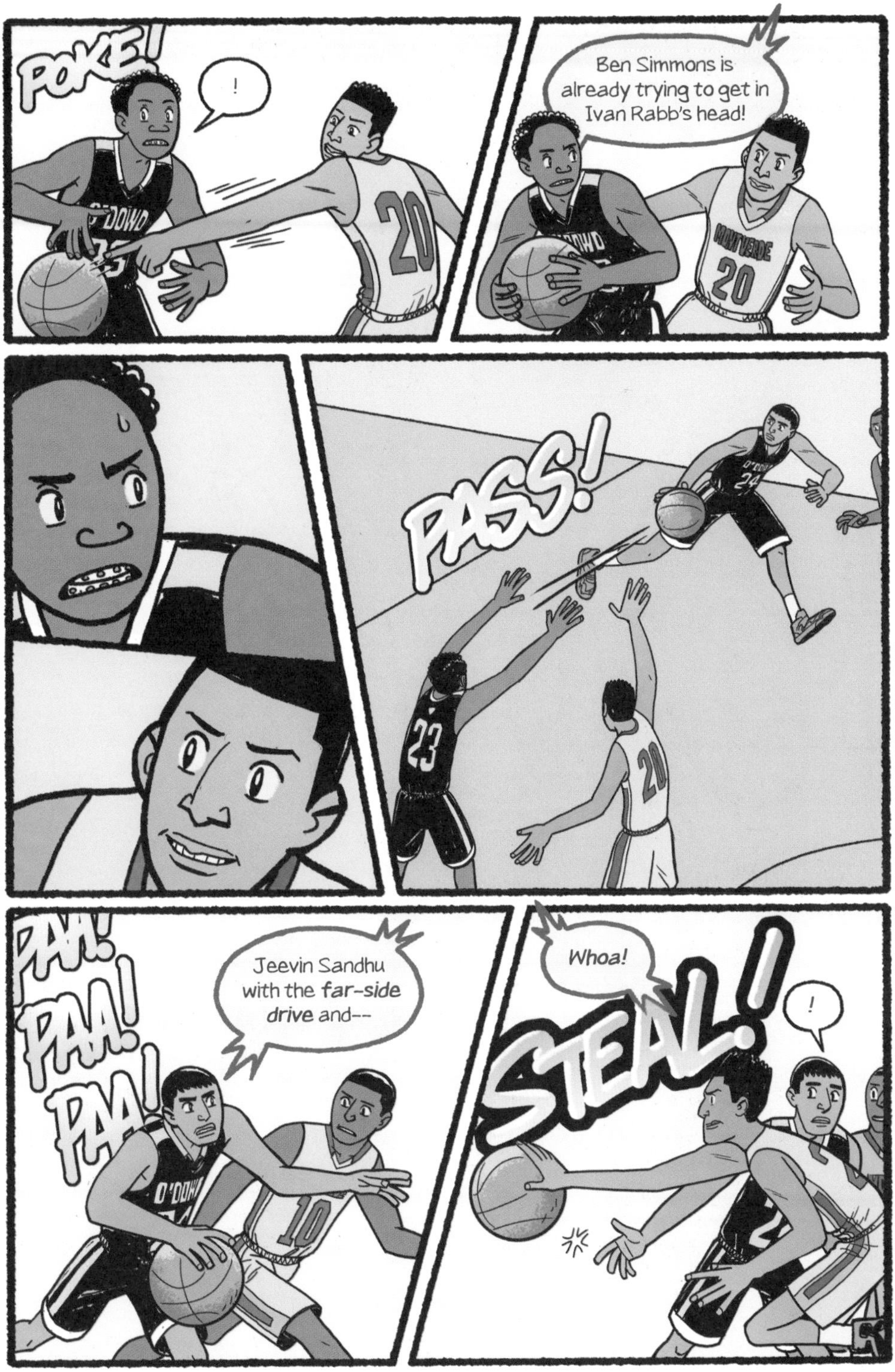
POKE!
!
Ben Simmons is already trying to get in Ivan Rabb's head!
PASS!
PAA! PAA! PAA!
Jeevin Sandhu with the **far-side drive** and--
Whoa!
STEAL!
!

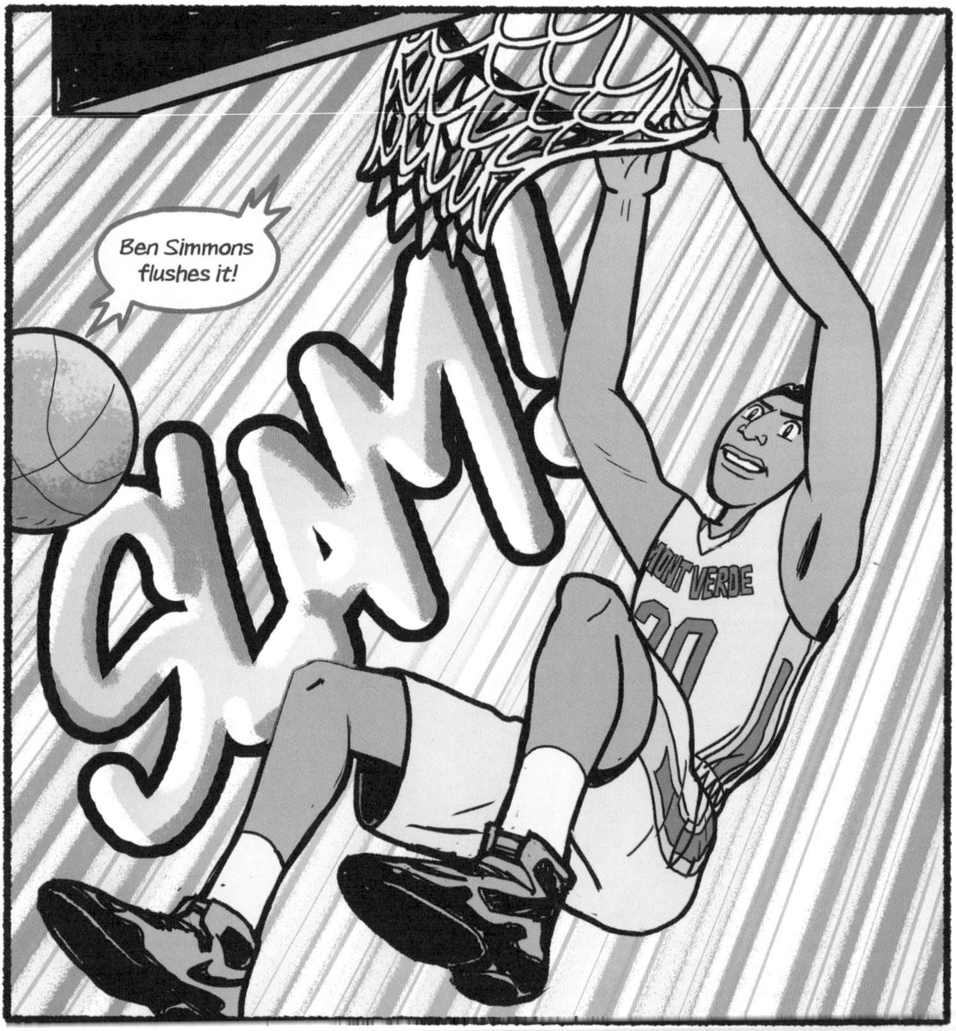
Ben Simmons flushes it!
SLAM!
MONTVERDE
20

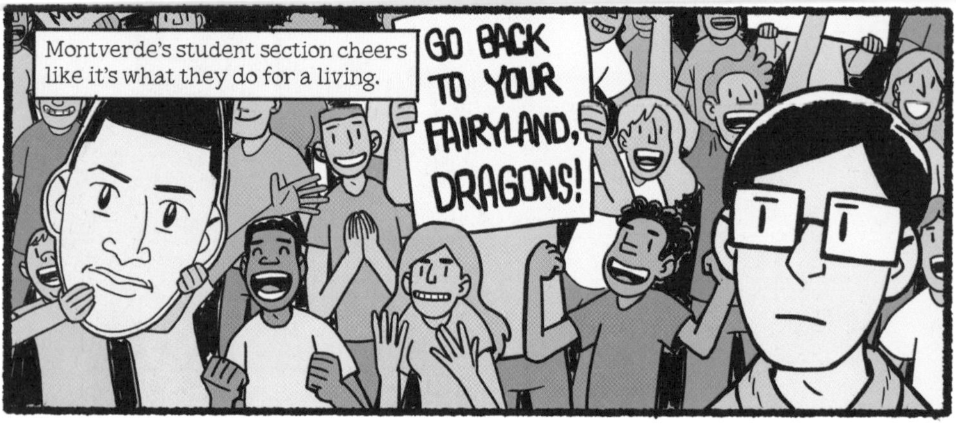
Montverde's student section cheers like it's what they do for a living.
GO BACK TO YOUR FAIRYLAND, DRAGONS!

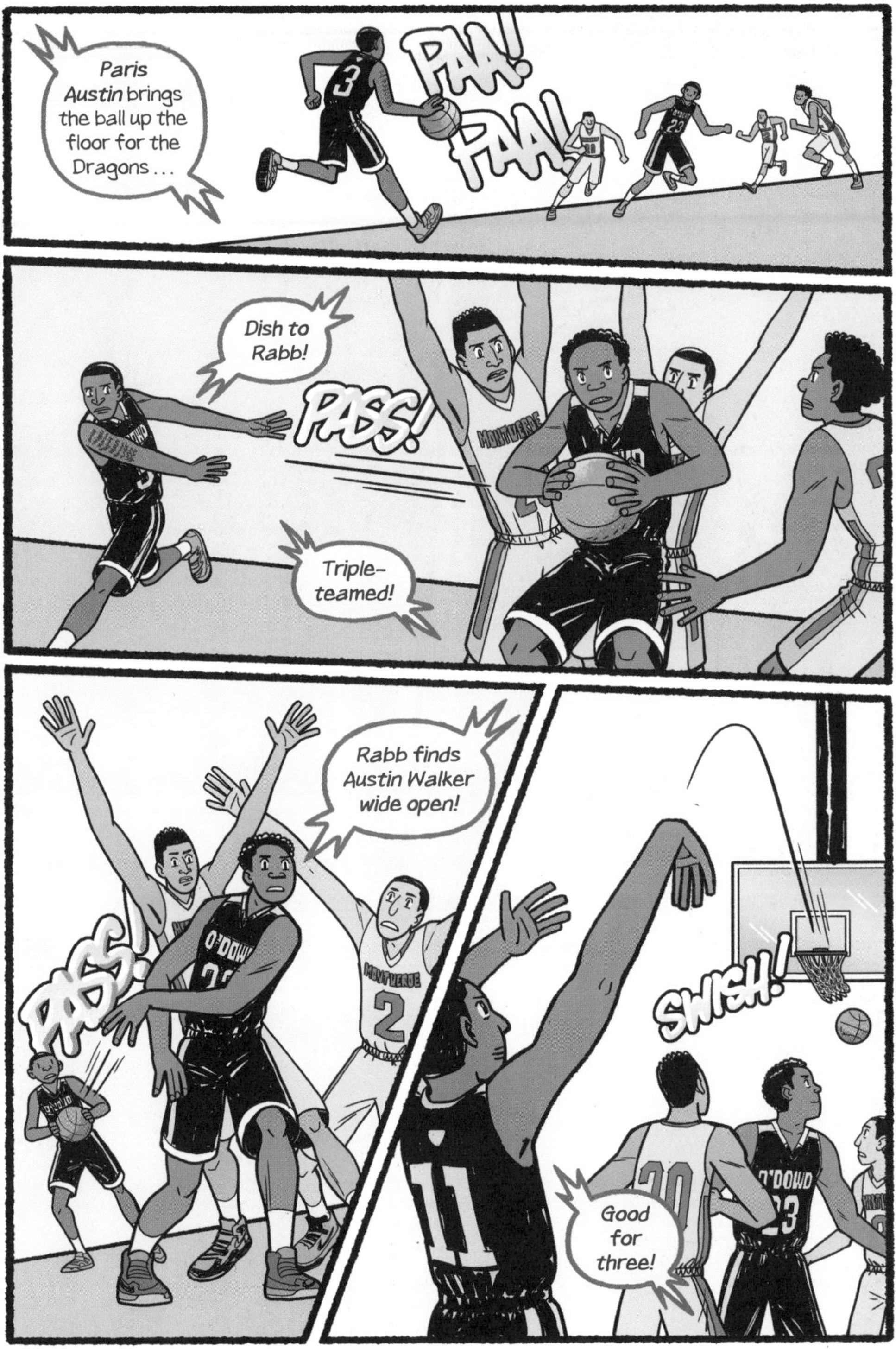
Paris Austin brings the ball up the floor for the Dragons . . .
PAA!
PAA!
Dish to Rabb!
PASS!
Triple-teamed!
Rabb finds Austin Walker wide open!
PASS!
O'DOWD
MONTVERDE
2
SWISH!
O'DOWD
Good for three!

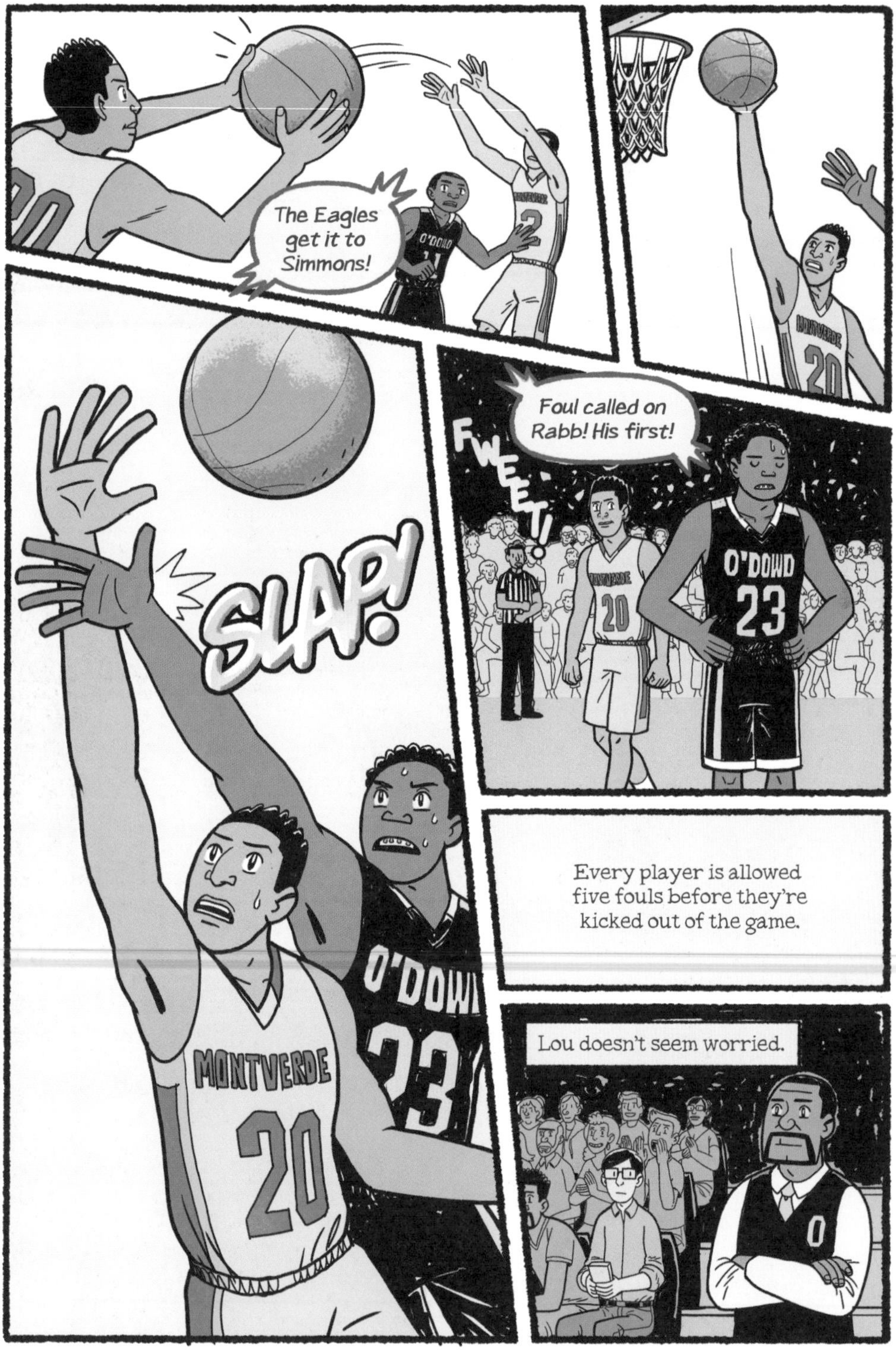
The Eagles get it to Simmons!
SLAP!
FWEET!
Foul called on Rabb! His first!
Every player is allowed five fouls before they're kicked out of the game.
Lou doesn't seem worried.

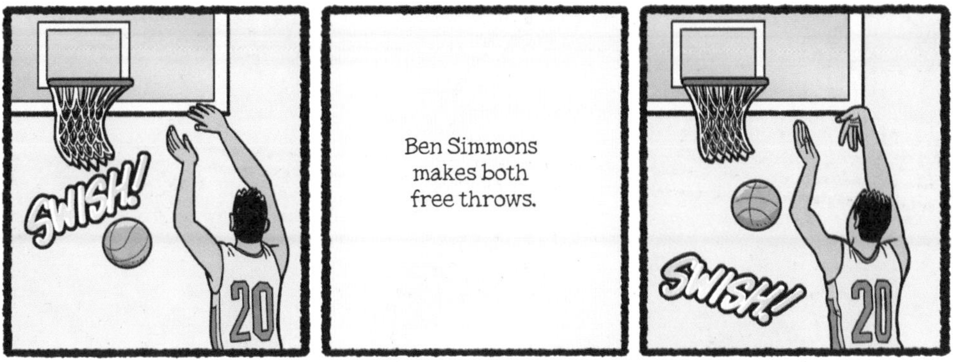
SWISH!
Ben Simmons makes both free throws.
SWISH!

The first quarter ends with the score all ***tied up.***

BISHOP O'DOWD DRAGONS	17
MONTVERDE EAGLES	17
0:00 PERIOD	1

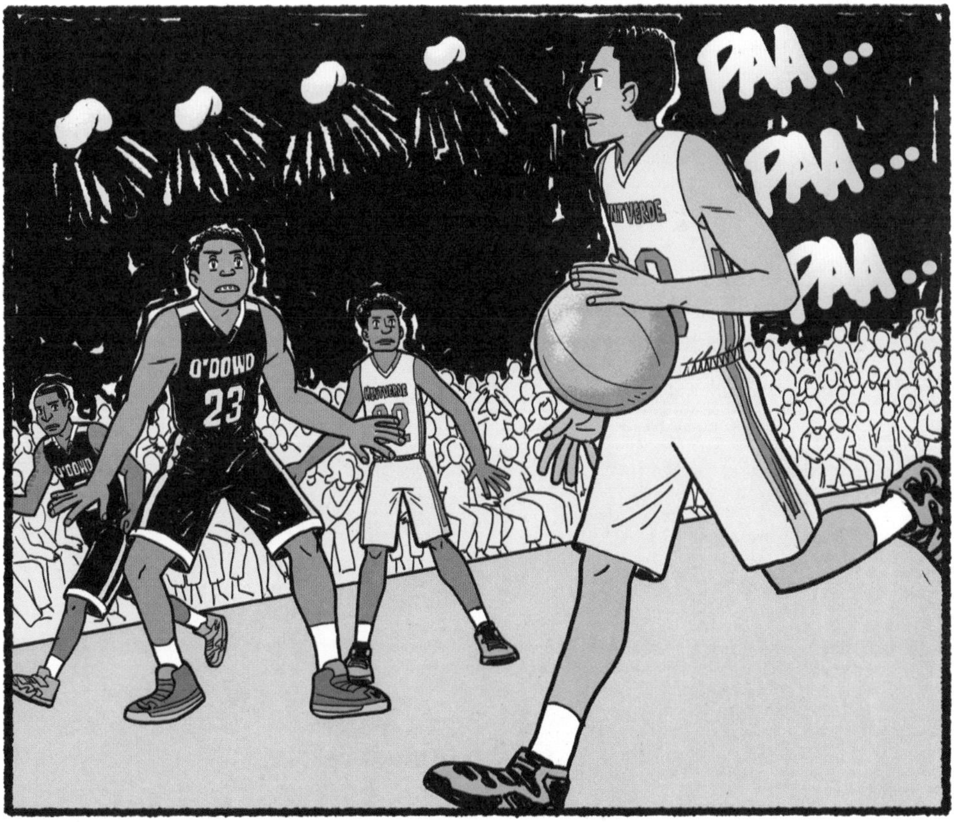
PAA...
PAA...
PAA...

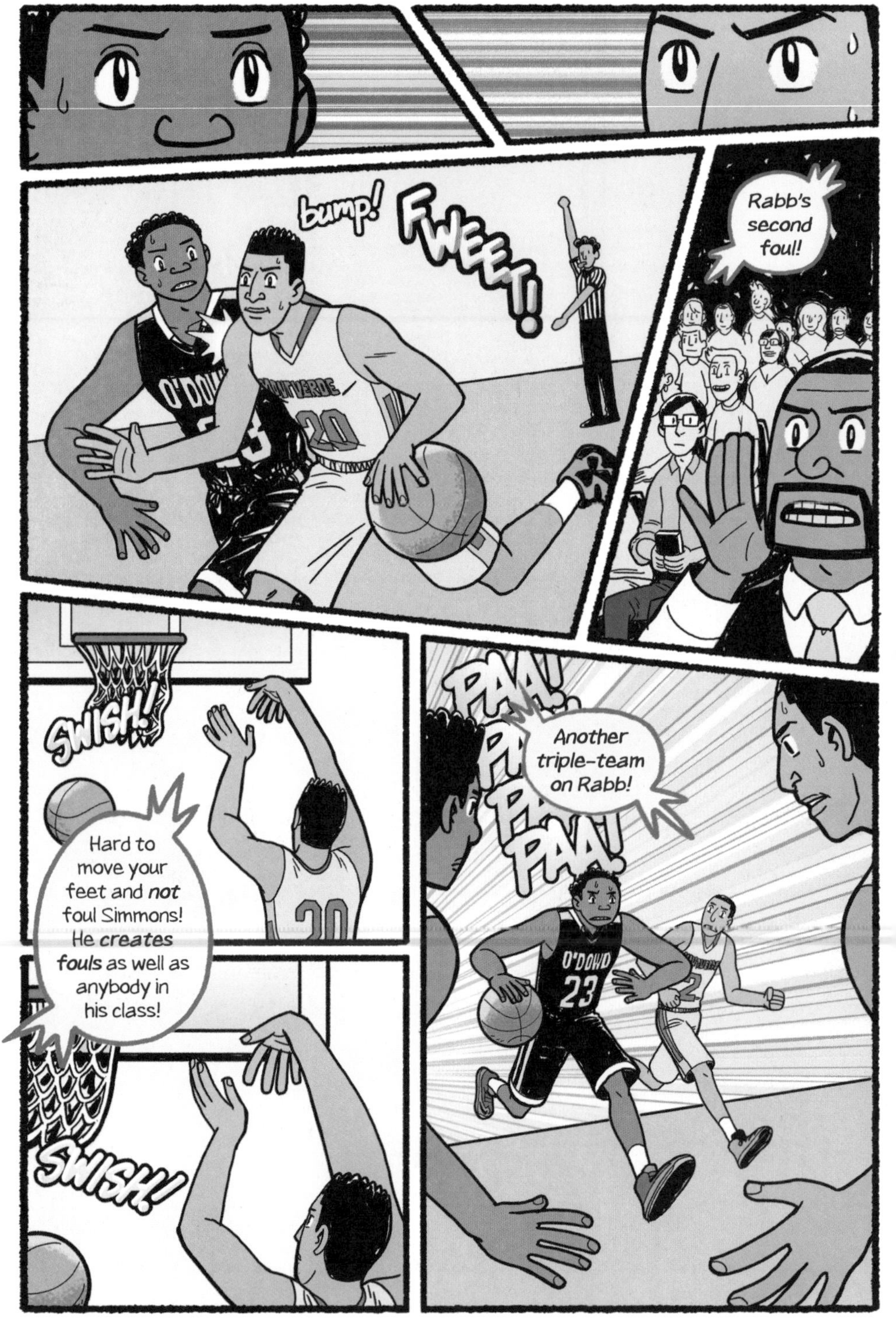
bump!
FWEET!
Rabb's second foul!
SWISH!
Hard to move your feet and *not* foul Simmons! He ***creates fouls*** as well as anybody in his class!
SWISH!
PAA! PAA! PAA! PAA!
Another triple-team on Rabb!

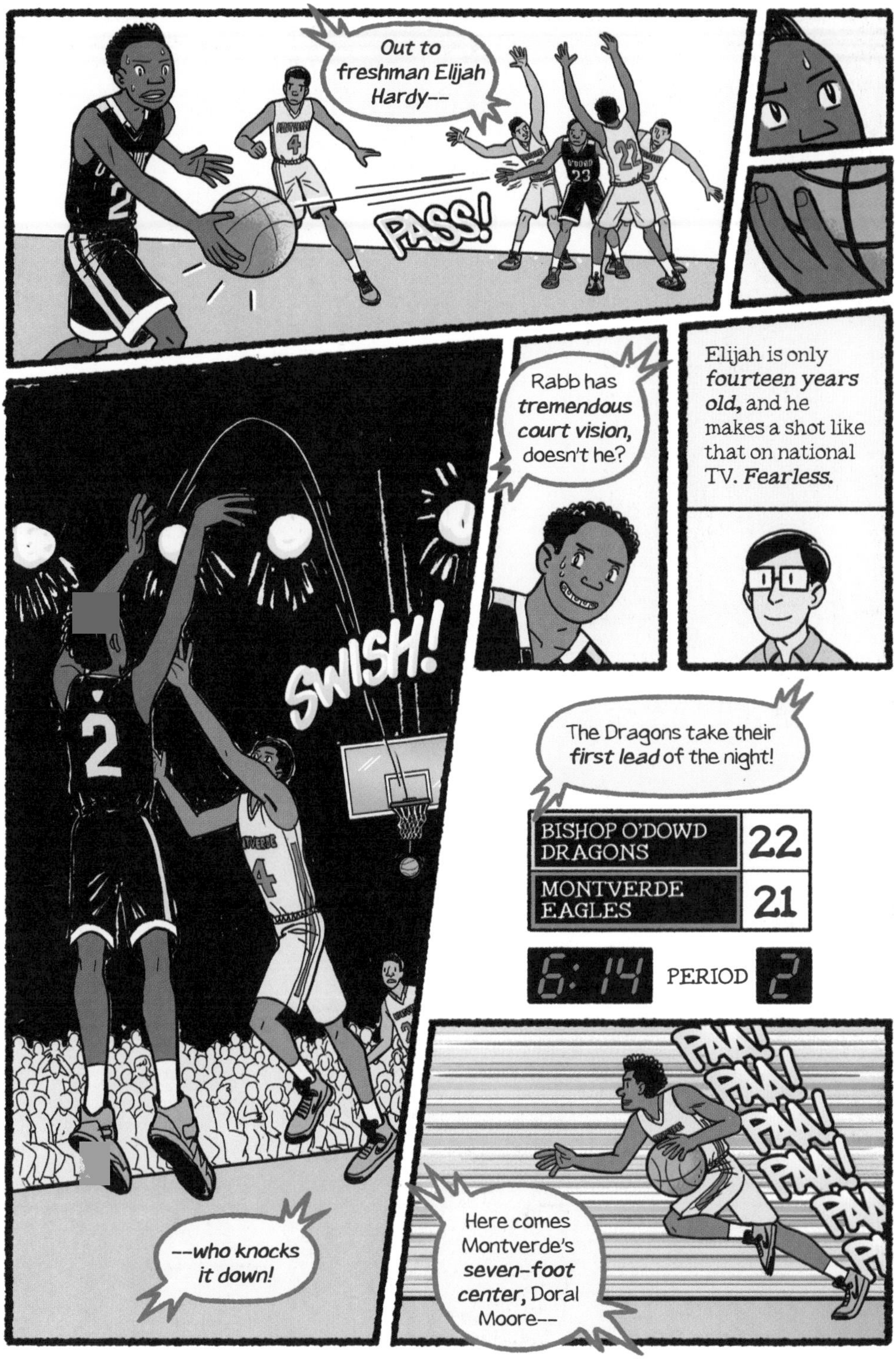

Out to freshman Elijah Hardy--
PASS!
SWISH!
--who knocks it down!
Rabb has *tremendous court vision,* doesn't he?
Elijah is only *fourteen years old,* and he makes a shot like that on national TV. *Fearless.*
The Dragons take their *first lead* of the night!
BISHOP O'DOWD DRAGONS 22
MONTVERDE EAGLES 21
6:14 PERIOD 2
PAA! PAA! PAA! PAA! PAA!
Here comes Montverde's *seven-foot center,* Doral Moore--

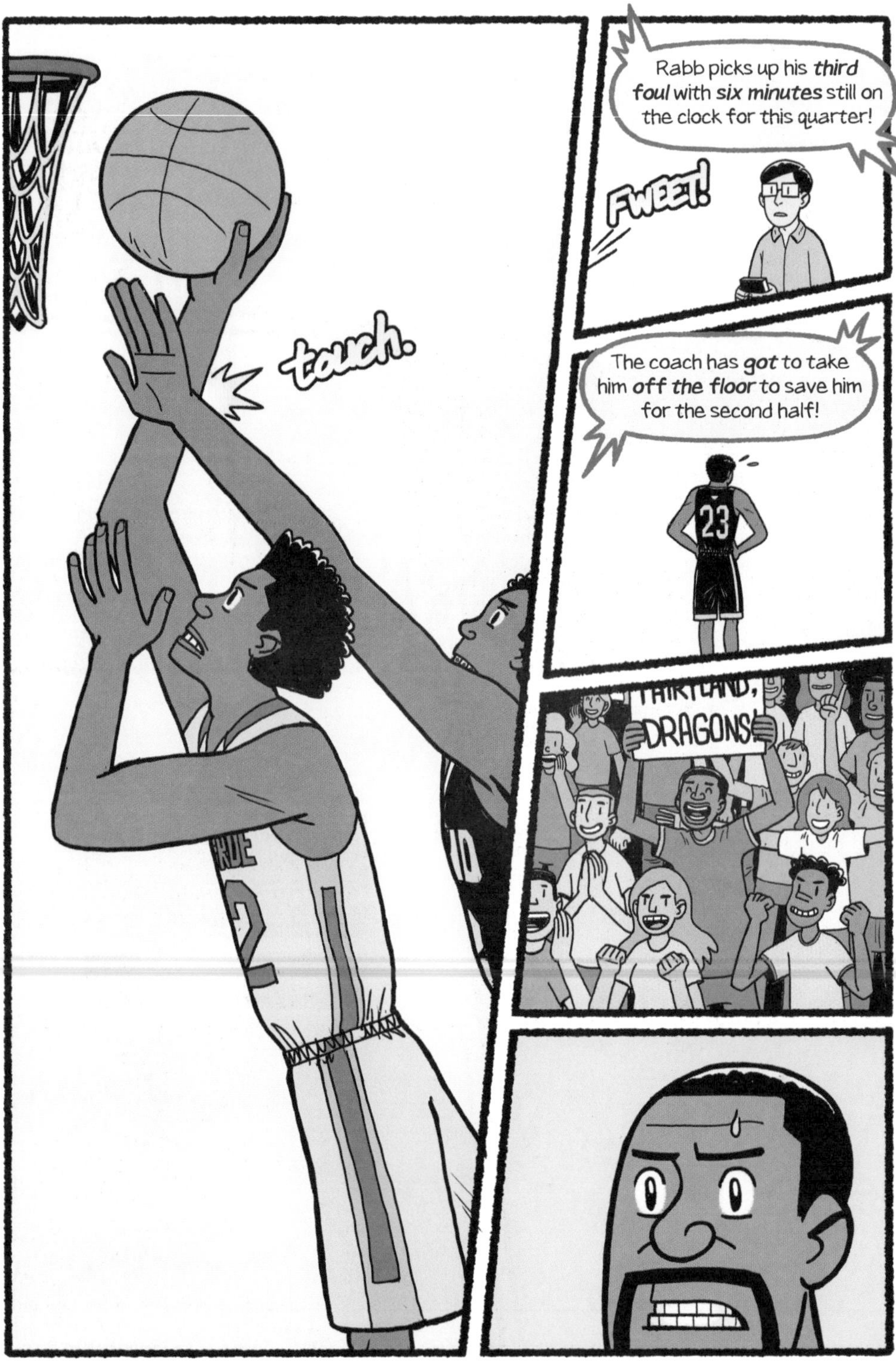
touch.
Rabb picks up his *third foul* with *six minutes* still on the clock for this quarter!
FWEET!
The coach has *got* to take him *off the floor* to save him for the second half!
23
FAIRYLAND, DRAGONS!

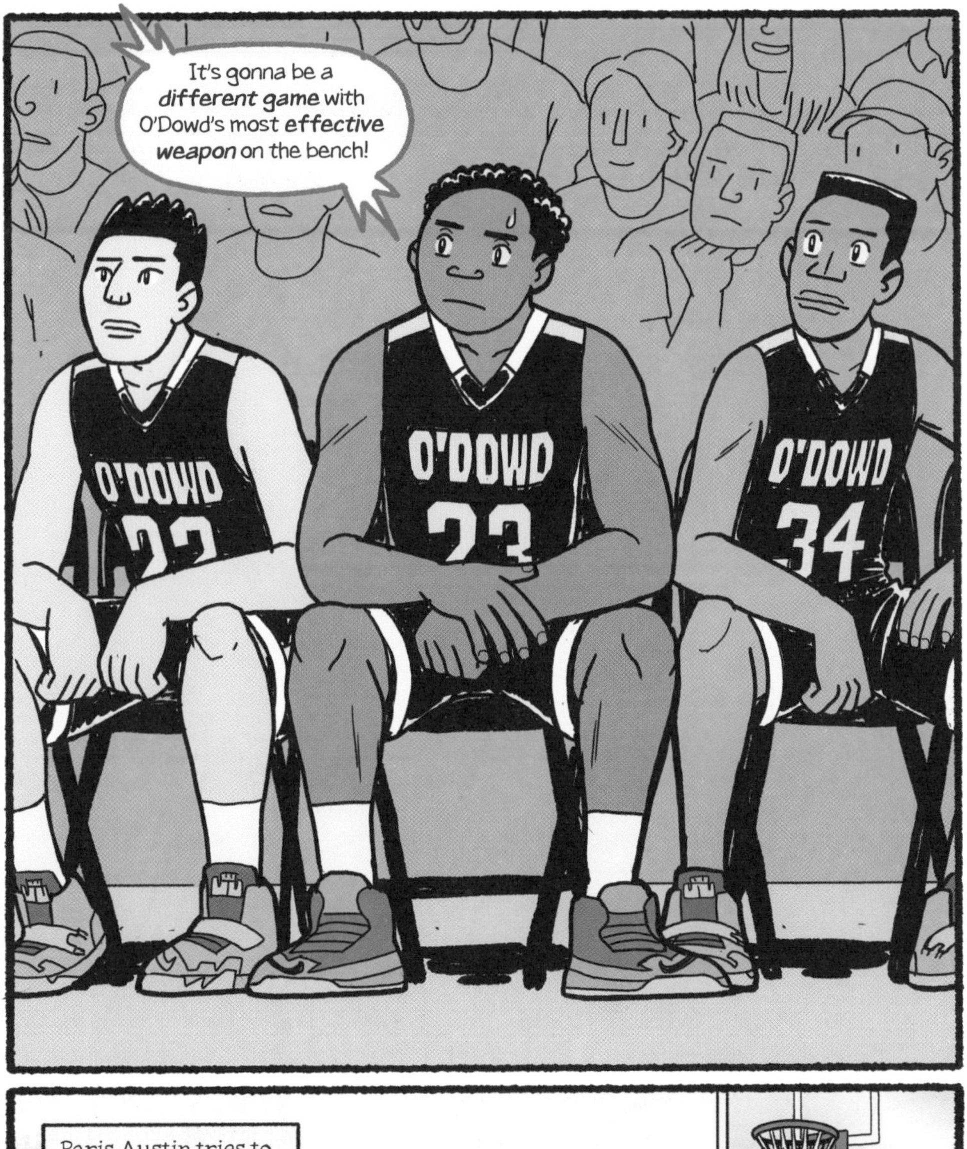
It's gonna be a *different game* with O'Dowd's most *effective weapon* on the bench!

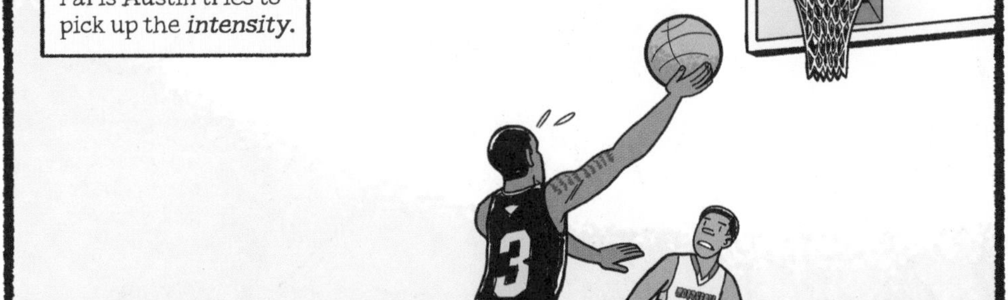
Paris Austin tries to pick up the *intensity.*

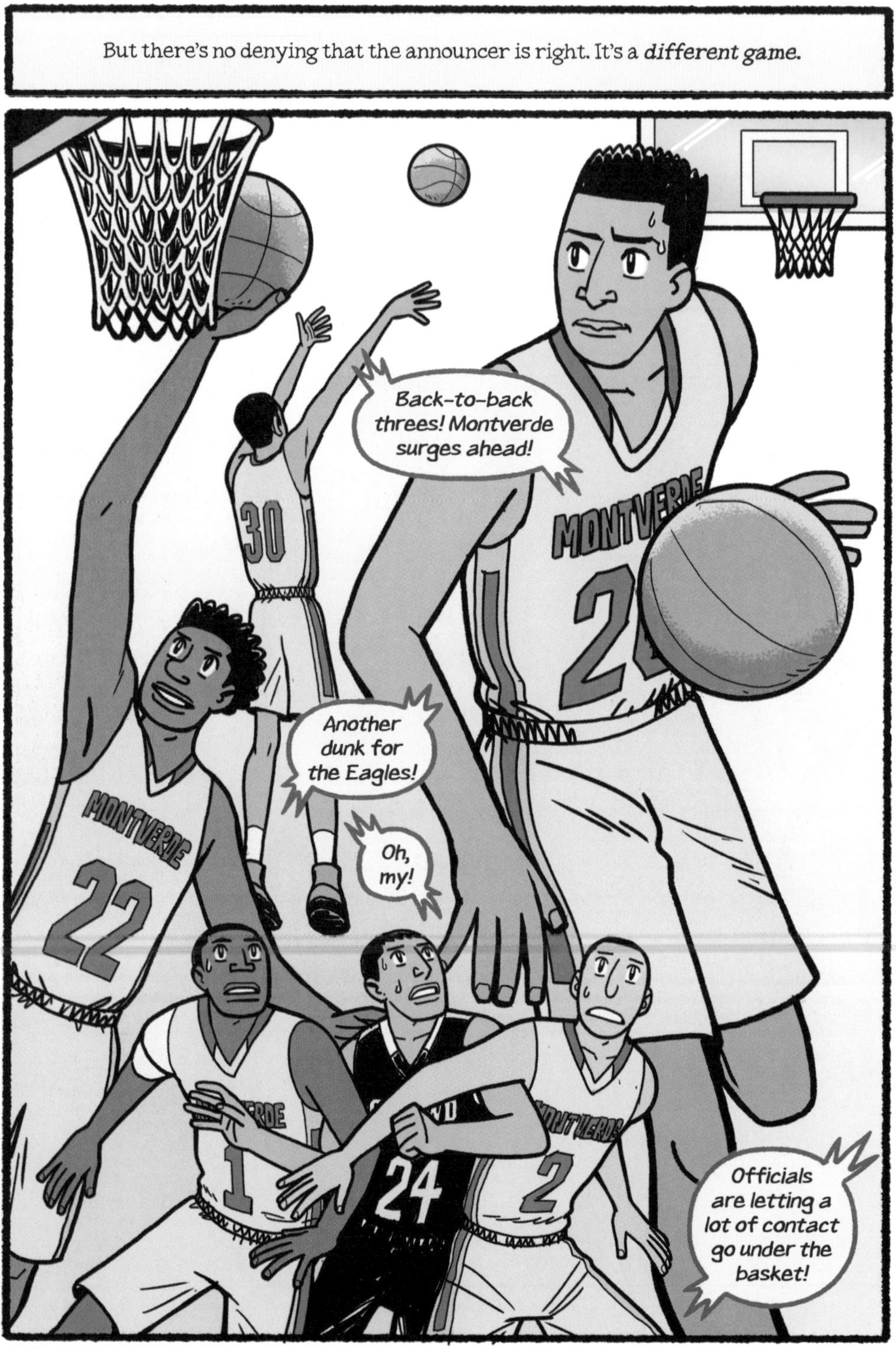
But there's no denying that the announcer is right. It's a *different game.*
Back-to-back threes! Montverde surges ahead!
30
MONTVERDE
20
Another dunk for the Eagles!
MONTVERDE
22
Oh, my!
1
24
MONTVERDE
2
Officials are letting a lot of contact go under the basket!

The Eagles have a *decisive lead* by the end of the half.

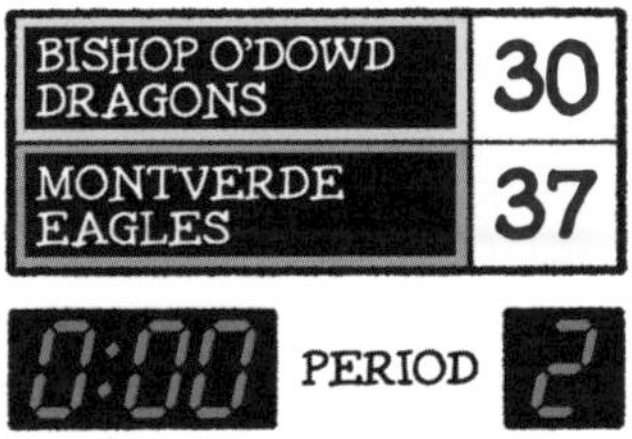
BISHOP O'DOWD DRAGONS
30
MONTVERDE EAGLES
37
0:00
PERIOD
2

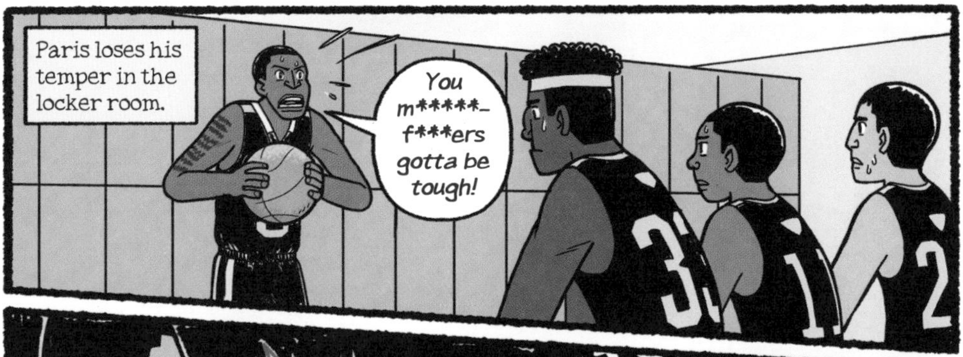
Paris loses his temper in the locker room.
You m*****_ f***ers gotta be tough!

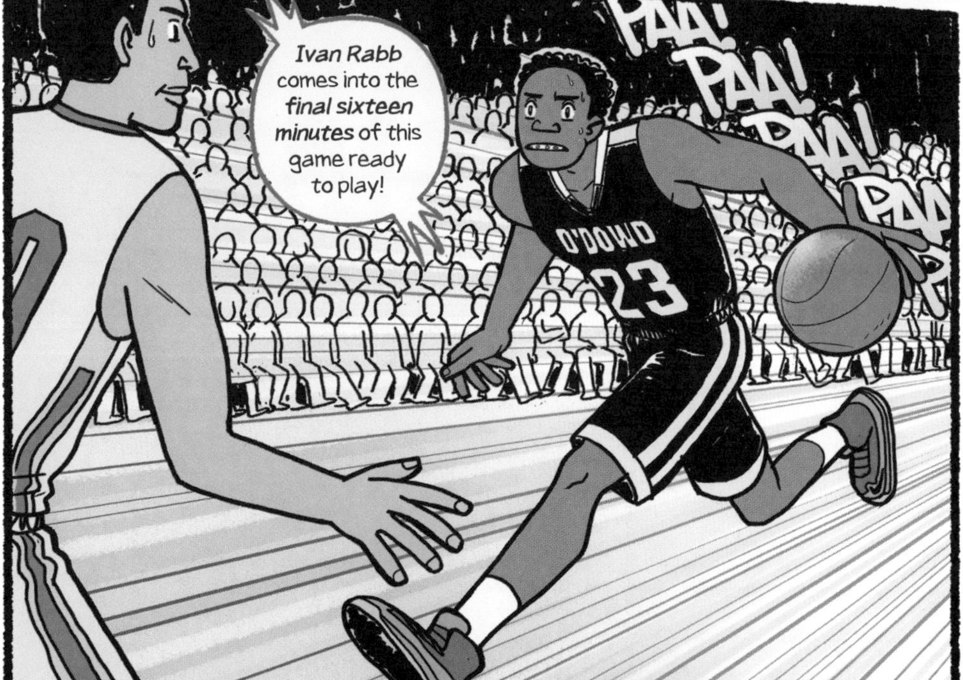
Ivan Rabb comes into the final sixteen minutes of this game ready to play!
PAA! PAA! PAA! PAA!
O'DOWD
23

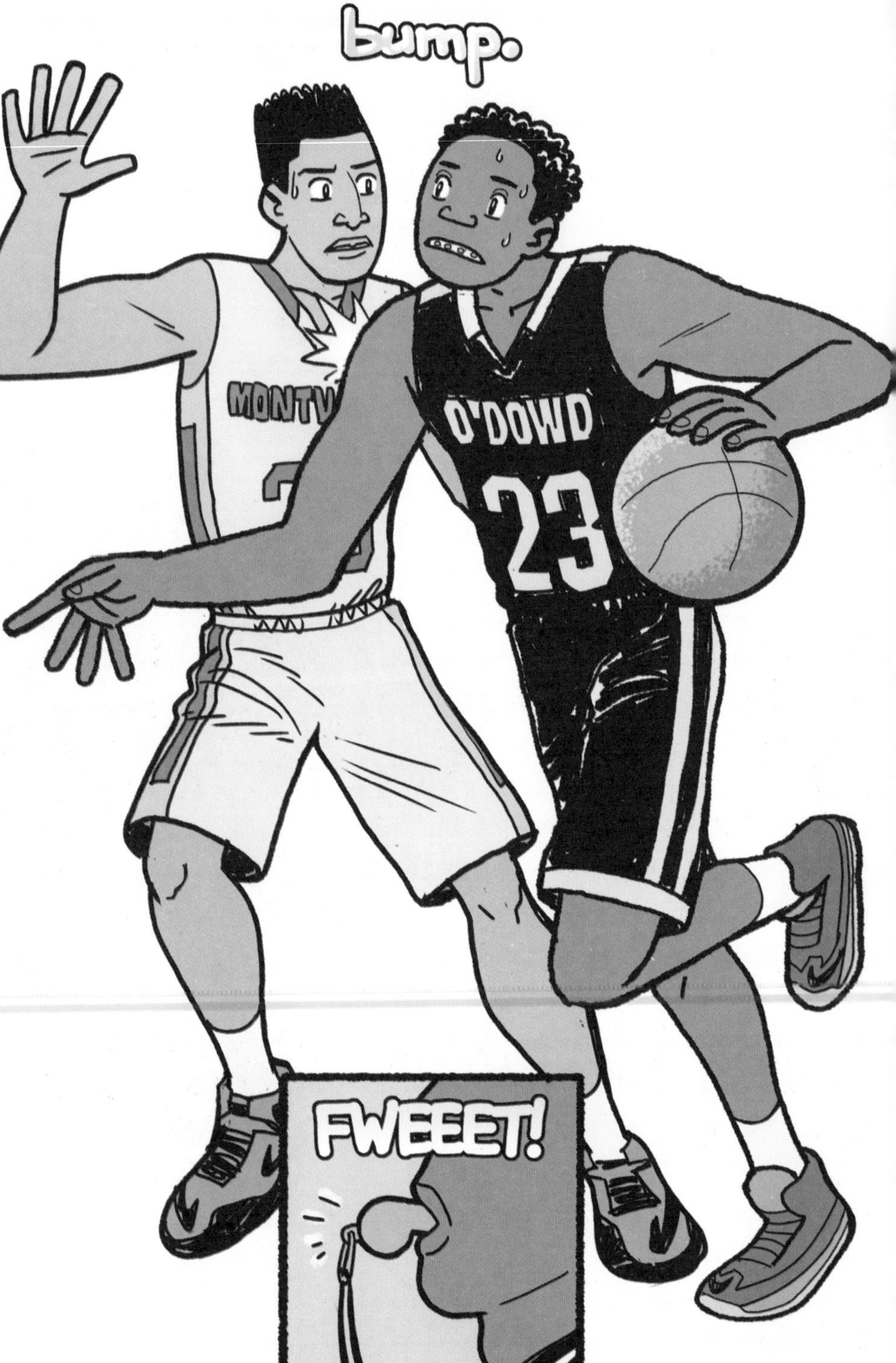
bump.
MONTV
O'DOWD
23
FWEEET!

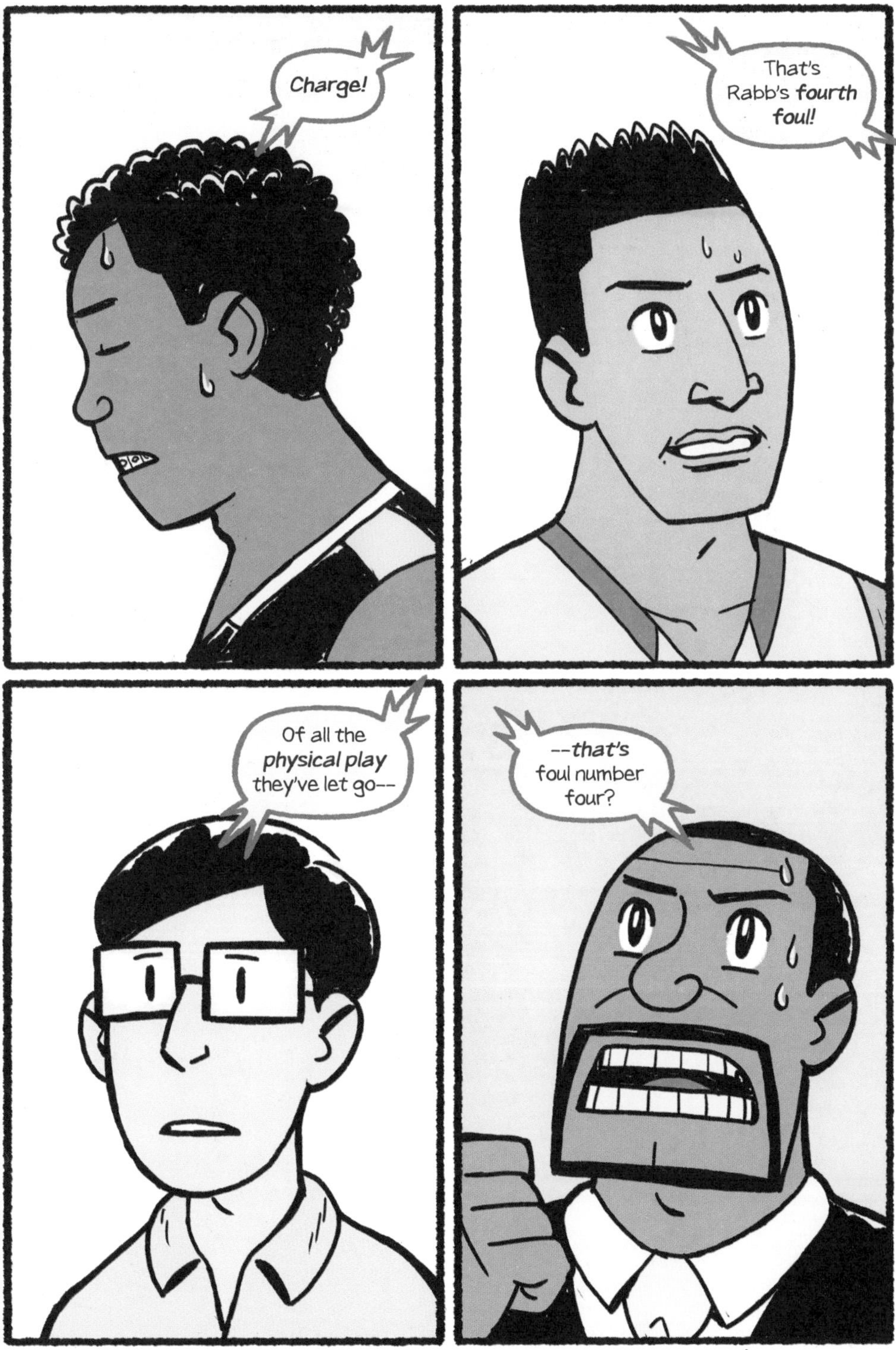
Charge!
That's Rabb's **fourth foul!**
Of all the ***physical play*** they've let go--
--***that's*** foul number four?

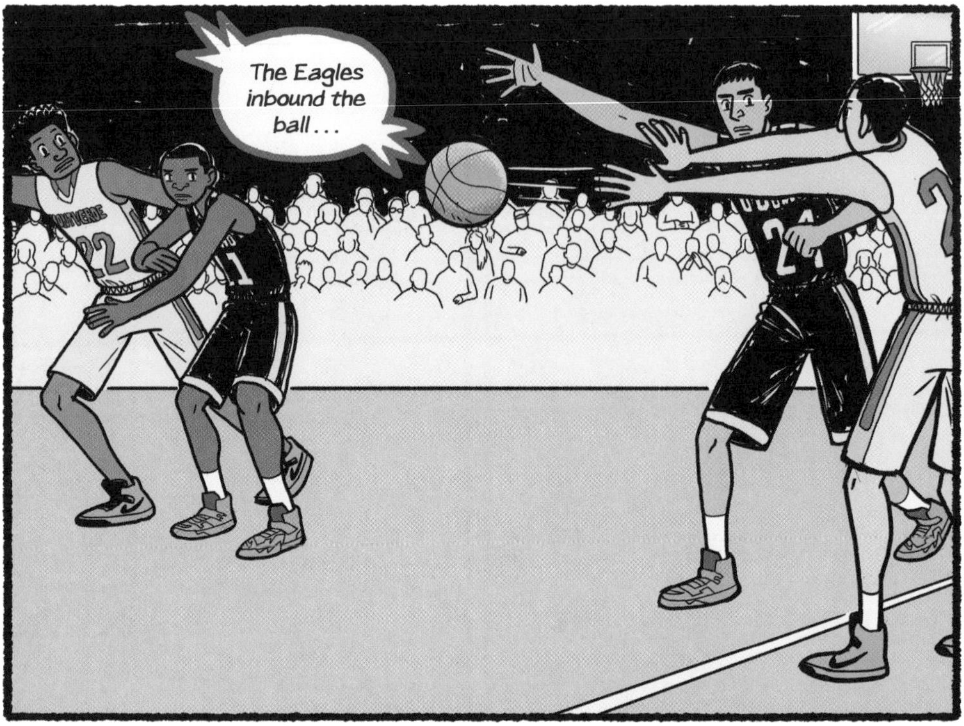
The Eagles inbound the ball . . .

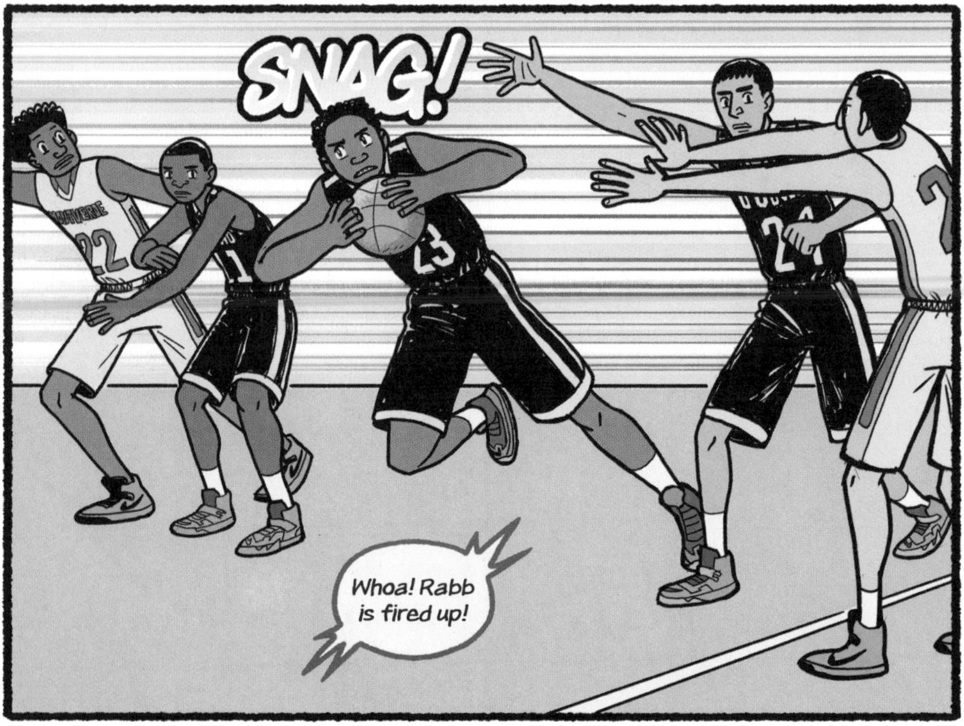
SNAG!
Whoa! Rabb is fired up!

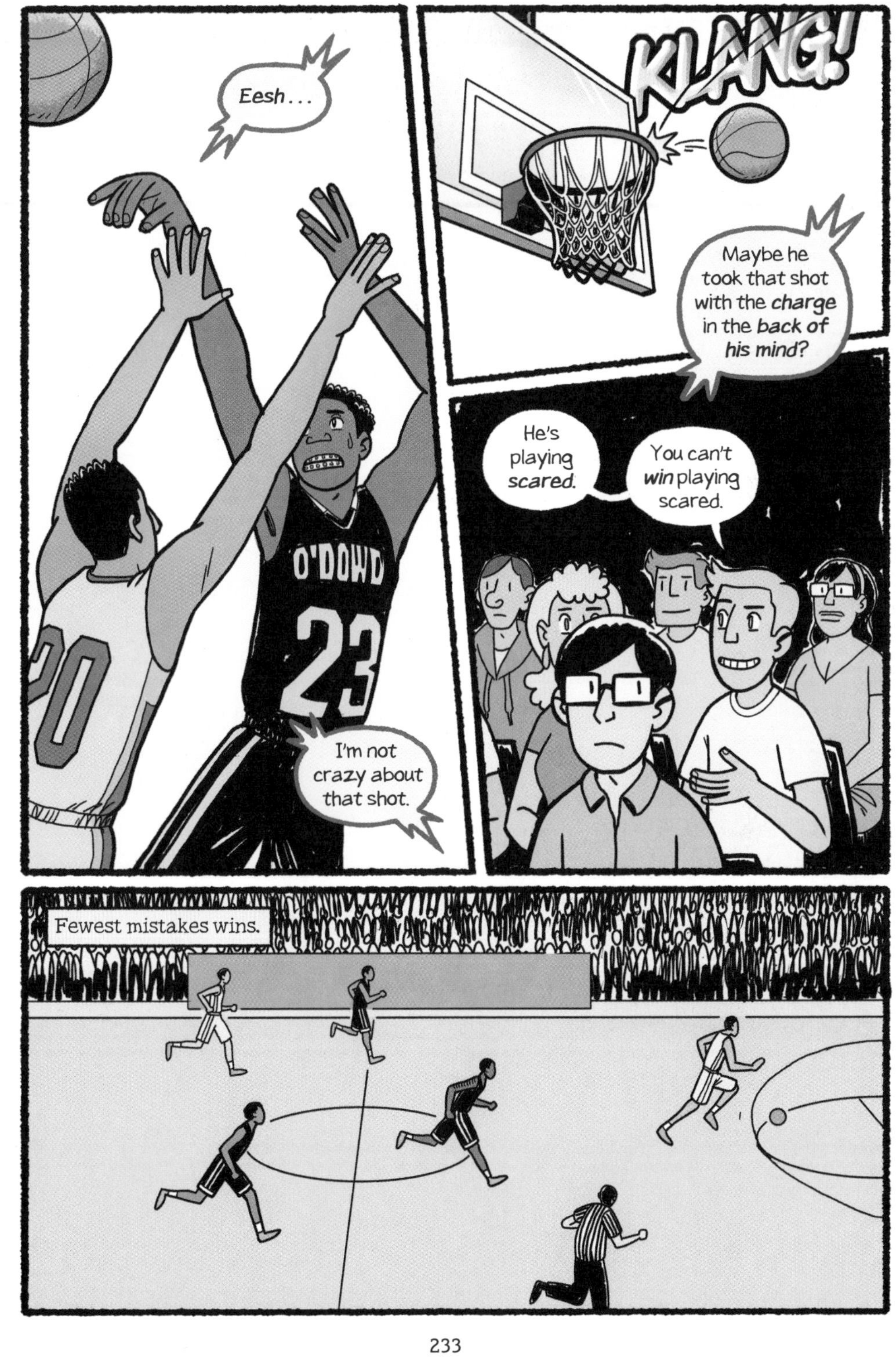
Eesh...
O'DOWD
23
I'm not crazy about that shot.
KLANG!
Maybe he took that shot with the *charge* in the *back of his mind?*
He's playing *scared.*
You can't *win* playing scared.
Fewest mistakes wins.

BISHOP O'DOWD DRAGONS	64
MONTVERDE EAGLES	78

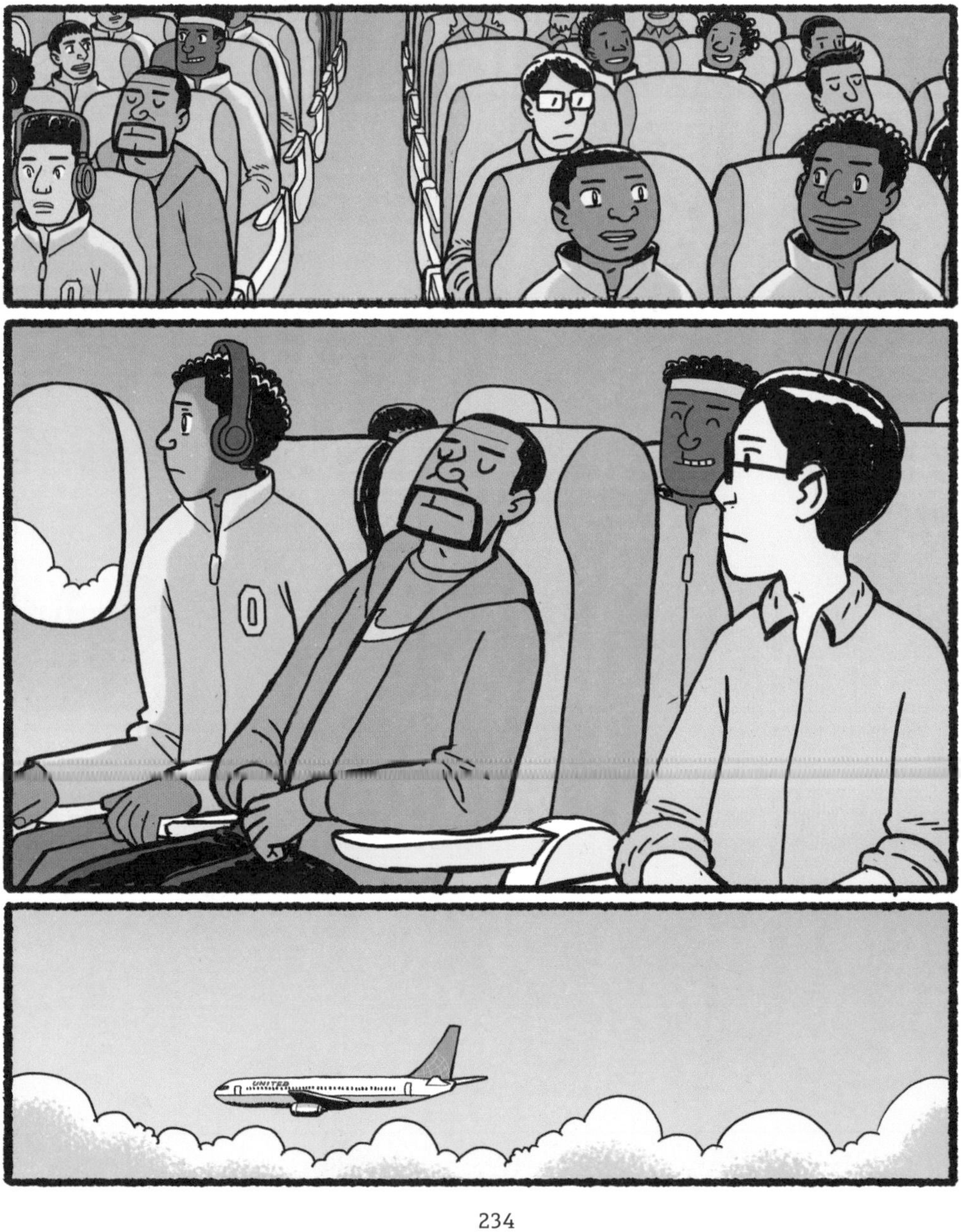
UNITED

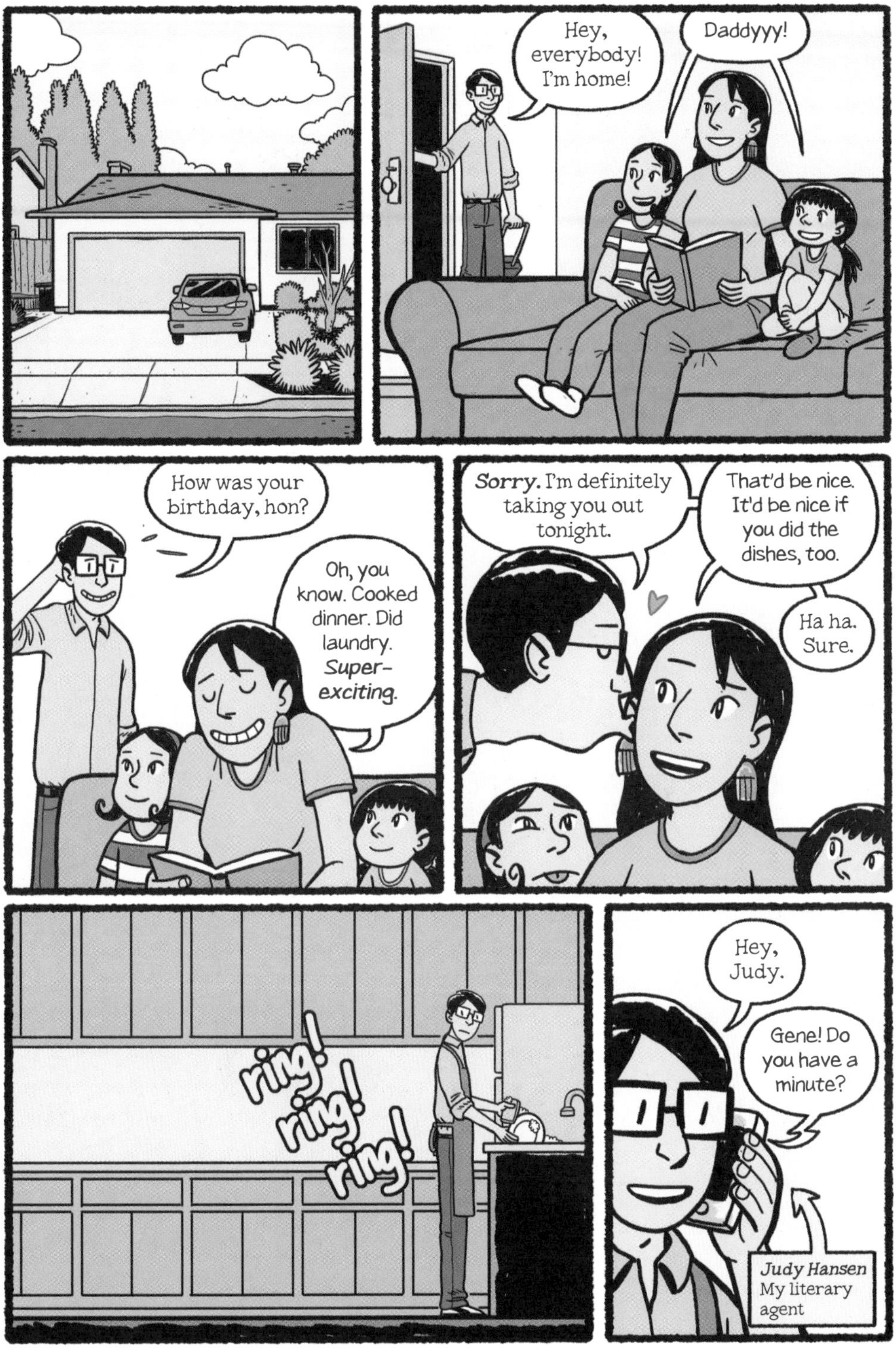
Hey, everybody! I'm home!
Daddyyy!
How was your birthday, hon?
Oh, you know. Cooked dinner. Did laundry. *Super-exciting.*
Sorry. I'm definitely taking you out tonight.
That'd be nice. It'd be nice if you did the dishes, too.
Ha ha. Sure.
ring! ring! ring!
Hey, Judy.
Gene! Do you have a minute?
Judy Hansen My literary agent

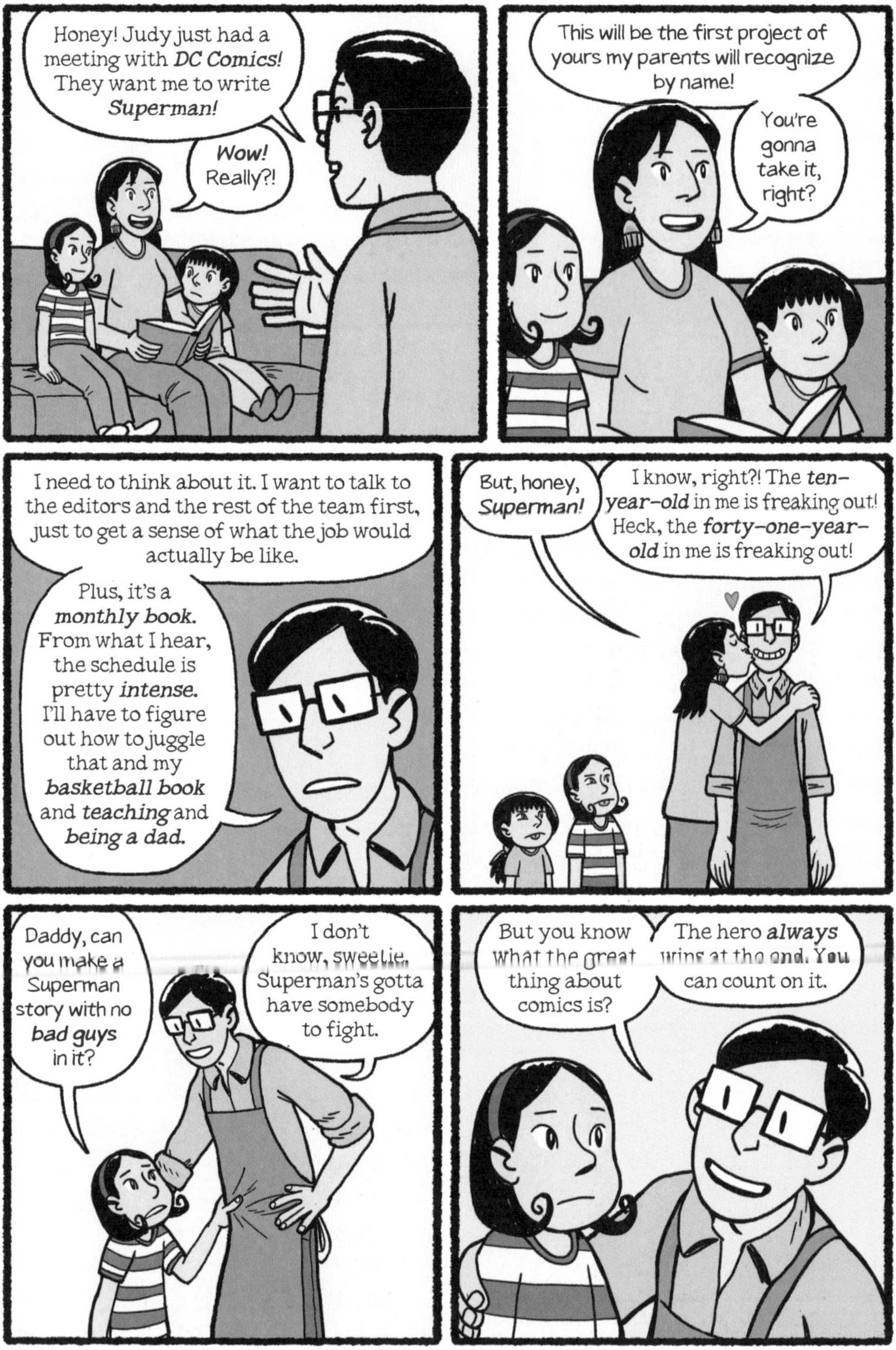
Honey! Judy just had a meeting with DC Comics! They want me to write Superman!
Wow! Really?!
This will be the first project of yours my parents will recognize by name!
You're gonna take it, right?
I need to think about it. I want to talk to the editors and the rest of the team first, just to get a sense of what the job would actually be like.
Plus, it's a monthly book. From what I hear, the schedule is pretty intense. I'll have to figure out how to juggle that and my basketball book and teaching and being a dad.
But, honey, Superman!
I know, right?! The ten-year-old in me is freaking out! Heck, the forty-one-year-old in me is freaking out!
Daddy, can you make a Superman story with no bad guys in it?
I don't know, sweetie. Superman's gotta have somebody to fight.
But you know what the great thing about comics is?
The hero always wins at the end. You can count on it.

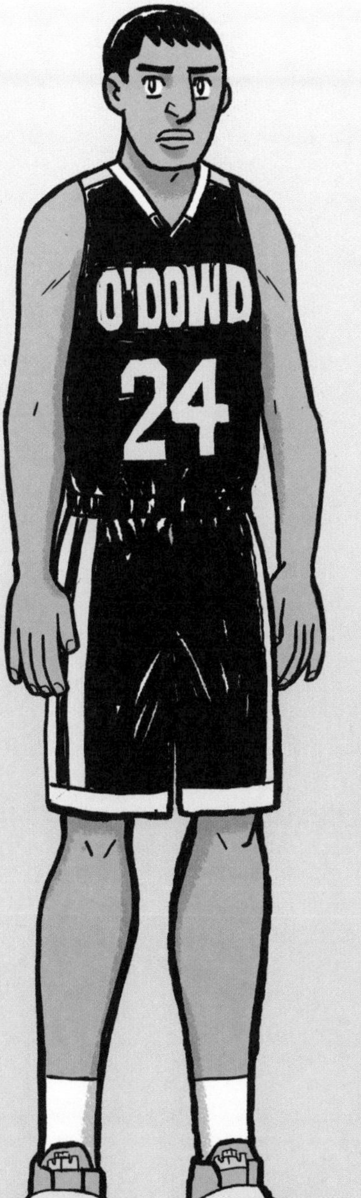
O'DOWD
24

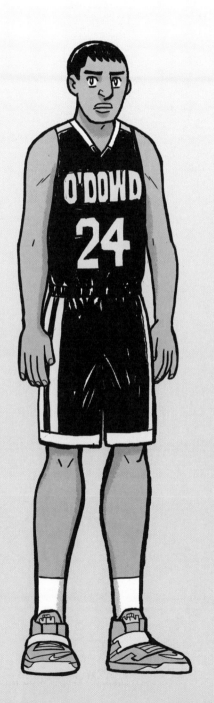

CHAPTER 8:
JEEVIN

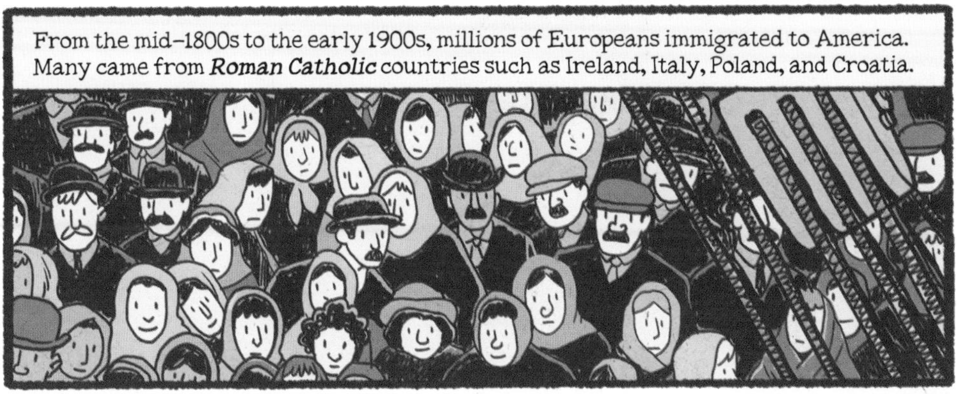
From the mid–1800s to the early 1900s, millions of Europeans immigrated to America. Many came from *Roman Catholic* countries such as Ireland, Italy, Poland, and Croatia.

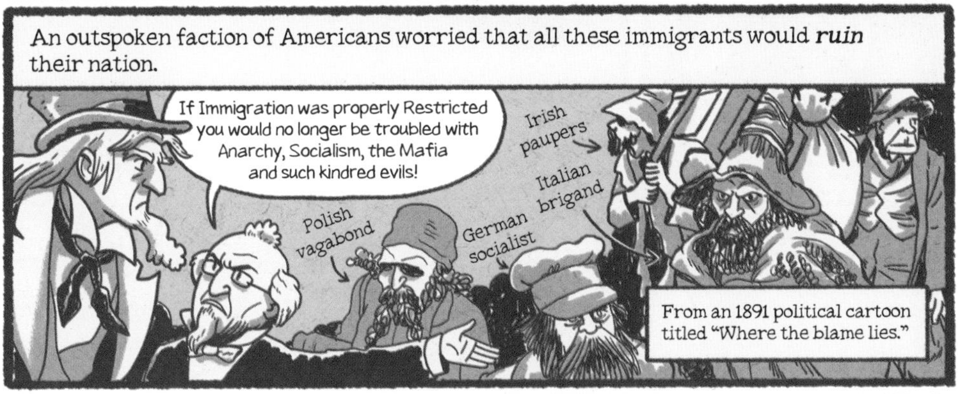
An outspoken faction of Americans worried that all these immigrants would *ruin* their nation.
If Immigration was properly Restricted you would no longer be troubled with Anarchy, Socialism, the Mafia and such kindred evils!
Irish paupers
Italian brigand
Polish vagabond
German socialist
From an 1891 political cartoon titled "Where the blame lies."

Some proposed using ***public schools*** to teach the immigrants' children how to be "proper" Americans.

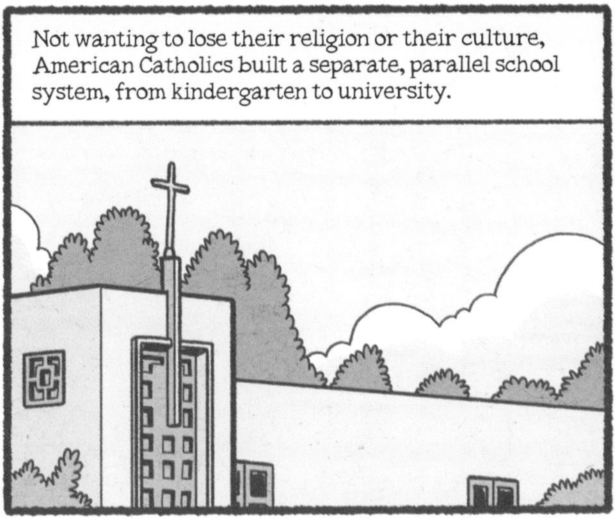
Not wanting to lose their religion or their culture, American Catholics built a separate, parallel school system, from kindergarten to university.

Early on, the Catholic schools were as ***poor*** as the communities they served.

They didn't have the same resources as their public and Protestant counterparts, so their athletic programs needed a sport that required ***little equipment*** and ***no grass.***

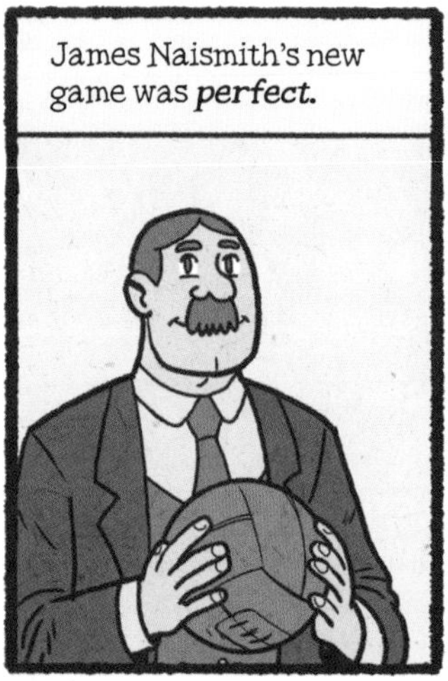
James Naismith's new game was *perfect.*
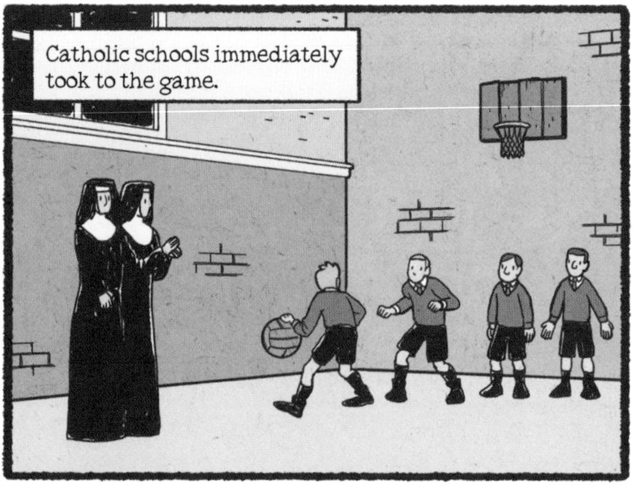
Catholic schools immediately took to the game.
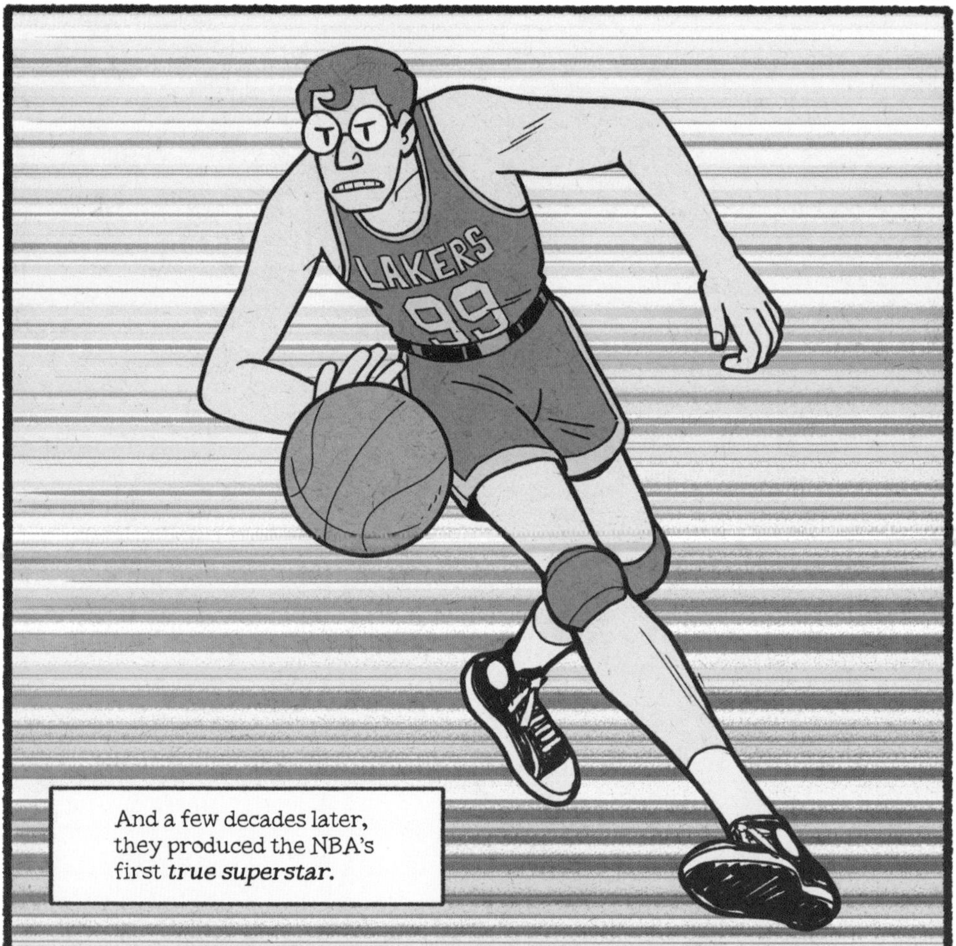
LAKERS
99
And a few decades later, they produced the NBA's first *true superstar.*

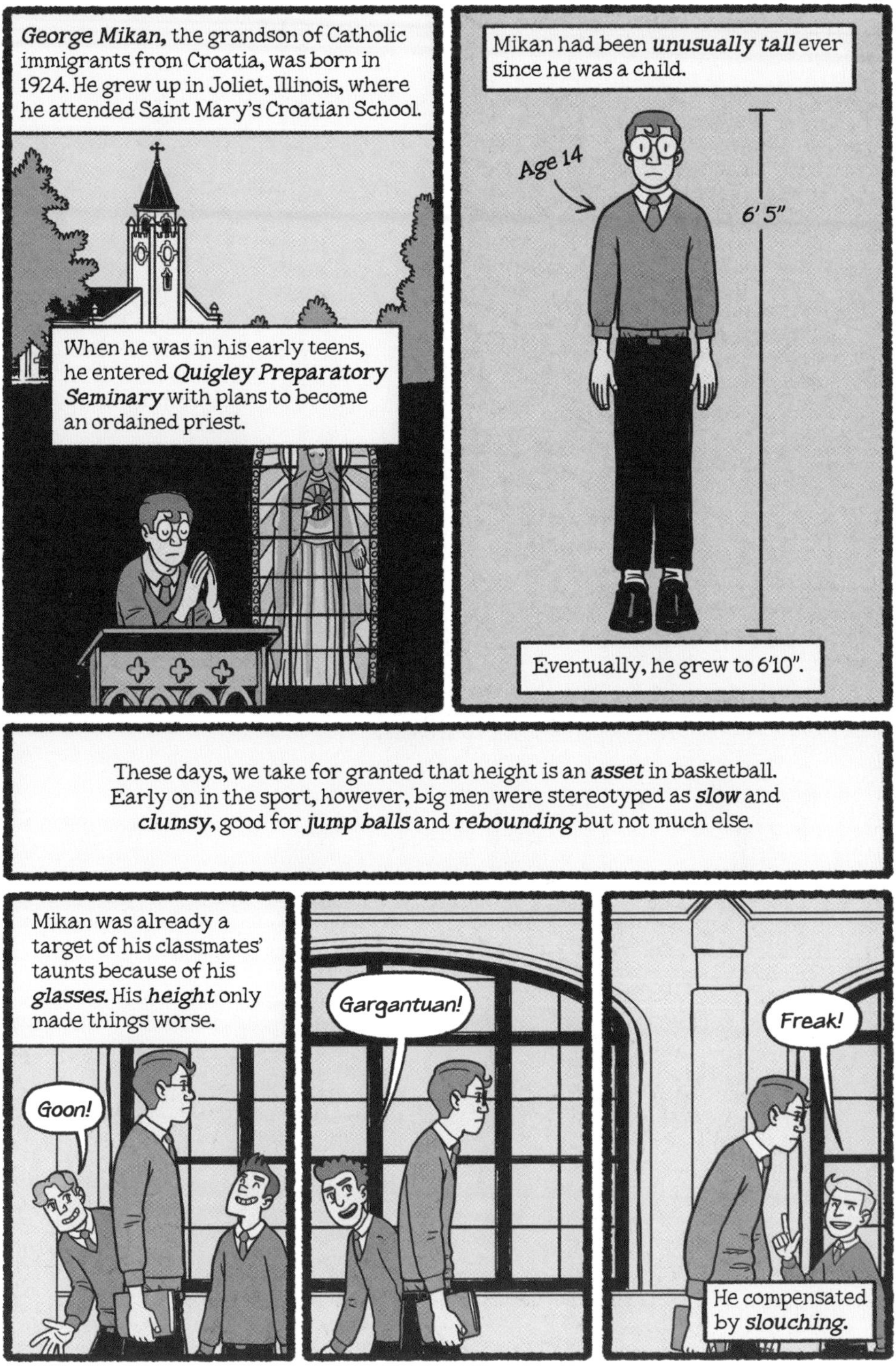
George Mikan, the grandson of Catholic immigrants from Croatia, was born in 1924. He grew up in Joliet, Illinois, where he attended Saint Mary's Croatian School.
When he was in his early teens, he entered Quigley Preparatory Seminary with plans to become an ordained priest.
Mikan had been unusually tall ever since he was a child.
Age 14
6' 5"
Eventually, he grew to 6'10".
These days, we take for granted that height is an asset in basketball. Early on in the sport, however, big men were stereotyped as slow and clumsy, good for jump balls and rebounding but not much else.
Mikan was already a target of his classmates' taunts because of his glasses. His height only made things worse.
Goon!
Gargantuan!
Freak!
He compensated by slouching.

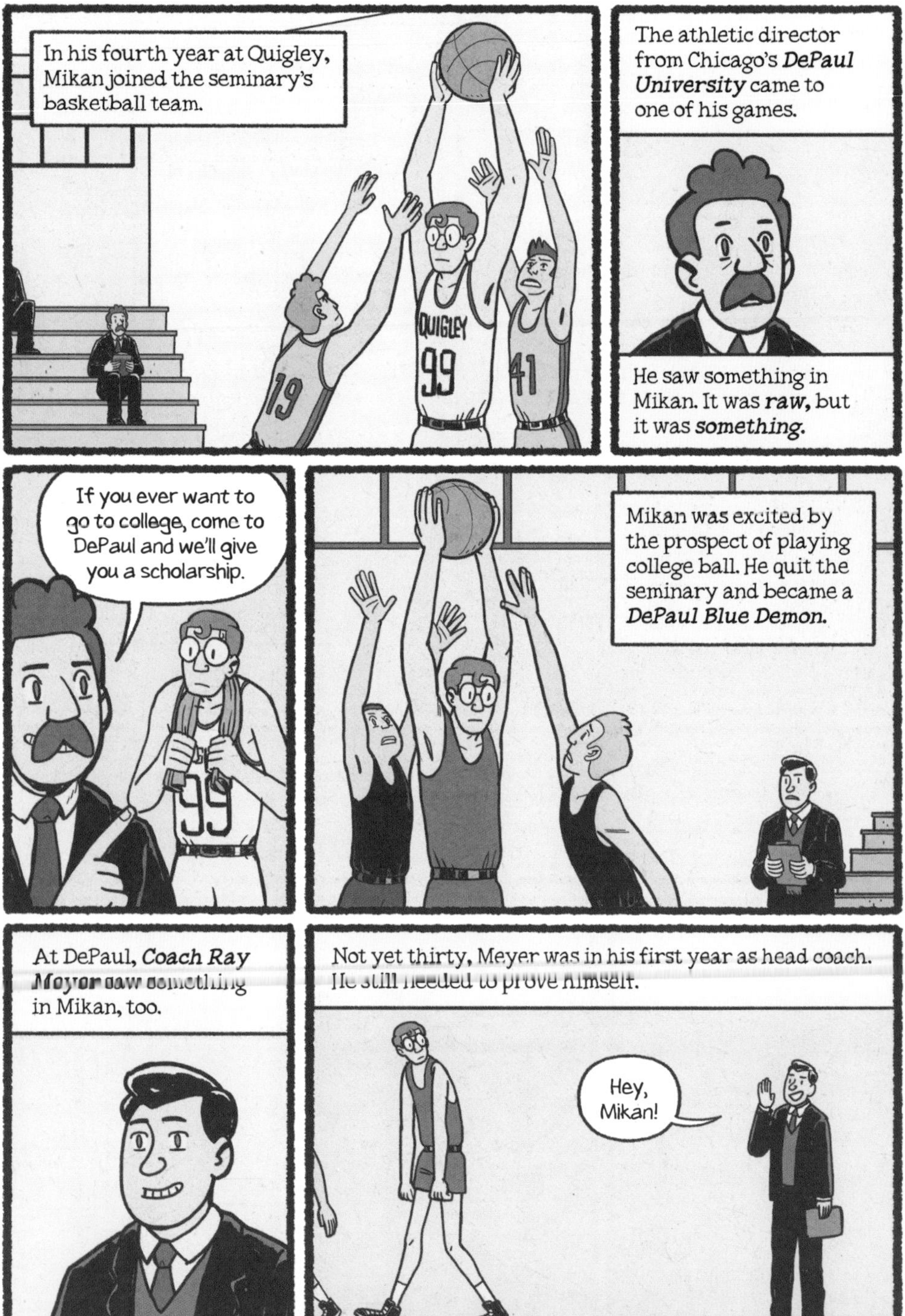
In his fourth year at Quigley, Mikan joined the seminary's basketball team.
QUIGLEY
19
99
41
The athletic director from Chicago's DePaul University came to one of his games.
He saw something in Mikan. It was raw, but it was something.
If you ever want to go to college, come to DePaul and we'll give you a scholarship.
99
Mikan was excited by the prospect of playing college ball. He quit the seminary and became a DePaul Blue Demon.
At DePaul, Coach Ray Meyer saw something in Mikan, too.
Not yet thirty, Meyer was in his first year as head coach. He still needed to prove himself.
Hey, Mikan!

And he would do it by accomplishing the *impossible.*

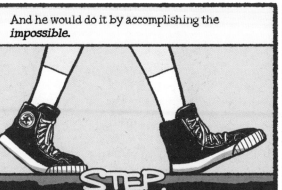

STEP.

He would get his *big guy* to move like a *little guy.*

Yeah, Coach?

You up for a special workout program?

Meyer designed an *unorthodox training regimen* just for Mikan.

This will make you *agile!*

This will make you *coordinated!*

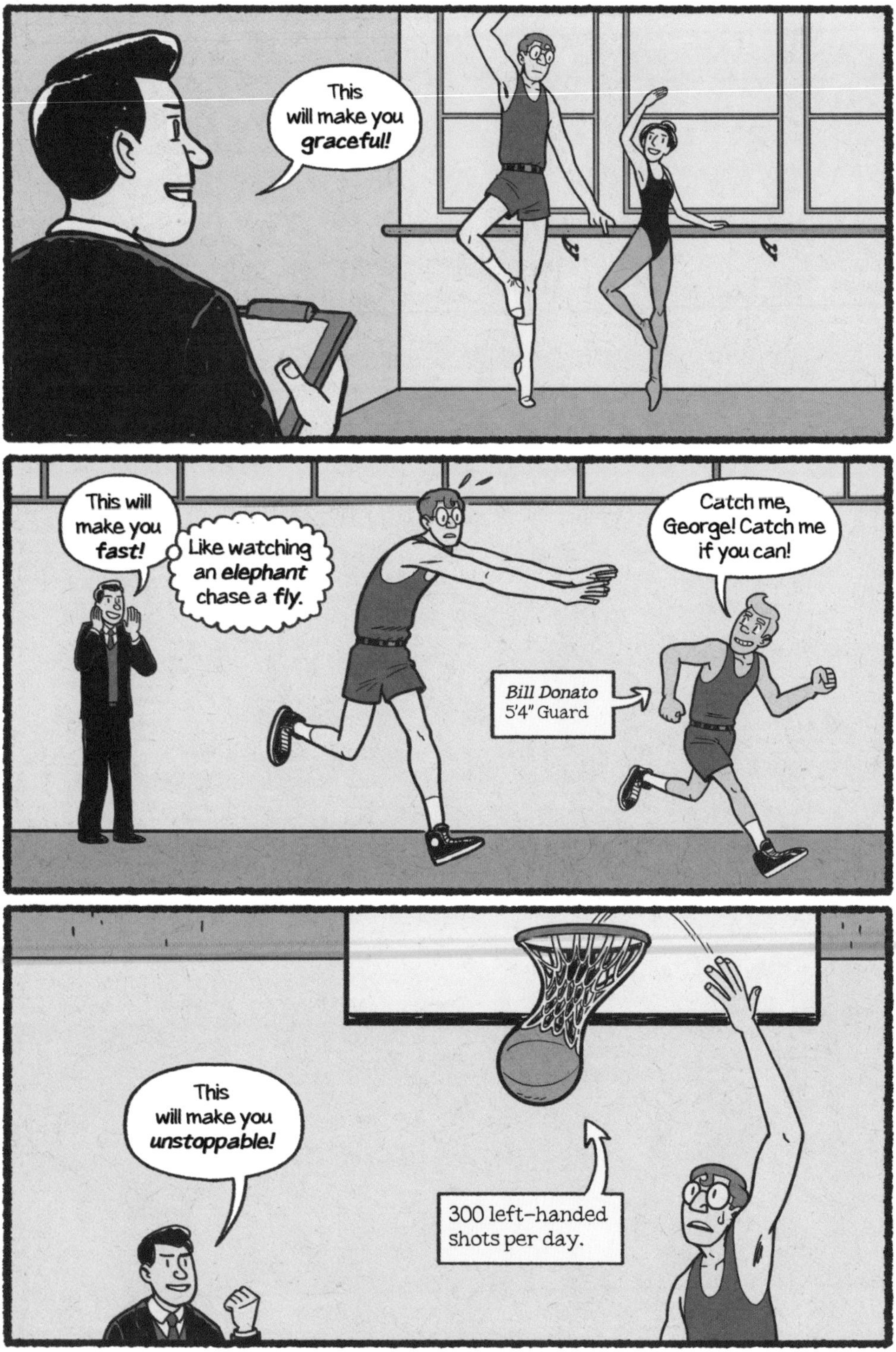
This will make you *graceful!*
This will make you *fast!*
Like watching an *elephant* chase a *fly.*
Catch me, George! Catch me if you can!
Bill Donato 5'4" Guard
This will make you *unstoppable!*
300 left-handed shots per day.

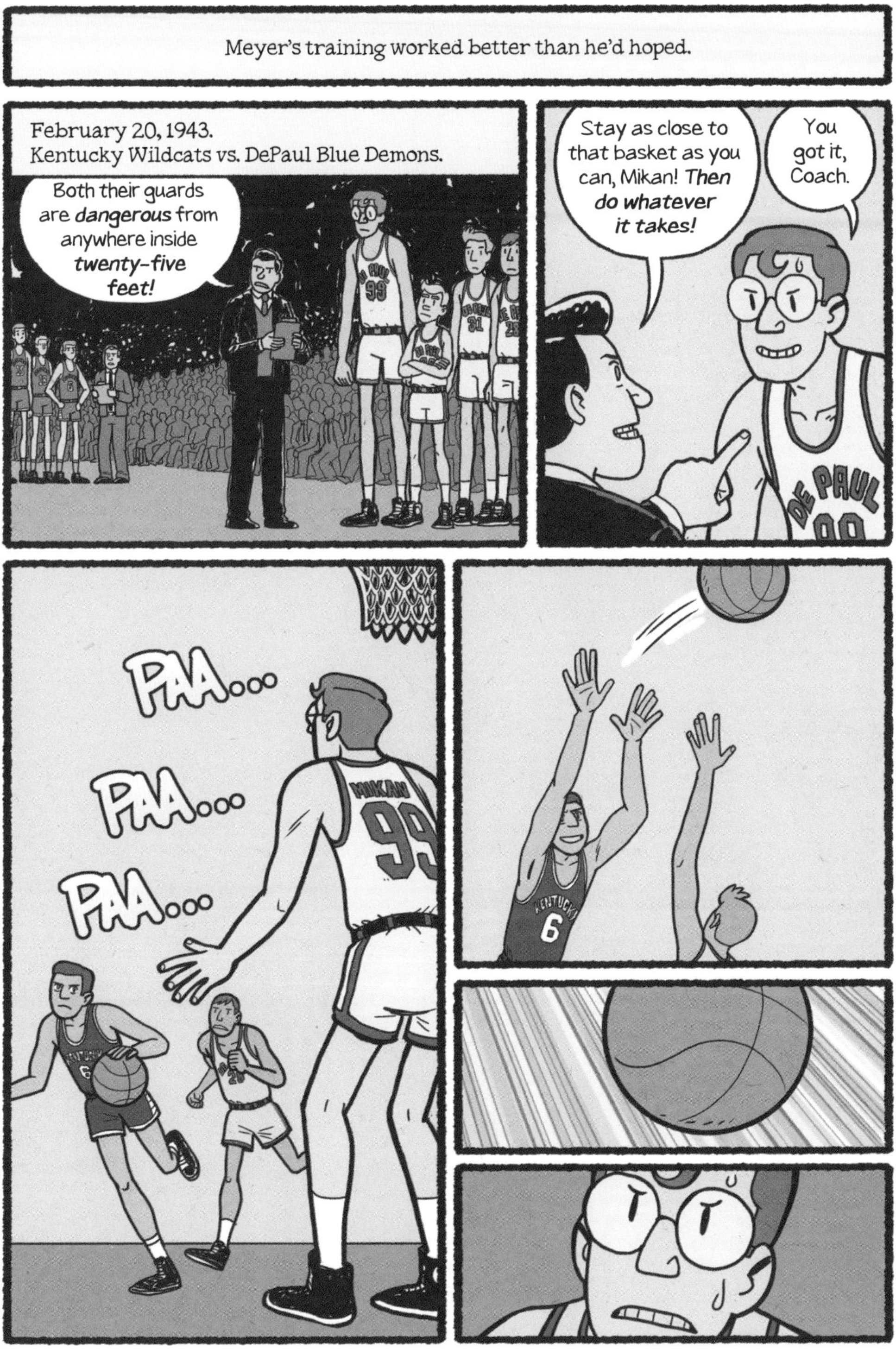
Meyer's training worked better than he'd hoped.
February 20, 1943.
Kentucky Wildcats vs. DePaul Blue Demons.
Both their guards are *dangerous* from anywhere inside *twenty-five feet!*
Stay as close to that basket as you can, Mikan! *Then do whatever it takes!*
You got it, Coach.
DE PAUL
PAA...
PAA...
PAA...
MIKAN
99
KENTUCKY
6

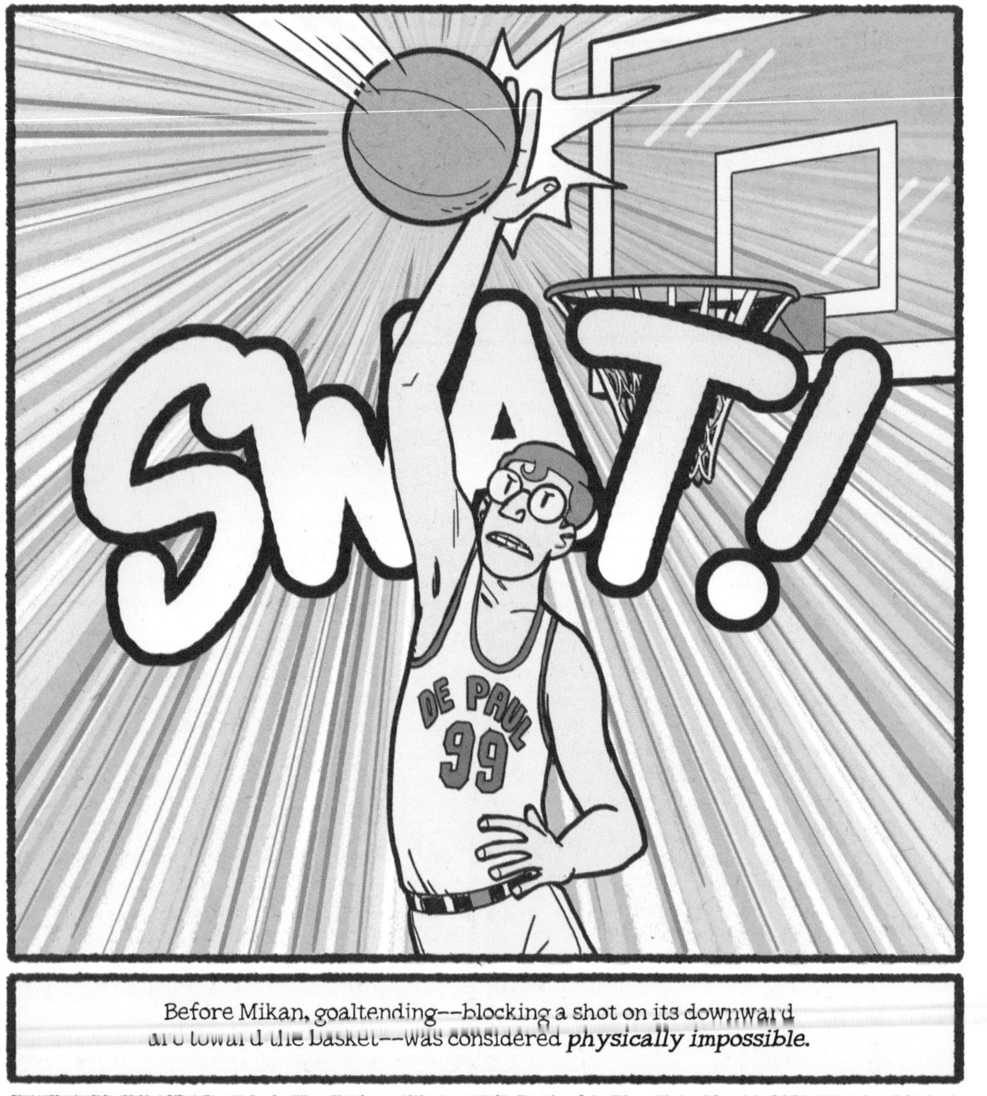
SWAT!
DE PAUL
99

Before Mikan, goaltending--blocking a shot on its downward arc toward the basket--was considered *physically impossible.*

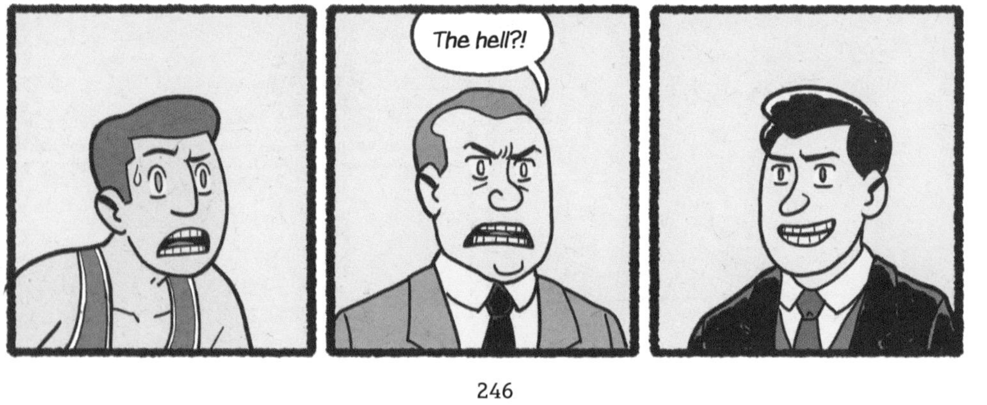
The hell?!

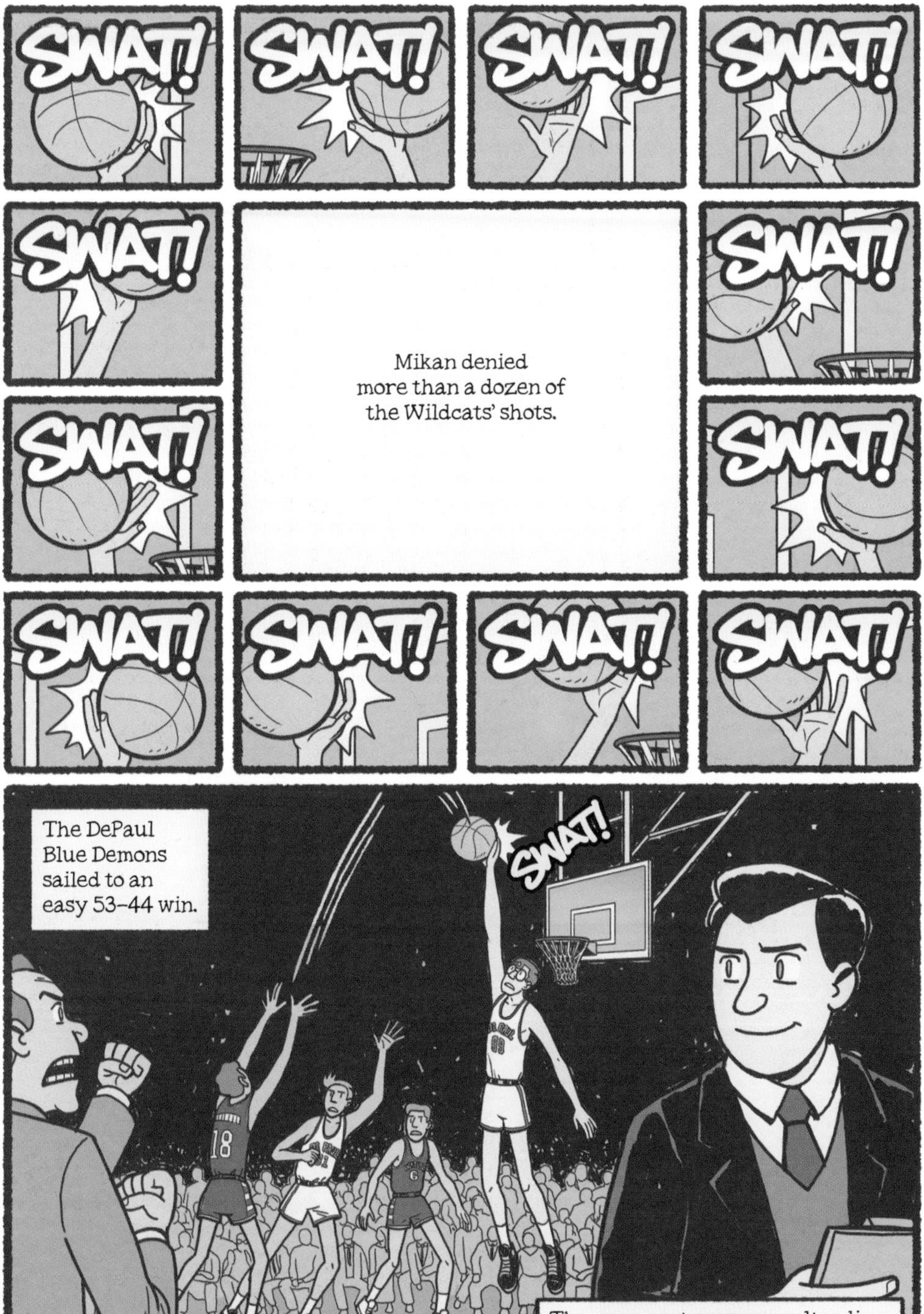
SWAT!
SWAT!
SWAT!
SWAT!
SWAT!
SWAT!
Mikan denied
more than a dozen of
the Wildcats' shots.
SWAT!
SWAT!
SWAT!
SWAT!
SWAT!
SWAT!
The DePaul Blue Demons sailed to an easy 53–44 win.
SWAT!
The very next season, goaltending was declared *illegal.*

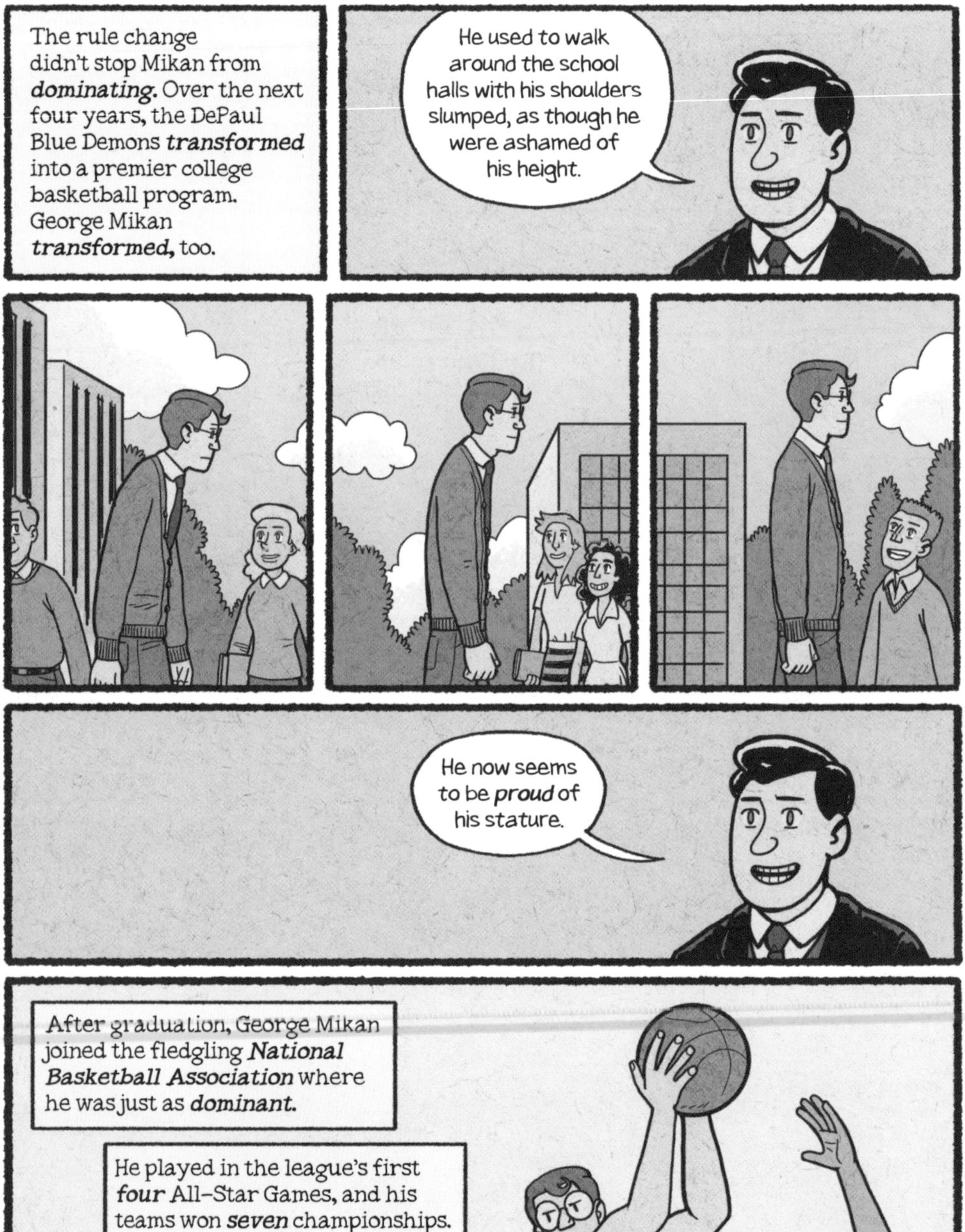
The rule change didn't stop Mikan from *dominating.* Over the next four years, the DePaul Blue Demons *transformed* into a premier college basketball program. George Mikan *transformed,* too.
He used to walk around the school halls with his shoulders slumped, as though he were ashamed of his height.
He now seems to be *proud* of his stature.
After graduation, George Mikan joined the fledgling *National Basketball Association* where he was just as *dominant.*
He played in the league's first *four* All-Star Games, and his teams won *seven* championships.
LAKERS
99

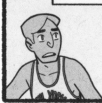

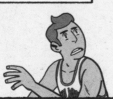

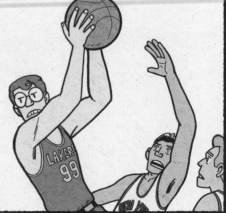

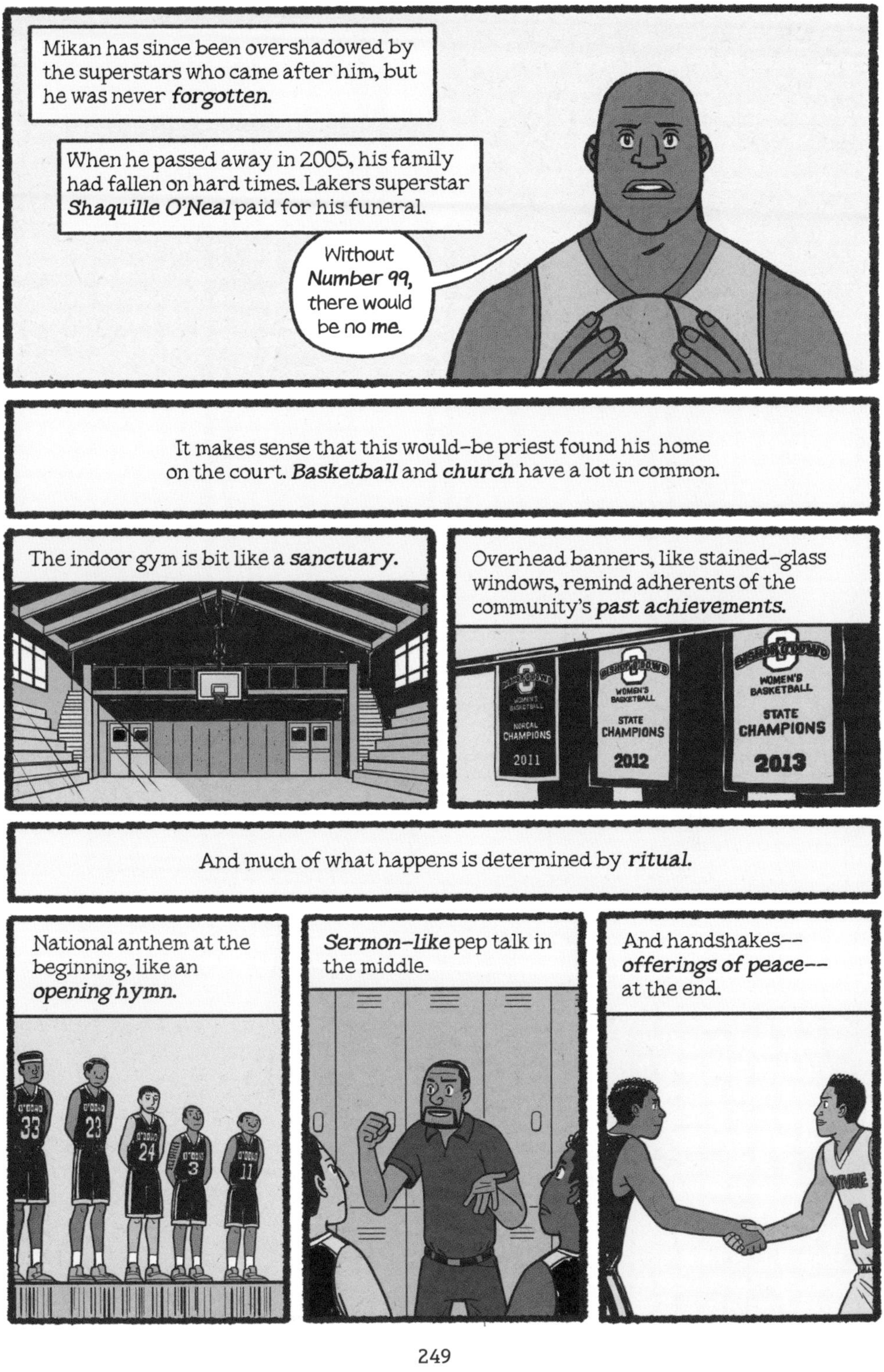
Mikan has since been overshadowed by the superstars who came after him, but he was never **forgotten.**
When he passed away in 2005, his family had fallen on hard times. Lakers superstar ***Shaquille O'Neal*** paid for his funeral.
Without **Number 99,** there would be no **me.**
It makes sense that this would-be priest found his home on the court. ***Basketball*** and ***church*** have a lot in common.
The indoor gym is bit like a ***sanctuary.***
Overhead banners, like stained-glass windows, remind adherents of the community's ***past achievements.***
WOMEN'S BASKETBALL NORCAL CHAMPIONS 2011
WOMEN'S BASKETBALL STATE CHAMPIONS 2012
WOMEN'S BASKETBALL STATE CHAMPIONS 2013
And much of what happens is determined by ***ritual.***
National anthem at the beginning, like an ***opening hymn.***
Sermon-like pep talk in the middle.
And handshakes-- ***offerings of peace***-- at the end.

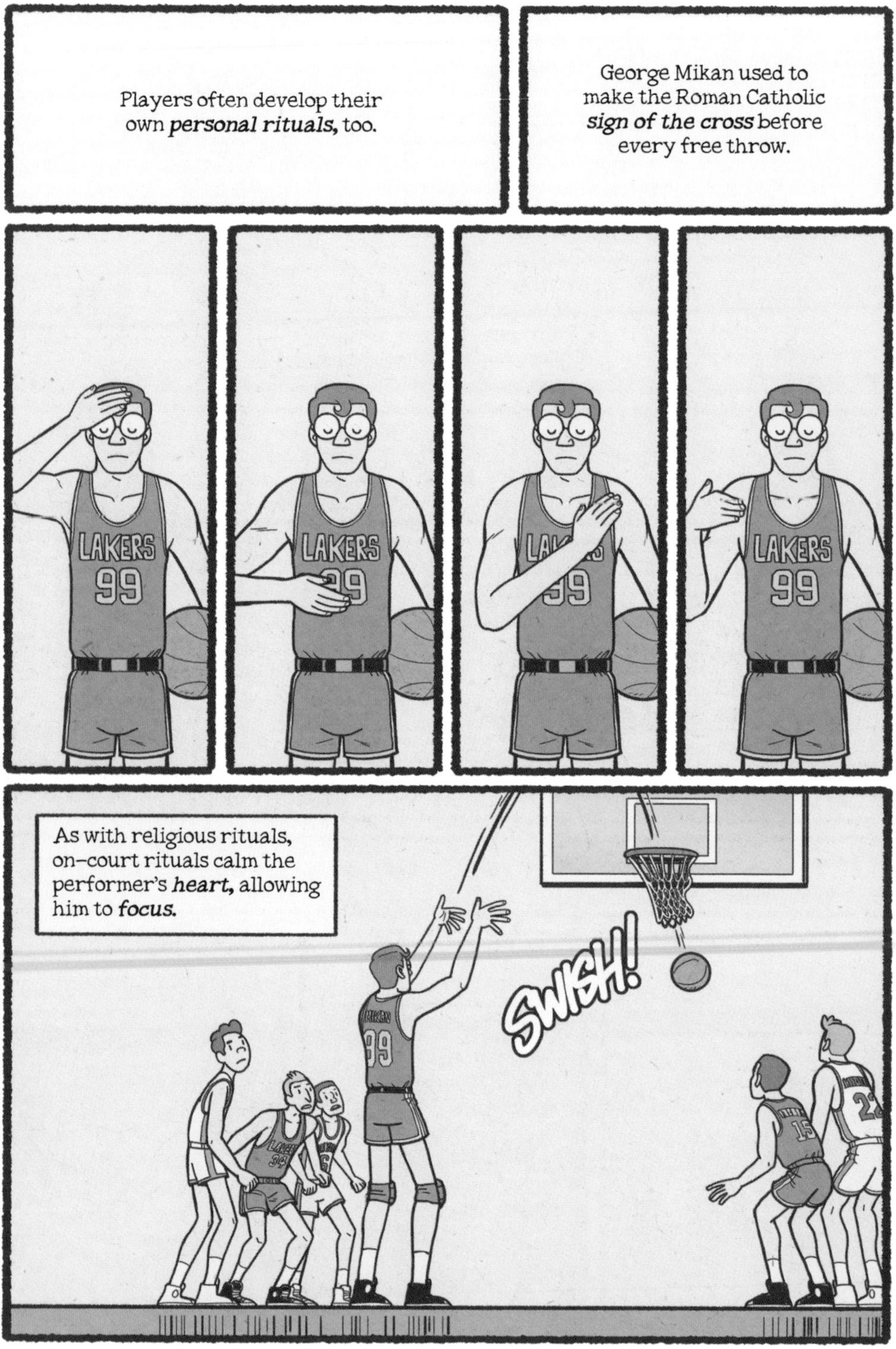
Players often develop their own *personal rituals,* too.
George Mikan used to make the Roman Catholic *sign of the cross* before every free throw.
LAKERS 99
LAKERS 99
LAKERS 99
LAKERS 99
As with religious rituals, on-court rituals calm the performer's *heart,* allowing him to *focus.*
SWISH!

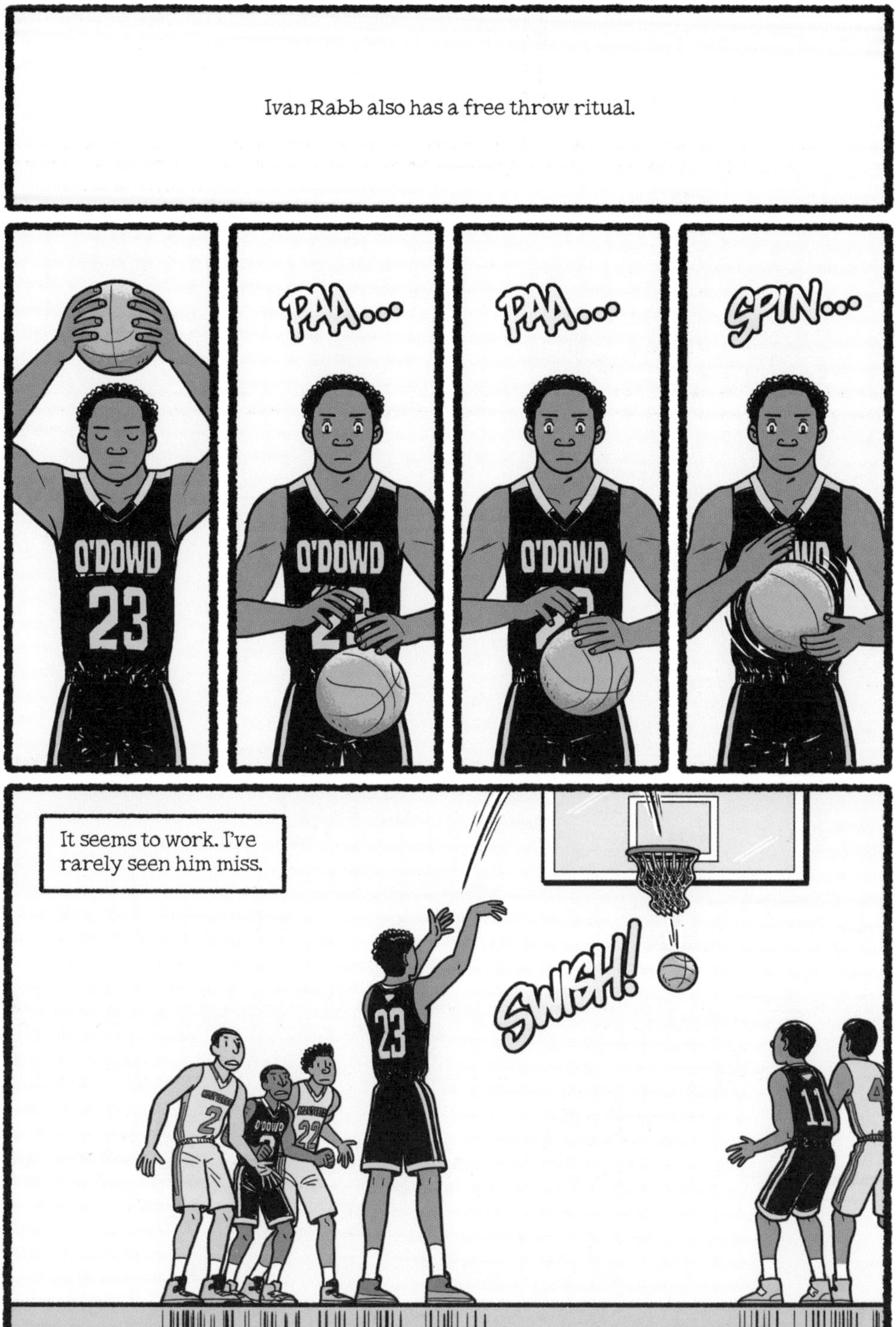
Ivan Rabb also has a free throw ritual.
O'DOWD 23
PAA...
O'DOWD
PAA...
O'DOWD
SPIN...
It seems to work. I've rarely seen him miss.
SWISH!
23
O'DOWD
11

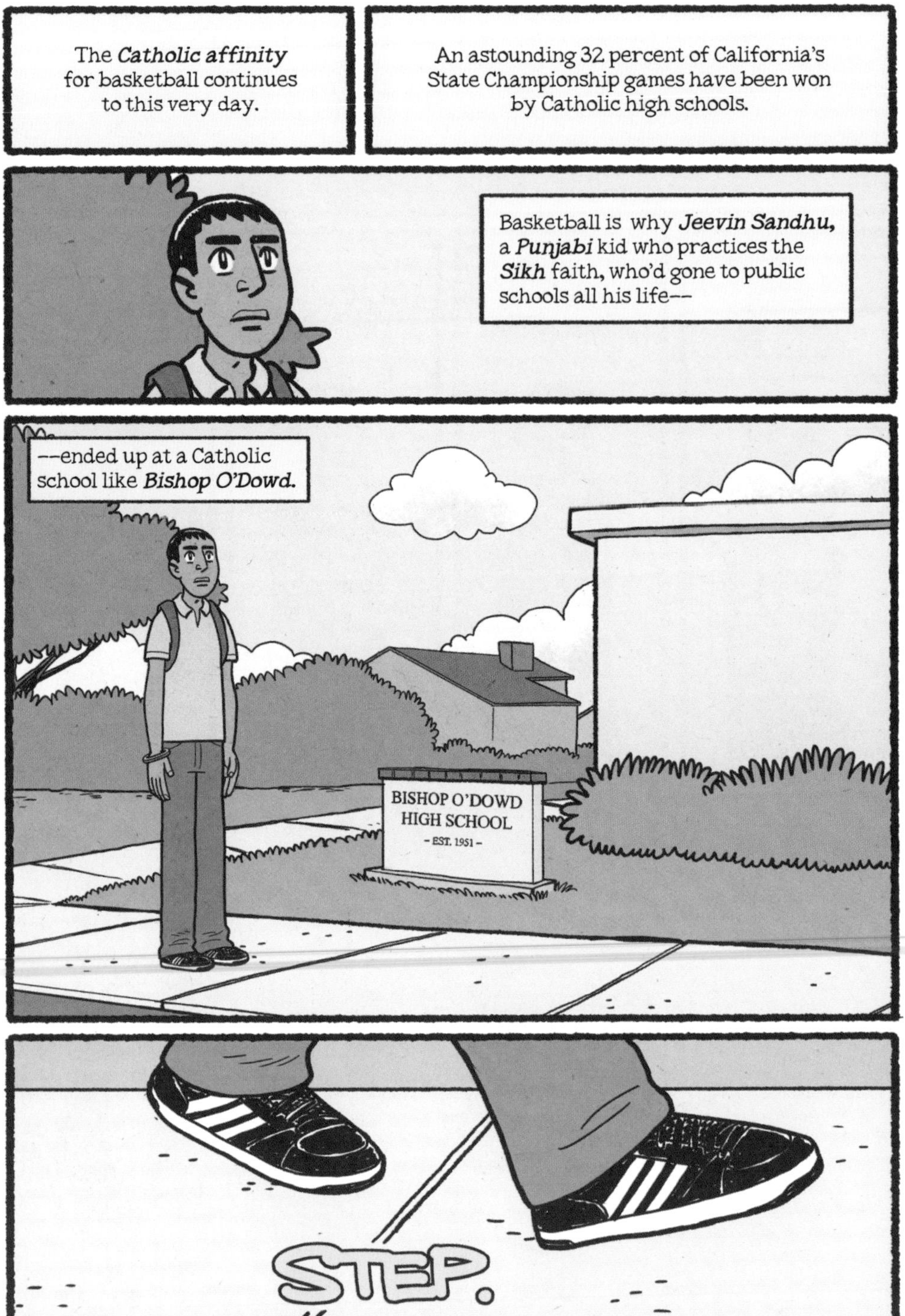
The *Catholic affinity* for basketball continues to this very day.
An astounding 32 percent of California's State Championship games have been won by Catholic high schools.
Basketball is why *Jeevin Sandhu,* a *Punjabi* kid who practices the *Sikh* faith, who'd gone to public schools all his life--
--ended up at a Catholic school like *Bishop O'Dowd.*
BISHOP O'DOWD HIGH SCHOOL
- EST. 1951 -
STEP.

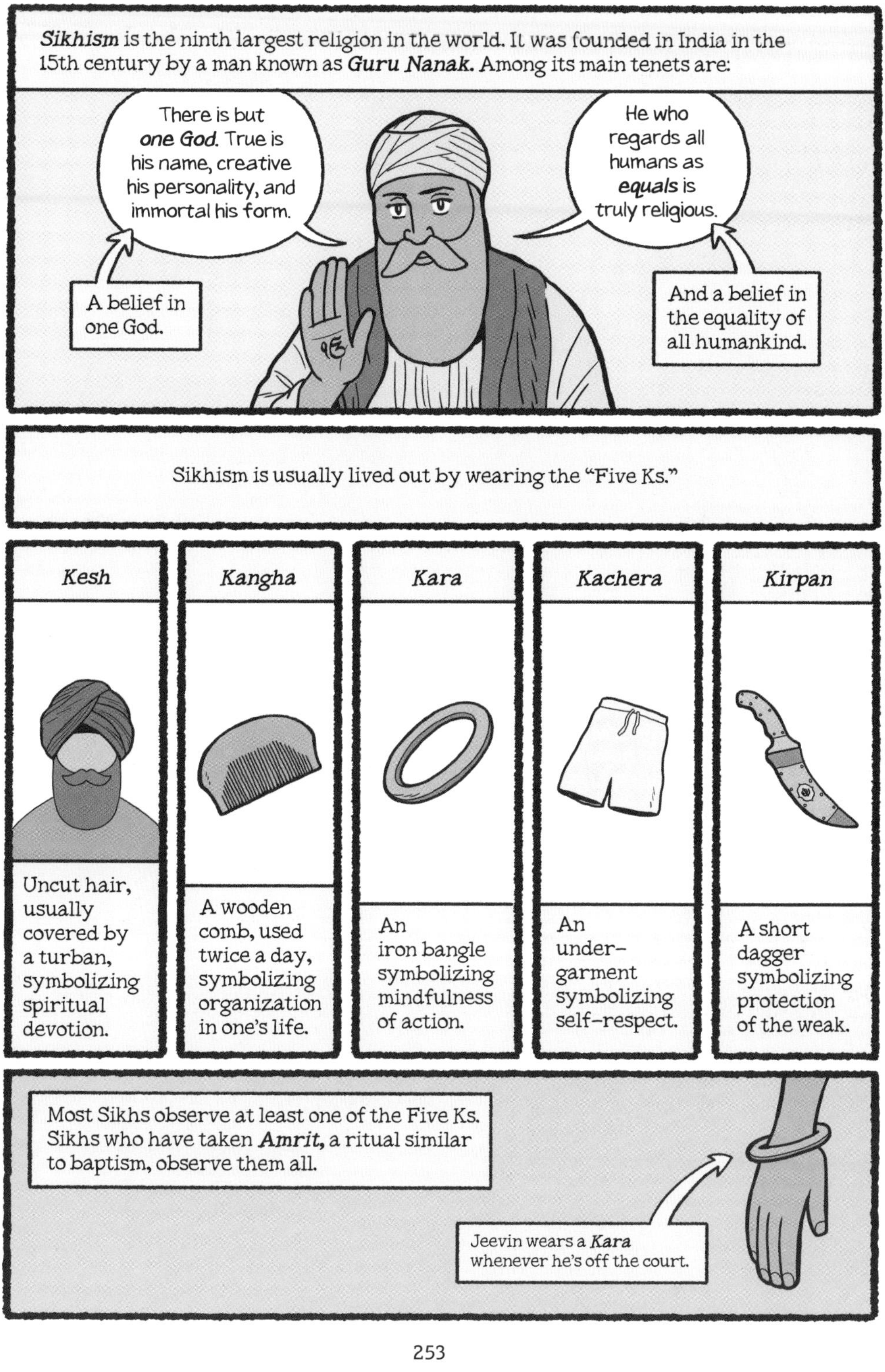

Sikhism is the ninth largest religion in the world. It was founded in India in the 15th century by a man known as *Guru Nanak.* Among its main tenets are:
There is but *one God.* True is his name, creative his personality, and immortal his form.
He who regards all humans as *equals* is truly religious.
A belief in one God.
And a belief in the equality of all humankind.
Sikhism is usually lived out by wearing the "Five Ks."
Kesh
Uncut hair, usually covered by a turban, symbolizing spiritual devotion.
Kangha
A wooden comb, used twice a day, symbolizing organization in one's life.
Kara
An iron bangle symbolizing mindfulness of action.
Kachera
An under-garment symbolizing self-respect.
Kirpan
A short dagger symbolizing protection of the weak.
Most Sikhs observe at least one of the Five Ks. Sikhs who have taken *Amrit,* a ritual similar to baptism, observe them all.
Jeevin wears a *Kara* whenever he's off the court.

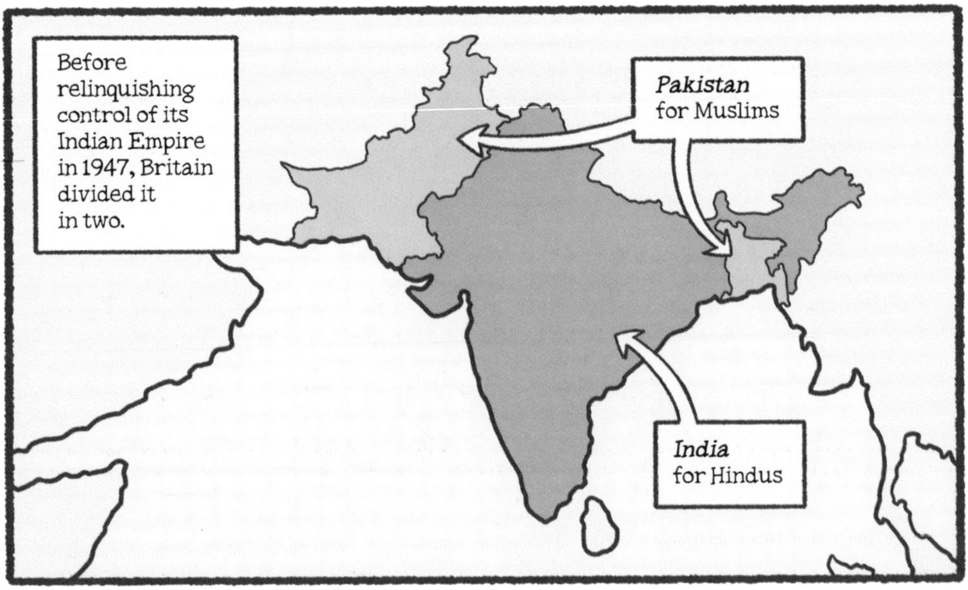
Before relinquishing control of its Indian Empire in 1947, Britain divided it in two.
Pakistan for Muslims
India for Hindus

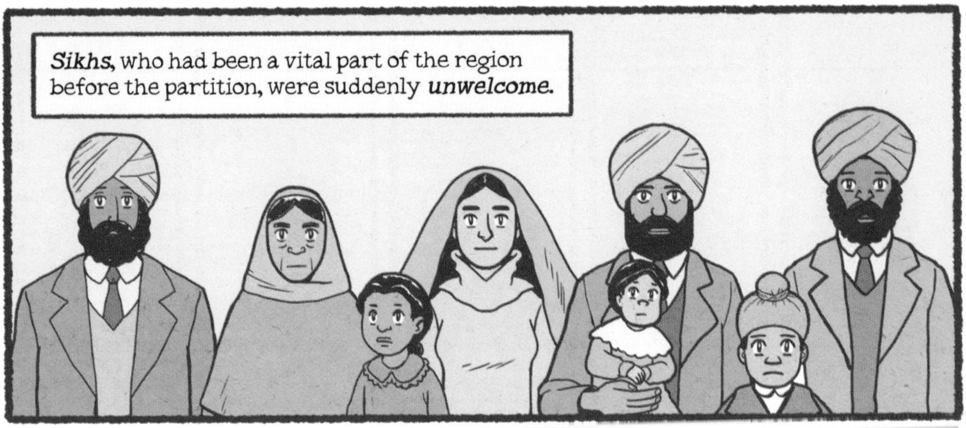
Sikhs, who had been a vital part of the region before the partition, were suddenly ***unwelcome.***

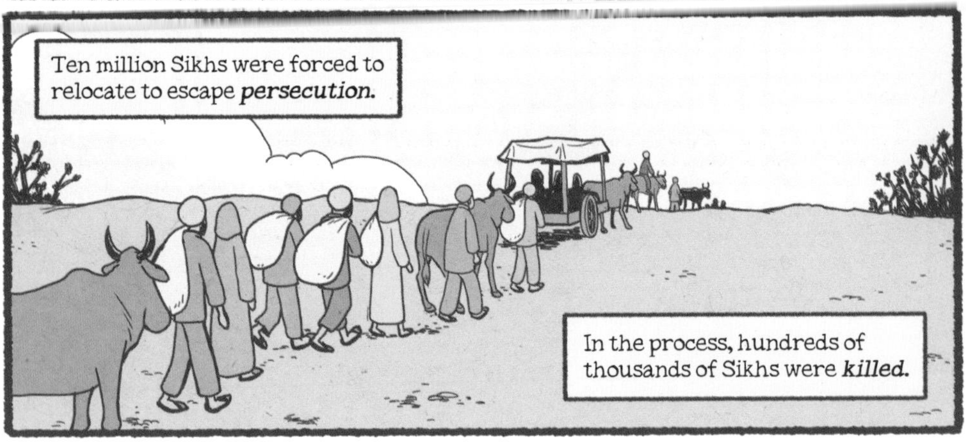
Ten million Sikhs were forced to relocate to escape ***persecution.***
In the process, hundreds of thousands of Sikhs were ***killed.***

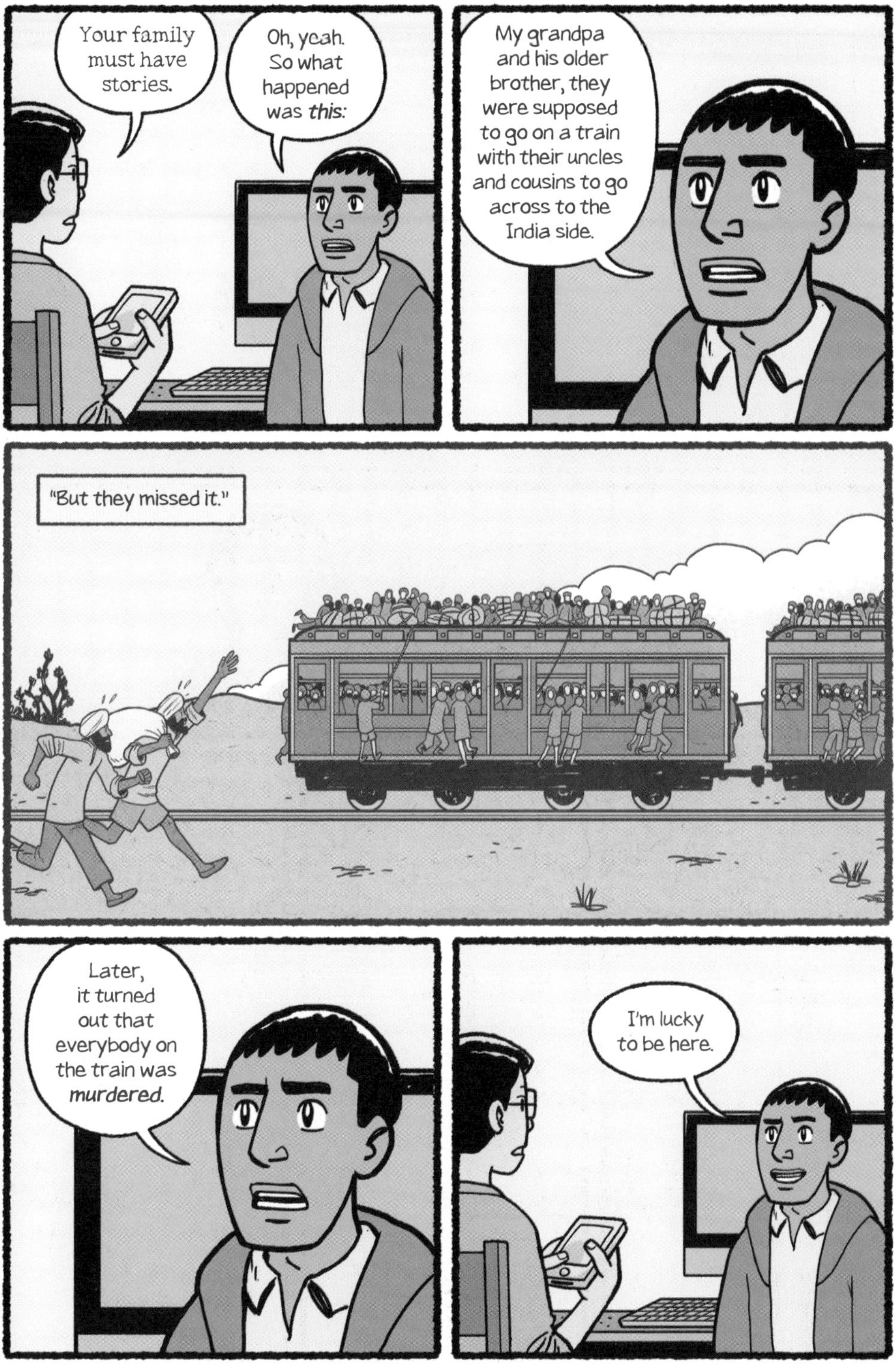
Your family must have stories.
Oh, yeah. So what happened was *this:*
My grandpa and his older brother, they were supposed to go on a train with their uncles and cousins to go across to the India side.
"But they missed it."
Later, it turned out that everybody on the train was *murdered.*
I'm lucky to be here.